The Winter's Hero

Generations of Winter

The Ticket to the Stars

Half-way to the Moon

The Steel Bird and Other Stories

The Island of Crimea

The Burn

Say Cheese

In Search of Melancholy Baby

THE NEW SWEET STYLE

VASSILY AKSYONOV

The New Sweet Style

A NOVEL

TRANSLATED BY

CHRISTOPHER MORRIS

RANDOM HOUSE

NEW YORK

S

Grateful acknowledgment is made to Spirit One Music o/b/o Irwin Levine Music and Peer Music for permission to reprint an excerpt from "Tie a Yellow Ribbon 'Round the Ole Oak Tree," by L. Russell Brown and Irwin Levine. Copyright © 1972 by Irwin Levine Music and Peermusic III, Ltd. Copyright renewed. All rights for Irwin Levine Music controlled and administered by Spirit One Music. All rights reserved. International copyright secured. Reprinted by permission.

Library of Congress Cataloging-in-Publication Data
Aksenov, Vasiliĭ Pavlovich.
[Novyĭ sladostnyĭ stil'. English]
The new sweet style / Vassily Aksyonov;
translated by Christopher Morris.
p.   cm.
ISBN 0-679-44401-7
I. Title.
PG3478.K7N6813   1999
891.73'44—dc21   99-13313

Random House website address: www.atrandom.com

Printed in the United States of America on acid-free paper

24689753

First Edition

Book design by Caroline Cunningham

In an idle hour one day we read

the delightful tale of Lancelot.

—Dante,
Divine Comedy, The Inferno
Paolo and Francesca (da Rimini)

CONTENTS

PART VIII

PART IX

THE NEW SWEET STYLE

PART I

1

THREE STEPS

On August 10, 1982, Alexander Zakharovich Korbach set foot on American soil for the first time. As he was standing in the massive queue at passport control in the Pan Am terminal, the date kept buzzing in his head: there was some further meaning in it. It was only once he was past the checkpoint and alongside the baggage carousel that it came to him: it was his birthday! Every year on this date, he "turned" something, and just now again he had "turned" something: forty-two, was it? No, forty-three. If he had thought a year ago in the Crimea that in a year he would "celebrate" his birthday in a New York airport! August 10, 1982. Forty-three years old—head hurts from last night—an H-1 visa—fifteen hundred dollars and three thousand francs in my pocket, I don't feel anything but a "simoom of sensations."

His first encounter on American soil happened to be a pleasant, if not a liberating, one. Suddenly, his suitcase arrived, among the first ones—came leaping out of the netherworld, displaying a strange agility, not to say excessive familiarity. Looking at the suitcase, Alexander, a man with a penchant for inadequate reflections about insignificant things, thought: Why, here it is, this battered little suitcase, and it's somehow endearing. The heart of the matter, after all, as it turned out, was this: someone killed a large animal somewhere, they made a case out of the hide in Latvia, and now everything "beastly" about it has vanished, and the suitcase has been transformed into an object of nostalgia.

The case went by, collided with a Hindu bundle, and fell over on its side. The next time around Korbach snatched his belongings from among the other bags and took his place in the line for customs inspection.

Customs Officer Jim Corbett was eyeing him from atop a high stool. While it is impossible to examine all the junk coming into the USA, there does exist a system of selective checking, which the professionals have mastered. The customs specialist reads faces, gestures, any movement. The potential violator is always spotted from a long way off. For example, the balding, finely featured head. An individual difficult to put in a category. The shoulders were twitching strangely—too much, somehow. A drug smuggler doesn't give little jumps like that. Let the head and ears go by, or check him out? It's always a toss-up. "Please open your suitcase," he asked politely, and added: "sir." The individual thrusts a piece of paper at him: "Declaration! Declaration!" Doesn't even understand English! Jim Corbett makes a gesture: a sharp turn of the wrists followed by an elegantly proportioned raising of the palms. "If you don't mind, sir."

There is nothing attractive, but nothing particularly repulsive either, in the suitcase. Among perspiration-stained shirts is a book in an old binding, embossed with a large gold *D.* Obviously no false bottom. Corbett glances in the passport: you don't get many of them, these Soviets. "Got any vodka?" the officer jokes. "Only in here," the new arrival jokes in reply, tapping himself on the forehead. Great guy—Corbett laughs to himself—it'd be nice to sit with him at Tony's.

A Russian must carry a lot of interesting stuff around inside, Corbett went on thinking for several minutes, allowing potential violators to pass without a check. A country of exceptional order, everything under control, no homosexuality—how do they manage it?

Meanwhile, Alexander Korbach was making his way in a crowd toward the entrance to a yawning tunnel, at the other end of which, in fact, the land of freedom began. A body that has just flown across an ocean might not yet be at full strength. Maybe the astral threads, all of these chakras, idas, pingalas, kundalinis, had to reassemble themselves into their natural order after having been transported at a speed so unnatural to human creatures, he mused with a melancholy chuckle. The shuffling of feet doesn't mean anything yet—it's just the movement of indistinguishable mechanisms wanting to end up in America. It takes time for old passions to rekindle.

Beyond the crowd Alexander Zakharovich could make out three steps of varying shades: the first white and of marble; the second rough, of some scorched-looking stone, purple to the point of blackness; and the third of fiery scarlet porphyry. The crowd silently flowed into the tunnel.

A second crowd, this one quietly waiting to greet the arrivals, came into view at the end of the cavern. The lights for the television cameras were already jutting out over their heads. Keep your cool, Korbach said to himself. Speak only Russian. No humiliating attempts at the local lingo. I'm sorry, gentlemen, the situation is unclear. For the moment, the theater still exists. The question of my position as artistic director is up in the air. There are creative forces in the United States with whom I feel an intellectual and stylistic kinship, and the purpose of my visit is to establish contact with them.

Well, then, while our five-feet-four-inch-tall protagonist, a man of not unattractive appearance, in the mold of that nineteenth-century poet and novelist Mikhail Lermontov—though with the receding hairline of the twentieth-century poet and novelist Andrei Bely—approaches the television cameras, we can use the opportunities provided by the novel's wide open spaces to leaf through his curriculum vitae.

2

CURRICULUM VITAE

*I*n 1982 a Soviet man had no idea what he was dealing with in these two badly pronounced words. He didn't know, of course, the abbreviation CV, whose pronunciation would only have reminded him vaguely of *sibyl,* a woman who can divine the future. There is some sense in this, since the CV, a cross between an information form and a biographical sketch, while relating to the past, always contains in itself the hope of positive changes in the future. Essentially, it is nothing other than an advertisement for an individual drawn up in such a way as to attract a buyer.

An advertisement ought not to deceive, however, and, in view of this, the author in his role as framer of the scene should reveal at the outset that certain aspects of our hero's CV were somewhat unclear, if not ambiguous. For example, that ever alarming "fifth item" in his Soviet passport: Alexander Zakharovich Korbach was identified as a Jew in all of his papers. Yet he had not always been one, we have to admit. His surname had not always ended in a guttural Hebrew sound. Moreover, his previous patronymic, Nikolayevich, had once resonated more sweetly than Zakharovich in the Red ear.

In childhood and early adolescence, our hero had walked through the world in the guise of Sasha Izhmailov, a Russian lad. He had a father suited to the role, Nikolai Ivanovich Izhmailov, who limped along with the support of a massive walking stick, a hero of the Great Patriotic War. And Sasha was suitably proud of his father. For his part, Nikolai Ivanovich treated Sasha with a restrained severity that could have been taken as a reserved expression of love, and it was only when he was deep in his cups that by some logic known solely to him he referred to Sasha as a mongrel, after which Mama would shriek, "I'm dying! I'm dying!"

Working in the nomenklatura—the upper Party hierarchy—Nikolai Ivanovich raised his standard of living, and his family lacked for nothing, as they say in Russian folktales. In the postwar years, Sasha's life was enriched with a little brother and a little sister. Nikolai Ivanovich would often frolic on the carpet of his office with all three of them, and only occasionally, taking Valerka and Katyusha in his arms, would he warmly whisper, "Mine, mine," with great emphasis.

You and I, dear reader, can now guess—the boy at the time did not understand—why his admiration for his "father" changed over the years into a sort of ill-defined vigilance.

Meanwhile, Grandma Irina, who was seemingly called by this name only, yet not simply for reasons of age, was always present on the fringes of this rather complicated household. She would try to turn up on those days when Izhmailov was off on his important business trips. At first she brought Sasha toys, later ice skates and hockey sticks. She would gaze at him lovingly and have chats with him about American Indians or captains of frigates or the world political situation for hours on end.

"Granny" was unusual. A military doctor, she had spent the entire war in field hospitals. She walked with the decisive stride of an officer, a Kazbek cigarette invariably between her teeth; her large spectacles reduced her whole aspect to the basic category of those women promoted in the 1930s, during a period of affirmative action. To top it all off, throughout Sasha's childhood, Granny drove her own car, an Opel Cadet that had been seized as a war trophy.

The boy did not understand how this remarkable character had come to be his grandmother—he felt as though the family had somehow been twisted out of shape, but he didn't want to get into the details. From time to time he would hear Grandma Irina and Mama begin talking in what might be called raised voices. Granny seemed to be claiming some right over him, and his mother rejected these claims with resolute fervor. It was only in 1953—that is, in Sasha's fourteenth year—that everything was explained.

One day, when he was visiting Grandma Irina in her large room on Starokonyushenny Street, he noticed something new on the wall—an enlarged photograph of a young serviceman with a miniature military insignia in his buttonhole. Who was it? He sensed the approach of some sort of dizzying turn of fate, but he resolved to ask the question anyway. "He's your father," Granny said firmly, and enveloped herself in deep blue Kazbek smoke. She was expecting an argument, but none was forthcoming. "Do you see, that's your face—the ears that stick out, the ear-to-ear mouth, the laughing eyes. As for your birth certificate, it's not true that it was lost in the evacuation. This is your father, Jakob Ruvimovich Korbach— my son—and you're my grandson. I insisted to Liza that your father's name be put on the birth certificate, even though he was already in jail at that time."

From that day on, Sasha stopped calling Nikolai Ivanovich Izhmailov Papa, despite the stubborn insistence of his mother, who seemed to sense a rift in the family: "Go and see your father," she would insist—"ask your father, get your father's advice."

Instead of a face-to-face meeting, there occurred one day a stunning turn of events. Nikolai Ivanovich was on an official trip (in those years he was in charge of nourishing the Donbas coal-producing region with the wisdom of Marxist gospel), Sasha's mother had taken his younger siblings to a matinee at the children's theater, and Sasha was sitting alone in the dining room poring over what was probably a physics textbook and listening to Kabalevsky's *Kola Brugnon* overture on the radio. The whirlwind of that musical evocation of an uprising swept over him, and he was filled with a desire to dash off to join those rebellious harquebusiers. Just then a heavy chandelier in the Stalin empire style fell from the high ceiling and landed right on his head, and he lost consciousness.

Later on he tried to remember his feelings at that moment, or at that tiny fraction of a moment, or in that pause unmeasurable in time. Consciousness, of course, was cutting its way free even before the pain reached the receptors; that's why you don't feel pain. Where is the soul during that interval? Is it in that interval that it's to be found? He remembered that this pause was broken off by a flash of monstrous compression and rupture, after which everything seemed restored—he opened his eyes and saw those of Izhmailov over him, flashing with a furious joy as they met his glance. "Nikolai Ivanovich," he whispered, and Nikolai Ivanovich broke down sobbing. What sort of unbridled existentialism and idiotic nondeterminism was this? You're sitting at the table, listening to *Kola Brugnon,* and at a given moment a goddamned chandelier falls on *you,* and not on some empty spot.

It would not be given to Alexander Zakharovich for decades of life to learn that that moment of compression and rupture had, after all, been determined by some previous developments. The fact is that no chandelier had fallen on him at all. Exercising the rights of the author, we could pass over even this in silence; however, observing the rights of the reader, we find it impossible to keep up our smirking secrecy.

The fact is that at the culmination of the overture, the newly returned Nikolai Ivanovich had come into the dining room. His leg, the one that was shortened and reinforced with a pin, was causing him terrible pain that day. The recent passing of Josef Vissarionovich had plunged the entire apparatus of the Central Committee into a pigsty of gloom, and Nikolai Ivanovich was no exception. Even in the Donbas he had felt a sensation of nausea. It was in this state that he saw before him the back of the hated boy's head. That damned offspring of Yashka Korbach, who'd had Liza, who had considered himself Nikolai's best friend, and whom Nikolai had denounced to the secret police. How could he call himself a reliable Party man if immediately after Yashka's arrest he had started forcing himself on Liza, staggering her with his lust? How could he forget it if there was always this new and growing Yashka before his eyes? Choking with rage, Nikolai Ivanovich now raised his boxwood walking stick and brought it down with all his might on the boy's head.

To the credit of Comrade Izhmailov, it should be pointed out that he did call the ambulance immediately and only later set about pulling down the chandelier to simulate an existential catastrophe.

The misfortune somehow reconciled Sasha to his make-believe father. The need for an explanation was silently put off by everyone, and he began calling his stepfather Nikolai Ivanovich. Even Mama said to him one day: "Nikolai Ivanovich is a very good man—after all, he married me when I was already pregnant—that is, with you, Alexander." And he, in spite of the manliness that was increasing in him every day, wiped his eyes and stroked her hair.

A face-to-face meeting perhaps no less dramatic than the one that had never taken place came three years later, in 1956, when Alexander was in the tenth grade. One day after dinner, Nikolai Ivanovich had a fit of temper over his newspaper covering the events in Hungary: "The swine! The swine! They hung Communists upside down!" The explanation, of course, could have waited, and the moment of nervous tension been skipped over; Alexander, however, having gone pale, pushed his plate away and made an announcement: "Mama and Nikolai Ivanovich, I want to inform you that I'm taking my father's surname and . . . and my real nationality."

"Why, you're out of your mind!" his mother cried immediately. "You're only one-quarter, after all!"

An agonizing silence fell. The younger children were sitting with their mouths wide open. Katyusha automatically carried on with her disgusting habit of slopping the soup from her spoon back into the bowl. "Get out of this house!" Nikolai Ivanovich finally said.

"That's the third thing that I wanted to announce to you," said Alexander. "I'm moving to Grandmother's place."

Mama buried her face in her napkin. Korbach's eyes met those of Izhmailov. The latter silently waved him off: Away with you! Go!

Having thus decoded such formal points of the proffered Korbach CV, we are obliged to point out other, perhaps not so important yet still essential, features of the terrain.

For example, under the heading "Education," we could write simply "college," but we could be more precise and mention not just one institution but a whole list: the philology department of Moscow State University, the Shchukin Theater Institute, the directorial department of the state film school, screenwriting courses. This list, however, would not get us anywhere except into confusion, since our hero didn't get a degree from a single one of these institutions.

They were ready to give him the boot from MSU after the very first semester for "revisionist views"; they did it after the second, however, and for a different reason: "expelled for unsatisfactory attendance." He threw himself into the theater school headlong, like a diver from a high tower sending up a spray, in laughter that was born again as "clowning," and he quickly clowned his way to the explanation "expelled for ruining the class play."

The saddest and also perhaps most dangerous period of Sasha's education turned out to be the film school. Fascinated by the possibilities of the "hidden camera," he made a documentary about summer military training camps. What he had meant as gentle humor led to the fury of the colonels on the military faculty. The film was confiscated, disappearing into the bottomless belly of the KGB. The liberal dean advised the young man to go away somewhere for a year. Society might not forgive him his violation of the "holy of holies," the patriotic duty of youth. To make a long story short, our hero was tossed out of the state film school without a degree and managed to get a place in the screenwriting course with the help of some hard-drinking friends only so that he wouldn't be hauled off to an army barracks and shaved bald like all the other recruits, or slapped with a parasitism charge or sent beyond the 101-kilometer limit.

To hell with them, with these Soviet schools, Sasha thought then. A real education nowadays comes not from the official system but in the catacombs: from forbidden and forgotten books, from Western intellectual journals, from underground art exhibits, and, most important, from associating with the still living stars of the Silver Age.

When he had thought the idea through, he headed for Leningrad and managed to beg an invitation to Akhmatova's flat, and to read her not less than a yard or so of his verses. "Now, this bit wasn't bad," the empress of the Silver Age said graciously, and out of the whole lot repeated one line that he wasn't especially proud of, and that he had tried to mumble in reading: "The bumblebee of boldness bundled a bunk." "Like in Khlebnikov," she added with a smile.

A friend from the days of his unfinished studies in the philology department introduced him to two eminent old men who lived in the writers' co-op at the Aeroport Metro station, Mikhail Bakhtin and Leonid Pinsky. The old men, not exactly spoiled with attention by the young generation, received the youth with curiosity and undisguised pleasure. Sasha's reverence before these giants of erudition never let up. He even tried to adopt the manners of the old intelligentsia from them, not always guessing that a deep impression had been left on these manners by exile and the camps—the men's ferocious licking of their spoons, for example.

More important was the way they lit in him a fire of interest in the Renaissance, and he realized that the word was often misused by Russians to mean the rebirth of something that had already been born once and had for some reason withered away into obscurity for five hundred years, or a thousand. Seen from that angle, to speak of the "renaissance" of Russian philosophy at the beginning of the twentieth century might be taken to mean that Russia had once created an Aristotle and a Plato. In speaking of a renaissance, one obviously had a general creative upsurge of a nation, a group, or an entire civilization in mind.

The stunned young man listened as the old-timers, who were forever lighting each other's cigarettes, talked quite naturally about the literary scene of thirteenth-century Florence, about the *dolce stil nuovo* (the new sweet style) that came from the two Guidos, Guinizelli and Cavalcanti, and about how the young Dante made a powerful entrance into this school. Three centuries before Shakespeare! Six centuries before Pushkin! Seven centuries before Sasha Korbach! And does that mean that before this "new" style there had already been an "old" one? Well, of course: the eleventh century, the troubadours of Provence! The style came to be called "new" because its proponents were desperately keen to revive the "old" one, all those outpourings, those chansons of Bertrand de Borgue, Raimbaut de Vaquieras, and other wandering courtiers girded with swords.

The human carnival procession with all its masks of laughter and horror passed before Sasha, led by Mikhail and Leonid, the "wise men and poets" of the *Opoyaz* who only toward the end of their lives, after arrest and the camps, had succeeded in carrying away their "extinguished lights" to their cooperative apartments. These were the people of the second Russian Renaissance. With the approach of the twentieth century, there burst forth in the country a mighty current of creativity, which two incarnations of "positivist thinking" named Lenin and Stalin dammed up.

Now there's a worthy goal in life, Sasha, yesterday's guitar player and the idol of Soviet young people, decided—to work toward a third Renaissance! And so, relegating his guitar to his grandmother's closet, the twenty-six-year-old Korbach, with his unfinished studies in the philology department of MSU and the Shchukin Theater Institute, walled himself off from the life of young people with philosophical tracts and volumes of the classics. He began visiting his mother again after a long interval—she was working in the manuscripts department of the Lenin Library and had access to the special archives.

His living space in those years extended like a cocoon behind the massive bookshelves of Irina Stepanovna Korbach, *née* Kropotkin—yes, yes, one of *those* Kropotkins—and the old lady never stopped delighting in the intellectual evolution of—as she put it—"not the worst representative of this unexpected generation."

Sasha earned a living by working shifts in the boiler room and didn't even shrink from reselling books that were in short supply. He decked himself out in a black pea jacket, which, naturally, had its own story, presented here in condensed form.

Western Estonia, Keila-loa. The restricted zone. Telegraphic prose in full flower. The abandoned Volkonsky-Benkendorf estate. Headquarters of a tank brigade. In the park, the remains of bridges on the remains of chains. The remains of idylls. A waterfall. Headstones tossed up by Caterpillar tracks. The tank drivers were looking for gold.

Going down to the sea. The droning rustle of the pines. Radio Free Wind. Greenish, foamy rolling water. In the shallow water a black pea jacket, like a man's upper half. Verbs and adverbs join in. Grabbed hold of it. I drag it. Heavy. Got tired. Turned it over. Fantastic. Flash of a double-breasted, not one of ours, from Stockholm!

The pea jacket, as heavy as a sea lion, was stuffed with gravelly sand. The young Sasha scooped the sand out of the sleeves and pockets. Brought to Moscow, this article was another three months drying out and finally came to life, lay on the shoulders like a densely woven soft second skin. A pea jacket of Swedish cut— there's not another one like it on the Arbat. It was this strange garment made for huge Swedish shoulders that he took a liking to knocking about the city in, all the more since there was room for piles of books in the seemingly bottomless pockets.

In this CV that we have concocted there is still another extremely confusing section—to be precise, "work history." At this point began all sorts of zigzags, spirals, sudden jerks, and, most important of all, A. Korbach's principal "credit": work as both an actor and an artistic director in a Moscow theater. This period would appear to be a fact known to everyone—but don't try to find the theater on the rolls of Muscovite temples of culture. Don't try to find the titles of Korbach's once much-talked-about and even scandalous productions in newspapers or dissertations—they're not there. All that's left is to rely on the conversations of the people of Moscow, and on private reminiscences, which is what we are intending to do.

Before we do that, allow me to go back to something that accidentally slipped from my pen about fifty lines ago or so, to Sasha's coast-to-coast fame as a singer and recording artist. For all its curious aspects, it, too, comes under the heading of "work history."

He first appeared in public with his guitar at a Komsomol song competition and immediately went against the grain of the "romantic spirit of faraway roads" and stood out sharply as an independent "bard," a rooster crowing in the dawn of the sixties. Sasha Korbach's song "Purgatory" was recorded in all eleven time zones, even on the oldest and creakiest tape players. Everywhere, the heads of girls were spinning from the romantic blues tune "Figure Skating."

Sasha Korbach's concerts were never officially sanctioned. Still, they took place, and often in the most unexpected locations: at a tourist camp in Balkaria, in the "political enlightenment" room of an electric lamp factory, in a miners' pub, in the dormitory of a vocational school for training salespeople, and then all of a sudden in the stylish Beethoven Hall of the Bolshoi Theater, on a set at the Moscow film studios, and after that on a sardine trawler in the Sakhalin port of Kholmsk, immediately followed by something in the West, at the Lvov Polytechnic Institute, for example, and in a cinema fan club in Riga. And everywhere he went, a whiff of denunciations followed him: he dropped political hints, dressed defiantly, seduced innocent girls. "We appeal to the authorities to take expedient and appropriate measures . . ."

Now he comes out, just a stripling, skinny but with an athletic spread to his shoulders, tosses his Beatles bangs back from his forehead—that style still existed back then, so how did he lose it, why did it disappear so quickly?—thumps the strings, strikes up the tune in a hoarse voice, and: delight, goose bumps, and let's get out of here, out of this muck, farther toward the sea, higher up into the mountains!

And then, suddenly, the darling of the public disappeared. It was rumored that he had defected to the West, that some *urkas* (convicts) in Yakutia had cut his throat, that he was hiding from seven women, and so on. It would scarcely have occurred to anyone that he might be at his grandmother's place on Starokonyushenny, sitting around on a sagging couch reading books and writing poems, and yet, as we already know, that's what was going on.

One day the current of human events rose around him again. At the time he was keeping company with some young men who were involved in the human rights campaign. We need to convince people that the state is violating its own laws. Without human rights, no renaissance is possible, my dear guitarist.

It was 1967, and they began gathering material for the White Book of the Ginzburg-Galanskov trial, organizing vigils around the courthouses in which the state was violating its own laws. One day a "fighting Komsomol cell" picked them up and took them down to the police station for questioning. The *druzhinniki* (volunteer police) all gathered around when they found out that among the "anti-Sovs" was Sasha Korbach. What's all this, Sasha? We sing your songs, and here you are with this human trash? What, do you feel closer to Jews than to the youthful masses of the people's and workers' scientific and technical revolution? All right, get lost, you're free, we'll sort out the rest of them.

He refused to leave, but some good citizens immediately made "the necessary calls," as a result of which there appeared in the police precinct the person most hateful to him on earth, his stepfather, Nikolai Ivanovich Izhmailov, a member of the upper ranks of the nomenklatura.

In theory, the hateful man could have put a stop to all this nonsense of the arrest of a bunch of layabouts. Over the years of alternating "thaws" and "frosts," Nikolai Ivanovich had turned into one of the most "balanced" functionaries in the Central Committee. It was no secret that there were stronger advocates of the "tightening of the screws" in Izhmailov's department. However, after meeting with utter rejection of his goodwill by his already grown stepson, this important state personage backed away and let matters run their natural course. This course led all of those detained into court, where they were given fifteen days each, and then to the Butyrka Prison to serve their time.

Sitting in a huge, stinking cell, Alexander suddenly felt the colossal boredom of this human rights work. Woe is me if my fate consists of idiotic judges and dreary sentences. Somehow I don't see myself in such a setting.

He hummed some melody to himself, mumbled out some rhymes. The result was "The Ballad of Butyrka Jail," a takeoff on Wilde's poem. In this way he hummed and muttered up his next twist of fate. Had she not been waiting close at hand to this pathetic example of a jailbird, he might have skipped right over Anisia Pupushchina. As it was, he didn't skip over her: the girl came toward him, radiant with all of her gifts like the antidote to jail personified. The girl's father, an old friend of the Izhmailovs, had recently fallen into bureaucratic disgrace and been sent to the "fiery continent" (Latin America) as an ambassador. Well, Anisia became her own boss in a big flat on Alexei Tolstoy Street. What, you never go there, Singer? He dropped by and saw as his future wife's guests a gathering of young Moscow bohemians, several—Tarkovsky, Vysotsky, and Konchalovsky—standing out in the crowd.

They were drinking heavily and speaking weightily, but unfortunately all at once, everything flowing together in a muddle of sound, so you couldn't tell right away that they were having, say, an existential debate about whether it was better to die like Socrates or hold out like Aristotle. Along the way there was some chatter about the Cannes festival, someone had some harsh words for Goskino Assistant Chairman Baskakov, while someone else said that he was "a man with guts all the same." They agreed to meet up in Yalta in the winter and got themselves into quite a lather, as though it were there, in Yalta in the winter, that everything would be decided.

He had known them all for a long time, and they all knew him. Come on, guys, let's belt it out, like we did back then: "Where are my seventeen years on Bolshaya Karetnaya!" Andrei said to him: "I remember when you were rehearsing *Galileo* at school. That was some interesting production you worked up, pal. Tell you what—come along tomorrow to Set Number Six, we'll give you a screen test."

No matter how Sasha Korbach tried to run from his popularity, it started to come back to him again. Just like that, out of the blue, within a couple of years he became a famous film actor and then made a huge hit with a detective miniseries on TV. He even got contracts to play a few roles on the stage. In addition to everything else, he turned out to have great agility. At the Taganka Theater, Sasha gave excellent demonstrations of a new version of Meyerhold's "biomechanics." Playing the part of Kerensky, Russia's last pre-Bolshevik leader, in the stage version of

Ten Days That Shook the World, he would do a series of pirouettes and tumbles with a closing reverse somersault. One could say that this small role grew into an event. The critics of the journal *Yunost* said cautiously that Korbach was bidding to become the embodiment of the modern young hero (and that in the role of Kerensky!). Somewhat more serious types, even some who were close to dissident circles, wrote that there was "something to say" for this actor, meaning that he was pouring out no small amount of bitterness on the man he was playing for not having managed to defend fledgling Russian democracy.

At the beginning of the seventies, that "decade of iron and concrete," the era of endless celebratory gatherings with banners and satanic chorales, the days of the stifling of the human rights movement and the flourishing of the hypnotic spectacle of figure skating on television, Sasha Korbach again surprised everyone: he founded a theater troupe called the Buffoons. He was director, principal actor, and author of the first play, *Spartak-Dynamo.* The show, in the style of a burlesque, turned out to be a highly ambiguous retelling of *Romeo and Juliet,* in which the Montagues were a street gang of Spartak fans, while the Capulets supported Dynamo; in other words, it made it seem as though the natural elements of Moscow, dockworkers and market sellers, were opposing the "policemen's club."

The show, of course, was closed immediately after its premiere. The unauthorized Buffoons, however, continued performing their musical in the Moscow equivalent of off-off-Broadway—in clubs where, of course, "everyone who was anyone" gathered. Then a miracle took place: a certain pillar of Western culture, who all his life had been oscillating between various shades at the red end of the color spectrum, from pale pink to deep crimson, came to Moscow. At that moment he was moving in quite pale, if not entirely White—i.e., counterrevolutionary— circles. The internationalists of the Central Committee decided to ask the Buffoons to stage a performance of Russia's unofficial art. The "pillar" was delighted: theater troupes like this one, comrades, would give the lie to tons of bourgeois propaganda!

All of a sudden, the Buffoons received quasi-official status. They were even given a cellar venue with a hundred seats—and a director from the Party, along with a well-stacked woman censor; in other words, they brought Korbach's black sheep into the normal Soviet fold. *Spartak-Dynamo* got several positive reviews under the subtitle "Antibourgeois Satire." The progressive elements at the Moscow film studios offered to make a feature-length production of the show, and in general the whole affair worked out in a way that was incredible for the times. The talk around town was of "Korbach's cinema." There were predictions of a Palme d'Or and a Lion d'Or. There, however, everything ended: the authorities would not let him go abroad. Receiving the lowest Goskino rating, the film's distribution stagnated just like all the rest of the Russian backwater.

Thus began the story of Korbach's Buffoons studio, the ups and downs of which could be plotted like the temperature of a malaria patient: a feverish rise— articles, trips to the Edinburgh and Avignon festivals, film versions of shows— followed by an arctic chill—silence from the authorities, cancellation of premieres and tours, closing of the theater for "major repairs," even freezing of their assets.

Nevertheless, something was always worked out. Gudok, the director, turned out to be amenable to good conversation over a frequently replaced bottle. All the male members of the troupe screwed the censor, a pretty girl from the Komsomol, and she turned from an informer into one of the fiercest partisans of the Buffoons, prepared to do literally anything for the home side. Several Marxists, reputed to be liberals even though they wrote speeches for Brezhnev, were put on the theater's advisory board, along with a couple of pillars of Slavophile art, to whom they proved that the Buffoons were not at all the product of decaying Western culture but rather pure inheritors of the time-honored tradition of Russian *skomorokhi*.

Finally, that principal bulwark of progressive Soviet art, world public opinion, with its shock troops, the foreign press corps in Moscow, wasn't forgotten either. Not a single show was put on without the presence of overseas guests, who considered it an honor to make the acquaintance of the "buffoon in chief," the one-of-a-kind Alexander Korbach, who, with his sharply sloping forehead and disheveled locks falling over his temples, his "satyric" (from the word *satyr,* that is) eyes, and his simian smile, looked a symbol of the avant-garde being reborn. American visitors from Broadway shook his powerful, guitar-callused hand. "Oh, Alexander Korbach! That's a big name in the States!" Foreigners in the midst of the atrophying conditions of "mature Socialism" were stunned to suddenly find themselves in the company of these lively and cheerful fellows, modern-day *cabotins* embodying Meyerhold's idea of theater as farce.

There were twenty-five actors in the troupe, and every one of them knew the overall secret strategy. The show was rehearsed in private. Then they would give a look-see to "the moms and the dads," and right away rumors about wild indignation in the upper echelons of the authorities, and about possible draconian measures, going almost as far as the disbanding of the troupe, would get started. The lazybones at the Ministry of Culture don't even have time to scratch themselves before they're getting calls from *Le Monde, Le Figaro, La Stampa,* the *Post,* the *Times, Frankfurter Allgemeine Zeitung. . . .* Could the ministry confirm rumors of the ban on the Buffoons' new show? Telephones of the cultural bureaucracy began ringing all over town. The heavy artillery of the "liberals" in the apparatus was brought forward, along with all sorts of big names, pillars of patriotism, daughters of Central Committee members—even Kleofont Stepanovich Sitny, Moscow gourmet and general in the secret service, moved himself into position, lured out by the female contingent. This pre–opening night artillery barrage reached peak intensity when radio announcers began their coverage of the latest crisis in the Moscow theater world by broadcasting reverse translations of Russian correspondents' reports. One got the impression that the whole world was watching with bated breath as the mind-boggling events unfolded. The weary regime began to yield under the massed pressures. All right, all right, take your Korbach, take your Buffoons, it's not exactly likely to make our power crumble. Go on, put on your— what is it again? *Zangezi Rock* or something? Just take out the anarchism, add a bit of patriotism . . . Oh, and change the name, too.

So, by the midseventies, the Buffoons' repertoire had been formed. It contained no fewer than half a dozen shows: *Spartak-Dynamo,* adapted from Shakespeare; *Mineral Waters,* adapted from Lermontov; *A–Z,* adapted from the phone book; *The Grandmother of the Russian Roulette Wheel,* adapted from Pushkin and Dostoevsky; the above mentioned *Zangezi Rock,* under its new ultra-Russian title, *Budetlyanin,* meaning "future seeker"; and an original play by one of the pillars of native soil culture with the title *Oats.* The last work, in which the author had difficulty recognizing his text, all the more so since the actors playing collective farmworkers were forever improvising in French, was considered to be more or less the ideological centerpiece of the Buffoons and an indicator of the depths of the group's national feeling.

By the end of the decade, though, this seemingly established stability had become a little shaky. First, the pillars of patriotism left the creative council, at which point the author of *Oats* took his name off the play. "With my hand on my heart," he wrote, "I have never much cared for your hinting at a spiritual and intellectual waning among our people, who are so alien to your essence." (It is interesting to point out here that the letter did not contain a single word with a Latin root.)

Then the secret liberals from the Central Committee and Party Institute of Philosophy stopped coming to the council's meetings as well. At that point even Kleofont Stepanovich Sitny struck a weighty, serious tone: man does not live by pâté and female companionship alone in our stern times. It looked as though somewhere at the very top, possibly at the level of Andropov himself, the decision had been made to have done with the Buffoons once and for all.

One day Comrade Gudok, the director in chief, called the artistic director into his office and announced that the ministry had formed a commission to investigate the situation that had arisen in the Buffoons theatrical troupe: "Among other things—you'll forgive me, Alexander—they'll be looking at excessively free morals in the sexual domain. There have also been reports of certain chemical substances."

Korbach looked at Gudok's brow, furrowed to make it clear that he was distancing himself, and realized that the theater was finished. Now they're probably even going to notice the picture of Marx in the director's office. On his birthday the actors, who had chipped in a ruble apiece, had bought him a portrait of the founding father. Over a year, neither Gudok nor any of his visitors had noticed that Marx's chest was decorated with the Order of Lenin.

"This commission, Yeremei Antonovich," the artistic director said, surprising even himself, "will be able to work only inside your office. We won't allow them onto the rest of the premises."

The air raid began, and the answering antiaircraft fire. There came a letter on embossed letterhead forbidding rehearsals of the play *The Sky in Diamonds* (an adaptation from Chekhov and Beckett). In reply, the Buffoons decided in a general meeting to continue working. Suddenly the electricity was cut off, and "emergency repairs" paralyzed the telephone switchboard. They carried on rehearsing by candlelight. The fire inspector fined them a backbreaking sum, but the electricity came back on. Just before the dress rehearsal, the side streets leading to the theater were jammed with foreign cars of correspondents and diplomats. The stars of cultural bohemia and of the bureaucracy jammed the aisles. It was a smashing success. At the press conference, which took place at 3:30 in the morning, the reporters gave Korbach and his troupe a round of applause. Three days later, Minister Demichev called the director. "It has reached my ears that the studio is putting on an interesting show. I think we ought to get acquainted. Come on now, comrades, let's not kick up a fuss—let's try to create a constructive atmosphere."

Diamonds was permitted in the end, but the term *constructive atmosphere* was obviously understood differently by each side. The Buffoons were more or less firmly established as a creative entity in the capital scene. It was only their founder, the wily Sasha Korbach, who was in doubt. The KGB rumor mill went to work. Every day he learned some bit of news about himself: he and his wife were divorcing because he'd been exposed as a homosexual; he put hard currency from foreigners in his own pocket, slapped actors around at rehearsals, snorted cocaine, was anti-Soviet and played into the hands of Western propaganda, had no talent, stole others' ideas, and, most important of all, he was unpatriotic, a Jew, earning credits for himself in the Russian theater to pave his way to Israel.

A brick came through a window on the tenth floor with a note attached saying, "The sooner, the better." At the Kuznetsky Bridge two gays invited him into their car with gestures of their hands and lips. On Pushkin Square, an expensively dressed Middle Eastern type asked him to change a "grand," a thousand-dollar bill. Once they brought a bag filled with banned books to his door, supposedly a parcel from a certain Karpovich in Virginia. At least three times a day someone phoned him and asked with a heavy Jewish accent when he was leaving. Invitations from relatives in Tel Aviv, Jerusalem, Haifa, and Kiriat Shmona arrived daily in the post. Three bespectacled types set about unscrewing the wheel nuts on Korbach's car right outside his window. He came racing out with an air pistol, but they were already driving away in a black Volga sedan with a flashing light, laughing and calling out, "Say hello to Uncle Benya!"

The timing for all this could not have been worse, since the forty-year-old Korbach had just parted, painfully, with his family. Anisia tried to turn their children, ten-year-old twins named Lyova and Styopa, against him. She shadowed his short-term girlfriends, called them, told them vile stories. She demanded more and more money. They were constantly dividing up property: the stereo system, their library, half a dozen paintings, all his pathetic accumulated savings. Then, all at once, they would have a flash of reconciliation, if it's possible to say that about an attack of sexual romanticism. She would come to the theater, still a beautiful young woman "who could turn it on," as the Muscovites respectfully put it. The household would be put right again for a few days before collapsing with an even greater crash and even more of a stink.

The harassment by the authorities also interfered with a matter even more important than all the nonsense at home, that of the approach of the "fundamental" production of his career. Plans loomed before his eyes and gleamed like the kitschy palace that appeared to Gogol as the second part of *Dead Souls.* For several years Sasha had been "muttering out" dialogue and sketching with a finger in the air the staging for a grandiose version of the life of Dante.

It had begun in the midseventies, when he had been added at the last minute to

the Soviet delegation to a meeting of the theatrical section o
Florence. The idea was the same as always: We'll send Korbacl
see that their views on Soviet art are pri-mi-tive! And he him·
able state of excitement, didn't have any understanding of wh
main thing was: "I'm going!" The main thing was: "It's on ⌐
hill! What's important is that I'll see those Peter Brooks and Peter Steins а...
the rest! What matters is to tell them about the Buffoons!"

The first person he met at the hotel turned out to be an old friend, the chubby, walrus-mustached Slavist Gianni Buttofava, who spoke Russian with a Leningrad accent, in the Brodsky to Naiman manner. "If you've never been in Tuscany—you haven't, have you?—then you don't know what eating is," he said. "Come on, I'll teach you to feed the Tuscan way!" When they had eaten and drunk their fill in a little cellar restaurant on Ghibelline Street, they went to look for the nightlife. The moonlight was splashing thickly on the walls, playing up the masonwork of the hewn stones. In a niche beneath a picture of the Madonna, a tiny *fiammetta* wavered in a little glass. "Just imagine that everything here looked exactly the same seven hundred years ago," Gianni said. "With some small additions, yes, around you is the Florence of Dante." Alexander gasped with excitement. All the neon lights and road signs disappeared, even the Baroque period wavered, giving way to the Trecento's Florentine Gothic.

They walked along the wall of the Borello Castle, with its iron rings for hitching posts—which judging from the crosslike form in which they were hung must have been used for chaining up criminals—and its huge gates of blackened wood and high latticed windows, on the other side of which extended vaulted, echoing halls. Across the street rose the walls of the Badia Church, some of whose stones were laid in the same way as in the castle, while some of them were covered with yellow stucco. They crossed the street and craned their necks to see the crenellated summit of Borello. The severity of the architecture seemed to have anticipated Dante and Giotto. Cars rustled by like ghosts breaking through from another dimension.

When they had gone around the old town, they passed beneath a gloomy archway and came out in a narrow lane covered by stone slabs of different sizes and mismatched colors, polished to a gleam. "You see how exactly they fit these stones against each other," Gianni said. "You mean that all of this has been here since then?" Alexander asked, dumbfounded. "Well, of course! Seven hundred years isn't such a long time for these stones. And it was in this church here that Beatrice Portinari was crowned." Gianni pointed to a small building with the same pattern of stonework, a round window, and a tiled canopy over the entrance. The doors were open, and they went in. Candles wavered in the crepuscular light by the altar. Several worshipers were kneeling on wooden kneelers, their elbows resting on the railing. "They married her off here, yes, to Simone de' Bardi, yes," Gianni went on, playing the role of tour guide. "And Dante may have stood in the crowd of curious onlookers, feeling something indescribable—even for his pen, I mean."

The lanes around the church seemed not to have been touched by the High Renaissance: stern walls and towers, simple right-angle peaks. One of these houses is in fact, as everyone here supposes, yes, none other than Casa Dante—that is, the family redoubt of his line. From the facade hung the Alighieri flag, with its coat of arms in the form of a shield divided into fields of black and green by a white band down the middle. "Listen, Gianni, how did the idea of writing about a world beyond the grave come to him?" "You know, Sasha, I think that he was simply there, and then tried to express in words the inexpressible." Gianni produced a bottle of Chianti from his bag. "We ought to drink right here, okay?" . . . They emptied the bottle in several swallows and left it beneath the flag.

Over the remaining few days Alexander wandered around Florence by himself. He made an effort not to notice anything later than Trecento. The fountains, for example. They didn't make such sumptuous feasts of marble and bronze in those days. Instead, there were round wells of polished stone, each topped with an arc from which a bucket was suspended. Sometimes, this arc would be supported by two Doric columns as a cautionary reminder of antique culture. He would stand before such a well on a tiny square closed in by a wall topped with right-angle crenellations. Even swallowtails had not yet come into fashion at the time. Let's try to imagine the quiet of such a night seven hundred years ago. In the silence resound the footsteps of several poets come for a drink of water. Cavalcanti, da Pistoia, Dante. What strange clothes: legs covered with threaded breeches, each of them wearing on his head a sort of cap with earflaps. Dante turns and stands in profile, as in the only the portrait of him, the work of Giotto. What sternness, what sharp angles! Theoretically, after all, he was not only a poet of the early Renaissance but a knight of that age as well. If the times demanded it, he would don armor and strap on a sword.

> *When I see how float*
> *the banners, striking the eye amidst the foliage*
> *And hear the neighing from the stables*
> *And the sound of the viols when sing*
> *The jugglers entering their tents*
> *The trump and horn call me*
> *To sing. . . .*

"Listen, friend," the leader of the delegation said sotto voce to Alexander one morning after breakfast. "I'm hearing reports about these strange nighttime absences of yours. You're writing poetry? All right, that's what we'll write: 'The poet is composing verses.' He's fallen under Dante's spell. Looking for his own Beatrice, right? And what was all that nonsense you were talking at the roundtable discussion last night? They reported back to me that it was some sort of full-blown mysticism, anarchism, modernism, obscurantism, who knows what. Don't you realize who is in this delegation with us? Don't play the hothead, or you'll have to stop at every light." Alexander, squirming as he listened to this rubbish, looked silently at the leader. The leader, "not a bad guy on the whole," looked at him. Then he shrugged his shoulders and turned away.

On the last day of the conference, they were all taken on an outing to San Gimignano, the very city to which Dante had been sent in 1295 as an envoy to reconcile the feuding clans and guarantee a strong ally for the Republic. They got there by bus in an hour, while he must have ridden for an entire day. It was an unforgettable moment—a turn in the road, and there, on the peak of a distant hill, the high, narrow watchtowers of the clans appeared above the city walls.

In the plane on the journey home, Alexander, his eyes closed, tried to turn over in his mind the patchwork blankets of the Tuscan valleys, the sky blue hills, the cities on the hills, the terra-cotta of the rooftops, and the gray stones of the walls. There won't be a green light to go abroad anymore, must carefully re-create these scenes so as not to forget them when I'm mounting a production, and later maybe even a film.

We won't dare to try to follow Dante and Virgil, Korbach had thought all those years. We'll stay on the surface, in Tuscany. The main subject of the play, and later maybe even of the film, will be his love for Beatrice. Things were not as clear-cut as they seemed, though. He had met her beside the Ponte Vecchio when she was twenty and he was twenty-five. He wasn't the innocent, dreamy youth described by the poet Nikolai Gumilyov: "Pensive, like a girl." He was already married, and a father. Marriages were not made in heaven then, being more often than not the outcomes of complicated political maneuvering between the clans. His father having died when he was quite young, he'd had to become the man of the Alighieri house. It could not be said, though, that his marriage was an unhappy one. He clearly loved his Gemma, loved to sleep with her, and probably knew her body just as well as Alexander Korbach knew that of his scandalous Anisia.

The appearance of Beatrice shook him like a surging memory from somewhere outside life, of love without lust, and of that nonexistent world where a man can love a woman without doing any violence to her. At this point it would be difficult not to establish a link with the Petersburg of the Silver Age and the poet who wrote "Verses About the Lady Beautiful." Like all the Russian Symbolists, Alexander Blok tried to read the sunsets and in his youth murmured after the manner of Vladimir Solovyov:

> *It is not the triple-crowned Isis*
> *Who will bring us the spring,*
> *But the radiant, eternal*
> *Maiden of the Rainbow Gates.*

A love from somewhere in the beyond, one that filled the entire being of the poet with unheard-of joy, the inexpressible happiness of life that is not life, which seemed to him a concept incompatible with the fever of the flesh. This love appeared in sunsets like reflections of gleams and flashes akin to those described in the third book of *La Divina Commedia,* like a reflection of what we might call "The Radiance of Beatrice."

Of course, all of this is at odds with the aesthetic of the Buffoons, but he was already well fed up with this aesthetic, quite independent of the criticisms from the Party. Of course we'll dance around the irreconcilability of the Guelph and Ghibelline political factions and other images of *The Inferno,* in which the greatly respected audience will recognize something, but the main theme will be love, the essence of earthly love and the nonessence of divine love. He thought along these lines for several years and, when he was alone, would compose the dialogues half-aloud and draw staging directions with one finger in the cigarette smoke.

Now everything was coming to an end, and he would have to say good-bye to these dreams. He never said a word about "The Radiance of Beatrice," not even at the troupe's meetings. A (anonymous) note dropped in his letterbox said that his entire "team" was riddled with informers. I've ripped out all this anonymous trash, tossed it to the wind, but trash still does its work, I don't even dare talk about Dante at meetings with my friends, when there's no one closer to me on earth than they. Instead, I'm giving them a play by the Communist yes-man Marquiset Guera Filatelista from the—how is it again? the "fiery continent" to read. Even though it's a repulsive compromise, it's still not as repulsive as it could have been: Filatelista may be scum, but he's not entirely without talent.

One day, however, in early 1982, Kleofont Stepanovich Sitny called. "Listen, Sasha, let's have a chat about business, okay?" The meeting took place in the small room of the National Restaurant. The flat features of the civilian general beamed goodness, comfort, an excellent appetite. "Sasha, you know you have talent, and those blathering assholes from Radio Liberty go on about you every day. The word here is that your nerves aren't exactly in great shape. Are they? Well, that means that our comrades are overdoing things a bit. I was just thinking that maybe it's not a good thing for an artist like you to be the talk of the town—there's no reason for you to shame yourself with the likes of Filatelista, you're not exactly the smallest fish in our cultural pond, after all. There are people who worry about you, who think about your artistic plans. 'The Radiance of Beatrice'—do you want to elaborate? Fine, let's get down to brass tacks. Some of these good people are thinking, Why doesn't Korbach look after his nerves, have a change of scenery for a while? There, there, don't turn your back, no one's pushing you to go to Israel. We're only talking a simple trip to civilized Europe here. Get a bit of fresh air, get in touch with the old values. Have you tried these mushrooms here, the ones *à la russe?* Fuck 'em, you say? Well, that's not the Russian way. . . . In a word, there's a choice. If you want an invitation, just ask your friends in the West for one—it doesn't have to be from a specialist, it can be just from people in artistic circles, you don't need me to give you a lesson. And I'm not hinting at anything either, I was only talking—what I had in mind was journalists, and not at all the ones that you were thinking about. Or there's a second possibility, an official trip, under the auspices of the All-Union Theatrical Society. That probably wouldn't suit you, would it, Sasha? Well, in the sense that then you'd be breaking ranks with the dissidents, so to speak. No, this is no provocation, Sasha, it's just thinking out loud—we've knocked back quite a bit of vodka together, haven't we?"

Another month went by after this meal in the Gilyarovsky manner. Everything remained the same: people openly tailing him, rumors about a decision to take extreme measures against the anti-Sov Korbach, statements to the Western press as the sole means of defense. Even his friends no longer had any doubts: go abroad, Sasha, they're just going to wear you down here.

He began to have attacks of inexplicable panic—right now, it seems, you're going to go over that fence—not over the one everyone has in mind but rather over one no one seems to have thought of. He began to go on benders, and one day, all of a sudden, he spotted his old guitar hanging on the wall. A curious thought came into his drunken head: Here's what'll save me! He tuned it up, banged the strings with his whole hand, and began singing again, like a hoarse rooster, so that even Volodya Vysotsky, his unforgettable friend, would have been proud of him if he had still been alive.

There suddenly appeared on the underground rock scene a new group with an old name—the Buffoons: Natalie the Battery, Elozin the Bronze Wizard, nutty Shurik, Lidka the Rattler, Tiger Cub, Port of Odessa, Boozy Mark, and, finally, the lead vocalist, our old idol Sashka Korbach, who hadn't gone anywhere, on the contrary, he's back with us, sticking his thumb right in the Commies' collectivist ass.

The authorities were beside themselves. The splashing of vocals and rhythm came to a sad end. A fire broke out in the club during a concert. In the panic, people broke God only knows how many bones, and a girl in the ninth grade was supposedly trampled. An investigation was launched, and they made Korbach sign a paper saying he wouldn't leave the country. After that he called up Sitny: You win, take care of the formalities for leaving. The investigation was immediately called off. The visa office sorted out his passport in record time. The All-Union Theatrical Society put in for an official trip for the director Korbach to France, "for artistic purposes."

Everyone around him looked at him as though he were a dead man. Women with whom he had "had a thing" wiped damp eyes: Remember him, remember him! One of them, the most recent one, whispered to him: "Fare thee well, and if forever, then forever fare thee well!" He got angry. He was fed up with everything, and now Byron in Russian translation. He still wrestled with panic attacks in public; his nights turned into a long series of deaths. In May he found himself in Paris.

Now he's coming out of the Charles de Gaulle Airport. A traveler. A celebrity. A tennis racket is sticking out of his bag. The lights of television cameras come on. Some people are waving to him like they know him. Sasha, do you recognize me? You jump back in spite of yourself: Lenka Cooperstock, the defector! *Monsieur Korbach, que voulez-vous dire au public de la France?* A young, roly-poly fellow—that is, a roly-poly youngster—quickly translates into Russian. "Comrade Korbach, we're from the embassy. Be careful, there are agents from Radio Liberty here. Look at their disgusting jackal eyes." They take him to the Crillon, where for three days he's the guest of Antenne-2. Encouraging glances from Western "specialists." It's nothing, it's nothing, he'll soon be himself again, right now he's just got culture shock. Yes, sure, he'll be fine, he says to himself, thinking of himself in the third person. You could cure him with a flatiron over the head. The umbrellas of Cherbourg or Bulgarian umbrellas—what difference does it make?

And, in fact, culture shock did soon begin giving way to realism with his morning coffee and well-baked croissants. Make an attempt on my life? Not likely. The intelligence services don't give a damn about some theatrical type. The Sovs—he soon learned this word from the émigrés—didn't give a damn either about his long-winded pronouncements on "the incompatibility of carnival theater and barracks mentality." They'd chucked him out of the country, made a check mark by his name, filed a report, and that was it. No reason to turn a squabble with a small theater into a worldwide sensation. In any case, the Parisian theatergoers don't see any tragedy in it.

He received invitations from the Odéon, the Chaillot, and the Comédie Française, and from small troupes performing in disused warehouses and bathhouses as well. The audience would applaud him before the show: bravo, Monsieur Korba! It was his old friend Antoine Vitez, who was probably the only Parisian director fluent in Russian, that he told of his idea for "The Radiance of Beatrice." A big idea, Antoine said, and with energy in his thin fingers began drawing something in the air. I'm not the only one who scribbles like that, Korbach thought, smiling. We'll think about it, Antoine said, and in the meantime—his face lit up suddenly—"why don't you put on two plays with me right away? One Russian, *The Seagull,* and the other Irish, *The Heron*—a modern reworking of Chekhov? Both plays could be staged with the same sets and the same cast. A two-night show, understand? After all, the Russians, when you get right down to it, are just as much drunkards as the Irish."

He was well-paid for his interviews with French, British, German, Danish, Swedish, Italian, and Japanese newspapers, and could take his time now to think over Vitez' proposition. On the whole, things weren't going at all badly, until, all at once, a new Soviet attack. First, the *Literaturnaya Gazyeta* correspondent Pyotr Bolshevikov—a notorious KGB type but well-known in the role of high-living playboy—approached him. "Listen, buddy, it looks like they're getting ready to strip you of Soviet citizenship. Somewhere they've prepared a selection of your statements for the Politburo. The patriarchs flew into a rage, especially Andropov. Over there, you see, concepts like the class struggle are alive and well. It's in this framework that, word has it, they want to have done with you."

Korbach drew his simian mouth up tightly, trying not to give anything away to the agent's piercing stare. The dreaded expression, however, had already got under his skin, and the artery beneath his collarbone was pounding. He wanted to shout out hysterically: Have done with? And what right do you have, you red swine, to condemn a man to death, even if he's a monkey? Still, he didn't cry out, didn't even twitch—but why had Bolshevikov gone away looking so satisfied?

The day after this visit, Kleofont Stepanovich Sitny phoned direct from Moscow. He spoke in a tone of unprecedented iciness, as though all of Siberia were contained in it. "See here! Have you lost your mind there, Korbach? How dare you say that carnival theater is incompatible with the barracks mentality? You reduced our entire society to a barracks? Have you sold out to those forces trying to undermine us? Well, you've only yourself to blame! I'm washing my hands of you!"

What can you say—the Bolsheviks' technique for a war of nerves was well-refined. Three days later *Sovetskaya Kultura* printed a piece entitled "Korbach the Buffoon at the Fair of Vainglory." The KGB nom de plume A. Nikolaev told in a rather smooth style (it was probably Petka Bolshevikov himself who had written it) of how this pathetic little actor, mad from thirst for fame, was selling out his motherland. The article was accompanied by a wrathful letter from leading figures of Soviet culture. A dozen signatures with titles: Honored, National, and so on.

Not one that he knew, apart from the actor Strzhelchik, who had long ago learned to make himself available for the intimidation of dissidents.

The broadcasters of the Russian-language radio stations were reminded of him again. Pumping himself up with Scotch from morning onward, he hacked out answering invective into the telephone. He was so uninhibited in his expressions that even the broadcasters would grunt, "Isn't that a bit harsh, Sasha?" "Don't worry about it—let them know that I'm not afraid."

Of course he wasn't afraid. After all, you can't call morning gloom fear, or the desire to either squeeze oneself into an immobile chrysalis or roll around in all directions like mercury. This is called depression, plain and simple. He would mutter lines from Dante, particularly

They know not that we are merely worms
in which are being formed a moth imperishable
soaring up to God's judgment from their darkness.

This helped, along with the Scotch.

One day his old pal Igor Yurin came to see him. He had defected from a Soviet deputation three years earlier and married a Moroccan woman. You know, one of the local Commies just asked me the other day with a disgusting smile: "They say your friend Monsieur Korbach died in a car crash—is that right?" Where, I say, did you get that information, and the Commie grins even more disgustingly: "Our comrades just flew in from Moscow." Well, there you have it, take it for what it's worth. Don't you get it? Want some advice, Sasha? Get out of Paris. They'll finish you off here with their agents of influence. Go where? Why, go to America. If I had your fame, I'd plunk myself down in America right away. Vitez won't be able to give you work forever. You know, the Russians in the States say they feel totally distant from the Sovs, they can't even stand to smell the bastards' stench. Personally, I dream only about America, but what can I do there as an unknown with no English? Besides, you speak pretty good English.

Curiously enough, the day after this conversation, in windy weather with flying hats and scarves, he bumped into the American diplomat Nikita Afanasievich Mauriac, whom he had known in Moscow as a great supporter of the Buffoons, always ready to help with getting letters and plays across the sacred border. Wearing a pince-nez with a dangling cord, the man embraced him. Fancy meeting you! I've been working in Paris for six months already, but I know all about you. They went into a café at the Carrefour du Bac.

"You know, I feel a sort of strange nostalgia for Moscow." Mauriac looked on with sad attention as Korbach ordered one double Scotch after another. His face lit up when he found out that the man across the table from him was going to America. "Fabulous idea, Alex! They'll roll out the red carpet for you there. Well, that's just an expression in English. All in all, they'll give you a great reception. For my part, I can guarantee you an H-1 visa, and in a year you'll get a green card." "Instead of the green snakes I see after drinking too much?" Korbach quipped. Mauriac slapped him on the back. "You'll sort yourself out there all right. Believe me, America is a long way from the Central Committee of the CPSU!"

By way of conclusion to this greatly abridged Korbachian CV, we will use the utterly banal sentence "Thus it happened that on August 10, 1982, Alexander Za-kharovich Korbach set foot on American soil," and we return to the crowd walking through the uteruslike Pan Am passenger tunnel toward the television cameras trained on them.

3

ONE HUNDRED DEGREES FAHRENHEIT

*I*t was only as he approached the barrier that Korbach realized that the cameras, photographers, and TV people were not intended for him at all. The curly head of a famous tennis player protruded from a clutch of lights and recording devices.

The other people waiting were looking for their friends and relatives among the arrivals. It was at this threshold that the transatlantic phantoms of passengers materialized. A process somewhat akin to the retrieval of his luggage, only with joyful emotions expressed in a more demonstrative form. No one, however, was in a hurry to retrieve Korbach the director. He walked by the cardboard signs bearing the names of those the signs' bearers didn't know by sight: Vernet, Schwartzman, Zoya Betancour, Kwan Li Zhi—his name wasn't there.

Maybe journalists were meeting him at some other exit, and the little shits got things mixed up? He walked through a huge hall filled with a phantasmagoric babble, of which he could not understand a single word. From time to time he was almost deafened by the paging system, which he couldn't understand either. Porters were talking among themselves in an absolutely incomprehensible language. Well, it seems that I don't understand English at all, if that's English. "Information," he read. Now, that I understand. Must ask where they're meeting the director Korbach here. Three fresh-faced girls in Pan Am uniforms were sitting behind an open counter talking with one another. When he got closer, he realized that he couldn't make out a word of their chatter. One of them turned to him: "Sir?" He averted his eyes and walked on by. She watched him go with an understanding expression on her face. Probably an East European. Polish and Czech refugees are often ashamed of their English, unlike the Tamils, Senegalese, and Burmese, who aren't.

Korbach dragged his suitcase on its little trolley around the terminal for no less than an hour and drank water from a fountain so that he wouldn't have to order a Coke in English, until the staggering thought hit him: No one is meeting me here! Yet Mauriac told me that they would! That there had been loads of reports in the American press! Every American he met had exclaimed: "Alexander Korbach! It's a great name in the States!"

He emerged from the building and saw before him a giant sea lion breeding ground, sleek and gleaming in the sun. From time to time the males would slowly begin to move. An overripe Daliesque sun hung over the supine herd. It was a vast car park.

You're soaked in sweat right away. Goddamned humidity. *Humidity* or *humanity*? Whatever it is, I don't matter to anyone in this place. "Mr. Korbach!" rang out at that very moment. A short, pudgy man in an untucked, loud, short-sleeved shirt was approaching him. A handshake, an exchange of perspiration. "Igor Yurin called me up this morning, asked me to meet you just in case. Stanislav Butlerov. Well, just call me Stas—we're the same age, after all."

He led him straight into hell—to the far end of the parking lot. "I'd started to think that you weren't coming: no signs anywhere of the journalists meeting you. I can't call your image to mind, sorry—in three years I've almost forgotten what heroes of the fatherland look like. I was just about to leave when suddenly, there he is, in the flesh." He quoted a song that Korbach had written what now seemed like a hundred years ago, and the composer felt a sudden upwelling of revulsion for his own creation. Well, there they are. A big yellow taxi was standing there.

"There's no driver," he said.

"I'm the driver," Butlerov said with a grin.

They drove along the highway, four lanes in one direction and four in the other. The stream of cars in all shapes and sizes was rolling along at the same speed, as though they had all been wound up with a single key and set in motion. They slid by nondescript houses and protruding cubes of brick without the slightest signs of an architect having worked on them, nothing but walls, windows, doors, windows—and what else? That's enough. Here and there a billboard rose over the rooftops: an ad from an airline or a man with a wheat-colored mustache and his Camels. A crowd gesturing for some reason with its fingers in the same direction flashed by on a corner, but on the whole everything was deserted.

"Where are you headed, anyway?" Stas Butlerov asked. He was quite correct in his manner—on the whole—but from time to time a slight expression of sarcasm flickered from beneath his eyelids.

"To the city center, I guess," Korbach answered with a shrug. Too bad he'd not had a drink at the terminal. That might have made everything look better now.

He wouldn't have had to squirm at every turn when the sun, overstuffed with raspberry-colored magma, appeared over the stacked bricks of the houses in the gray immobility of the sky.

"That means Manhattan," Stas said, intoning the words with a strange cunning. He steered in a broad semicircle onto a ramp leading to an elevated highway. To the left, skyscrapers stood pressed to each other like a phalanx about to go into battle.

"Strange sight," Korbach muttered.

"That's the Jewish cemetery," said Butlerov.

I must be going crazy, Korbach thought. I take a nearby Jewish cemetery for faraway Manhattan. I should have had a drink at Pan Am.

"Now then, this here is Manhattan," said Butlerov. He was trying with all his might to keep a triumphant tone out of his voice, but in the end he failed.

The sight that evening was magnificent and foreboding. The stagnant hundred-degree heat lent a feeling of some vague inevitability, an approach of something fundamentally inhuman, to the whole mass of stone, glass, and steel. Clarity was introduced only by the ball of the sun hanging over the rows of buildings in a murky stew of urban pollution, in the American, and in no way the Russian, sense of the word, which means "wet dream."

"Is everything clear?" Butlerov asked. It was difficult to say which there was more of in his voice, sarcasm or pride.

"Perfectly," laughed Korbach. "Like in a film," he went on, still laughing. "Like in a dream." And he kept on laughing.

I. THE PROCESSION

Did something push it, or did he break away on his own?
The sting of love, or did a steam iron
Come tumbling down? Well, here it is—he exited with a joke,
Strode over his own madness, collapsed, fell silent.

From Taganka, through the Yauza, to Solyanka
The mournful procession still stretches,
His soul is still soaring over it, a fugitive
In the vapor of sadness and the excitement of Celsius.

The body is drawn to the luxuries of botany,
To the burial park of the nomenklatura.
Thus "titanics" sink into the deep,
Their fires snuffed out, their steam exhausted.

Music lights up with Mozart,
But fades in a plaintive cacophony.
Farewell, disturbing kingdom of acoustics.
Farewell, manias, and with them phobias.

Everywhere lurk security detachments,
The monstrous water cannon looms blackly in a daze,
And the crow, its maw wide open,
Portrays the flight of witches.

A crowd 100,000 strong sways with corpulence,
As though thirsting for a pathetic revenge.
The cement of Russia crumbles beneath it,
As salt crumbles on the banks of the Sivash.

Floats low over the catafalque
His energy, or that which he called
His soul, having left the dumping ground,
Will not yet break away to depart for the astral spaces.

She still gazes on the remains
Of his short, endlessly dear life,
Not yet strong enough to see with her own eyes
The throng of Russian souls above the roofing tin.

The sad remains knew how to somersault
From a galloping horse

And hold out staunchly in the marathon
with the other "chariots of fire."

They once caught fire with passion—
Thus an Israelite burns with faith in the temple.
They knew no suffering, suspected not old age.
Like birds that sing, they flew with purpose!

The cells were saturated with hemoglobin,
The life process seemed eternal,
When suddenly all of the rivets burst,
As though Perseus had suddenly set the harpies loose.

Now their only role is "poor Yorick."
On the last journey of a buffoon and ham actor
Let four Soviet majors carry on
Like the four captains in Denmark.

The astral spaces stand before him like a canvas by Filonov,
An accumulation of forms outside classes and nations,
As though the whole painting had been begun again
By a consumptive titan, a connoisseur of innovations.

The energy of the earth still draws to itself
All the names of flowers, saints, and planets;
From Andromeda to Sergius Most Holy,
Though those names ring silent without air.

Words have departed and essences arise,
The Torah's divine starry vault
Sparkles like unseen hundreds,
For the joy of the angels and devils in the mountain.

Good-bye and farewell. Over the high spire—
Stalin Baroque, palazzo of the Ministry of Transportation.
The singer soars, alone in extraterrestrial calm,
And at his feet glides an obedient dog.

So, at every coming of a new being
Kindred spirits hasten in their descent,
At times to the very limits of corporeal horror,
Like nimbuses of light in a cathedral vestry.

At the bottom comes the turn of the glass.
Spilled over with grief, dried out with vodka,
Moscow! She rolls along in a staccato
And drinks to the memory of the soul.

PART II

1

ANISIA IN NEW YORK CITY

*T*his was not the first visit to New York by Korbach's ex-wife, Anis, née Anisia Pupushchina. In the early seventies, after successfully dousing the "fiery continent" with the kerosene of Communism, her daddy, a bigwig in the Ministry of Foreign Affairs, had been sent here as deputy chief of the Belorussian Republic's mission to the UN. He did, after all, have a certain connection to Belorussia, in the form of a characteristic pronunciation of the sound *ch*. This gift, it should be said, was passed on to Anisia. One day in primary school, the teacher had her say a series of words containing the suffix *-chka*. The innocent child with the big bow in her hair was somehow unaware of the Great Russian way of softening the sound in the middle of such constructions. *Dochka-tochka-svechka-pechka-nochka-tochka.* The class fell about laughing, and even the teacher smiled: You're our Belorussian, Pupushchina!

As was the case with all Soviet people, the family roots of the Pupushchins could not be traced very far back, so it was not impossible that there were some "White Russians" (the literal meaning of *Belorussian*) somewhere out there. Later on, when she had grown into a young woman with a stunning mane of fair hair, people began to take Anisia for a Scandinavian. Right now, in fact, as she walks along Fifth Avenue in the wind, in a colorful outfit and high Italian boots, with her well-turned superwoman figure, men's jaws are dropping: She must be Swedish!

It's an exaggeration that they've all turned into homos in America. A lot of them are just crazy about women. They walk alongside you, chase you, muttering something—this damned *eengleesh* just doesn't take with Anis—that makes it sound like they're making indecent propositions, without breaking stride, as though she were some young tramp rather than a forty-year-old Soviet woman.

Yesterday, one of them had thrown all restraint to the wind. The creep rushed at her as though he had seen his dream. Eyes and teeth gleaming in a black face with a hint of purple. Large, velvet lips protruding. Long fingers with rings sparkling on them. Was he some sort of gangster? "Where are you from?" she asked. He gave the name of a country that she didn't know—Haiti. He shoved gifts at her: a Mont Blanc with a gold nib, a jeweled Rolex, a heavy crocodile-skin wallet, a tiepin—want it all at once, madam, everything, for just one night? She laughed: Maybe you'll give me your shoes, too, señor? He immediately began to undo the laces on his thousandth pair of crocodiles. An exotic someone . . . oh, yes, Albert, with a surname that sounded like "Chapeau claque." He walked her to the mission building, and at the sight of the Soviet sign opened the alcove of his mouth in amazement. Anisia, embodying the dignity of Soviet woman, disappeared beneath the seal with its ears of grain.

This time around she was a Soviet woman in spades. The fact was that she had come to New York as a member of a delegation of the Committee of Soviet Women. At various lunches, chewing tasteless triangular sandwiches, drinking watered-down wine, she and her friends pulled the wool over the eyes of blue-haired old ladies: peace on earth, we're all in the same boat, and so on. True, they occasionally ran across sharp-tongued Jewish girls in men's jackets who worked for Helsinki Watch or Freedom House. This sort immediately began machine-gunning them with questions: Why did you break up the Leningrad feminists? What did you have against the magazine *Maria*? What feminists? And what *Maria*? Well, what do you say when you've simply never heard anything about it?

Finally, today some thug from the First Department, a Soviet agency that managed to combine personnel functions with counterintelligence, had led her off to one side. Today, Anisia Borisovna, at 3:00 P.M. or so, you need to go for a walk on the sunny side of Fifth Avenue. It's entirely possible that you'll meet someone there. And now here she is, strolling obediently, but for some reason with a stride that is a bit too quick for a casual walk. She is reflected in the shop windows that are in shadow, and disappears almost completely in the sun's reflections.

After a quarter of an hour or so of such walking, there appeared from the crowd moving toward her the man for whom she was waiting—the one who had put her through years of torment. The bastard, I can't forget, to hell with feminism. Her legs felt their forty years, and she slumped against a lamppost. Korbach was about to keep on going, then stopped and began to look around worriedly. He was not alone. Next to him, a gloomy figure looking the typical Russian muzhik was slicing the air with his palm. Anisia could hear: "Mediocre minds! Moral infants! Degenerates!" She saw Korbach grab his hand, as though wanting to stem the flow of invective, as though trying to break through the stream of curses to a turn of fate, if one can ascribe to fate a scenario worked up outside the novel by idle and vulgar directors. Having finally spotted her by the lamppost bearing the green sign 35TH STREET, he pushed away his traveling companion and ran toward his ex-wife.

2

THE ABSENTMINDEDNESS OF FORTUNE

*B*y this time he had been in New York for two weeks and was living at the home of the only person to meet him at the airport, Stas Butlerov. The moment he stepped over the threshold of the Butlerovs, he had been put in mind of Moscow by the smell of eggplant frying in the kitchen. Stas's wife, Olga, a plump intellectual, and her mother, Frieda Gershelevna, covered the table according to the Russian principle "anything from the stove will do." In one corner of the living room, beneath a portrait of the genius Pasternak and a picture of Oskar Rabin with some herrings on a copy of *Pravda,* stood a twelve-year-old violinist, the "hope of the family," with an adenoidal expression of genius. The family lived mainly on the salary of Olga, who was a computer programmer, and also on the food stamps that Frieda Gershelevna received through a program for immigrant senior citizens, which made her, too, a programmer of a sort, as she liked to joke. Stas, meanwhile, feeling reduced to the level of a beast by his failure to pass the bar, sometimes took shifts for a taxi-driver friend and sometimes stood in for another who was a night watchman. He had been a connoisseur of the arts in Moscow, had known all the theaters and loads of celebrities, had even crossed paths with Korbach, though the latter was damned if he could remember it.

"I can't believe it—Sasha Korbach himself!" Olga exclaimed in English. "Shut up, Mama!" her husband said, cutting her off. "Only Russian in the house!"

The meal concluded at 3:00 A.M. Stas, who had taken on a load, was cursing history and the present day, Russia and America, and was proposing an eternal friendship of the "exiles of the spirit." The proposal was accepted. Korbach collapsed onto the bed prepared for him right next to the dinner table, his face to the crudely embellished ceiling. I don't want anything, don't see anything, don't hear anything, don't say anything. I'm going round at the edges, or, better yet, I'm spreading out in space. I'm lying supine. You weren't strong enough to go to the camps, so now, stretch yourself out in the void.

What had actually happened? Why had no one on American soil met this celebrity, over whom, after all, a fair bit of fuss had been made? He would have come out for half a dozen interviews at least, anywhere you like, at least for the Russian-language papers of the Big Apple. I'm afraid that he'll never find out that all that had occurred was a small misunderstanding. Well, it won't cost us anything if, exercising our arbitrary authorial rights, we tell the story of this small misapprehension.

The fact is that Nikita Afanasievich Mauriac's secretary in Paris had been mistaken as to the date by all of one day. When Meg Patterson, a staff worker at the headquarters of Freedom House, received the telex saying that Alexander Korbach, dissident of the Soviet theater world, would be arriving at JFK on the eleventh of August, she immediately set about calling various newspapers and television stations, because she already had quite a lot of experience in the greeting of Soviet dissidents. Channel 13, ABC World News, *The New York Times, The Washington Post, The Wall Street Journal,* and even *Time* magazine, which had just found a small spot in the "People" section in between Barry Fonvizin's marriage and Larry Cranchlaw's divorce, all expressed an interest in sending someone.

Naturally, no one there had ever heard of any such director, yet in a strange way that will be explained later, everyone understood that "Alexander Korbach is a great name in the States."

Of course, if Meg Patterson had had the sense to call around to the big names in the theater, like Bob Boss or Julio Solovei, who had seen more than one Buffoons show, Korbach's name would have become a big deal anyway; she didn't go to the theater, however, as her dissertation took up all her time, and she didn't know their names.

So it was that exactly twenty-four hours after the arrival of our hero, just at the moment when he and Butlerov were getting ready for another dinner party of herring and eggplant in Queens, a respectable crowd of American newspaper and television people, along with a few characters from the local Russian press, had gathered at the end of the Pan Am tunnel. After not meeting anyone and getting in quite a temper, the journalists all went home. Knowing this crowd, we are within our rights to suppose that an insult like this would have lit a fire under them, and that they would have taken off in one large pack in search of the lost Muscovite; that very evening, however, the news broke that some Arab "enthusiasts" in the Middle East had seized an American airliner. The drama swallowed up all the columns in the newspapers, and they immediately forgot about the "dissident of the theater."

A sad story, to be sure, particularly for a depressed Soviet celebrity at the end of his rope, and all the more since history knows no celebrities as such—there was nothing left for him from it but an emptiness resembling heartburn. Nothing left to do but engage in self-flagellation. The Soviet critics were obviously right: Vanity has burned me. All of my dreams of a third Renaissance were nothing but convulsions of vainglory. And all of my *dolce stil nuovo,* and all of my "Danteana" with "The Radiance of Beatrice"—why, all of this was dreamed up as a way to raise a fuss in Moscow. My fame itself, be it Soviet or anti-Soviet, is just petty vulgarity. Fame in general is just vulgarity, vain effort, cheap exaltation, the most indecent of things. Being forever in an unnatural state, cheap numbers for showing off one's modesty, or arrogance, or merit, in turns. It's just a ridiculous condition. Once you're on the merry-go-round, you can't jump off anymore. They forget you, and you just carry on flirting with the whole world and think that the world's flirting with you.

Got to use this sobering belch, even though it feels like it's burning up my insides, to break away from the whole goddamned circus farce. Head forward, tear yourself out of the round dance of whores! It's a shame that I don't know how to do anything except write useless songs for no one, put on farcical plays and dances with acrobatics. Then again, maybe I could drive a cab, like Butlerov, a mouthpiece of the Soviet kangaroo courts. On weekends we'll knock back half a gallon of Smirnoff, walk along the boardwalk bombarding the artistic bitches and the political elite, and gradually turn ourselves into Brighton Beach crazies.

Meanwhile, Butlerov, inspired by his unexpected friendship with *the* Sasha Korbach, continued taking him to the apartments of people he knew. To tell the truth, he was amazed that a superstar would unconditionally accept any invitation and, instead of going to cocktail parties in the real American New York, sit for entire evenings around cramped tables among engineers working as unskilled laborers, doctors who could not get their Soviet qualifications accepted, journalists, lawyers, and university lecturers who had become masseurs, waiters, pretzel vendors, T-shirt printers—that is, operators of the presses stamping pictures and signatures on the most widespread article of clothing in this country, collarless shirts with short sleeves.

These people, in fact, were what in "the theater" in Russia were called "the audience," and in their time they had made the popularity of Sasha Korbach. After two or three shots, they began to sing his old songs, slyly looking at him, and after a fourth would come right out and shove a guitar at him: "Come on, Sasha, let loose!" He obediently did precisely that, and they nodded to him approvingly: "You've got it all, old pal—the voice, the style, and the passion!" In their eyes he could see that they felt sorry for him, as a man of the past.

Rumors, though, were already going around "Russian New York": Korbach is in town! One day he and Butlerov wandered into the Kavkaz restaurant, and before they had even had their first drink, the whole establishment was on its feet with their glasses raised: Sasha Korbach is with us! Let's drink to Sasha! A Gypsy lady fluttered the hem of her skirt: Our beloved Sasha Korbach has come to visit us, the dear man! A revelry in the pure Muscovite spirit started. From the Kavkaz they headed for the Ruslan. From there to a huge, dimly lit loft, the refuge of artistic bohemia. But there was another type, the highbrows. They made no particular ecstatic gestures to the genius, though—on the contrary, the whole evening it was as though they were paying no attention to Korbach, letting him know that over there in the land of the Soviets he was somebody, but here things went according to the real scale of quality. Here we don't count your past honors. Some tipsy girl tried to make her way to him, but she was taken out behind the potbellied stove and slapped across the face. "All right, Stas, I've seen enough, let's go, we're out of here!"

That night, New York, for the sake of variety, had shaken off its sticky humidity. Canadian air descended in a solid wall from the stratosphere to the crushed beer cans and began to blow a fresh wind through the tired metaphors of Manhattan—that is, through the stone canyons, or maybe through the stone labyrinth. What "stone labyrinth," though, if even a drunken monkey couldn't get lost in its numbered geometry? The night was, in a word, enchanting, long, white clouds tossing across a black sky like university rowing sculls. One moment, and I'll fall in love with this city. The moment slipped away.

"You know, Butlerov, when we were evacuated to Kazan, we lived on Butlerov Street. I was just a tiny thing then, but I still remember the tumbledown wooden houses and the rumbling streetcar." "That Butlerov, Korbach, was a famous chemist, a professor in Kazan, and one of my ancestors—no more, no less." "Listen, Butlerov, I just don't know what to do." "I realized that, Korbach—I just go out of my mind when I see what these bastards have done to you. Why, in the old days you used to crackle with inspiration like a torch! If you want, I'll go to *Newsweek* tomorrow and I'll make a scene: You write about any little shit, and a Russian genius you don't even notice!" "I appreciate this outburst, but you don't get my meaning. I just need to get away somewhere." "Where else is there to run to, pal? There's nowhere else."

The night was humming. The Korean shops were open. The wind was blowing freshly over the fruits in their sloped stalls. Three half-naked Americans of Babylonian origin passed by. As a matter of fact, they were three lions with permanent-waved manes. By the Chelsea Hotel, some hanger-on novelist was horsing a woman around. A streetwalker with no pants was wrapping her bosom in a mink stole.

"You know, Korbach, I want to run off myself. Olga's found herself some Puerto Rican ten years younger than she is. We've always been proud of our progressive views on sex, but it turns out that I can't stick to them." "Butlerov, that revolution failed, too. We're threatened with sexual totalitarianism. Come on, then, let's take off somewhere. Isn't there some state next to California that sounds like *Ochichornia,* or is there no such thing?" "Don't know about that, Korbach, but I've got a friend in Los Angeles who's doing well. He's got a share in a parking garage. He'll find us a job."

For the rest of the night, Korbach tossed and turned on the couch just beside the dinner table, which was spread with uneaten saury, a Pacific fish from a Russian shop. From the bedroom he could hear Butlerov howling while Olga sang her Spanish song, he at the top of his range and she in a thin, happy mezzo-soprano. Things could also be heard falling down: now it was books on the floor, now plastic bottles of diet Coke. Male hysterics, however, were powerless before the ringing word *corazón*.

Our hero was woken by the ringing of the telephone right in his ear. The device, as it turned out, had fallen onto the pillow during the night, but the receiver had managed to stay on the hook. "May I speak to Mr. Korbach?" asked a voice saturated with Leningrad courtesy. The man who had picked up replied with a heartrending cough. "Good morning, Alexander Zakharovich," said the voice, as though it had been waiting for no other answer. "I saw you last night at the Ipsilon. This is Arkady Grebenchukovsky of Radio Liberty speaking. Would you like to be on one of our broadcasts?"

"On what topic, Mr."—Korbach still stumbled over these "Misters"—"Mr. Grebenchukovsky?"

"Why, on any topic at all!" the radioman exclaimed. "It seems to me that to shut up the agents of disinformation and cheer up your friends, all you have to do is go on the air. Rumors about you are going around over there, one after another."

"Oo-oo-oo-oo," Korbach said, imitating the sound of jamming.

"Even so, millions listen to us," Grenbenchukovsky replied with some warmth. "Come on over to our studio, Alexander Zakharovich, and we'll record a chat—and by the way, we'll pay you a cash honorarium."

The voice is pleasant and the arguments convincing, Korbach thought. Must go on one more time before disappearing. The word will get around Moscow: Korbach is alive. And his mother will know it. And Anisia and the kids. Then I'll vanish. Vanish in the midst of life.

The call had come during that short phase of the morning after, when he was in a good mood, which would be succeeded by a prolonged neurotic phase. He had barely managed to write down the address and phone number of Radio Liberty when that fucking second phase kicked in. He suddenly felt a momentary twinge of nostalgia for his mother—about whom, to be honest, he rather seldom thought—tugging at him. Mother, the poor woman, is retiring, losing her "high importance to the state." Izhmailov just sits there like the painting *Menshikov in Exile*. Valerka and Katya are living with their families. Grandma Irina died two years ago. Of her own mother—Grandma Raisa—she's somehow ashamed. Poor, frightened creature, the parent of an "enemy of the people"!

Just then there was another ring, some guy blathering something in English in a deep, drunken voice. This language is impossible to understand, Korbach thought in annoyance, and he asked, putting clear spaces between the words: *"Vood-yu-pliz-spik-slouli?"* Plumber, plumber, the man's voice in the receiver said hoarsely. *Ich bin plumber.* A rosy Olga Mironovna rolled in like a fresh, romantic breeze after a sleepless night. Why, it's that German plumber, he's just the one I've been waiting for. Korbach understood from a few glances that the presence of the "Russian genius" was already becoming a bit of a burden in the family. With the exception, of course, of its head, who was finding the family itself a burden.

At three in the afternoon, the friends were engaged in their favorite activity, strolling through midtown Manhattan. They were talking about California. Everything will be fine out there. It's a whole other world. They say that the air there smells different from everywhere else. "I remember," Korbach said, "the smell of some other dream that wasn't covered with shit yet." "Beg your pardon"—Butlerov was surprised—"but in the first chapter, you know, it said that this is your first time in America." He doesn't know everything, Korbach thought, and grinned. "We were showing a picture there ten years ago at a festival. I went along as an actor. Just for a week, you know. Slept with some chick. Some actress named . . . what was it—Capablanca, I think. From Mexico, you know."

Butlerov scowled: Not a word about Latins in the cuckold's house! "Oh drop it, Stas, you're not the first and you won't be the last. My wife slept with God knows who, too." "Yeah, and you got a divorce." "Right, and you're getting one, too." Butlerov brightened. "You're probably right—after all, the barricades of the sexual revolution are behind us." Korbach shot a sidelong glance at the meaty runt. He doesn't look much like a barricade fighter.

There was only an hour left before the appointment at Radio Liberty, so they had only one drink—a double gin each, truth be told. "In California, Stas, you'll forget about your sorry diploma, and me about my shows and films. We'll become normal forty-something guys." "Right you are, Sashok"—no one had ever called him Sashok, but he liked it just now—"we'll become . . . blue-collar workers, they call them, right? And no contacts with artistic bohemia, with those cheap snobs, those mediocre minds, always pregnant with betrayal, like that shit Mitka Ipsilon."

The crowd on Fifth Avenue was becoming more and more cheerful in the Canadian wind. Manes of hair were flying about, neckties and pigtails as well. It seemed to Korbach that many people were watching him, as though they recognized him as a celebrity, the way people had in Paris. Smiling mockingly at himself, he saw people's smiles and glances of recognition again and again. "Just look at that babe over there staring at you," Butlerov said. "Obviously she knows you!" This simple-hearted guy, he always knows how to draw out just what I'm trying to push down. Korbach looked at the tall, beautiful woman at the intersection. And recognized in her his ex-wife. And was all at once engulfed by a feeling of unbearable love for her.

3

OH, SAMOVAR LOVE!

*T*hey hadn't had the slightest contact in perhaps two years, and now it was all rekindled! Well, Sashka, thought Anis, as she eyed her former husband. He's got hotter than ever. He's turning me on; that's what they do with a samovar, after all—they stuff burning coals inside it and pump it up with a bellows. Oh yes, I'm turning into a samovar, I'm going to boil over any minute, start spitting steam, he'll burn up everything for himself.

What's happening to her? he wondered as he screwed the woman. You close your eyes and you feel like you've got some twenty-year-old babe in your arms. Everything's rocking and trembling. Hey, I'm not going to get in a spiral of excitement like the Tower of the Third International. And now I'm soaring, like that pterodactyl Letatlin with his prey. Where do such foolish thoughts come from when you're having it off with someone? She's bending over, shaking all over; she always was quite a looker with her samovar steam, her rocking back and forth, and her whirlwinds of hair—you feel like you're doing it with some fantastic filly instead of a woman. All she needs is the tail. Finally they stopped and fell into a wordless embrace, panting and sobbing from love. Then they sat up, and, with their backs to the shaky wall of the lousy little motel, lit up cigarettes in the best tradition of their youth. Then he asked: "How are the kids?"

"You must be praying for them every day, they're doing so great." She smirked.

"They're here with you?"

"No, right now they're with their grandparents in Nizhnaya Oreanda."

"You mean you're not staying with your dad now?"

She jokingly put on an expression of haughtiness, which looked rather ridiculous for a naked woman. "No, sir—think a bit higher! Before you sits a worker for Soviet culture, a senior script editor at a film studio, and a member of the delegation of the CSW."

"Council of Soviet Whores?"

"Almost—Committee of Soviet Women."

"That's great," he muttered in a faltering voice. "But why haven't you got a tail?" he asked, stroking the corresponding spot. "Who took your tail off?"

She resisted weakly. "All right, Sashka, all right—that's enough for you. I know these tricks of yours about the tail."

He didn't answer, and she was silent, giving free rein to his fantasies. Here it is, your tail, take it, it's just as magnificent as it was before. If you'd only known before how much love was piled up in it! Alexander, what are you doing with a forty-year-old woman? As it happened, she said the last sentence aloud.

"You're not forty, you're thirty-nine."

She stroked his hair. "If you knew how glad I was when I saw you on the street! You threw yourself at me for sex, but I just saw in you someone dear to me."

"Ah, now the Belorussian mush starts," he said with an affectionate laugh.

"You know . . ." Anis ran to the bathroom, came back with a towel between her legs, and continued her sentence: "You know, I didn't believe it, but they always spread such dirt about defectors in Moscow. Well, they went around telling everyone that you'd died in a car crash. And suddenly, here you are, alive, my precious!"

"The eagle of the steppe, the bold Cossack," he crooned the words of a popular Soviet ditty. She sang along in her former ironic way: as though she was a teary-eyed village girl, he a Muscovite full of bile. Suddenly, she turned to him seriously, with the genuine face of a "Soviet woman." "Sashka, what do you say we start all over again? Imagine how happy it would make our kids, Styopka and Lyovka!"

He looked at her seriously. "How do you picture that, Anis? I was practically banished from the country, an enemy of the people. Milkmaids and steelworkers are demanding my head in the newspapers."

"Oh, that's all rubbish!" she said with a dismissive wave. "You know how it works! *They* can turn everything around in a minute!"

"And what makes you so sure?" he asked—a question that, as he would later reproachfully tell himself, immediately shattered their love, so recently rekindled in such mysterious fashion.

On her face, her two basic masks were changing back and forth rapidly: that of the stern editor, member of the creative council, which he couldn't bear, and that of the crazy woman whom he loved so much. "What do you mean, what makes me sure? I got it from *them,* of course. Did you really think that they wouldn't approach me? Your ex-wife and the mother of your children?"

"So they gave the go-ahead for the reconciliation?" Throwing his legs out of bed, he began to pull on his boxer shorts—his socks and trousers were lying in a heap on a zebra-striped mat that looked as though it had been trampled by a hippopotamus.

"No need to reduce things to a primitive level," she said in her editor's voice, tossing her hair the way she always used to. "Well, you know what they say now. We don't want to cut off all oxygen to Alexander Zakharovich. He still has a chance to regain the trust of the motherland."

"Were they precise?" he asked, already in his trousers.

"They hinted at things, of course. An interview, an admission of mistakes, of excessive vanity, the usual guff, but, most important, the unmasking of the secret services of the West, all of this trash that's boring everyone to death. You tell the lies they want, and they'll leave you alone."

From his jacket pocket he took a flat bottle of Chivas, gulped down nearly a third, and, in an automatic gesture, held it out to his partner. She also took a good swig. And seemed to pluck up courage.

"They guarantee you a return to the theater with your old position and a 'green light' for your projects. They mentioned some Dante show, or maybe it was Petrarch."

He was in a mad whirl: head spinning, rage, heartburn, rage, nausea, and rage, rage, and rage. So, even this explosion of love had been rigged by the KGB! They're trashing Dante with their greasy fingers! "And they made a good job of it with you, too!" he said. "They shoved you in a delegation and even took you to Fifth Avenue, calculating my route. No, we still underestimate the 'knights of the revolution.' They've always been able to turn beautiful women, any sort of high-quality ass—they've got the method down to a science!"

"Shut your mouth!" she shouted, so loudly that a television on the other side of the wall fell silent from fright. "How dare you? The mother of your children! Bastard, bastard, bastard!" She was already rushing around the room, snatching up her scattered underthings, her breasts flopping, tall, absurd—for the first time he noticed that her stomach shook like a handbag being taken over potholes.

This sort of scene, he thought coldly, ought to be done up in costume. Some say that the *nu* in such situations is strengthened by postmodern totality. I don't agree. Listen, dear friend, what we see in these dialogues of naked bodies is what the Americans call redundance, or what Russians call fabrication. At any rate, it's all an invention.

4

THE NETHERWORLD

*I*n the gathering twilight, he slowly trudged toward Times Square. In those days, the huge Camel man was still blowing out perfectly formed smoke rings. A stream of red fire poured out on the broad heights of a wall of yellow fire, to be replaced by one of blue flame, after which the Assyrian word *Nabisco* appeared. *The French Lieutenant's Woman* was playing at the movies, if memory serves. The ground floors shone with their hundreds of brightly lit caves—in one, a thousand cameras; in another, a thousand radios; in a third, a thousand suitcases. A helicopter sending out groping beams hung amid the skyscrapers, though all of their light was dispersed in the perspiration of the lower orders. The crowd wandered here and there, looked at itself, looked for something sweeter. Up there, on the ledge of the fiftieth floor, it would be good to join that Symbolist dwarf with the fiery tongue stuck to the sky. The people will think: What are they trying to sell with that supertongue?

He walked aimlessly into a cave burning with the lights of a thousand television sets. Baseball, soap, drama, an explosion, a fight, a bit of leg, lips sucking on a sweet, a tire, several faces displaying a burning interest in some vital question, flickered simultaneously. A woman's voice cut through everything else: "I always have sex with my clothes on, and out of my bedsheets!" Like most Russians, he couldn't hear the difference between *sheet* and *shit,* and wondered what excrement had to do with all this, but, then, doesn't everything eventually come to that anyway? A knot of the Middle Eastern owners of the shop watched him attentively as he passed by the screens. Not everything is complicated here, he thought— you've just got to fumble around until you find the key to the secrets, the key in the sign of a serpent wound around a column. Then again, better not to fumble, better just to walk on by, at least to try to miss it all, or else the answers fall on you like a crystal chandelier. The Asians turned away: This man is just looking. Tie a yellow ribbon round the old oak tree, if you still love me, if you still want me, if you're still waiting. This old local melody, like a bit of news from home. From home, where bands of traitors live and lady stool pigeons flourish. Nothing opens up to me, here or there, except bottles.

They used to sing: "And his passion was at the bottom of a bottle long ago, long ago." Where was that from, anyway? Suddenly it came to him: The first year after the war, the crunching of snow under felt boots, trampled-down snow like marble beneath the moon, he's seven years old, he and Mama are coming back from the theater, happiness wrapping itself around everything, little leaps and dashes, sliding along smooth expanses of ice, I'm singing just as the hussars in the theater were singing: "Long ago, long ago!"

It was not just a memory. That winter moment had simply come back to him there in the middle of Times Square. He suddenly found a place for himself in the middle of Purgatory, and he didn't seem to be disturbing anyone. He was somewhere outside of time. The chain of the never-ending trickery of moments rushing by from the future into the past. He remembered the epitaph in the Peredelkino cemetery: "Waves of time flooded over us, and our lot was momentary." Time can't sink us, it doesn't exist when we don't exist, it's something else that drowns us. The moment of a winter of his childhood that had appeared was not a moment. I feel like I'm riding along on some ultimate point. One more nonmoment and I'll find myself outside of time. If I'm still in it now, that is, he thought with a shudder.

Suddenly the feeling struck him that he might not even be among the living. After some moment or other in Moscow, this is no longer life that's happening to me, just the aimless movement of a store of not yet dissipated energy. It's not impossible that the KGB has killed me with an iron across the head. Or they smashed a dump truck into my car. Maybe it happened even without the KGB—after all, a chandelier fell on my head when I was child. The body had probably been seen off by all of Moscow; Moscow hadn't seen such an outpouring of emotion since Vysotsky's funeral. A harbinger of revolution. As for me, I—that is, my beam of energy—was projected into space, into the zone of reflections, and whole peoples flowed with me like a throng of shadows, into America and into Purgatory. Only Virgil is lacking, unless you count Stas Butlerov. Am I throwing off the shadow? Right now in Times Square I'm throwing off dozens of shadows, but that still doesn't mean that I'm corporeal in the usual sense. I drink vodka and nibble cucumbers, but I don't feel the taste. Everything has gathered together and been reflected by a myriad of mirrors. My personal proof of this is my grotesque sex with Anis, and the most apparent thing from among the unapparent is the return of that winter night from my childhood.

In the whirlwind of this staggering revelation or—dare we suppose—in an acute stage of nervous breakdown, he hadn't noticed that he'd turned off the triangle glittering with commercial blandishments into one of the soberly lit side streets. Now he was moving along it, at one moment striding like the Futurist poet Mayakovsky, at another shuffling along in the Beckett manner, now bursting out with joy in the face of the cosmic sense of what was happening, now trembling like a frog in fear about his own absence. Just have a look in a reflecting mirror—don't you see anything? There was the reflection of a man covered with sweat, in a short jacket, a bulging forehead like on a Boeing 747, long locks of hair clinging to his cheeks, and in his long mouth there might even have been a red tongue that could roll out to cover half the sky. Or the complete absence of a tongue.

I'm just under an absurd amount of stress, came the saving thought, I need tranquilizers. Suddenly there appeared to him a sight in the center of which, in huge, burning letters standing out against a dark sky, was his own name: ALEXAN-DER KORBACH. Well, that's it. My time has come. They're calling. Everyone meets his own Apocalypse. Everyone goes through his sufferings on the Day of Judgment alone.

Meanwhile, Neuvo Yorkers were passing by, some elegantly attired and some in cheap shirts and what looked like boxer shorts. They were coughing, yawning, guzzling their drinks, checking the time on their wrists. That's how things go—everyone's moving along, and one is being called by terrible letters in a dark sky. A woman with the face of a humanities major came out of a bakery. She was carrying a brown bag from which two baguettes protruded. The man under judgment lurched toward her. "Madam!" Even at that moment he couldn't bring himself to speak English, and began to babble in broken Français. *Est-ce que vous voir cela au-dessus?* She shrugged her shoulders. *Mais quoi! What's the matter, monsieur?* He clapped a palm to his stomach to calm the intestinal and vascular turmoil. *Qu'est-ce que c'est, madame?* I'm begging you, *qu'est-ce que c'est?* She gave another shrug. *Just "Korbach," sir! Un grand magasin!* And with these words and with her head turned away, and with astonishment in her eyes, she got on a bus. God bless the little lady, let her enjoy breaking her French bread today!

In his pocket, he remembered, he had an unfinished flask. Sitting down on a stoop next to a bum and resting his head against a shaky skyscraper, he took a swig from the flask and looked at the evenly illuminated letters of his name. They did not blink, and they did not change colors like a Times Square chameleon. With a calm, yellow, electrical light, they confirmed it: "Alexander Korbach is a great name in the States!" Smells of the evening meals of various communities wafted along the street: mushu pork and wonton soup from the Chinese, sweet basil from the Thais, truffle sauce from the Provençals. An everyday civilization, New York.

5

THE CABINET OF DR. DUPPERTUTTO

*A*rthur Duppertat, a young and promising employee of the giant corporation Alexander Korbach Retail and general director of the celebrated New York department store, was not among those who slip away from their desks as soon as the whistle blows. On the contrary, he loved to work late at his desk with his cup of coffee steaming away and his computer switched on. He loved his job, was very proud of the huge responsibility to which he had been promoted at the age of twenty-seven, and for that matter he liked his office itself.

The office was indeed worthy of rapturous admiration: a large room with three French windows overlooking the western crest of Manhattan, with Virginia oak panels, portraits of the founders, armchairs with dark yellow upholstery, a huge old globe in a sturdy copper stand, and with a smell of expensive cigars that had lingered down the decades, and of even more expensive ports and sherries. And here I am, standing on my head in the *sirsasana* pose, on a springy Persian carpet, a kid from a low-income family with its nest behind a pizzeria in a tough neighborhood of Baltimore. Wouldn't you say there's something to be proud of?

Art Duppertat didn't look bad upside down, all the more since he was now crowned with two first-rate Church shoes, an English make. The idea was that a man in this position should not think about anything at all, so as to attain the desired meditation. We must admit, though, that, even standing on his head, Art could not get away from pleasant thoughts about his life and his career. On the contrary, the increased flow of arterial blood to his brain was an even greater stimulus to the generating of ideas. At the very moment of the reader's introduction to this character, a new idea was racing around the latter's head with the speed of an atomic particle: And-what-about-Stanley-Korbach's-younger-daughter-pretty-intelligent-she-likes-me-ought-to-marry-her!

After his having imagined such a thing with regard to the daughter of the all-powerful president of the company, we might well banish Art from the glorious generation of American yuppies of the eighties and fling him back into the past, into Dreiser's gallery of soulless heroes, those careerists and violators of innocent girls; for the sake of fairness, however, we have to say that he bore no resemblance to people of that ilk. He was pure, happy, and ingenuous, and the fact was that he was simply mad about Sylvia. No whiff of a mésalliance here, ladies and gentlemen, particularly if one considers the ever-decreasing number of men getting married in the last few years on this side of the Atlantic.

And just at the moment of the conception of this happy idea, Ben Duckworth, a hefty black fellow built like a lineman for the Washington Redskins, and chief of security for the store, came into the director's office. He looked unusually excited. "Sorry to bother you, Art, but some strange character wants to see you." Without changing his blissful position, Art asked who it was. Duckworth told him what had happened: "We were getting ready to close when I spotted this guy in Perfumes. He was talking strange, I tell you, going up to Iris Rabinowitz and a few other girls and talking like a nut. I asked him into my office, but he said he wanted to talk to the manager himself. 'With your director' was the way he said it."

"Why didn't you just put him through to me on the phone?" Duppertat asked.

"Problem is, he doesn't really speak English. Chatters like a machine gun, without anything coming out that you can make sense of. To tell you the truth, at first I wanted to chuck this damned Frenchman out, or Hungarian, or even a Bolshevik, if you don't mind me saying so."

"*Pardon,* but I do mind," his boss interrupted. "Allow me to remind you of our recent conversation. All of our employees have to demonstrate an unimpeachably cosmopolitan attitude toward all our customers, or potential customers. We mustn't show any signs of American superiority!"

Duckworth laid a hand of no small breadth over his heart. "My God, Art! You know perfectly well that I know many non-American folks. I saw loads of them in non-American countries, when I was serving in the Hundred and First Light Cavalry. The cosmopolitan spirit took root in me when we were based in Germany, near Wiesbaden. . . . What are you smiling like that for, sir?"

"I was just imagining you in a light cavalry unit, Ben," Duppertat said innocently. At this, the head of security sighed deeply. "What amazes me, sir, is that a lot of our clever and stylish city boys, even the ones who got their education at Harvard or Yale, that is, at colleges with a lot of possibilities for studying our country's history, still think that the men of the Hundred and First Light Cavalry ride around on horses. Our unit, sir, got the name a hundred and thirty years ago and has carried it proudly as a sign of respect to military tradition ever since. As for me, I served as a senior instrument specialist, sir."

"Well, all right, Ben, I take your point, but just what did you observe over there in Germany?"

"A simple thing, Art. I realized that for all the good qualities of overseas countries, not one of them can hold a candle to the USA. Even Germany, Art. I'm not particularly delighted about it, Art, but even the Germans, try as they might, are still way behind us."

"In what domain, Ben?"

"In every domain, Art."

"Even in music, Ben? And in philosophy?"

"Especially in music, Art. And in philosophy, too."

"Hmm . . . ," said the manager, but the head of security only nodded vigorously in reply to this interjection. "As far as any other country is concerned, what can we expect from them if not even Germany can keep the pace? Take, for example, this Hungarian who can't even string a sentence together and calls himself a director in the theater. His clothes don't look like they've ever seen an iron, but the most pathetic thing is that he's drunk, sir!"

Mr. Duppertat smiled. "If I may be so bold, my dear centurion, there's one domain in which overseas countries can still challenge the United States of America. I've got a hard time imagining the head of security in a large German department store bringing a drunken visitor to his boss's office."

"I was expecting you to hold that against me," Duckworth said sadly. "Maybe I really do deserve a telling-off from the highly respected, although very young, directorship, but how could I not introduce a man named Alexander Korbach to the directorship?"

After saying this, the monumental figure moved to the ancient globe, and with a nudge of his indestructible finger set the slow, creaking rotation in motion. Australia, he guessed silently. If it stops on Australia, everything with my job, our company, our city, and the whole country will be fine. The result of this secret wager was somewhat ambiguous. The globe really did come to a stop on the spot where Australia ought to have been, but alas, that small continent had not yet been discovered when this noble geographical apparatus was being constructed, so that instead of the land of the kangaroos, it was a rusty patch of sea that met Duckworth's gaze.

At that moment the general director came out of his *sirsasana* and changed to a more natural *Homo erectus* position. "Amazing!" he cried. "You're sure, Ben, that this fellow has the name of our company and that he's not American?"

"I checked his papers," the officer replied. "There in the middle of some gibberish in French was 'Alexander Korbach.' "

Art opened the door himself and invited the mysterious visitor in. The latter entered under the escort of two young security men, Jim and Ricardo; the general manager took pride in the fact that he knew all 812 of the store's employees by name. The foreigner was neither young nor old, neither tall nor short, quite bald, yet at the same time attractive, with his well-outlined chin and his strikingly blue eyes.

"These gays," he said, indicating his guards. "Not p'lite."

This nearly knocked the wind out of the manager. "These *gays*? You said 'gays,' sir?" Everything became clear to him. "You probably meant 'guys,' sir? It's no wonder that the guys weren't 'p'lite' with you, sir!"

A comedy of mistaken identity, Alexander thought. Usually this sort of thing ends with a good punch to the jaw. "It's my fucking *eenglesh*."

The young manager asked the guards to leave him alone with the foreigner and motioned the latter to a sumptuous bourgeois chair. There appeared on the table a cut glass decanter containing a dark red liquid, the very sight of which revived almost extinguished hopes of a turn to triumphant humanism.

"Question"—it came out as *kveschin*—said Alexander. "Kveschin, kveschin, kveschin." With a horror that had a faintly comic edge to it, he realized that he had forgotten all of his English verbs. A few nouns still jumped out here and there, but the verbs were rolling away like mercury through the holes in his trousers.

"I'm all attention," Duppertat announced cheerfully and even drummed his palms lightly on the green cloth of the tabletop.

"Alexander Korbach," Korbach said, and jabbed himself in the chest with his index finger. Then he made a broad gesture that took in the oak-paneled room. "Also Alexander Korbach. What? How?"

Art shook his head in still greater amazement. "I understand your confusion, Mr. Korbach. To see your own name on the top of a huge commercial enterprise in New York! Like something out of science fiction, wouldn't you say? Of course, if you were American, it wouldn't have surprised you. We've probably got hundreds of Ralph Laurens and thousands of Hechts, Sakses, Exxons, and other people who have famous names. At the end of the day, this country is the land of opportunity, or at least it thinks it is. But you, as I understand it, came from overseas, without knowing our great names. Where are you from, anyway, Alex?"

From this whole speech Alexander had managed to catch only the last sentence clearly.

"The Soviet Union," he said. "The union of dicks. Moscow, the capital of cunts. New York fucked up the ass. Theater. Director. Street. Sky. My name. Hallucination?"

The verbs were still making themselves disgracefully absent.

"Listen, Alex," Duppertat said patiently. "I'm going to speak slowly so that you'll understand better. Alexander Korbach is a big name in our country. It belongs to a gigantic commercial and financial corporation, which was founded a hundred years ago by a man named Alexander Korbach. Here before you on the wall is a portrait of the gentleman in the prime of his life. As far as I can tell, he posed for this painting right here in this office, in which you and I are having this stimulating conversation."

Alexander took a darting glance at the painting in its golden frames with its thickly applied oil brushwork and found there a cold-eyed gentleman with a mustache à la Kitchener and thin, light-colored hair crowning a narrow head. His marsh-toned velvet jacket was painstakingly rendered; there was a pin in his tie and a ring on one of his fingers, which surprised one with their callused quality.

Art Duppertat went on: "In the beginning, this was a company that dealt in retail, and our department store was its flagship. Can you imagine, friend, how proud I was when they appointed me general manager of this national treasure?"

Alexander interrupted him. "Jew?" he asked, nodding toward the portrait. "Russia?"

Duppertat smiled gently. Educated at a liberal Ivy League school, he had maintained a tolerant attitude toward the stranger's brusque manners, ascribing them to Russian backwardness. "As far as I know, sir, Alexander Korbach came here from Warsaw or from Berlin and founded here a great American dynasty of tycoons. Good news for you, Alex: the dynasty controls the corporation as it always has, and you have a chance to be introduced to our president, Stanley Franklin Korbach. Can you imagine that?"

"Vat? Vai?" The deep parallel grooves that appeared on the forehead of the great American's namesake reflected his confusion. "I don't!" Thus his first verb managed to jump up to his tongue. "Vai? Vat for? I don't imagine!"

Duppertat, in a generous mood, extended a hand across the table and patted his interlocutor on his rather damp shoulder. "Well, all right, I'll try to put it another way. Do you want to make the acquaintance of the president of our company, Stanley Korbach, himself?"

Alexander shrugged his shoulders. "Vat for? No, I don't."

It seemed to Art that some sort of suffering had flashed in the eyes of this clearly not entirely normal man. "Listen, dear friend, you don't seem to have understood. Stanley Korbach is one of the richest men in this country. Access to him is closed to practically everyone. You, however, my stranger of a friend, have got a one-in-a-million chance. First of all, you're the namesake, first and last, of our founder. In the second place, you've had the fortune to meet me, to meet a man with personal ties to Stanley and one who feels a certain sympathy for you that can't be explained. And third and finally, I learned during a round of golf not so long ago that Stanley has an obsession with genealogy. I'm sure that he'd be interested in talking with you about your line of Korbachs. Understand? This gives you enormous possibilities . . . well, for the search for enormous possibilities. Get it?"

Korbach stood up and offered his amiable host a farewell handshake. "How old are you, Dr. Duppertutto?"

"Twenty-seven," Art replied with modest pride, as if his age were something like an inherited gift. Then he gently corrected his visitor. "However, my name's Duppertat, not Duppertutto."

The visitor suddenly laughed in his most carefree manner. "Sorry, I don't want to . . . er, oh hell, you insult. Doctor Duppertutto . . . from, you know, Hoffmann, Meyerhold, you know, commedia dell'arte."

The manager was a bit offended all the same. "Art, for your information, is just a diminutive for Arthur. So, then, do you want to take advantage of this once-in-a-lifetime opportunity?"

Incidentally, he refused to admit even to himself that the offer of this "once-in-a-lifetime opportunity" to the doubtful foreigner gave him a "once-in-a-lifetime opportunity" to bring himself to Stanley Korbach's attention, and once there— who knows?—get an invitation from this demigod of a sort.

"And how about another glass of this drink?" Alexander asked in Russian, making an expressive gesture to indicate his desire.

Art immediately filled their glasses with his exquisite port. And froze, dumbfounded. The stranger drained his glass in one gulp and gave a grunt. "Wonderful!" he exclaimed, still in Russian. "This hooch brings a man back to reality. The *Divine Comedy* turns into commedia dell'arte!"

Art showed his guest to the door, throwing an arm around his shoulders on the way. To his surprise, he discovered the strong muscles of an acrobat beneath the shabby cloth. "Where are you staying in New York, Alex? In a hotel? With friends? Relatives?"

The visitor seemed to be understanding English better by the minute.

"I stay right now in my own body," he said with unexpected elegance.

Art beamed with friendliness. "In your own body, ha, ha! Why, you've got a great sense of humor, Mr. . . . er, Korbach! How old are you, by the way?"

"For now, the usual," the visitor said with a smile.

Art guffawed. "That's even better! You're just a joke machine, sir! How about dinner on Saturday?"

"Thenk you, Art, you good boy—me, I fly California, new life, self-realization—good-bye, you nice guy." With these words he slapped the general manager on the back and was gone.

Duppertat went back to his desk, turned off his computer, and "disconnected" himself for a second. When he had come "back on," he found himself gazing at the elongated rectangle of space among the steel and glass walls. The rectangle was now and again sectioned by the beams of police helicopters and the lights of airliners approaching the airport. "Commedia dell'arte," our young and promising manager muttered to himself. "With my Yale diploma, I really ought to be able to get my mind around things like that faster."

Strange as it might seem, the shy visitor who had appeared from some asymmetrical, disharmonious, and illogical plane of existence had made an encouraging and stimulating impression on the well-balanced mind of the "young urban specialist." This yuppie wanted less than anything to see himself among characters like the heartless, sad careerists of Dreiser. He hungered after something else, perhaps a wind from those lands from which the eccentric with the same name as his store had appeared.

6

THE INK BLOTTER

*W*hile all of this was happening in the life of her former "faithful companion," or, as she was now calling him, "the scum of the earth," Anisia Korbach-Pupushchina was wandering with her tattered emotions through the shopping arcades of the Big Apple. Everything was driving her mad this evening, she couldn't pick up anything for herself, either the prices irritated her or the cut—just American shit. They think a great deal of themselves, but they just don't understand style. In her mind she kept returning to that damned Sashka: The bastard, the bad coverage in the newspapers was right, he'd learned all of the anti-Soviet tricks right away! Screwed blue and tattooed his dear wife and starts accusing her of being a stool pigeon! Piece of shit of a genius, who needs you? We lived without you before and we'll get along without you now, so just go and get pissed in your bourgeois jungles!

New York, meanwhile, had gone over to its nocturnal regimen, with wells stretching up into the dark while signs burned brightly at the bottoms. She was already approaching the Soviet mission when she saw at the beginning of the block a long, silver limousine. Someone had rolled down one of its four reflecting windows, out of which wafted sweet Latin music. For some reason, she stopped and stared at this whore's dream—an entirely inappropriate occupation for a member of the CSW. It seemed to her somehow that this heap had something to do with her. And she wasn't mistaken. Alongside the limousine, looking at her, stood two men: one ordinary young American, and the second a not-at-all ordinary someone, slim and gangling, in a suit the color of the car and with skin the shade of the school ink of her childhood. Well, there it is, my destiny has appeared, she thought, running the frightening thought slowly through her mind. This future destiny of mine has started in the form of a cheap vaudeville act.

Suddenly she recognized him, the inky one. It was that same Albert—what was it? Blancmange, or something like that?—who the other day had tried to pick her up on the street, offering her riches for just one night. Having spotted her, he somehow went limp, sat back against the rear of the limousine, and for some reason pushed the Ordinary Young Man forward. The OYM suddenly began to speak in the Russian language that was so familiar to her.

"Greet me! I is the translator for Mr. Albert Chapeaumange, the Baron Vendredi. We to wait for you more than five hours already. The baron give me job of to invite you for delicious dinner. He to love you magnificently and sleeps to know your name."

"Well, hello," she answered, as though she were talking to a member of the Party. "My name's Anis." The Baron Vendredi touched her by no means weak hand with his long-fingered one. Contact was made. Well, all right, Bolshevik patriarchy, now we'll show you that the traditions of the Russian feminist Alexandra Kollontai haven't been forgotten yet. You're all used to looking at a woman like some article of bedding, sending her to spy on her own husband—well, now the Bolshevik patriarchy's going to get a forty-year-old—sorry, thirty-nine-year-old—Young Communist League greeting!

Albert cackled like a West Indian rooster in one of the Creole dialects. Anis caught only *amour, jamais,* and *trésor* from the fountain of words. The OYM was devotedly earning his generous emolument. "Monsieur Chapeaumange, Baron Vendredi, promised for vous all the trésor of the island of Haiti. For the most part he always anticiperated this rendezvous in particular of all the life."

"Where are we going?" she asked.

Passion opens its velvet mouth right down to the larynx, the vibration of the vocal cords is visible, a tremolo. They're going to the Plaza, and here they are at the Plaza. The rooms of the Presidential Suite, a staff of Filipino servants, silver-covered platters, magnums of champagne at six hundred dollars a pop. She, of course, didn't know the prices of these things, but we do, and we have no wish to keep the reader "within the limits of reason." "All right," she said to the enamored baron. "Let's go to the bedroom!"

There, in a draped alcove, the purplish black ink of her schoolroom days swept over her in a flood. She suddenly became like an inkwell, like one of those who, with their conelike innards, no matter how you twisted and turned them, kept everything within themselves. At one time she had drawn tiny Georgian bandits with features like Chapeaumange with this sort of ink. Now this *Zhigit* had turned out to be pick of the whole set, with a long drawing pen with a number ninety-six nib, with which he screwed her in a frenzy. Ink blotter, purple stream, shaking, wobbling, the ceiling is spinning. Freedom appears fleetingly in Anis's weary mind.

II. THE BOULEVARD

At the hour of your birth
I must have been at the cinema,
A ten-year scalawag playing hooky.
I shuddered when a rook shrieked as I left.

It was a morose day, and the clouds bulged
Like the bellies of Moscow watchtowers.
At the traffic light there was a bleating
Of horns of BMWs—war trophies.

The cowboy film, the rook, the heavy clouds,
And a gray-coated Stalin standing on the corner.
Somehow everything had changed, but how?
Then, abruptly, behind Trubnaya Square,

The sea seemed to roar,
As if the film had not yet ended,
And I knew:
Loneliness was over.

PART III

1

YORNOVERBLYUDO COUNTY, MARYLAND

*I*t was not until the end of October that Art Duppertat managed to wheedle an invitation to visit his revered president, Stanley Korbach. This had been preceded by several attempts to bring himself to the attention of His Omnipotence, but all of them had come to naught. It wouldn't have been much easier for the lad to get through to Deng Xiaoping in Beijing. The operators informed him that the boss was somewhere out of communications range, perhaps in Greece, perhaps in Indonesia. Art, however, suspected that he was just sitting in his library, playing with the latest bee in his bonnet, genealogical research.

One day, Art simply scribbled a postcard in which he told his boss that he had some confidential information that could be useful for widening the branches of the Korbach ancestral sequoia. For a long time there was no reply—the bastards probably throw all letters into a special high-tech shredder—but then one day the phone rang, and it was none other than Stanley himself on the line! In his usual hoarse, bluff, I-don't-give-a-damn manner, the boss asked: "Why don't you just come down, Art? It's not so far from New York to northern Maryland, after all." What do you know, he's being invited right into the heart of the empire, to Halifax Farm, on the outskirts of Alconost, Yornoverblyudo County, boys and girls!

Once the invitation has come down, that means we're out of here! Art rented a car, and not just any old clunker, but a Cadillac Seville. He wasn't bothered by expenses, since they were tax-deductible for the recently founded Doctor Duppertutto & Co. Art would not have been a superb representative of the yuppie generation had he not founded a fictitious corporation in his own name as a tax dodge.

The leaves were already beginning to show yellow, as the words to a popular song ran, ladies and gentlemen. And to turn scarlet, kind people, and the grapes were taking on a deep cognac hue in the depths of the groves, in case anyone is interested. A record corn crop the height of guardsmen stood along the sides of the winding roads of Yornoverblyudo County. Art looked at it in amazement. He had quite forgotten somehow that before its transformation into popcorn, this . . . er, this stuff stood as a green host festooned with ears like antitank grenades. White clapboard houses with verandas completed the harmony of the hilly expanses. How can one avoid clichés? Ought to just chuck everything and settle down on that hill over there! One can't avoid them, but one can pass by them. Closer and closer to reality.

Reality for Art Duppertat at that moment was a dream, and its name was Sylvia Korbach, his boss's eighteen-year-old daughter. He remembered how, the previous spring, she had jumped out of the water in Palm Beach. I don't know what the birth of Aphrodite was like, but that was obviously how the men on that Florida beach imagined it: a raid by a high surf, a foamy, rubbery boom, crossing the time barrier, and the embodiment of youthful femininity leaps out at you on a slippery board!

Like many beauties of her age, Sylvia was in love with her own body, was ashamed of this feeling, and averted her childlike eyes so as not to blush. Art had tried to attract her attention to another body, that is, to his own, with a demonstration of resilience and flexibility. She had suddenly gasped with delight when she found out that he too, too, too was a fan of those old-timers the Grateful Dead! For a quarter of an hour, no less, they strolled alongside the ocean talking about the genius of Jerry Garcia, singing his songs and breaking into little dances. Could anyone forget it? Impossible, Art was thinking as another meeting came nearer. Hard to imagine that a girl like that still doesn't know about my decision to have her for a wife. After all, such strong thoughts must be transmitted at a distance.

The marvels started right at the approach to the estate. He was driving slowly along a golf course, suddenly saw a golf cart with two passengers approaching a crossing point through the road, and immediately recognized in the two passengers the people for whom this journey had been undertaken: big, broad Stanley and his delicate little daughter Sylvia. Art lowered the window of his Cadillac and asked in a strong un-French accent: *"Est-ce que vous avez du Grey Poupon, monsieur?"*

"Mais oui!" boomed the boss and handed him a flask containing something not bad at all. *"Mon Dieu!"* Sylvia exclaimed and began to glow, leaving not the slightest doubt that strong thoughts are transmitted at a distance.

After a round of golf, this company of somebodies installed themselves on the terrace that surveyed the green banks of an Anglo-Saxon embodiment of the dream of earthly harmony. Art kept staring at his future spouse. She had changed a great deal over the past few months; in any case, she was trying with all her might to show that her childish gusts of emotion had long ago been transformed into an elegant reserve. In keeping with this new direction, she had changed her wardrobe as well: jeans and tank tops had given way to long, wide tweeds. Sylvia was constantly winding a broad silk scarf around her shoulders, then her waist, then her bottom, as though preparing some magic trick. Then again, it was not impossible that things were the other way around: the new wardrobe had summoned up a change in manner. Daddy, of course, held the latter view. Leaning over to Art, he whispered: "She went to visit her big sister, and look at the changes." Art fixed a deep stare on the company president's chin. Stanley—he transmitted his one strong thought to him—I don't need any dowry, no millions, all I need is your Sylvia. The magnate nodded.

Their old servant, Enoch Agasf, whose age of course could not be reckoned, brought everyone tall drinks and stood in one corner of the terrace like a Sumerian Babylonian sculpture of Hammurabi. Let's run through the cast of our mise-en-scène, then. Let's start with the guests. The young soon-to-be relative—so, at least, his intuition told him—Arthur Duppertat. One more quasi relative—that is, simply put, a distant cousin of Stanley's on his mother's side, Norman Blamsdale, a roly-poly, slightly gloomy, middle-aged man, a glance at whom would immediately make our reader say "Now, there's a typical insurance agent!" were he or she not to read to the end of the sentence, the chief aim of which is to impart the information that Norm is a multimillionaire and president of the corporation Blamsdale Brokerage, which is at present expressing a strong and, consequently, suspicious desire to merge with Alexander Korbach, Inc. Also before us is the owner of the property, the massive fifty-five-year-old Stanley Franklin Korbach, with one magnificent leg crossed over the other, no less monumental one, humorously scratching the piebald undergrowth on the crown of his head, steadily, swallow after swallow, dispatching his "vodkatini" to the nether regions of his body, a process helped along superbly by the movement of an Adam's apple supporting a pelicanlike craw with its small age spots. Next to the owner was Marjorie Korbach, the lady of the house, a forty-five-year-old girl with a mane of luxuriant blondish hair with purplish highlights, hair that she had brought up to an unheard-of splendor, constantly running through it pretty little fingers that were also capable of expertly pulling a rifle trigger, for the fingers' owner was a Maryland state shooting champion. Nearby, of course, was the daughter of the owner and his wife, the subject of our, and Art's, sighs, Sylvia, a student at Pennsylvania's Dickinson College, who was preparing to leave the local pastorales of higher education in order to join the wild herds of students at Columbia in Manhattan. Next to his half sister, in a determined pose, that is, leaning against a column, stood Marjorie's son and Stanley's stepson, twenty-three-year-old Anthony Arrowsmith, of the breed of latter-day Byrons—that is, one of those young people who are not about to pay their own way in later life. The latter had just returned to dry American land after two years of solitary sailing, and had graciously agreed to resume his studies of Shakespeare at Harvard. The most improbable member of the cast, at least as far as Art Duppertat was concerned, was the head of security at Alexander Korbach—that department store that we already know so well—the handsome, dark-skinned Ben Duckworth. It's curious to note that Art, who was in a state of unimaginable excitement, at first paid no attention to him, and it was only just before dinner, when he bumped into him at the fountain, that he not so much asked as exclaimed: "And how'd you come to be here, Ben?" to which the reserved light cavalryman replied that his family had tight connections with the Korbachs, so much so that they were almost like relatives.

Having observed this selection of characters in stasis, we must now, of course, introduce some dynamic energy, and toward this end we need to add to our cast

Lenore Yablonsky, Norm Blamsdale's "just happened to drop in at Halifax Farm" niece, known in these rural surroundings as a young woman "with a complicated story."

The conversation moved along sluggishly at first; everyone seemed to be looking at Duppertat—what's he going to say? Art sensed this mood, and without any self-consciousness—to his credit, it must be said that he was never tongue-tied in the presence of the powerful of this world—lightly slapped a palm that he had worn out playing golf to his forehead. "By the way, friends"—at this point Marjorie Korbach and Norman Blamsdale exchanged imperceptible glances that were perceptible all the same—"I've been saving a funny little story for you. Imagine this, a couple of months ago, I learned from a strange visitor that my last name has a connection with commedia dell'arte, in fact to a character created by Hoffmann, a Doctor Duppertutto."

"How nice!" Sylvia cried with a clap of her hands, and became a bit flustered when she caught Mom and Uncle Norman shooting glances at her that were fleeting but still did not escape her entirely. Daddy burst out with one of his winning laughs. "Really, Art, you only found out about that two months ago?" Art parried right back: "Do you mean that you knew about it when you made me director, Stanley?"

"Well, naturally," the boss said, and everyone laughed. "When I looked over the list of possibilities, my friend"—at this form of address, Marjorie's rosy lips formed an elongated O—"I just tripped right over your name. Aha, I said, there's Doctor Duppertutto, and an Art at that! That's my boy, I said, and, as we see now, it was the right choice!"

He applauded Art, and everyone else followed his example. Of course, the splashing of the young college lady's claps and the booming cannon shots of those of the security specialist stood out from the general hubbub.

"I wonder, is there so much as one bottle of champagne in this house?" Art asked, and then thought that this time he may have overstepped his bounds a bit. Not a bit of it. The boss simply turned to his old servant. "What do you think, Enoch, have we got a bottle of champagne around somewhere?"

"Of course, sir," replied the old Semite and immediately moved off.

So that we don't have to come back to it again, we'll say right now that about ten minutes later he came back with half a dozen bottles of Veuve Clicquot '62.

Art explained: "I asked for champagne in the hope that everyone would drink to my commercial success with this 'commedia dell'arte.' "

"To your success . . . mmm . . . Art?" Mrs. Korbach asked in surprise, without disturbing a single one of her very few wrinkles.

"Pardon me, Margie," the insolent young man corrected himself. "I meant, our commercial success in general."

"Maybe you'd like to explain?" Anthony Arrowsmith asked haughtily. This was the first time that he had seen this overly familiar type, and he was surprised at how the fellow seemed to get away with anything in the presence of Mom and her stern close friend Norman. Anthony despised yuppie parvenus with every fiber of his neo-Byronism.

"Well, of course, don't worry, old man," Art said to him. "Listen and learn while I live. Now then, after this strange guest who had told me about Doctor Duppertutto left, I switched on my information system and tried to learn as much as I could about these Italian comedies, whose roots go back to Dante's day—you know, all that folklore business. Everyone knows, of course, that they developed particularly in eighteenth-century Venice. Yes, there were two Carlos, that's right, Sylvia—Goldoni and Gozzi—and they were the ones who got this stuff seriously rolling. I ordered up some visuals, and soon there were various old masks lying before me. And suddenly I had a brilliant idea. Yes, yes, Sylvia, brilliant, I don't have any other kind. Then again, I ought to say, obviously, that this idea, all boiling over with thunder, came on me like some dark purple storm cloud in the middle of a stuffy day. No, Margie, dear, your servant here doesn't write poetry, but I think I could. On what theme, you'd like to know? Why, on the theme of eternal love, of course, dear lady. For me, ladies and gentlemen, love isn't castles in paradise. Love sends a signal that the motor of the heart is switched on again and firing on all cylinders, madam. Let's get back to this story of commercial success. My idea was as simple as this bottle of champagne. I decided to make a line of large dolls along the lines of the amazingly funny characters of commedia dell'arte, all of these Pantalonis, Pulcinellas, Brighellas, Colombines, Harlequins, Pierrots; the Captain, braggart and coward, who claims to have sailed around the world; Tartalli, the boring pedant; and also the old chatterbox, my ancestor, Doc Duppertutto, created by the great Hoffmann—in other words, the heroes of all of these immortal *fiabe*. You know, of course, that the tired old Barbie doll is still one of the most reliable sale items in the world. Why don't we try to beat her with our new characters? I thought. A risky venture, you say? But doesn't our head office teach us the art of risk? Am I right, Stanley, or not? Why not give it a try, after first making careful calculations as to the conditions, and then letting rip all of the devices of aggressive marketing?"

Stanley nodded. "Interesting idea, Art! I'll give you the okay, you can have a try."

"I already have," Art admitted modestly. "Using funds from my own company, I ordered the first shipment of these dolls from a clique of young artists in SoHo, super guys, free from any clichés or stereotypes. Then we put the shipment in Alexander Korbach at prices that wouldn't run over mass-production prices. The results beat all my expectations! The dolls sold out in three hours! The customers snatched the dolls like crazy people, grabbing them from each other! There was almost something like a riot when we announced that our stocks were exhausted. The 'riot,' by the way, was very tactfully handled by our security guards. After this first test, we doubled our order, then tripled it, then increased it by ten. At the present time, the goods are coming in on a regular basis, and the number of buyers keeps on growing. Believe it or not, ladies and gentlemen, they line up every morning before the shop opens to pick up these Artie-Dartie-Italianos, as they call them. According to the figures for the first three weeks, we've even beaten the Cabbage Patch Kids. That's how things look!"

"I saw a big headline in *The Village Voice* the other day," Lenore Yablonsky put in suddenly. She was straddling the railing of the terrace, a clement breeze from the Atlantic lightly ruffling her dark hair. "The headline said: 'Doll Craze in Alexander Korbach. Dr. Duppertutto's Records!' "

Having said this, she lowered her eyes, as though she were embarrassed by the momentary general attention, and as if until then she hadn't noticed that young Arrowsmith could not take his eyes off her. There's a slut for you, young Arrowsmith's mother thought at that point.

"Oh, I'd really like to see these Artie-Dartie-Italianos!" Sylvia cried. "I'm going to New York tomorrow!" Everyone turned toward her, and she in her turn was no less embarrassed than the experienced Lenore, and even blushed a bit. Hmm, Art thought. The local mademoiselles are remarkably timid. Hmm . . .

"Don't worry, baby!" he said. "I brought you a whole bag of them!"

He rushed, arms forward, to one corner of the terrace, sliding on his stomach like a football player on the tile floor. There he got a densely packed Adidas bag that he had brought up beforehand. A flourish of the zipper, and the previously mentioned characters began to appear, each one no smaller than a good-size cat.

Even the skeptics—and there were at least three of them on the terrace, including that old fox in business Norman Blamsdale—were won over. Excitement reigned. The soft dolls were passed from hand to hand, kissed by dry and wet mouths alike, pinched on their cheeks and chests. Sylvia cuddled them like a child. The mighty Stanley had Brighella and the Captain doing a little dance on his athletic shoulders. Marjorie kissed the frivolous Colombine on both cheeks: "She looks like me, don't you think?" When the tumult had subsided, the young manager came out with his prepared little speech: "I still can't believe, ladies and gentlemen, that for this commercial, not to say aesthetic success, I'm obliged to none other than that very strange visitor with his chaotic manners. And now, guys, hold on to your seats, the name of the visitor, a recent immigrant from Russia, is Alexander Korbach!"

This was the cue for the beginning of a "freeze," fully in keeping with the traditions of the founder of the Russian school of the grotesque, Nikolai Gogol, in his play *The Inspector General.* Only Ben Duckworth smiled, tapping the floor with a polished heel and giving silent thanks for his unusually restrained character. It's a good thing Art brought this bit of news to them, and not me. It would have been one stupid idea for me to do it. For several reasons—more about that later—it would have been tactless.

The first to speak, prying open her frowning mouth, was the lady of the house: "I beg your pardon, Art, but it seems to me that you're putting on one of your commedia dell'arte scenes for us, as if we were nothing more than a company of fools for you. Are you sure you've not missed your calling, young man? Maybe you ought to be in the theater, instead of in a business enterprise?" With each word, she moved farther and farther away from the image of Colombine.

"You're wrong, Marjorie!" Art said. "This is all quite serious!" He began to tell the story of the strange man with the large bald spot but youthful features who had seen in the night a lit-up sign advertising their huge store, had experienced something along the lines of an existential shock, and had staggered inside, frightening the entire perfume department.

At this point the owner of the house interrupted him. "If you don't mind, Art, you can tell me this story personally in my study." Excusing himself to the others, he firmly took his "retail genius" by the arm and led him into the interior of the castle.

2

HALIFAX CASTLE, NOTHING SPECIAL

*W*hile they're making their way through the tangle of corridors and halls in the direction of the study, we can spare a few pages for the story of the dwelling and, in passing, give the reader some idea of who the second principal character of this saga is, the man whose lot will be to decidedly cramp the style of our nervous Sasha with his *dolce stil nuovo,* so appropriate to the trash heaps of New York . . . sorry, but we seem to have lost the beginning of the sentence, making it as crude as the trim on the ceilings of Halifax, under which young Duppertat and his aging boss are now making their way in the direction of the latter's study.

Of his numerous residences scattered throughout America and the world, Stanley Korbach felt the greatest attachment to this Maryland nest, perhaps because it had been right here that he had come into the world. This hilly land with its bluish green pines had been bought precisely a hundred years before by Alexander Korbach, the founder of the business dynasty, on the occasion of his marriage to Cecilia Daugherty, of whose non-Jewish ancestry he had been so proud in those naive days. In addition to her ancestry, there were other reasons for pride—to be precise, Cecilia's solid dowry, provided by an old Irish clan that had struck it rich in the railroad business. It was this dowry—as well as, naturally, the new ties of kinship—that had contributed to the rapid rise of the already respectable fortunes of the Alexander Korbach retail business and had led to the building of a gigantic, by the standards of the era, department store just off Broadway. Taking advantage of the cheap labor of his recent comrades in immigration—that is, providing an example of the most rapacious sort of Marxist capitalism—Korbach soon built a branch store in Baltimore, as well as this "English castle," in which we have introduced the reader to his great-grandson. By our use of quotation marks, by the way, we are not placing in doubt the English origins of the castle. As was the fashion then, Halifax was brought to Maryland almost stone by stone from a faraway shire where the young couple had seen it on their honeymoon. The stones and the wood were seventeenth-century, though the originals had not been enough for their nouveau-riche tastes, which was why garish imitations had been added on. The result was a dwelling rather ungainly in appearance, with Tudor facades and Moorish arches, decorated with sixteenth-century tapestries and, above them, kitsch, brought back from hunting, in the form of huge deer heads—with wide windows in the Parisian style and pseudo-Scandinavian towers, which still gave an aftertaste of the spirit of commerce of the late nineteenth century.

Each generation of Korbachs had made its own contribution to this hodgepodge. Stanley's grandfather Robert had built an Art Nouveau guesthouse on a nearby hill, with stylized eagles at each corner of the numerous terraces that could hardly fail to remind our reader of the style of *The Great Gatsby*. The school that had followed it, Deco, in combination with Constructivist elements brought from Russia and Germany, was used by the architects of Stanley's father, David, to build a one-of-a-kind orangerie cum garage, in which to this day are parked collector-quality Bugattis, Hispano-Suizas, Rollses, and Daimlers, as well as two beloved 1956 Cadillacs, one white and one black, which the eighty-five-year-old patriarch likes to drive—the black one or the white one, depending on his mood—through the nearby towns, pretending to be an ordinary farmer and flirting with the girls. Everyone in these parts knows him, of course, but everyone plays along with this familiar pastime of Yornoverblyudo County.

In the forties Dave Korbach founded a stud farm, through which several generations of stallions and mares had passed and which turned out a valued breed of racehorses that sold for millions. In the sixties, when David Korbach retired from the financial world to concentrate in the main on various forms of debauchery—he was one of the pioneers who blazed the now popular trail to Bangkok—his son Stanley took his place at the head of the company and of the splendidly burgeoning clan. Of course, he had done his bit for the growth of Halifax Farm. His second wife, Malka Rosenthal, in whose Italian Jewish beauty all the pride of the Mediterranean seemed to seethe, had been a great appraiser of modern art. The architectural celebrity Mr. Pei was called in and built for her his latest masterpiece, a telescopic art gallery, which had quickly been filled with visions of artists of the Chicago School. The inspired figures themselves made frequent trips to the area around Halifax for plein air exhibitions and never missed the opportunity to gather around the castle's mahogany bar; oh, the sixties!

Now, in the early eighties, the farm more often than not went calmly through its daily routine in the absence of its owners. Art experts had compiled catalogs and sent the masterpieces to exhibitions; the breeders looked after their *gungs* (see *Gulliver's Travels*); the servant population increased through inbreeding and watched televisions in the inhabited wing of the dark palace.

But lately, most frequently in the autumn or at a Seder supper, the Korbachs had been entertaining, and the castle windows were ablaze with light, as in the old days. The first two generations, alas, were already beyond the reaches of the financial world. The third generation was represented by the old king, David, the fourth by the reigning prince, Stanley, his wife (the latest one), and his sisters and their husbands. With the fifth generation—that is, the Korbach children, aged eighteen to thirty—all the raging racket of young modern America made its way into the castle, just the sort of thing that one might hear entering a bar in George-town on a Saturday night. A sixth had already appeared—growing children whose peeping sounds foretold the next link in the chain, so long as the union of free states that so recently, all of two hundred years ago, was such a sparsely populated continent still stands.

Arriving at Halifax, Stanley sometimes would open the door to the room in which he was born and stand on the threshold. The bed, brought along with the stones from England, had not changed a bit since then. Here, between the spread legs of his mother, through her distended vulva, one more scrap of human flesh, this one bearing his name, had wriggled out. The birth process clearly, in a certain sense, imitates the primeval rising of life from the ideal, a certain inflation of what is now called DNA—that is, the formula of original sin, the temptation of what is sweet, dragging all biological life writhing in pain after it. The formula from the very beginning grows ever more complicated, gives birth to the "secret of being," then begins to simplify itself—that is, to die—and in the final analysis decodes it-self, as it were, into dust, into the simplest elements, beyond which stands the "se-cret of unbeing."

When he stood on the threshold of this room, Stanley nearly always remembered August 1945. The rocking deck of the aircraft carrier *Yorktown*. Huge sunsets in the Pacific, on the approach to Japan. He had turned eighteen at the beginning of that year. To his mother's horror, he had volunteered for the Marines. He had gone through half a year of training in Norfolk, Virginia. Now they were heading west to get to the Far East, and to finish off a country that not so long ago had been so mighty. In the gathering dusk, gigantic flashes of lightning illuminated the smelt-ing furnace of the sunset for a few moments. The men were quietly saying that probably every fifth man, and maybe even every third man, would die in the land-ing.

One day he caught a sergeant who was usually a crude and bellowing loud-mouth looking at him with sadness and affection. This look seemed to say: Are they really going to kill this kid, too, so tall and well-built? At that moment the ship began to execute some maneuver and pitched even more than usual. Stanley felt an existential terror. He realized that it had nothing to do with the coming battle. He simply felt the instability of existence, that moment between two dark secrets. After that, strangely, fear before battle disappeared. There was present in the world something in the face of which the storming of Japan seemed a simple and even invigorating affair. After the sixth of August, they landed on an island paralyzed by the atomic revelations. No one in their unit died. Only Dick Duckworth strained some ligaments trying to be the first to get to shore.

The aircraft carrier *Yorktown* is permanently anchored in a quiet bay near Charleston, South Carolina. The deck no longer rocks. Tourists capture their mo-ments on the flight deck with Kodaks and Minoltas. Photography confirms reality. Or does it mock it? Stanley Franklin Korbach, fifty-five-year-old president of

Alexander Korbach, Inc., is one of the symbols of the stability of this great country. One would never imagine any skeletons of existential self-doubt in his closet. No one even guesses how little he gives a damn about his presidency. All the business of the firm, including the increase of its assets and the reductions of its liabilities, investments in Silicon Valley, in television, in retail, in Kuwaiti oil, negotiations with the Blamsdale group concerning the merger of two giants in the name of unimaginable progress—all of this seemed like the whining of marmosets in comparison with that moment on the threshold of the room in which his mother had once groaned as she freed herself of her burden.

They passed by "the room" and climbed a spiral staircase into the tower room with large windows that was Stanley's study. Art took in the details of the room with a clear eye, in order to either instill them in his own life or reject them categorically. A bust of Aristotle—now there was a piece of work! A bronze heron with the round eyes of a silly young girl—that wouldn't do: just kitsch. The owner of the house removed several books from the shelves and took out a decanter of port from behind them. Judging by the color, it beats my stuff by a long shot, the young merchant thought, not without regret.

"Believe it or not, Stanley, that Russian Alexander Korbach knocked back a whole bottle of Churchill in my office in fifteen minutes."

"I can easily believe it," said Stanley and thought: Maybe even in five.

"Well, all right, tell me the story, and don't spare the details," he said. He sank his backside into his armchair and raised his knees to the level of his chin.

Art began to tell him the story that is known to the reader from the last chapter. We'll not repeat ourselves here, seeing as how we told the story from the point of view of our fine, upstanding young man, from whom we expect no falsehoods. The narrative technique that we employ often excludes the possibility of lying. We'll add: Or it immediately exposes it. We ask the reader not to notice the devices of the literary craft, but we wouldn't object if he were to take what has just been said and wash it down his gullet together with the booze.

"Well, I thought that it might seem important to you," Art said, finishing his story. "He's an exact namesake of the founder, after all."

"Important?!" Stanley said excitedly. "What could possibly be more important?!" The merger with Blamsdale Brokerage ought to be, thought Art.

"The B.B. merger is a piece of shit compared to this!" Stanley seemed well and truly agitated. He stood up sharply from his chair. The old man's got one springy backside, Art noted. Stanley was already pacing back and forth his round, spacious study. "We've just started working out the Russian branch of the Korbach family tree—there are some gaps in it—and now a discovery like this! This Alexander Korbach could turn out to be none other than the son of Jakob Korbach. The Russians have a middle name called a patronymic. From his full name we can know the name of his father. Tell me, Art, did the word Zakharovich come up at any time in your conversation?"

Art, unfortunately, couldn't remember. He had wanted to keep the fellow around, even put him in the Plaza on his own account, but the guy had suddenly waved him off and left. "He's a strange one, this Alexander of yours, Jakob's son. Seems to be one of those artistic personalities that rock the boat. What do I mean? Well, when you realize that he doesn't do things like everyone else, you start to ask yourself, Why do I do things the way I do them? That sort of rocking the boat."

Stanley rubbed his hands together the way his grandfather before him had done. Never mind, we'll find him anyway! With the advance of the years, he had suddenly developed the Jewish habit of rubbing his hands together vigorously when excited or concentrating on something. "A genealogical team is working for us now, three highly qualified specialists. One's a bookworm who digs in the archives, one's a detective, and the third . . . well, he's just an English spy. They'll start digging right away!"

Art was pleased that the boss thought so highly of his news. Nevertheless he asked: "What are you doing this research for, Stanley?" The magnate was momentarily flustered, scratched the back of his head, then spread his hands wide apart. "I'm sorry, Art, but I don't want to talk about it with you right now, at your age and in this exuberant mood of yours. Sorry, I don't want to offend you, but I can't answer your question just now." He began pacing again. "In fact, I've got a question for you that has to do with your age." He silently circled the office for some time, giving Aristotle a slap on the head, stroking the heron as though he were going to say something to it, and then he would come to a sudden stop—"Art!"—and then continue circling, until he sat down directly on the arm of his guest's chair, that is, towering over Art with all his own body of a rower on Columbia's famous 8 Team from the fifties. "It's not even a question but a request—that is, a question in the numerator and a request in the denominator."

When did he find the time to get so potched? thought the young merchant. "Listen here, Italian, how would it be if you married my daughter? You ask which one, and I'll answer that it's my youngest, because the three older ones are already married, it seems. To Sylvia, the one you were flirting up a storm with today."

"All right, all right," Art said, trying to bring him to reason. "You've had your joke with a poor young man."

"I'm not joking," Stanley said severely. "You know that she's enrolled in Columbia University, and you know as well as I do what Columbia's like, just one long orgy. All they think about at Columbia is how to get through thousands of bucks, getting stoned and screwing in attics and cellars. Sweet Sylvia will be easy prey for that crowd. She'll read her poems, play her cello, and then she'll get seduced and she'll come down with some disgusting new disease. Am I making myself clear? Fall in love and get married! You'll be happy—forgive me for getting mushy—and you'll bring me grandchildren!"

With that, the head of the firm, losing his balance in all senses of the term, slid down from the arm of the chair and gave his future son-in-law a bear hug. Art Duppertat wiped the tearful eyes of his future father-in-law with his sleeve. The fate of a nearly grown young woman was being decided. Would he agree? How could one refuse a suffering father? How could they leave her at the mercy of the sex maniacs at Columbia?

3

STANLEY KORBACH IN THE FAMILY
CIRCLE AND ON HIS OWN

*T*he dinner table was set on the terrace of the guesthouse beneath the eagles and beside the stone maw casting a crystal stream of water into a decadent cup. The diners seated around the table—and there were no fewer than a dozen of them—took no particular notice when the owner of the house and his young protégé joined them. General attention at that point was concentrated on Lenore Yablonsky. That beauty was one of those people who know how to turn a perfectly planned meal into utter confusion. Her simple checkered shirt could have thrown anyone into confusion. In the first place, it was buttoned perilously on her chest, and in the second place its simplicity was underscored by her recherché spectacles, sitting on her well-turned nose in the role of a dragonfly of discord.

There were stories that Lennie Yablonsky had led the radical students to mount the barricades of Berkeley in '68 like Anka the Machine Gunner. Maybe the stories were false, maybe not. She seemed to have calmed down since then, had even wanted on several occasions to start a family, but there was still something intimidating about her from those revolutionary days, and interested men always chucked her once they noticed that bile sometimes clouded her magnificent eyes. No pun about "the apple of her eye" is intended here, because Lenore didn't know that her name meant "apple," and anyway in English eyes are referred to as "balls." Let us add one more interesting detail: The aging appearance of her hands didn't fit with her youthful-looking neck, as though she really had pulled the trigger of a machine gun on the barricades and had hatched explosives in the basement at home.

At the moment when we, along with Art and Stanley, were approaching the table, just to know what the rich have for dinner, Lenore was telling an off-putting story with a wicked smile. It seemed that a former friend of hers, who, like our Anthony, had always been obsessed with the glories of seagoing adventurers, had also set out to circumnavigate the world in a thirty-foot yacht. However, unlike our brave Anthony, he didn't set off across the Atlantic right away but sailed along the American coast from north to south and, after several prolonged and very pleasant stops, made it to Nassau. He stayed there for a month, smoking dope, while local underage girls got to know the springiness of his gangplank.

Our Anthony, as everyone knows, made his first extended stop in Morocco, while this one, after leaving the Bahamas, sailed along through the Windward Islands, stopping for a week or two in Aruba, then on to Sint Maarten, drifting around these fashionable resorts and never forgetting to visit the casino.

In the end he got to Guadeloupe and was absolutely knocked out by the beauty of the Creole girls. He spent almost six months there and went regularly to a nudist beach incognito, always a drink under his belt, or even several. Once every two weeks he would get in radio contact with a mutual friend of ours, a member of a yacht club, and would let him know that he was, say, entering a storm front around Cape Horn, and so on. On these solitary sailing expeditions—our Anthony knows more about this than I do—you can lie your head off without any risk to your reputation. Isn't that true, Anthony? Well, what are you getting so steamed up about? If it's not so, if there really is some way of checking these things, then just tell us, people who aren't in the know . . . why get so hot under the collar?

Everyone had already begun to get tired of all this when Anthony stood up sharply, pushed away his chair, and ran down the stairs into the darkness of the park. Lenore sighed and spread her arms in a gesture of despair—it's so hard to find mutual understanding.

Stanley, meanwhile, putting away fish with a salad, had almost sobered up. He was looking with satisfaction at his daughter and young Duppertat, who, it seemed, had already agreed about how to avoid the temptations at Columbia. He also took no small pleasure in failing to notice his wife's significant glances. With advancing age, the old girl had begun to often show a strange indignation at everything happening around her. It seemed to her that everyone was living off us, that no one paid enough respect to us. And yet what a slut she'd been not so long ago! You were already on her territory at ten paces, and you couldn't get away without banging her in some convenient place. Or in an inconvenient place. In an inconvenient place often enough, oh yes! In a forest, for example, in the thorns. On a coral reef. In order to get back to her own essence, she always had to have her sights trained on a new penis. If I'd been open with her, I'd have told her to always aim for a new penis. But not for Norm Blamsdale's, all the same. That sort of thing makes you a little sick. Of course, she feels comfortable exchanging looks with him, but it would still be better for her to try for another one, so as to blaze out with her old electricity. Stanley remembered that the negotiations for the merger of "SK" with "NB" would get under way the next day, and he felt a bit sick himself.

Anthony suddenly emerged from the darkness and sat down beside Lenore. They quietly struck up a conversation about something. Lenore had not looked at Stanley once the whole day. Goddamned women! He wasn't about to start playing these tedious games. He only gives what he can. And that's quite a lot! Quite a lot! No need at all to just turn up without warning in the family circle, even if you are a distant relation, to attract attention to yourself by telling sarcastic stories, and to needle a kid fourteen years younger than you are. He deftly avoided eye contact with Margie once again, stood up, and walked off into the park.

There was a musty, autumnal smell of oak and elm in the air. From the top of the hill, from a bench knocked together by someone as far back as Grandfather Robert, he saw the lit-up terrace and the young people around the table. Art was playing the guitar and performing like one of his dolls. Marjorie, by the way, was right—he put us all on today, like it was a play. Well, this play at least we'll remember. Everything that doesn't get into dramatic art tumbles into the abyss. Then again, dramatic art, once it gets unsteady on its feet, falls in, too. "Waves of Time" doesn't enter into it here. There is no time outside of us. No sooner do we shake off our skin than all time comes to a stop. The past, and the present, and the future. What's more, this whole idea of an orderly march is pure fiction. Motion, in principle, comes back. A moment of the future immediately becomes the past. All moments, without exception: the swirling of the leaves in an Atlantic breeze, and the falling water, and the immobility of the stone eagle, and picking the strawberries out of the ice cream, and Duppertat's little song . . . everything from the future becomes the past. They say that we are the hostages of eternity, captives of time. No, we're captives of something else.

He came down the hill and walked along a tree-lined path, beneath the soft leaves of chestnut trees drooping out of the twilight. He walked past a capricorn lit by a bright lamp. Hi, Dad! Everyone here seemed to notice a resemblance between the statue and David, the family patriarch, but no one said anything out loud. I'm walking away into the dusk. I'll appear again in a band of light beside the little house that Enoch Agasf has lived in since the "Korbach era" started a hundred years ago. The windows were open there. The young generation of the great Semite's offspring were watching TV—on the screen, the arbitress of thoughts hosting the chat show, lips, brows, and noses all protruding. The sound of her voice reached him: "I want to ask you, victims of sexual violence! If a rapist at the request of his victim uses a condom, can we consider his actions rape?" Outburst of emotion in the packed auditorium. He was going back into the dusk. Everything is moving forward, that is, into the past. Steps, as always, lead into the past. Darkness also goes into the past, it doesn't have forever to be dark.

At the end of the path is a gazebo like the *hermitages* of old Russian country estates. According to motifs of the Russian classic *Eye*-van *Tooor*-genev. There beside it, at one time, just before the period of his Third Disappearance, he and Enoch had buried bottles of cheap booze. A repulsive period of his life, it must be said. Margie and her retinue searched the whole garden, sent spies even to the local dives. Outright persecution, that's what it really was, but according to the family mythology, she "saved him."

It made him sick to his stomach to remember those lunches to which she'd invited some famous psychiatrists in the guise of new neighbors, or realtors, or distant relations. He had to hear only one sentence to know who was sitting at the table and drilling his little professional eyes into him on the sly, earning a fee.

In order to lighten the pronouncement of their diagnosis of a midlife crisis, he began to read "In the midway of this our mortal life, I found me in a gloomy wood . . . ," and laughed loudly when he realized that he'd hit the nail on the head.

She proclaimed "dry law." Who do you think you are, feeling sorry for me, or is it yourself you're feeling sorry for—it's disgusting, downright idiotic, he ranted. Afraid they'll kick me out, that you'll lose your title? You stupid woman, what the fuck do we care about this title? I sit in the president's armchair only because they can't make a single decision without me. Walking computers can't say yes or no.

She chased off people I sent out for booze. Everyone was cowed—it was totalitarianism, pure and simple. Only the Eternal Jew out of all of them buried a few half-gallon bottles of Gallo's California rotgut for me. A vital thing, I must say. Swallow a few gargantuan gulps and you feel like you've seized this fucking nonexistent moment by the bridle.

I'll bet there's still a bottle of the stuff around here somewhere, maybe even two. Three years after the Third Disappearance, he remembered that there were still bottles left here, but now he was coy with himself, pretending that he was looking blindly. Finally, he pushed away a few bricks in the foundation and thrust his arm into a dark hole. Now some goddamned filthy creature's going to rip my hand off. His hand calmly ambled along the necks of the bottles. He pulled one out, tore off the moldy sealing wax, and unscrewed the plastic cork. He had a swig of the contents of the three-year-old survivor. Eh, not bad!

So, let me have a look at myself objectively. Stanley Franklin Korbach, great-great-grandson of a Warsaw furrier, sits with all of his still muscular behind on one of the highest American thrones. He sits, but he squirms. What the hell is he sitting there for if he can't settle in? Let's not just dismiss the question, particularly since my head seems to be strangely enlightened.

Well, he sits there, as we've already said, simply because without him this whole *meshpukha*—the family and the company—would come tumbling down right away. He sits here like Gargantua, or like his son Pantagruel, benevolent tyrant over slobs and clods. He'd felt something Gargantuan in himself his whole life, ladies and gentlemen of the reading audience and members of their families. A strange inclination toward gigantism had always slumbered within him, and had sometimes been aroused. His throat felt the need for huge swallows. The Homeric appetite appeared out of nowhere. Just today, for example, he'd furtively eaten a two-foot fish. Moderation in sex was replaced at times by a gigantic drive; he would do it with six of these Maryland German babes, one right after the other. At times it seemed to him that, I'm taller than my oaks, I'm dragging myself along, looking over the golf course and the farm, with a crown of birds circling my head. Fortunately he'd gotten down to manageable Rabelaisian dimensions, and he was opening a normal bottle. To your health, O great Gargantuan!

Three years ago this half-gallon cost $3.19—the number was fixed in his mind, because he'd had to borrow money from the servants. These days, to judge from the state of the New York stock market, you wouldn't get off for less than a fiver for a bottle. Still, that's not a high price to pay for an attempt to separate two flattening walls, the future and the past. His old drinking buddy, Rabbi Dershkowitz, says that booze won't save you from the gloom. *Tfila*—that's the best antidepressant, he says, but knocks it back as well as Gargantua. Never argued with him, and I'm not going to start. Always believed in all the gods, and I believe in them now, and of course in the One God. I believe in the burning bush, and in Mt. Sinai, and in Moses' prophetic tongue-tiedness. I believe in God the Son Jesus Christ, sent to separate us, the lambs of the universe, from our sins. I believe in the Latter-day Saints and in heavenly Mohammed. I believe, yet I suffer just the same, because my faith lies in time, and time doesn't exist.

Is it because I belong to America and it's here in America I'm living out my life that I'm squirming so much? The people of Gargantua and Pantagruel felt immortal, and every decomposition saw a new composition. Perhaps homogeneous nations have preserved this spirit of bodily unity right up to the present—all of these French, Japanese, or Poles. Either America or Russia, these communicating courtyards of multinational rabble, have not yet discovered this idea of infinite reproduction or else they've lost it irretrievably.

I consider myself a Jew, and I don't even understand what a Jew is. Being an American, I'm always hearing the siren song of cosmopolitanism. A man of planet Earth, I can't imagine myself as its tiniest particle. That's why I try to grab hold of the umbilical cord of my people and let myself get dragged back into the uterus. You're mad, you'll say, madam, and you'll be close to the truth. Diagnosis: chronic alcoholism. Vegetative dystonia. Psychasthenic syndrome with manic-depressive tendencies. Midlife crisis.

There's no point in talking about the middle of life anymore, ladies and gentlemen. My skin is being implacably speckled with age and drooping. The tragic Jew is constantly peering through the mask of a grinning Yankee. Final third crisis, at best. After an eruption of his libido late in life, Goethe banished mortal flesh to Mephistopheles. Mephistopheles buys a soul with only one aim—to divide it from the body. He has no use for the soul, he wants to have mastery over the human body, which, obviously, was the whole point of original sin.

Another philosopher, however, would say that the body is a holy vessel, in which, after all, the soul travels—which means that it, too, is sacred. Are there souls with flaws, or are they irreproachable? The warping of a personality—does it consist only in a deal that the body strikes with the devil? Doesn't irreproachability abolish the very concept of personality? Impersonal perfection seems monotonous to us here in our earthly estate. Or are we simply shrinking in the face of the incomprehensible? Let's recall Signor Alighieri's songs from Paradise, that pure beaming of joy, "monotonous" in comparison with the torments of Hell and the severity of Purgatory. The modulation of the radiance on Beatrice's face speaks only of love, but the world of heavenly love is far more incomprehensible to man than the torments of Hell, because it bears no relation to the body. In the third and most improbable of the books, Dante repeats over and over: Can't understand, can't grasp it. Beatrice tries to lower herself to his level of understanding:

My beauty, which the loftier it climbs,
As thou hast noted, still doth kindle more,
So shines that, were no tempering interposed,
Thy mortal puissance would from its rays
Shrink, as the leaf doth from the thunderbolt.

Lowering himself to the floor and leaning back against a column of the gazebo, Stanley Korbach took another swig of the hard stuff and continued to blissfully mutter what he remembered of the *Divine Comedy:*

In color like to sun-illumined gold,
A ladder, which my ken pursued in vain,
So lofty was the summit; down whose steps
I saw the splendors in such multitude descending.

The entire park seemed to him just now like a part of the universe, not even needing to be covered with a layer of air, and he himself was a part of the universe who didn't even need to be in his aging skin, perhaps was even just a step away from the "means of transport."

His eternally old manservant Enoch Agasf was sitting alongside him now with a cigar. He whispered or thought to a conclusion anything that, as it seemed to him, the "kid" had forgotten or left out through absentmindedness.

4

A SUCCESSFUL NIGHT

*P*erhaps we should close this section on a youthful note. It seems as though the cook who started the soup ought to lap the rest of it up. It was 4:00 A.M. when Art Duppertat, absolutely exhausted from his success, dragged himself off to the room that had been prepared for him with its Napoleon-era bed under an Egyptian canopy. Just before collapsing onto this most impressive of berths, he remembered to clean his teeth thoroughly with an electric toothbrush that had only just appeared on the market.

While he was brushing his teeth, something unforeseen occurred. A large, gleaming, pearly bubble appeared from his mouth. For no less than five minutes, Art stood before the mirror with a bubble between his lips. He realized that the grotesque sight before him was a symbol of his success. He was afraid to move, to frighten it away. Finally he took hold of himself and turned out the light. In the darkness, the bubble made its way back inside, filling him with the joy of being.

He lay for a long time with this joy, all of his limbs quivering. Sylvia, Sylvia— why, she's just an absolute angel among our young people! Hard somehow to imagine that it's possible to possess this treasure, to stick my member in her. Through the open window wafted the frost-tinged, starry October air. Suddenly the door creaked, a bare shoulder peeped out into a band of moonlight. A put-on tiny peeping voice said: "Doctor Duppertutto, Colombine is visiting you, her little head hurts, please cure it, kind *signore*!"

What an angel among our young people, though, he thought, filling with passion. The unimaginable was now presenting itself as an entirely real prospect. And it was only in the close quarters of the infinite possibilities of nakedness that Art realized that he was a captive not of the "angel" but of that battle-scarred sexual warrior Lenore Yablonsky.

III. THE PREMIERE

All of life might be Rome, which
Without liberties or waste
Puts you in an actor's platform shoes
And crows: Let the show begin!

Night. In a well-lit side street
Stands a demanding beau monde.
Foppish girls chatter there like jackdaws,
And snobs smoke Belomors.

It's just about to begin. The thunder of the prologue
Will shake yesterday's recycling center.
A four-span chariot will burst with a cart
Into the great modern style, totally mad.

You begin. The thunder of the ovation
Addles your head like cocaine,
Your talents and your sly people
Are seething everywhere, wherever you look.

You're a leaf in the wind, with a gust of laughter
You jauntily fly off into the distance,
But with a heavy slap in the face
You're challenged to a duel.

Clown and buffoon with the build of a tramp,
Life for you is like a slice of watermelon.
You've died onstage so many times,
Not thinking seriously about death.

My competent caballero,
Hero of the Promenade des Anglais,
There, someone switched the rapiers,
Rhyming poisons and the call of the naiads.

Such a small error
Will cut off the oxygen in a moment,
And you, like a sunk submarine,
Will be drawn into the ocean depths, my lord.

In the hours or in the moments of waning,
Alas, the pun will go out,

The hacienda will put out its lights,
And the logs in the fireplace.

The lights will dim in Parisian ballets
And Copenhagen's cellars,
While versifying fades away in Cobuletti,
Where he so blissfully boozed.

The propaganda of the grove flies away,
And the slope of the High Tatras fades.
The last thing that disappears—
A theater shining in the night.

PART IV

1

THE HOTEL CADILLAC

*S*omeone back in our third act fell asleep, and here in our fourth, someone is just waking up. Don't think that the event is occurring the next morning in the same place: the "chronotope," kind ladies and gentlemen, has changed.

Once he was awake, our protagonist, Alexander Zakharovich Korbach, tried to write down an inspiration from a dream on a lousy cocktail napkin from a disco that he had unwound in the night before. After crumpling the bit of paper into a ball and tossing it through the open bathroom door, he followed it himself, clutching his empty stomach. The title "bathroom," in point of fact, was only an honorary one, as there wasn't any bathtub there, only a wrinkled rubber teat of a shower hanging from the wall. There was also a window the size of a transom—a transom without a window beneath it, let's say—and through it, through its dusty glass, was visible a patch of eternally blue California sky, a scrap of an antenna, and perched on it a white seagull whose tail reminded one of the spots on a domino—to be precise. No, this isn't a forced comparison, he thought, addressing the "kind ladies and gentlemen": the black tail displayed the three white spots from each side. Perhaps in flight, this tail spreads out and the comparison is lost, but for the time being we see: it's a "six"!

During these observations, the morning ablutions were going on. Then he thoroughly, but quickly, cleaned his teeth and swished some mouthwash around in his mouth, which was tired from kisses. Usually we shave after breakfast, but we get into our jeans before breakfast. Now we do it during breakfast. Crossing the room, he glanced at the bare back of his bed companion. What's her name—Maxine or Lavonne? He'd picked her up last night at Le Jaws, a nightclub on the outskirts of Venice. The club was named after the film about a shark, but with a French definite article—that is, with a hint at a "French kiss." There was nothing easier than picking up babes in those jaws, because they were picking up "billy goats"—to use the Moscow slang term literally—themselves. It was a singles bar; no one was putting on any particular act. To hell with it, I'm not going to Jaws anymore, I'm going to go a month without chicks and booze. Shuffling over the lumpy floor of the Cadillac Hotel, past the warped doors on the other side of which the old men could be heard farting, he stumbled out into freedom. Oh, God's world in its Californian variation, how good you are! How your breeze cools and invigorates the "crown of life"! Positivist philosophy sometimes surges back like a belch of peanut butter, but the sea is glistening, dark blue—there's a real masterpiece for you! To top it all off, the palms were crackling their plumage at him. It is July 1983. Eight months have lurched past since Brezhnev kicked the bucket. Andropov is reigning in Moscow. America is preparing to stand up to the Soviets in a "final and decisive battle." The seagull flies away from the antenna. What looked like its tail turns out to be its wings. So much for all allusions to dominoes. A huge beach stretches before our hero. Half of it is paved and painted with stripes for a parking lot. Right now it's empty.

In the middle of the emptiness was a queue to nowhere. All among their own, bums and panhandlers. There were black ones, red ones, light brown, dark blue, green, and yellow ones. "How ya doin'?" Kastorzius asked, poking his birdlike German nose out of a skein of cloth. *"Normalno,"* our hero replied. The figures of late arrivals appeared in the sand from the cardboard apartment blocks and made their way to the line. Finally, breakfast appeared—that is, a van operated by the Catholic Brothers organization, with breakfasts for tramps. A hospitable rear bumper rolled up to the head of the line. Brother Charles, his face frozen in a smile of horsey magnanimity, began to give each bum a brown packet containing a hamburger and french fries, with a large paper cup of steaming coffee. What sins is he atoning for, this bringer of morning charity?

"For two," Alexander Korbach said, and held up two fingers. Brother Charles halted his dispensing hand for a moment. For two? Sasha Korbach nodded decisively: "Friend lying down. Very sick. Very unhappy." A shudder of mighty compassion ran down the diagonal lines of the long face; the hand extended two packages: "Enjoy your breakfast."

Munching his hamburger and sipping his coffee as he walked, Alexander stopped beside a *Los Angeles Times* dispenser. He didn't have a quarter in his pocket so as to pull out the heap of text. Just then, a gentleman in a Panama hat put in his quarter and drew out a paper. The Competent Worker (as Korbach often referred to himself) managed to stick a pencil in between the closing door and the dispenser. The closing was stopped, and he took out a free copy of the paper of record of the large country of California. Thus charity corrupts. Gods of the Pacific, why, something dramatic is happening right here on the first page; is fortune singing, are the Erinyes circling? A large picture showed Andropov, the new general secretary, hanging limply on the arms of two bodyguards. The text said that rumors that Yuri Vladimirovich was having health problems seemed to be true.

Korbach suddenly felt unwell. After all, Brezhnev had just kicked the bucket! What's happening to them, those ruling pagan priests? Maybe the job itself had become hopelessly decrepit, had depleted its energy, was yawning before some black hole? What'll happen to that country, my motherland, if its ruling thugs, one after another, go on hanging disgracefully on the arms of their healthy but ultimately stupid bodyguards?

He tossed the heavy newspaper into a trash can and walked on, quickening his pace. Mustn't be late today—he was taking over the shift from Gabriel Lianoza. You turn up five minutes late, his Marxist ass begins to stink. A good jump onto the front porch of the Cadillac. There's your morning exercise. One leap like that, and you take ten years off. I'm thirty-three or thirty-four again, like always. I fly in with the gleam of my second youth—not a word about any third! "Hey, Maxine, get up, baby! Breakfast's here!" Quick shave of the young cheeks, whistle something—oh, let's say, Mozart's Twenty-first—or whisper something in the *dolce stil nuovo.* He considered various nuances of the Russian translation of the term in his mind and was sure that one would not find them in other languages. Without meaning to, he found himself swelling with pride in the Turgenev GMJF, as some writers ironically called the great classic's "great, mighty, just, and free" Russian language. What am I doing playing the intellectual so early in the morning—me, a hustler of Catholic hamburgers? He dabbed his now even younger cheeks with Savage cologne. The previous night, when she'd seen the bottle of cologne in the bathroom, the woman had whistled. "Wow! You use Savage, I see!" He glanced from the "bathroom." Maxine was already chewing her Catholic hamburger. The sight was not exactly an inspiring one: cheeks rubbed bare, lips bedraggled, her raven plumage hanging down wherever it wanted, in a word, the apotheosis of *tachisme.*

"Don't look at me!" Last night, though, that truck driver's voice had had a touching chirp in it. "Don't even think about calling me some fucking Maxine! I've got my own name!" "And that is . . . ," he said, delicately putting an ellipsis in his voice. "Denise!" she growled. He nodded respectfully. Denise Davidov. Why yes, in fact this girl did have something in common with the guerrilla leader of the 1812 war. She burst out laughing. "Damned fucker! Fucking loveski! Doesn't remember the girls he sleeps with! Got a beer, loveski?" He shuddered with self-revulsion: she's calling me "loveski"! That means I was talking that rubbish about the Stanislavsky method again!

2

THE WEST WOOD

*S*tuck in the usual morning traffic jam on the San Diego Freeway, he was listening to the radio. There was nothing about Andropov's health on the news. There had been a drive-by shooting downtown last night: three killed, seven wounded, two critically. A truck carrying toxic materials had overturned at the sixty-two-mile mark of the Santa Monica Freeway. The nearby town was being evacuated. In North Hollywood a barber stabbed his sister's boyfriend. A fire in a warehouse on Sunset Boulevard. Arson for reasons of extortion was suspected. The normal news of this healthy version of Arkhangelsk. Having recently come up with the idea of renaming Los Angeles Arkhangelsk, he was trying in his thoughts not to let the possibility slip away.

The news went on. In Beirut, a fanatical Shiite had driven a truck filled with explosives into the Marine barracks. The scale of the disaster was still being established, but already it was clear that several dozen of our boys were dead. The artist Tracey Claude Marmour had bought a "historical" lobster named Jonathan for fifteen hundred dollars at the restaurant Andrew's and set it free in its native state of Maine. We know what conclusion to draw, Alexander thought somewhat obtusely. There are still occasional flickers of compassion in the world, not everything is lost.

Now at a standstill on the freeway, he had to step on the accelerator from time to time so that the engine wouldn't stall. On arrival in the area, he'd bought a Fiat 124, slightly rusted out on the bottom, for eight hundred dollars; apart from the rust, there was practically nothing to distinguish it from his Zhiguli in Moscow. A good Italian pony, no doubt about it, picks up the morning news perfectly. In any case, I understand it perfectly.

In his eleven months in America, Sasha's English had gone through curious changes. In the beginning, as we remember, he was losing all of his verbs. Then the verbs came back to him. He began to build sentences, which, strangely enough, were almost comprehensible to those around him. At first, news broadcasts flowed over him in one murky stream, but soon they began to break up into isolated, understandable words, and from them it was sometimes possible to guess at the meanings of the sentences. Then the understandable words began to join up, and all of a sudden, at some point, the world assumed fairly intelligent outlines. Now he could already talk to the general public, even if it was at the level of a semimental defective. At the First Bottom bar, anyway, everybody could understand Lavsky. Sometimes a group of fellow drinkers would gather around him to laugh at his studies in "reincarnation."

Of course, it was still GMJF running through his head, but partisan detachments of English were constantly breaking through these flowing fields; and my tongue, sly and sinful, always somehow pressing against the roof of my mouth in a certain way, even trying—you Russian lout—to make a difference between a *d* and a *t* at the end of a word, while all around the unbelievable hodgepodge of local people is tramping along: all these Chicanos and Caribbeans, Asiatics and Caucasians, the latter sometimes being called simply "white trash."

It was a quarter to eight when the Fiat finally managed to get off the freeway and head for Wilshire Boulevard. There were still a few traffic lights before Westwood

Village. The upper stories of the steel-and-glass buildings gave off a utopian gleam in the rays of the sun, perhaps even hoping to give the chaotic metropolis a surface layer of futuristic harmony. Savage mercantilism, however, always forced its way downward.

Now he was turning left in front of a large cafeteria called Ships, for some reason in the plural. At this eatery one could stock one's hold twenty-four hours a day with shrimp salads, ribs, T-bone steaks, cheap fish fillets, fruit jellies, chocolate pastries. In spite of the early hour and the slaughter in Beirut, the mood in Ships seemed normal—that is, exultant. Mouths were exchanging jokes while finely wrought optimism gleamed on fingers.

Then he drove by the little Clairmont Hotel, which, with its two light-colored potted saplings and its striped canopy, somehow always reminded him of some sort of false memory of good company supposedly having gathered here around the bar to sit out a thunderstorm.

Another two or three turns, and here he was at his place of work, the sturdy concrete Colonial Parking, six floors up and three underground, with spaces for 1,080 cars. The attendant on shift, Gabriel Julio Lianoza, a representative of the "fiery continent," who might never have done any burning himself but who often smoldered in a Marxist foul temper, was waiting for him in the changing room. At one time—in a tight black suit with little bells on the shoulders and silver embroidery on the chest and between the shoulder blades, in a sombrero the size of a UFO—Gabriel had propped up the limestone walls of the city of Morelia, gently rested the leg that he had injured playing soccer on the side of his beloved instrument, the tuba, with which he provided the rhythm for his band of street musicians. Large numbers of these musicians stood along the walls there, ready to play a madrigal, a tango, or a funeral march if the price was right. All of them were Marxists, of course, and complained about the lack of interest in talent on the part of the "world of cash." Gabriel was angrier than the others, although his tuba supported the household: two old grannies; his wife, Claretta; her two sisters, Uncia and Terzia; and seven—or however many there were—children.

Everything would have been fine if Claretta had not gotten carried away with black magic one night and jumped out a window in order to join a throng of witches flying over the mesa: basically, just the way they teach it in Latino-Marxist magical realist circles. "Sleep with Uncia," she sang every night to Gabriel through the smokestack. "Or with Terzia!" The call was heeded, he began to sleep with both of them. For all his good intentions, this turned out to be a violation of revolutionary morals. His union drove him from the city for imitating the imperialist gringo. What else was there to do? Crawling, and sometimes jumping, this man who had built up a huge chest through years of blowing on his tuba, and who had grown shaggy brows with the help of ideology, crossed the northern border, and now he's parking the gringos' cars, so that they can all burn in the war of liberation!

When Korbach came in, Lianoza was eating his enchilada. What grammatical gender is *enchilada* in Russian, anyway? In addition, he was scooping beef in chili sauce from a paper plate. "*Buenos dias, músico infernale,* or whatever they call you," Sasha said to him. "Fucking Russo," Gabriel greeted him in reply. "Late again, *burro calvo!*" With these words he threw the plate with the remains of his chili out the window of the partly underground floor. A second earlier and it would have been perfect for a pair of light gray trousers going by. "Off your fucking head, amigo?" Sasha asked him. "Sauce out the window?" Lianoza shrugged shoulders that were like singed hams. "Was that sauce? A lousy imitation." His eyes suddenly clouded over dreamily. "If you want to eat well, Sasha, we'll go down to Morelia *juntamente,* you and me. Eat and sleep, amigo, we'll eat and sleep. You'll sleep with Terzia and me with Uncia. Then the other way around."

He was half a head shorter than the not overly tall Korbach, and a shoulder broader. The "imitation food" must have put him in a good mood anyway—how else to explain the fact that he had shared useful information with the Russian? A lady in an Oldsmobile Cutlass was parked next to the meter by the street, the motor running. Come on now, take a look, come and help. And he pretended to blow a few bars of the Torreador March on the tuba.

Finding himself alone, Alexander hung up his Paris sport coat and put on the silver jacket with the badge reading ALEX. This procedure always irritated him. In this jacket and baseball cap, he looked like some repulsive adolescent. That was the style of the management here, though: the attendants had to personify youth, and if it was a forty-four-year-old good-for-nothing, no one would care. So, in the jacket, get a move on, like a youngster, hop over to the dispatcher's!

As luck would have it, one of his own—the shift cashier Aram Ter-Aivazian, an Armenian dissident—was there today. Next to his high stool, however, sat the boss, Tesfalidet Khasfalidat—Ted, that is—in an armchair. Tearing himself away from the previous day's takings, he took two rapid glances: one at Alex approaching at a run, and the other at his watch. The handsome ebony computer with fine gray curls on the top silently noted the seven-and-a-half-minute tardiness.

The parking deck, located in an entertainment district, was run by the Armenian-Ethiopian mafia, which imparted a certain informality characteristic of the ancient civilizations located on the periphery of the Fertile Crescent. They're not going to get up your nose about being seven minutes late here, but they won't forget it if there's any trouble in the future.

At this early hour on a weekend, the bulk of the customers were parishioners of the large Baptist church next door, who were as strikingly distinguished from the nocturnal clientele as the crew of a cruise liner is from that of a pirate ship. No sooner had Sasha Korbach's turn at the stop line come than a silver Lincoln of early sixties vintage pulled up. In this enormous clunker sat the ideal couple, two old Anglos, the man with a fine line of a mouth on a set of Gothic features and a little scarlet flower between two pincushions, his eternal spouse a bulwark of Puritan kindness and good sense.

Alex looked at their license plate and thought to himself in English: Jesus, they're from New Hampshire! Grandma was behind the wheel, naturally. He helped her to extricate herself from leather depths, in which, apparently, no one had done much sitting. "Thank you, my boy," she said in an enchanting voice. "You'd better help Philip—he needs it more." Philip turned out to be a more complicated case: there was a folding wheelchair to be taken out of the trunk and un-folded, then they had to install two enormous batteries in it, secure it in its work-ing mode, and only then seat the old man in it. "You drove the car from far away, sir," Alexander said to him. "It was Emmy that drove," he replied severely. "I don't drive anymore, but this little girl is great at it." "Bravo!" Sasha exclaimed. "From New Hampshire to California! It is a long way indeed!" He had long had the feel-ing that all he had to do was add an *indeed,* and he would begin to sound like a genuine American Anglo.

"Where're you from, my boy?" Emmy, the curious sort, asked. Now, how is it that they know as soon as I open my mouth that I'm "from somewhere," and not just a local "boy"?

"From Russia."

"Oh yes, that's a bit farther than New Hampshire," Emmy said with disarming surprise.

He rolled Philip down the parking lot ramp to the street. The old lady clattered along vigorously in her high heels next to them. She was extremely grateful for such kind assistance. Many had told them that the people in California were very kind, and now they were seeing that it was true. It should be said that they had en-countered kind people along the whole route. It's still possible to travel in this country, in spite of the reports on television. They'd come here to see Philip's older brother Matthew on his way. Yes, yes, Matthew's leaving soon. For where? For an-other world, my boy. At the moment, they were in a hurry to get to the beginning of the service at St. Martin Cathedral, to address a few important requests to the Almighty.

In the dispatcher's office, Ted tore himself away from his calculator for a sec-ond and watched the procession with an approving glance. The seven-minute tardiness, obviously, had been canceled out. Philip watched the parking deck staff, who were so different from the inhabitants of New England, with great at-tention. Mokki, Sossi, Khozdazad, Trifili, Varuch, Pavsikakhi, Varadat, and Eikaki Ekakis, racing by with rings of car keys, were showing the dynamism of modern man. "Interesting folks, don't you think?" the old man asked with a force of ex-pression that was extraordinary for his ailing body. "Very! Very!" his best friend replied, already having taken the chair over from the "kind boy." "Now you see, Philip, that the trip here was worth it!"

After saying good-bye to the enchanting couple on the corner of the street, Alexander set off to see what was happening with the Cutlass. The motor of the powerful machine was still running. From time to time its entire body was shaken with the convulsions of a sick man. The gas tank was full. The water temperature was approaching the critical point. Gabriel Lianoza's prediction came true almost immediately. A tall, attractive woman in a floral dress was racing in a panic be-neath the palm trees to the car. She'd have looked a bit like our ex-wife, Anisia, if it weren't for her dark skin with its hints of purple. "Gosh, what a mess!" the lady cried. "He'll never forgive me, I'm such a fool! Oh God, our love's finished! Fin-ished for good!" Even these exclamations might have reminded him of the woman he had once loved, and who had cheated on him with the apparatus of the state, if the professional in him had not announced itself. Every attendant in the garage was equipped for such occasions with a steel "slim-jim," which, when inserted in the crack between the window and the door, opened the lock without any trouble. "Voilà! No need to get so worried, ma'am!"

His reward was an impulsive kiss on the cheek. This function of the mouth was followed by nervous activity in the fingers, and a bill leapt from her handbag. Then the hand, with a fifty-dollar bill, crept into the tight pocket of his jeans. "Not a word to anyone, young man! You deserve it! You've saved my generally positive view of modern society!" Deeper, deeper, stop! Well, thanks, hope to see you soon, all the best! He was left with a fifty in his pocket and a business card in his hand: Lucia Cornovalenza, professor of sociology. A strange feeling of things being not entirely real. For an extended moment, if there is such a thing as an extended moment, unless it is a sequence of unextended moments. For that matter, do any "moments" really exist at all in the expanse of life, unless one counts a pun between the Russian word for "moment"—*mig*—and the mass-produced MiGs of the Soviet Air Force? What's happening? He addressed the question to his chronotope, but just then things re-formed their normal connections and snapped back into place. There's a miracle on its face for you, the instantaneous reestablishment of the United States of America as a political and anthropological given.

At the end of the street, among the slowly advancing cars, there appeared the figure of a seldom seen animal, a Harley-Davidson with an enormous rider in the saddle. For some reason it seemed that the motorcycle had turned up at that "moment"—"here," that is, either in the middle of this page or on the noisy street, to make off with his soul. For the time being, there is nothing left for us to do but take our next time-out in the following description.

3

TIME-OUT

*A*nd so, a whole year has gone by since the luckless arrival of the Moscow exile in the overseas *fortezza* of the free world. His twilight adventures in New York, about which the reader, we hope, has not yet forgotten, lay behind him. After that, everything had gone more or less according to the exile's plans, if one may suspect him of having had any. He and Stas Butlerov somehow arrived in the Californian version of Arkhangelsk. When we say "somehow," we're referring not only to the two friends' constant state of intoxication but also to the storm that had blown up in the Butlerov household when its head announced his decision to take off in "free flight." For several days the sobs and shrieks of his wife and the tragic scraping of his daughter's violin raged in the apartment. His mother-in-law, though she kept her mouth shut, constantly dropped dishes, meaning that she made no small contribution to the aural uprising. His wife rushed to the spilled borscht with a rag, and in the same rag buried her swollen face.

The houseguest, in her opinion, should have played the role of arbiter. Sasha, it's unbearable, simply unbearable to think that Stas, with his intellectual level, turned out to be such a monster of jealousy! To throw away everything that they'd been through together just because of her little affair with that charming Salvadore from the third floor, an affair in which there had been more platonic romanticism than promiscuity, my dear friend. As the master of the minds of our generation, as the lawgiver of the morals of Russia's struggle against—I'm not afraid to say it— tyranny, you ought to explain to your friend that a "female partner" has a right to excesses of mixed-up emotions! Why don't we all just sit down at the table, next to the stove: you, Stas, we three generations of women, the young Salvadore, and, let's say, our neighbor up on the fifth floor, that quiet and thoughtful Vikram Tagor, why don't we have a group therapy session on the question of relations between the sexes in apartment blocks? After all, a modern group of people in the USA in the eighties of the twentieth(!) century can easily arrive at a common denominator, Sasha—don't you think?

I don't need your common denominator, Stas howled. For some reason, it had never entered the mind of Olga Mironovna that her spouse, the very man she had cheated on, would now commit a fundamental act of betrayal. Having once made up his mind, he had come to hate all these stewed eggplants, and for that matter everything connected with the family, and was now dreaming only about "free flight" to the Californian land of kind and carefree women.

"I'm not taking anything from you," the demagogue yelped. "I'm leaving everything that you squeezed out of me! Only give me back my honor!" Finally, almost tearing their suitcases out of the hands of the three generations of women, the men beat it or, if one prefers, departed. For five hours they boozed it up in a United jet, and then there they were in L.A., if the time has come for abbreviations.

———

Butlerov's friend, a still quite young Muscovite by the name of Tikhomir Burevyatnikov, always added the word *cinematographer* to his name in introducing himself. Their friendship, if one could call it that, dated from the days when Stas was working as a legal consultant to Mosfilm studios. Burevyatnikov's history in America was fairly simple. For all his comparative youth, he had ten years in the Party under his belt and was his own man in—well, on the Committee of Youth Organizations, let's put it that way. A year and a half earlier he had been named assistant director of the Red Roosters film group and had arrived in revolutionary Nicaragua to formulate the general line for joint leadership in the conditions of an overall goddamned mess.

Practically speaking, the idea of the film was fairly gut-wrenching: to reflect in artistic images the Nicaraguan love for Communism. The realization of the idea, however, ran into difficulties, above all in the person of that fucking genius, guys, the director Oleg Pristapomsky, national artist of the USSR, laureate of every Soviet prize, and member of some fucking committee of the Central Committee of the CPSU. You can believe it or not, but it had long seemed to Tikhomir Burevyatnikov that Oleg Venyaminovich was not entirely what everyone took him for. On the outside, you couldn't get anything on him: large, gray-haired, voice like a trumpet—why, simply a classic of socialism—while in fact he turned out to be a first-class foulmouth and a skirt chaser. It wouldn't have mattered—one can always close one's eyes to amorality, a man's a man—if not for one problem: creative contact just didn't happen. He'd adopted, you understand, the swinish habit of roaring all over the set, at the drop of a hat: "Burevyatnikov, I don't want to hold you up." And his whole miserable group had taken up the phrase. About the broads, there's nothing much to say there—they turned the man with a respectable Komsomol and Party background into a laughingstock.

It was because of this that everything happened. One day, Burevyatnikov set out for Managua to pick up a load of hard currency in the diplomatic pouch. With the money in his rucksack, he was walking around the revolutionary capital and suddenly began to shake with anger. I'm thirty-four, I've been their hired hand all my life, and you'd think that just once they would have put me in for a state award! Just then he felt something urging him to visit an establishment called Havana Libra, where a large number of members of the organization turned out to be having a get-together. They greeted him as one of their own, without any rudeness. Ironically, these people, foreign to him, understood him better than his own, even though not all of them had learned Russian yet. Going on from there, *Cherchez your chick,* as they say. The popular Komsomolist Mirelle Salamanca, the "angel of our poetry," as they called her, appeared. All the macho types fired their Makarov pistols at the ceiling—"Viva Mirelle!"—and she whispered in Burevyatnikov's ear: "Let's get out of here before it's too late!" He gathered up all his male dignity in a tight spring. He left a note in the bar for Pristapomsky: "I respect you as an artist, I despise you as a human being! Don't think badly of me, Oleg Venyaminovich!"

And there they were, running, the goddamned grass and leaves rustling, the fucking moon shining away. "You've turned my whole life upside down, *russo!*" Mirelle Salamanca squealed. They'd bought a car from a soldier—a dear old Soviet jeep—they were driving it along, something never to forget! Now it's day, now night, here they're just bumping along, there they're racing. Mirelle's stream of poetic inspiration is inexhaustible.

At the Costa Rican frontier, Burevyatnikov himself did the explaining to the cop: "*Poquito libertad. Communisto nicht zusammen.* They'll cut off our heads. Understand?" He understood perfectly and let them through. At the American embassy, of course, they were met with open arms, because they wanted to win over as many young artists from the Socialist camp as possible.

Tikhomir wiped his face with his own shirt, since he had already been sitting bare-chested at the table for some time. That, guys, is the short version of the details of the deepening of this émigré friendship. Emigration—it's a hard test of a man's character, comrades. Where's Mirelle Salamanca, you're wondering? Vanished, as they say here, into thin air—got it? The bag with the money vanished as well, which is natural, and you should never regret, guys, something that brings you satisfaction for at least a short time of your constantly growing needs, like they taught us at school.

The big-boned, robust Burevyatnikov had made over his wardrobe entirely in denim in the land of his political asylum—jeans held up by denim suspenders, denim shirt, denim cap, denim moccasins. In his person, one of the chief fantasies of the Komsomol was embodied. In this way he used to make his way around the San Fernando Valley, a mysterious smile on his face, two fighting paws dangling at the ready. I'm the friend of my friends, but a man has to be on his guard.

Well, he went through all sorts of things, guys. One day he just felt himself sinking into the slime. He was dreaming about a T-bone steak. Without steak, he couldn't even get his penis in the air, not to mention the intellect of his existence. At that point, on Hollywood Boulevard, he ran into this one who's before you now, Aram Ter-Aivazian, with whom he had once taken training courses for lower- and middle-echelon Party cadres. Aram, even though a nationalist, was still a genuine first-class Soviet lad from the twilight days of the totalitarian empire. He looked at him point-blank and gave him a shoulder to lean on.

Now Burevyatnikov himself was looking at Korbach intently, as though he wanted to ask: Are you the son of a bitch that you're trying to pass yourself off as? Something too simple, somehow, about what's happening here—don't you see? Sasha Korbach himself turns up to help, along with Stas Butlerov, who passes himself off as a descendant of Russian advanced chemistry.

Well, come on, Sasha, old friend—he took his seven-stringed girlfriend down from the wall of his apartment—scratch out one of your famous numbers for us, at least "Chekhov's Sakhalin"! The group, as they say, was sitting pretty. Genuine Soviet sausage, chopped up on a copy of the émigré tabloid *Panorama* with an excellent short sword ordered through *Soldier of Fortune* catalog; wheels of Camembert had gone runny in the heat; in a frying pan, Jewish dumplings were swimming in grease; pickles doing figures in a jar like embryos; a half gallon of vodka was nearly killed, with a second assuming a combat stance.

Korbach, wincing, but understanding that it was necessary, sang "Sakhalin" and a couple of other hits from his twenty-year-old repertoire. When he'd finished singing, he saw that the émigré bastards were crying. "This is just between us, fellas," he said to them. "For everyone, I'm dead—I exist only for a select few." He couldn't have put it any better. Everyone—Stas, Tikh, Aram—kissed him three times.

The last had been an influential figure in the parking business for some time already. It was no problem for him to find jobs for another couple of people at Westwood Colonial. Of course, the American H visa that Korbach had on his passport—the so-called preference visa, designated for people capable of making a contribution to the scientific or cultural life of the country—somehow didn't forecast that its bearer would labor in the field of auto service, but the Ethiopian fraternity, refugees from the bloodthirsty Marxist Mengistu Haile Mariam, found a way out of this ambiguous position. On the advice of Tesfalidet Khasfalidat,

Alexander went to the INS and filled out a form requesting "political asylum." With that, in fact, his ties to his homeland were cut off and those to his new homeland established.

The Ethiopians were paying him $5.50 an hour, and half of his tips were sacrificed on the altar of the Ethiopian counterrevolution. In all, he was making around eighteen hundred bucks a month, which allowed him to rent a so-called studio at the Hotel Cadillac, an establishment fairly well-known among the lower strata of Los Angeles society, where in those days old Jewish pensioners, young transvestites, and middle-aged alcoholics lived. There on the backside of the village by the sea of Venice, he lived without problems and complaints, with a minimum of memories and a maximum of morning-after heartburn. So as not to have to come back to the question, we'll tell you that after a year, political asylum was granted.

The most complicated thing about the parking business was the endless variety of makes of cars. Emergency brakes engaged and disengaged differently, headlights and instrument panels were switched on differently, depending upon the model. You won't work out right away that the maws of some of these crocodiles are lit up by the turn of one knob around another knob, which in its turn rotates around its own goddamned shaft—no, you won't.

On the other hand, there was nothing simpler than dealing with the customers. Everything came down to four or five phrases—"Are you staying long, sir/ma'am?" or "Thanks for the tip, have a nice day," usually nothing else was needed. Sometimes a customer wanted to be sociable—that is, to make a joke. In Southern California, social contact and joking are practically synonymous. So as not to make a gaffe in English, you just laugh, and you're almost never wrong. When we say "almost," we'd be happy to forget the few times our hero put his foot in it, but our professional ethic obliges us to give the reader at least one example.

He's yours, ladies and gentlemen. Midnight. Sasha Korbach is bringing an off-white Porsche with an aerodynamic tail up out of the bowels of the garage. The customer's sky blue hair is flying in the wind like the flag of the United Nations. His companion, wearing a dress with thin straps (the sort of dress that would have been called a slip in earlier times), just slips out of his arms, her eyes bulging, her neck twitching with some sort of hiccups. Alex the attendant politely opens the door, hoping for a dollar. "Listen," the customer says to him, "the bitch is ODing again. You see how she's rolling around? Call nine-one-one, help us out!" Not having understood, Alex laughs politely. The customer is stunned. "What are you laughing at, you dumb fuck? She's dying, can't you see? I love this piece of ass, understand? I don't wanna lose her!"

Tossing his girlfriend into the arms of the attendant, the customer runs to the telephone himself. The lady commences to collapse on the concrete. Her legs are twitching in their wrinkled stockings. Five minutes later, an ambulance arrives from the nearby UCLA hospital with its siren wailing.

The girlfriend is quickly revived, and now everyone can laugh. The blue-haired gentleman gives Alex an easily understood look in parting: Where, it says, do these stupid motherfuckers come to us from?

The most remarkable thing about this job was that after one day on duty one could forget about it for two. On these free days, through the good offices of Tikh Burevyatnikov, there would sometimes turn up a cushy job, usually with a roofing company that worked on émigrés' houses. Tikhomir had quite a knack for picking things up in this domain. In this "Americania," he would say, only a lazy man doesn't cover his roof. You run down to Hechinger's lumber and hardware store, get yourself whatever you need for a roof, everything's measured and cut to fit, and the roof itself just lies there like a Spanish girl. They would form a foursome, always the same ones, and go off on commissioned jobs, sometimes to the San Fernando Valley, and sometimes to Fairfax, where quite a few of "our guys" already owned homes, where they mended the roof for fees lower than the Arkhangelsk norm. And in the tradition of Russian laboring men, the crew would sit in the garden after work, at a table covered with aspics, vinaigrette, and, of course, what one always has with such snacks.

They had quite a good time sitting around like this, pretending that they were simple blue-collar workers—the lawyer, the artist, and two Komsomol workers with considerable experience as political informers behind them. Blue-tails flew over them and among the flowers, looking like brushes for scrubbing narrow articles of dishware. Sometimes a curious visitor would even stick its snout out of a bush as if asking to join the group: a coyote. The housewives tried not to let their daughters out into the garden. The lads weren't much interested in these little girls, though, since after these meals they would usually head for Jaws to pick up older ones.

Unfortunately, after six months the roofing business, and with it the accompanying sessions around the table, came to an end. Tikhomir Burevyatnikov had no further use for roofing, since the man who was the brains of the outfit headed for the greener pastures of a more interesting job, about which we'll say more later. An unexpected turn of events also occurred in Stas Butlerov's life.

It was mentioned earlier that the biggest pain in Stas's backside was caused by his unaccredited law degree from MGU and his unrecognized passing of the Moscow bar. Suffering from the process well-known in the pertinent literature as an identity crisis, Stas could dream only of getting his brilliant documents accredited and joining the American class of his profession, where they get paid—imagine—by the hour, like highly qualified welders.

Being occasionally sober—something that wasn't true of him very often, as the attentive reader will have noticed—Stas began to study the American legal code and even went to the exam a couple of times. After failing with gusto, he would collapse on the couch, the one right beside the stove, with a half gallon bottle of Popov vodka in his arms. "I don't want to be a second-class citizen!" he would grunt like a beached seal, fall silent, shake all over, and then raise another bearlike roar—"Third! Third-class!"—and then fall facedown again into the monastery of rags that reeked of Granny (she liked to rest her bottom there). Olga, shaken by the suffering of her "outstanding nature," would sometimes go up one floor and sometimes down one, which helped her to survive the latest drama. His daughter, not moving from her usual spot, kept on improving her virtuoso technique and sometimes sang in a reedy voice: "The years and days run by in a senseless stream, each races along a thorny path to the grave." "My dear little monster." Stas wept gently, and then fell asleep.

In Los Angeles, where the new arrival catches the smell of the perennial grapefruit even at the airport, Stas felt a surge of new energy. He became a mover in émigré circles and finally went out after what he was looking for—that is, to see several colleagues who had already succeeded in establishing their credentials. With one of them, a most excellent gentleman from Riga by the name of Yura Zimbulist, he established a good business relationship and suddenly climbed up to the next highest rung on the local hierarchical ladder. In making his own a certain rather curious specialty that was quite unknown in the USSR, namely ambulance chasing, he achieved maximum proximity to his beloved profession.

California, as everyone knows, is packed with cars. Several tens of thousands of former subjects of the great Soviet Union—that is, a group of not overly bright individuals—are already circulating in the flow of its traffic. It doesn't take a genius to figure out that the rate of traffic incidents among them is constantly increasing. Maybe some gray-haired Jew hits someone in the ass, or maybe some California dreamer makes a hash of his tail. This, you understand, is the most innocuous possibility where metallic violence is concerned, never mind the head-ons, the ones who get hit in the side, or the ones who flip over entirely! In all of these episodes, the shaken individual—often with broken bones, compressed vertebrae, partly scrambled gray matter—doesn't understand what's going on around him and as a result receives only minimal compensation from the insurance company.

Unless, of course, some noble friend, unceremoniously known in these insurance companies as an ambulance chaser, gets involved. The sphere of activity of such a chaser is strictly in accordance with the basic principle of American business: be in the right place at the right time. A well-wisher of this sort, speaking the native language of the victim and knowing him as he knows himself, immediately takes over everything, offers as much help as possible in explaining the laws, sends the victim to "our Russian doctor," Nathan Souloukhin, for examination, and then to a prominent attorney—also one of ours—Mr. Zimbulist. The amount paid by the insurance company triples as a result of these measures. No losers. A fat check is better treatment for the stressed-out victim than any psychotherapy. Souloukhin and Zimbulist get their solid fees, and the "wave runner," as Stas Butlerov had begun calling himself, pockets a nice commission. The interesting thing is that the insurance companies aren't bothered about it, since high payouts greatly increase the size of their clientele, and, as everyone knows, American business is interested in profits, not in economy.

Of course, malicious rumors do circulate in this California version of Arkhangelsk that Stas Butlerov sometimes stages his own accidents, but civilization's noble idea of the presumption of innocence has obviously never so much as spent the night in such circles. These evil tongues also speculate that this trio is overly taken with the diagnosis of brain concussion, but would you be so kind as to tell us who in our times can boast of an undisturbed mental apparatus?

In a word, Stas had set himself up not at all badly for a deeper foray into American jurisprudence. He'd forgotten all about that Popov rotgut, and had gone over to fine wines, but most remarkable of all was the fact that here he had even found a woman with outstanding qualities!

The former Shura Fedotova, now Shirley Fedot, gave off in all of her appearance a glow of optimism akin to the ads that Oil of Olay was using at the time. Her skin was a masterpiece of resiliency and feminine outlines. What she had to say was always upbeat and to the point. The slight gleam of an easy lay in her eyes shone hope into the heart of every man, and even to women it sent a message of encouragement: Not all is lost, girlfriend! Her bright, loosely fitting clothes had Rodeo Drive labels on them and teasing Belorussian motifs as well. It was said that Shura Fedotova's unexpected departure from Minsk had raised a huge fuss in Party and government circles, which contributed to the further slide toward the historic dissolution. As far as her tidy California income was concerned, it was purely the result of her personal positivism and spirit of enterprise. No one was better than she was at convincing a nouveau-riche *émigrée* of the necessity of "discovering a new age within herself," that is, of getting a face-lift by a famous plastic surgeon like Igor Gnedlig, Oleg Ospovat, or Yaroslav Kassel. In fact, it was in medicolegal circles that Shirley and Stas found each other. By the beginning of our fourth section, that is, early in July 1983, they were already living together in a condominium on San Vicente Boulevard and were thinking about buying a town house in Marina del Rey.

Caught up in the maelstrom of such changes for the better, Stas Butlerov often completely forgot that he belonged to the "protest generation," and rarely even thought about his friend, the once famous protester. This was how it happened that Korbach suddenly found himself in an environment from which all the Russian oxygen had been banished. Sometimes he would go for weeks without speaking a single word of Russian. The only survivor of the old group still in sight, Aram Ter-Aivazian, preferred to speak English. Or, if possible, Armenian. I'm only thirty-five, he would say, there's still time to forget all of that Komsomol jargon—that is, Russian.

Well, that's just great, thought Alexander, endlessly tossing back and forth between Venice and Pacific Palisades along the water's edge, I'll stay all alone with my jargon, just as Ovid stayed with his Roman jargon in Dacia. For that matter, he should have been wandering along the Black Sea, and the elegies began to fly out of his ears in the form of flowers and birds, and pollen of different colors that was snatched up by the wind and flew away, alas not to dissolute Rome, so dear to my heart and member, but in the opposite direction, over Pont, to Kolkhida, to Meskheti, as though perishing but in fact hastening to arrive in time after a thousand years to fertilize the court of love of Empress Tamar, where a bookkeeping knight, or the treasurer of the exchequer, as they called them then—a certain Shotta Rustaveli—began plying his trade of writer just in time.

Perhaps the only thing that distinguishes me from Ovid is the fact that I don't have the energy to create anymore, to produce truly artistic work. Apart from that, we're almost alike. They banished him to the steppes for the "science of love," and me over the ocean for the science of laughter, but was there really ever any love without joking? My friend, you say, joking helps us to heal ourselves of the past, but why do you moan about it so pathetically, egghead? We wear almost exactly the same shoes, Publius Naso, only you wrap a leather strap around your shin, and I stick my big toe with its crumbling archaeological nail into the loop of a sandal. I envy you your tunic—it flaps in the wind, lets your entire body breathe; your balls are in free flight while mine are constricted by shorts. You, the chief buffoon of an empire, the progenitor of the *dolce stil nuovo,* twelve hundred years before its birth, you ended up left by the roadside. Augustus's mind didn't stretch as far as understanding the *Metamorphoses* or *Saturnalia,* because he hadn't read Bakhtin. He knew how a man is transformed into an emperor, but he couldn't work out how Jupiter could become a bull and then a majestic constellation. Nevertheless, he understood with an emperor's sixth sense that irony marks the twilight of one civilization and bombast marks the birth of another. Maybe that's why Dante, so tightly tied down by woolen stockings, chose Virgil as a guide rather than you. Forgive me for being immodest, but you're better suited to me, even though I, too, once dreamed about "The Radiance of Beatrice." A thousand apologies, but even under your leadership I wouldn't be able to get out of this overseas Purgatory, just as you couldn't get out of Dacia despite your plaintive letters to Augustus. And you can bet I'm not writing to Andropov—he's no Augustus, after all, our top-secret graphomaniac.

The ocean, meanwhile, was occupied with its primary task—the underscoring of human insignificance. The surfers were taunting the giant anyway, hopping from one of its trillion waves to another. How does it go? How did Pasternak phrase it—"Days pass, and thousands and thousands of years. In the white zeal of the waves, hiding in the white spice of the acacias, only you, sea, you bring them, bring them to naught." Every wave, though, is different, and we look like fools again. The water illustrates our futility, something that Tarkovsky understands very well—you won't squeeze the water out of his screen. Do the bookkeepers of the "dream factory" grasp the metaphysics of water? Does the second viewing of the same film mean that you've stepped into one and the same current twice?

He sat on the sand for a long time with a can of beer in a small paper bag. For finishing up an almost empty can the beach patrol can fine you here, but no one has the right to stick his nose in a paper bag—privacy, one's personal life! He ran his palm over his forehead, as though he were stroking the croup of a racehorse. Funny, why did I go bald so fast at twenty-eight? In photographs, his father was distinguished by his excellent curly Jewish mop. Maybe that Czechoslovakian Central Committee chandelier was to blame? Had it crashed down on some related area of the head and programmed it for premature baldness? At the same time, maybe it taught him to sing, to write poems, to act, to stage plays? Creatures from other planets are sometimes shown with foreheads like this. Perhaps out there, in the depths of space, they encourage every child with a smack on the head as a ritual akin to Jewish circumcision. And after the procedure, they all become bards and buffoons, and those few who can't put on plays get sent to their own version of the United States of America.

As sunset approached, the strollers began to appear against the ocean's backdrop. Along the asphalt trails winding among the dunes came the knee- and elbow-padded Rollerbladers with a forceful rustle, wearing half-moon sunglasses, bandannas, little antennae of their private means of communication sticking out of their ears. Flocks of sky bluish–pink old ladies emerged squawking from the Longevity Center, its gloomy mass planted firmly in the very surf: Come on, girls! Joggers trotted efficiently along the fringe of the densely packed sand. A business traveler in a three-piece suit carrying an attaché case wandered along through the half-dressed crowd. Girls of the "sun and fun" sort were stretching their legs and rubbing them with oil—a sight for everyone to behold. The writer Graham Greene used to come down from the Hotel Shangri-La and make notes on his pad: "One has difficulty in distinguishing the beaches of California from the camps of the Gulag." Those who have been here with Kolyma forced-labor camp experience under their belts have been in no hurry to join the writer in his paradoxical opinion.

One day a Russian-speaking group walked by Korbach and suddenly turned around. Whom did they just spot back there? he wondered. The people reminded him of that stratum of society known in the Soviet Union as techies. Through the twilight potpourri, their voices reached him: "That one looks like one. A Negro. Not at all. Looks like one to me. You've got a fever, ladies and gentlemen!" The group continued on. He looked over his shoulder. There was no Negro there. They must have taken me for a Negro. Holy cow, to think that not so long ago I was the ideal of these techies!

He remembered a show that they had put on in, oh, maybe 1977, in Chernogolovka. The theater had almost been done away with by a decree of Demichev, but the Chernogolovka Progressive Union, issuing a challenge to the thickheaded party-liners, invited him and the Buffoons to their club. They put on *A–Z,* with no sets, among chairs that had been set out. After the show, the jocks didn't leave, they staged a sort of impromptu demonstration, yelling, "Hands off!" The wonderful young mugs of those jocks, the laughter, the shouts, the bacchanalia of the native language. Suddenly, all of this, now abandoned, swept past him on the beach at Santa Monica like something living, like a slanting wall of rain. Fall on my face, cut my way out of this moment, and cut my way into that one?

The sunset over the ocean was thickening, growing darker. Sasha quickly walked along the water's edge in the direction of home. Someone running up ahead of him stumbled, yelled, "Shit!" slipped as though he were on ice, regained his balance, and carried on running. A second later, Sasha himself put his foot in some sort of bag of slime that was on the move. A huge, half-crushed jellyfish was agonizing there. A life-form fairly alien to enlightened humanity.

All things crushed and agonizing stick in the memory, the way bats find their way into white shirts. One day, a big reddish black cat had jumped out onto the freeway. No one could put on the brakes. A van up ahead knocked the cat onto a spiral off-ramp. The cat flew in an arc and landed on its side between a Honda and a Volvo. It should have just lain there, the fool thing, without moving, but, stunned by the blow, it was trying to get to any safe corner and ended up under the wheels of another oncoming car. What was left of it went on twitching in a senseless struggle for another few seconds of existence, then it was gone from view. The mighty iron demons all flew along the freeway at the same speed, reducing the remains of the cat to a smear.

He burst into tears at the wheel and went on shaking for a quarter of an hour, even forgetting about both the cat and the freeway demons, any one of which could be squashed and smeared the same way in a moment; forgetting about himself, and about his sons, whom he had left to the Central Committee for their upbringing. He wept and trembled as though he were somewhat outside himself, and there, within himself, some sort of psychiatrist narrowed his eyes and stated with Leninist reason: "Hey, old boy, I see you're under quite a bit of stress there!"

This reasonable voice often drove him to the First Bottom bar, saying that he needed to relax. There, in one corner, was a little old guy looking just like all the cinematic clichés about the "black musician," named Henry Miller—no joke— and singing in a hoarse bass:

If you treat me right, baby,
I'll stay home every day,
But you're so mean, baby,
I'm sure you're gonna drive me away.

It looked amazingly like a real American bar, as though it weren't in fact a real American bar. Sit at the counter like a boozy foreigner in a genuine American bar. By midnight, the place was filled almost to the point of turning people away, but everyone got in. Our Sasha already has quite a few acquaintances here, if not almost friends. For example, Matt Shuroff, a mountain of a man with tattooed arms, the boyfriend of the supervisor of several residential establishments in Venice, including the Hotel Cadillac flophouse, and the no less imposing Bernadetta Luxe, who walked around the neighborhood with curlers in her hair at all hours of the day, straightening her shoulders beneath the tasseled cambric top that she always wore.

Matt is a long-distance truck driver and when he comes back from his trips goes for weeks without doing a thing, waiting only for First Bottom to open; there he first looks at the newspapers, then the television, then shoots pool with the Vietnamese, gradually getting loaded, before assuming his definitive position like a sculpture on one of the barstools.

Two friends over whom Matt is good enough to watch invariably set down

anchor next to him: a refugee Vietnamese general named Piu, who has earned a
reputation as the best plumber in the area, and the Hungarian refugee Bruno Kastorzius, who turned into a genuine bum a long time ago. They're often joined by
Melvin O'Massey, a young, well-turned-out fellow from the business community.
All four of them wait for the incomparable Bernadetta to appear; they all benefit
from the good graces of Luxe from time to time, though no one disputes Matt
Shuroff's priority status. Alex Korbach, nicknamed Lavsky, the fifth member of
this club, keeps himself a bit off to one side, though even he, we'll admit, has managed to get acquainted with the secrets of Bernadetta. From time to time the supervisor of the building opens the door to his studio with her master key and
without hesitating falls on the puny little clod with all the warmth of her ocean-
side ego. "Where's my cutie dickie-prickie? Let me cover it up with my veggie-
meggie."

Everyone at First Bottom knows what it means when Lavsky's had his third
shot of Stoly, how he starts talking some nonsense about some Mr. Stanislavsky
with his method that the whole world supposedly knows about. That was how the
nickname started: Stanis Lavsky. Very witty they are, the people in our country.

"It's still not clear who was more of a Formalist, Meyerhold or Stanislavsky,"
he's saying, talking to someone directly in front of him—that is, more often than
not, Frankie the bartender. "Really?" is Frankie's polite reaction.

"Trying to imitate life to the maximum degree, Stanislavsky wanted to isolate
himself from your 'really,' Frankie—that is, to create theater as an end in itself.
Understand? Meyerhold, refusing the imitation of life, insisting on the theatrical-
ity of theater, dreamed, on the contrary, of making it part of those stupid utopias.
Understand, comrades?"

"Understanding, *to-vor-ish*!" Bruno Kastorzius said, dredging up what he
could remember of the occupying army's language.

Bernadetta applauded. There was a bright gleam in Lavsky's far from weak
eyes. "To take down the fourth wall, to unite the viewer and the show—that is, with
the street—it's tempting, but it's not as complicated as forcing the spectator to
bang his head against the wall between the oracle of the theater and the bazaar of
politics, to peep through the keyhole. Got it, Piu? Do I do go on, Matt . . . on the
mat! . . . or not?"

"Right on, Lavsky, just take your hand off Bernie's ass," said the number-one
man, whose epidermal covering had come more and more, over the years beginning with his acquaintance with the penal system of the state of Nevada, to resemble a Gobelin tapestry, where warriors with wings and crossbows represented
the forces of good, and mermaids swam off by themselves, like prostitutes' legs in
fishnet stockings.

Knocking back a double on the rocks, Korbach went on: "From this angle we
view the question of the actor as well, ladies and gentlemen. Improvising in the
key given by Meyerhold, the actor becomes a *cabotin,* a street ham—that is, a part
of those fucking people who can fuck themselves bloody red with all their cherished hopes. Stanislavsky, however, said: 'Transform yourselves! You're free of
your society, you're in the temple of characterization, they can't grab at you with

their dirty paws!' You, Piu, change yourself into Macbeth, right now! Forget about hightailing it out of Saigon and your shithouses over here—come on, Macbeth!" Piu, for some reason closing his eyes, began to make whistling noises. That, from his point of view, was how Macbeth would have whistled. "Magnificent!" Korbach howled with still irrelevant mad energy. "You're on the right track! You've already begun to 'hermitize' yourself!" Then he turned to Bernadetta. "And what about you, Miss Luxe? Here's your assignment—you're Ranevskaya! Say: 'Where's my cherry orchard?' " Coming unexpectedly close to other interpretations of the immortal drama, Bernadetta intoned in a deep contralto: "Where's my cherry pie?" The men around her exploded with sycophantic delight. Korbach let his arms drop and then put his head in his hands. The party's conclusion was taking place in his presence, but without his participation. Then Matt shook him by the shoulder. "Get up, Lavsky! Can you walk?" He made his way out of the bar and walked straight across the inordinately wide beach toward the white-capped billows of the surf, which was getting higher in the gloom. "The end," he muttered. "After this, just roar and foam. The rest is silence."

One day a young man in broad striped pants and a skimpy jersey came after him from the bar. Catching up to him on the beach, he looked at him from one side. "Excuse me, sir, for just butting in like this, but I happened to overhear you in the bar—you were saying something about the Stanislavsky method, weren't you?" "Go fuck yourself," Korbach said to him in Russian, and the young man naturally took the phrase as an invitation to continue. He was beside himself with excitement. "My name's Rick. I'd very much like to talk. If that's acceptable to you, of course. It seemed to me that you were talking about something important. I understand that you're a foreigner. Can I invite you to lunch?"

"Go fuck yourself!" Korbach shouted this time and gestured in the direction of the city. "Go, go!" The young man sat down on the sand and began following with his eyes the figure that was moving away toward the sea, its jacket billowing in the wind. It seemed to him that it was beginning to lose its shadow, and then it merged with the darkness, and only after that did it reemerge, outlined against the whitecaps. Got to wait, thought the young man, Poseidon is going to appear suddenly from the sea and grab him in his fist. There's got to be at least one witness.

Trying not to lay any traps for the reader of our tale, we'll tell you right away that this young man, Rick Quillian, was an actor in a noncommercial theater company, not a homo, as Korbach had supposed. In this company, incidentally, were people who had been to see the Buffoons in Moscow, and—let's not be afraid to use a high-flown phrase—had worshiped at the feet of their director. However, bad luck, in this case an alcoholic crisis, again distanced Korbach from his own.

How long is all this bullshit going to go on? he thought in desperation one morning after, when the coppery sunrise was not yet even gleaming on his hidden windowless transom. And why is everything around me all wet? Did I piss myself? Or did I try to walk into the ocean? Did I just imagine it last night, or did my shadow vanish? The spirits were able to tell Dante from their own by the fact that he cast a shadow. In this world, however, everyone casts a shadow. That homo who tagged along after me on the beach cast quite a long one. Still, America's not a very original Purgatory, just a paraphrase. Maybe I'm the only one here who doesn't cast a shadow. Horrified, he turned on the night-light and made rooster shadows on the wall with his ten fingers.

"Hey, old boy, I see you're under quite a bit of stress there!" Butlerov said, making a pseudojoke in a pseudo-Leninist voice. He'd remembered his friend after all and paid a call on the down-at-heel Cadillac, looking fit, well-dressed in a linen suit, accompanied by his splendid Shirley Fedot, a masterpiece of Art Deco in combination with the sumptuous primitivism of the jack of diamonds—there's a real woman of the arts for you! "My little Sashenka, I can see what you need, darling!" she said in a kind, carefree, and sweet voice that immediately put him in mind of Moscow, the theater, the unity of the premieres, the adoring glances, wet kisses—"Let's join hands, friends, so that we don't perish separately." This woman, Stas's new girlfriend, seemed to embody everything surrounding the theater, an amicable feminine zone of defense against Soviet pushiness, a milieu in which it was possible to decide all questions, in which everyone addressed him in this way: "Sashenka," "darling," and even "my sunshine."

"What you need, my sunshine, is a new girlfriend," Shirley went on. The pompous tone that one associates with heavenly beings evaporates in a friendly, everyday tone. "You need a beautiful Russian woman who can stand on her own two feet, and I've got my eye on just the one for you."

They began by going to Once Is Not Enough, a secondhand shop on Melrose Avenue that Shirley had scouted out during her combings of this sector of the Arkhangelsk commercial sea. Here one could happen on fantastic things at fantastically low prices. With a single motion, the hand of the experienced lady swept a light-colored ribbed cotton suit from a hanger. "Well, boys, what do you think? A Polo Ralph Lauren for $99.99, when the original price was $800, no less! Rich Americans often give things away here through their domestics, so that they'll have a reason to buy a new wardrobe. Well, come on, try it on, Alexander Zakharovich!"

Korbach felt a brightening of his mood, something that he had almost forgotten could happen. This stylish thing was going to be his. The suit was like new, except for a little spot about the size of a nickel inside the pants, at the crotch; when one held it up to one's nose it gave off a curious—not repugnant but still discouraging—smell. "That spot inside, we can put a patch over it," Shirley said encouragingly. When had she managed to notice this little stain? "The sleeves are just a bit long, but they can be rolled up—it'll be cool, my darling."

The suit transformed him. Instead of a pathetic bum, there stood in the mirror a nonchalant habitué of international festivals. Of course such people go through hard times, but they have, as everyone knows, their brilliant moments as well. Shirley was satisfied. "All right, boys, now let's go to Dvoira Radashkevich's— she's having a party today, as luck would have it."

The word *party* can serve as a shibboleth for distinguishing the real Americans from the *assimilated* ones. Not even an Englishman, never mind a Slavoid, can pronounce the *rt* in the middle of the word as something approximating a *d* and at the same time being far from it. Korbach looked at Shirley in surprise: she pronounced the word the American way—in any case, he didn't catch the difference.

They arrived at the three-bedroom apartment on Ocean Avenue. It was filled with a crowd of people drinking and munching away. Here, among the young emigration, the American style had already caught on, particularly "dipping"—that is, sinking a piece of carrot or a broccoli stem into a thick sauce. As for sex, it was practiced somewhat in the same way; in any case, no one made a big deal out of one-night stands. It even seemed that some of the Russies outdid the natives in this respect, especially the hostess, a dazzling little blonde with the walk of a ballerina.

Dvoira, recently a Leningrad Darya, was separated from a man who had struck it rich as an art dealer. In the separation proceedings, Mr. Radashkevich had left this beauty with a tidy six-figure sum leading off with perhaps a six, perhaps a nine. Buy a boutique, Dvo, her girlfriends—particularly that oracle of common sense Shirley Fedot—had urged her. Otherwise you'll blow it all. And now the boutique was bought, which was the reason for this extravagant party.

Korbach was staggered by the simoom of Russian after such a long lull. He moved from wall to wall and caught guests giving him strange looks. Did they recognize him? If they did, it was clearly without any great pleasure, perhaps even with slight contempt. He remembered that he had run into this sort of thing once before . . . oh yes, at the Ipsilon Studio, in SoHo. You're not going to foist the stale old Soviet idea of "hip" on an enlightened North American audience that's already been spoiled with the real thing.

At that point he noticed that at least two people were not regarding him with disdain. The hostess and Shirley Fedot had kindly smiles on their faces as they looked at the new arrival. He remembered why they had brought him here and went over to introduce himself. Dvoira staggered him right away with her first question: "*Eez eet true* . . . oh, sorry, I'm got English in my mouth all the time . . ." She went on in Russian: "Is it true that you're a great lay?" And she put her hands on her hips in delight at her "provocative question." She had an amusing little mug that changed expressions quickly: now she was a laughing monkey, now a mouse sniffing the air.

That night it seemed to him that he was playing hide-and-seek with the two masks. You get close to the sniffing mouse, and all of a sudden there's the monkey in front of you. You want to catch the laughing monkey's maw with your lips, and there's the mouse's sharp little nose. In the morning, one of the two whispered in his ear: "Listen, are you really *the* Sasha Korbach?"

When he woke up toward midday, he couldn't find his clothes in the bedroom. Dvoira came in just then, carrying his shirt, socks, and a suit that had been given a new lease on life, all pressed and even steaming slightly with unexpected freshness. "Listen, how come your trousers smell of Paul Newman's dressing?"

"It's his suit," he replied. "He loaned it to me for a couple of weeks."

"No, seriously?" she cried.

He nodded. "Alas, just for two weeks."

While he was dressing, she fixed him breakfast: a large glass of grapefruit juice, a stack of excellent toast, butter, jam, coffee.

She held up a bottle of Johnnie Walker by way of a question. Quick on the uptake, this one, he thought with gratitude. A bright mouse-monkey, technically well-prepared.

"You know what," she said over breakfast. "You've got to stop this fucking incognito business. Korbach is Korbach, for Christ's sake. We'll set up a press conference. I've got some guys at the *Times,* and the owner of *Panorama* is simply one of my best friends. We'll raise a tempest in this teapot. You'll get loads of invitations. The immigrants have already got the means to pay. We'll start with the Ataman, okay?"

He froze with the bottle in his hand. When he had finished chewing, he asked: "We'll start with what?"

"Don't pretend! The Ataman—it's a trendy Russian club on Sunset Boulevard! They'll give you an entire evening! Do you want me to make a call right now?"

Anger poured into him as fervently as the cold juice had five minutes before this turn in the conversation. "Not so quickly, my lady. You know, I wanted to tell you this last night, but I thought it would be tactless. You know, if it's a choice between the mouse sniffing the air and the laughing monkey, if I were in your shoes, I'd take the second."

She paled, as if she had immediately understood what he was getting at. "You scum! I knew you were a punk—lots of people said so! Get out of here and forget this place!" She let the whole last sentence go in English for greater effect.

Winding beneath the huge palm trees of Ocean Avenue in the direction of his vulgar Venice, he savored his freedom and scolded himself for his vulgarity. You just humiliated one more dame. Splashed her with a dirty, bohemian comment like used dishwater. She, a born ballerina, had decided to dance a magnificent duet with me, and I put her in her place and humiliated her. Trash is going where trash belongs, in Venice.

In this postmodern neo-Byronism of ours, he thought as he went along, we may be discovering something in the way of self-expression but nothing in the way of love. Each new generation gets demonized—"the superfluous men," "the Burned Ones"—we're playing the flirt with our own decadence. We never even get close to the simplicity and purity of the *dolce stil nuovo,* the seven-hundred-or-so-year-old poetry of Guido Guinizelli:

Cupid's bow drawn taut
ecstasy radiates
honeyed his vengeance
his tidings staggering
but heed his fabulous tidings
the arrow-pierced spirit
exonerates him
of impotence and
the ardor of new afflictions.

Instead of our spirits, kind ladies and gentlemen, the arrow hits us in the coccyx. Acupuncture of the erogenous zones. Everything else is just ill-fated flirting.

4

THE METAL LION

*N*ow it's time to return to Westwood Village, to the intersection where huge billboards advertising new movies hang. Sixteen pages or so ago, we left our hero here, standing stock-still at the sight of a slowly approaching motorcyclist. In keeping with our rules, we're not going to tease the reader with any speculative guessing; we'll say right away that the rider was none other than Stanley Korbach on a forty-thousand-dollar Harley-Davidson. Motorcycles had recently become the obsession of the fifty-six-year-old magnate, as a good means of distracting himself from existential suffering.

Alexander Korbach had no idea of this, of course. The last thing in the world he was expecting was the appearance of any Korbachs next to the Colonial Parking garage in Westwood. It wasn't likely that he remembered any of the particulars of the conversation that had taken place a year before in the department store that bore his own name. At best he could have remembered only his clumsy, if not shameful, entrance into the place, which he had taken at first for the gates of the Last Judgment. In any case, if he was ever even visited by memories of the event, he tried to shake himself free of them as soon as possible. Nevertheless, at that moment of stupor, he felt for some reason as though this unusual rider had come there looking for him.

The rider, with a gray mustache and an excellent crop of clean chestnut hair, gave him a quick glance that was full of humor and benevolence, then rolled past into a dark part of the garage. When Alex followed him inside, he saw that the owner of the bike was standing next to the dispatcher's office, having what looked like a friendly chat with Ted. The Harley was alongside, like the well-trained lion that had followed the Buddha.

"Hey, Alex, this gentleman wants to talk to you!" Ted shouted, seeing his employee walk by. One could have caught a note of surprise in his voice, as though he was immediately asking himself several questions: What's this gentleman got to do with our Russian? Do gentlemen even ride Harleys? Do Harleys allow themselves to be controlled by gentlemen like this?

To be sure, there was nothing Babylonian about the gentleman's appearance. He was wearing an ordinary leather jacket of the bomber classic type, and not at all in black armor crisscrossed with long lightning bolts; no fleshy mermaid on the gas tank; no gloomy grandeur in his face either.

"Mr. Korbach?" the guest asked excitedly, as though he could hardly believe his eyes. "Is that you?"

"Yes, sir!" Alex answered. "How may I help you, sir?" Displaying the standard politeness of the automotive hired help, he instinctively was on his guard. Not from *there,* is he, this guy? Not one of *them*? He meant the KGB, naturally.

Not wasting any time, the guest immediately dispelled any paranoia about the KGB. "Allow me to introduce myself. I'm Stanley Korbach. You could say we're related, in a way." *"Ni khuya sebe!"*—well, fuck me!—Alex murmured aloud. He remembered immediately that the name put him in mind of the young manager of the department store. The name of the president of a gigantic corporation, "a big name in the States!"

"You won't mind, Mr. Korbach, if I borrow you for a little while? What would you say to an early lunch, sir? I have something important to discuss with you."

Taken quite by surprise, Alex mumbled something almost incomprehensible. The words of his English vocabulary were hanging like half-dead flies in a spider's web. "It's so *neozhidanno. Ya na rabote.* Job, job." He finally managed to come out with an understandable sentence. "Thank you for the invitation, but I can't use it right now, because I just started my shift." Stanley beamed. This guy speaks pretty good English. Nothing nutty about him, and nothing pretentious either. A normal, not-too-bad-looking guy in the Korbach style—energetic, light on his feet.

"I hope that Mr. Ted will help us to find a way out of this situation." He turned to the boss, who had been watching the whole scene with growing amazement—which, however, did not show in the slightest on his ebony Ethiopian face. Three hundred-dollar bills lay on the counter in front of the boss. "No problem," said Tesfalidet with a wave of his hand, which was that of a pianist. "You can take an emergency leave, Alex—no problem." Aram raised his thumb at Alex and then made a gesture as if sprinkling salt on it for extra luck. Your ship's come in, old man, congratulations!

The Korbachs left the garage and headed for the nearest establishment, called Cafe Alice. They were just beginning to get the tables ready for lunch there. Stanley was much taller than Alex, wiry yet broad-shouldered, a giant of his race. A hard chin hung proudly over a turkey's pouch of flaccid skin. Alexander was pierced with a sudden, unexpected feeling of comfort, if such a feeling can be piercing. In the world, it seems, there exists a certain comfort and feeling of natural progression if you can go like this with a hypothetical relative to a nearby café in the morning. Stanley caught his eye and smiled with good-natured yet slightly diabolical humor.

In the restaurant, Stanley adopted the role of the absentminded provincial. "Are you hungry, Alex?" he asked. "Not very" was the reply. "As for me, I'm not hungry at all," Stanley said. "Shit, we've fallen into a trap. If we order hardly anything, they're not going to respect us much. And if we order a full lunch and don't eat it, they're not going to respect us at all. I say we start with a good bottle of champagne. Champagne's expensive, so they'll respect us right away, understand?"

Just what I've needed all my life—a wise older brother, thought Alex. "I like how you order champagne, Stanley," he said.

When the first bottle of Clicquot was finished, and before the arrival of the second, Stanley began his "important discussion." "Allow me, dear friend, to invite you on a short trip to a rather far-off country and to a not too distant past—shall we go?"

5

IN THE MENORAH'S LIGHT

*P*icture Warsaw in the seventies of the last century. A provincial capital of the Russian empire. It's forbidden to speak Polish in public places. Yiddish, as you can imagine, isn't well thought of either. At that time, the Korbach fur shop on the Stare Miasto was quite well-known. How long before that the Korbachs had come to Poland we're still trying to figure out—no need, though, to confuse the Jewish Korbachs with the Polish Korbuts, who've always been there. We can suppose on the basis of certain information that the Korbachs were actually the Kor-Beits, and that they landed in Poland via Holland after the Spanish exodus and adapted their name to the phonetics of Polish.

Gedali Korbach had a large, brooding brick house festooned with heavy shutters and, of course, full of demons. The master, a devout, well-to-do man, enjoyed great authority in Jewish society. In the house one was forever running into interpreters of the Talmud, along with worldly wise men in suit coats with long tales and velvet *kipas*. Then again, there were secular guests, too. Legend has it that even Baron Ginzburg himself used to visit the house and not only bought furs for his women but also discussed the fate of the people with the ponderous Gedali.

Baron Ginzburg, naturally, spoke French, but the everyday language of Warsaw society was a strange tongue, a stew of Russian, German, and Polish seasoned with turns of phrase from the Talmud. Colleagues of the owner of the house from the fur business would sit in the living room by the light of the menorah along with owners of tanneries and glove factories. A strong smell of mothballs prevailed throughout the house, and it seemed to the children the natural odor of nearby Hell. The furniture, of course, was kept under canvas slipcovers, which reminded one of the tents of the old nomadic camps. On Friday evening, life came to a stop; everyone sat covered with white talliths, reading prayers.

As in all prosperous Jewish households, the children were taught music—

meaningless daily torture. The despondent atmosphere that was characteristic of the East European Diaspora reigned here, a constant desire to hide from the outside world, as if they already felt even then that things would come to no good end. Gedali's wife, Dvoira . . .

At this point in the story, Alexander interrupted Stanley. "Dvoira? Did you say Dvoira?" Stanley nodded. "Yes, yes, that was her name, all right. What about it?" "Oh nothing, nothing. Go on, please."

She died when her oldest sons, the twins Alexander and Nathan, were fifteen. In the synagogue, they found the upstanding trader a new wife, Rachel, the widow of Fisk the grocer. She tried to make the boys like her, but nothing came of her efforts. The boys felt weighed down not so much by their stepmother as by their father's burdensome way of life. Outside the house, the interesting, intense life of the seventies was going on. From Petersburg and Moscow came rumors of liberating ideas. They began to say the words "Russian intellectual" with a particular meaning in mind. They smelled of the powder of homemade bombs. In Warsaw a new generation of conspirators was growing up. The newspapers printed stories about steamship passages to America. The boys saw only two alternatives for their futures: to go off and join the revolution or to run away to America. They tried to stoke the fires of their pseudohatred for the stepmother as much as possible to justify their unavoidable flight.

They were still a long way from sixteen when they made up their minds. The demons of the house, naturally, incited them to rob their father. One night they broke into the shop, snatched the week's takings, and filled two suitcases with Siberian sables. With these goods, it seemed to the boys, they would take America by storm. It was never explained where the sables were stolen from them—while they were still on the boat or at customs in New York—but in any case they found themselves among the first arrivals on the Lower East Side without a penny to their name—that is, just as it should be in a novel.

The likable twins—or *was hab ich doch gedaft,* as the Yiddish speakers called them—aroused sympathy among the trading crowd, and they soon managed to get jobs at an Italian greasy spoon called Downing Oyster House and Pasta Place. Alexander and Nathan probably had to open no fewer than a million oysters each in that place. What was even more ironic was that, according to the kosher laws, they were forbidden to eat mollusks. And do you like oysters, my friend? Well, what the hell, order half a dozen dozen! My thanks to the kosher laws. If it hadn't been for them, we might have inherited an aversion for these delightful little slugs.

It was a year or a year and a half before the twins moved out of the Italian cellar and over to respectable work in a Jewish establishment, the Fimmy Steak House. There they were waiters and got tips from coachmen, butchers, street vendors, and wholesalers. Fimmy's, by the way, is still there to this day. We'll have to have dinner there sometime. Only without champagne. It's absurd to order champagne in that sort of place. Got to order vodka. That's right! Let them bring it in a chunk of ice. That must be how it was done in Russia. They kept the bottles in some sort of Volga. It froze, then they cut up the goddamned containers with sabers, or whatever it is they cut vodka out of ice with where you come from.

"You're pulling my leg, Stanley! Stop it!" said Alexander, very proud of the fact that he'd used an idiom. "Oh my God!" Stanley shouted and glanced under the tablecloth. "I hadn't even noticed your legs, friend!" With a snap of his fingers he ordered another Clicquot.

Our twins were living near this temple of chops, on Orchard Street, almost a slum—which later, in the twentieth century, would be called Yashkin Street by the new waves of immigrants, so that the name change became quasi official. Go there now and you'll find the same opera playing as a hundred years ago: Kauffman's and Gorelick's shops, Sol Mosckot and Leibel Bystritskis kosher gourmet. The boys were lucky—by the time they arrived, the city authorities had ordered that the houses there be equipped with fire escapes, primitive ventilation systems, and also "private outside conveniences"—that is, one toilet with a little oval hole in the courtyard for twenty tenants. Until then, they squatted in the bushes.

At the end of the seventies something important happened in the life of the Korbachs, some sort of sharp rise in their financial status. There's a vague note in the diary of our founder—that is, your namesake, Alex—concerning this period. "Part of the furs has come back," he writes. "Profits in dollars." The figure is erased and scratched out with a nail. We can suppose that the lads worked out some sort of deal with the Jewish mafia that controlled the territory on the edge of the Bowery and the Lower East Side.

One way or another, they managed to rent an apartment with indoor plumbing on Seward Avenue. It seems that by this time they had bought forged documents showing that they had graduated from the czar's Russian gymnasium in Warsaw. Who in America would bother to check that not even their ages were right for these diplomas? It's known that Nathan took courses at Hunter College for several years and fretted over the idea of going to MIT. Alexander, meanwhile, became one of three owners of Fimmy's, where the brothers still worked as waiters. Then Nathan left the restaurant to work at some paper mill at the corner of Grand and Mulberry. He did extremely well at this job and in the end even patented a new process for making high-quality paper. Now came a crisis in the relationship of the two brothers.

You know, of course, that twins from the same egg have something like a feeling of double personality all their lives. Far from each other, they don't quite feel themselves; they always feel as though any step they take is somehow incomplete. The thought of a prolonged separation seems just unbearable to them. Our lads were no exception, in spite of the differences in their temperaments and interests.

Here's what we now know about the situation. Alexander was a typical extrovert, made friends easily, took risks, even big ones. New York, with its sudden cuffs on the ear and its no less sudden successes, had swallowed him completely, and he became a typically aggressive American businessman of his time. In Nathan's face we see a typical assiduous young man of the sort one finds working in a laboratory. I don't think he was much interested in "abstract subjects," yet in the library that he left, alongside the physics and chemistry books you'll find Dickens, Balzac, and Longfellow, not to mention novels by Tolstoy and Dostoevsky, the kings of fiction of the time, ordered from St. Petersburg.

It's doubtful that these guys, caught up in the excitement of the New World, were good Jews, yet they kept the Sabbath, of course, and went to the synagogue on festival days. In Nathan's books I found, among other things, the chronicle of Josephus Flavius, which means that he was interested in the history of Israel. Alexander Korbach, I'm afraid, never read anything except the stock market reports in the newspapers. He was a generator of commercial ideas and a fashion plate. And, of course, he had good contacts with the heads of the mafia.

Strange as it may sound, the riskiest scheme of them all came not to Alexander but to Nathan. In 1881 he announced to his brother that he was going back to Russia to start a factory to make paper according to his own method. From the writings of our future great-grandmother, then Alexander's fiancée, we know that Alexander was beside himself with rage. I think he was not only enraged but frightened to death. The second half of the egg had never gone so far away before. It seems that he never forgave his brother this rupture. It also seems that Nathan always carried a certain feeling of guilt around—how was it his fault if all the nostalgia intended for two had landed on his side of the egg?

In those days, Russia and America may have been far from each other, but they were still parts of the same world—unlike today—connected by fairly reliable steamship lines. The brothers only very occasionally, but steadily, corresponded. Alexander sent dry letters, and cards on the occasions of Jewish holidays. He usually dictated to his secretary, so copies have survived. We've never managed to find any messages of congratulation to him on his birthday—curious, don't you think? Nathan's letters have so many lyrical passages and descriptions of landscapes that they sound like a novice writer trying out his pen. With each year he used more and more Russian, though my expert has found quite a few mistakes of grammar and syntax in them.

So, in one way or another, the brothers were well-informed about each other's lives until 1917. Nathan knew that Alexander had married a rich Irish girl soon after his departure. The couple brought two children into the world, including my grandfather, and also a large department store, which to this day bears the noble name of the sable kidnapper, that is, your name, Mr. Alexander Korbach, which has so remarkably resurfaced again after two generations.

Nathan Korbach, meanwhile, bought a small paper factory in Riga and redesigned it his own way. Soon he got married to Rebecca Slonimsky, the daughter of a piano tuner, and they had a son, your grandfather, the greatly respected Ruvim Natanovich, who, it seems—at this point our information starts to get a bit murky, and we're hoping for your help—studied painting and sculpture and married your grandmother Irina Stepanovna Kropotkina, something that the part of the clan that had stayed in Warsaw was very unhappy with, since she was a shiksa.

In one of his letters, Nathan gives a rather witty description of the circumstances of his marriage to your great-grandmother. You've probably never heard about any of this. I didn't think so. Here's what happened. As you can probably imagine, the return of Korbach—not bad looking, well-off, and young—from America threw the unmarried young ladies of Warsaw, Riga, and Vilnius into an uproar. At this point, something strange happens. For some reason, the matrimonial affairs of an entire branch of big Jewish families were in the hands of the well-known sculptor Mark Antokolski. This man, who was forty and a bit at the time, was considered the most successful member of the community, since his fame had spread beyond the Pale of Settlement. All of our Korbachs and Slonimskys, and the Ginzburgs, Rabinoviches, and others, too, treated him like a patriarch, and he, as I understand it, was only too happy to accept such an honor. It was with a letter from this very same Mr. Antokolski that the young Korbach appeared in the Slonimsky household, where two daughters were dying to get married. Even here, though, not everything was so simple. Solomon Slonimsky, Riga's greatest specialist in pianos, had married a woman older than himself after the death of his first wife—the mother of your great-grandmother Rebecca—and that woman had two daughters of her own. It was these two daughters who were reckoning with getting married, and it was to them that the patriarch Antokolski had sent young Nathan for a look-see.

A banquet was given with an endless succession of *kreplakhs, knubli, knadels,* and *tsibels,* followed at the end by a stunning Viennese strudel, which the girls had made themselves. Everyone listened, hardly daring to breathe, as Nathan talked about America. To them, he was an impeccable gentleman from New York. They could hardly have imagined him in an outhouse on Orchard Street. The family was on tenterhooks, watching to see which of the two girls he would prefer.

And all the while he was secretly following with his eyes the third one, who only occasionally sat down at the table, helping the servants most of the time. This was the eighteen-year-old Rebecca. At a moment when she was carrying out some dirty dishes, Nathan quietly asked: "And who is that girl?" There was an awkward silence. Then Madame Slonimskaya said in a casual, worldly tone: "She's just a relative." Rebecca dropped the dishes and shrieked: "Not a relative, but the daughter of her own father!" And rushed away into the kitchen. The young gentleman followed her with the light tread of an East Side mafioso. Everything was clear.

Antokolski the sculptor was extremely annoyed by the fact that the meeting had not gone according to his plan, though later, when he had got to know the young couple, his anger turned to kindness, and he even took their growing son, your grandfather Ruvim, under his artistic wing. It was in fact under Antokolski's influence that the youngster entered the arts and subsequently became an important figure in the Russian avant-garde, which would, of course, have completely disgusted his former patron, had he lived to see it.

"I heard something about it from my grandma," Alexander said. "He joined the group Jack of Diamonds, and then Oslinyi Khvost. How is it in English . . . Donkey's Tail?"

"Monkey's Tail?" Stanley asked.

The café had been filled for some time with people who had come for lunch. In the center of the room, a group was energetically making their salads. Other customers were whispering to each other, glancing at the rather odd, somehow ill-matched pair of men knocking back Clicquot at that hour of the morning in a corner of the veranda beneath a lemon tree. A strange pair indeed: the older one has a shock of perfect hair, the young one is bald; the old one in the brown leather jacket is crossing one of his long legs and shaking it back and forth, so that you have to go around it with a bowl of salad in your hands, and the young one in a silver jacket that has COLONIAL PARKING written on it is smoking one cigarette after another—that is, he's damaging his own health and indirectly the health of everyone around him; judge for yourself what sort of people they are.

Stanley went on: After that, the story starts to blur. We know that the Riga factory turned a good profit. In one of his letters to Alexander, Nathan proposed that his brother invest in an expansion of production. Expanding production was all that Nathan ever thought about, of course. They were close to an agreement, but for some reason it never came off. In 1908, Nathan cut back all operations in Riga and moved to the Volga, to the city of Semeria—oh, thanks, *Samara*—and took up the production of paper according to his Manhattan formula again.

All this time, the brothers were intending to see each other, making plans for trips, but in 1917 all these plans fell through, and the correspondence stalled as well. To this day we don't know what happened to the Volga Korbachs. They were a long way from Auschwitz, fortunately. Their factory was probably nationalized, but as for Nathan's end, we haven't got the slightest idea. Maybe you can remember something, Alex? I'd be very grateful to you for any information about your family. We already know something about it. Believe it or not, you and I are fourth cousins.

His story finished, Stanley felt strangely awkward. It was hard to tell how this guy—this "fourth cousin"—would act henceforth. Would he suddenly start asking for money? There was, of course, something absurd about the whole meeting. The absurdity was heightened by the entrance into the café of two muscular types, our magnate's bodyguards. Somehow they had managed to follow him on his impulsive motorcycle jaunt. Professionals, no question about it.

Alexander, shaken to the ground by what he had heard across the table—the longest monologue that had ever been addressed to him in English—shook his shiny head slowly from side to side. *"Nu i nu . . ."*

"What does *nu i nu* mean?" Stanley asked. Alexander made a gesture with his hands that signified "Well, well." "Can I ask one question?" "The more questions, the better," Stanley answered with a nod, then barked to one side in a voice just short of rage: "I know! Tell them, I know!" It was because one of the bodyguards had strolled by their table and had added a meaningful glance at his own watch, which looked as though it had been filed down from a lump of coal.

"How did you manage to find me here, Stanley?" was, naturally, Alexander's first question.

His fourth cousin smiled. "This country, Alex, is a citadel of freedom. A citadel, understand? After Art Duppertat of our New York store told me about his meeting with you, we got in touch with the Immigration and Naturalization Service and learned that the Soviet citizen Alexander Korbach had actually come to this country on an H-1 visa. Then we got in touch with the L.A. office of the same organization, since you'd told Art that you were planning to go to California, and without any red tape they told us there that you'd put in a request for political asylum. With that information it wasn't hard to find your Social Security number. Beg your pardon, I even wrote it down here in my notebook." Saying this, Stanley took out a tiny computer, pushed a button, and showed Alexander nine numbers that, on Stas's advice, he had learned by heart, so as to be able to say them even in his sleep, if need be: 777-77-7777.

Stanley went on: "Everything else was perfectly simple. We got your address and phone number, and today they were kind enough to call and say that you'd gone to work for Westwood Colonial Parking. So, you see, they're wrong in the USSR when they say in the papers that America is at the mercy of fate. It's at the mercy of computers, more likely."

"I don't mind," Alexander agreed. "Even better that way. After all, we're not on the rubbish heap, right? Sometimes you even get a free breakfast." Saying that, he meant the Catholic Brothers, but Stanley took it to mean himself and guffawed. "Well, cousin, computers still haven't helped us to figure out who you are. They don't give preferential visas to parking garage attendants, you know." "Oh, I'm from the theater," Alexander said with a dismissive wave and then fell silent. Stanley realized that he had no intention of elaborating and cautiously added: "Alex, you're new in this country, and maybe you haven't noticed yet that over here you can't just sit and wait for success. Here you've got to sell what you have to sell, and do it with energy. Aggressive marketing, they call it." "Business terms aren't in my line," Alexander noted dryly. "Listen, Stanley, it's better if I tell you what I know about my relatives. I never knew my father, he was shot in nineteen thirty-nine, a few months before I was born. No one ever said a word in the family about any relatives in America. I'm not even sure that anyone knew about your part of the Korbach clan. To tell the truth, I didn't even know anything about my great-grandfather Nathan. Grandma Irina sometimes hinted at some 'Samara Korbachs,' but then she would change the subject.

"In the seventies—I was over thirty by then, and she was more than seventy—they performed a successful operation on her eyes, they removed some cataracts. After that she somehow began to remember the past, even lots of clear details, as though her memory had cleared up along with her vision. In one of the stories that she told then, the 'Samara Korbachs' came up again. Not long before the revolution, Ruvim went to Samara to see his relatives—his 'half brothers,' as he called them. I don't remember whether she mentioned my great-grandfather or not, but even if she did, it wasn't in a way that a man of the theater would remember.

"Wait a minute, I just remembered something: the photograph! She was always rummaging in her photo albums then, remembering her old life and suddenly pulling out large photos, mounted on stiff board with some sort of embossed seal at the corners. Look, Sasha—here's Grandfather with the Samara Korbachs! I was always hurrying somewhere then, so I didn't have the photograph in my hands for more than two minutes. The picture had been taken in a studio with typical luxury curtains in the background. There were at least a dozen people, as I recall, the older ones sitting in armchairs, the younger ones standing behind them. Maybe I'm making a mistake under the influence of your story, Stanley, but in the middle there was a proud-looking old man with a mustache à la Wilhelm. Well, he seemed an old man to me at the time. Yes, it was clear that he was around sixty. It's possible that that was Great-grandfather Nathan.

"I should tell you that Soviet people have completely gone off the habit of digging for their families' histories. People wanted to keep their genealogy in the dark, not reveal it—no telling when some 'enemy of the people' might jump out: a priest, a czarist officer, a kulak, a small businessman. Hardly any of my friends could trace his descent past his grandfather. The revolution created a sort of colossal wall in Russian history, a border in time. Everything on the other side of it is like the days of Nebuchadnezzar.

"I remember that two haughty young men in that photo caught my eye—the younger half brothers of Grandfather Ruvim, Nolya and Volya. Grandmother told me in a whisper that they had gone over to the Whites during the Civil War. In Samara there was a multiparty government of supporters of the Constituent Assembly; a voluntary regiment there was taking Jews. The whole group, I have to say, surprised me by its bourgeois gentility. Good clothes, relaxed poses, bold, confident looks in their eyes. A complete absence of the 'Russian spirit,' and no great abundance of the Jewish one either. Two or three characteristic faces, but on the whole, the family looked quite European.

"I must admit that before this meeting with you, I'd never really thought much about my Jewish roots. I only found out that I was descended from the Korbachs when I was fourteen, and before that I had my stepfather's name and was registered as a Russian. It was only at the age of sixteen that I made the demand for the return of my family name and nationality, but I didn't do it out of any Jewish feeling, only out of disgust for everything Soviet; in the circles that I lived and worked in—the theater, you know—no one concentrated on anything exclusively Jewish. The Jews made up a sort of humorous Odessa vein. Strange, but even the subject of the Holocaust didn't come up much. The Communists managed to reduce religious devotion to a minimum, and when the religious revival began—also more as a protest than as a deep feeling—everyone started wearing crosses. Many Jewish lads went over to the Orthodox church. Pasternak's philosophy of assimilation in Russian culture was closer to them than Israelite antiquity; the New Testament spoke to them more than the Torah. You also have to consider that we were blended into the population to a large degree. Your newly discovered 'fourth cousin,' Stanley, is only one-quarter Jewish, you see."

At that point, Stanley gently interrupted Alexander. "Alex, I'm afraid that you're more Jewish than you think. Last winter my assistants Fuchs and Lester Square were working in Moscow, and they managed to find out that your grandmother on your mother's side, Anna Mikhailovna, née Gorsky, was Jewish, too." He laughed, seeing the amazement on Alex's face, and gave him a sympathetic pat on the shoulder: Chin up, my friend, he seemed to say, there's nothing particularly terrible about this bit of news.

Alex tried hard to remember Anna Mikhailovna, the most modest of people. He had seen her only a few times, when she would come from Sverdlovsk to see her grandchildren. These visits were always the cause of a certain ambiguous feeling in the Izhmailov family. It was obviously taboo to ask Grandmother's nationality. In all probability, Mother had not mentioned her half-Jewish origins in filling out the pertinent forms and all her life stubbornly considered herself a full-blooded Russian. My poor mother, a secret archive employee, an unhappy Soviet liar.

6

THE HIMALAYAS AT SUNSET

"Tell me, Stanley, why are you doing this research?"

Instead of answering, the tall man stood up, now looking at his watch himself. The bodyguards, their happy faces like pears, hurried to the exit. When the two Korbachs came out of the restaurant, a limousine half a city block long was waiting on the side of the road. "Unfortunately, I have to fly to Seattle right now," Stanley said. "When's your flight?" asked Alexander, not without relief. There had been enough revelations for him today, not to mention the fact that his tongue was painfully tired from speaking English. "As soon as we get to the airport, we take off," the large man replied. What am I asking for, thought Alexander—he must have his own jet. "Let me give you a lift," Stanley offered. "I want to see how you've gotten yourself set up in America. And your good Mr. Ted will drive your car home for you later."

They bounced along on the limousine springs for a while in silence. Then Stanley asked: "And where might that family photo be now?" Alexander shrugged. "Most likely it got left behind in my flat in Moscow." "You've still got an apartment there?" Stanley asked, greatly surprised somehow. "Well, I had one, anyway," Alexander said with a sheepish grin. "I understand," said Stanley.

He understands everything, don't you see, Alexander thought with some annoyance. Billions don't always help to understand everything, Mr. Cousin-Playing-President, or rather Mr. President-Playing-Cousin. The entire recent lunch now appeared in hypertrophically distorted form, and his cousin inflated to Pantagruelic proportions. He swallows oysters, dozen after dozen, half a dozen dozen, a dozen half-dozen dozen. They haven't got enough food at Alice's, they've got to run to the Bazilio for help. He knocks back all the French champagne in stock and then switches to Californian while they're bringing up new cases of Clicquot. When he's noticed your amazement, he brings up to your nose his gigantic hand, in the palm of which, between the lines of life and fate, lies a clear salt crystal. "Open your mouth, Alex!" He laughs and tosses the crystal into your mouth, which you've opened willingly. A thirst for champagne immediately takes hold of you, an unbearable and unquenchable thirst. A very strange meeting indeed after centuries of separation!

Stanley didn't catch the slight twist in the mood of his happily discovered "fourth cousin." His own mood was something else entirely. An inexplicable warmth was growing—without even any limits in sight, it seemed—for this neglected, bald youngster with his mangled English. I've got to help him, he thought. Not because I'm richer, but because I'm twelve years older than he is. Of course I feel awful placing myself above him, but there's no other way—I have to help him. "Listen, Alex," he said. "You're still a newcomer here, and you've got through what might not be the most brilliant time of your life, so I hope that you won't stand on ceremony too much if I—"

"Thank you, Stanley," Alexander interrupted, and thought: He's a good guy after all. "Thanks, I'm very touched, but I don't need anything. Everything's okay."

They drove up to the Hotel Cadillac just when it was sticking its cracked head out into the hottest part of the day. On the terrace a few old men were playing cards. One of them, with a well-chewed and extinguished cigar stub in one corner of his mouth, took his attention away from the game for a moment and glanced at the limousine with his one good eye, its bandit flame suddenly blazing to life. A handsome means of transportation, that's for sure, was the thought swimming up to him from his still living American dream.

"What've you got here?" Stanley asked.

"A studio," said Alex with a smile.

"With a bathroom?"

"What, you need to take a leak?"

"How'd you guess?"

In the lobby, Stanley surveyed the pride of the condominium—a large painting showing a mermaid getting caught in a large net, with some large Huguenot fortress in the background. Not even Bernadetta Luxe knew anything about the origin of the painting, though many detected a resemblance between the features of the mermaid and those of the owner herself. "Inspiring," was the financial and industrial magnate's short summation.

He only made up the bit about the toilet so that he could see the poverty I live in was what Alexander thought. Stanley hadn't been fooling at all, though. He had certain problems with his urinary tract, especially a need to brace himself against the wall behind the water tank with both hands in order to let fly with a steady stream. He emerged from the "bathroom" with a brightened expression and more automatically than out of interest took a book from the flimsy bookcase that Alexander had found not long before on a Santa Monica sidewalk. "What's this?" Obviously, he couldn't read a word in the Cyrillic alphabet. "Dante," Alexander said. "The *Divine Comedy*." Stanley chuckled. "Looks like we have the same bedside books." He recited the beginning as if he were reading it:

In the midway of this our mortal life,
I found me in a gloomy wood, astray
Gone from the path direct.

"It sounds better in Russian," Alexander said.

"Well, of course!" Stanley laughed. "So long, Alex! Hope we'll see each other soon."

When he had gone, Alexander went out onto the porch and lowered himself into a crudely made rocking chair from which much of the paint was chipped. In front of him was a side street bathed entirely in sunshine and seemingly completely white. A row of Dumpsters, each one the size of the Trojan horse, diminished in perspective. In the distance was the ocean, and on it several sails. Over the ocean was a cloudless sky, into whose omnipotent, spot-cleansing blueness an enormous jet rose powerfully, its course set for Japan.

He closed his eyes and shut himself off, as it were, and when he opened them again, he saw majestic cloud formations set against the gleaming copper screen of the vault of the Pacific sky. All of this together formed an image of his Young Pioneers childhood. The clouds were imitating the Himalayas and inviting him to their snowy slopes, on the other side of which breathtaking adventures awaited the young Leninist. The sun, meanwhile, was on a downward trajectory, and the lower it dropped, the more dramatic the cloud front became, and the more the observer on the terrace of the Hotel Cadillac grew up. The deep blue with its fiery fringe represented Sasha's early adolescence, calling him to a crusade for a "bonanza" in the West with its inspirational gleam. Gradually his youth turned into young adulthood, of which the heaped-up clouds accumulating a violet eroticism spoke eloquently. The sun completed its unimaginable trick and touched the horizon of the sea. Now Korbach's carnival was reaching its high point before his eyes. The whole of the atmosphere was shot through with the *dolce stil nuovo,* which with every moment was sending freshly minted images right across the bottle green sky—a scattered herd of camels, a squadron of Baltic skiffs, or a maelstrom of masks dancing around a fountain. Alas, all this didn't last long. The camels were quickly transformed into a pack of wild mongrels, into baby rabbits with two heads and three ears, into the taillike snout of a crocodile, into a family of dirty mushrooms, into an overturned statue of Lenin with his backside overgrown with weeds, into all these signs of a midlife crisis, filled in with the secretions of age spots. The darkness was deepening; early stars sprinkled across the sky like dandruff announced the end of the concert. The last emerald ray flickered like the words "The End" in a cheap film. The "tender night" had arrived, but it was from another opera entirely, as from a vacuum.

He got up and went inside. In the lobby the usual crowd of "people of advanced age"—old folks, that is—was sitting in front of the television. A popular opinion maker, the hostess of a talk show, was introducing the day's talking heads to the audience: adolescent homosexuals and adolescent "straights." The old hags giggled as they listened to the young people's witticisms. The warped floorboards of the corridor creaked beneath Alexander's sneakered feet. He went into his "studio."

To his surprise, the television in his room was switched on, too. On a different channel, another discussion was droning on, this time on the problems of masochism. A middle-aged lady, her spherical tits almost popping out of her décolleté dress, was confessing to having surprising sexual inclinations: "I've got to say that even Madonna looks modest compared to what I do with my guys. I start out by choking them a bit, until they start to wheeze, then I start stroking them passionately, then I whip them with a belt, I slap their mugs, I pinch them and I bite them—sometimes I alternate, sometimes I do both at the same time. Now, don't you think that's an example of female superiority?" The woman's chortling and the furious agitation of the audience verged on destroying the little visual box, which was also, by the way, sort of picked up at a garbage dump.

Alexander sat down on his bed, which still bore the traces of the previous night's struggle with that hussar of a woman, Denise Davidov. Turning the sound off, he decided to watch the entire program without even trying to imagine the sway of public opinion, not understanding a thing, receiving only the sensation of a strong, pleasant smell of lemon coming into the Cadillac from a neighboring garden. A sleepy feeling of warmth and comfort came over him, as though Grandmother Irina had sat down next to him, gazing at him lovingly and sometimes running her fingers through the hair behind his ears. No reason to worry about anything if Granny's here—if she smells so nice, like a lemon tree. . . .

How long he slept, he didn't know. The television had somehow switched itself off, which rarely happened. There was a knock at the door. He leapt from the bed and opened it. Before him stood Stanley Korbach. "I suppose you were already asleep, Alex?" he asked with some embarrassment. "Nothing of the sort, I just woke up," Alexander answered. "What about you? You didn't fly to Seattle?" "No, no, we just got back," Stanley muttered. He sat down on the edge of the table. In the dim light of the room, he looked like a young man. "You know, I flew back here to answer your question, but I forgot my answer along the way."

"What question?"

"Well, you asked me why I'm interested in looking for the Korbachs and genealogy in general."

"Forgive me for the stupid question."

Stanley grinned. "There is no answer, but there is a stupid confession. I simply can't live because of death. Do you know that feeling?"

Now it was Alexander's turn to smile. "How would I live without it?" Stanley peered at him intently. "How did you get over it?" He shrugged. "I hammed it up in the theater."

All at once, a commanding knock at the door interrupted the developing dialogue between the descendants of the same egg fertilized in 1859. A turn of the door handle, and into the room came none other than the incomparable Bernadetta Luxe, her forceful curves visible through her peignoir of crumpled silk. "Hey, Lavsky, how're things, babe, so sweet and so lonely?" It was as though all the hubbub of the bar—and with it, the smell—had come into the room with her. Wonder of wonders, between her breasts on this night was a nearly ideal creation, a tiny

Chihuahua that couldn't have weighed more than half a pound. Its little ears were sticking out, its eyes darting back and forth, the cradle of the bust that was the living miniature's reliable support was rocking it back and forth.

"Why, there's another little boy in here!" the landlady cried at the sight of the towering figure of the guest.

"What a wonderful surprise!" rumbled the magnate. "Providence is sometimes kind to its fools after all!"

"This is our Messalina Titania," Alexander explained.

"Missed again, Lavsky!" Luxe wagged a warning finger carrying a ring with a turquoise the size of a sample bar of soap, after which she extended a powerful hand to the "other little boy" and introduced herself: "Bernie-Thorny." Stanley clicked his heels together. "Stanley-Smoothly." After the handshake he offered a palm to the passenger of the enormous sand dunes. The Chihuahua leapt nimbly from the cleft onto Korbach's line of fate and established itself firmly as a quivering masterpiece with aroused miniature prick. Bernadetta lowered her eyes and said in a rumble that came from her depths: "Some guys go loopy for dogs, and some of 'em for girls." The happy Stanley said with a loud laugh: "There's room enough in my heart for you both!"

Alexander took a blanket and left the room. His departure seemed to go unnoticed. On the beach, with a newspaper for a pillow, he stretched out on the sand and wrapped himself in the blanket. "A Hard Day's Night" had finally come into its own.

In the morning, he was first in line for the Catholic Brothers' breakfast. Brother Charles handed him two packages. "How's your friend, my good man?" "Keep praying, Brother Charles, and everything'll be great," Alexander answered, thanking him seriously. "Looks like he's feeling better."

IV. THE TERRACE

Where in Washington can you soften up a hangover
With free booze—that is, like a real bum?
That's what the homeless people ask,
The ones with only chewing gum under their cheeks and not a cent in their
*   pockets,*
Who have a lax conscience but wily wisdom.
Well, here you are on the terrace of the Kennedy Center
At quarter past four in the morning with the dawn's first rays.
The main thing is to come out as the one and only!
The willows are rustling like children's dreams.
The morning world in an upside-down eyepiece
Presents its most important plan—unfinished drinks.
Last night they cooed over Rostropovich here,
And at the intermission the sophisticates sipped champagne.
Lanky women hid the experience behind eyeglasses,
The filigree of their teeth playing gently.
A lot was left undrunk during the conversations,
Or perhaps fell prey to a bum.
Half a dozen goblets—there's a pint for you,
You can substantially increase your joy.
Highly respected Mstislav Leopoldovich—
Slava to you—thanks for the matinee!
The marble is slippery, it's as though you were trudging on ice,
A shadow spreads out on the wall.
Then the shadow of a panther looms up,
And you, insolent, salute,
But then, behind the mirrored, rhythmic spats,
A monster awakens with leftist zeal.
Right after that, the spawn of the fallen trees with disheveled withers,
In crow's feathers from the tail up to the clavicle,
Like a herald of the Holocaust,
The greediest of the she-wolves springs out
The reflections of ghosts, the nightmares of a fortune-teller,
It reflects in the buttons of a general's tunic,
It's the most decrepit of old ladies
Riding over Georgetown in a wheelchair.
Her massive legs are covered with a high-quality poncho,
A full beard trailing over her shoulder like a polar fox,
One general's shoulder strap is still gleaming,
A thousand-peseta cigar gleaming in his teeth.
Picking up a couple of glasses by the fountain,
An old woman squints, as though she's heard the command to fire.

The specter of revolution and the phantom of Marxism
Take aim at capitalism once again.
Well, let's say it, it turned out well, this morning tipple!
Who are you, old woman? Don't squirm, answer!
What are you doing here with your smirk—
Are you the swill of theory or the terra firma of practice?
Is it true, that in an unfinished glass
Thoughts remain, and if that's so,
What was this crowd, soaked through with spirits,
Thinking about here through worldly beat?
The general laughs badly in Spanish.
The stamping of Budyonny's cavalcade sounds.
They think only about the Inferno.
All of them see only a dumping ground and Hell.
She moves away with a long wink,
The sun has risen over the bridges of the Potomac,
And as she goes into the distance sings like Domingo,
Dragging the notes out of her knapsack.
You stand there, a timid bum,
Emptying twenty plastic cups,
You whisper: God, All-merciful God,
Let me lie down awhile beside your harvest.

PART V

1

AGAMEMNON'S SHOP

*T*ikhomir Burevyatnikov had decided to try on a new suit, or, even better, a *costumenzzia,* since ordinary words are hardly adequate to describe true masterpieces of the tailor's art. If everything used to be cut to fit tightly, as if to show off the wearer's body, now the cloth falls from it (the body, that is) in broad folds. That's the style now, Tikh, the salesman on Sunset Boulevard told him—everything's cut for someone else's shoulder, for someone else's behind. These days, my friend, you don't show your business card right away: its glorious kilogram is hidden by a pleated fly.

Tikhomir had reason to believe Agamemnon Grivadis, and not only because show business stars rolled into his shop from time to time and picked up a dozen suits and two dozen shirts on the run and a garland of silver-tipped slippers—there were other reasons for his confidence. He was his own man, after all, completely his own. The features of a good Soviet boy—we'll put it that way—showed in all of Agamik's face. His papa had fought for socialism under the colors of General Marcos, and Agamik himself was no dime-a-dozen jerk-off: he had gone through a serious Komsomol school in Tashkent, and when the time came he had skedaddled from the swamp of socialism for the free world. Even though Burevyatnikov had nothing against the Jewish and Armenian emigration, he somehow had more confidence in one of his brother defectors.

Agamemnon led his customer-pal into the fitting room and offered him three suits to choose from: one sky blue, one moss green, and one chocolate-golden brown. A man of taste, Burevyatnikov opted for the last. The shopkeeper went out, the customer divested his torso of a jacket with a heavy inside pocket (that's right, sir, a Browning) and had only one leg out of his jeans when Agamik's head, with its well-tended, pencil-thin mustache, poked itself into the fitting room. "Sorry, Tikh, a comrade wants to talk to you." Immediately after this polite interruption, a man of rather nondescript appearance, his right hand beneath his left armpit, entered the room. "Well now, Mr. Bur," he said, using Tikh's current surname, one that was not very well known to those who knew him. "Greetings from the Soviet government!" There was no point in reaching for the weapon in his jacket hanging on the wall. Burevyatnikov began to climb back into his just-vacated trouser leg. Better to die with your pants on than with a half-naked ass! The new arrival grinned. "Steady on, traitor to the motherland." Agamemnon returned with two folding chairs. "Bring you a couple of beers, boys?" "It wouldn't hurt," Tikh said dryly. The stranger called back over his shoulder: "And an ashtray!"

"What department are you from?" Tikhomir asked. "N," the stranger replied. Jesus fucking Christ, Burevyatnikov thought. They sat down on the chairs. The stranger laid an attaché case on his lap. They looked at each other in silence for some time. The representative of the Soviet government smiled, showing a gold tooth. "Any more questions?" he finally asked. Burevyatnikov wagged his chin negatively. "Agamik, where're those fucking beers?" he shouted.

Agamemnon came in with a six-pack of Grolsch and a jar of Jewish pickles. After he had opened the bottles, he stayed in the fitting room, as if to show that he was no Judas, just doing his duty. "A decision has been made," the representative said. Burevyatnikov took a swig from the bottle of Grolsch. What could taste better than an ice-cold beer just before being shot at point-blank range? "Doesn't look like we made a mistake," said the representative to the owner of the shop. "Not at all, Comrade Zet," Agamemnon confirmed. Tikhomir downed the rest of the bottle.

Comrade Zet slapped his attaché case. "In here is five hundred thousand dollars. It's for you by decision of a group of competent authorities. Now you have the opportunity to atone for your guilt before the fatherland."

"No 'wet jobs,' " Tikhomir answered right away. "Soak them yourselves."

"Shut up, you bastard!" said Zet in a shout that was not very loud but still threatening. "You've picked up a lot of American horseshit about the KGB! Who do you take us for, killers, hit men?"

"You know, I'm not used to that tone anymore," Tikh said sardonically. "I've been in a normal society for two years now, you see." He was surprised at himself, wondering where this hardness had come from. From movies, probably. He'd seen quite a few films here with men of iron as the heroes.

Some sort of contest between systems was going on. A motor-rifle unit seemed to run down the newly arrived comrade's face from his ear to the corner of his mouth. "You ought to ask first, Tisha, and suspect the worst later," Agamemnon put in, trying to be conciliatory. "All right, I'm asking," said Burevyatnikov. "What's the dough for?"

Zet outlined the task for him in a hostile voice. "The money has been sent to you to start a business with. Your primary task is keep up a good bank account. Is that clear?" Tikhomir put a second bottle to his mouth. "I would advise you not to refuse," Zet said. Tikhomir looked at Agamemnon out of the corner of his eye. "I wouldn't advise it either," the latter immediately confirmed.

"You'll burn me alive?" Tikhomir inquired. "Like Penkovsky?" Comrade Zet put the jar of pickles on his half million. "Just as the Japanese imperialists burned our comrade Commissar Lazo." He chuckled. You can't get away from these bastards anywhere, Burevyatnikov thought with bitterness, and agreed: "Give me your 'half mil'!" Agamik and Zet immediately beamed with human kindness: say what you like, the Komsomol is still the Komsomol!

Closing the store, they got down to serious drinking. They were sitting now in the wholesale hall, among racks of male and female vanity, surrounded by piles of sequined designer vests and displays of high boots that reminded one of the fourteenth-century peasant wars. There were things here that could be used to strangle a man if the need arose: belts of various lengths and sizes, some of them with jeweled buckles that could crush any Adam's apple.

They quickly polished off a good bottle of Jack Daniel's, with a champagne chaser for each of them. By now well in his cups, the superspy revealed his real surname, which was Zavkhozov. Continuing with his revelations, he told them that the calculations on Tikhomir Burevyatnikov in the Lubyanka had been done with an IBM computer the size of a department store. "You owe your life to that big bastard, Tikhomir. Without it, it would have been the supreme punishment in absentia for you. All of that cybernetic crap tells us, sorry to say, that our system won't last. So that means we've got to change directions. But that doesn't mean that everyone has to perish in the ruins, is the conclusion that a group of competent authorities came to. Human reason is still more powerful than a heap of clever iron, isn't it? In principle, the process will go on in the spirit in which Lavrenty Pavlovich Beria, that visionary Georgian mountaineer, conceived it even in his day."

"What a lot of smart people you've got in N," Burevyatnikov said with an unpleasant laugh. "Shmart as shwhistles."

Zavkhozov's glare bored into him through the bottom of his glass, and he gave a mocking snigger. "In this fucking America of yours, most people think they're just walking around free, when in fact everyone's under surveillance. For example, there's that slut in the liberation movement, Mirelle Salamanca. Big deal! Half of X has fucked her." Tikhomir ground his teeth à la Pugachov. I wonder why they didn't give you any training in mounting professional provocations. Can they really stand up for themselves, those animals, those corrupters of young people?

The lights of the shop with all its fabric were extinguished, Sunset Boulevard went dark. In its place, the sunset of personality began to unfold, the downfall of existence. Soft fabrics were mashed in its fiery teeth, and finger- and toenails were snapped off in quantities greater than the twenty given to every person. Suddenly, some little green dot appeared on the periphery, something tiny and much loved, like mommy-granny. Everything that hadn't been devoured rushed in that direction: Save yourselves, save yourselves! A string sounded in the little dot and—it survived! The store with its trappings and mirrors appeared again, and Tikhomir saw his own reflection in the long yawn of a mouth and all its facial muscles. Agamik smiled amicably. Zavkhozov, in a voice of modest triumph, said: "Now you see, Tikh, what they teach us in the N."

Another glass each of Johnnie Walker, or "Iochny Valker," as Zavkhozov called it, was poured. "Don't they teach you English there at all?" Burevyatnikov said, still playing the dissident. "What the fuck for?" Zavkhozov asked in surprise. Agamik ran down a sausage with a large knife—rat-tat-tat!—not bad training there either. "Put down some food, guys, or else you'll never make it to your cots!"

Chewing with the solidity of a Party man, Zavkhozov continued to develop the concept of the collapse of "everything dear to us. We can't permit the cadres to corrode, after all, but they're very tired just the same. Take just me, guys: I carry around large sums, but my day's pay is peanuts. Per diems are a joke. Is that really what our grandfathers, the iron men of the Cheka, dreamed of for their offspring? A group of competent specialists have worked up different scenarios for a revolution of the 'organs' against the atmosphere of stagnation. Toward that end we have to use certain repugnant individuals. What? You say they don't teach us Russian either? You little shit! Go to West Berlin, you'll see how many of our people are in jail for black-market currency operations. The day of the collapse of national monuments will come, but we'll be armed to the teeth to meet it, so that scum of the earth like Sasha Korbach can't exploit the great changes. That's whose necks you need to put the question right around: Whose side are you on, masters of culture? Let's drink to the second birth of our friend Burevyatnik! You're the one to settle up the bastard, Tikh!"

A strange metamorphosis now began to take place in Comrade Zavkhozov. He hung there like an empty suit. The sleeves and trouser legs were dangling. The tie flapped around, tried to cut off his oxygen. Tikhoryosha Burevyatnikov pulled up on it with an ape's paw, looking into what was left of the face and an extraordinary head. "You bastards in your stinking N, how can you dare go after one of the idols of our generation?" "Cut it out, Tikh, don't compromise the organization!" Agamik tried to pull Zavkhozov down by his dangling boots. Burevyatnikov then tossed the man away with a semaphoric gesture. "Well, boys, shall we take a walk?" the representative of Soviet power offered. "I've been here for three days now, and I haven't seen the city, figure that. Have you got our women's groups here?"

It was hard to say what the lieutenant colonel had in mind, but there was a female presence on Sunset Boulevard. Over its flat rooftops, a popular woman writer at least eighty yards long lay on her side. Half a hundred copies of her novels, spines facing forward, supported her magnificent body. The slogan of the billboard—"You couldn't put it down, could you?"—shone out its double meaning with playfully flashing lights. Next to it, another popular item was on offer. From two bottles, one neck-up and one neck-down, emerged the word *Stolichnaya,* with the stress for some reason on the second to last syllable. Cowboys were converting their cigarettes into tarred butts in a nicotine idyll somewhere in Marlboro country. A tiger was leaping out of a stream of Exxon gasoline, *voilà!*

Taking a little leap on the empty asphalt, he rushed at the strolling threesome, a pitiless beast. "He's larger than life, guys!" Tikh roared. He was the size of death! Jump to one side, you stupid fucks! Up against the wall! You'll get squashed like the dry skin of a Neanderthal!

Zavkhozov was spreading out in a puddle of his own. Why, there're dozens of them here, there're hundreds of them. A thousand striped ones, they won't leave a scrap! There's America for you, there's your freedom! Well, go ahead—roar! Long live the motherland! And he headed straight for the wave of tigers.

"Come on, guys, it's just a hallucination!" Agamemnon Grivadis exhorted his friends. "It's not dangerous—completely harmless! Follow me, guys! Do like I do!" Tearing up a manhole cover, he disappeared beneath the ground just before the arrival of the harmless hallucination.

So they scattered in their various directions, the heroes of our nostalgic introductory chapter. Tikhomir, after hanging for a bit on the wall of ABC studios over the evenly moving traffic, jumped down and combed his hair sharply back and slightly to one side. He picked up the attaché case with the half million and, with a healthy grunt, headed off into the distance—a newly made capitalist.

2

BEETHOVEN STREET

*W*hile this historic (where the revelations of Lieutenant Colonel Zavkhozov were concerned) event was taking place, an event that had concluded with tigers hunting a man frightened by drink, at the other end of Arkhangelsk by the Pacific our main protagonist was wandering, as usual, along the ocean's edge, pretending to himself that he wasn't going to the First Bottom at all.

The day before yesterday yet another stunning incident had occurred in his life. Toward evening, while in search of a set of tires at the cheapest possible price, he wandered into the intersection of Pico and Bandi. There, over the concrete semicircles of the freeway, a large number of Mexican shops clustered together, with cardboard and plywood boxes that had not yet been carted away lying in heaps. The side streets in the neighborhood were all numbered, but one of them for some reason was called Beethoven Street. Turning into it, he saw a small theater, which was even called Theater on Beethoven Street. "Theater," he almost said to himself with a little smirk, and was already starting to turn his back, yet he didn't turn away, and didn't smirk. He stood spellbound and looked at the entrance of this *divadlo,* as the Czechs call it. A long row of lanky palm trees with punk hairdos marked the skyline. It was still broad daylight, but the lights over the entrance were already on. A bare, ocher-colored wall hardly reminded him of a theatrical building. It didn't look like anything other than a warehouse or a dry cleaner's.

It seemed to him that the whole street was staring at him now, watching him struggle with the pull of the theater. In fact, no one was paying any attention to him. In the open doorway stood two young actors—he and she, Romeo and Juliet, Daphnis and Chloe, Hamlet and Ophelia, Treplev and Nina—who were obviously the ticket takers. Suddenly they looked right at Korbach. In bewilderment, he bought "uno cola" and "uno hot dog" from a nearby Sancho Panza, as though he'd only stopped for dinner. The actors went on staring at him. "Hey, Bradley!" they shouted and waved their arms. Against the black backdrop of the opening, it was a nice effect: he, tall, in a white shirt and trousers, and she, slender, in baggy blue overalls. Perhaps it was the opening note, or perhaps the final one. "Hi, guys!" a voice rumbled behind Korbach, and a bicycle rustled past him with a gust— Bradley's broad back with the words HARD ROCK CAFE and a ponytail. Approaching his friends, he hit the brakes like a little boy. Laughter, high fives in the basketball manner. The little fat lady in a shapeless T-shirt that one invariably finds in such theaters came out the door. She was carrying a rack of wigs and beards. Three cars pulled up, one right after the other: a VW Bug, an old Continental convertible, and a van. A fairly large number of people got out of them, and immediately a theater crowd formed. A sort of emotional mucus joined itself to the half-chewed hot dog in Korbach's mouth. That's how our mob used to get together in Moscow's Presnya Theater, what should I do? Fall at the feet of Stepanida Vlastevnaya and sob: let me die in the theater!

"Another napkin," he said to Sancho Panza. The latter had no idea what he was talking about. "Servetta," Sasha explained. "I need to blow my nose." The Chicano beamed. If only everyone here would talk that way . . . He handed an entire paper bouquet to the likable gringo. Korbach forcefully blew his excess mucus into the soft cloth, after which he decided not to go crawling on his knees to Stepanida but simply to go into the theater as an ordinary spectator. Maybe they put on here the kind of junk that will knock the nostalgia out of my system.

He crossed the street and joined the crowd. They looked like Moscow's down-and-out beau monde, with one exception, to be sure: there ripped jeans are drama, here they're chic. "How much are your tickets, folks?" he asked the fat lady, who turned out to be the cashier as well. "Fifteen," she said, and immediately added: "Ten for students." He took off his cap and rubbed his bald head for her: "And how much for senior citizens?" The people around him laughed good-naturedly. Another emotive tie: these are my people—for the first time in America, I'm around my own sort of people! For "senior citizens" it was ten dollars, too. "What's playing today?" he asked the amiable cashier. She gave him more information than he had asked for: "For the moment, we only have one play—*The Man of the Future.* We're a young troupe, sir, we've only been around for a month. Oh, I'm sorry, I've got to put my makeup on!"

In the theater there were no more than fifty seats, like in the Buffoons' cellar in Presnya. There, however, a hundred people had jammed in every night, sitting even on the stage and not taking offense if some actor, overplaying, fell into the audience. Here, one-third of the seats were empty, but he could tell from the actors' faces as the troupe hurried by that they were all happily amazed at such an inspiring number.

At the back of the stage, a bass guitar began to rumble. An alto sax crowed. Someone played runs on a keyboard, after which that same actor–ticket taker in white jumped out onto the stage. He had added only a long gray beard to the outfit. He sat down on a chair as though he were mounting a horse, and began to croon:

Nickery, flickery,
Little stewball!
Coackery, catchery,
Tortury, mortury,
Matchery catchery,
witchery watchery—
Evens in heavens
As evening descends,
Nickery, flickery,
Little stewball!
That storm is a séance
That I can see,
Signs of a science
The eye can see.
Hello, freedom,
Good-bye, force!
Giddyap, giddyap,
*My good horse!**

There was something that sounded familiar to Korbach in this strange aria. The actor from time to time did an acrobatic trick on his imaginary horse. Then, pushing himself away from it sharply, he did a somersault and ended up in a split, and then, pulling down his beard, he said to the audience in a tragic whisper: "I'm sick of history. It's a dirty business, isn't it? Sometimes it seems to me that we keep a record of the wrong events and the wrong people, while the right people pass by unnoticed. Like me, for example." Then he wound his beard around his head and left it on the crown, like a wild punk hairdo.

I wonder if he's improvising or if it's rehearsed. Then again, he could wind the beard over to one side and turn himself into an outright monster. Such were Korbach's thoughts, and meanwhile, the show was becoming more and more familiar. Four girls appeared onstage: one in a hoop skirt, another one in the nude, a third in a camouflage jacket and no pants but with a hammer and sickle on her left thigh, and a fourth, the ticket taker, in the same blue overalls as before. From the flitting, half-meaningless dialogue he made out that before him were the Bluebeard Sisters, whom the guy with the beard on top of his head was in love with. Standing on one leg like a crane, he half-crowed, half-sang:

Willow tresses,
Oh, my amorous flu!
Sisters in their elegant dresses,
The eyes are blindingly blue!
Push it or press it,
Ya vas lyublue!

* From Velemir Khlebnikov, *King of Time* (trans. Paul Schmidt), Harvard University Press, 1990.

And he began to whirl around so quickly that it was as though a skewer had been run through him from his head to his heels.

Just then, Korbach was struck by the realization: why, they're doing *Zangezi Rock,* for which the Buffoons had taken so many lumps. Why, this kid was yelling *"Ya vas lyublue"* at the top of his lungs with a Boulevard Pico accent! And the Bluebeard Sisters—they're the Sinyakova Sisters, whom Zangezi-Khlebnikov was in love with! Why, even the staging looks a bit like it, and there are similarities in the costumes! With only the smallest of apologies, he snatched a program from the hands of the man sitting next to him, who was watching the merry goings-on with the sadness that comes with complete incomprehension.

"Zangezi, who are you, who are you?" the girls asked as they circled. "Are you very old, little one? Are you very young, hook-nosed warlock?" Alexander looked at the program and broke out in a sweat. *Man of the Future*—why, that's a direct translation of *budetlyanin.* Remember, we joked that you could translate it into English as "will-be-atnik." There was a group of young actors from California there at the time. Frank Shannon had brought them especially so that they could meet the Buffoons. "Adapted and staged by Jeff De Naagel." The bottom quarter or so of the program appeared to contain a postscript in small print.

Stepping over people, he crept up closer to the stage, where the illumination was better. The light, however, was constantly changing: a tropical sun, an arctic night, a whirling cylinder of multicolored lamps. They have a tighter rhythm than the Buffoons. Maybe that's because they drink less vodka. There were no more than ten actors in the cast, yet, by adroitly changing masks and costumes, they created the impression of a noisy crowd. Here and there, revelations of the "supersaga" broke through the dizzying chatter, but not often. The three sisters took off more and more of their clothes, as though striving to attain the perfection of the fourth. Finding a perch on the edge of the stage, he read the postscript.

> A few words need to be said about the history of this play. This adaptation is a paraphrase of sorts of a stunning show that was first mounted in Moscow by the Buffoons theater studio. That version was based on the supersaga *Zangezi,* which tells the story of a reclusive prophetic genius, who, as many literary experts believe, was the alter ego of the author, the legendary Futurist poet Belomor Khulepnikov, who died of a drug overdose while at the Caspian Sea. The play was written and staged by the director and leading actor of the Buffoons, Alexander Korbach. (Laugh if you want, but there are no Korbach stores in Russia.)
>
> As a result of this show, the Buffoons and Mr. Korbach himself came under withering attack from the Kremlin leadership. The troupe was broken up, and its leader forced to emigrate from the Soviet Union. Since his departure, no one has been able to determine his whereabouts. One cannot rule out a worst-case scenario, but his friends remain hopeful that he is alive and simply trying to hide from the long arm of the KGB.
>
> In presenting the American version of this outstanding show, which contains equal measures of tragedy and comedy, we would above all like to ex-

press our solidarity with our persecuted colleagues behind the Iron Curtain, and we sincerely hope that the spectators will like *Man of the Future* in the Theater on Beethoven Street—this manifestation of free expression, unrestrained fantasy, and all other forms of hoop-lah-lah-brou-ha-ha. Thank you.

Jeff De Naagel,
Artistic Director

After that, Alexander saw everything as patches of light in a muddled dream. By the end of the show, everyone's attention was concentrated on the trunk that the Beethoven troupe called the Zangezi Magic Box. Out of it jumped the prophet himself, this time wrapped in a leopard-skin tunic. Around him danced the sisters, by now entirely naked, accompanied by cymbal players in skintight costumes. They demanded answers to the accursed questions of life, and Zangezi, instead of answering, tossed doves and bouquets of flowers at them. "What is this shit?" some in the audience whispered to each other. But there was no shortage of applause.

When it was all over, Jeff De Naagel himself came out onto the stage. Alexander remembered him right away. This fanatic of the theater had once spent an entire winter season in Moscow, trudging around with moccasins on his bare feet. He disappeared backstage with the Buffoons, boozed with the lads from Sunstroke, fell in love with Natalie, and went completely stiff with reverence at the sight of Korbach. Heaving himself up darkened ladders, he dealt easily with the imposing dimensions of his stomach and buttocks. He's going to recognize me any minute now, Alexander thought in a panic, and quickly took off for the back row, putting on his cap and dark glasses. No one paid the slightest attention to him. Jeff thanked the audience for their attention to the young troupe, modestly boasted of the critical attention they had received, in proof of which he held up a small clipping from the *Los Angeles Times,* and asked those who wished to make a contribution, even a very small one—it would help to keep the theater afloat without having to resort to piracy. On that note, the evening ended.

For the next three days, not to mention at this moment in the novel, on his usual route along the ocean's edge, Alexander turned the evening over in his mind. To stumble on a hotbed of his own work beneath a freeway off-ramp, seemingly in the concrete bowels of the leviathan! To be so strangely afraid of being recognized in public! He shrugged his shoulders, like a faded spinster frightened by sexual overtures.

After Stanley's departure, he had again found himself completely alone. And had sighed with relief. He didn't seem to need anything anymore except this solitude of his. This thought was not a terribly uplifting one, either. I'm afraid of being recognized; it's like I really am hiding out from the KGB. I refused the help of that fruitcake fat cat, my "fourth cousin," now I slipped out of a theater in horror! A true artist surmounts these little bruises to taste and style—that is, to his vanity—so that he can get on with his own work. I'm not "true." I'm no good for anything anymore; time to forget about "The Radiance of Beatrice." Nothing left but some final convulsions, a few rhymes in my sleep. Of that bald, toothy windup monkey who could bring any audience to "raptures of creative ecstasy" there remains only a barhopping scarecrow.

So, let it be that way. Let these flashes of ambition stay in the past, and let them evaporate from the past as well. There is no pure art, only a shameful peacock's tail. Gogol was right to burn his manuscript—he realized that literature was just the strutting of a peacock, monkeyshine, the embodiment of original sin, and that talent is a trap. He shook all over and tried to get away from his vegetative state—not even the auto-da-fé helped him; he had been fleeing from himself all his life, but couldn't run away anywhere except death. And you, you monkey, you're still so smart, you're playing the wily fool, and your legs still carry you into a theater to see some pathetic show. It's a shame that you haven't got beside you Gogol's Father Matvey, the apostle of renunciation—I'd fall at his feet, cut myself off from everyone I loved, from Khlebnikov and Meyerhold, from Vysotsky, and even from Dante, and most important—I'd cut myself off from myself.

Remember Tolstoy now, with his disavowal of everything. To write morally instructive parables with his verbal sex, to turn himself into Father Matvey! Bow now before him, stop writing down dreams, kneel, knock your forehead against the floor, that's what this head bald as a cue ball was given to you for.

He was cunning right up to the end, though, the old count. At night he made his way like a cat—like Leo the lion, that is—from messianic preaching to Hadji-Murat, described how the latter shaved his head until it was blue, scribbled down his verbal theater, which refused to die.

Come on, admit that you can't get along without playing parts, without adultery! Sideshow entertainer, I can't do without you! Go to Jeff: fat boy, take me in! Don't tell anyone how famous I am, just let me drive nails for you. I'll stay up nights, driving out the roaches and the rats. An alcoholic isn't a sinner or a blasphemer, let me finish scraping out my tune here—me, an old Jew who's forgotten the Old Testament, that is, who never knew it, who never bowed down to any temple except the den of theater.

3

THE PROUD VARANGIAN

*E*xhausted, he found himself abeam the bar, turned from the densely packed, wet terrain onto loose sand, and shoved his feet into his moccasins when he reached the pavement. The First Bottom was flashing its anchor-shaped sign hospitably. Broad-shouldered shadows were rocking in the windows. One of them froze for a second, one with a protruding beard who looked like Kastorzius.

From the threshold you immediately plunge into an alcohol-filled aquarium. You're drunk even before you take your first swallow. Henry Miller, as usual, is pleading with his "Baby": "Come to me, my precious one, my vicious one!" What's she like, this she-tyrant of his? Must be a little chatterbox who loves to make a scene, with pointy tits and a protruding ass. The whole gang seems to be here today: Bernadetta is sitting on her stool with three new combs like boats in a waterfall of hair. She probably borrowed that mane from the hindquarters of Bucephalus. A tattoo on her bare shoulder: a little heart bearded with letters spelling MATT SHUROFF. The lucky possessor of such touching love stands next to her, his shovel of a hand resting on the steep incline of her hip. On the other side sits General Piu, one leg wrapped around the stool, the other dangling like a child's. One hand is constantly going for a stroll on the prima donna's knee. Mel O'Massey, minus his jacket yet with an impeccably tied tie, is showing his independence by watching the TV. The Rams are making war with the Redskins.

Now, of course, though, everyone will turn to him: "Hey, Lavsky, how ya doin' today?" No one turned. He sat on a free stool and said to the bartender: "Double Stoly, Rick, okay?" Rick looked up strangely and then whispered: "Sorry, Lavsky, but we're not serving Stoly anymore."

"Why's that, then?"

"A boycott of everything Soviet."

"What sort of bullshit is that?"

Now everyone turned and began to look at Lavsky. Matt's chest, as mighty as a bridge bastion, was decked out that evening in a green T-shirt with a drawing of a Sea Stallion helicopter. His eyes narrowed as though behind the sight of a machine gun. "You can't figure it out, Lavsky?"

Bernadetta laughed with sinister enjoyment. "The boy can't figure it out!" Piu made a clicking noise with his tongue like a jungle bird, then gave a masterful imitation of the whistle of rockets followed by an explosion. "Shooting, shooting!"

Mel shoved a swollen and already beer-sodden newspaper at Alexander. "Damned sorry, Lavsky, but your fighter shot down a Korean Air passenger liner."

"My fighter? What are you talking about, guys?" Alexander was holding the heavy newspaper in his hands, but for some reason it hadn't occurred to him to look at the headlines.

"Fuck you sideways, man!" Matt intoned threateningly. "Your fucking Russian jet killed a whole bunch of innocent people—understand, you fuck? Fuck Stalin and Lenin, and fuck you and anybody who looks like you, fucking Lavsky!"

Alexander pressed his fingers to his temples. "Rick, give me what you've got! I can't understand anything without a double shot!" "Hey, Piu, give him a double shot, why don't you!" The American working man laughed. "Show this Commie your famous 'palm strike'!"

"Easy does it, guys!" the bartender said in a half whisper and with half-closed eyes as he gave the Russian a double Finlandia.

Alexander hastily tipped the shot down. There's no difference between all these vodkas, they're all just the same strong rubbish that stirs up in the user any sort of filth like insulted dignity. Now he could read—not the newspaper headline but the ribbon of letters on the chest of the truck driver, immediately beneath the picture and over the turtlelike armor of his abdominal muscles: KILL A COMMIE FOR YOUR MOMMY. Piu meanwhile was knifing the air with his hands resembling little shovel blades. "Give it to him in the liver, brother gook!" Matt yelled, and then one of the blades, fingers forward, caught Korbach beneath the ribs. It's so painful, he thought, slowly slipping off the stool, opening and closing his mouth, as though he were trying to bite off a piece of air that he couldn't quite reach. It's not just humiliating, it hurts. Oh to hell with the "humiliating" part, if only it didn't hurt so much.

"Well, Lavsky, you're just a comedian!" Bernadetta Bucephalusova howled with laughter. Putting on a scowl for show, she took the Vietnamese "Green Beret" by the collar. "Where'd you hit him? Not in the nuts, I hope? When I'm here, guys, don't hit each other in the nuts!"

From the depths of the establishment, a bug-eyed Kastorzius popped up. "*Ambulanza!* Call an ambulance, boys! He's dying, our good Russian!" He had a bowl of thick chowder in his hands. Obviously someone was treating the popular panhandler. Drops of grease were falling on Korbach's upturned face.

"The best Russian's a dead Russian, am I right?" Matt Shuroff said to Mel O'Massey. "No, you're not right, friend," replied the young man in the computer business. "There are all kinds of Russians. This isn't Lavsky's fault." He left his stool and squatted beside Alexander. "You all right, Lavsky?" "That fucking Vietnamese busted a gut in me," Alexander said through a grin and tried to sit up a bit. "You get fed up with being a shield between the Mongols and Europe, and now America is still left standing out there like a cow." He got to his feet and began to turn toward the bar. A tiny, impassive face followed his every move. "Piu, you dung beetle, you should have planted one like that on Ho Chi Minh! You're all flashing the weapons after the fight's over, you abortions of history!" No one, of course, understood these mutterings in Russian, but everyone was watching to see what would happen next. Alexander giggled. Should I break the cinchona's arm? Jump all over it and break all the bones in it? No, Mr. Asian, we're going to go a different way. We'll strike a blow at the heart of the anti-Russian coalition.

"Rick, put a big draft beer on my tab!" Thanks a lot, you prostitute of alcohol, you've become the accomplice to a crime without knowing it.

With a single motion, he threw the whole beer in Matt's face and with his next move ripped the chair out from under the beauty queen's bottom. As a result the former Marine didn't see his sweetheart's disgraceful tumble. "I'm finished!" she wailed. "Good-bye, youth! My donut's broken! My god, I'm pissing like a horse!"

The stunned giant turned to the left and to the right, offering any comers a fist the size of a coconut. The principal comer, however, was no longer interested in him. Now he was hanging on the twitching Vietnamese. The shameful configuration of the battle would not allow him to get his quick little legs in motion. "Our proud cruiser Varangian will not surrender to the enemy!" he yelled drunkenly, the patriot awakened in him. By this time the football match had been interrupted and a special report on the tragedy over Sakhalin Island was on. The coconut accidentally plowed into the indelibly foreign face of Bruno Kastorzius, even though he himself was a victim of Russian imperialism, his flight from burning Budapest twenty-seven years earlier having put an end to his brilliant legal career.

Alexander released the Vietnamese from his grip and began to sob uncontrollably. Piu darted out of the hold, did a pirouette, and dispatched the sharp toe of one of his tiny cowboy boots toward the enemy's jaw. While this toe was in flight in the direction of his jaw, Alexander had time to think one more despised Russian thought: There it is, another crime of my motherland! I don't have the strength to be a Russian anymore—let them kill me! The blow broke off his train of thought. Everything went dim around him, though for some reason there rose up and froze in the darkness the frontispiece of an antique Italian book, with a U like a V written with a fine brush and in which were drawn, with still finer brushes dipped in gold or indigo, in azure and vermilion, cupids in the broad margins in threads of blooming branches, and where somewhere in the depths of a small architectural quadrangle was the dark blue sky of Tuscany, for the sake alone of which, for the sake of a possible reunion with which, coming back to consciousness was worth it, O Theophilus.

The whole tavern was already fighting, while the "hero of the occasion" was out cold. As always happens, the original cause of the punch-up had been forgotten, but passions were boiling over, chairs were being snatched up and sent flying through the air along with torn sleeves. An unhealthy atmosphere of hysterical anarchy prevailed, and beyond this atmosphere Russia, who had just made a sweep with her death-dealing wing over the Romeo international air travel route, stood like a dark wall. Saving the furniture, rushing around among snorting men and shrieking women, were Rick the bartender and his two helpers, Kit and Kif. The police were a long time in appearing, because fights for no reason were breaking out all up and down the waterfront that evening. Meanwhile, Henry the pianist, abandoning his usual repertoire, was giving a virtuoso rendition of one of the Brandenburg Concertos in his own interpretation—that is, dedicated to "baby."

So Alexander Zakharovich Korbach, heartened by the music, summoned up all his memories of his acrobat's past, rolled out the doors, and sprawled on the pavement. There were three of them—Jewish girls from the Hotel Cadillac, bluish wigs, pink, bell-shaped skirts, yellowish tights, 225 years between them, not counting the little monkey perched on one of the six shoulders. "You've got a package, Mr. Korbach," they said respectfully. "Express. It must be from one of your rich relatives."

He got to his feet. "Thank you, girls!" What the hell do they want from me? I don't want any packages, any relatives, any theaters, and least of all any Russia, with its Andropovs and its "andropoids," because of which they kick your guts in and break your jaw.

The stiff fingers, on which the soles of more than one shoe had trodden that evening, open the package. Its contents turn out to be rather curious: an invitation, ladies and gentlemen, printed in a quasi-Gothic font on excellent Vergé paper to the "Korbachs' All-American Reunion" that is taking place on the eighteenth of November at Halifax Farm in Maryland; a voucher for a reserved room at By the Creeks, the nearest hotel; a map of Camelyork (Yornoverblyudo) County, with the approach roads to the estate; a plane ticket from L.A. to B.W.I.; a check for a thousand dollars, and, finally, a note from Stanley: "Do come, Alex! It'll be fun!" scrawled in the best tradition of American millionaires—that is, nearly unreadable, yet legible just the same.

The plot thickens, thought our hero, along with, naturally, the readers. It keeps whacking him over the head, in the liver, walks over his ribs, and shoves in his maw a treat sweet enough to make his head spin: don't be afraid of diabetes, suck on it!

4

IN THE LAND OF THE HOUYHNHNMS

Six weeks after the "wet job" carried out by the upper echelons of the generalship of the USSR, and the subsequent brawl in the seaside tavern First Bottom, the scene now shifts to the arrival gates at the Baltimore/Washington International Airport. An elegantly dressed gentleman emerges from these gates in a crowd of ordinary—that is to say, not elegantly dressed—passengers. A soft tweed newsboy's cap at a rakish angle lends him a look of unobtrusive daring. His raincoat reveals a Burberry lining as he walks. The gentleman's scarf displays its kinship to the lining of the raincoat, and the jacket peeping from beneath the unbuttoned raincoat and the trousers swaying as he walks are clearly begging to be included in the same clan as the cap, while the heavy burgundy wing tip shoes moving so assuredly through the air speak for themselves—that is, they complete the dynamic range of his almost impeccable appearance.

The uninitiated might think, to look at this gentleman, that he's in the film industry, that we have before us some well-paid screenwriter, casually attired in his favorite, not quite new things, but our reader will have little difficulty in recalling the not excessively clever adventures of our last chapter, and will figure out with equally little difficulty that all of these items were acquired just before departure at the Once Is Not Enough shop with the collaboration of that very same Shirley Fedot at one-quarter of their original price. In a word, we see before us our hero, Alexander Zakharovich Korbach, a conclusion that is confirmed by a partly dissolved but still noticeable dark yellow hematoma in the right corner of his jaw; oh, my!

Following the instructions of Miss Rose Morrows, secretary of Halifax Farm, Alexander took a taxi, and then, after having been driven through Baltimore, considered one of the most authentically American of this country's cities, got out at the railway station. From the platform, he looked with pleasant surprise at the yellow crowns of the strapping mid-Atlantic oaks and poplars in the distance. In the time that he had been living in California, concepts like "autumn" and "leaves falling" had been swept right out of the lonely refugee's consciousness.

A bell rang, and a train with three carriages drawn by a locomotive with a massive, bulbous smokestack and well-polished copper fittings approached the platform. It was a memorial institute on wheels known by the letters TTT—the Tolley Trail Train—that had been hauling farmers and weekend vacationers out into the depths of the northern Maryland counties for a century.

There were no more than a dozen people in the carriage, all of them clearly knowing one another very well and Sasha Korbach not at all. The men were hatless, yet they seemed to take their hats off at the arrival of a stranger. The women were putting on fleeting airs as though imitating a curtsy. Have I landed in Jutland or something? A good-natured black conductor resembling the locomotive punched his ticket and asked him if he'd like a pillow for his head. "Sleeping through my stop is just what I'm afraid of most," Korbach joked. This sentence, of course, was formed in such a way that no one around him could understand a bit of it, but everyone smiled welcomingly. "A-a-a-ll abo-o-o-ard!" the conductor sang out, and everyone smiled again.

His place by the open window and the quiet speed of the train gave him the chance to survey the landscape. Indian summer was in full cry. The air smelled of smoke and frost. It seemed to Korbach that he was returning into the past, even if it was in a roundabout way, even if it was through literature about the old days of America and, therefore, home. Blocks of town houses gave way to detached houses, after which the TTT entered a corridor of vegetables, greenish yellow mixed with the crimson of beets, through which the Tolley Trail, named in honor of a dynasty of American admirals, ran. Here and there in gaps in the foliage rose the heights of the deep blue of an ocean of air, in which vapor trails from nearly invisible dots of jet fighters stretched out like strands of spiders' spit. Then the train again dived into a body-shaking darkness, and with it into a time when the skies of the motherland did not need such a strong defense. Sometimes the trees thinned out into nothingness, and gently sloping hills and shallow valleys swam into view, along with fields freshly plowed for winter or recently sown, among which stood white clapboard houses, red barns, and phallic silos. Every ten or fifteen minutes Mr. Cook, the conductor, would come through the carriage. "Glover Place, please! Ladies and gentlemen—Amy and Christopher. Mrs. Auchincloss, don't forget your personal items, thank you! Next stop—Carters!" The passengers left the carriage, executing some form of a bow and thanking Mr. Cook. Sometimes new passengers got on, inhabitants of the stops, extremely well preserved old men and flourishing children dressed for the season in inexpensive, rugged things from the L.L. Bean catalog. Korbach was touched: kind, commonsensical people, do you happen to need a Russian scarecrow for your vegetable garden? Just then, he arrived at his station, Chatlaine, and noticed as he moved toward the exit that everyone in the carriage, Mr. Cook included, was watching the "scarecrow" with undisguised curiosity, filled, naturally, with the best sentiments.

Heaps of dry leaves asked to be rustled about, as they should be, with his secondhand English shoes. The request was granted with pleasure. A large black-and-white cat with a collar sat on a railing in the tiny station. It was watching with keen interest the end of the platform, where a flock of birds numbering about fifteen souls had gathered. Not far from the station was an orange sign reading BY THE CREEKS.

Before he could even open the door, the sound of heavy heels pounding down the stairs facing it was heard. By her clothes and hairstyle, the woman, the personification of hospitality, could have run down the stairs in the same way to greet a guest a hundred years before. "Mr. Korbach, welcome! Your room is ready. Do you want anything to freshen up with?" Without his needing to ask, she took the guest's small suitcase from his hand and told him that a car would come for him in an hour and a quarter to take him to Halifax Farm, and that he could make good use of this time to regain his strength after such a long trip from overseas. "But I'm not from overseas, ma'am—just from California." The eyes of the lady of the house widened with surprise. She seemed to think that California was overseas. "Is it far from here to the estate?" he asked. It turned out to be only two miles. "Oh, well then, I can go on foot." "Oh no," cried Mrs. Creek, whose name in Russian means "shriek," thus providing a pun that just jumped out at us, but what can you do, since this hotel has belonged to the Creek family for a century and the present owner has a penchant for excited exclamations? "A fine automobile will come for you, sir! The Korbachs are famous around these parts for their fine automobiles, among other things!" Immediately sensing the excited, passionate tone of the conversation, Alexander assured the lady of the house that a walk was indispensable to him for regaining his strength. Capping off his eloquence with a gesture, he left the inn and set off on the indicated route.

Why, this is one of the unexpected pleasures of life, he thought—walking along and looking around as the narrow road winding before him disappeared over

the crest of a hill, only to appear before him again as he climbed. Traffic had almost ceased here. Large dogs behind fences greeted him with an expressive wagging of their tails. Here and there a hand was raised on a porch to wish a good
journey to such a surprising phenomenon as a lone pedestrian.

All at once he found himself in horse country. As far as the eye could see in
every direction, on manicured hills and beneath bouquets of magnificent trees,
moved, even raced, smooth and graceful creations of various colors, though most
were bay. Near a fence, eyeing the walker with a glance fraught with meaning, a
majestic stallion passed. "An enviable existence you have, my friend," Alexander
Zakharovich said to him, by way of striking up a conversation. "You've known
success, applauding crowds. The horns of marching bands were calling to you to
dance along in time with the beat of your four legs, each of which contained the
power of an antitank rocket plus a dolphinlike grace inaccessible to any rocket.
You felt triumph with every fiber of your being, old friend, in the tips of your ears
and in your elongated brain, and in your tail rushing along like the pennant of a
battleship. And then you retired from the arena, but not to any dumping ground,
batono, and not to a dirty barn in oblivion, but to the kingdom of love, to these
wide open hills, where you're respected, my noble czar of mares, for that remarkable staff that grows between your legs whenever it's needed, and where you don't
race into the distance anymore, but higher and higher! Accept my admiration,
mighty father!"

The stallion touched one of the beams of the fence with a hoof, as if he were
calculating whether or not it would be possible to put a stop to this blather. Two
mares, one bay and the other roan, came up, along with two foals. The wind was
blowing hard, tossing their tails and manes. The entire family of Houyhnhnms was
looking at Alexander Zakharovich with interest. The presence of ladies and children put even the sovereign in a peace-loving mood. Korbach was about to launch
into a new monologue, this one addressed to the entire family, when there appeared in his field of vision something that immediately struck him: by the grace
of God, a girl on a horse was descending from a nearby hill into his life at a slow
gallop.

The girl was galloping on a white horse with dark oaken dappling, her boots
in the stirrups pointing straight ahead like those of a Swedish cuirassier. Her chestnut hair was flying in the same direction as that of all of those present, with the exception of those who had none, and uncovering her sharply angled forehead, which
was a testimony to pure breeding, if it's possible to speak of such things in the late
twentieth century. Her eyes shone even through the haze of her protective goggles.
Her lips alternated between pursing into a ripe cherry and opening to reveal a natural crop of teeth like the white keys on a piano. Her extraordinarily lithe figure
merged with that of the horse. Good Lord, he thought—why, she reminds me of all
of them put together—Beatrice, Laura, and Fiametta! Dear God of mine, thought
Alexander, for some reason lapsing into the Odessa mode, why, I'm head over
heels in love! One stride after another, she's approaching. I've never been so in
love and never will be again. Why, that's her, finally—the one who was anticipated
by the adolescent in the days of the falling of the chandelier on his head. It's only

for her, you see, that I plunked on the guitar and played roles! Why, it was only in a dream about her that I managed on another occasion to tear myself away from the noisy horde and stare vacantly as the sunset illuminated all the windows of some twenty-story idol from one side. Or in the desolation of the Estonian beach Cloga Rand, among the waves crashing in, I turned toward a quiet inlet and saw there a gentle heron, only in a dream about her.

This was what flashed before his eyes in ten galloping motions of this play of knees and hooves. There remained an approximately equal number of strides when yet another thought occurred to him with piercing sadness: all of this is in the past, we didn't meet at the right time, she's twenty now, and I'm forty-four, a destitute monkey with a cracked noggin. If only she were even twenty-nine, O Theophilus!

Who's this, thought the girl on the horse, arriving on the fly—this not badly dressed guy fixing me with a simian smile? Pulling up alongside a fence, the racer danced in place, and an elk-skin-covered leg sailed over the saddle. Please let her not be taller than me, Alexander Zakharovich was praying at that moment. The prayer was heard: the young lady turned out to be shorter, albeit not by much. Take the heels off her and she'll be just right. Leading her young filly by the nose, she was right for the Houyhnhnm family. Olympus, you heard my cry—she looks twenty-nine! In a momentary flash of insolence, his eyes removed the stranger's clothes. And the shoes, kind ladies and gentlemen, the riding boots, too!

"What's going on?" she asked sharply but immediately, as if correcting herself in annoyance, adopted a more polite tone. "Can I help you, sir?"

"Oh yes, miss!" he replied, not with a happy feeling of cunning but, applying restraint, explained himself modestly. "I just stopped to ask the way to Halifax Farm."

"Of the horses?" she asked, smoothing her hair down.

"They look like intelligent creatures," he said.

She laughed. "Unfortunately, they can't associate with anyone on a level of cleverness lower than theirs. . . . Sorry, I didn't mean to offend you."

He laughed as well. "I hope the ones that ride them reach this level."

"You flatter me, kind sir!" she said with a guffaw and pointed with her riding crop to the crown of one of the hills, where a good-size American barn sat like a castle. "If you can wait for a few minutes, I'll take you to Halifax." She soared into the saddle, reached the barn in a fluid motion, unsaddled Gretchen, and went inside. Oh, she thought in the dusk, if only he doesn't go away in these few minutes. I can't just jump out looking like a madwoman and shout: Come here, take everything off me, melt into me, long-awaited fool! Measuring off three minutes on her luminous watch, she began to wait.

She seemed to him stern and a bit distracted when she emerged. She was sitting in a Jeep. He was climbing toward the barn. What's with his eyes? Is he blinded by my beauty? Taking off his hat, he wiped his enormous bald head with the sleeve of his raincoat. She gasped with delight: how about that!

"Are you Russian?" she asked on the way.

"How did you guess?" He was smoking and sitting sideways in the Jeep. I've got another Hemingway on my hands! He's probably already imagining all sorts of Byronic pleasures.

"I recognize the Russian accent."

"What, have you been there?"

"Three times . . . oops, four times!" She laughed, obviously in connection with the "fourth time."

A man could go out of his mind for her, he thought.

The gates to the property opened. The Jeep drove along a path lined with plane trees, went around a fountain, and drove alongside a pond. On one of the bright green slopes at least a hundred people were listening to the playing of a flautist and a clavichordist. "Who are those people?" he asked. She laughed. "Those are Korbachs. You're a Korbach, too, I suppose?"

"You guessed it. My name is Alex Korbach. Sasha in Russian—well, let's say Alexander Zakharovich." She repeated with unexpected ease the name Alexanderyakovlevich, so unimaginable to the American tongue. Just then he thought that she, too, might be one of the Korbachs and wondered with alarm whether this might be a budding case of incest. She looked at him with interest. There suddenly flashed in that look something that you never see in the eyes of a Russian woman, or even a French woman—something that is peculiar to the local "individuals of the feminine gender," some extra dash of activity. Here you hardly ever run into that Moscow whore's way of putting on airs that always did my head in. The woman is active, she takes matters into her own hands.

"And my name's Nora Mansour." "Well, thank God, I was getting worried," he muttered. She laughed, and in her laughter, in the wrinkles that gathered around her eyes, in the gleam of her pupils and the whites of her eyes, in the tossing back of her hair, all the "dashes of activity" were dissolved, and no "whore putting on airs" appeared, only a nymph splashing around, full of the joys of life and myth. As though she were saying: Come on, don't drag it out, confess your love, otherwise I'll confess mine!

Everything, however, continued within the bounds of propriety. They drove up to the castle and went into the large foyer, which, with its oaken sashes and lancet windows, was an almost pure example of the Tudor style and only distantly reminded one of a Bavarian beer hall. For some reason, there was no one there, though at the far end an apparition of a stooped old man of Semitic appearance went by. Nora walked up to a long table on which plastic cards bearing the names of the guests were arranged. "Here you are—'Alex Korbach, Moscow'!" She pinned the laminated tag to the lapel of his jacket, staying at the lapel a moment longer than was necessary for the pinning. Both of them felt the sensation of a kiss that had nearly happened. They moved apart but didn't leave each other, sitting down beside a medieval stained-glass window, through which was reflected a "carpet of beautiful bright and trembling italics," as Alexander Zakharovich did not fail to remember from Pasternak. She asked him for an item that had helped generations of lovers to overcome initial awkwardness—a cigarette.

"And what do you do, Alex?" she asked. Well, I can't tell her that I do valet parking in the concrete guts of a big city. Two little sables—anyway, her eyebrows—rose in surprise as a response to his silence. "Well, all right, I'll tell you about myself, my child." "What did you call me?" she asked in astonishment. "I called you 'my child.' I'll tell you the short version, my child, so that it will be harder for you to take it for lies. In that country that you managed to visit three or four times, I was the director of a small theater called Shuty, that is, 'Buffoons' in your language. We were incorrigible improvisers, my child, so the powers that be decided to teach us to play by the score as written. To make a long story short, I'll just say that they gave me a good kick in the ass, my child." "What do you keep calling me 'my child' for? You're not much older than I am, young man!" "That depends on how old you are." "Thirty-four, young man." "Only by ten years!" he cried out joyfully and added: "My child!" She smacked him on the wrist with her palm.

It was only now that they noticed that the hall was rapidly filling with Korbachs: obviously, the concert on the lawn had ended. Servants were bringing trays of cocktails around. In one corner of the hall a buffet with hot coffee had been set up. The serving staff was made up for the most part of young people, students to look at them, but they were taking their orders from an ancient man in a camisole, breeches, and gloves; this, of course, was Enoch Agasf from the chronicles of antiquity. "And what do you do, Nora?" "I'm an archaeologist—strange, don't you think?" A young voice called from the crowd: "Nora! Nora!" She left him—"I'll be right back, Alex!"—and this use of his first name stirred up his breathing as much as resurfacing after being underwater for a long time would have done. Twisting himself into a rather absurd posture, he followed her with his eyes as she glad-handed in the crowd, and, giving a studentlike shriek, rushed up to a young woman pouring coffee for the guests. The reply was another shriek and a hug. A shift in the movement of the crowd hid Nora and her girlfriend from his view, and by the time Alex had climbed out of the club chair, the girls were no longer in the hall. Thereafter, our aging youth, a bald Muscovite cultivating the *dolce stil nuovo* beneath a solid layer of obscenities, who only yesterday had imagined himself as a hermit in the American Purgatory, found himself in a loud, English-speaking crowd of his supposed relatives, or at least of people with the same last name as his.

5

THE THRONG OF RELATIVES

*T*here was laughter everywhere. Most of these people were meeting for the first time. They were walking around with glasses, eating tiny kidney bean–shaped sausages on toothpicks. It happened, of course, that some swallowed the tooth-picks along with the sausages—how else to explain the fact that the paramedics on duty for the occasion had to give more than one Korbach a healthy whack between the shoulder blades?

It would be difficult to say who invented the name tag that is pinned to the chest in order to make meeting people easier, but it's indisputable that the idea appeared in America. In conceited Europe, this custom was probably considered an insult to human dignity, until it was generally accepted even there. Now this democratic means of identification is successfully used even at writers' conferences. We re-member how once, at the Winter Bazaar of the International PEN Club, it was pos-sible, with rejoicing in the soul, to lower one's head slightly to read "Norman Mailer" or "Günter Grass" on a man, or raise it to the name tag "Kurt Vonnegut." Unfortunately, name tags are rarely used at Hollywood parties; sometimes it's a question of vanity, and sometimes, in the case of women, there's nothing to pin it on. It's a pity: after all, not everyone—far from it—is able to distinguish, say, Bar-bra Streisand from Raquel Welch at a glance in the hustle and bustle of modern life.

At this all-American congress of Korbachs, people casually exchanged glances at each other's badges and said warmly: "Nice to meet you!" then followed up with the two obligatory questions "Where are you from?" and "What do you do?" Nearly all the states of the east and west coasts were represented: from the heart-land, however, they were thin on the ground, so that Korbachs from, say, Kansas, were looked on as exotic fauna. Even more exotic were the few guests from abroad, particularly an American oil-drilling family from Kuwait who, after many years in that Arab kingdom, had come back to their home country for an extended leave. People treated these oil folk with some curiosity. Accompanying them to the memorable event were their Arab in-laws, namely their son's young wife, Aisha, and her parents, from enlightened, pro-Western royal circles. At home in Kuwait they considered the Korbachs with their cowboy hats the embodiment of every-thing American and were surprised beyond words, if not actually shocked, to spot a family of Hasidic Jews from New York in the throng of potential relatives.

The most exotic guest, however, turned out to be not the sheikhs but the ele-gant gentleman from Moscow, that is, our A.Z. By now, he was well-accustomed to the unvarying first question asked by Americans, especially Jews, about Russia: How did you get out? He usually answered: Nothing could have been easier, they threw me out! This time, everyone was still feeling the impact of the recent Soviet misdeed and asked A.Z. how the Sakhalin flier could have fired rockets at a pas-senger liner. I hope at least here they won't beat the shit out of me for Andropov, our hero thought. "Well, you know, ladies and gentlemen, what else was the guy to do? They make robots out of their soldiers." The curious were not satisfied by this explanation. Henry Korbach, a young dentist from Washington, got par-ticularly hot under the collar. "Listen, Alex, I'm sure that he did it with sadistic pleasure. Did you read the transcript of the radio intercepts? When he got the order to shoot to kill, he said something like 'walkie-talkie' and pushed the button." "*Yolki-palki* was the phrase," A.Z. corrected him. "Whatever, but that means 'fiddlesticks,' after all—that is, 'Oh, it's child's play, nothing could be easier,' or something along those lines." "Excuse me, Henry, something along those lines, but not exactly. *Yolki-palki* isn't 'fiddlesticks.' It's a euphemism for strong language. You can read a whole range of negative feelings into it, including horror at the cannibalistic order of his commander." Shaken by this unexpected interpretation, Henry Korbach retreated into deep thought.

Dentists, it must be said, are among the most serious analysts of political situations. It's possible that this has to do with the specific nature of their work. Perhaps for them, cavernous and rotting teeth take the form of destroyed cities. The drill approaches tender layers of flesh and demonstrates the defenselessness of what is animated before the inanimate, buzzing beginning of things. The use of prostheses, in contrast, shows the obstinacy of the human utopia. It was obvious that the argument about *yolki-palki* was not giving Henry Korbach any peace over the course of this joyful and even in some ways touching gathering. Running ahead, let's say, to the very end of it, when many of the Korbachs were already quite merry, he, perfectly sober, sought out Alex and told him that now he saw the enormous significance of a correct translation. "Your interpretation, my friend and cousin, throws a new light on the situation in the Soviet Army. When you start to have problems with your mouth, come to Washington, you'll save a good bit of money."

There were quite a few dentists in the crowd, but their number paled beside that of the lawyers, realtors, bankers, and brokers, the representatives of the great American class of middlemen, whom one segment of the population considered parasites and whom another saw as an indispensable engine on the road to the American dream.

There were even representatives of unusual professions here, in particular Mort Korbach, member of the American astronaut command, and Dorothy Berlinhauer (née Korbach), a professional fortune-teller from Atlantic City known by her professional name of Madame Fatali. The latter, with the springy step of a pioneer of the Jane Fonda aerobics movement, went up to our Alexander Zakharovich and, tossing back a soft-fibered strand of hair, whispered in his left ear, the one not yet overgrown with silver wires: "In three years, my boy, remarkable changes will begin in your country."

All of these people had gathered on the initiative of the most powerful Korbach in the world, Stanley Korbach, and thanks to the efforts of his three genealogical specialists—namely, Sol Leibnitz, who had left his job at the Library of Congress to do this work; Dr. Lionel Fuchs, Ph.D. in archival sciences; and Lester Square, former agent of the British secret services, to whose pen half a dozen controversial novels had been ascribed. Even now, at this hour of apotheosis, the trio did not stop working. They would gently approach one person or another, exchange pleasantries, then take out their tape recorders and ask questions along the ascending and descending lines of the family and the collaterals as well.

Significant complications arose from the fact that in the course of their American lives many Korbachs had ceased to be Korbachs altogether. Some, streamlining their names just as they did their cars in the races so much loved by our people, had lost the ending and become Korbs; others, seemingly as a result of being hit in the rear bumper, had changed the ending to an American form, and had become Corbetts, as, for example, one customs officer. Also present were a few isolated Corbells, Corbys, Corbins, and even one lady named Dolores Corbellini, who took some convincing to admit that she was simply Laurie Korbach, without any Spanish or Italian embellishments.

Curiously enough, at least a third of those present had not even suspected that they had any Jewish ancestry. This revelation produced varying reactions: some were absolutely delighted, others laughed nervously, and still others bridled, seeing in all of it some incomprehensible provocation. All, however, were reconciled by their unexpected ties to Stanley Franklin Korbach, president of the AK & BB Corporation, for in all of them the American dream was as alive as it could possibly be.

The three sleuths finally came to our A.Z. The tiny Fuchs jumped up to the height of Alexander's lapel with a magnifying glass and let out a sound of delight that resembled his own last name. Leibnitz, a perfect specimen if one discounted a sagging right buttock, approached briskly. Like one of their own people, as if he weren't British at all, Les Square slapped him on the back. "Alex Korbach from Moscow! Just the man we were looking for, mate!" After several minutes of conversation, A.Z. realized that, since his meeting with Stanley, the specialists had managed to dig up quite a bit. His membership in the ranks of Soviet underground celebrities was no secret to them. They knew that he had been stripped of his citizenship, but that wasn't what interested them at the moment. "You know, Alex, we're stumbling a bit over your grandfather's younger sister Espheria. What did that woman do, whom did she marry, were there any children?"

He happened to remember something about Espheria Natanovna. Grandma Irina had spoken about her with pride on more than one occasion. Phera, as she was called in the family, had followed in the footsteps of her older brother and become an avant-garde artist. She was one of those Jewish girls about whom Yesenin, forever playing his peasant role, said that, without them, Russian poetry would be without readers. She studied at the Petersburg Institute of Applied Art and Sculpture and sat at first at the feet of Malevich, then Filonov, then the leading women artists of the time: Rozanova, Popova, Pestel, Mukhina, Tolstaya-Dymshchitz, Udaltsova, Stepanova. Just as her older brother had taken a shiksa for a wife, she married a goy, the literary critic Verkhovo-Loshadin. With the improbable triple-barreled name of Korbach-Verkhovo-Loshadina, Espheria took part in the celebrated O,10 Supremacist exposition. They had a son, Konstantin, that is, the cousin of Sasha's father, Zakhar, who became an electrical engineer. Professor Verkhovo-Loshadin was shot for aesthetic formalism—yes, gentlemen, for aesthetic formalism—but his son survived, and with Grandma Fira . . .

At that moment, the man telling the story had the impression that he had heard the sound of Nora's voice in the babble. He unceremoniously put off his interviewers. She was nowhere to be seen, however. The blasted Korbachs were mingling with great intensity, complicating his search. I wonder what my remarkable archaeologist is doing on this estate? Maybe she runs the department of prehistoric

Korbach bones. Suddenly he noticed her and realized that she had already appeared in his field of vision more than once but had passed unnoticed. She'd changed her outfit, that was the trouble. With a businesslike air, she was walking along the far periphery of the hall with a group of young people, carrying some sort of a vase, then an armful of flowers, then a chair. The equestrian woman of a few hours ago had disappeared. Parading around in her place was one of the shock troops of *la vie mondaine:* hair gathered beneath a tight-fitting knit beret, a flowing Art Deco dress that reminded one of the Russian film *Funny Kids* and the book *The Great Gatsby.*

A gong sounded, the elaborately carved doors opened, and all the Korbachs poured into the dining room. Toward them, from another set of doors, came the sovereigns of the place. First to appear was the patriarch, a ruddy-cheeked man of an advanced age, as they say—eighty-five-year-old Dave Korbach. He was leaning on a cane but more as a fashion statement than out of a need for support. He was joking, firing off rejoinders over his shoulder to the second banana of the procession, Progressive Congregational Rabbi Sam Dershkowitz (a Korbach on his mother's side), waving with a hint of flirtatiousness at the young ladies in the room, who seemed to be old friends of his. Stanley Franklin Korbach, the real master of ceremonies, occupying only the third place in the hierarchy, wore a tuxedo, with a red bow tie and cummerbund, a huge figure with a modestly combed head of hair that seemed to say: Don't pay any particular attention to me. On each side of him he held one of his sisters by the arm: Judy, the elder one, who already had something of the old woman about her, and Jane, the younger one, a magnificent, still youthful lady. The husbands of these ladies were escorted by the lady of the house, the utterly irresistible Marjorie Korbach, décolleté and all. Somewhere in the background, behind Marjorie's shoulder, loomed the face of the powerful new business partner, runty little Blamsdale.

The hosts and the guests applauded each other energetically, after which Rabbi Dershkowitz invited everyone to take seats at the tables. "The years of labor have fallen away, my friends, and now before us is a time for celebrating and socializing. Enjoy the food, wine, and good, heart-to-heart conversation." He knew what he was talking about. Everyone began to take seats at the tables, checking the place cards. Alexander found his table but not the desired face at it. What, has Nora forgotten about me already? He saw her now, diagonally opposite him at the far end of the hall, at one of the numerous tables in the company of some pleasant young people, and in immediate proximity to a well-coiffured lad with movie star looks, the sort who, with the ankle of one leg resting on the knee of the other, gives casual interviews to Diane Sawyer or Charlie Gibson. Oh no, Nora, it's not going to be as easy as that! Just let me finish my wine and I'll come right across the room to you! The pretty boy will be finished. Who said that a head of hair does more to make a man handsome than a nobly gleaming bald pate?

Taking a panoramic view of the hall from Alexander Zakharovich's table, we would seem to be narrowing the angle of view of our narration, but who is to prevent us from exercising the author's right to be arbitrary, to skip over the rest of the room and spy a bit on Nora; all the more since this is probably what the reader desires. What a fool I am, she thought angrily, now and again glancing at the spot beyond the clustered heads where the golden egg was gleaming. I should have moved his card to my table. Then at least he wouldn't have ended up next to that fire-breathing old bag from Oklahoma. Russians must adore fat women. Oh no, my darling Alex, today you're going to have to reexamine your tastes! Who else is that next to him? Why, that's none other than Art Duppertat with his newly pregnant Sylvia. Just let me get a couple of drinks down, and with the third I'll walk across the whole room as though I'm coming to them but will actually be to him! To him!

Let's get back to him. The model employee of a California parking garage was, in fact, at his first American formal dinner. He supposed that the toasts would begin any moment, at first solemn, and then more and more chaotic, and then he would make his way over to Nora in the confusion. He was not aware that these dinners were arranged according to a different principle: talk played not the role of an appetizer but rather that of a tablet to help digestion, and therefore was relegated to after dessert.

Rabbi Dershkowitz had a severe, religious appearance, yet in his sermons to his congregation, and, to tell the truth, in his personal life as well, he maintained a more liberal concept of Judaism. Gazing sternly at the people around him as they ate and drank, he addressed to them a mental *bracha* along the following lines: Eat, my children! Feast on your artichokes stuffed with fresh crab! The Talmudic codes won't be shaken by a little violation of the kosher laws! Why shouldn't you pamper your stomachs with a bit of excellent Gruyère after a veal chop? Be good to yourselves, my children! And I'll drink to you once, twice, and yet again, until my soul sings a hymn to the Lord with even greater strength! And as if heeding this outwardly ascetic spiritual leader's interior monologue, the entire gathering indulged itself enthusiastically, and the waiters, for the most part students from the local colleges, unrestrainedly poured wine into the rapidly emptied glasses.

"Hey, Alex, I see that you don't recognize me even when you look right at me!" a young man with a longish Italian nose inherited from his father's side, and full lips from a Jewish mother, shouted to him from across the table. "Take a better look—now, doesn't my face remind you of commedia dell'arte?" A.Z. peered at him, by now ready for any wonders on this Earth that had so recently seemed like a tile-floored desert to him but that was now saturated with an odor of freshness so strong that it sometimes made him feel ill. "I'm damned sorry, sir, but your face reminds me of several images at once, Harlequin and Pierrot—strange, isn't it?—but most of all, I hope you won't kill me for it, our unforgettable Pulcinella. . . ." The stranger, taking no offense, called out: "You're wrong, old chap! Wasn't it you who gave me the name of Doctor Duppertutto a year ago?" The thunderstruck Alexander even forgot about Nora for a while. The demonic skies of the New York night, with his own name among the lowering clouds, that dazzling den of a department store, the girls from the perfume department, the security guards, and finally this young fellow here who had poured him a glass of life-giving port, all swam upward from the depths of his memory. Why, he was the one who had mentioned him to Stanley! The news about the new Alexander Korbach had come from him. "There's a lot I need to say to you, Alex," Art said with a grin, "but first, fess up, what's happened to your English? Have you spent all this time in Oxford?" Alexander didn't have time to answer in his "Oxford English" before the speeches began.

The speech of Rabbi Dershkowitz was significantly drier than his fatherly, reformist thoughts, so full of love for his "children," had been. His basic theme was that this gathering of the American Korbachs was part of a worldwide movement toward the search for ancient Jewish roots. "For generations, our people were concerned with only one thing—how to survive in the ghettos and shtetls. Persecuted and despised, we lost the threads running through our history and often could not trace our ancestry any further back than our grandfathers. Those days are gone forever. Our traditions are no longer part of withered provincial dogma. The Jewish people are the bearers of a humanism and culture embedded in their religion.

"Today in this hall we see the realization of optimistic ideas. Let's thank all of those who came to this celebration, and also the master of ceremonies, my old friend Stanley Korbach!"

After rising to his full imposing height and quieting the amortizing movements of pairs of applauding hands, Stanley made a short speech to those gathered in which he went even further than Rabbi Dershkowitz in the vein of overcoming dried-up dogma. His idea, as he laid it out for the Korbachs, consisted not of a distinctly Jewish heritage but of an attempt to project the human molecule as a part of the universe. (At this point Marjorie Korbach barely managed to restrain a nervous yawn.) "Scientists are still not able to answer the question of whether or not genes die, of whether or not DNA disappears into oblivion. Our genealogical researches—my outstanding collaborators Leibnitz, Fuchs, and Lester Square and I are now into the Spanish period of our diaspora—could help them in the future to arrive at new discoveries, and more importantly to the broadening and deepening of memory as a phenomenon to resist the merciless march of time. Nevertheless, the Jewish people and their history are our cornerstone. Having lived for twenty centuries of our era among other people, not to mention the centuries of Egyptian and Babylonian captivity, the Jews have contributed more actively than others to the construction of the human molecule. The most remarkable thing, however, is the intersecting of ethnic lines—I ask you to forgive me for my none too orthodox point of view—in the creation of the pan-human cosmic element, capable perhaps of breaking down the wall of our universal isolation. The codes of the holy books of Judaism, Christianity, and Islam, the neighboring teachings of Hinduism and Buddhism, contain numerous lights calling us to them, and we should not only contemplate them but go toward them. For all of our weakness, we can still suppose that no one and nothing disappears without a trace. Let us have no fear of endless empty wastes and let us rejoice! Mazel tov!"

The speech of the head of the Korbach household confused a few, though the majority simply took it as empty rhetoric and answered Big Korb with applause, whistling, raised glasses, and their own shouted mazel tovs.

"Well, what'd you think?" Art asked Alexander with the slightly ironic tone that was characteristic of the boss's young friend. "Deep." Alexander nodded. "Not too deep?" "Intelligent and touching," Alexander reassured him. Art wanted to develop the conversation and ask Alexander if it didn't seem to him that Stanley might be dragging out this whole story, or in any case some of its characters, to the point of no return, but the ceremony was continuing now, and Sol Leibnitz was presenting the oldest Korbach to those assembled. It turned out to be not David but 104-year-old Zacharia from St. Petersburg, Florida. With uncommon ease, he rolled out onto the dais in a wheelchair holding a bunch of colorful balloons over his head as if it were these balloons, and not a perfect set of batteries, that set him in motion.

Then came the turn of the youngest Korbach. A plump young woman took a nine-day-old creature, baby Diana, out of a large bag that she was wearing over her front and that resembled a kangaroo's pouch. The next number on the program was entitled "The Highest-Rising Korbach," the astronaut Mortimer Korbach, Ph.D. Tanned, as though all they did in outer space was lie on the beach, the scientist cracked a pretty good joke, saying that the feeling of weightlessness didn't free him from his family ties. "Well, now, of course, they're going to call up the Korbach who fell lower than everyone else," Art Duppertat joked in the dissident manner. "That means me." A.Z. sighed.

"There is here among us one unusual Korbach," said Sol Leibnitz, as though the preceding one had been perfectly ordinary. "He arrived in America quite recently and naturally had no idea that he had so many relatives here. Our research team had a difficult time tracking this man down. In his home country, in Russia, he was a famous singer and actor, sort of a cross between Bob Dylan and Woody Allen." At these words, the hall burst into a roar of laughter. Sol went on: "In the United States, this man prefers to lead a more modest life. Let's give a hand to Alexander Korbach and ask him to give us a sample of his art."

Before the eyes of A.Z., who was stunned by the unexpectedness of it all, the heads of the crowd gradually turned into faces with little wings of applause fluttering beneath their chins. Among the faces, at the far end of the hall, there was Nora's, with two shining "mirrors of the soul." A thrilling tumult boiled up within Alexander Zakharovich. He had never been so on edge in his life. He stood up and showed his hands as if to say: I haven't got a guitar. "Duppertutto," never without a scheme, immediately handed him his. Had he deliberately stashed it away? Nora, having leapt to her feet, was waving both arms. A bit too much enthusiasm for someone your age, madam, if you're really thirty-four. Abruptly, he took the guitar and literally sprang onto the dais. He took off his jacket and tossed it on the piano. He caught sight of Stanley's face, with its frozen expression of childlike amazement. Well then, kind Korbachs and Nora Mansour, who has joined forces with them, now you're going to see an example of Moscow's garret and cellar arts scene. I'll pull out all the stops, with the same dash that I had at the first Buffoons' premiere when I was young!

He began by quietly running his fingers over the strings, then struck up the song with a "genuine Russian" howl:

Oh Russia, our great motherland
One-eyed, though many-visaged

Oh our long-sufferer, our silent one
You toil beside your shores.
Wolf calls have begun to weave along in your tracks and
Deceivers have begun to play tricks amid the rotting haystacks.

No one in the room understood a word, of course, except perhaps Lester Square, from MI-5, but everyone assumed a respectfully serious expression: here she is, Russia, the age-old bitter misfortune of mankind! Nodding his head as if under-scoring the thoughts of the enlightened audience, Alexander went on wailing:

Oh, and in the saddest grassy steppes of our motherland
Only shadows swim, flocks of mournful shadows
Here, a small ray of sun doesn't seem . . .

He fell silent and lowered his head, then struck the strings with his full hand and roared: "And suddenly, down come the Buffoons by parachute!" His face broke into a smile like that of the king of the apes. His guitar was working in a rock-'n'-roll rhythm. His legs began to shake violently. In a hoarse voice, partly frighten-ing and partly joyful, like Vysotsky's, Alexander now cried out:

Buffoons with parachutes
Are dropping from the sky!
Fireworks and rockets
Make the flames leap high!
The vigorous pounding of a tap dance,
a leap with a scat.
Somewhere a potbellied thunderstorm went for a walk
Head over heels! Over we go.

And he did a backward somersault. How many years is it now since you've made such abrupt movements, and now love itself is twisting you right around! Here's Russian merriment for you, even if it is the rock-'n'-roll kind, and in a squatting dance, too!

The stunned audience gazed at this universal *cabotin* incarnate: first he sings something that doesn't seem entirely proper, then he does some tumbling, then he hammers out some tap-dancing that's as good as the masters from the Cotton Club, and all of it done to the rhythm of a *trepak* in a swinging syncopation.

I know "right" and I know "left,"
Ich marschiert to the beat of the drum
I'm from Geneva
captain in the musketeers!
In the fields of Europe
the fever of cannons.

Stallions gallop.
Guten Tag, Mein Tsar!

Swept away by this stream of nonsense, completely caught up in what they used to call an outpouring, A.Z. did not forget to act, giving in flashes an extremely curious demonstration of the Stanislavsky method. Abandoning the guitar, he suddenly attacked the piano, letting go with another act of clownish fidgeting:

The wolf is in the little boat, the little boat, in the little boat he sails.
The fox in its new little boots is walking onshore!
The wolf keeps rowing, rowing, rowing toward the shore.
The fox keeps sweeping, sweeping, sweeping with its tail toward the little boat.
And they never meet, never kiss . . .

The sugary old Russian style, but we can see the arches of Verona and the galleries of Venice in it all the same.

The audience didn't understand any of it, yet broken down by the crushing pressure of the farce, the merry-go-round of *chari-vari,* they stamped their feet and made highly approving noises and shouted "Oh, yes!" Alexander raced up and down the keyboard like a hurricane, combining themes from "Rock Around the Clock" and *The Barber of Seville.* Finally, he glanced at Nora. Her eyes seemed to say: Very amusing, but that's enough. All right. He stood up, serious, put on his jacket, took up the guitar, and walked to the microphone. In a pleasant, pensive baritone, he finished his performance:

What is there left for you to do with the Buffoons?
Force them to drink vodka to the point of black melancholy?
Break their throats so that they don't sing like waxwings?
Decorate them with a medal, buy them off with a bullet?
No, dirty scoundrels,
Watchmen of poverty
You don't frighten them with executions!
The Buffoons joke with all their might!

Again the smooth soles of his shoes shifted into the staccato rhythm of a slow tap dance. With half-closed eyes, like a hungover Gypsy, he brought his bacchanalia to a close.

The beam of a television light that had been constantly dancing reflected off the polished head, now sunk in a deep bow. In the hall, a tropical storm of thunder and lightning broke. Now *there's* an artist! He hadn't expected such an eruption, hadn't thought that he would be able to repeat an "outpouring" that he hadn't done for twenty years. He raised his head to catch a glimpse of the one for whom he had been jesting, both now and back then, when she was fourteen. She was no longer in her seat. Meanwhile, the importunate Art Duppertat sprang onto the dais. "Hey,

Alex, that was something! You won over this whole audience! Listen, you could do a first-rate show with all this stuff of yours: singing, dancing, guitar, piano, acrobatics! Do you want me to be your agent, *starik*?" he crooned, showing off that he knew the Russian slang expression "old man," used when speaking to friends of long standing.

Alexander cautiously pushed the young financial genius away. Many years of artistic experience had taught him that after a successful performance it was practically impossible to get near any girl in the hall. That was what had happened in Kharkov, must have been back in '66, when he sang the whole evening just for one little Babette in the third row, and she was practically swooning with happiness, and then a crowd of student clods separated them forever. The same thing is happening in America now. Various Korbachs are coming up to him with congratulations and questions about Russia. I don't give a damn about Russia, America either! Where's my Nora Mansour, the enchanted horsewoman?

Suddenly, His Majesty Stanley came right up to him. "Alex, I knew you were an artist, but not such an artist! I have to admit I never dreamed that there were artists like you in Russia." He put a powerful arm around his shoulder and led him off. "Hey, people, beg your pardon, but I'm kidnapping this guy for a while!" Drawn away by the king, he nonetheless managed to spot Nora, who indicated with a few gestures that she would wait for him in the drawing room. He beamed, and, seeing his glow, she beamed in reply. Stanley led him along numerous staircases and passages, past highly significant artistic treasures, to his tower, where the trio of specialists—Leibnitz, Fuchs, and Lester Square—was already seated in casual poses around a table. "Congratulations, congratulations, great show!" the troika exclaimed. "Quite in the spirit of the old Buffoons," Square said in Russian. "I saw lots of your shows, you know, when I was serving in Moscow, at the British embassy."

Stanley put a hand on Alexander's shoulder, so tired that it trembled beneath the gargantuan palm. "I brought you here, Alex, in order to toot my own horn. Fuchs, be so kind as to show my cousin our latest discovery." The tiny Fuchs, who had a bushy mustache of the sort that grows under the noses of painstaking bibliophiles and masters of filigree, removed a large antique photograph mounted on stiff paper from a good-size album. Well, well, it's that very same picture of the Samara Korbachs from Grandma Irina's archive! The same embossed seals on the mat, even the company logo was legible: "Sizyakhov Elektrovelografia, Samara," and in the background, the luxurious drapes and the "Swiss" appearance—a European Jewish family positioned on chairs and on a sofa. "How did you manage to make such a copy?" Stanley burst into laughter, very pleased with himself. "Well, well," he said, almost in Russian. "*Nu i nu.* This isn't a copy. This is the original that you told me about in L.A. Now it's yours, my friend!"

It turned out that after the meeting of the descendants of the identical twins, the whole research team had taken off for Moscow. They were able to find out a lot. First the bad news, Alex. Your apartment was sealed off by the "organs" last year when you requested political asylum. Before that there was a search; they took away a lot of papers. It seems that they wanted to try you in absentia, like

Rudolf Nureyev in his day, but something went wrong and the trial didn't take place. Now the good news. The Buffoons, imagine, still exist and are even doing fairly well. The fact is that in the time you've been here, your actress Natalya Motalina has become the Kremlin's favorite singer, and even, they say, the mistress of one of the Kremlinites. They invite her to sing folk songs at the official concerts every time they have a jubilee of some sort. That's why the theater is still going. Your guys even managed to keep two of your shows in the repertoire, without your name credit on the posters, though. All of the Buffoons send their greetings, they're all cheery and daring. We even recorded something. From his briefcase, Lester Square produced a tiny Dictaphone of the sort that dissolves in the mouth if its owner is captured, and turned it on with the mons veneris of his left palm. The sound of the whole troupe speaking in a chorus was heard: "Our beloved Sasha Korbach! We haven't fallen into a hole! We're clowning as best as we can, and we're letting the liars have it." Alex, Alex, what's wrong? I didn't expect you to be so . . .

The agent of the British services, as reliable as the Rock of Gibraltar, was looking at the bald man, who had all at once burst out sobbing. A.Z. buried his face in his hands, his shoulders shaking convulsively. Fuchs just sat there, for some reason with an index finger to his lips. Leibnitz leafed through the pages of some historical folio in embarrassment. Stanley, not covering anything up, was wiping his brimming eyes. That Alex, he thought—what a guy, you old so-and-so. "I beg your pardon, gentlemen," A.Z. said very soon after that. "Everything connected with the theater puts me in some strange hysterical state. I lose all control. So, how then did you get that photograph, gentlemen?" "We just bought it," Leibnitz said. "From the KGB?" Alexander asked in amazement. "Why does that surprise you so much?" "Well, they are the 'knights of the revolution,' after all." "There's no one in Moscow with a greater weakness for dollars than those 'knights,' unless you count the boys from the Komsomol. That bunch is ready to sell Lenin's corpse."

Fuchs turned off the lights and switched on the slide projector. The Samara Korbachs were sharply outlined on a white section of wall between an original Dürer and a shelf of trophies won by the lord of the manor when he was on the Rowing Eight at Columbia. "So then, Alex, in the middle is, indeed, your great-grandfather Nathan. The resemblance to the great-grandfather of our boss is striking. It seems that the brothers grew big mustaches at the same time, which made them indistinguishable from each other. That man on his right with the ironic smile is the brother of his wife—your great-grandmother, that is—Benjamin Slonimsky, a well-known journalist on the Volga. On the left is Nathan's cousin Kasimir Korbach, either an important functionary or a co-owner of the Mutual Credit Bank—that remains to be seen. Right here, in the group of the older generation, we see the wives of the three men: Rebecca, Ksenia, and Matilda; hats with feathers in them. The second generation is distributed along the sides and among them—on the left, of course, is your grandfather Ruvim Natanovich, and his sister Espheria Korbach-Verkhovo-Loshadina, Petersburg artists of the new tendency, to which Espheria's scarf and Zakhar's jacket over her shoulders testified. The third generation was represented by children in new sailors' suits, your future grandmothers and grandfathers, and even two youngsters in white summer double-breasted jackets, Volya Korbach and Nolya Slonimsky. That year, those two graduated from a private high school and were getting ready to get past the percentage quota for Jews for admission to Kazan University and the Petersburg Conservatory. You were right when you told Stanley that both of them joined the Volunteer Regiment of the Constituent Assembly and emigrated. There's evidence that Nolya, that is, Arnold Slonimsky, settled in Paris, where he was a pianist in a few movie houses, and then, strange as it many seem, a local pioneer of American jazz. As for Volya, that is, Vladimir Leopoldovic Korbach, he, not getting as far as Paris, settled in Teheran, worked there in a British oil company, and married a local Jewish girl named Miriam Korbali."

While Fuchs was telling this story, his mustache and sideburns had gone quite fluffy and his eyes had begun to burn, like those of a cat on the prowl. "Well, that'll do for now," Stanley said to him. "You'll end up in captivity in Babylon looking like that!" Fuchs went quiet. Square laughed. "And why not?" Stanley went out onto the balcony, taking with him a bottle of port that had held out well—in other words, for at least thirty years. He turned in the doorway and beckoned Alexander to follow him. Together they emerged beneath a starry sky. "Alex, do you remember what the Lord said to Abraham? 'Look up at the heavens and count the stars—if indeed you can count them. So shall your offspring be.' Those stars, Alex, were not just a metaphor, were they? It was no accident that the Lord included stars and human generations in the same saying, was it? What do you think?"

Oh, *yolki-palki,* Alex said to himself and remembered the death-dealing pilot over Sakhalin Island. I can't talk about the stars of the universe right now when only my personal star is beckoning to me. "It's our fatherland, dear cousin," he intoned, and rather unceremoniously jabbed an index finger at the fatherland. "I hope that we'll have another chat about 'human molecules,' but right now I'm in a hurry, please."

That Alex, thought Stanley—there was a smell of whoring in his room, yet even here, he's having visions of some adventure. He nudged him with an elbow and asked: "How's Bernie, eh?" A.Z. remembered Bernadetta tumbling from her stool in the bar: her mane with its combs, a hank of mother-of-pearl, her clips weighing a pound apiece, her legs in their white stockings with the pink garters. "Great," he said. "She asked to be remembered to you, sir." "Really?" asked the delighted tycoon. "What a sweet girl! The sweetest creation I've ever had to deal with!" Just whom did he deal with before her? Alexander thought, and headed for the exit. Stanley watched him go. I'm not just watching him for no reason, he thought. I'm watching over him like an older brother. I see right through him. I wouldn't be surprised if Lenore grabbed him right by the knob. Go, go, descendant of one and the same egg! Just don't run into a dirty comet in this galactic mess!

6

THE SHY FILLY

*N*aturally, Alexander got lost in his amorous rush. He flew up and slid down Tudor staircases, drumming past almost at a run the enfilades of rooms with their portraits and fireplaces. Suddenly he found himself in the heavenly groves of an Art Deco orangerie, but, not finding his temptation there, his—he was sure of it—other half with her hot desire for him, and finding instead a large flock of parrots watching him intently, he rolled out into a telescopic, supermodern exhibition, where in the main hangar a gigantic orange robot, a creation of the geniuses of the Chicago School, raised one of its levers, perhaps its penis, perhaps a third leg. Then he jumped out into a Moorish-looking gallery, sprang down from it, and ran along in the darkness through a grassy expanse irrigated by a large number of sprinklers; he gave himself a good irrigation, too. Soaking wet, he tumbled into the reception hall, where the rendezvous had been arranged, but didn't find what he was looking for. Instead of her, Korbachs were roaming around, getting drinks at the bar, shooting pool, and talking in loud voices. Well, it goes without saying that he bumped into Art Duppertat again.

The latter was dancing there, doing the waltz with some young beauty or other; the "ideal couple" as they say. Catching sight of Alexander, Art abandoned his lady and hurried toward him as if he were an old friend. The computer generation thirsts for an immediate, even if unilateral, exchange of information. Hey, Alex, how'd you like Pantagruel our king, my fantastic father-in-law? Well yes, I'm his son-in-law, and this is his daughter, my lovely wife, Sylvia. Get acquainted, guys! Sylvia, this is the very guy who made me rich. Alex, do you realize that I owe you some hefty royalties? What do you mean, for what? For your idea of the dolls! Come to our room, I'll write you a check! What? Later? Sylvia, did you hear that? What, money doesn't interest you? It does, but not right now? My darling, something is going on in the world—people have appeared in it who are interested in money, but not right now. Not at the moment, understand? Watching the "Russian Korbach" running across the main entrance hall in the direction of the lit pond, Sylvia laid a bare elbow on the shoulder of her husband. "Can't you see that he's in love?"

A number of guests were sitting at tables by the pond. Many of them invited Alexander to join them, but he didn't even favor them with a reply. Wild agitation, if not panic, had him in its grip. Nora lost forever! Like the biggest schmuck out of all of these schmuckish Korbachs, he'd lost the woman of his life. Having resolved finally to say her name aloud, he turned to the old servant, who even at this late hour was still serving drinks. Trying to make his chin stop shaking, he stood up to the appraising Jewish glance and received a polite response. Of course he knows Mrs. Mansour. Yes, he saw her just a little while ago. Not more than a quarter of an hour ago she drove off in a car. No, he doesn't know where. Somewhere in that direction.

"You mean, into the darkness?" Alexander asked inanely. The old man nodded seriously. Yes, sir, off the farm, into complete darkness. No, she wasn't alone, she had company. It seems that Mr. Mansour was behind the wheel. No, not her father, sir. Her husband. The husband of Mrs. Mansour, Mr. Mansour. The old man was just about to offer his help in getting a message to the Mansours, but the "Russian Korbach" was already shuffling away, twitching like a soldier after delousing. Yes, my lady, I know what I'm saying: like a soldier after delousing.

For some reason, it had never once entered Alexander's mind since meeting her that she might be married. "What a rotten turn of events," he muttered, twitching. As though someone out there in the goddamned darkness had just let him have a load of this goddamned gravel now crunching beneath his feet right in the mug. An animal husband of a human woman, like some vile centaur grazing among thoroughbreds in a paddock! No, I can't live with this! Why can't they leave me alone? Why does fate keep throwing the theater or love up in my face? My God, all the resentments of the past: the absence of his father, and the chandelier crashing right down on his nut, and separation from the motherland, and his recent beating for the sins of that bitch of a motherland—it was nothing in comparison with the appearance of that beast of a husband. These thoughts had stirred up all the moisture within him, and he was now sobbing loudly, trudging along the dimly moonlit gravel path, among the accumulations of clouds outlined by the tops of the Maryland trees.

All of a sudden, the clouds parted, everything brightened, the stars poured out their light on the now revealed enclosures of the land of the Houyhnhnms. He recognized the places where they had met a few hours before. The contours of the huge barn, beside which her bright yellow Jeep was parked. Yellow is compatible only with green; combined with red it becomes the color of betrayal. Put on yellow light, Nora, your husband will be in red. Must forget her name! In the distance, the sad figures of horses ambled along the hills. A medal winner would not allow any outsiders here. I can't even protect my one and only woman. Resting his elbows on the fence, he soiled the sleeve of his jacket by wiping his face on it, and feeling almost entirely emptied, having cried away almost all of his Nora—I'll blow my nose a couple more times, and the rest will splash out along with the snot—with a nearly calm, or more accurately, usual, disgust with the rubbish heap that was his life, he moved off in the direction of the By the Creeks Hotel.

The paved road began. Now and again cars went past. Some of them stopped: Need a lift? In America, the sight of a man walking often summons up a desire in people to help. Or to pull out a gun. Sometimes both. He sent them on with a wave of his hand: Go ahead and shoot me if you want, just don't try to help me.

Beside the hotel was a streetlamp putting out a weak light, illuminating only the windows of the lobby, where a lone television was shining kaleidoscopically.

The sign gleamed faintly, too. The roofs of half a dozen cars in the small parking lot were reflecting the light of the moon. In a darkened corner, a dappled white mare tied to a tree was stamping. He recognized her immediately. She was the same one that had brought Nora to him today at a powerful gallop. Now she was watching him in embarrassment, inexperience, and innocence itself. Had she really never yet been touched by a magnificent sire? What are you doing here, pussycat? In reply she turned her head away slightly and looked at him from the corner of her eye with tenderness and shame. The wind was rustling her mane in a way that took Alexander's breath away. The chest, which by day had seemed an agglomeration of muscles, now looked meekly like a bare chest. You know that I love the woman who galloped on you to me today. How can you admit that so openly, sir? was just what the flickering motion of the legs seemed to say. It seemed as though she wanted to turn away, but she was afraid to show the dappling on her croup to a man. Even if this is how all this is going to end, then even for these moments beneath the rustling leaves, I thank you, Lord! So he thought, even though he already realized that the *dolce stil nuovo* was beginning to penetrate the moonlit night.

"Gretchen, pussycat, who are you flirting with there?" he heard over his shoulder. For a second he still pretended not to have understood and was afraid to turn around lest he jinx her. The boards of the porch creaked. He turned. Nora was standing there in a very strange outfit indeed—ball gown, boots, and a leather jacket thrown over her bare shoulders. "Well, there you are, finally!" she called out happily, then ran down the steps and embraced the dumbfounded nocturnal faun as if he were her property entirely.

V. THE SONG OF THE OLD WOMAN

I always knew that I was like her
Scampering through the struggle's annals,
Handsome like her
But not her!

They said, "Fidel!" to me,
Faithfulness to the ideas of the Leader
I kept—in purity?—
Until the last rain.

When the people
Forbade me to smoke,
The days were stormy,
Like the fate of the Kurils.

An archipelago of teeth
Flickered in the mirror of the age
Amid the generals' goiters,
Spotted like matzos.

I downed a goblet of rum,
Listened to a pounding march.
The banners, fuck them, fluttered
Like a scar on skin.

I leapt into a litter chair.
"Give me in exchange for cattle,
Motherland of all cigars,
Blessed nicotine!"

An ancient tribute to flight
I paid in my youth,
As Imre Nagy would have,
Raced on a raft down the Danube.

Brows and shoulders I raised
As though I had entrée into the spheres.
Thus I left the Saynod
Of large-caliber mugs.

Now let the one whom I resemble
Excuse me.

PART VI

1

THE MOMENT OF THE OPENING

OF THE MOUTH

*T*he reader may have noticed that we don't often depart from the chronological sequence of the most important events. We do, of course, permit ourselves to leap over two or three years, but only forward, as befits a realist writer. Then again . . . all right, let's not only praise ourselves but admit to something as well. Better to do it oneself than to be caught red-handed. We do take leaps, even into the past, within our chapters—modernism is a contagious disease, ladies and gentlemen! Even stalwart Socialist Realism might have caught on in the end had it managed to stay in good health for another ten years. On one occasion, a professor of Socialist Realism from the first workers' and peasants' state in the history of the world was holding forth publicly on his theory of how to uncover hidden and potential modernists. The chronology gives them away, dear comrades! Make a diagram of his chronology, and the modernist is caught! Put the events in the sequence of the story on one axis and the time of the action on the other, and the notorious modernist "chronotope" will turn out to be so jagged that it would make even the peaks of any lunar mountain range gasp! With this stool pigeon of a professor in mind, we hope that we won't find ourselves guilty of such an affront, though now and then we find ourselves dying to leave some character with his mouth open, in midsentence, for a minute, and during that moment of the opening of his mouth, and during that fictional minute to recount the events of the last three years, and to display all sorts of artistic devices in it, and even to alarm the great with allusions and parallels, and to go off on a tangent about some philosophy or other, before closing that frozen mouth, offering the chance to complete its sentence.

Just such a moment has now arrived. In between the fifth and sixth parts of this novel, three years slipped away unnoticed. It was November 1986. Still the same parking garage in the middle of Westwood Village. Night. The last showings at the movie theaters finished an hour earlier, but the restaurants were still languishing from handfuls of patrons who seemed to be dug in for a long stay. One can hear the palm leaves crackling in the wind. At this hour, the night "valet," slender like a palm tree, although without its hat of foliage, forty-seven-year-old Alexander Zakharovich Korbach, was standing by the entrance and staring vacantly at the intersection with its three lights, whose changing, though obtuse, always seemed to be beckoning to some unknown place.

A huge, very strange car appeared in the intersection and went through the red light. A.Z. would have said that it was a 1939 Soviet ZIS-101 limousine had he not known that it was impossible. However, it was indeed a ZIS-101, from the garage of the collector Leroy Wilkie. The short version of the car's story is this: it was brought to California over a sea full of floating mines. It had been brought for the opening of the first session of the UN General Assembly. Full of gas, the engine turning over, the apparatus was able to transport the head of the Soviet delegation (obviously Molotov or some other creep) from his villa to the assembly hall. This was its only successful mission under the red flag. In the post-Stalin years, space was needed in the garage, and the head of the Soviet mission flogged this unique machine off to Leroy Wilkie's father, Vince, who came from the spy city of Monterey and had started an automobile collection. Strange as it might seem, the name of the administrative manager—*zavkhoz* in Russian—was actually Zavkhozov, and he turned out to be father to the present agent for special assignments.

Making a pal of Vince Wilkie, Zavkhozov winked at his comrades in the mission: this is the way to do it! Wilkie, no fool either, would let slip, seemingly accidentally, stories about Zavkhozov in the Chez Seals bar. In the late 1950s, Vince Wilkie set the fashion in Monterey and Carmel, where in the evening he would pick up girls in his jaw-dropping "Molotov-limo." He brought the machine up to near-ideal condition with his own hands. We say "near-ideal" because no amount of effort made it possible to install a reverse gear in the transmission. The Soviet automobile went only forward. When the need arose to put it in reverse, Vince put the car in neutral, and the girls would jump out and push its imposing front with their bottoms.

The present Wilkie, Leroy, had surpassed his dad. Stuffed with modern technology, the Molotov now moved both forward and backward. Some snobs in Beverly Hills and Bel Air offered him a cool million for the machine, but Leroy had enough millions as it was. He simply wanted to live as happily as possible for as long as he could. The backseat had been removed from the car long before, and the floor covered with springy mats and soft carpeting. At the moment, a group of Californians in young middle age was sprawled on this floor, no fewer than seven bisexuals. They were heading somewhere but had decided to drop by the Westwood Colonial first to ask about an attendant named Alex. They stopped among the concrete columns of the first tier, swept by the night wind. A figure in a silver jacket appeared. That must have been the very same Alex who had been recommended to them.

The latter approached the car and could not believe his eyes: that's a ZIS emblem on the hood, all right! A couple of girls in their second youth emerged from the interior. The wind was fluttering the broad silk trousers on their shapely legs, trousers that would have been called pajamas in the ZIS era. After them followed a youngish male extremity that stretched a long way, until it reached the fringe of a pair of cutoff jeans that looked as though they'd been chewed by a cow. Then came a gangling man with faded hair done in a trendy style, with a slanting fringe and the back of his head shaved. This design made him one with the ZIS era: the Komsomol activists had walked around looking that way then. Hanging on the young man of middle age as a complement to the shorts were a five-hundred-dollar jacket and a Dior tie that hadn't come cheap.

"Are you Alex?" he asked, aspirating in the British way.

"At your service, sir," our hero answered right away in a businesslike tone. He looked at the man closely—that is to say professionally. There was something familiar about this lanky fellow, but among the other Ecstasy fanciers, he didn't seem to stand out.

"Anchorage, Alaska," the lanky one said, using the password for the week.

"It's not as cold as expected," Alexander replied, opening the lock. The lanky one smiled foggily and produced three crisp hundred-dollar bills from his jacket. Alex had the corresponding amount of powder ready in his pocket. The deal was sealed with a handshake, and just then, at the moment of the shaking of the long hand, something quite remarkable happened. The eyes of the gangling sensualist flashed with a heat unusual for this sort of visitor: more often than not these sluggish folk crawled for the latest dose.

"No!" he shouted. "I don't believe my eyes!" after which he indeed froze with his mouth open for the duration of our "minute." At this point, we, the filmmakers of this novel, began to pull the camera quickly back as if not even concerning ourselves with the rapidly shrinking figures of the moment: silk trousers fluttering in the wind, a flickering long-in-the-front fringe, puffs of pipe smoke from behind Leroy Wilkie's bulwark of a jaw, Alexander Zakharovich's jacket billowing like a sail . . . that's about all that would arrest one's attention for a second.

The aim of this headlong dash seems fairly simple at first glance: we need to show, after all, how our noble Korbach has fallen so low as to be a front man for the narco business, if we may be permitted to translate the capacious American term *drug pusher* in this way. We say that love is to blame for this, ladies and gentlemen, and, having pointed out this circumstance that would not matter much to a court but that goes a long way toward softening the blow for the reader, we pull back to the end of the preceding chapter, that is, exactly three years earlier.

2

COPPER ETCHING

"*O*h, Alex," Nora whispered, when he approached her again and again in the tiny little room of the Maryland hostelry, where the moonlight reflected by Gretchen's trembling white croup beamed richly through an open window. "How can you do it again and again and again without taking a break?"

"But it's your fault, Nora," he said with mock self-justification. "It's you, after all, who keeps kissing me, touching me with your breasts, taking my dick in your hands. It's you, after all, who won't give me a rest, my love." "I wasn't wrong, you're a faun," she murmured, again and again raising her legs and winding her gentle arms around his back. "As soon as I saw you among the horses, I thought: He's a faun, he's on the hunt, he's dying to turn me into a nanny goat–nymph. Now, confess, you sweet monster, how many women have you tormented like this?"

"I've never tormented anyone the way I have you," he fibbed. "I've never fallen in love so quickly and so goddamned wonderfully with anyone as I did with you. Most of my life was wasted on silly things," he went on, now without lying. "I don't know what to compare this with except the meeting of Dante and Beatrice on the Ponte Vecchio." She laughed hoarsely. "Now, there's a comparison! They never even screwed, after all, and right away we . . ." And she took his member in her hand again and brought her mouth up to it.

"Is that really what you call it, my dear?" he whispered. "Maybe that act has another name in our case?"

The autumnal anticyclone outside had reduced the temperature to thirty-two Fahrenheit, that is, zero degrees to a Russian. Perhaps everything in the world that night had been reduced to nothing, leaving them with a clear field of action. Only the old house occasionally creaked, perhaps from their labors, or perhaps from age, and Gretchen pitifully whinnied from time to time, perhaps out of jealousy, and perhaps out of concern for her mistress. Only the dawn with its graphic display calmed them, unless one could call it an etching on copper, for the Atlantic was heaving by their bed with a mass of predawn radiance.

It was time, however, to come back to reality. She invited him to stay with her in Washington. "Alas"—he sighed—"I've got to get back to Arkhangelsk." She laughed loudly. "Los Archangeles! What's the hurry, my dear?" He would gladly have come right out and said that Ted had been too kind already by not dropping him from the shift schedule, and that if something like this happened again, he would be out of the Ethiopian Komsomol like the cork from a champagne bottle.

Instead, he muttered almost inaudibly that his departure was already written into this play. "I could come with you!" she exclaimed. He managed to shut down the "treacherous circus of mimicry"—that is, his face: all I need is for her to show up at the Hotel Cadillac. "But I can't," she went on, "because tomorrow I've got to start that fucking freshman seminar foisted on everyone by the Subcommittee for Core Curriculum at lousy Pinkerton." Aha, so this beautiful lady teaches at prestigious Pinkerton University! "I'll fly out to see you in a week, Nora." "Really, Alex, do you promise?" "We won't be able to hold out for more than a week without you, Nora." "Why are you using the plural?" "Because I'm speaking not only for myself but for all of my organs as well. We simply won't be able to stand it without your company." "There it is, I knew it, it's starting again. It looks like I'm threatened with spermatoxicosis, and it's your fault, my darling buffoon!"

Even harsher realities began to take shape after his return to L.A. If I'm going to fly to see her in Washington, what am I supposed to use for money? Maybe I can scrape together enough for a round trip from the rest of that thousand, but that'll be an end to these amorous adventures. There's no way I can admit to her, the professor, that I live on pathetic tips. We could convey the ensuing chaos in his "practical considerations" only with a confused mass of punctuation marks. I'm a bum waiting in line to go nowhere! His Soviet life experience didn't suggest anything that seemed very promising: do I tell her everything? She'll feel sorry for, give money to the "faun" out of pity; the idea of selling . . . there's the Ponte Vecchio for you! They sold something there in such circumstances, though: was it a radio or what? Remember—back in the USSR he sold off a twin-bed ottoman. In America, I've got nothing to sell except my own . . . I know: my Fiat . . . who'll buy it? Kiss it good-bye, that rustbucket. The Washington Beatrice with the ways of an experienced hetaera—maybe she could call up Sweden so they'd give him an advance on "Letters from Exile"—where did she learn all that? Who remembers me in Sweden? And from a distance, after all, she looks like a freshman; he'd have to explain to the Swedes who he was and why; you're out of your head for this chick; you're in exile? What's the catch? Admit to yourself that hetaeras are the only ones you've ever liked! Maybe I could borrow it from Butlerov or . . . from Dvoira . . . Stanley's worth something, after all—she sits there on her subcommittees with the innocent expression of a learned archaeologist on her face she's not an archaeologist she's mine all mine my B-girl and my Beatrice—it would be ridiculous to ask Stanley for a loan—she's sitting there: that convex Anglo-Saxon forehead—when he could give me a million dollars for a film and not even blink— a receptacle of academic knowledge—if only I ask, but I won't ask! Just the word *receptacle* makes my head start to spin. . . .

In this way he thrashed around in his thoughts, and at the same time the feeling of some possibility that had gotten away wouldn't leave him. Suddenly a thought came to him: Art Duppertat had offered him some money that night! Well, Sasha Korbach is in his repertoire! Fortune wouldn't smile on the absentminded with such a gift twice. The reasonable reader will ask: why not? Would it really be so complicated to write to New York and remind the young tycoon of his impulsive gesture? The reasonable person, however, still hasn't gone very deeply into the character of our protagonist. Of course it's complicated for him or, more simply, impossible.

He called Nora every day, usually from a phone booth in Venice, on the edge of the sand and the pavement. Every day he got the answering machine. A brisk, formal, feminine voice said: "Hi! Your call will be returned if you leave your telephone number. Start talking after the tone." Even this almost unrecognizable voice seemed to set his entire body levitating: his member loomed up, his lungs expanded, his heart tried to leap out of his chest, sweat broke out on his forehead. It seemed to him that in her rapid speech he could hear that note of sweetness that had been addressed to him personally that night. Though maybe not to him, but to someone else? Without even realizing that he was jealous, he saw the sky over the beach swelling with something unbearable. Finally, he left a message on the confounded machine: "Nora, this is Alex! I can't get through to you! Where have you disappeared to? I'm just dying without you! Nora! Nora!" The next day, instead of the formal, brisk voice in the receiver, there was different one: "Alex, why, what a fool you are! Why didn't you leave your number? Do you remember Gretchen? She's dying without you, too! Leave your number, and everything will be all right!" The telephone company intervened: "Please deposit one dollar, twenty-five cents to continue."

But he was already rushing along beneath the darkening clouds in a jacket billowing from the wind, sliding past the swaying streetlights like an albatross. Taxi! To the airport! Half an hour later he was already ambling through the glassy corridors of the airport. After buying a ticket from United, he had exactly one twenty-dollar bill left in his pocket. He had a beer in a bar and asked for five dollars' worth of quarters for the phone. He had a ten left. What could be better than a beer before a flight, before a flight like this one? What cozy bars they have here! And these airport bartenders, the picture of dignity and amiability!

Everyone in the bar was watching the television. A nationwide discussion on sexual themes of the 1980s was on. Four transsexuals were sharing their experiences with an excited studio audience. Two had become women, two, men. One, to tell the truth, had already had the operation to become a woman earlier but was now a man again. "It's good being a woman," he was saying, "but it gets a little boring. Our enlightened society still hasn't attained equality of the sexes. It gets a little boring always being a second-class citizen." That was where the desire to return to the "men's division" had come from. The jaws of the people at the airport bar dropped. Even Sasha, in spite of the amorous fog that he was in, was surprised. Was it really possible? It was possible to imagine how a male creature could be reformed as a female—you know, they take away the bits that hang on the body, cut a hole, pump up the tits with hormones—but how would you go back? After all, the effect of sculpture on marble shows up, doesn't it, ladies and gentlemen? After all, you can only take away from marble, you can't add anything to it or glue anything on. "There's nothing simpler," said the two-time defector. "In our day, the surgeon is becoming a sexual sculptor!" Thunderous applause.

The emcee of the talk show, as always, rose to the occasion. "So, Richard, in

the end you decided to return to the sex of the masters?" he asked. "Won't you become a misogynist now, my friend?" There's a question for you, right at the Adam's
apple! That's what they pay this emcee for! The two-time defector began to make
flustered self-justifications. No, no, and again no, Jill! The experience of having
been the "underdogs" will only help him to fight for their equal rights with the "top
dogs"! At this point, A.Z.'s thoughts suddenly moved off in an entirely unexpected
direction. Not long ago in a supermarket tabloid he had read that the network was
paying this host $12 million a year. That meant that if that guy were to fly first-
class from L.A. to D.C. every day, in a year he wouldn't spend half of his monthly
salary! That's how they pay a really worthwhile person here!

"What, do you really believe this circus?" the skeptical bartender unexpectedly
asked him. "How could I not believe it?" asked the surprised Korbach, whom emotional harmony had rendered quite stupid. "There it is, the proof's right in your
face!" "I don't see any proof," the bartender said severely. "It's all deception. Unhealthy manipulation of the public's strange tastes."

Just then the flight for Washington was announced. Sasha, immediately forgetting about this earthshaking argument, leapt down from his stool. He spotted a
pay phone by the boarding gate and tossed a coin into it. I want to delight in her
voice. I'll make my way in with the stragglers in the crowd, for now I'm going to
delight in her voice. There was no chance to delight, though—the crowd was moving quickly. In reply to the ever so *dolce stil* of her latest recorded message, he had
time only to say the number of his flight.

He had counted on drinks on the airplane—it was assumed that the stewardess
on a transcontinental flight would offer beer, and wine, and good cognac—but not
this time. At this time of year, the skinflints at United charged three dollars for
every drink.

From the dusky Californian realms the plane began immediately to plunge into
the nighttime skies of the East. Fearful thoughts came with the darkness. What am
I flying for? Wouldn't it be easier if we just filed the business away under the heading of one-night stands, as so often happens here? Among other things, she's married. He's a Lebanese Arab, she'd said. It would be easier if he were some fat old
pasha who'd paid money for her. More likely, though, he was a man with a Sor-
bonne education, excellent professional references, a partner of the Korbachs—
how else could they have turned up on the farm?—a person of progressive views
who calmly allowed his wife to have her little adventures—there are such people
among the Arabs these days. He knows that she'll come back in the end. That's
how men in trench coats talked in the old films. The influence of Hemingway
hasn't received its proper due. He must have influenced Lebanon as well.

At Dulles, a single reasonable thought finally occurred to him: I can't even get
into the city with my last tenner. He walked along with the crowd to the exit and
noticed with surprise that the passengers were putting on coats and winding
scarves around their necks as they walked. Why was everyone so cold all of a sudden? If she hadn't come to the airport—and most likely she hadn't—he'd have to
ask the American people for help. Help a refugee from the USSR, ladies and

gentlemen! He's got no money, but he's full of love. And I'll recite something from *La Vita Nuova*. It can't be that there won't be one person in this crowd with a good heart.

No sooner had the doors opened than Nora surged up out of her total absence. He saw her pale face, her disheveled hair, and her broad jacket that seemed cut for someone else. Spotting him, she flushed and bounced up and down, as if the fire rushing into her cheeks had tossed her in the air. Many in the crowd looked back in interest at this beauty passionately embracing this none-too-representative, even curious gentleman.

All right, well, all right, stop, not here, after all! She turned out to have a convertible, a Mercedes or something. As they were driving into the city, the heavy weather was getting worse, or, more correctly, was getting heavier. In any case, at first there was snow, then rain mixed with snow, then the reverse, and then snow was simply pouring down, or rather, it was flying at their heads in fierce volleys. Nora swore: the mechanism for raising the roof was jammed. They pulled over, tried to do it manually, couldn't manage it, only one thing to do—to kiss like honeymooners! Some of those driving by had time to point a finger at them and laugh. They drove on and arrived at the house with snow pies on the tops of their heads. Sasha's "pie," however, immediately slid down onto the parquet floor of the entrance hall. "Please don't worry, sir," said the doorman, who, it seemed, had been waiting only for them to kowtow before.

The farther they went into the building, and the higher in the elevator, the fewer details Alexander noticed. It was only later that he would recall how expensive every object had been, from the elevator to the door handle, but not of the sort of expensive quality that cries out to be noticed, rather of the sort that would not seem to admit of any other possibility. The tenderest of all the precious objects in the building he held in his arms. Lust and tenderness, what's all this, sisters? This was his thought, and she answered in the English manner: But of course!

The next morning, he woke up well after midday, that is, he dispensed with morning. The bedroom was still partly in darkness, but through the blinds one could hazard a guess at sun and blue sky. In a mirror across the room—too bad he hadn't noticed it the night before—he saw their bed and the naked Nora, who was peacefully sleeping, lying on the beloved extremities of her right side and breathing from one of the odd-numbered organs of her head, that is, her nose and mouth, directly into one of his even-numbered ones, that is, in his ear. The poet had said it once, after all: "To love others is a heavy cross to bear, but you are wonderful without a curve," he remembered. I'm going to get into a debate with you, Mr. Pasternak, love is nothing but a winding road, with sharp turns just like this one, from start to finish. Then she woke up and asked: "What's this? Do you really think that love is a curve in the road?"

"Well, it's not a straight line, anyway," he said, explaining himself.

"I love it that you're bald," she confessed. "I can't imagine you not being bald. It gives your face a strange sort of youth. In ancient cultures, in Egypt, for example, the nobility shaved their heads right up to the crown."

"I'm flattered," he said. "Even more since you remind me of Isis. Especially when you sit on me with your legs drawn up."

"In what way?"

"You know what way."

"You mean like this?"

"Exactly like that."

"And that reminds you of Isis?"

"Does that surprise you?"

"Not at all. I knew it."

After this excursion into ancient Egypt, the blinds were opened, and it turned out that two of the room's four walls were glass. We're up at the very top, as it turns out, in the penthouse. On the other side of the glass, the late Washington autumn was playing its divertimento. The muscular river flowed along, changing colors over the range from bottle green to blackish blue. Blazing with autumnal self-expression, Theodore Roosevelt Island divided it into two branches. The area on the other side of the river stood beyond it like a glass wall. Now they could open the sliding door and go out onto the terrace. Why, there's as much room here as on a bastion between two fortresses in Jerusalem! A whole troop of heavily armed men could form up for an attack against the rebellious riffraff. Washingtonians rolled along below on the intersecting freeway ramps. On the side streets of Georgetown, rooftops were twisted into warped shapes. Good old colonial territory, why did you separate from the Crown if you were going to preserve the British spirit right up to the present day? On the left, however, loomed something in its own style, gray, steep-sided, very familiar—why, it's none other than the center of American scandal, the Watergate fortress! And beyond it, a center of artistic fame, the gigantic temple of Rostropovich's glory in the shape of a box with sixty-six gilded iron columns—the Kennedy Center.

That, roughly, was the setup. The lyric poem, that is, the dynamic, of the moment was created by a wind from the Atlantic, fluttering flags, a large airplane slowly descending toward the airport, and, flying in the opposite direction, a flock of geese whose trumpetlike cries were enough to make him grab himself by the gaunt belly and cry out: "Glory be to thee, O God!"

"Breakfast! Come stuff yourself!" Nora called. There remained from the night before an untouched tableful of crab claws, Persian caviar, and champagne. It was rolled out onto the platform of the bastion. We're going to eat the way Sulamith and King Solomon ate over Jerusalem, although we're not keeping kosher! She laughed as though she'd already managed to take a nip somewhere. We've even got appropriate clothes for it! She and the beloved put on fluffy, floor-length dressing gowns. Snow from the day before still lay in the corners of the bastion but was quickly melting beneath an autumnal sun that, leaping out from behind a cloud, managed to create the illusion of the blazing heat of Jerusalem.

They had scarcely raised their glasses when another couple came out onto the terrace, a blonde so tall she seemed otherworldly and a dark-haired man of almost equal height. Good young people we've got here, any veteran of big business would have said, looking at them. "What's going on, Omar? It's occupied here, I see!" said the billowy, childlike lips that looked almost absurd atop such a gorgeous figure.

"It's no problem, Jennifer, we'll find something else just as good, but first say hello to Mrs. Mansour and her new friend," said the dark-haired man with a French accent.

"Hello-Mrs.-Mansour-how-are-you," the girl said through clenched teeth, the same way that her forty thousand sisters would have said it.

Nora emptied her glass before replying. "Hello-Jessica-oops-Jennifer-how-are-you?"

The brunette walked across the previous night's snow in his bare feet, shook Alexander's hand, and said warmly that he was glad to see Mr. Korbach again. "Your surprising performance at Halifax Farm, Mr. Korbach, made an indelible impression." Having said this, he went back to his blonde, and they retired from the scene, she pouting, he obviously satisfied about something.

"They have an apartment here, too?" Alexander asked.

"Oh, the whole building is his," Nora said with a wave of her hand.

"How did he come to be at Halifax Farm?"

"As a relative."

"He's a Korbach, too?" Alexander asked, surprised almost beyond words. Nora looked at him in even greater surprise. "Do you mean you don't understand, Alex? That's Omar Mansour, my husband."

"My goodness!" he exclaimed. Of all the American exclamations, he had for some reason picked this one up first. "He looks so young!"

"And why wouldn't he? What, am I too old for a husband like him?" she asked playfully. Then she laughed out loud. "Well, of course the bastard is four years younger than I am. Poor Alex, I guess you thought that the Lebanese husband of your beloved was a fat old pasha, am I right?"

"Nora, for God's sake, you said that he was a relative of the Korbachs—what does that mean?" She peered at him with great attention, as if trying to determine just how dense he really was. "Officially, he's still my husband, so, therefore he's a relative of the Korbachs." Cautiously, he came closer. "And you're related to the Korbachs, Nora?" She pounded herself on the forehead. "I'm an idiot, then! Do you mean I didn't tell you that Korbach is my maiden name? Did no one in Halifax tell you that I'm Stanley's daughter?" "No!" he howled in the soap-operatic tradition.

At that moment, a handful of burning cold drops of rain hit him from the heavens. Dark forces were closing a ring around the nation's capital. The sun disappeared, apparently for the rest of the day. The next portion of raindrops flew down from a giant's palm by the feel of them. Nora and Alexander took no notice of them. They were looking directly at each other. You're shaken, my friend, he read in her eyes. You feel as though you're caught in a trap. You can't imagine yourself in a romance with the daughter of your fourth cousin, right? Just like that, you're ready to flee our Ponte Vecchio in a panic?

The icy rain was already lashing them with its full force. The upper tier of the storm system was playing out its indomitable demonic quality in pompous, purely Wagnerian style. Meanwhile, in the lower tier, shaggy clouds were sweeping along almost at the level of the ridges of the roofs like the embodiments of the petty demons of rock 'n' roll. Looking up at the heavens, Alexander intoned in Russian: "I grew up, misfortunes and dreams carried me like Ganymede." Then he tried to translate these lines from Pasternak for Nora. He filled their glasses. "You know, of course, that Ganymede was a sommelier. Let's drink this to the bottom, so that the rain doesn't spoil the Clicquot!" She smiled, relieved. "You Russians are filled with your poetry like a Christmas goose with stuffing."

He banged his fist down on the table, directly in a puddle formed by the folds of the tablecloth. "How do you know what Russians are filled with? Why did your young husband call me your *new* boyfriend? So you had other boyfriends before me, then? You, the sinful daughter of my fourth cousin, you, a lioness, forced me into shameless incest? I'm sure that among your old boyfriends there were Russians, 'filled with their poetry like a Christmas goose with stuffing.' Admit it on your own, or I'll have to punish you without mercy!"

She laughed like a madwoman. "You jealous monster, you bigmouthed Russian buffoon! You haven't even noticed that I sacrificed my innocence for you! You, you lusty old fifth uncle, you defiled your fifth niece, a little girl who's never had any boyfriends of any kind, let alone Russians stuffed with their own poetry! You've befouled the symbol of inexpressible purity!"

As wet as if they'd fallen into the sea, they laughed and threatened each other. Then she suddenly turned and rushed into the bedroom, a good part of which had been flooded by the heavy, slanting rain. He moved quickly forward and caught her the way that fauns catch nymphs in Attic oak forests. Having caught her, he pulled her into the bathroom, removed her wet dressing gown, twisted her body into the ideal knee-to-elbow position, and began coupling with her in a way that really was a severe punishment for a naughty girl. She was whimpering and shrieking, the lying little bitch, or rather, first-class sex actress. Suddenly a treacherous thought bored through him. This lewd bit of theater might be the beginning of the end. Jealousy might become an indispensable part of our love, and an agonizing lust will sweep over everything, and all of our *dolce stil nuovo* will evaporate like a sad little cloud.

"What's happened, Uncle Alex?" she asked in an innocent, melodic voice. The bitch's mug was looking at him from the various mirrors in the bathroom. The treacherous thought vanished, and everything was as it was before, an expression of complete and mutual playful sincerity. They prolonged their pleasure for as long as they could, until they collapsed in total exhaustion.

Only after that came true innocence and tenderness. They were sitting together in a steaming tub amid mountains of bubbles, as though they were at the top of a heavenly cloud. "So, tell me about yourself, my love," he asked. "What would you like to know, honey?" she asked. "Honey" admitted: "Everything!" She began way back when, before the Flood, that is, in the days before she was born.

3

TINY NORA

*T*he late forties, postwar euphoria, Hollywood. Stanley Korbach, at the peak of his playboy fame, was often combing the West Coast in search of new games. He was only twenty-one then, but he had already landed in Japan and was considered a World War II veteran. So, he negotiated the turns on the Pacific Coast Highway in his collector's item Hispano-Suiza bought from Vince Wilkie himself. Well of course all the doors of Malibu were open to the young prince of the Alexander Korbach Retail line.

Pay attention, a historic moment is coming up. The irresistible youth meets Rita O'Neill, the movie star. Rita O'Neill, *the* Rita O'Neill! Then again, I don't suppose that you knew this famous name on the other side of the Iron Curtain.

Just imagine, Nora, people knew Rita O'Neill even in Stalinist Russia. We were allies during the war, after all, and films with this girl in them played in our country: *Fifth Avenue, The President's Sister, A+ in Math.* After the war they were taken off the screens, of course, but when I was growing up, we used to attend semiunderground showings of American films in people's apartments. As a lad of fifteen I was in love with that dazzling Rita O'Neill. I hope you don't mean to say that she's your mama?

That's exactly what I mean to say. When my parents met, Mom was twenty-five, that is, four years older than my dad. That's right, the same difference as there is between me and Omar, but there's nothing symbolic about that. Stanley fell in love, and Rita was good enough to take him in. A year later little Nora was born, and then they got married. You see how it works out, darling: as a young man you masturbated over Mama in the shadow of Stalin's monuments, and now you're sleeping with her daughter in the shadow of the Washington Monument. All right, I won't be so cynical anymore. I'll go on. Are you interested in the ethnic makeup of the newborn? Well then, let's work it out. The name O'Neill, naturally, was thought up for Mom in Hollywood. In those days, American names sounded like pure gold to the Jews out there. Mom was one-quarter Jewish, one-quarter Czech, and half Mexico City Spanish. So, from Mom I got one-eighth Jewish blood, which together with five-sixteenths from Dad makes seven-sixteenths. So, let's add up the sixteenth parts: your tiny Nora is seven-sixteenths Jewish, two-sixteenths Czech, four-sixteenths Spanish, one-sixteenth Italian, three-sixteenths Yankee. There's one part too much, I don't know why—well, to hell with it. We're Americans, after all, we need a surplus of everything.

For five years my parents enjoyed a happy family life. They may have broken the record for happiness in Hollywood in those days. Then came the breakup, and when the dust settled, their happiness lay in ruins. Even now I don't know exactly what happened. Mom's usual answer to the question is that Stanley killed not only the woman in her but the artist too, but she won't go into details. It seems to me that she thinks it was my father who kept her from joining the ranks of the giants, like Greta Garbo and Ingrid Bergman. Sometimes she even says something along those lines. "I could have been the new Garbo, but certain circumstances in my personal life kept me from doing it." Pause. Close-up. Violin playing in the distance. She's treasured her grief for a long time now. She's still one of the most influential women in Hollywood, but she wants to have something dramatic in her past, something preordained—you know, something elusive. Would you like to meet her, Alex? Just say yes, and you'll be breathing down Hollywood's neck.

"No, no," said A.Z., "there's no need."

Stanley never said anything mean about Rita, only once, in connection with his first marriage, he remembered a pair of lines from Shakespeare: " 'Tis brief, my lord / As woman's love," from which I gathered that he didn't consider himself the only home wrecker. In those days, though, hitting back at women wasn't the done thing among sporting people.

Tiny Nora stayed in her mother's house and lived there until she went to college. Her father dutifully visited her and swam with her in the pool. It's to him that tiny Nora is indebted for her perfect swimming style, which she hopes to demonstrate to her new Uncle Alex in the near future.

When she was a teenager, Nora, with the full consent of her enlightened mother and her friends (there was always a council of friends there watching over the fragile Rita O'Neill), visited her dad on the East Coast, that is, either at Halifax Farm or at Newport, where his fleet of yachts was based. It was wonderful, to fly east alone, to take on such a pose of worldly nonchalance that it made the stewardesses go around on tiptoe. Daddy would meet Nora at the airport; there was always some beautiful woman with him whom he usually introduced as his "best pal." How wonderful it was to display a casual, worldly attitude toward the objects of Daddy's passion. One of those "best pals" turned out to be that slut Marjorie, but that's neither here nor there.

There was an amusing paradox in Nora's life in those days. As an artist, Alex, you ought to be able to appreciate the benign madness of the situation. In her mother's house, Nora saw the most brilliant and inaccessible people in the world all the time, all of these Orson Welleses, Frank Sinatras, Stanley Kramers, and Burt Lancasters, whom she called "our club" and considered crashing bores. Visiting her daddy's empire, she would meet people whom she considered "different," that is, who stood out from stereotypes: sailors from the yachts, mechanics, horse breakers.

Until Grandpa David gave up the presidency of AK Retail, his successor, Stanley, led an eccentric life. Mama, fortunately, didn't know that Nora often took part in Daddy's escapades, otherwise she would have taken away his visitation rights. A dozen nice postcards were prepared in advance for Mama, and Dad's servant, the "Eternal Jew" Enoch Agasf, would send one every three days to Bel Air. The daughter, meanwhile, was crossing the Atlantic, outracing the ocean liner *Ile de France* with her daddy on a small but powerful cutter, so as to take part in the hot-air balloon races on the Côte d'Azur.

"And what about the horses, darling?" Alexander asked.

"Well of course there were horses, and horses and more horses!" About your plans for your life, daughter, her permanently tipsy father would say in the evenings—why don't you concentrate on show jumping? Father, you've got me mixed up with someone else, she would usually reply.

It goes without saying that Mother had other plans for her only daughter. Nora was supposed to attain in Hollywood what Rita had not been able to. She was supposed to leave all the other stars in the shade through her inimitable megashining. The "council of friends" was planning the creation of a new idol in jeans and an undershirt, who would be an American answer to the overseas beauties like the then all-powerful Bardot and Deneuve, who was already preparing to take the former's place. The idea was to create not simply a young beauty but a new type of personality, a representative of the "thinking young." They began dragging Nora to dance classes, music lessons, acting workshops, and karate lessons, without which not even the daughter of "the incomparable Rita O'Neill" could count on a successful career. Each of the friends considered it his duty to share his experiences in the film business with the girl, and it was all quite unbearable.

All of this foolishness crumbled into dust. The girl rebelled. She declared that she wasn't about to imitate the "thinking young" but simply wanted to become part of them. In other words, she was intending to go to college, to take courses in history and foreign languages, particularly French and Arabic, as well as classes in ancient culture and the Renaissance, so as to enter her own chosen—once and for all—profession: archaeology.

Up until now, one felt sorry for Mama: she was simply devastated by the decision of her daughter, who was, it seemed to her, her image and likeness. To prefer the rotting smell of libraries, the world of some pathetic scholars, to the brilliant lights of showbiz, the only existence worthy of the name! Moreover, to show such foolish disdain for her friends, for the whole world of the "rich and famous"—that is, of those gifted ones singled out by fortune to form the tastes and the minds of the public! To despise those who were leading the whole world toward the dream! "I'm sure that your father had something to do with this!" she cried out in the spirit of some memorial theater or other.

"Nonsense, Mom!" Nora parried. "My pop is a first-class sportsman and a charming man, but he's still an inseparable part of those superrich *meshpukha,* and I don't have the slightest respect for the 'fat cats' of the East Coast."

Rita tried to insist that she at least go to the "right school." For God's sake, anything but that scandalous Berkeley! At least go to Stanford! Nora promised, but she didn't keep her promise. She joined the "shock troops of Red Berkeley" in the autumn of 1967.

"Because he was from Berkeley," Alex the wise supposed.

You guessed it, my imaginative friend! Jealousy really is the key to a lot of mysteries. You've earned a reward, so I'll tell you that they met in the Louvre, his name was Danny, and he was an archaeology student from Berkeley. He was almost ten years older than Nora—that is, your age, Alex. He'd been trying to get his M.A. for a long time because he was from a poor family and needed to work for a year or two here and there to pay for his studies. He was a Marxist, of course, and a Trotskyite to boot. He hated the establishment of the USA and despised the USSR because it had not been able to start a worldwide conflagration and had built a police state instead. So, Nora came to hate the establishment of the USA and came to despise the USSR, too.

It ought to be said that her rebelliousness was not only a result of her enthrallment with the first man in her life. Even as a child, the girl had sensed that the order of things was not how things were supposed to be, as well as the artificiality of the life of her mom and her circle, in which they drove unnatural cars, counted up their money in sums inaccessible to most of the population, who in their circle were known as "the audience." Fed up with famous faces and their curious habits, the girl began to yawn in irritation every time the subject of movies came up. I don't want to be a marionette in this puppet theater! Her greatest pleasure was to flee on a bike into Westwood during a street festival, to jostle her way through crowds, eat cotton candy, and drink Cokes from the bottle. At school she concealed who her parents were, and one day even blew up at the principal when she asked her in her sweetest voice if the incomparable Rita O'Neill couldn't grace their establishment with a visit. Even Stanley, with his racers, sailors, and balloon pilots, paled in the eyes of his daughter after she met Daniel Barthelme. Her father's world no longer seemed "different" to her. He uses the outrageous advantages of a superrich man, walks around among his daredevils like some medieval suzerain. Aimless adventures, a meaningless existence!

In those days she rejected any nuances. Danny banged his fist on the table in Parisian cafés or London pubs, or in their first run-down apartment in the middle of the Oakland ghetto. Nothing could be dirtier than the enormous wealth that your parents possess! It's simply an amoral, monstrous, rotten way of life! Millions of simpletons in search of new pagan gods have created a false aristocracy for themselves out of these Hollywood dolls and dimwits. And those who accept this situation as the most natural thing in the world see themselves as divine beings. As far as your daddy is concerned, not much good to report there, either. The Korbachs try to look like working merchants and bankers, when in fact they're nothing other than repulsive nouveau riche, some sort of line of new Jewish pharaohs. Listen, Nora, if you want to be a normal human being, you've got to forget about your parents! Look at what's going on around you! History has never seen a revolution of young people on this scale. The University is becoming the headquarters of the uprising. Then Factory and Farm will join us. And we'll win! Our people are everywhere—in Paris, in Germany, in Japan, even in Czechoslovakia—they're storming the pigsty of this world, whose wire is choking not only the Vietnamese but all of us, too—our dreams, our thoughts are always being choked by this fucking belching behemoth of a world!

Then Danny would begin to shake and couldn't stop until he had indulged in at least one of three "emancipating" acts: knocking back some dollar-a-gallon rotgut, smoking pot, or screwing Nora.

My God, they were so magical, those days in Berkeley! Stendhal once said: "Unhappy is he who has not lived just before a revolution." Now, after so many years, we can paraphrase this idea: "Happy is he who has lived just before a revolution that never happened." Morning was breaking before the walls in an endless *dazibao*. Students were yelling and singing to the sound of guitars. Meetings were going on where resolutions were accepted either on the abolition of exams and grades or on the question of the creation of the People's Democratic Republic of San Francisco Bay with Comrade Kim Il Sung, leader of the Korean people, at its head. The crowd would march down Telegraph Avenue chanting:

> *In San Francisco, the day will come*
> *when we'll be embraced*
> *by Kim Il Sung!*

The smell of pot was everywhere. To this day, that odor is nostalgic for me. In the evening, mobs of kids would fill all the bars along the little streets of downtown. The whole spectrum of the cultural revolution was represented there: ancient beat poets like Ginsberg and Ferlinghetti—imagine, they were over forty!—and new boys and girls from the London "flower power" movement—Danny hated their slogan, "Make love, not war!" "Make war on war!" was his slogan. Alongside them marched militant anarchists, Maoists, Che Guevarists, Black Panthers, homosexuals, lesbians, gurus of Eastern cults, and the bums and the narcs, too.

Our little Nora found herself right in the thick of this crowd, since she was working as a waitress at the Rooster Cafe. The regulars knew about her boyfriend's explosive temper, and this restrained the outbursts that were fairly traditional for this sort of café. Nora became a sort of favorite of the revolutionary movement, Miss Red Berkeley, all the more so since she was ready to sit down at the piano at any moment and sing "Blowin' in the Wind" or "Try to Make It Real" (to which the whole bar would thunderously reply, "Compared to what?"). I wonder, did anyone know those songs in Moscow then?

"Maybe a small group of Stateniks did," Alexander said. "We had a Joan Baez and a Bob Dylan of our own. In Russia, everything is upside down in relation to the West. I was Dylan there, on the left, because I was against socialism." "Yes, but not for capitalism, right, Alex?" she asked, as if emerging for a moment from her own eyes, in which the smoke of Red Berkeley mirrored the entire surface. "Precisely for capitalism," he growled. And stroked her hair. "Never mind, never mind. Continue your story, reckless Nora."

In a word, university life for Nora became a never-ending vagabonds' ball. God, how happy everything was on Telegraph Avenue in '67–'68; it was enough to make your head spin! Not long ago she had gone back there for the first time in twelve years. It was fantastic: the street hadn't changed at all—the same smell, the same sounds, similar faces. She'd even noticed a few old friends, sixties rebels. They'd become street vendors, their wares spread out in front of them: pins with the daring slogans of those years, cheap jewelry with Navaho turquoise, Bolivian ponchos, Tibetan bells, selections of desert grasses, powdered gadflies—you know for what; by the way, you don't need any. Capitalism co-opted the revolution, too, and your side won, fifth cousin!

She walked around for a long time in a big cap and dark glasses. Something *was* new about the place, she couldn't work out what, until she thought: how pleasant the fluttering of the leaves is, the shadow of the leaves gives this street even more color! Then it came to her: there were no trees here then! It seemed that one day the mayor, driven to distraction by the demonstrations, smashed windows, and barricades, had ordered trees to be planted, but they were just pathetic seedlings that no one paid any attention to, no one except our dogs, who ran around them as a free commune. And now Nora's youth was over—the revolution, too, and Danny had already been on the run for a year, and the trees on Telegraph Avenue had grown and established themselves, rustling with their foliage; excellent Swiss plane trees.

"If I start going off on another lyrical tangent, pinch my ass, Alex, okay?"

"You said that your Danny was on the run—what does that mean?"

Nora falls silent for a while, and the author makes use of this pause to put in a rather tactless reminder. The fact is that all of the preceding conversation, or more accurately journey through the past, took place in a bathtub. At this moment—a thousand apologies—the temperature of the water was passing out of the comfort zone, and then under the general influence of some perhaps mysterious or perhaps entirely simple causes—maybe she pulled the plug?—the water began a noisy egress from our chronotope into the corresponding aperture, leaving two naked bodies in patches of foam of rather shameful configurations. Fearing that Nora in her patches would put him in mind of something mythological like bathing on Cyprus, A.Z. leapt from the tub and brought two dry bathrobes. She looked distracted and tired. He couldn't bring himself to repeat the question. On the one hand, he wanted to know more about her first lover, who had obviously left a deep impression in her mind; on the other hand, he saw that, in remembering her past, she was moving away from him, and he felt pangs of jealousy toward that idiot Danny, that monstrous rabble in the Rooster Cafe, and even the trees on Telegraph Avenue. She glanced at him and smiled sadly as she returned to her story.

Well, by the end of the first academic year, that is in April 1968, the whole carnival had come to an end. The cell made the decision to resort to the tactic of revolutionary violence. Nora didn't know anything about it because Danny wanted to protect her from these dangerous activities. It was only after the action that she found out all the details from that bitch Lenore Yablonsky. Alex had met her at Halifax Farm, of course. No? That's strange. In those days, she was screwing her way through every person in the cell, regardless of sex. She was the strongest supporter of the action, but somehow managed not to get her hands dirty.

In a word, the Trotskyites held up the Perpetual Bank, in a rich neighborhood on the other side of the Bay, in broad daylight, cleaning out the vaults and shooting two cops in the process, maybe out of necessity, and maybe just for kicks. The ideal in the cell at the time, by the way, was the young Russian revolutionary-expropriator of 1905. The year 1905 was considered the height of purity. The successful revolution of '17 considered a model for the antiestablishment commune. "The lessons of Kronstadt" was the subject of lots of meetings. For some reason, no one pointed out that it was none other than the revolutionary idol Lev Trotsky who had bathed the rebellious island in blood.

When Nora was arrested, she shouted at the FBI agents: "Long live the youth revolution!" and only later started climbing the walls. "Where's Danny? Give me back my Danny!" The investigation showed almost immediately that she had nothing to do with the holdup of the bank, and they let her go. A huge storm blew up in the press, of course: the beautiful freshman, the daughter of the incomparable Rita O'Neill and Stanley Korbach, the powerful East Coast business magnate, was closely tied to a group of armed rebels, whose leader, Daniel Barthelme—in all probability Miss Korbach's lover—had been arrested a few days ago, charged with murdering two policemen and robbing a bank, but managed to escape from a maximum-security jail.

Rita and Stanley immediately came running to the scene of the revolutionary drama. For the first time since their divorce, they found a common language. They were both shocked by the poverty in which their beloved "kid" had spent her first year at college. Without having agreed on it beforehand, both were nothing but tactful, and entirely sympathetic to Nora's ideas and sentiments. "Anyone who wasn't a socialist at eighteen becomes a bastard at thirty," and other pearls of wisdom along those lines. Both of them—not cooking it up between them, God forbid—offered Nora a long trip abroad so as to be out of the law enforcement agencies' line of sight for a while, and for other reasons as well. At the time, both of them were calling her by her childhood nickname of Hedgie, short for hedgehog.

Nora turned them down. Instead of traveling, she decided to register for the summer semester and to plunge herself into archaeology. "It's your life, Hedgie," her parents said. "You do what you want." In the end, Rita did manage to make her daughter laugh hysterically by saying: "You've come through a great trial, darling. In spite of all the unpleasantness, this story could be the basis of a terrific film. Why don't you think about selling the movie rights? You could even play yourself in a film about the 'thinking young.' It's a super project, don't you think?"

"You're incorrigible and delightful, Rita O'Neill," said Stanley, who had been sitting in on this conversation, and he kissed the hand of his ex-wife.

Of course, Nora was still hoping that Danny would come back. One night, the outside screen door creaks, and then someone bangs a knee into the locked inner door. She rushes along in the darkness, her pounding heart throwing her off balance. And there she is on his chest, leaning right into an iron object in his pants, a pistol. Oh, my darling, my Danny!

Months, however, go by, and Mr. Barthelme still hasn't appeared. Some of the surviving members of the cell dropped hints to her that the agents had bumped him off a long time ago, and then started the rumor about his escape. It was not entirely fanciful that she suspected that these members wanted to take the place of Danny in her bed. Without a moment's delay she gave them a good kick in the backside and immersed herself in archaeology. One had to give Danny his due—penetration into the cultural dust of the planet existed right alongside the revolutionary dust in him. He was well-grounded in the subject, and had experience in the field. There, in the Egyptian section of the Louvre, where they'd met, this lanky Yank had given Nora the impression of just that calm dedication to his chosen field; his revolutionary fervor had flared up only later, in the café. After the ugly drama that had played itself out so quickly and Danny's disappearance, Nora remembered that the best times of their life together had had something to do with archaeology. Forgetting about the time of "the order of the day," they had quietly talked about, say, the difference between the Egyptian and Mesopotamian civilizations. The Sumerian and Egyptian conceptions of life beyond the grave differed from each other as dramatically as the calm flowing of the Nile, with its strictly regulated high-water periods, did from the murky currents of the Tigris and the Euphrates. In the midst of their majestic stone constructions, the Egyptians seemed already to have found the harmony of eternal life. The Assyrians and the Babylonians in their clay dwellings, which would be destroyed several times in the life of one generation by unpredictable floods, were more inclined to believe in Hell than in Paradise. Danny talked about Gilgamesh as though he had known him personally. He would talk about the cosmic meaning of archaeology. Departing into the earth, humanity would become an accumulation of cosmic objects.

***

"That sounds like Nikolai Fyodorov's *Philosophy of the Common Cause*," said Alexander, "except that he went further than the cosmos. He said that the principal task of humanity was the return of departed ancestors. Their return from the unknowable realms to the flesh. The cosmos for him, it seems, was only a border region." "What did you say his name was, 'Nicholas Fodora'?" she asked academically, squinting in his direction; it even seemed to him that he could see the glasses on her nose. "He's a Russian? Over here we don't know this philosopher."

He grinned. "We don't know him in our country either, except in samizdat."

"Oh yes, these 'narrow circles' of yours."

"How do you know about our 'narrow circles'?"

"What do you mean, how? From Russian lovers, of course. Who can a woman find out about anything from?" In the breathing spaces between screwing sessions, lovers had told her about the narrow circles and about samizdat, but for some reason they never mentioned this philosopher.

Meanwhile, dusk was gathering in the room. In two hours they would have to go the airport. Nora rolled over onto a heap of pillows and took a pack of cigarettes from the night table. Alexander had the impression that from time to time she was shooting him inquisitive glances, as though she really did want to know more about Fyodorov. "According to Fyodorov," he said, "Almighty God expects every generation of the living—that is, the 'children of the air'—to work for the resurrection of all the dead, that is, for the return of cosmic and esoteric objects to life by means of science and technology. This is the principal idea: overcoming the enmity of nature through the resurrection of the fathers. The starry sky speaks to us of distant worlds, but it says more about the tremendous search for the 'father' by the grace of God."

"Did he influence you as an artist?" she asked. He became strangely flustered. "At first, yes, but then some resistance sprang up. He has ideas about art that say nothing to me at all. Fyodorov considers prayer the beginning of art, which I have no quarrel with, if dance can be considered prayer. But then ideology comes into his thinking, and even something like the politics of the day. He divides art into 'theoanthropourgical' and 'anthropourgical.' The first consists of the discovery of God through a vertical, prayerful state, that is, with the building of a monument to the dead. The second is worldly art, on the one hand frightening, on the other, sensually attractive. Prayer is replaced here by the exhibition." She passed a hand over her brow, pressing firmly, and said: "That's right." Alexander shrugged. "Too right for my taste. Art has one more important goal. It's aimed against the most important enmity, which comes not from nature but from time. Complete destruction comes from the racing of time, and art tries to turn it back, to catch the uncatchable. Before there was art, everything fell into the abyss; now, from time to time it seems that at least something remains. Maybe it's in that something that the Holy Spirit appears."

"Where can you get this book?" she asked. He shrugged. "I've never seen Fyodorov in book form. It was just piles of cigarette papers that the intellectuals passed around among themselves. It's not likely that the Bolsheviks will publish him: after all, he talks about things that make dialectical materialism sound like the babbling of infants."

He looked at his watch. She followed his glance. "Yes, we ought to get dressed. Turn your back!" He snorted. After the sort of closeness that they had only just been engaging in, such modesty all of a sudden. A glowering look. So that's what it's all about, she's drawing me into her trap again. "What, you won't let me get dressed in peace?" A slow but ever growing arousal. "Well, here you are again, sir," she said, as though trying by some languorous bit of trickery to shift the responsibility for something that she herself was guilty of onto him. He had already noticed that she called him "Mister" and "Sir" during sex and used the subjunctive mood of the verb *will*. "You were getting ready to hear more revelations from poor Nora, sir." "Nothing's stopping you, ma'am, continue with your story," he said, beginning his "again." She raised her eyebrows. "Do you suppose that I can continue with the story of poor Nora when you spread me out underneath you this way, like a frog?" He was insistent. "I have to know everything about this poor little girl who does so much to torture men!" She started to go on.

In principle, the most dramatic chapter of the story had already been told. There remained only a routine academic career and archaeological expeditions to the Fertile Crescent. Four years ago, on Cyprus, Nora met a young man from Beirut named Omar Mansour. They went to Paris together and got married quite suddenly.

"Do they have children?" he asked, pressing her somewhat. "She has a ten-year-old son; he's being brought up in Switzerland." "Who's his father?" Another convulsion of jealousy ran through his body from head to toe. "Nora wishes she knew!" she murmured. "Maybe the driver from an expedition." This woman certainly knows how to drive me crazy! "And what's the boy's name?" "She gave him her own name, he's Bobby Korbach, if it pleases you." "I'd like to be his father," he said, surprising even himself.

She let her face fall on the pillow, her fists clenching and unclenching, her body shaking—she was trying to suppress a howl. Meanwhile he continued to press his amorous dispute, and the thought of bringing it to a conclusion never entered his head or his member. "Beg pardon, sir," she whispered, panting. "Do you suppose that you could envisage the possibility of the completion of this overwhelmingly long copulation? In the first place, you might miss your flight, and in the second place my vagina's bleeding, I'm afraid. Were you really this powerful with other women, sir, if I may ask?"

"Absolutely not," he replied. "A most rare phenomenon is to blame, madam. I've simply met the woman for me, and she's shaken loose all of my secret corners, obviously. It seems that I've completed my subconscious search for the female half of my ontological essence, that's all. I simply love you with all of the tiniest cells of body and consciousness, ma'am."

When all this finally came to an end, they both glanced at the clock and saw that they had about twenty minutes for innocent cuddling. She kissed and caressed the damp, slippery slope of his head. "My dear chosen one, if only you knew how much I love all of you, but particularly, for some reason, your bald head!" "You know, I began to go bald very early, when I was still quite young. It seems to me that a curious incident in my adolescence was to blame. I was nearly killed, my darling, when a heavy chandelier fell right on my head." She took him by the hand, gazed into his eyes, as though she could see this drama of existentialism with her own, and demanded the details. With a wandering smile, in a half-serious tone, he told her how he had been sitting at the dining room table with his goddamned physics textbook and listening to Kabalevsky's *Kola Brugnon* overture, when he suddenly blacked out. She shuddered. "What's wrong, then, darling?" he asked, frightened. "It wasn't a chandelier, Sasha"—for the first time she used his Russian diminutive—"don't you understand that it was someone behind you who wanted to kill you with a huge stick?"

He shouted, or more accurately howled. Now it was his turn to look straight into her eyes, as though wanting to see there what he had evidently always kept in a corner of his subconscious: Nikolai Ivanovich Izhmailov approaching from behind with a stick. "How could you see that big stick? Are you a clairvoyant or something?" He told her about the boxwood stick. The Russian word for "boxwood"—*samshit*—caused a bit of difficulty by its resemblance to "some shit," but together they successfully extricated themselves from this linguistic trap. Nora suddenly embraced him like a mother or a big sister. "That's never happened to me with anyone before. Sometimes I feel as though I read you without words, read even what you can't read yourself."

Well, all right, it's all over, and an hour later their meeting, too, came to an end, at Dulles Airport. The boarding for the United flight had already begun. In the crowd Nora spotted a group of people she knew, men and women who were giving the lovers extremely curious looks. "The Pinkerton people are here— physicists and geneticists," Nora said. "Want to meet them?" The physicists and geneticists for reasons of their own were being devoured by curiosity; they were approaching. "Hi, guys! I'm just seeing my friend off," Nora said to them jauntily. "I'd like you to meet Alex Korbach, a famous theater director from Moscow!" "Oh, the Moscow theater!" The educated people sighed with respect. "Sorry, guys, we need a moment alone," Nora said in the same tone. The physicists and geneticists didn't have to be asked twice; they immediately retreated, their faces beaming with curiosity satisfied.

What could be more beautiful than Nora's lovestruck face and her figure in a tweed jacket, with a scarf thrown over the shoulder? What could be sadder than parting? "See you next Sunday," he said, and for his part couldn't even imagine being able to live through the seven days of the week without her. "Will you really come?" she whispered. "You can count on it."

With some tension in her voice, she asked the question that she had had on the tip of her tongue for some time: "Sasha, have you got any money?" He joked: "Do you know a single Korbach without any money?" On the note of that not particularly successful joke, they parted.

4

THE UNION OF THE RICH

Swimming over the clouds from east to west, he gained several hours, and as a result even managed to catch a nap at the Hotel Cadillac. In the morning he shaved, savoring the call that he would make to Nora at Pinkerton from the Colonial. Then he ate the sandwiches that she had put in a small Pan Am bag for him: Spanish ham that was nearly black, layered with Belgian endives, salmon with pickles—on the whole, better than the Catholic Brothers. While he was eating, he kissed the flight bag several times. With this bag over his shoulder the previous evening, he had looked like just an ordinary traveler, and not like some idiot. Inside it there was something else besides sandwiches. Delving to the bottom, he found two first-rate shirts, in all probability from Mr. Mansour's wardrobe. The next time he would have to try to be a bit more unbiased where he was concerned. On the other hand, maybe he'd borrowed a dozen pairs of panties from his wife's drawer for his blondie. We're even, then, Omar—we can dispense with the open-mindedness. Digging even deeper, he found five hundred dollars in crumpled bills. She'd stuck it in at the last minute, cleaning the house out of every bit of cash on hand. Rich types like Nora Mansour didn't walk around with cash. On the other hand, it might cause unexpected problems. Something to pay a gigolo with for a good lay. You can't write out a check to some cunt chaser. You creep, he said to himself—you're a real pig, Alexander Zakharovich. You just can't help pissing all over everything around you, including your own happiness—you're a mongrel, a pervert, you don't even value human love and a woman's inclination to protect her beloved.

All the same, he said to himself with a grimace that was grotesquely reflected in his teapot, all the same you can't accept any help from her, can't give her the slightest opening for thinking, even against her will, that she's helping some fading Russian neurotic with his love life. Again he was seized by a feeling of complete helplessness. If I want to see her every week, I can't get around revealing my pathetic life—that is, total humiliation.

Alexander went into work that morning oppressed and plunged into gloom by these thoughts. Everything's finished, there's nothing left of my youth, even love was submitted to a withering interrogation from everything that his shuddering car met along the way: palm trees, the skyscrapers of Century City, billboards with their playful abracadabra. He didn't know, of course—just as we didn't know until a previous page—that with every mile he was coming closer to a new turning point in his American destiny.

The first thing that he saw that morning at the Colonial was a brand spanking new Lincoln Town Car, from which protruded the just as brightly beaming, if not new, face of his Chicano friend Gabriel Lianoza. "Like my car, a real Fucco-Wulf?" "Where'd you expropriate it, Zapatista-fuck-me-sideways?" Alexander asked. He had been noticing for some time that the former musician, corpulent in a crablike fashion, had begun flaunting various chic, well-used items: here a snakeskin jacket, there crocodile shoes.

It should be pointed out that Korbach had recently struck up a real friendship with the Mexican. He seemed to him the personification of Latin American magical realism. A hidden folk wiliness, a clumsy dance to the rhythm of a tuba seemed to be permanently at play in his lying red eyes, in his abundant facial hair, in his huge hands, those of an obstetrician or a baker. Gabriel did indeed like both to bake bread and to coax a newborn out of the expanding birth canal of his wife into the light of day—that is, out of his own seminal tubes.

Often after work they would hit La Cucaracha and feast in the garden on mutton and heaps of any kind of peppers you could think of, seasoning it all with gallons of cold Coronas, which gave Gabi even more of a belly, and Alex grew more gaunt. Lately, Mr. Zapatista-fuck-me-sideways had been refusing to let his friend Mr. Fucco-Wulf go dutch with him. Undoing wads of dollars, he would bare his wrists as thick as shrubs, from which gold bracelets and chains were hanging.

Alexander thrust his head in the automobile that reeked of wealth and said: "Listen, Gabi, I'm in love, I need money." "What, you mean she won't do it without money?" Señor Lianoza inquired. "Something like that." Alexander nodded. "I see you've gotten rich lately—let me in on the secret. How're you making the money?" The Mexican looked at the Russian for some time without saying a word. The tungsten threads in his eyes, those harbingers of peasant revolutions, were already beginning to heat up, but then they went out and he burst into good-natured, though not very pastoral, laughter. "You've really gotten stuck on some high-grade piece of ass. Listen, Gabi Lianoza can't tell you anything, but as one artist to another, he can give you a piece of advice: ask Aram the same question."

Aram Ter-Aivazian was sitting on his high stool as usual in the cashier's booth. As always, or even more than before, he was extremely serious and self-contained; he could have been a member of the Armenian government in exile. Even as he was coming near, Alex noticed things that he hadn't paid attention to before: Porsche smoked-lens sunglasses, a Versace tie, a Cartier watch. A man's sitting behind the cash register in a parking garage with goods like that! Damn it all, I want into this strange rich man's club, and Aram has got to share the secret with me—after all, we've downed a lot of vodka together!

"Listen, Aram, I need to make a few more bucks. Couldn't you recommend me to the ones who know how to do it?" Aram was an unusual sort of Armenian: hair black as coal and bright eyes the color of oysters. The oysters narrowed at Korbach's questions, as though they had been sprayed with lemon juice. "You know it's dangerous?" Korbach silently nodded. The oysters widened again and even seemed to acquire an outer film of amiability. "Okay, pal, in the afternoon I'll introduce you to some important people who can examine your request. Or who might not even spit in your direction."

On a stifling, smoggy afternoon—the Californian curse, the Santa Ana wind, was making an out-of-season appearance—Alex and Aram arrived in downtown Los Angeles, that cluster of skyscrapers thrusting up from a sea of low, formless buildings. The elevator of one of the skyscrapers took them to the thirty-eighth floor. Springy carpet, doors with brass handles and nameplates. One of them read with unheard-of modesty: HORNHOOF & BENDER, LTD. The strikingly beautiful secretary smiled generously at the visitors. "Hello, Natalie," Aram said. "Mr. Hornhoof is expecting us." "Please have a seat, gentlemen," came the most delightful of replies. She murmured something soft and tender into her intercom, then stood up and walked to the boss's door. Her walk was perfection itself, a quite unobtrusive demonstration of everything that was absolutely wonderful. Through the slightly opened door Korbach heard a familiar voice, yelling down the phone with a marvelous Russian pungency: "You tell him to fuck off, Semyon! He can suck me, that Azeri cunt!" Mr. Hornhoof turned out to be none other than the Soviet Komsomol activist Tikhomir Burevyatnikov.

Tikh was now hovering over the canyons of L.A. in the role of some sort of flourishing pterodactyl. I wrenched myself free from the ghetto of Soviet deputies, and now I'm just hanging around, hanging not badly at all, fellas! His horsey mug was covered with a tennis tan, the general impression one got was almost from a Deineka painting of a healthy man in his thirties, although, true enough, his finger trembled slightly from the use of various sorts of whiskey. After the first investment, made through Senior Supervisor Zavkhozov, Department N, extremely satisfied, began to send electronic transfers from God knows where—some from Hong Kong, some from Bilbao—to Hornhoof's account and quickly brought his bank balance up to seven figures. Making active use of the motherland's largesse, Tikh broadened the scope of his own business, the income from which naturally stayed under another shelter. Friendship's one thing, you Red bastard, but you can get your own snuff.

"Hey, guys, am I glad to see you!" Tikhomir said with good Soviet bonhomie. "Remember how we used to tear it up last year, you two, me, Staska Butlerov! There was a real 'team spirit' with us! Remember how you sang 'There's a Lot of Us in Our Foursome,' Sasha? You don't remember. Well, I remember—some things you don't forget, buddy! And then just a year ago something scattered us! No, brothers, there are some things we just lose in the world of cash!" Having tossed up enough Komsomol exclamation points, Tikhomir stopped talking, as if by way of asking them to tell him what they'd come for. Real suffering could be read in his eyes.

"Listen, Tikh, Sasha needs money," Aram said.

"How much?" Burevyatnikov yelped. He opened a drawer of his desk, shook his head in some sort of strange gesture of condemnation, took up his checkbook, scribbled on a check, tore it out, and tossed it over to Korbach. "Fill in the amount yourself!" "You didn't understand me, Tikh," Alexander said. "I don't want a permanent loan. I just want to make money like Aram, like Gabriel Lianoza, and like I don't know what other guys in the garage."

"You're barking up the wrong tree, Sasha," Tikhomir said sadly. "You don't need to get involved in this business. They're interested in you, still monitoring you. No, Aram, old pal, we need to keep Sasha Korbach out of it, like the Decembrists did Pushkin. What do you need that sort of danger for, Sasha?"

Sasha suddenly had an inspiration and stood up. "Listen here, Tikh, I'm not Pushkin, and you, you're no nobleman—I'm just a joker, my dear man! There's a similarity in terms of the Semitic blood—he was part Ethiopian and I'm part Ashkenazi Jew—but even so, there's no need to protect me. Boys—Aram, Tikh, and you, the absent Butlerov—you know it's not greed that's pushing me into the chase for the green stuff but love! In my life, in the clouds above this country, a spectacle of ultimate inspiration is whirling around, and if I let it get away, then shame on me!"

"How beautifully he puts it!" Mr. Hornhoof exclaimed.

"Is that from some poem?" Ter-Aivazian inquired dryly.

Alexander definitely knew how to talk to Komsomol militants. Hornhoof stood up sharply and paced around his office, decked out with a silk-screened reproduction of a Van Gogh. "Somewhere in the larger scheme of things I understand you very well, Sasha!" He went over to the large window, through the blue-tinted glass of which, miles away, the California desert could be glimpsed. He stood for some time in silence, then stretched his whole body in one strong movement. All his joints cracked terribly, like the rapid fire of a platoon. "Oh, how I'd like to break through!" Burevyatnikov's voice moaned. "Break through all of these windows and fly, fly, fly!"

———————

That evening, with a hefty ill-gotten advance in his pocket, Alexander dropped in at the First Bottom. Here it is again before you, the relativity effect. So much had happened to him in the two months since the brawl, and here the same slow, boozy atmosphere still reigned. Everything stretched out into infinity, and time passed unnoticed. Boredom is the greediest devourer of minutes. Love is the strongest fighter for their prosperity.

He went in and immediately received a welcoming gesture from the play-by-ear pianist. He was still running his ten fingers up and down the keyboard and singing some plaintive song in a hoarse voice to Baby, just as he had been two months ago. Bernadetta was sitting at a corner of the bar this time, so that you could see her august profile, and, beneath a tower of swept-up hair, her perfectly sculpted ear was reminiscent of the ocean frigate of His Majesty King George sailing for the New World with good news. Matt Shuroff was sitting next to her, his muscles bulging more than ever—those on the left arm more than those on the right, however, thus introducing an element of imbalance into the staging. By contrast, the giant of the working class fit in well with the two political refugees: General Piu, whose hand, as usual, was hovering like a seagull over Bernadetta's hip, which resembled the sloping deck of a nuclear submarine; and Bruno Kastorzius, looking, as always, like a pile of scrap paper left out for recycling. The group was, as usual, completed by Mel O'Massey, who in his Saks Fifth Avenue suit seemed to embody a cool breeze and who as usual was sitting two feet from the others, as though he weren't with them at all, though everyone in the First Bottom knew perfectly well that the young specialist was only waiting, trembling slightly, for the incomparable building manager to turn to him. The five of them made up an ideal Pop Art composition, and at this quiet hour it could seem as though the folds of their clothing were saturated with sculptor's grease, which had the effect of uniting this mortal mob with eternity.

"Look who's here!" Rick the bartender announced, and his two assistants, Kit and Kif, applauded. "Lavsky, my little boy!" Bernadetta turned to A.Z. with the grace of a sea lion. "A double Stoly for our Lavsky!" The bartender set down a glass of the already rehabilitated Soviet rotgut in front of him. "I knew he'd come back!" The giant of the long-distance haulers was immediately all sweetness— he must not have had any rest from remorse these two months. Everyone moved, letting Lavsky come closer to Bernadetta's body, which was radiating love and friendship. Letting all of his emotion out, Mel O'Massey was slapping the prodigal on the back. General Piu was sensitivity personified. He gently stroked the area of Alexander's liver and even kissed him on the jaw. Bruno took something genuinely dear to himself—a whole hotdog with a generous garnishing of mustard and relish—out of his pocket. Handing this object to Lavsky was his way of demonstrating the solidarity of Eastern European anti-Communism. Everyone was happy: Lavsky's back!

Now I can see that they didn't want to kill me that night, they just wanted to teach that damned Russia a lesson, that's all. They wanted to hurt me, but not kill me, of course. Break my jaw and a couple of ribs, that's all. People have good hearts when you come right down to it. They can even make mistakes in choosing their targets.

Hugging him, Bernadetta called out: "Now don't you feel loved here, you young punk! Guys, our Lavsky's loved! His thing isn't reacting to my mammary glands! Admit it, Lavsky, you're all romantically screwed out!" Henry the pianist at that moment struck up a bravura rendition of Vivaldi's "Spring," in his own arrangement, naturally—that is to say, with yet another reference to Baby. Lavsky, otherwise known as Sasha Korbach, put three hundreds down on the bar and said that he was buying a drink for everyone who wanted one within the limits of that amount of money. "Listen, Lavsky," Matt said to him confidentially, almost in a whisper, "we've all been missing your Stanislavsky method here something awful."

Alexander, who, as they say, had already been brought around, began to demonstrate the technique of "reincarnation" to the whole group, and then to the whole bar. Let's take an easy one, say, President Reagan. You've got to catch his most important characteristic. Everyone knows that he used to be a movie actor, so he's always looking, even when he's not looking, in the direction of the movie camera. You know, almost like a Japanese actor who's always trying to figure out where the eyes of God are watching him from. Ronnie has a particular relationship with his god—that is, the camera. He's always concerned with whether or not he looks all right. He always wants to comb his hair, but alas, he can't always do it.

Comrade Brezhnev is another matter. Before me is a man who's always afraid lest something drop out of him. Look here, you drunken bastards, how I, Brezhnev, go to the podium to make a welcoming speech to the Leninist trade unions, while all the time I'm afraid that something's going to drop out of my trousers. Here you are chowtling, comwades, and yet it's a gweat human twagedy.

He went on playing roles to the general laughter of the First Bottom, and with each new wave of repulsive moisture he found new nuances in the reincarnation system. Give us Johnny Carson, the regulars roared. Meanwhile, Bernadetta was demanding that he remake himself as a woman. Well, certainly, sister! Before you, dear ladies (he actually said "bladies," but not even Kastorzius, the local Russian expert, caught this nuance) and gentlemen (he actually said "champignons," but the meaning of this refined touch escaped even him), before you is the embodiment of the archaeologically well-known "woman with a tail." Historically, this type was represented as an empress—you know what I'm talking about, you blockheads. He moved along majestically, hardly sticking out his backside and thrusting out his left breast, which, as many knew, drooped more than the right one. Then he threw himself on his back and set his tail, his mane, some sort of train of hair flowing down the empress's back from her head to her heels, in permanent motion. "I'm dying of jealousy," Matt Shuroff said, "but I still love that son of a bitch Lavsky." Bernadetta was howling with laughter. "Too bad that son of a bitch has a belly full of love. I'd reward him like a king today for that sort of work!"

It's a land of enormous possibilities, what can you say? No need ever to throw your hands up in despair. When you get up in the morning, look right away to see where fortune is smiling on you from. Yesterday you were as poor as a church mouse, and suddenly, just like that, you join a criminal gang and your pocket's bulging with bucks. That doesn't stop you from playing the bohemian artist for the woman you love, all the more since you're separated by three thousand miles, and the circles in which you move have about as much chance of intersecting as wolves have of meeting dolphins.

So, the forty-four-year-old A. Z. Korbach, former leader of a Moscow theater troupe, bard and all-around, if outrageous, actor, joined the none too small army of California drug dealers and stayed in it from November 1983, when he came back after his first transcontinental meeting, until November 1986, when, on the night shift, he handed a bag of cocaine to a long drink of water whose necktie was flapping in the wind like a magpie.

On the surface, everything looked fairly straightforward: he heard the password, handed over the goods, took the money, put it in a metal box under Mr. Tesfalidet's chair. His friends didn't let him in on any more than that, perhaps because they really were staying in line with the favorite Russian legend of how the Decembrists "protected" Pushkin. One way or another, though, twice a month, in addition to his usual paltry check from Colonial, he would receive an envelope with extra "dough," sometimes two thousand and sometimes three. Now it was no problem at all for him to fly to Washington for romantic meetings, which he did almost weekly. Nora quickly picked up on changes in Alex's behavior, and he stopped finding hundred-dollar bills that had just had happened to end up in his shoulder bag.

He got used to airplanes, and hardly anyone in United's friendly skies even noticed him anymore. One day, the head stewardess asked him if he wanted to join the frequent flier plan, which was new at the time. "Given your work, sir—that is, your commuting from coast to coast—you can easily accumulate enough miles for a free flight to an island in the Pacific or Australia." He was happily surprised; he never thought that this "job" would bring in any profit. The stewardess, though she didn't understand, chuckled. Among the ways of Americans is this pleasant trait—laughing at jokes they don't understand.

Time no longer seemed so slow on the flights—that is, it decided, in the underhanded way that it has with its customers, no longer to seem slow to him. Once he spent the whole five hours to Washington mumbling a dozen lines of poetry to himself. More often, however, he didn't mumble but only sat there filling up with more and more heat at the prospect of the tryst. The seat itself brought forth the first trickles of this heat. The flights were almost always late ones, and for him the atmosphere of the deserted airports merged with an almost forgotten feeling of Florentine romanticism. Here, then, ladies and gentlemen, if you're not fed up already, is another cursory little sketch of our seeker after the *dolce stil nuovo*. While his files in the "corresponding agency" in Moscow are filling with dispatches, while the KGB's writers look for places in their articles where they can aim yet another kick at the "sellout to the secret services of the West," the man in question is wandering in his elegant rags down an endless airport corridor, past already shut souvenir shops and still open but nearly empty snack bars, with their flickering screens on which the debates about the sex lives of the American people so characteristic of the eighties never come to an end; shuffling along with his carry-on bag, perhaps young, perhaps quite old, maybe American, maybe not very.

He insisted that Nora no longer meet him at the airport every time. She objected. You want to deprive me of one of my greatest pleasures, it means so much to me, that moment when you emerge from the faceless crowd as though you're being hatched from an egg; I see you and experience a feeling of immediate surrender—you know what I mean. But he persisted. What do you want to drag yourself to the airport every time for? Sit at home in your chair with your Campari and Haydn and wait until I show up. There was something masochistic about this insistence. Sometimes it seemed to him that he was hoping to catch her cheating. Of course he understood that she loved him, and more and more as their relationship grew closer and deeper. Subconsciously, however, he couldn't imagine that a woman like Nora could go through a single day without becoming the target of male aggression. I know, I know, but her sensitivity was already well-known to him, and he could easily imagine her "immediate surrenders" in a crowd of greedy . . . if not apes, then Cro-Magnons, all these Washington singles—lawyers, pols, military types, spies, and diplomats. Everyone knows that despite its surplus of women over men, the District of Columbia suffers from a shortage of attractive females—in such conditions, then, Mrs. Mansour—a woman without prejudices, possessed of a remarkable gift for arousing magical heat in the testicles of a man even at long range—will be the dream of the whole city.

At the beginning of 1984, he finally moved out of the Hotel Cadillac, was seen off with warm kisses from the girls of the Jewish Senior Citizens in residence and with slaps on the back from the guys who were pushing ninety and who sat on the porch of the fleabag day in, day out, discussing the fluctuations of the stock market. Bernadetta and Mel O'Massey, who by that time had become one of the most influential leaders in the real estate business in Santa Monica and Venice, found him a first-class studio next to Marina del Rey. The right sort of place for our Lavsky, all the regulars of the First Bottom agreed. He'll be able to jerk himself off with his Stanislavsky method here to his heart's content.

The spacious deck of the apartment overlooked the promenade, beyond which, as it did everywhere along this stretch, extended a beach two football fields wide. Farther on could be seen a considerably wider area, which enveloped half the globe with its watery turmoil, created by the Lord for some reason that was entirely unknown, if it wasn't for constant enjoyment.

Alexander couldn't get used to the new place. Every time he crossed the threshold and saw the silver or purple of the ocean outside the huge window, he thought: An idiot's dream has come true, you finally live the way that people with their eternal Soviet head colds imagine life abroad. How simple everything seems—all you've got to do is join the mafia, and life turns its rosy side to you; a load of sea ozone sweeps in and blows the miasmas out of your gloomy subconscious; man is born for happiness as a bird for flight (Was that Gorky? Sholokhov?), as a shark for swimming, as a dragon for breathing fire. Theoretically, the same thing had been offered him in Russia, when Comrade Sitny and his generals had advised him over vodka and smoked salmon to turn up the patriotic volume of the Buffoons, to strengthen our uniquely Russian element, to strike a blow at the class enemies of the Great Russians—the merchants, the priests, the landowners. The principle was the same: just be a member of the gang and everything will be fine.

Nowadays in this country, though, there is an alternative to the totalitarian monster, a band of merry swindlers. It doesn't look like there's any way for a man to extricate himself from the shit without some sort of con as an alternative. Open these sliding glass doors and breathe: this is your place now.

In addition to the main room of the studio, there was a so-called loft, with a small spiral staircase leading to it. He rigged up his bed there, just beneath the skylight. A seagull with a domino pattern on its tail feathers often perched on this window. He was sure that it was the same one: the creature had obviously gotten used to Korbach and had followed him in his move.

Looking down from the loft, or from what in Russia they would have called an *entresol,* he never ceased to be surprised by how much living space he had. This place is just the right size for a theater with a dozen seats. You could make the stage deeper at the expense of the terrace. So far, he'd bought an umbrella with the

Stolichnaya logo for the deck. Another six months of criminal activity and he'd have enough for a piano, and then keyboards with electronic programming, on which he could write the musical accompaniment for his show "The Drug Bust." Life, as always, helps art along. It would have been easy for the police to search the studio: the corners weren't full of junk. The seaside studio of a major artist ought to be filled with the karma of the ocean. All the same, I should keep a suitcase packed in case I'm arrested. I wonder if Zakhar Korbach had a case like that stashed away? The idea of running away, of course, would never have come into his head—how do you run from the "organs" at home?—but he must have been ready to be picked up, like any Soviet man in those years.

Until then, though, he'd just have to enjoy his new life, and he enjoyed it. He even cut down on his visits to the First Bottom. He sat for hours on the deck, following the aimless movements of the yachts. For some reason, large ships never came into view, but jumbo jets bound for Japan, Hong Kong, and Sydney would rise mightily and evaporate in the skies. Beneath the terrace, a two-directional stream of tourists gurgled along regularly. Sometimes the gurgling sent up a fountain of laughter. Baroque music was always wafting lazily from a small CD player at his feet. These harpsichords, violins, and violas of Vivaldi, these dramatic surges of his—as though he regularly began to flutter in a gust of something penetrating and elusive, as though someone in a Venetian cocked hat would come in, holding a mask at a distance and announcing: Things won't be this way forever, they'll be different! How had the century managed to survive without Vivaldi? What sort of stupid rhetoric is this, Korbach? Ezra Pound introduced Vivaldi to the twentieth century and then became Mussolini's radio announcer.

I must have a talk with Nora about ancient music. What did they find in their excavations, what sorts of instruments? Did the Greeks and Romans have musical notation? With such a colossal network of theaters they must have had professional musicians. If I ever put on "The Radiance of Beatrice" in the theater—even better, as a film—the subject of the music of the ancients will come up. The classical poets were the forerunners of the troubadours, and they stand out colossally in the culture of the ancient world. After a millennium of decay, they were reborn anyway!

Let's imagine a scene like this: Cavalcanti, Dante, and da Pistoia are sitting around a cask of wine. Some youth will show up, say, the young Giotto. He's brought an extraordinary copper flute, which he unearthed in the ruins of the ancient forum at Fiesole. This is a flute of the ancients, says Guido. Alas, we'll never know what sort of music they played. Dante tries the instrument, which has been cleaned with vitriol—some sort of wheezing comes out, a few squawks, and suddenly he begins to play a Miles Davis concert.

And now Alexander caught himself, for the first time since his emigration, thinking about "The Radiance of Beatrice," and thinking "creatively" for the first time at all. This "ocean studio" was obviously having a good effect on him. He felt so sound in his new place that he even let the weekly flight to Washington go by. When he realized it, he shuddered with jealousy. No doubt about it, his absence would be compensated for by someone's presence. He rushed to his loft and picked up the phone: he had his own phone now, of course, and no longer had to hang around on the beach with a bag full of quarters. "Don't worry about it," said her voice, so soft, so kind. "You can't fly every week. Of course you've got a lot to do in your wicked Venice. Now it's my turn to arrive without warning."

Having said that, she was suddenly afraid that she had given her own jealousy away, and tried to cover it up with carefree laughter. The thought that she too might be jealous had never occurred to him. "Do you love me, babe?" "More than ever!" she whispered. Her voice alone drove him out of his mind. "Can I undo the buttons?" "Please, undo them." "What are you doing now, my love?" "For a start I'm putting up a light Atlantic breeze to calm down the Pacific pirate in his red hat." "And what's next, kitten?" "You know what's next." "No, tell me!" She told him and, panting slightly, told him to say something too, with language as close to that of Soviet barracks as possible. He didn't have to be asked twice, after which all of the smut vanished into thin air, giving way to just disordered romantic mutterings on both ends of the satellite connection. "I-love-you-baby-I-love-you-so-much-so-so-so-much-much-much-babe-babe-babe-love-love-love. . . ." That time, then, was playing its usual game with the human race—that is, the jumping of moments from the future into the past—was unknown to them, since passion had become synonymous with the present for them. "What are you doing with me now, Artemis?" he finally howled. She came right back with "I'm just trying to pussify your ironclad battering ram, Hermes!" Then both lovers began letting out wails that could have disturbed the grandeur of all the objects orbiting the Earth at that moment. "Phew, wow," Nora whispered after the explosion and put the phone down. "I can just imagine the bill from Pacific Bell," the becalmed A.Z. murmured, and fell asleep.

When they next met in Washington, Nora asked him, her eyes averted: "Don't you have the feeling that we committed some sort of outrage against time and space?" He reasoned with her gently: "Leave time alone, it doesn't give a damn about us. As for space, well, maybe it really was degraded."

5

NORA'S FLIGHT

A few more weeks passed in the usual rhythm of meetings and partings. Sometimes Alexander would fly in on days when she wasn't teaching and would roam in the vicinity of her building, pretending that he was just out for a walk, not even admitting to himself that he was spying. He saw Omar Mansour hurry from the building one day dragging a suitcase behind him. The youngster jumped into a limousine, the case landed in the trunk with a thud, and they took off immediately.

Alexander watched the entrance driveway from his rented Ford on the other side of the street for an hour. Now comes the unmasking. The husband is off on a business trip, the lover is three thousand miles away, now comes the third man. He couldn't get this hateful nonsense out of his head. After exactly an hour a yuppie in a Jaguar drove up and walked through the doorway without taking his mouth or his ear away from his mobile phone. Now I'll catch her, unless, of course, the doorman gets in the way. Doormen, those bastards, minions to rich scum, they're always trying to put you off your stroke, to cover up whoring with a screen of respectability. They don't always succeed, of course—no, not all the time. He found Nora all by herself, her table piled high with books, her computer switched on, her favorite dragonfly spectacles on her nose.

"How come he's started coming in the middle of the week?" She scanned the face of her beloved intently and caught a sign of something dishonest. Just so he doesn't start spinning some yarn about the theater business: everyone in the family knows about Colonial Parking. Where does he get the money for these flights? Maybe Stanley's giving it to him? After all, they're friends, they're always corresponding about the Korbachs' rotten roots and their lousy branches. So why has he started coming in the middle of the week? Maybe he's got some chick out there who it's more convenient to see on the weekends? What, can't other chicks feel the incredible sex drive in him? Why should I think these bitches he meets at "readings" and on "drives," no matter how mythical they may be, will have any consideration for the fact that he belongs to another woman? How can I suppose that he doesn't get visits from all sorts of nymphs and nymphettes, goddesses and heroines from their Russian literature that manages to be straitlaced and mind-bogglingly decadent at the same time? Could I really have forgotten that in that fucking Venice all he has to do is whistle from the balcony, and—*voilà!*—any of those disgusting "reincarnations" is in his bed! If I see one of those whores between his sheets, I'll kill her on the spot—bang! bang! bang! I still remember the Trotskyite training camp in Ochichornia! My God, what idiotic thoughts go through your head!

On one of the days filled with such thoughts, she raced to the airport and caught a plane coming through Washington from Geneva and heading for L.A. Naturally, she tried to fool herself: I need to get away from the college routine for three days, she told herself, and to see my mother, and to see with my own eyes how Sasha lives, have a serious chat with him, and make him finally understand that love isn't just about screwing. She's no Beatrice, of course, yet all these illuminations, radiances, and flashes of lightning that motivated art were not entirely unknown to her, either. If he thinks that archaeology has no poetry, no theater, then he's just an ass. This was what she kept telling herself, and all the while the jealous monster was perched on the wing of the aircraft and staring her in the face with an unblinking yellow eye. A trap was lying in wait for her: love and jealousy, aren't they sisters, after all? Aren't they Siamese twins that suffocate each other in their meaningless interweavings?

In Los Angeles she occupied herself with running about her mother's house and socializing with the "circle of friends"—among whom that day was Marlon Brando, sitting there like a Chinese idol—and swimming in the pool as well, whiling away the time until nightfall. Do you know the California night? she thought nervously in some strange Russian vein. No, you don't know the California night! Once that night used to blaze all around, and I would dance in it like a salamander; now everything inside was burning her without even having caught fire yet.

We'll wear all black things from the old supplies. I haven't gone fat at all! Don't spare the makeup! Hat angled to one side, bag over the shoulder, we'll toss one of Mom's many revolvers in the bag—Rita O'Neill, honored member of the NRA!—just for fun, of course, nothing serious, not really to kill some fat-assed Brünhilde. Just for fun, for a little date with her bald little boy; a teensy-weensy pistol in her teensy-weensy bag.

She drove up to the promenade around 1:00 A.M. This damned Venice still wasn't asleep. Rollerbladers were circling on an asphalt lake in the middle of the sand. Standing out among them was a hefty woman with a tail billowing like that of Bucephalus, and with arms that had obviously been borrowed from the Venus de Milo. Behind her, keeping up the pace and copying all of her movements, rolled four men of different heights and builds, including a tiny Vietnamese with whiskers like a mouse. Well now, Maestro Korbach, it looks like you've got quite a nice troupe here.

Here's his apartment block. Three stories with glass-sided terraces and sun-decks open to the sea. The building was shrouded in darkness. That means they've already turned out the light and they're going in for love acrobatics by moonlight. For some reason, in her mind's eye she kept seeing that same healthy-looking Rollerblader, who could still be seen in the distance with her suite of followers, as Sasha's partner. A solidly built kid in a sleeveless T-shirt came up to the door. A blond fuzz on his shoulders. He glanced at Nora, standing beneath a streetlight in her melodramatic outfit. "Want to come up to my place, babe?" "I need to go to Number Eight," she muttered. "My key's bent, it won't go in the lock." "That's tough when it won't go in." The kid nodded and held the door open. "Go on in! You don't want to come to my place, go see anyone you want."

This loser will be an unknowing accessory to a crime. When they pick me up, I'll tell the cops right away who let me in, Mr. Blond Shoulders! She went up the stairs to Number 8. She hit her knee against the door slightly, and it opened. This building is simply forcing me to commit a murder out of jealousy! The two-tiered room was filled with moonlight. The glass door to the deck was open. Shrieks rising from the "skating rink" and the muffled splashing of the surf could be heard. A television was blazing silently in one corner. Artificial sex organs were on the screen. Surely he's sleeping already, holding someone in his arms in the same way, sleeping sweetly like he does with me après? She took off her shoes and noiselessly climbed up to the loft. There was a large bed there, or more accurately a king-size mattress, innocently covered with clean sheets. A big Russian book lay beside the lamp, two pairs of glasses, my love, on the floor a small tape recorder and three cassettes: Vivaldi, J. S. Bach, and "Pulcinella" by Stravinsky, or Stravi as he calls him. Oh, my love, the very picture of purity and intellectualism!

But where's he gallivanting at this time of night? He could be just about anywhere—maybe he's sitting in a jazz café or doing the night shift at his parking garage, or maybe he's at one of those mythical theaters. I'll wait for him here. We'll see what time he drags himself in. And with whom. I'd just like to know: when and with whom? There won't be any dramatics, just a surprise. And I'll throw this teensy-weensy revolver in the sand somewhere across the promenade. I'll take the bullets out now, just to be sure that some guy with a snootful doesn't blow his own head off. Or from jealousy. A wild feeling, old girl, a wild feeling. You used to think that it was like fire or the music of Bizet, and now, having experienced it yourself, you see that if fire it is, then it's the fire of darkness. Don't expect any apotheosis from it. A black, greasy oil is burning, clinging to everything and destroying.

With these thoughts running through her mind, Nora took a step out onto the balcony and immediately saw Korbach, Alexander Zakharovich, lying there on a chaise longue. The fringe of the blinds had hidden him from view until that step, and now he appeared before her, skinny legs, proletarian belly, and all. And with a look of simian suffering on his face. And also with a spot of moonlight on his forehead shining like the roof of a car. Having spotted her, he shuddered, his head slipping past the upper edge of the chaise longue and bobbing backward. Forgetting about her own sufferings, she rushed to him. Everything became clear in an instant. He'd been sitting here all alone and thinking about her, because there was no one else that he could think about at this hour. He was thinking: Can she really be lying beside someone right now, and is she really putting her head on someone's chest the way she puts it on mine, with the same trust, with the same gratitude for the pleasure? They weren't even thoughts, just a slow convulsion of every cell in his body. And suddenly this convulsion materialized in the form of her body emerging from the darkened room into the moonlight. As though he had given birth to his own convulsion.

"You can rest easy now, you little fool," he whispered, hugging her and shaking all over. Little fool. *Idiotka,* in Russian. Idiot-*ka*. These Russian suffixes are equipped with the ability to sometimes change the structure of a word to the point where it's unrecognizable. The glowering idiot of jealousy with its bloody intentions in its handbag is transformed into an easygoing scatterbrain, as lovestruck as a cat. Scatterbrain—*sumasbrod. Sumasbrod-ka.* As they were stretching out together on the chaise longue, and, after its collapse, rolling together along the floorboards of the sundeck, he explained to her the meaning of another word, made up of a noun, a verb, and two particles: out-of-mind-ka, that is, more or less the same: *idiotka.*

After that night, a great deal changed in their relationship. They realized that their love was threatened, and that the threat grew out of love itself. If we suppose that the thirst for love means one half looking for the other in the infinite chaos of souls and bodies in order to unite in some pre-Adam-Eve wholeness, then the case of Alex and Nora might be something approaching that ideal, along the lines of Samson the Israelite and Delilah the Philistine woman. Or of any love, alas, where betrayal is lurking nearby, and the proffered biblical example is no exception. For Alex and Nora, jealousy was synonymous with betrayal, now advancing toward, now retreating from them like the army of the Philistines, whirlwinds of chaos.

So let's get out our own sort of vacuum cleaner against jealousy, okay? Let's confess everything to each other, and the more often the better. "Let me go first—I confess that since we met I haven't slept with anyone else." "And I haven't slept with anyone," he said. "And I can't even think about anyone else anymore." "And I can't even look at another woman." Both were just the tiniest bit—it was absolutely trivial—insincere in their confessions, since both of them had had to round out previous relationships one way or another. It was as though they were tacitly trying to lower the temperature of their love, and at other times to lead the huge, overly demonic passions to the bucolic pastures of friendship, mutual attachment, and concern about the circumstances of each other's lives, all lightly peppered with a bit of what the French call *les amis comme cochons*.

One day, Nora revealed to Alex her "little secret," which sent him into a state of shock. It turned out that she had managed to visit Moscow for three days, that she had met his mother in secret, and had also made the acquaintance of many of his friends, among whom were quite a few more or less attractive women; you slept with them at one time or another—"Admit it! Admit it, you priapic monster! All of these people expressed their love for you and their enormous respect for your talent. The Buffoons were broken up after all, but they get together here and there for underground shows, in apartments or abandoned warehouses—once even in a morgue where one of them works as a security guard. I listened to a pile of cassettes of your songs, and they even made me cry, like some teary old American slut. They showed me films—of terrible quality, they were—of two of your shows, *Spartak-Dynamo* and *The Telephone Book*. World-beating stuff! I was bursting with pride at the idea that such a genius chose me as his faithful concubine. In short, Uncle Sasha, I learned as much about Comrade Korbach in three days as I could have pulled out of you with tongs in three years. Besides all that, I managed to bring out a manuscript of *Philosophy of the Common Cause*—can you imagine? Now I'm getting ready to hire a Russian writer, some guy named Vassily who lives in Georgetown, to do a line-by-line translation for an American publisher."

After that day, everything was different. Nora had decided to look after her lover. The fugitive Danny Barthelme and the Lebanese tycoon Omar Mansour might be able to tell stories about similar periods in their relationships with this woman, but they'd just have to be content with the subjunctive mood; nobody's asking them to tell their stories. Now Nora was crossing the country first-class on weekends, and from the airport rushed not to Beverly Hills but to Venice, which was closer. If things had gone like this earlier, I wouldn't have had to join the gang, our drug dealer thought from time to time. He had not yet revealed this secret to his solicitous sweetheart. Have to leave at least something for the future. It'll be better if she learns about these dirty little dealings after I'm in jail.

The reader may already have noticed that we're trying not to play on his nerves with the aid of cheap silences, yet we have to point out that not all of Nora's secrets had been revealed yet, even in this "period of trust." This isn't because we want to whet the reader's curiosity, not at all; rather, it's simply in accordance with the rules of composition, and Nora knows it perfectly well. It sometimes works out that composition is more important than a clear conscience, but what can you do? If anyone doesn't understand that, let him not read novels.

At the moment, the rules of composition allow us to reveal one of Nora's little secrets, the existence of which she could not bring herself to admit to her lover. The fact was that the time for her purely academic activities was running out, and the time for what archaeologists call the field was approaching. In a few months, Sasha would have to approximately quintuple his flying distances in order to reach his trembling beloved.

In the meantime, she was reorganizing his studio, buying sound and video equipment, filling the refrigerator, throwing out bottles of cheap booze, and lecturing him about the civilized consumption of fine wines that lead not to marasmus but to an ennobling of the taste, as though she herself had never rolled in the gutters of Beirut and Old Jaffa.

6

BUBBLES OF THE EARTH

*O*n one of her trips she decided: Sasha has got to meet Mom, at last. Well, Sashka, we're going to go and see Ritka! Without having learned Russian yet, she had already acquired a feeling for *-ka,* that strange addition to the root of a word. Norka to take Sashka to Ritka. *Kak tak, kak a cock, s'il vous plaît!* She couldn't get up the nerve to invite him home to meet Mom: she'll think that I want to get him into the "circles." A foolish, un-American pride was tormenting her darling, yet she did in fact want to get him into the "circles." It would be enough for Rita O'Neill to make a call to anyone in the "circles," and they could sign a contract with him for a screenplay, and then, you'll see, they'll ask him to put a film together. If only he could shake off his complexes!

Listen, do you want to go over and visit with some of my school friends tonight? There won't be any fat cats there at all, just my unpretentious gang, some beach volleyball fanatics. What should you wear? Don't make fun of me, Sasha! We'll go as we are, you in your sport coat, to which you're indebted for making me fall in love with you at first sight. "An unperishable commodity," Alexander said, and they were off.

Nora hadn't lied, her school friends really were beach volleyball fanatics. She had simply neglected to mention that since graduation sixteen years earlier Jeff Crappivva had made a brilliant career for himself in those very same circles that one of the parking garage attendants in Westwood Village had so much contempt for. Following in the footsteps of his father, an influential producer, he had outdone the old man by far. In the early eighties he had managed to raise a record budget on the order of $50 million for a sci-fi disaster film, as a result of which California became its own planet in the solar system. The film was a complete flop, and Hollywood suffered catastrophic losses. The young Crappivva, however, gained an unshakable reputation as the man who had raised a record budget.

In the gathering dusk, they drove up to a beach house in Malibu. Alexander noticed neither the group of liveried chauffeurs standing beside the Rolls-Royces, nor the beefy bodyguards, nor the people of his own profession, valet parkers, scampering around in purple vests. Setting his chin in an independent posture, he strode behind Nora's silk dress, which was reminiscent of a flowering garden in a high wind. The doors opened, and cries of "Nora! Nora Korbach! As young as ever!" went up.

It was then that he saw that behind the modest facade was, as they say, a world of wondrous plenty. It's not quite clear where you've landed, in a residence or in the Academy of Science's greenhouse, inside or outside. The guests were standing beneath sturdy-looking palm trees, yet here and there among the palms hung a chandelier. A little hill crowned with an abstract sculpture showed the planner's touch; alongside, however, semi- and surreal pictures were displayed on entirely real walls. Grapefruits and sweet lemons were hanging on branches, and some of the guests were picking and eating them. Moving a bit farther down the main path, you nearly stumbled over an extraordinary bubbling reservoir, which seemed to promise the presence of a crocodile, though several laughing faces were looking out of it, a hirsute chest rocked back and forth pompously, and a hand holding a bottle of champagne protruded. As a backdrop to this panorama, a foamy barrier of ocean surf was stirring; here it had been put directly at man's service.

I've fallen into a trap, thought Alexander Zakharovich, while Nora was glad-handing with her school friends. That broad, that spoiled child, dragged me into a trap. Should I get out of here now, just dump the twit? The backs of the heads of the humming crowd looked to him like a gathering of Persians at the walls of Jerusalem. Finally Nora came up to him with the owners of the house. A quite young couple, but of course ten years older than their classmate. The guy really did look like a beach volleyball fanatic: a haircut like that of Karch Kiraly, hero of the recent Olympic games, and dressed in the quintessential California style—tennis shirt, faded jeans, and the very sneakers that I always want to find but somehow never do. The girl was a bit on the plump side for volleyball, but it suited her. Black T-shirt with a nuclear disarmament symbol, a string of beads around her neck, shorts, white cowboy boots with turquoise inlays—fine handwork, each boot was unique, a separate artistic creation. "Guys, this is my boyfriend, Sasha," Nora said, beaming. Cringing, he was expecting the ad campaign to begin at any moment: genius, great director, suffered under a tyranny. It was managed without any show or flash, however: "He's Russian," Nora said by way of completing her introduction. Jeff and Beverly, who were clearly no standouts in terms of arrogance, shook the Russian's hand. "I was in your girlfriend's class at school, Alex. Gramercy School, what a madcaps' refuge. Your girlfriend looks younger than all of us now, and she looked older than all of us then—funny, isn't it?" Have to make a joke, got to say something funny at this point. "Anyway, I was already playing teacher in those days, but now I only study." They didn't understand the joke, and neither did he, but everyone laughed. "Sasha, please, don't reveal our secrets." "What do you think, Sasha, will Gorbachev get far?" "You for that crack pay," Nora said to Alex. She obviously wanted to flaunt her Russian. "And you'll pay for this entire evening," her uncle replied. "What's the matter?" She pretended not to notice Superman and Superwoman making their way through the palm trees, a couple of James Bonds and the French Lieutenant's Woman, Catwoman and E.T., as well as several miragelike figures; standing out among them by virtue of his rippling muscles and lovely Teutonic smile was America's new hero Schwarzenegger, whose name yields a euphonious Russian translation: Chernochernov, i.e., Blackblackovich.

Jeff Crappivva was distinguished by an extremely quiet, intelligent voice. With that voice he beats megabudgets out of the Hollywood bigwigs! And with this voice he was seriously asking about Gorbachev's prospects. Where will he go? "To China," our hero responded immediately. "How do you mean that?" the surprised host asked. "America's too strong for him, so he'll come down on China." "Where did you learn such great English, Alex?" asked Crappivva. "From Nora," A.Z. said, now with almost no levity. With her elbow, she nudged him with a gentleness that forgives everything; it was her tender palm. What's with the three martinis in a row, sweetheart? Is that supposed to be forbidden, honey? While you can still walk a straight line, come and meet my mom.

It's for the birds, Hemingway was supposed to have said after seeing his film with Ingrid Bergman, and went away to have a few more. Postwar blues. Astral salt, lunar eggs. On the lemon-grapefruit path stood Rita O'Neill and Gregory Peck, cocktails in hand. Objectively speaking, the path ended at the washroom, from which men were emerging in a steady stream, but that detail can easily be left out. Nora brought Alexander up to the living legends. Mom, this is the man that I was telling you about. The man about whom she had been speaking was delighted to the point of trembling. Gregory Peck was old and handsome. Rita, though sixty, in the dim moonlight of the lemon tree path (leading to what—the toilet, or a scene from the unforgettable *Hawks of Gibraltar*?) looked as young as ever, and touching, of course—simply a wonder of wonders: svelte and wearing a décolleté gown.

Before Nora and "the man" arrived, Rita and Gregory had been discussing an offer that she had just received from Paramount, the role of an old nun in a convent in a Poland rife with the struggle against Communism. She intended to turn it down. "I can't play an old mother superior, Greg!" Peck, as one of her "circle of friends," was trying to persuade her to accept the offer. "You'll look irresistible in a habit, darling! Just tell them that they have to rewrite the screenplay a little. There's a place there for a powerful scene between you and a general of the KGB. They loved each other twenty years before, do you see? A few well-placed flashbacks of you looking young and in love. It'll be the return of the great Rita O'Neill!"

She extended her hand to this strange lover of her baby Nora. Kissing hands had long been out of fashion, but he did it anyway—these Russians! "Greg, this is Nora's friend. He was a great artist in Moscow." "Are you Jewish?" Peck asked, and, after getting some incomprehensible answer to this simple yet important question, immediately evaporated in the moonlight as he had done a thousand times in his brilliant screen career. "I see that you're really in love, kids," said Rita with undisguised phoniness by way of a beginning to her "wisdom of your elders" étude. As though replacing the withered old Peck, a fleshy, freckled man seized her in a manly embrace. "Oh Rita, how wonderful to see you, my dear! You look like you've joined the company of the gods, an eternally youthful Eos!" Shaking his sides and buttocks, he filled in the space between the film star and her interlocutors on his own. Who's that, then? Alex silently asked Nora. The latter shrugged.

"Listen, Nigel, as a poet it ought to be interesting for you to meet Alex—he's a poet from Moscow," she said in a nasal twang, as though she were acting in a satirical antibourgeois play on a Muscovite stage. "Don't worry, Nigel, he has pretty decent English."

"I'm afraid that my English, ha-ha, isn't very decent," he said, cuddling up to the diminutive Rita like an overgrown, pampered cat and paying no attention to the others, yet still extending a hand to one side to greet his fellow poet. Alexander didn't take it. "And what does this asshole write?" he asked Nora in Russian. "No one knows what he writes, but he's a poet laureate," she answered, and shook the poet's hand in place of Alex. Satisfied, the poet's hand retracted into the depths of his body. "Well, I'm off, girls," Alex said, and started to go. Nora held him back. "Where are you off to?" "To observe the morals of this collective farm," he replied, lurching to one side as though falling out of a boat.

Out of everything that was going on here, and out of all those present, his beloved seemed to him the most perfect embodiment of *mauvaise foi* of all. She walks around here with a condescending smile for this mob stuffing its multiple faces, an apostate who has attained the heights of archaeology, eyeing everything with an academic smirk that no one in this ignorant fraternity will even know how to read, and at the same time clumsily tries to introduce her lover, this thick-lipped ape with the bald dome as though he'd been put together in a Hollywood makeup room, when she's actually ashamed that he's Russian, so that she has to introduce him in a crowd where everyone's famous. Building up more and more bile for Nora and thinking up more and more rubbish where she was concerned, he made his way through the crowd that grew more densely packed the closer he got to where the food was. Several times he nearly took a header into a bubbling Jacuzzi; either he didn't know where the hell he was going, or there were a lot more than one of them here (what's the grammatical gender of *Jacuzzi* in Russian, anyway?). Along the way he snatched martinis and glasses of champagne from trays floating past and got thoroughly drunk.

"You know, I liked your Russian Korbach," Rita O'Neill said to her daughter. "He's one of us, an artist. Vain, just like me." Nora worriedly watched Alexander walking away. "I'm afraid that he's going to make a scene here tonight." Rita smiled. "So what?"

Suddenly Alexander spotted the only worthwhile person in this crowd. Cassidy Reynolds! This broad-jawed square-shooter character had got himself noticed in the Dom Kino, the national film society of Moscow, way back in the sixties. The connoisseurs immediately set him apart from the crowd of shoot-from-the-hip cowboys. Just look at how he walks, Cassidy Reynolds! How he looks, how he keeps his mouth shut, that Cassidy Reynolds! Too bad I haven't got a Cassidy Reynolds for the leading role, young directors of the "new wave" like Tarkovsky and Konchalovksy said to each other. When they chose someone for a screen test, they usually explained: as close to Cassidy Reynolds as possible.

Sasha Korbach looked at this guy from three feet away. Hollywood still hasn't come up with a decent screenplay for him. They still haven't come up with a decent director, either! He still hasn't played his greatest role, and it doesn't look like he ever will. . . . Cassidy Reynolds! This guy had for some reason seemed like the embodiment of the masculine ideal for the Soviet and Polish filmmakers of the sixties generation. I'll never forgive myself if I don't have a word with him.

"Hey, Cassidy, my name's Sasha Korbach—how's it going?"

Reynolds, with sagging jowls, stomach, and kidneys in a permanent tremor, foggily saw in front of him a stranger with a glass of something desperately desired but forbidden. His face, well-known in Eastern European circles, had long ago turned into that of a retired geisha; of his famous walk there was not much left but a drooping backside, which he tried to drag along with dignity, like a Japanese war criminal signing the capitulation papers on the deck of the battleship *Missouri.* "Go, go," he forced out of himself and gestured with an index finger over his own back: Get lost, stranger!

"Listen here, you jerk," Korbach said sincerely. "You think I'm bugging you because you're *kak* a celebrity, but I'm bugging you because you're a mirage from my youth, okay? Our whole 'new wave' in Moscow used to idolize you: Vysotsky and Tarkovsky both—that's how, *kak,* it was!" Reynolds had never heard of any new wave, and the names of Vysotsky and Tarkovsky ran through his addled head like the humming of tires on the road. The only thing that stuck was the oft-repeated word *kak,* which means "so" or "how" in Russian. "You're a cock yourself," he mumbled to the stranger. Well, fuck you, too, Korbach thought, and exhaled loudly. One more ghost has ridden off to Marlboro country! If you're such a goddamned mess, what're you doing hanging around at parties, Cassidy? You ought to sit at home, sucking down TV.

Making his way around the idol of his youth, Alex found himself again on the brink of the bubbling tub. Suddenly amazement almost knocked him off his feet. Avreli, a well-known Muscovite, the creator of the multiseason series *Altai, My*

Altai, the winner of the Lenin Komsomol prize, was climbing out of the Jacuzzi. Stretching, he held his arms out for some time, as if offering the crowd the chance to admire the broad sweep of his shoulders, and the Orthodox cross the size of a man's hand on his hairy chest. A laughing mouth beamed out of his curly beard, a pair of gold crowns representing the solid reserves of the USSR. A sudden shift, and Avreli jumped out of the Jacuzzi in a spray. Sashka! He rushed to him in delight, not even shaking off the spermatozoa and Tampax smears that had clung to him in the hot tub. An embrace—since when do Soviets rush to give warm hugs to "enemies of the people"? "Sashka Korbach, well blow me down, what're you doing here? What a *cucaracha*! It rhymes in Russian, you know: *vstrecha*—meeting—*cucaracha*! So how are you, how are you? You are *kak* yourself? Just a minute, let me put my pants on!" "Go ahead, I can wait." He got into his Versace trousers and pulled on a Gucci jacket over his naked torso. "At least tuck the cross in, Avreli, you blockhead!" "Hey, Sasha, I see you're behind the times!" "What times am I behind?" "From the new spirit." "Let's drink to this meeting, there aren't enough of us, we can be two, remember?" "No, no, there are more of you, a lot more."

Avreli led Korbach to the buffet. On the way, he fondled the bottoms of some women, demonstrating the Soviet libido, as ever-wakeful as the KGB! The wet spot on his jacket between the shoulder blades was reminiscent of the Island of Crimea. "A lobster-tail for you and a lobster-tail for me. Take another one! Take three lobster-tails at once! Did you see that bottle I snagged? It's Stoly—it beats the whole world. So what? So stick it in your mouth! This Crappivva, he's a multimillionaire, fuck his soup! Let's have a drink, to our generation, to the new freedom, fuck it by its udders!" "So then, Avreli, you punk, freedom to you is a cow?" "Yes, it's a cow!" "You're lying, you fucked-up motherfucker, freedom is a winged creature, it's the *dolce stil nuovo*—so let's drink to that!"

When the emotion of the moment had subsided a bit, Avreli slurred out his story. He was now in Los Angeles to stay. Anyone who thought he was a defector, though, was dead wrong. He's living here as a free man, period. The wind is blowing in a new direction now. He's got a woman here, that's all. A volcanic woman, rich and crazy, like Croesus. She sells her designer crap on Rodeo Drive, got it? He picked up a pneumatic brunette in a bikini trimmed with fox fur. "Sasha, you're such a genius, if you knew how much our generation loves you! How did you manage to survive, to avoid the Soviet bullet, the poisoned chalice, jail, the asylum? Let me whisper something in your ear." "Beg your pardon, sir, my ear isn't an hors d'oeuvre." "Sorry, but I'm not chewing on your ear, I'm talking into it." "So repeat what you said, then, but without the touching bit, okay, goddamn it." "You've turned strange, somehow, Sasha, you're not one of ours—but listen to me anyway. There's been a secret decision to have done with it." "What do you mean—have done with what?" "The historic experiment. It didn't work. It's been decided to take a new direction, to save what's still left, got it? Responsibility for carrying out the plan has been given to the KGB and the Komsomol. Gorbachev has secretly met with Reagan and the Pope to inform them. Apologized for the attempts on their lives. Said that the guilty parties would pay. What it boils down to, *starik*, is that the USSR will soon cease to exist. Are you chewing on that? Taking it all in?"

A.Z.'s head was spinning. As luck would have it, a palm tree was growing beside the buffet. He grabbed it and began trying to slither down it. Avreli continued to drone in his ear without touching it. "Don't get all grief-stricken, *starik*. The USSR will crumble and Russia will pull itself out, that's the kind of horse it is." "But I am grieving," Korbach panted. "I spent my whole life in the sinister USSR—what have I got to be glad about? Avreli, prizewinner, without the dirty Soviet motherland, I can't . . . I'm dying."

Nora found him lying beneath a palm tree. His chin was twitching. Avreli was heatedly explaining something to the guests who had gathered around. One of them, a recently empowered movie broker, observed the dying man with interest. That guy has exactly the same sport coat I had three years ago. Suzanne gave it away to some secondhand rag shop.

The remainder of the evening and part of the night Sasha and Nora spent in the First Bottom, sitting on a couch that had been through the wars, in the part of the establishment that was known as the living room. You introduced me to your people, and now I'll introduce you to mine, he was saying, having calmed down and almost sobered up, stroking her back. My love's back is just as nice as her chest, he thought. And my love's stomach is on a par with the just mentioned bit, and her nose has no reason to envy her navel. She's not just a beautiful woman but a collection of beauties. Every look of hers is a beauty, and her voice is a beauty, of which we got confirmation over the telephone. In this place you need to tell lies, and I'm going to lie. We'll be together, as we have been, we'll never cool off to each other. If jealousy doesn't devour us, Nora thought in reply. What does it mean, "We'll always be as we have been"? And in the Florence of "White Guelphs"? And beyond the boundaries of "existence in the air"? In the given cosmic conditions, in pre-Adam wholeness? What, then? Look for yourself then, fistulas in archaeological strata of the earth. She smiled. It's better not to lose yourself.

The First Bottom was in a state of half-waking drunkenness. Henry, nodding off, was running off roulades from Chopin in his own interpretation—to Baby. A melancholy Matt circled the pool table, cue in hand, taking a measure as though he was hunting a fly, and then delivered a deafening blow and smiled at Nora: everything's under control. Bernadetta, rising like a fortress tower, was languorously dancing with Piu. Mel O'Massey was sleeping peacefully in a half-collapsed armchair. Bruno Kastorzius, obeying the feeling of solidarity that was well-developed in him, was here as well. He was playing solitaire and smiling with his uneven—to put it mildly—teeth. "You see how idyllic it is, Nora," Alex said. "And yet these bastards almost killed me one day at the height of the Cold War."

"You've slept with that female centaur, of course?" Nora asked. "Could it have been otherwise before your appearance on the scene—my Renaissance?" replied

Alex in his rhetorical "sweet style." Bernie meanwhile had approached them from behind, licked Nora's ear, and whispered: "I love your daddy, sweetheart." Henry suddenly fell asleep at his keys, and in the subsequent quiet, the television's latest announcement reached this point: "Seventy percent of Americans are dissatisfied with their sex lives."

It was a sweet night on the edge of the American double continent bearing a vague resemblance to an hourglass.

7

THE MOMENT OF THE CLOSING
OF THE MOUTH

*A*t this moment, we begin again to fiddle with the chronology of our story and with the gaping reader, but only slightly, it would seem, and not in accordance with our own wishes, rather with the rules of modernist composition. We yell, "Cut! Cut!" and quickly pull the camera back (or is it forward?) . . . well, anyway, it's the autumn of 1986, in the Westwood Colonial Parking Garage, where A.Z. is standing in a jacket stuffed with hundred-dollar bills and packets of cocaine. It seems to us that at this very moment we can close the mouth, open in amazement, of the young man with the lock of hair and the necktie fluttering in the wind. Why at this moment and not another—why didn't we continue the story of the three years that had to come in between these two fixed points? Well, in the first place because that story in its full length might fill up our whole Macintosh, and in the second place—and more important—we don't want to disrupt the rhythm of our story.

So then, the lanky fellow let out an unthinkable howl of "Sasha Korbach!" and then shut his mouth. Now, after the reestablishment of our chronotope, by way of a conclusion to the part, we begin recounting the events in lapidary style. The long-limbed sugar-powder lover turned out to be a certain Rodney Pomrette, a fanatic of modern theater, who, about a hundred years ago, had gone to Moscow with Frank Shannon's troupe to get acquainted with the work of the Buffoons. The cocaine-inspired languor in the beanpole evaporated and yielded to an explosion of memory. Over the few minutes that followed he peppered Korbach with the maestro's own quotations. He sent Leroy Wilkie after the theater people. An hour after the spotting of a great director of the modern era, that is, four years after his arrival in the USA, a welcoming party began on the roof of the parking garage. The only car on the top level, as it turned out, was the beautiful ZIS-101. No fewer than two dozen people had gathered: some from the Theater on Beethoven Street, some from the Back Pocket, some from the Argo, and so on and so forth. Everyone embraced the maestro, whom they had supposed to have shuffled off this mortal coil long ago. Many were weeping. Sasha let down his guard, laughed loudly, and wiped away a tear: I'm finally with my own people, among the avant-garde, the nonmaterialists. Toward morning they heard that Frank Shannon was flying from New York with his students, and a representative of the Theater Communications Group. Korbach, the Meyerhold of our times, had been found!

Over the next few days the newspapers printed several articles with pictures. One photograph came out particularly well: a greasy crepe perched on Alexander Zakharovich's polished head. The journalists, of course, had never heard his name before, nor Meyerhold's. The big story turned out to be not Pomrette's discovery but the fact that a Moscow director, and one bearing the name of one of the largest corporations in America at that, had been working as a valet parker in Westwood for four years. "You've 'made news,' my friend," said Shannon, a gray-haired acting teacher, beaming with happiness. "You know how it goes here in America: if a dog bites a man, that's not news. It's news when a man bites a dog." Alex nodded. "By that logic, then, an American parking-garage attendant who became a director in Moscow would be news, right?" He scratched the back of his head: it's a good thing the newspaper people didn't find even juicier details for this story.

Either way, a sort of modest sensation occurred, and Alexander, who by that time had already become fairly well Americanized, waited for offers from the theaters (from, say, Arena Stage, or Cocteau, or La Mama—just name them yourselves), or even from Broadway or Hollywood to come in. He wasn't Americanized enough yet after all. It was only later that he understood that the people who make the "offers" never read news stories about parking-garage attendants.

Nevertheless, the local theater, Argo, asked him to put on something of Chekhov's for them. He had long before gotten a bit sick of endless stage variations on sisters, uncles, and tea with cherries, but he got himself moving just the same and replied with an offer to do a postmodern production in the spirit of Chekhov. Unfortunately, the "argonauts" wanted something more traditional—that is, something that was more of a moneymaking proposition, after all. And for that they were offering Maestro Korbach an amount of money that he could earn in a week with Tikhomir Burevyatnikov. An idiotic situation resulted: it was impossible to go back to the parking garage after the "sensational discovery," yet to feed himself without the garage was also impossible.

Everything worked out in unexpected fashion. Nora, gathering all the clippings from the newspapers, worked up a first-rate résumé for him and went with it to the president of Pinkerton. Oh, these American "résumés," so incomprehensible to the Russian mind and heart! A Russian, after all, is used to disparaging himself, to self-effacement, to lowering his eyes. He's always hoping that someone will spread superlatives about him behind his back so as not to embarrass him. It's hard for him to understand that here in America you've got to display your wares directly in the customer's face: yes, he's a genius, yes, he's effective, no, not old at all, yes, he's got a sense of humor, yes indeed, he'll be a good colleague. Either way, there suddenly came for Alexander Zakharovich a letter on university stationery with an embossed seal and the personal signature—definitely not a copy—of President Millhouse, one of the pillars of the American educational process, whose prestige might be envied him by some of those elected to sit in the White House.

Dear Mr. Korbach,

Knowing you to be one of the most prominent directors in the world of the modern theater, the President and the Board of Trustees of Pinkerton University are honored to offer you the position of Director in Residence for a period of three years (with full possibility of extension) and with a yearly salary of $70,000 (negotiations for the increase of this sum are possible). Naturally, the contract will provide for all additional benefits, in particular health insurance and a pension fund.

We sincerely hope that you will accept our offer, and that the academic community of our university, as well as that of greater Washington, will be enriched by the presence of such a highly valued colleague. We are eagerly looking forward to the new shows in our experimental theater that will be created under the influence of your theatrical, poetic, and philosophical ideas.

Nigel Tabbac, Chairman of our Theater Department, will send you a more detailed letter.

Sincerely yours,
Benjamin F. Millhouse,
President

That evening, Nora called. "Did you get it? Ask for eighty-five, they'll give you eighty. What—you still haven't decided? Sasha, can't you understand that there's nothing for us to do on the West Coast?" Staggered by this "us," he stood on his sundeck and said his farewells to the purple ocean, along which a strong southern wind was sending Mexican ripples. Well, Ocean, old buddy, of all the beings of the New World, you were the kindest to me. I'm going away to be with your brother, not as broad in the belly but maybe a bit longer. Don't be offended—after all, you're joined to each other, like Siamese twins.

And so, at the end of Part 6, at the beginning of 1987, our hero marks the halfway point of the novel by moving to the nation's capital, Washington, D.C., which the Russian émigrés who have settled there call *Nash*ington. He rented and later bought an apartment near Dupont Circle, an area swarming with all possible human types. Now, from his window, instead of his old buddy Ocean, which had treated him so well, Sasha could see the Dixie Liquors storefront, along with the cafés Zorba and the Childe Harold, the multipurpose self-service bookstore Lambda Rising, and Kramerbooks, too, where one could drop in at 1:00 A.M. and get a beer.

Before bringing this part to a close, we should say that the first person who called Sasha was not even Nora but her father, Stanley Korbach. In the first place, he wanted to congratulate his fourth cousin on his successful departure from L.A. (as for what he meant, we'll leave that up to our perspicacious reader). In the second place, he told him that he was calling from the hospital. In answer to the question of what happened, he replied jauntily, "The normal process of dying out has started," after which he changed the subject and talked about new hypotheses concerning the migrations of the Tribes of Israel.

On that note, we close Part 6 and move on to the second half of the book.

VI. THE LION IN THE ALIOTO

A sea lion plays near Fisherman's Wharf.
For the third time in five years I come to the Alioto Restaurant.
They haven't forgotten me here, they remember I'm not a thief.
Last time, a certain Señor Axelotl greeted me here.

Since then that sea lion hasn't grown old,
A zealous refugee of the sea, and perhaps a cheeky one.
You couldn't say, though, that he's terribly young.
At times he's even comical in his courtesy

Toward the lionesses of the San Francisco Bay.
You want to remind him as one shaman to another:
You might be a hooligan, batono, *but you're still no plebeian,*
To pretend to be an ataman for a band of whores of this bay.

Where have you scattered your seed, your posterity, all drops of your jism?
They might ask him at a time of alcoholic brittleness:
Could you estimate the value of your life the Komsomol way—
The one that you splashed away in the ocean depths, knowing no peace?

Could one find a better refuge for a retired stud?
It would be hard to find a merrier channel in the domain of pacifism:
Salads, herrings, beauties from herds of whores—
In a word, everything that streams out of the local restaurants.

Maître Axelotl comes up as a type from my major oeuvre.
Buon giorno, *Alessandro! Greetings to you from Grappelli.*
I see you're occupied down there with this Major Morzhov?
You're probably drawing ambiguous parallels?

He comes here, always inebriated, once in a year or two.
It's a bit like the visits of an experienced seaman,
A week of debauchery, and he dives down into emptiness—
In other words, sir, into the spaces of the peaceful ocean.

Don't tell me, Axelotl, you can distinguish him
From the millions of sea lions in their hedonistic frenzy.
Not by their mugs, surely, always smashed?
How can you pick out that ever-cheeky mug?

Listen, Alessandro, have you seen his left fang?
The maître d'hôtel bows, mysteriously illuminated.
His left fang is gold like a Saudi tank.
That's the sign by which we can always recognize him.

Shortly after that dinner, by the time of sunset,
When the lapis lazuli and indigo frontispiece
Was reflecting all the great trembling ocean light
On the glass sides of central San Francisco

Somebody double-clicked his Apple,
Time flashed by like the reflection of a reflection,
And with a piercing feeling I spied the golden fang
Of a sea beast swimming away into the open spaces.

He is leaving behind, my friends, these opulent shores
Departing gluttonous piers and dirty plums,
Increasing his speed as if being spurred on,
The tooth, however, gleams in a farewell "All the best!"

He's pretending he knows his new destination,
As if he knows not only the means of getting there, but the goal.
There, on the other side of the ocean, purified geishas
Will dance for him the apotheosis of Giselle.

His chest, still powerful, spreads the currents,
He swims toward the horizon, where time sways like the funnel of a tornado.
His golden tooth is radiating luminescence,
He is going, going, going, mafioso and merchant . . . Gone!

PART VII

1

PAIN AND ANESTHESIA

In January of 1987, Stanley Korbach turned sixty. No one, neither in the family nor in his office—that is, in the headquarters of the empire—noticed the approach of the date. For that matter, he took no notice of it himself. Of course he was aware that the boundary between middle age and what the French elegantly call *le troisième âge* was approaching, but the date slipped his mind. All things considered, something like the following scene was proposed for the novel: perhaps in his jet, or on the tennis court, Stanley strikes himself on the forehead and exclaims: "Why, I'm already sixty, my good and faithful people!" After that, he was supposed to turn the page of some report or hit a ball with a racket, or, in the most likely scenario, pour himself a Scotch, and forget about the celebration. As far as the "faithful people" were concerned, the concept of old age was incompatible with the image of Stanley Korbach, a boss who existed outside of time, the benevolent Gargantua of his commercial fiefdoms. That's how things were planned in the novel, but things turned out quite differently.

On the morning of that day—outside was the dreadful stew of a Washington winter, snow or icy rain, wind and flying leaves—Stanley was visited in his hospital room by Sister Elizabeth, a Catholic nun. She crossed herself before the crucifix hanging in the corner opposite the television and said gently: "Good morning, Mr. Korbach! You're sixty years old today, sir. Congratulations, with all my heart!" She looked at him with her forget-me-not eyes, encircled with a dear ornamentation of wrinkles, and smiled with the gentleness of a model child. It was obvious that everything she was saying was indeed coming straight from the heart, since she belonged to that small number of souls unspoiled by existence. "Today you might have to undergo a serous operation, and I'll pray for you, my dear Mr. Korbach, sir."

Stanley was moved almost to tears. He took one of his arms from beneath his blanket and asked her: "Please, touch my arm above the elbow, my dear Sister Elizabeth." She did it willingly, but then suddenly jerked her fingers back, as though there were something in that arm that she could not pray for. Stanley went on, not noticing this tremor: "Thank you for your promise to pray for me during the operation. I'll be praying, too, though I've no idea for what—maybe for myself and my operation, or maybe about something else. I'm starting to pray right now, and I'll keep on until Dr. Hertz puts me under the anesthesia. Do me a favor, Sister Elizabeth, stay with me for a few minutes. Just sit in the corner, my dear, and I'll pray—maybe like a Jew, maybe like a Christian, maybe like a Muslim, and maybe even like a pagan."

The nun silently nodded and looked around for a place to sit. For an instant it seemed to her that some representative of one of the non-Christian faiths was sitting with great dignity in the room, but the moment passed, and she calmly took a seat beneath the well-carved small wooden crucifix that hung in sharp relief on the severe white wall.

Stanley Korbach began to mutter something unintelligible. He was retreating further and further into this muttering, and it seemed as though he himself no longer fully understood its meaning. Sister Elizabeth sat with her head bowed and her hands in her lap. The monotonic murmuring was interrupted from time to time by what was almost a wild cry. At those moments the nun raised her head, her face illuminated by such a lively expression that one might have thought she understood all the gibberish of a mind—or of a subconscious—clouded by strong painkillers. Making use of our authorial rights to arbitrariness, we will try to present our respected reader with a picture of what Stanley Korbach was muttering in his strange "prayer" before an operation in the surgical wing of Washington's Holy Cross Hospital.

The Babylonians had destroyed the Temple and put the city to the torch from all sides. And the inhabitants of Jerusalem were racked with terror and sadness. In the darkness many of them tried to flee the city and take refuge among the rocks of the Judean mountains. At that hour, King Nebuchadnezzar entered the city, where pillaging and murder were still going on. Zedekiah, king of Judea, and his family were taken captive. They were tied to the foot of the Babylonian king's field throne. Zedekiah was forced to watch the execution of his children. After that he was blinded with a dagger and chained to a column. By then, there had already appeared crowds of Israelites, driven with whips and spears into slavery.

A craftsman whose shop in a narrow side street at the foot of Mount Moriah had just been looted by Babylonian soldiers was trudging along in the crowd of prisoners; his name was Kor-Beit, which in Hebrew means "cold house." Suddenly he caught sight of his king in chains, howling savagely in unbearable pain. Kor-Beit could not stand such humiliation.

"I know that Kor-Beit was my ancestor," Stanley muttered. "I see it all, like in a film shot twenty-five centuries ago. I've already seen this Kor-Beit, or another one, every time I've taken morphine. I've seen how he drags hides up from the cellar of his 'cold house' and makes protective vests and high boots from them. And now at this moment, when I'm praying before an operation on my own genitalia, I see Kor-Beit bolting from the crowd, snatching a sword from a guard, and trying to run it through King Zedekiah to spare him further suffering. I see the Babylonian soldiers catching up to him and dragging him to the feet of Nebuchadnezzar, who is sitting on the throne that follows him on his campaigns, on the befouled terrace of our Temple; his mantle is stained with the blood of Zedekiah and his children.

" 'You wished to deprive him of feeling?' Nebuchadnezzar asked Kor-Beit, and my ancestor replied, 'Yes, sir,' very politely. The king was very gloomy on that day of his triumph over Judah. He was well-grounded in astronomy, and he had a more or less personal relationship with Astarte. From the configuration of the stars, he knew that the goddess did not approve of the bloodbath, but he also knew that he had no choice in the matter. The problem of anesthesia once and for all disturbed him. He asked Kor-Beit which he would prefer, feelings or absolute tranquillity. 'Feelings,' answered Kor-Beit, as a good Jewish craftsman. 'As you have said.' Nebuchadnezzar nodded and ordered that a good lash be cut from his skin, and that with this lash he be given fifty sound blows, not sparing any parts of the body.

"My Catholic Sister Elizabeth, what do you think about this Judean story? It seems to me that I can see the sky of that night over Jerusalem, the unfathomable transparency of the heavenly vault and two stars, seemingly moving toward us, toward me and him, my ancestor, who is crawling among the heaped corpses to his 'cold house.' He survived, Sister, and kept his own balls—otherwise you wouldn't have to pray right now for this fucking sinner Stanley Korbach. He howled the whole night through and for another full month, but now and then there suddenly appeared before him in his ravings, between a wall full of pain and a wall full of anesthesia, a momentary image of a flock of birds scudding across the blue sky in a movement so well-synchronized that they seemed to be a single creature."

Stanley Korbach was muttering and occasionally bellowing all of this, or less than all of this, or more than all of this, until the door opened and Dr. Eddie Hertz, his own Nebuchadnezzar, came into the room. A crowd of young doctors, nurses, and medical students brought up the rear. This was standard practice for the morning rounds, and no exceptions were made for rich patients, even if they could buy this entire prestigious Catholic hospital without batting an eyelash.

"Hi, Stanley!" Dr. Hertz said in the tone of a college athlete. A respected urologist, he looked like a track and field champion. "You look great today!" He always treated his patients, at least during the morning rounds, as though they had nothing more wrong with them than a minor sports injury.

The problems of Big Korby, as his partners sometimes called him behind his back—he hated it!—began almost literally out of the clear blue sky. One day, during a flight from Paris, he noticed a curious anomaly in himself, one that might seem absolutely ludicrous in the context of securities and capital investments, in which he had been dealing all week. He was unable to take a piss, the fact that his bladder was about to burst from excessive deliveries from his kidneys notwithstanding. He spent two of three hours of the supersonic flight trying to squeeze from himself half a glass of the liquid that had been wont to leave him in a mighty, faintly ringing stream. The passengers on the Concorde were surprised to discover that one of the two little rooms at the rear was constantly occupied.

It turned out that he was suffering from hypertrophy of his male gland, the prostate, which normally sits behind the bladder and quietly produces its secretion but which, when enlarged—something that happens in the "third age"—can compress the bladder, and all of this had nothing—or ever so little—to do with the world's financial situation.

By the end of that day, Eddie Hertz, whistling Vivaldi's "Spring," had inserted a flexible catheter into the penis of the megamultibillionaire, who was in agony, and freed the bladder of the extra weight. What pain, and what relief—you should know them, peoples of the world! Here's a world of feelings and sensations for you—pain and bliss sometimes exist right alongside each other. Aren't they sisters, Sister Elizabeth?

After a series of tests and analyses, Korbach was given a long plastic container, which joined the catheter and was attached with special adhesive strips to the patient's left leg. He would be able to walk and, in addition to this remarkable capability, would be able, by lifting a trouser leg, to observe the accumulation of the cranberry juice from his traumatized urinary tract. "Please, Stanley, avoid any form of sexual excitement," the doctor advised him earnestly. "Does that still exist?" the patient moaned softly. The doctor smiled mysteriously. Easy to say, hard to do. Almost every night in the hospital, Korbach was visited for some reason by colossal erections, which caused him pain that was positively Babylonian.

The more the scope of the tests done by Eddie Hertz's team broadened, the more complicated our giant's physical condition became. It was revealed that his coronary arteries were blocked with cholesterol formations as dense as the Babylonian and Philistine patrols on the mountain paths of Judah. Given the conditions, it would be difficult to decide in favor of a "surgical procedure," as Hertz put it. Fortunately, Stanley did not yet need an open-heart bypass; he could get by with just an angioplasty, that is, a cleaning out of the arteries. Unfortunately, there was one more serious complication in the scenario: even with modern equipment it would be risky to do an angioplasty when there was a history of prolonged bleeding. And finally, there was still the most threatening danger of all: the enlarged prostate could be the result of a malignant process. In that case they would have to prepare for a major invasion of the abdominal cavity.

First of all, then, they would have to perform a biopsy, which, of course, constituted a "surgical procedure" all by itself. If Stanley was lucky and the swelling turned out to be benign, then they would still get at the gland that he diffidently called his creamery without opening his stomach, through that same old organ that stubbornly objected to the idea of being considered simply a part of the waterworks. "Full speed ahead, Doc," said Stanley. "Do everything that you need to do with this far from perfect boat for a voyage of the soul, as one of my Russian relations puts it."

Hertz went over all the details with Korbach as the strategists of the Pentagon might have discussed the cleaning up of Panama. They decided to do the angioplasty first, and they did it. After our giant had recovered from that procedure, they sent him to the operating room again and removed a section of his enlarged prostate for analysis. Then, several days passed as several years, or several minutes, in something like a state of near death, while Stanley waited for the results. Matters were complicated by the fact that all of this had coincided with a long weekend occasioned by a national holiday, when all the university laboratories were closed. Of course, AK & BB, Inc., could have opened any lab in town and paid anything to do it; our patient, however, objected strongly to this approach, telling his wife: "At this stage of life, little girl, I want to be just like my brothers, experiencing agony and hope. Agony and hope, my friend—that's all." On the big day, Eddie Hertz didn't make him wait. Striding efficiently into the room, he announced the good news. No cancer, the swelling is benign.

The entire week before this, lying in a bed with needles poking into the principal highways and byways of his internal galaxy, he had gone on thinking about the two questions that seemed to him the most important at the time: feelings—that is, existence—and nonfeeling—that is, nonexistence. The tranquilizers, analgesics, and also some drink that the Eternal Jew had brought to him had dug a strange sort of mine shaft in his consciousness: he didn't know if he was having astonishing dreams or if it was some new form of space and time travel. He was sure of the existence of ontological parameters beyond the boundaries of life, and was not afraid of death. Nevertheless, when, just before the biopsy, he received a powerful dose of a general anesthetic, and woke up the next instant and realized that the "surgical procedure" was over and had in fact contained an incalculable number of instants during which he had simply not existed, the fatal idea of the total absence of any ontology, the absence of anything beyond the boundaries of instants of feelings—in other words, the absence of God—had pierced through him. The idea of total horror gaped before him, and they left him embracing this idea to wait for the laboratory results over a long weekend in the capital of the United States.

―――――――――――――

"So, we'll start preparing you immediately for a procedure on your prostate." Dr. Hertz asked for a piece of paper, and, in the best traditions of American surgery, began to use a felt pen to draw for the patient what they were going to do to his poor flesh. The chief aim of this fairly new technique is to avoid a major operation for the removal of the "creamery." "Instead of removal, we're going to apply part of the tissue to your bladder, so that in the future your 'factory' will be able to start doing its work again, at least partly."

Stanley nodded and asked how long it would take. Ninety minutes was the answer. "And what about the anesthesia?" "What about it?" "There's a well-developed anesthetic procedure for this sort of operation. What's wrong, Stanley?" "I don't want general anesthesia, Eddie, even if it'll be painful. At least leave me partly conscious, okay?" "This operation doesn't require general anesthesia," Hertz said dryly, and left the room. He didn't like patients who ordered anesthesia as though it were a garnish in a restaurant.

His amiability came back to him in pre-op, though, when he saw Stanley hooked up to every tube going and surrounded by a team of anesthetists. "Mr. President, I guarantee you that the stock of AK and BB will take a big jump tomorrow! Come on, come on, think about the stock market, tennis, your sailboats, women, anything but Nebuchadnezzar and Torquemada!" We forgot to tell the readers that doctor and patient became friends after a week spent together on the tennis courts on Martha's Vineyard.

Soon after this send-off, Stanley Korbach began the descent (or ascent) into a cloud of blissful, slowly revolving travels within himself, or around himself. He could see nothing but the pleasant waves of something wave-shaped, and could hear nothing but snatches of medical terminology intoned by some good spirits. From time to time in the midst of this beatific state, someone would pull or yank on his member, but this did nothing to reduce the feeling of overall harmony. On the contrary, it added to it. He smiled, showing that these movements were familiar to him—he had already experienced them there, where he had recently been, in his life, in that very thing that was now lying just beside him. There's nothing harmful in these tugs on his penis, nothing demonic—it's just the innocent games of creatures who were once—and still are!—called people.

Later, the field of his vision, if we can call it vision in the usual sense of the word, split into segments, and in these segments he could see, or foresee, or remember various details of his life, magnified or reduced, and even whole panoramas, focused or blurry, and all of it together was wonderfully dear and close to him: suddenly, a little elbow protruded from a rosy rose of lace, then there appeared a sturdy paving stone from a street at the end of which stretched out the flatness of a dark blue sea with whitecaps along its entire width, someone was walking beneath dark archways, he was proud of his new boots, he was approaching some turning point in his life, a small white spot in the corner of the cement was quickly transformed into a fluttering canvas, a carriage appeared, drawn by two shining light brown horses, the clip-clop of their hooves was mixed with the tapping of his heels, the door of the carriage opened, a small rose-colored spot suddenly blossomed into a huge rose, all silk and lace, and a feeling of youth, beaten like cream, mixed with the sorrow of parting; forever, then, farewell! A small ball of gloom bounces across the stage, dragging a wire tail. Spit out a lump of saliva and mucus! Drink some water, wine, or milk, walk up the gangplank, swallow the sea, swallow youth, triumph, don't believe that they'll beat you like a Jew when you return, enjoy your assignation, and say to those lips and fingers and to all the other parts of the rose: Señors, do it any way you want, I'm all yours.

"What's his pressure now?" Hertz asked his assistants. "Katy, add a sedative to the IV, would you? Thanks."

The segmentation of the circle disappeared, in the same way that the circle itself dissolved into the cozy warmth of the narcotic quasi Nirvana of a Washington Catholic hospital.

2

ACCESS TO THE BODY

*H*e began gradually regaining consciousness, once in his room. The first thing to come into sharp focus, naturally, was the television, bolted firmly to the ceiling. What a humane way of addressing the needs of the bedridden patient! The strange playfulness of his mind reminded him of the first stage of a hangover. What does a postoperative patient desire most to see after a trip into the inner astral spheres? Why, reality, of course—that is, a television set. And after he wakes up, his hand automatically gropes for the remote control.

On the screen, as usual, the sound of a talk show was droning on, with a popular hostess who couldn't seem to decide which image suited her better: a capricious baby with pouting lips or a bespectacled hag with a keen mind. The audience was discussing the eternal hot-button issue of incest. He was already looking forward to half an hour of the great national pastime when someone switched off the beckoning screen.

"My poor boy, my darling," he heard, and out of the corner of his eye saw his lawful wedded wife sitting beside his bed and weeping decorously and touchingly into a handkerchief that had undoubtedly been carefully chosen for weeping at the bedside of a wounded husband. How beautiful she is, he thought. What a fine Barbie doll I hooked up with twenty-three years ago. How can we dare tell her that we see in her face the grandmother of the two-year-old Mr. Duppertat Jr.? "What do you want to drink, dear?" Elegance asked. "Mineral water, chicken broth?" He smiled. "What I could really go for right now would be a bottle of Grolsch." "You have to forget about beer, darling," she said with a tearful note in her voice. In keeping with all the time-honored traditions, she tucked a pillow just behind the giant's head and bent down ever so slightly, intending to cool his fevered brow with a kiss. "Take it easy, Margie," her spouse warned her. "Hertz said that I have to avoid getting sexually aroused, as long as there's rubber hanging out of my johnson." She sighed, and a glimmer of her constant and habitual indignation flashed in her eyes. "Why, how can you say such things right after an operation? And why does everything have to be humorous—why can't you ever do without the irony? Why is it that even after this painful procedure you won't allow yourself normal human feelings, my brave darling, my precious Stanley?" He waved his hand weakly. "No, no, Margie, I'm not making jokes, I'm not trying to be ironic, God forbid. I'm just talking about beer, sex, and a catheter in my business end, that's all." With those words, he fell asleep.

The day after, he felt better. On the third day the catheter was removed. Eddie Hertz would appear, and, as playfully as ever, give Stanley a briefing on what was happening on his downstairs floors, as it were. "As far as your virility is concerned, Stanley, sir, there are two possible scenarios: a good one and a not so good one. Considering your exceptional nature, we're within our rights to hope for the best. You'll have normal erections and nearly normal orgasms—in this day of ecological catastrophes, that's already something. As far as ejaculation goes, don't expect what I suppose were the gargantuan outpourings of the old days, my friend. So just don't think about it, don't talk about it with your sex partner, and you won't see it, period, unless you . . ." At that moment, Dr. Hertz eyed his patient with the mischievous expression of any *yidische mama* looking at her incorrigible child.

Stanley admitted then that he had already conducted a small experiment like those that had been carried out forty-two years earlier in a Marine barracks in the Pacific theater of operations. Everything was indeed in good shape where the orgasm was concerned, but he had almost burst into tears when he saw the tiny drop of watery liquid that was the result of his exertions. "Don't worry, Eddie—I'm not going to sue you for malpractice. You performed a first-class operation and I'm damned grateful to you. It's just sad, that's all, like any sign of deterioration." "Stanley, Stanley!" Hertz remonstrated with him for his premature experiments on his organ that had already suffered so much. "That sort of thing will get better, of course—just don't expect any volcanic eruptions. Keep your libido alive, but try to be more moderate, and go for more simplicity in that domain." What a simple story, sad, according to the norm, sighed our tycoon.

He stayed in the hospital for another three days. It might even have been that he enjoyed lying around without a care. He watched TV and read the newspapers (every part of them except the business section) and received visitors. He smiled at these pilgrims and flashed the V for victory sign. At times it seemed to him that he was looking at his visitors from the enormous distances outside the physical dimension of his recent "travels," from the place where it doesn't matter if you're alive or dead, whether you existed, are existing, or will exist, or don't exist and will never exist; from the place where Kor-Beit the tanner crawls like a ragged lizard among the heaped corpses on a Jerusalem backstreet at the same time that an old Jewish woman who was a stranger and yet somehow dear to him is sitting on a high bed, from which her legs didn't even reach the floor; sitting, her eyes lowered, and the nose between them seemingly trying to reach the end of her chin; an old woman, stock-still in inaccessibility and in stony sadness. These moments, however, passed, and it was not without pleasure that he returned to the aerial medium, to the physical boundaries of existence.

Among the first of the visitors was, of course, his most important partner and his distant relation Norman Blamsdale. He asked for fifteen minutes and got them. Looking at him, Stanley reflected on the fact that illness did have its positive side—most notably that he had completely forgotten about the existence of Norman Blamsdale. Now he was sitting on the bed in the lotus position, whereby he positively towered over his vice president, who sank in an armchair. "You look good, Stanley," Norman said. "You too, Norman," said Stanley. They smiled at each other hypocritically. Blamsdale shot a sidelong glance at the wall mirror. That goddamned super-Korbach was sitting in his hospital gown like an emperor. I might think that the whole scene was staged especially to humiliate me, if I didn't know that that sort of thing would never cross his mind. Everything is going perfectly naturally. The bastard just has a natural predisposition for towering over decent people. Stanley followed the movement of his eyes and smiled. "Sorry that I'm above you, old chap: this is a hospital." "Don't worry about it," Norman said.

You're a swindler and a pain in the ass, thought Stanley. I could put up with your shady deals, if you weren't such a bore. I wonder, what did Marjorie ever see in this lapdog? Maybe he's a good lover? Norman opened his briefcase. "Let me give you a brief rundown on our activities during your . . . er, medical activity. Frabinda canceled its order for the Syracusers, but then it offered seven hundred million more for twelve million shares of Ismail Ladda. So as not to cause a panic, we decided to raise the rate to fifteen percent, thinking that Kibbles Quantra can't buy more than twenty percent of our Compaq Oracle—you must remember that deal—according to the conditions of the poison pills provision of the bylaws." Norman raised his head from the papers and saw that Stanley was yawning. Outrageous! He has no respect for the corporation, and none for the hundreds of people who are working hard to find the right decision. How many of these yawns, which he doesn't even hide at board meetings, have we got to put up with? "Okay, okay," Stanley drawled, and then knocked him flat: "And have you talked to Kirk?"

"To Kirk?" Norman opened his mouth and forgot to close it.

"The first thing you need to do in this situation is call Kirk," Stanley said, with an expression that showed he was both fed up and bored. "Next item. We've got to keep our rates from going up, otherwise there's going to be a panic. Third item. Offer a billion for the Ismail Ladda shares. That's all."

Norman closed his mouth and chewed on his tongue. As an experienced broker, he understood right away that the approach proposed by Stanley, and in particular the allusion to a possible collaboration with Kirk Smetten, his personal friend and fellow S.O.B. of nearly the same rank, would immediately clear up the situation and lead the corporation in the right direction. Everything was so simple now! Why hadn't anyone thought of it before? "Simplicity," Stanley would usually repeat at the board meetings, "that's what our age needs, when armies of mediocrities are tearing our economy and financial system to bits." Well, you've got to give his decisions their due—they're like saber strokes. "You know we can't do that—you're not the Ashurbanipal of AK and BB!" Stanley shuddered and looked at him with a glum smile. "Do you mean Ashurbanipal or Nebuchadnezzar?" Norman jumped out of his humiliating chair. "Everyone knows that you're a direct descendant of the founder, that your personal fortune is the largest segment of our budget, but even so, you know, you're the head of a corporation in the late twentieth century—this isn't some medieval manor, after all!"

"Seven," Stanley said. "What do you mean, seven?" Norman roared, almost non compos mentis. "I'm sorry, Norman, but you've only got seven minutes left. A man recovering from an operation has to rest with Rabelais in front of him." The mention of a book, and for that matter a writer, whom his interlocutor had never heard of, drove the vice president right around the bend. The S.O.B., he's always pretending to be intellectually superior, that Stanley—there's a philosopher for you, and a historian, and now, he seems to think, a highbrow bookworm! The running of a corporation was just a minor matter—what really counted were these lofty subjects, like genealogy. You see, an aristocrat has turned up, the reconstruction of the past! Blamsdale couldn't contain himself anymore. "I wouldn't be surprised, Mr. President, if questions were raised about your leadership at a meeting of the board soon. The modern financial world is too complicated a structure for us to allow ourselves to have at the top of the pyramid a man who's irresponsible, not to say not entirely . . . not entirely, that's just it . . . a man!"

Stanley roared with laughter. "Not entirely, that's right! Entirely not entirely!" Norman had the impression that he'd gone too far. "Well, that's just what I heard about you recently. As an old friend and a close relative, I only wanted to warn you about these rumors—they're a long way from harmless. Don't forget, we're all under a giant magnifying glass!"

"Norman!" Stanley yelled.

"Yes, sir, we're under a giant magnifying glass!" the VP shrilled. For a moment his eyes popped out of their orbits as though they were photo lenses.

"Under a giant one?" the delighted president exclaimed. "I'd like to believe it's true."

He's talking about something else, thought Norman, and went on: "Stanley, I'm ten years younger than you are, we're from different generations of Americans, but I'm still the son of your mother's favorite cousin!"

Stanley raised an index finger significantly. "Aunt Deborah was in good form when she had you." Norman waved the phrase off like a bothersome fly. "Don't interrupt me, please! I've only got five minutes left, and I still need to talk to you about one more important thing. Or rather not about a thing, but about a person. Yes, I insist—about a person! I want to say one thing to you about one person. That's right, Stanley, I'm talking about Marjorie! Marjorie's not only a beautiful girl from my generation, she's the most sensitive and delicate individual I've ever met! And I want to emphasize, Stanley, that you're treating your wife badly, my friend. The other day she came home from the hospital in tears. She was complaining that you'd given her the cold shoulder. She tried to reach you with all her heart, and you responded to her with your usual irony. Irony in response to compassion, Stanley, that won't work. You shouldn't treat the mother of your children that way. Stanley, it's only our friendship and our family ties that allow me to bring up this question. In my heart of hearts, I dream that our Korbach-Blamsdale clan will become the very picture of love and harmony, Stanley!"

The president was now looking intently at his VP. So, he's not such a lump after all. He sleeps with my wife and he dreams about family harmony. Perhaps he's "not entirely" too? Or is it the specific sort of operation I had that's given him so much spunk? This thought was not the least bit pleasing to the president. He could feel himself starting to snarl. I'll show him, right here and now, the real lion's roar of Ashurbanipal and Nebuchadnezzar. The roar began on a low note, as if from the very depths of antiquity. With every second it gathered force, as though someone had started the engine of a Tomcat fighter in the room. "Get the hell out of here, you crook!" The thunderclap had not entirely died away before the room was empty. Well, now the bastards know that the lion's still alive. He stretched himself out on the bed and buried his nose in the volume of Rabelais, which was open to the scene of the battle with the armies of King Picrochole. Oh God, warm me with your magnifying glass—just don't burn me, please, Creator!

The next visitors were much more agreeable. Alex Korbach and Nora Mansour, his own daughter by the muse of the cinema, appeared. Her father had known for some time that Hedgie had got involved in a serious romance with the representative of the Russian Korbachs. He wasn't opposed to it. The blood relationship was such a distant one that no one could have called their love incest by any stretch of the mind, kind ladies and gentlemen. On top of everything else, he didn't like Nora's husband. He obviously knew more about that refined Parisian than his daughter did. No sooner had the newlyweds arrived at Halifax Farm seven years ago than he'd ordered a dossier on the young man from a highly qualified private agency.

Omar came from a large and very wealthy family of Lebanese aristocrats. Some of them Muslims, some of them Christians, these people considered themselves not Arabs but Phoenicians, claiming that their roots went back to the quasi-mythic merchants and seafarers of the ancient world. That's fine—you want to be Phoenicians, be my guest. What was worse was Omar's highly dubious connection with the most extreme elements in Middle Eastern politics. There were even rumors (unconfirmed) that he had commanded a small private army in the fighting in Beirut under the repulsive nom de guerre of Putak. Stanley Korbach, of course, had no intention of making public his information about this swarthy, well-built man who looked like a male model in an ad in *The New York Times Magazine;* however, kind sir, you can, of course, reserve the right to receive further information, contrary to the original information about Cyprus.

The solicitous father had even managed to sniff out the fact that Nora and Omar had first met in Paris in the late seventies, at one of those left-wing bohemian parties where the guests went significantly silent at the mention of Action Directe. Of course he saw that his beloved daughter had entirely immersed herself in archaeology after the Berkeley hysterics, but he also knew that to this day Hedgie's breathing still quickened slightly at the word *movement.*

It was reported to him that on the day after this party, a remarkable coincidence occurred: the two young people met up with each other on an El Al flight to Israel. Fate itself, it seemed, had directed their peregrinations. Omar took a room at the Tel Aviv Hilton, while Nora set herself up at the archaeological camp at Ashqelon—that is, just thirty miles away. Knowing Nora, the reader can easily imagine the course events took. That's all clear enough, thought Stanley, turning the pages of the agents' report—the only thing I don't understand is why they got married. Maybe he was carrying out an assignment to infiltrate the corporation?

Korbach had come to feel an aversion to Mansour. He didn't like the way his son-in-law looked at him across the table or on the golf course with a rather insolent expression on his handsome face, as though he had his own file on his father-in-law. Now and again a strange expression of undisputed superiority typical of the movers and shakers of the Middle East would peep through his gallant Parisian manners. They look at you as though they hold the key to some mystic, merciless power that would be capable at any time of reducing the "Western infidels" to shreds. The most disagreeable thing of all was that Stanley somehow could not even imagine how Hedgie slept—or had slept—with that guy. On the other hand, he could easily, and with approval, picture how Hedgie slept with Sasha. What could be more natural? Copulate to your heart's content, kids!

"Well, how goes the Rabelaising, Your Majesty Pantagruel?" were Sasha's words of greeting to Stanley. "By your prayers, Your Majesty King of the Buffoons!" Super-Korb replied. It was the first time that Nora had seen them together. How do you like that, the guys get along like a house on fire! When did they have time to get so friendly? She didn't know that in the three years that had gone by since the beginning of the affair, Stanley and Alex had met many times in L.A. and spent hours discussing Dante, Rabelais, Josephus Flavius, Ovid, the Roman Empire, and little Judea, with its strange, stubborn struggle against the triumphant legions; discussing the nature of Judaism as well—should it always be as strict and ascetic concerning earthly delights as it was in the days of the Yavna School?— talking about John the Baptist, too, and the ablutions of the early Essenes . . . Can I tell you some of the other topics of their discussion, O Theophilus? With pleasure: New York as the "new Rome" with its barbarian hordes; Moscow as the "new Rome" in its Socialist version with its own barbarians thirsting to consume but for the time being standing in half-starved queues; the sunset of empire and the decline of the Earth as such—it won't go on existing forever, after all; time as a trap for mortals and travel beyond the limits of this trap under the influence of certain substances; airspace—will we always have enough air and will people in extraterrestrial colonies be able to produce air and keep it around themselves; the wind, that fantastic gift of God, without which there would never have been any lyric poetry—does that mean that in these outer-space colonies there won't be any poetry; yachting—do you think we'll beat those damned Aussies next season; the Soviet obsession with sport as a manifestation of an inferiority complex; the Russian Jews who helped to fan the flames of the revolution in 1917, only to become its favorite victim—now there's the real Jewish way of making history; Pasternak, who became more Russian than the Russians, who with his own "sublime malady" expressed the keen emotions of the Russians where their land and extended families were concerned, who as an apostate from the faith of his fathers called, like Josephus Flavius, for assimilation into the majority population, for which he was universally sent to the whipping post; the subject of ethnic purity and mixed marriages—why the Israeli zealots of purity so stubbornly insisted that only a person whose mother was a Jew can be a Jew, and whether or not this created some deep ambiguity, also considering the Sumerian ancestry of Abraham, Father of us all, and all of the Canaanites, Amalekites, Ammonites, Philistines, Greeks, and Romans whom our people had to live among; is our people chosen by blood, or by faith in one God? The One Omnipotent, Invisible God Whose Name Must Not Be Pronounced is incomprehensible to mortals, and perhaps that's why mankind throughout history has tried to humanize the idea with a multitude of pagan gods, and then in the form of prophets and saints; man is the sacrificial lamb of the universe, and to encourage us God sent his incarnation, Jesus Christ, showing that he was going through our sufferings with us; aren't all of these anthropomorphic images of pagan mythology God's creations? The Olympian throng is the carnival poetry that helps man to hang on; how magnificent they are in the context of the worldwide amphitheater, the monsters of mythology, and where would Hercules be without the Hydra and Cerberus. Humor and laughter are God's most precious gifts to the human race, and without them we all would have been turned into gloomy, self-destructive idiots; sex, which seems to address itself directly to original sin, and at the same time contains within itself consolations and inspirations; wine, which was given to us as one more holy consolation (Clicquot champagne) but which was defiled by the Unclean Spirit and became a curse (Stolichnaya) . . . What else?

At this point we'll pause for just a moment to catch our breath. The literary device has begun to drag. I'm writing these lines sitting in a room with a view of the sea, at the top of a basalt hill, in the old fortress of Visby, on the island of Gotland. Just in front of this hill, underscored by the backdrop of the sea, stands the light gray cathedral of St. Mary, with its gargoyles and a gilded rooster on its spire. My room is at the level of the upper windows of the cathedral, so that I can see the square in front of it and its doors from a harpy's-eye view. The brick red rooftops of the little town, slanting downward, huddle up to the sea, which, in the light of the setting sun, changes its colors every time I look up from my manuscript, from fine, rose-tinted watercolors to thick, dark oils on which bold strokes of the brush have scattered the sails of yachts. There's a tableau for you, one worthy of a ten-minute break: a second wind is already furrowing the western waters, and I'm going on.

They spoke more than once about the misconception that most Americans had about Russia. Russia was considered a dull country for some reason. You feel sorry for us, the "poor Russians," but you suppress a yawn. You don't even try to understand what an astounding thing it is to be Russian! One would say this, and the other would nod in agreement.

Let's talk about the Russian understanding of America now. You treat us like crude, pragmatic cowboys, devoid of any refined feeling, or of any sense of tragedy or nostalgia. One would say this, and the other would nod in agreement.

They also talked about cars, horses, dogs, cards, drinking sprees, prostitutes that they had known at various times in their lives—in other words, they talked like friends.

In the course of their conversations, after they had got quite drunk, drinking more and more until they nearly felt reduced to shreds, they would come to the subject of mutual respect. Real men should experience this feeling for each other without any superfluous words. Entirely without them. No surplus words at all. Get a gun and mow them all down, these surplus words. Wipe them out like roaches. Throw them in the Potomac, so that they don't float belly up in our drinks. Instead of these useless words someone ought to play jazz. Having agreed on jazz, they made their way to Blues Alley. Having spotted a couple of bow-legged girls, they talked about ugliness. It couldn't block out the inner light. No, it doesn't conceal inner beauty. Chicks, meanwhile, were pissing between trash cans, smoking, and laughing, laughing, laughing.

Everything previously stated could not, however, eliminate a certain censorship in their talk. Two subjects were taboo, and they had a tacit agreement not to bring them up. One of them was how Alex would get himself set up in America. Nothing would have been easier for Stanley than to help his fourth cousin find his feet in his new country with a maximum amount of comfort or to arrange protected status for him in the movie business, or both. Alas, their friendship was such that he didn't even try to hint at the subject. "Hey, man, I see you're doing all right," he would sometimes say as an introduction, and would then fall silent, as though leaving some breathing space for complaints, or at least for some heavy sigh. And each time Alex would reply: "Can't complain," and they would pass on to one of the previously mentioned topics.

The second off-limits subject was Nora. Even if his behavior was rather unusual for a multimillionaire, Stanley was, at the end of the day, a multimillionaire, and those people always want to know everything that's going on in their entourage, never mind their daughters' love lives. It goes without saying that he was aware of their romance almost from the very beginning, yet he never broached the subject. He didn't ask Alex why he came to Washington so often, as though there were nothing strange about a parking-garage attendant from California visiting the nation's capital at least twice a month. He also kept mum about what Nora told him concerning her feelings. It was only recently, from the hospital, in fact, that he had called Alex at his new apartment in Washington and thus "legalized" the "Nora question." An approaching operation sometimes helps you sort out any awkwardness in your friendships.

Either way, they entered his room, graceful, amusing, casually dressed, beaming at each other with love and humor. "Listen, brother of mine, king of the Buffoons, why don't you marry this princess, your niece five times removed?" Stanley asked in a loud voice, and unexpectedly even to himself. They sat there openmouthed for not less than a minute, then burst out laughing. "I'm sure you've already thought about it, you rats—you just haven't had the nerve to say it out loud in so many words," Stanley went on, relishing their embarrassment.

"What an interesting, positively Homeric idea!" Alex said.

"Positively Homeric, you say?" Stanley asked heartily.

"Yes sir, positively Homeric."

Nora intervened. "Beg your pardon, gentlemen, but are you really intending to marry off a married woman?" She sat there with a prim, if not puritanical, expression on her face. The imperial palm of her father's hand made a gesture of refusal. "The sooner you send your 'Phoenician' packing, the better. We Jews have to back each other up, and the Korbachs all the more."

"Wisdom speaks through your lips, Your Majesty!" Alex said. "What could be more natural than a marriage between an uncle and his niece? Wisdom worthy of Yehudi Kha-Nozi, head of the Sanhedrin!" Nora had already changed from a puritan into a woman of the world from the era of *The Importance of Being Earnest.* "I'm afraid we've overlooked one point in our conversations about the new happy family. The groom also seems slightly married, doesn't he?" Alex hit his forehead with the heel of his hand. "I thank you for that reminder, my lady. I heard that my lawful wedded wife, Anisia, got married to a Haitian prince. They now live in a luxury villa in Port-au-Prince."

"They're to be envied." Nora sighed.

"I hope they don't drink the Port-au-Prince tap water," Stanley said with concern.

"As far as I can remember, she never drank tap water," Alex said innocently.

"Okay, even in the context of the Cold War your marriages don't mean a thing, kids," said Super-Korb. "Let's get down to brass tacks." "He means our wedding, Sashka," the incorrigible Nora explained. "I realized that!" Alex growled in reply. "Enough joking! That'll do for irony!" Stanley yelled in irritation. "Humor and irony are the mind's debauchery. The mind ought to be serious, as someone explained to me not too long ago. So, let's talk about the matter at hand.

"First of all, why I'm interested in your marriage and why I'd like for it to take place as soon as possible. You know that the American and Russian Korbachs were begun by the fertilization of one of Dvoira's eggs by two of Gedali's spermatozoa. We must have been all one clan, but then the Russian Revolution like a miniapocalypse scattered everyone and threw up an insurmountable mountain between us. Are you kids listening to me? Stop giggling! Now we've got a unique opportunity to conquer this mountain, to escape the consequences of the catastrophe and, by unorthodox methods, create a new metaphysical feeling of union. Metaphysical union, that's what interests me in your case.

"You're not exactly young, to put it mildly. Alex is forty-seven, though he looks thirty-seven, and you, Hedgie, you're thirty-seven, though you look fifteen years younger. No, Hedgie, not twenty, fifteen exactly! You love each other, and, as I understand, love to get off with each other, which means that if you decide to stop using pills and condoms one day, you could conceive and give birth to a nice new Korbach, like correcting a historic injustice.

"Now for a few practical questions that I have to bring up as a financial magnate, or, as Sasha's countryfolk would say, 'a shark of Wall Street.' I know you spit on the disgusting wealth of your father and future father-in-law. She already has her own steady income, her professor's salary at Pinkerton University, and solid royalties from her book *The Hygiene of the Ancients,* in which the description of Cleopatra's bathing procedure made our enlightened people tremble.

"As far as Mr. Alex Korbach is concerned—perhaps I should say Professor Korbach—he, having received a portion (small for the time being) of his future great calling, has also become a man who disposes of a steady university income. Of course, this income might be not so very hefty compared with what the Westwood parking attendants make (attention, reader!), but it's free from risk and from the feelings of foreboding peculiar to the parking business."

Eh, what's that? Alexander looked Stanley right in the eye. The latter nodded and took a sidelong glance at Nora. She definitely didn't know about the extracurricular activities of her friend, who had been staked out by AK & BB, Inc.'s secret service. There was no need for her to know. He went on: "So, I have before me two hardworking intellectuals. For all my respect for your independence, however, I want to tempt you with a nice little dowry . . ."

"What?" Nora howled. "Are my ears playing tricks on me? You're offering me a dowry? Are you—" "Shut up!" her father interrupted, not without noticeable anger. "Yes, I want to give a dowry to my daughter, just like all my ancestors hundreds of years ago did! Take for example Señor Samuel Corba de León—he gave his daughter a dozen superb horses, three trunkfuls of velvet-and-lace gowns, three trunkfuls of fine china and dining room silver, an oceangoing ship, a hacienda . . ."

"Father!" Nora whispered pleadingly. "Excuse me, Stanley, but where did you see this dowry of Señora Corba de León?" Alexander asked. "In what archive?" Stanley glanced at him with an almost hunted look. "It doesn't matter where—I saw it, that's all!" He laughed with relief. "I only mean that it's my right to offer a dowry for my daughter, and you, of course, have the right to refuse it. So, then, I offer the crown jewel of our empire for her, the Alexander Korbach Department Store in New York. That's right, my friend, that very building you took for the gates of Judgment Day at the beginning of the book."

"How wonderful!" Nora clasped her fingers together as in an old-fashioned melodrama. "What a generous father I have! Alex, honey, could you ever have thought that that temple of light and luxury could become our property? Just picture our dear little children, Korbachs on both sides, riding up and down on eighteen elevators day in and day out, up and down, up and down!"

Stanley laughed. "That's funny—Korbachs on both sides and eighteen elevators!" Nora went on with the joke. "And what about your favorite, Art Duppertat? Is he included in my dowry?" Stanley suddenly became serious. "Don't worry about Art." Then he looked at his watch meaningfully, flopped back on his pillow, and closed his eyes.

"Well, what do you think about all this?" Alexander asked, as soon as the newly "engaged" couple had driven out of the hospital parking lot. Nora sighed. "I'm very worried about him. I hope it's just the aftereffects of the anesthesia, and that all this business about 'Korbachs on both sides,' dowry in the form of a historic department store, allusions to 'Catalonian forebears' are just flying out of him as part of the recovery process. He doesn't know that I was at his bedside when he was delirious. I suddenly felt strange, listening to his mutterings. I know that Margie and Norman are spying on him. They're carefully trying to get talk going that he's out of his mind. You don't know the story of his three 'disappearances.' It looks like he's getting ready for a fourth."

Trying to maintain the distance between the author and his characters, we're still prepared to thank Nora for mentioning Art Duppertat, that energetic representative of the "yuppie" generation, which replaced the "hippie" generation and thereby made a constructive contribution in many areas of our life, not to mention the notorious "crisis of the cities."

I hope the reader won't object if we direct his indulgent attention to a small phonetic detail in our chronicle. All three of those little words that just sprang onto the page, *yuppies, hippies,* and *Duppertat,* have a double *p* in the middle. This strange phenomenon, in our view, lends a specific plosive energy to them, no? Always stress the double *p,* darling, is Art's advice to his charming and still quite young wife, Sylvia. Don't chew on them like one last strand of spaghetti, press on them, underline them, almost like you're sneezing, because it's the pepper of our family!

Characters, characters, oh, these characters, we'll say in Mr. Gogol's style of "lyrical digression." Isn't it a bother for a novelist to keep them in mind all the time, to make them interact, to display at least some logic in their actions, to find new traits in them—that is, to describe them in development, to drag them up to the mirror from time to time so that they'll take a look at themselves, or to suddenly open a window onto a world of freedom, air, and birds before them—that is, not to leave them in dark storerooms decked with cobwebs, like abandoned marionettes, to drag them out from time to time, give them a good phonetic shower, a good, healthy breakfast, a beer over lunch, champagne over dinner, to treat them well on the whole, as equals, or otherwise you might discover one day that they've run away from their moldy corners and raised a rebellion against you in the distant provinces so as to demand a larger role in the book and even to insist on the abdication of the author and the establishment of their own hippie-yuppie-pepper-puppet-Duppertutto-abracadabra republic.

And then if you show complete respect for your characters and attention to their ideas of limited autonomy pronounced in their storerooms, you might in the final analysis turn your authorial sufferings into a joyful carnival where the characters behave themselves in accordance with the demands of the book, enter and exit on time, and if need be dance around our and your philological fountains, dear creative reader. I haven't made a slip of the tongue and I'm not trying to curry favor—I really do divide readers into the creative ones and "the others," and it's that creative reader, and not some Mr. Skameikin, that I consider the real coauthor of the book. Speaking seriously, every act of reading creates a new version of the book, as in jazz. And God save us from the mechanical "bench-sitting" reader who would grind up even filet mignon into Swedish meatballs, but that's from another opera, esteemed ladies and gentlemen!

Permit me now to raise the curtain a bit, so as to expose a few literary contrivances and some backstage fuss. Then again, you've surely already guessed on your own that we're turning the round of visitors to Stanley Korbach into our own sort of parade of *les personnages,* having as its function to remind the reader of the principal characters of our story.

The Duppertats come in. The thirty-two-year-old head of the family. Still the same springy walk. The same amiable features. Complete readiness to take up any joke, work on it for a few seconds with the help of all the microchips in his brain, and immediately return it enriched. "Hey, Stanley, you look like the fittest father-in-law in the world!" He still doesn't know that his next big takeoff is waiting for him just around the corner, but as a general rule he's ready to take up any assignment at any time. Well, what else is new? That's right, dear reader—a mustache! A remarkable acquisition, à la General Kitchener, with two lightly turned-up tips pointing at any time in the directions of opposite sides of the world. The two sensitive antennae no longer put us in mind of the Pulcinelli of before but rather Basilio, the master of the love potion. And what else within the bounds of common sense, gentlemen? So that I don't look too self-assured, I can't not mention Art's outstanding commercial success. Having firmly established himself with his "toys for aging children," which for some reason had once been so fiercely sought after, he became an important shareholder of AK & BB, Inc., and his own company was getting bigger from year to year. Now, to respect our rule of not playing cat and mouse with the reader, we're going to reveal a secret that is ready to be revealed. Preparing for his "fourth disappearance," Stanley Korbach came to the decision to make his son-in-law one of the most influential VPs of AK & BB, Inc., with a yearly salary of . . . oh . . . enough, no need to rub salt in so many wounds . . . and, with a percentage of the gross, of course. That's how our America treats its favorite sons—if she's decided to make a man rich, then there's no containing her.

Considering all these circumstances, it would seem that there's no need to worry about Art, but for the time being we're going to worry anyway. At times we find him in a strange state of distraction. It seems to him that with each passing year he loses something more important than the "heaping up of wealth"—some alternative, that looming chaos of life that he had once met with in the face of the drunken Russian jerk who by the time of the writing of this sentence had nearly become a relative. These concerns of ours, it seems, are shared by Art's dear wife, his sweetheart Sylvia, who doesn't even admit to herself that she has doubts about Arthur's "stability."

We would say, "Your fears are groundless, Sylvia," if we didn't know that her husband has developed a hankering after new territories—after the Russian earth, in fact, and even more precisely, after Moscow, where he has already gone twice under the guise of "business research" and from where he had returned in a bedraggled state, like a cat after the roof-fight season. From what some of the members of the Buffoons (we'll have the occasion to meet up with them again in the course of the vicissitudes of the novel) have said, we know that Art has flabbergasted more than one girl in the capital of the socialist world with the curious declaration "Russia is in my heart. I need her like I need repentance."

As far as our young beauty is concerned, I myself have to repent before the indulgent—I hope—reader. After meeting her in the second part, we were all of us ready—isn't it true, good sir?—to fall in love with this superb fruit of the Korbach tree but under the influence of some hazy reminiscences preferred more mature women. Now we see that Sylvia has become absolutely irresistible in the domain of tender, Beatrice-like feelings. We ought to qualify this statement, however. From time to time, her face, which had been impassively wonderful, would be visited by some new expression. This expression could lead you with your rapture far beyond the platonic boundaries. With this expression, and also with Baby Harold on her knee, she looked not only like a beautiful woman but like a mildly offended beauty, which turned the heads of gentlemen on the island of Guadeloupe, where she often took her growing child for his upbringing.

At moments like these, a reader inclined to deeper penetration into the world of the character might read the following on Sylvia's face: yes, you take good care of me, thank you, you pulled me out of the lecherous crowd of students at Columbia, you rid me of a few nasty habits, I'm very grateful, you gave me happiness in Baby Harold, you gave me love and protection in the form of your hands and your slightly too hairy chest, but why, kind sir, don't you see me as a person? You know, the way it always is with these insatiable females.

Now it's time to turn our attention to Baby Harold, who has already been sitting on the right shoulder of his grandfather for some time. Together, the two of them form a truly mythological tableau: the aging giant with a cherub on his shoulder. "Now here's a real Jewish boy!" his grandfather exults.

"Begging your pardon, dear patriarch," Art noted, "but Harold has fifty percent Italian blood, not to mention a few other ingredients. Does that tell you anything?" "Absolutely nothing at all." The giant melted under the little buttocks, and his hair stood blissfully on end, snatched up as it was in the controls of tiny fingers. "Harold is a Jew because his mama is a Jew, and because her mama is one-quarter Jewish on her mother's side, and her mother's mother's mama was one hundred percent. Naturally, then, no case of infidelity on the part of this chain of women will be taken into account in our definition of Jewishness, isn't that right, Harold?" *"Mais oui,"* replied the little tyke, who had only just returned from his Creole nanny in Guadeloupe. "Now that's too much for a two-year-old kid!" his delighted grandfather boomed. *"Voilà,"* said his father with a modest bow. His mother said nothing and took the baby down from the tower. She was on the verge of tears.

As they were leaving, Stanley asked Art to stay behind for a minute or two. "Listen, Art, it's clear that I'm going to disappear pretty soon." He was surprised to see his son-in-law looking at him with love and concern, head lowered but eyes up. "Don't say things like that, Stanley! I asked some questions, sir. Everything's okay with your stuffing." His father-in-law laughed loudly. "That's just why I'm disappearing, kid! Right now, time itself is vanishing into thin air." "Your Fourth Disappearance?" Art guessed. "That's right!" said Stanley with the expression of a man who feels completely liberated. "I'm going to leave my fucking business and my whole acquired snooty aristocratic routine. I feel ready to do anything worth doing down here in the kingdom of the air, until I turn into some cosmic object. And you, Art Duppertat, will be my man on the AK and BB board. You've just made first vice president—congratulations, you lucky pup!"

"No, no, Stanley, no! Please, don't pull my leg!" Art begged, rocking back and forth as though he was in the midst of a hurricane. It was a minute at least before he came fully to his senses and asked in a whisper: "Do you want me to keep an eye on Norman?" "You're a bright lad. I never doubted it." His father-in-law smiled.

The parade of characters went on. All of them seemed to have agreed to show Stanley that the world was unshakable and that Atlas was alive and kicking, inasmuch as his arms were busy holding up the globe. Among others, the apple-cheeked Rose Morrows, office manager for Halifax Farm, Maryland, turned up. She was accompanied by her coworker, the pale and buxom Lu Laroq. The ladies brought lots of good wishes from the neighbors in Yornoverblyudo County, including six women, Trudie, Lizzie, Laurie, Milly, Lottie, and Ingeborg, who at one time, before their sweet-smelling marriages, had made up the rock group the Singing Mermaids. Rose took a picture of Lu with her boss and asked the former to take two pictures of her with the boss.

Benjamin Duckworth came down from New York with his fourteen-year-old adopted son Rabindranath. They ran into the aforementioned ladies in the doorway and asked them to wait at the reception desk. "Very glad to meet the chief of my father's crew," Rabindranath said to Stanley Korbach. By way of an explanation of his words, he held out an issue of *Sail and Motor* from 1970, on the cover of which was a picture of two members of the crew of the large yacht *Australian Nightmare,* two American giants, one black and one white, one Senegalese by ancestry, the other Jewish. With their log-size arms around each other, both were laughing, as though their yacht had nearly overdone it trying to clip the nose of the *Australian Star.*

Stanley was quite touched but didn't forget about the matter at hand. "Keep on your toes, Ben," he said to the son of his old war buddy—that is, as though to his own son. "It could be that I'll need you urgently." "Anytime, Stanley" was the immediate reply of the former airborne soldier.

Duckworth and his adopted son Rabindranath had not even left the hospital room before another pair of visitors came in: it was none other than Lenore Yablonsky and Anthony Arrowsmith. That beautiful woman, who had never faded a bit, was a picture of magnificent femininity even now. Hey, she's happy, you know—absolutely happy, happy with no strings attached, everything's great!

Anthony, who was twenty-seven and a bit, didn't look bad either: a black cape was draped over his shoulders, a broad-brimmed hat cast a shadow on his face, his immaculately gloved left hand held the right glove, which he had just removed, and his right hand was extended toward his stepfather. Stanley for some reason was expecting to see a deck of cards in it, but he was mistaken—the hand was held out for a handshake.

Wonder of wonders, Lenore Appleovsky (the Russian version of her name) looked almost shy that evening. At times, she would give Stanley looks that seemed apologetic, as though she was saying: No, no, Stanley, nothing's forgotten, not one of our passionate nights (and mornings, he would add) has dropped into oblivion, but what can I do, darling Stanley, I've fallen for this boy, be nice to him!

Sex, Stanley thought, is an interesting phenomenon, isn't it? Why do people make such a big deal out of these couplings? Why do they think that having it off automatically brings feelings of closeness and warmth? I've copulated with my wife, Margie, countless times, but not once have I felt any closeness or warmth. Take a stroll beneath the echoing arches of the classics, where our Sasha wanders, and you'll see the youth Dante gazing at the young Beatrice. By the time they met he was already the husband of Gemma and a family man, but the idea of having sex with the radiant new beauty never crossed his mind. It was an incomprehensible passion of a different order, from another realm, and not a single sexual impulse visited him or his cavernous body; that's how it sounds in poetry, in any case. As for us, nonpoets but not beasts either, we dress up any lust, any lay, in some foggy costume of nostalgia. What we call romanticism is just a cosmically distant reflection of true love. Even romanticism is beyond our reach, so we thirst after warmth and closeness. Even this forty-one-year-old girl with her impressive record of missions behind the lines in the American sexual revolution looks at me shyly: Stanley, please, don't think that everything's forgotten!

The reason for Lenore and Anthony's coming was quite simple. In the first place, of course, they wanted to offer their sympathies to the recovering patriarch, and to wish him a return to his usual magnificent state of mind and body, and also to his well-known and noble liking for the ladies [sic!]. And let us wish you a happy birthday, too. Many happy returns! In the second place they wanted to inform the head of the clan of their decision to get married. The twelve-year difference in their ages (fourteen-year, Stanley quickly corrected in his mind) doesn't mean a thing if you love someone so all-consumingly and so selflessly. Tony's mother is making trouble—that's the problem. She and Uncle Norman blew up at our decision. Looking desperately for support and warm, mutual understanding—yes, warm, mutual understanding—they had decided to seek Stanley's blessing. They needed his wise advice, as well: how should they act in such circumstances, how could they hold out against the hostility of the family?

There's nothing simpler, my dear children, Korbach immediately replied, at the same time asking himself if they punish people in heaven for this sort of cynicism. Question 1: the sought-after blessing is granted! I couldn't ask for a better wife for my stepson than you, Lenore. Question 2: to rid yourselves of Mom's nagging and grumbling and Uncle Norman's bullshit, you need to take off on a trip around the world on a good old-fashioned honeymoon. Choose whatever you like: charter flights or the famous yacht of Tony, that seafarer. If you need money, get in touch with Art Duppertat at our headquarters; he'll take care of that for you.

"Art Duppertat? At our headquarters?" Anthony exclaimed with an intensity that was somehow out of place. "Ah, Art Duppertat," said Lenore, drawing out the name as though she were remembering something from the movies. "Why not—he's easy to talk to." "I don't doubt it," Stanley said, and dismissed the couple with a regal wave of his hand. And the betrothed headed off into their stormy and unforgettable family life.

The next evening—the night before his discharge from the surgical monastery—one more unexpected visitor for Stanley showed up. This one was not even announced by a bell at the reception desk, which was very strange indeed in a well-run establishment. The door simply opened, and across the threshold, in rubber boots, strode Bernadetta Luxe, the heroine of his almost desperate postoperative dreams. We refer readers who are eager for the details of these dreams to Moscow writers of the younger generation. In addition to the boots, Bernadetta was sporting bright blue overalls and a bright red jacket. This ensemble explained perhaps why the girl hadn't been challenged. The staff had obviously taken her for a plumber. "Stanley Smoothly!" she said in a stage whisper and opened her Venus de Milo arms wide for a huge, loving hug.

"Are you okay? Is everything okay? We were four days and four nights driving here from L.A.! Just imagine your sweet Bernie-Thorny behind the wheel of a huge truck on I-70! Matt couldn't get me away from the wheel! You know, he was crying! The poor guy kept on repeating: 'I respect your feelings, girl, but you need rest, girl! You need to kick back a fifth of Seagram's, have a good screw, and sleep a bit, girl!' 'Shut up,' I'd yell at him. 'I need to see my big baby, he had an operation, he needs my love!' So we drove on day after day, only stopping to fill the tank and unload the tomatoes. Your little friend Cookie"—she reached in a lightning motion into the pocket of her jacket, and right away a tiny little face with a short little nose, a pair of quivering ears, and bulging eyes leapt out—"the poor little thing had to do his business right in my lap sometimes—it doesn't matter, his drops don't add much to the general stink in the world."

Cookie, meanwhile, leapt from the pocket, kissed Stanley on the mouth, and began to rush around on the bed, sniffing here, sniffing there, terribly excited from the different olfactory nuances inaccessible to the overgrown nostrils of modern man. The little creature was most attracted by the toes of Mr. President. He bustled around them, sticking his sharp little nose between them, and finally curled up behind them, regularly sticking his little head out like an elite Chihuahua guard on a crenellated rampart.

"Bernie, dear," Stanley said in a tragic tone, "I've got the greatest esteem for your faithfulness and courage, but alas, kindest of damsels, my recent operation will hardly allow me to respond to the outpouring of your emotion with my former adequacy."

"That's nonsense!" Madame Luxe replied firmly. "It can't be that simple! Come on, Cookie, my boy, let's go to work! You lick our hero's Achilles tendon, and I'll look after the battering ram!" She remembered the curious connection between the two phenomena from her school curriculum.

The blowing of Hellenic breezes, the rustling of zippers, the smacking of lips, the odors of smoldering volcanoes, all the aromas of the Mediterranean expanses, including harvests rising from the depths of Atlantis; what bliss, the reviving Achilles groans, what a wonder this she-monster is working with me!

It goes without saying that after this sinful action we need a spiritual leader, and now, O Theophilus, we already hear his crisp steps in the resounding corridors. Into the room that the healer of bodies has just left comes Rabbi Samuel Dershkowitz. Yes. He's here with his faith, in spite of our ecumenical shortcomings.

Sam Dershkowitz was already described in Part 4 as a man with the severe appearance of a religious fundamentalist. Now we'll add two or three other well-worn stereotypes to this description in the form of a long beard and *peyas*— ringlets twisted into small pigtails at his temples. His outer appearance notwithstanding, he was in his heart probably the most liberal shepherd of any Jewish flock in the Middle Atlantic states. He had a splendid body and the firm stride of a well-conditioned athlete, which not even his liking for strong drink did anything to harm. Having said that, we can't retreat from this subject without saying a few words about his boxing past.

He grew up on a tough street on Manhattan's Upper East Side, and he spent his childhood in fear of receiving a blow from a baseball bat to the top of his head, or the word *kike* in his ear. These troubles led him in the end to a boxers' gym, and before long the street was respectfully calling him Mr. Punch. He even won several trials and was taken on by the Golden Gloves team, but soon after that he quit boxing. I simply can't hit human flesh, much less the receptacles of their thoughts, these heads of theirs. And with the perseverance of his days in the ring, he plunged into the bottomless annals of Jewish wisdom, concentrating on the ancient works of Simon Bar-Yokhan and Yehudi Kha-Nasi; on the *Mishnah* and its parts "Galaki" and "Agadda" that refresh you like good wine, my friend; on the works of Amoriah; on the Babylonian Talmud; on the Masoretic texts; and also on apocryphal works, including Moses Maimonides' *Yat Kha-Khazan*.

In those postboxing years the young man often came back to one fundamental idea, which had sprung up in him as a result of his studies of Jewish history. All the centuries preceding the destruction of the Second Temple, with the exception of the blessed years of the Kings David and Solomon, were times of bloodshed, cruel power struggles, or resistance to occupiers. And only after the humiliating collapse of the state did the remnants of the Jewish people enter into an epoch of humility and reflection, of intensive research into the holy texts and writings, in the day of Zakai and Gamaliel, when philosophy, poetry, and mysticism flourished, and when the nearness of the Mashiakh seemed palpable.

Stanley and Samuel were sitting opposite each other and smiling at each other. The rabbi said: "Stanley, I've known you for almost thirty years, but to this day I don't understand why just looking at you makes me so thirsty." Stanley laughed. "Unfortunately, Rabbi, I can't quench it right now within these walls." Dershkowitz took off his glasses and peered at Korbach's face. "You old sinner, you look like you've just had a very good date!" Stanley jokingly waved him off, but the rabbi insisted. "Admit it. I've come to know you very well in thirty years." Stanley gave a roguish grin. "Twenty-eight years, to be exact. We met at the Yacht Club. You'd just moored your *Tveria,* and you struck up a conversation with me about spinnakers. God bless you, Teacher, but it was on a Saturday."

"That couldn't be!" the rabbi said heatedly. "People can say whatever they like about me, even that Rabbi Dershkowitz sings *niggunim* in the synagogue, but I still absolutely claim that I've never sailed on the Sabbath!"

Stanley went on teasing him. "You were on vacation at the time, Sam, and it's easy to get the days of the week mixed up when you're on vacation." The rabbi smiled. "Do you mean we're both sinners?" "Your words, *mon maître.*" They laughed. Dershkowitz changed the subject. "Either way, I see you're in good shape, that you're coming back to your life, and that you're getting ready to disappear again." Dividing this sentence into three parts, he became more serious with each one.

Stanley was somewhat taken aback. "How did you guess?" The rabbi spread his hands apart modestly. "What, are you against my running away?" "No, I'm not. I just want to tell you one important thing that has to do with it. Please, listen carefully.

"I know, Stanley, that you're always itching to run. In spite of your huge financial successes, you're not a businessman by nature. Well, most people do something that doesn't really suit them, pass their time doing things that aren't for them and at the same time have a vague longing for some other job, some other life, and of course for other women. They're all shackled by a lack of will, and there's a connection between that lack of will and the religious impasse on the question of free will and predestination. Is it worth my trying to attain anything, if everything is already predetermined?

"Other people are of a slightly or strongly 'demonic type,' the ones who in literature are called Byronites—they throw down the gauntlet to fate, but then they throw up their hands, thinking that even these challenges were predestined. You're of that very type, Mr. President.

"Of course, I don't know your true calling. Maybe you were born to be an artist, or an adventurer, or a kind of 'messiah.' I use the word in quotation marks and with a lowercase initial letter, because most of the time we're dealing with so-called false prophets. They're almost always outstanding people, and we've known quite a few of them in Jewish history, from the great Bar Kokhba to the not very great David Alroy. Often they reach such a high state of exaltation that they seem to themselves like divine envoys. Others are caught up in megalomaniacal ambition. This phenomenon is as old, or as young, as the human race. Unfortunately, in many cases, it has cost the contemporaries of these 'prophets and messiahs' dearly, ravaging minds and populated lands. I know that your 'disappearances,' which go by Roman numerals in your family, are your search for yourself, some sort of ontological essence of yours, and for that reason I beg you to keep away from the idea of worldwide happiness for all, from any megalomaniacal Homeric *tsdaki*. The world can't be happy. However prosperous it might be, it's all a reality of earthly being, a turning into dust. I know that you've got a reliable guard against megalomania, and that's your sense of humor, well-known to every yachtsman on the East Coast; we know, however, that might and power can often corrupt a man, and I'm afraid for you. I love you, my friend, and I pray that your humor won't desert you!"

The shadows in the hospital room were lengthening. The wind outside suddenly plastered three lemon yellow leaves against the window, and they clung to the wet surface, forming a strange configuration, an unreadable harbinger. Stanley laid the log of his arm on the stone of Samuel's shoulder. "Tell me, friend, do you still feel thirsty in my presence? Then have a snort!" Dershkowitz didn't have to be begged; he took out a flat flask. Megalomania, Stanley thought. Why, I'm just trying to run away from the feeling of my own insignificance. It's the same with me, thought the rabbi, and so I'm clearing off from this text until at least the last chapter. Take my *brakha* and . . . see you!

3

THE FOURTH DISAPPEARANCE: GONE!

*T*he last in the chain of visitors, of course, was the head of the staff of servants at Halifax Farm, Enoch Agasf, who had been almost visibly present in the room already, and whose fleeting passage had been noticed by Sister Elizabeth in particular. This time he appeared with two of his great-grandsons—for that matter, they might have been great-great-great-great: add as many *great*s and hyphens as your heart desires—and the three of them, without asking any questions, quickly began to pack Korbach's belongings in some sort of bottomless sack that gave off a smell of badly tanned oxhide and shepherds' campfires from Jewish settlements. Stanley, meanwhile, was decking himself out in velvet trousers, a flannel shirt, and a warm jacket. With half an ear he listened to the mutterings of the old Semite: "The earth also was corrupt before God, and the earth was filled with violence. And God looked upon the earth, and behold, it was corrupt; for all flesh had corrupted His way upon the earth."

"We're ready, boy," he said finally to his beloved master. The hitherto invisible Sister Elizabeth emerged from her corner and made the sign of the cross over the vanishing ones. Agasf gave only a twitch of his shoulders. A large white limousine was waiting for them in the darkness of the parking lot as though on a drifting ice floe in a blizzard-swept night.

In February of 1987, Alexander Korbach was beginning his first semester at Pinkerton University. As one might expect, the new arrival received a generous selection of invitations to receptions and dinner parties in his honor: a "wine & cheese" at the theater department, a "brown bag" luncheon hosted by the members of the core curriculum subcommittee, dinner with the board of trustees, a "Russian carousel" laid on by the old playboy Professor Steve Iglokluvov, and so on and so forth, and finally lunch with the president himself, a lanky "Anglo" with watery blue eyes, filled with the basic ideas of the Enlightenment—never fall out of context.

Having no experience of academic life, Alexander was expecting that some sort of examination of his creative and pedagogical intentions would be made during this round of social events—he was even ready for an explanation of his philosophy of theater. Nothing of the sort, though, happened. People were nothing but friendly, said, "welcome aboard," looked at him as though expecting him to tell a joke, and asked questions that concerned mostly the parking business that the newspapers had talked about, the thing they seemed to consider the most humorous period of his life.

"For God's sake, darling, take it easy," Nora would say. "These people teach philosophy, history, physics, astronomy, archaeology, whatever you want. They don't want to talk seriously at receptions, they want to chat, make dumb jokes, and clown around. What's more, let me tell you frankly that no one on campus takes the position of 'director in residence' seriously, no one's expecting a revolution from you. In a way, they see in you a bald comic artist that the university can afford. So you see, honey, everything's come full circle: you're a Buffoon again! Isn't that wonderful?"

Well now, my love, my one and only, you're not terribly tactful, are you? he thought. He might even have been cut to the quick by this apropos rejection of a significant role for him in university life. Okay, let's see what'll come of this in the end. If they want to have a laugh, why don't they look for their target in the archaeology department?

Meanwhile, he was still finding his feet in his new surroundings, in Washington, D.C., that box of surprises, lashed onto a hump in the state of Virginia right beneath the paunch of the state of Maryland. In contrast to L.A., it was a real city, where people congregated on street corners, called to each other from across the street, held on to their raincoats flapping in the swirling winds of the urban labyrinth, grabbed at their hats to keep them from flying away, ran after these hats that had flown away anyhow, pursued them right up to a triumphant end or to a bitter defeat—that is, to complete bewilderment at an intersection, to hatlessness in the middle of traffic raining down on them suddenly from nine directions (a peculiarity of Dupont Circle), in the intermingling of all the winds, resorted to clever tricks to evade greasy drops of chili sauce or ketchup, burst into cozy hole-in-the-wall coffee shops, caught their breath, asked (begged) for anything warm and friendly, listened with horror to the latest news from Panama, did a little dance so as to look like regulars, had a piece of cake from a display of baked abundance, smeared their faces with blueberry cream, put in their two cents in "pro-life, pro-choice" discussions, took a bullet in the stomach and returned fire wide of the mark, kissed the target inside and outside, shoved it down on their heads, then continued following it on its way—that's a real city for you, not the endless plantations of Los Angeles.

One morning he woke up with a lovely feeling of urban Gemütlichkeit. Got to devote this entire free day to the needs of my city life. To putting in all sorts of devices—gadgets, they call them—without which life is impossible: radio hi-fis, boom boxes, TV-VCRs, all of those things in all of their techno-glory. In theory, I really need to turn this one-bedroom into a nice little burrow for a bachelor artist who has yet to sell his freedom for the multimillion-dollar dowry of countless young ladies. Having decided on this, he began hanging pictures of Nora on the wall, no fewer than a dozen, framed: as a child, smiling, flirting, swimming like a dolphin, digging up our archaeological planet, getting cross, beaming at the Sight of Guess Who, waiting for SOGW, riding Gretchen, dancing, wearing glasses, drunk as a skunk, waiting to get laid, trying to lie, demanding the truth. Well, what else? Must lay a carpet opposite the fireplace—a dark blue Tunisian rug that Nora had bought on an expedition to Quok Island, shaggy and soft; now you see how everything's turning out, Comrade General Sitny, you asshole, who predicted ruin in the "soulless West." The oval writing desk, made to Nora's order for a thinking director, will go right here in the den with a window looking out on Dupont Circle. And why not stroll around the neighborhood and pick up a couple of table lamps? Walk around town with an umbrella serving as the walking stick of an urban gentleman, and ready at any moment to turn into the umbrella of an urban gentleman, indeed. How wonderful to live on Dupont Circle, where everything is either across the street or around the corner! Take the Childe Harold café, for example, and here's Kramerbooks with the Afterwords Cafe attached, and there's the Janus cinema—four-faced, in fact, A.Z. jokes without forcing it, since four masterpieces play in its four halls at the same time; and let's toss out a few other storefront signs to give the reader an idea of the quarter of the city that we have chosen to live in for the time being: Rabelais, Zorba, Frontline, and Lambda Rising to boot.

It's nice to live in a real city, he thought, and even better to be out of the reaches of that parking-garage business, where you thought every knock at the door was a visit from the Bureau of Alcohol, Tobacco and Firearms. At that very moment, his thoughts were interrupted by a loud knock at the door, produced by the lion's head of Korbach's very own knocker. He looked through the peephole and saw a burly man in a uniform just outside. He could, of course, turn out to be an ATF agent, but he looked more like a general in the Soviet Army. Could the Reds have taken the city in the night?

"Mr. Korbach, sir," the "general" said with exemplary politeness, "Mrs. Marjorie Korbach apologizes for this unannounced visit, but extraordinary circumstances force her to ask for a confidential audience with you." Alexander Zakharovich opened the door and saw a Silver Ghost just beyond the file of cars parked along the sidewalk. A second later, a slender, eternally young lady with a pair of large, dramatic eyes and a sad mouth popped out of the limousine.

A.Z. had long been used to the fact that no meeting in America, be it for business or for love, could take place without an offer of some drink to ease the possible sufferings of a parched throat. "What would you like to drink, Marjorie?" he asked. "Tea, coffee, mineral water, beer, Scotch?" The answer was most unexpected. "Thank you, Mr. Korbach, beer will be fine." And it was. The picture of Marjorie Korbach among the clutter of the undecorated apartment with a can of Bud in her hand was worth remembering.

"Yes, ma'am." He was sitting across from her, his interlaced fingers over the knee of a crossed leg—his left, to be precise. In the USSR this had been his preferred "rehearsal posture." Nora loved to comment on this pose. "Look at the master's hands, dear readers! Look at the nervous trembling of the fingers! It reflects a greater artistic nature!" He looked at his guest and thought that her "Mr. Korbach" was to give him to understand that she considered him a relative from neither the one nor the other side of the family. All right, then, his "ma'am" signals his full understanding of the situation. "Alex!!!" one of the best girls of the fifties generation suddenly shrieked with three exclamation marks, and all the unexpressed hurt of that generation seemed to sound in the cry. "Stanley's disappeared! They were supposed to discharge him from that dreadful hospital, but he disappeared in the night! He left unnoticed by anyone! I'll sue them for ten million! My dear husband has disappeared!" Eight phalluses, that is, exclamation marks, kind ladies and gentlemen—you don't have to count them—sounded in the drawn-out wail of the unhappy woman. Alex Korbach wiggled his artistic fingers, as though trying to reduce the level of exaltation.

"Don't worry, Marjorie! He wasn't kidnapped, don't expect any ransom demands—I'm sure that he disappeared by his own decision."

"This is the fourth time it's happened," Marjorie whispered. A whisper like that could curdle blood in the veins. "The fourth time in the twenty-three years of our marriage. He alway joked about his 'disappearances,' but I take them seriously. It's dangerous, Alex! He's not normal! He's visited by people from the past! With the levers of financial power that he has at his control, he could do something terrible! He could wreck our home, our family, our corporation, the whole country! Please, Alex, don't pay any attention to my gawking, it's just Graves' disease, that's all. You know, I'm ready to sacrifice myself for the sake of my family, Alex Korbach (I'm stressing it, Kor-bach!) but I don't want to sacrifice my family, our entire clan for the sake of some arcane ideas that are the result of male menopause!

"Yes, we're rich, but the rich are people, too—they can cry, despair, sacrifice themselves for their loved ones, like I'm ready to offer myself up for Stanley! Everyone knows what comes of those lousy egalitarian theories: Nazism, Bolshevism, terrorism—you know it better than I do.

"Alex, you were my husband's closest friend for three years. I even got a bit annoyed at the constant mention of your name. Alex here, Alex there, Alex said this, Alex said that . . . Yes, yes, please, another beer, thanks very much. . . . In theory, you're even a distant relative of ours, aren't you? You know, I've never been against your romance with Nora. After her stormy life, she's finally found a quiet port. Alex, let me say this frankly: you're the only one who can save our family from disgrace! I'm sure that Stanley will turn up on your doorstep soon for a drink and a chat. Please, just let me know that he's alive! I don't even dare ask you for a huge favor, but maybe even so you could try to talk him out of this ridiculous escapade?"

She buried her face in an exquisite handkerchief; her shoulders shook slightly—at that moment, she looked like a college student in some classic film. She's only two years older than I am, thought A.Z. In order to suppress emotions that had no place there, he looked away from Marjorie and began to watch the city life outside the window.

It was getting dark, putting the picture in sharper focus. In a crowd by the Metro a gangling, brightly dressed Jamaican was breathing a long tongue of fire from his mouth. A few passersby fell to their knees before him: Have pity, Zarathustra! He was waving into the distance with both hands, as if saying: Congratulations, Sashka the Buffoon! You've become a character in a real soap opera!

VII. MIRACLE IN ATLANTA

One day a demon dropped me off
At the Atlanta airport.
Drawing one in with his hugeness
He was akin to Atlas.

To a merchant,

The one whom our ball drew
Into the arena of commerce,
And there he stands, not having moved,
And not having set prices.

The vendor is good!

Everything here was from a giant's shoulders.
To capital cities in order of importance
An underground train was hauling
Crowds of passengers,

Playboys, spendthrifts.

To glimpse some Peruvian llamas,
To catch the sound of bells' ringing,
Of Tibetan lamas, and airplanes
Taking off on business.

Shalom to all of them!

In a bag hanging on a shoulder,
I was dragging my gear along
When suddenly an extraordinary event was triggered:
The central computer failed

On one of the mornings.

The crowd's shouting is like the cawing of crows.
Chaos whirls like a hellish dervish,
A maelstrom at all the gates:
No takeoffs, no landings!

Surge forth, people!

All the popcorn was already eaten.
A donkey fell into a gloomy mood,
And on the floor among the columns
People sprawled like swine.

There're the swings for you!

In addition to that, my friends,
There blew up stormy weather
From those that I don't dare
To rhyme with together.

Farewell, visions!

Like the shaggy locks of a black beard,
The whole neighborhood began to sway.
With a huge mass of water
Appeared typhoon Hugo.

It tore off the reins.

It seemed that the sky's arch would crack
And blueness gush out of the cracks,
And the whole airport would collapse
Like Atlantis Station,

Crushing the sinful.

In the Irish Pub I took an oath
Of loyalty to the Free Earth,
When suddenly the bartender signaled
And shouted: No more beer!

Without etiquette.

The beer's run dry! Who could imagine
This dive parched?
Shake the earth, acid smog—
Everything would be simpler.

Where can you find a beer?

Suddenly, to the bar, among the tipplers
Came a young lady,
Wise like a throng of old women,
Fresh like Adam's daughter.

And the rustle of trousers!

All the world went quiet, having spied the beauty,
Forgetting about the lightning's brawl,
A parachute, gleaming, descended
From Portinara's gondolas.

She had a Campari.

A hundred lime trees trembled,
Horseshoes clattered,
And suddenly some guy began to sing,
A juggler from the counties of Moscovia,

Hoarse and husky.

"The system of saturated vocal cords
Is no good for cantos,
And just the same, brothers,
My song sings for the Doña."

So inspired

By her divine beauty
And the nobility of her gestures!
Thus an old cuirassier dreams
About a young maiden:

He's not made of tin!

We have not met these eyes
For perhaps seven centuries,
And he who is overly inclined to obscenity
Will be punished with the lash.

So I've had my say.

O thou, purest of women,
Accept my music!
I am, you see, struck by amour,
Though I shriek here roosterlike

Beneath a starry sign.

The Pleiad warms the vault of the heavens,
Instill heat in a man.
Is it not there, the world of holy freedoms—
Are they not there, all of the reasons

About which we shout?

You see, our life is vulgar.
The meaning of distinction is lost.
Say whence you descended,
Holy Beatrice,

To our perishable slag heap.

He looked around. Everyone
Prayed silently—
A suntanned beach bum from Miami,
A farmer from Alaska,

Devotees of physical love.

One venerable gent,
A Windy City venerologist,
Extended a dumpling on a fork,
When suddenly a solo burst out

Following the juggler.

He sang of the tricks played by love,
Venereal pranks,
Of how little nightingales
Care about dragonflies,

And about splinters.

Holy Lady, he prayed,
Send us heat without gnats,
Sacred syrup without tar,
Gardens without pubic parasites,

And some stale pastry.

The whole club of men joined in singing:
A builder, a con man, a lecturer,

A driver of mules and donkeys,
And a homicide detective.

So many words!

Holy Lady, show
The road back to preancient days,
Where knives were not set in motion
By jealousy, the murderer of love,

The sister of lie.

After that came the moment of parting.
The Irish den trembled.
A mime leaned over in alarm.
A poet bent down, curving inward,

Exhausted by melancholy.

A Parisian barber shrieked,
A pagan priest of science began to cry.
Just then, the first flight was announced:
United, to Kentucky.

Be kind to us!

Without having said a word,
She got down from her stool,
White as a mountain goat,
Light, not stooped,

As though blown away by the wind.

And anyone who was harsh in life,
And those who had a weakness for the sensual,
Watched, as through a gleam of spheres
She walked to the boarding gate.

A noiseless explosion

Shone in her Campari.
Noiseless were the howls.
A fountain was surging up and dying down.
Everyone received a drop.

And dreams died.

PART VIII

1

"PINKERTON"

Ten months have passed since the end of Part 7, and "Fall '87," to use the language of academic semesters, has begun. The sets have changed substantially. The campus of Pinkerton University, with its expansive grounds and inspiring layout, has entered the novel. Pseudo-Gothic towers exchange shouts with postmodern buildings, lending a certain quality of mystery to the expanse. In keeping with the new trends, the century-old statue of the school's founder—apparently some colonial ancestor of the famous Scottish-born detective—with all the usual trappings, such as a cocked hat, wig, a craw that looked like a dove's, a walking stick that he had so often wanted to lay across the backs of the students, those lackadaisical Virginia louts, and also stockings and shoes with buckles, turned out to be on a sharply sloping square, forming the center of somebody's "conception of shift."

Well, what else is new? A huge number of characters have been added to the story in the form of twenty-five thousand Pinkerton students. Here they are ambling from parking lots the size of pastures to the classroom buildings, some dressed in rags worthy of that Chairman of Planet Earth and Futurist poet Velimir Khlebnikov, and some according to the rules of their clubs: blazers and ties, shorts, ruddy knees like guardsmen's chins. If you ask any of them what they're going to do after graduation, they'll answer: Work for the CIA. Others will say: Join the worldwide revolution. There are quite a few Iranians in the shuffling crowds. It's a curious thing: they curse America as the "Great Satan," and they send their children to Satan for their studies. Our kids ask these newcomers: Is it true that drinking's not allowed over there, guys? They answer: Not during the day, but at night, if the doors are well-locked. And is this fucking revolution of yours going to go on for a long time? The Persians laugh. If a mullah mounts an ass, he's not going to dismount until the ass kicks the bucket. Like our Soviet motherland, the director in residence thinks as he walks among the students, only he puts the question differently: Who's going to kick the bucket first, the ass or the mullah?

Paths wind among fastidiously mowed rounded hills. It's not a short walk, and you hear all you want of all sorts of things along the way, even Persian jokes. The roads gradually merge as you go along, and there are more and more people, but the single largest crowd is outside the Student Union. The country is fighting nicotine, but here everyone is smoking. Hey, man, how's it going, didn't fuckin' see you last night! Didn't fuckin' see *you,* either. Long fuckin' time since I've seen you, man! And it's been fuckin' ages since I've seen you, man! How ya fuckin' doin'? Doin' fuckin' great! Why the fuck didn't you come to Tracy's? I was at fuckin' Susie's last night, you dumb motherfucker! (Now, for you Russian readers of this version, if you think that the most often used word in this dialogue has anything to do with the word *faculty,* we hasten to disabuse you: only in part, ladies and gentlemen.)

And after four years of standing around like this, they turn out to be great specialists of "the relative" and "the absolute," Alexander Zakharovich thought with groundless venom as he passed through the crowd, even though he understood perfectly well that not all the students were standing there, and that those who were standing there didn't always stand there, and that there wasn't always a crowd standing there anyway. After his first year of university work, A.Z. had little reason for sarcasm; on the whole, everything was going well for him, but that's the eternal Russian dissident spirit: don't expect any joy from it, just the gloom of a piglet contemplating its future, and by the truckload.

He entered the huge cafeteria, where half the people present were scattered around the hall eating, and the other half were standing with their trays in line for the Korean cashiers. He often preferred the cafeteria to the faculty club, where one always had to find something clever to say. You go quickly to the salad bar and pour some healthy food—beets, carrots, broccoli, beans, something else, I don't know its name and patronymic—onto a paper plate. Then over to the vats of hot soup, ladle a dab of chili into a plastic cup, and there you go! Take a little packet of fried onion rings off the shelf for courage, pour yourself a big glass of diet Coke, and you're set. Now you get in the line for the cashier. You jerk off with a few lousy ethnic generalizations: they're brainy guys, but procrastinators, these Koreans! In point of fact, however, there's really no one in the world who can add up the price of the food you've chosen faster than the Korean cashiers at Pinkerton—no one in the world!

At the far end of the room a rock group is playing, to ensure that no one can eat in peace. The lead singer, a long-limbed, round-shouldered type wearing what looks like long johns that have seen better days and with a hairdo out of *The Prisoner of Chignon* is belting out a refrain mighty in its mournfulness: le-bee-ts-kaya-sssiiilllaaaa! The drummer, for some reason nattily dressed, with a bow tie, is hitting the nail on the head with every syllable. Natty dressing ends with him: two others in moth-eaten T-shirts, the kind that people here both sleep and go to class in, are extracting from their crotches electronic roulades worthy of Elton John's band. These guys aren't howling in Russian, are they? No, of course they aren't, it's just the usual stuff they're singing, don't be silly, it's just A.Z., sensitive to everything Russian, imagining he hears his own native rubbish. The room, meanwhile, is chewing, flipping through fat catalogs, no one paying any attention to anyone, even if you're the smartest guy going, like our Alexander Zakharovich. Then again, even here there are five girls swooning before the hacks, since even these swineherds haven't been deprived their fair share of female admirers. A.Z. mutters to the vegetables that he's eating: That's the world we live in, that's the world we sin in, heights and depths are reached by bums, just fuckin' around and bangin' drums.

Suddenly, a voice comes from all the way across the hall. "Sasha, Sasha, we've got an emergency!" Rolling in between the tables like a hat in the wind is Korbach's greatest fan, Lyusha Beaujolais, assistant director of the Black Cube and a relative of foreign wines. What's the matter, Lucia? I suppose Harry Pons and Robby Flook are under the gas again? They didn't come for their costume measurement? Let's hang the scoundrels from the mast!

From a distance, the Black Cube resembles the Holy Stone of Kaaba stood on one of its corners. Close up, and particularly inside, this resemblance disappears. You find yourself in a labyrinth of staircases and galleries, spheres and cubes that suddenly lead into a hall for an audience with a stage that can be hauled up and down, to the left and to the right—when you come down to it, you could hang it on your ears if you wanted.

The appearance in the theater department of the "director in residence," the Russian daredevil with the out-and-out American name, was greeted benevolently, if not joyfully. No one had ever heard of him, of course, or of his Moscow Buffoons, but everyone had read the "résumé" Nora had worked up for him from newspaper clippings and now pretended to be completely au courant. It's wonderful, Sasha, that you can carry on your Moscow explorations with us, at Pinkerton of all places! What would you like to start with, *starik*? Department Chairman Nigel Tabbac, who passed for a classicist, encased in a heavy hand-knit cardigan, with a big ruddy face framed by graying sideburns, shone with the soft hues of a watercolor palette.

Alexander began cautiously taking the measure of things from a distance. They say that there was once a city called Florence. Not quite the Florence that millions of tourists litter with pizza crusts these days. In *this* Florence, if three men walked down the street after sunset, their heels clattering, there would be conversations about an uprising of the "Guelphs" or "Ghibellines." It was there, seven hundred years ago, in the glow of early courtly troubadourism, that the *dolce stil nuovo* was born. Two poets, two Guidos, talked endlessly about love, not having in mind exactly what today's mobs of tourists meant by the word. They spoke also of the music of the golden Greco-Roman age: What was it like, were there songs about love, was it in the right key? One day, he was shyly approached by a young man from a family of "White Guelphs," Alighieri. In the ruins of the palace of Marcus Aurelius he'd found a flute that was a thousand years old. So, that's the beginning. What do you say, folks?

"I don't much like that era," Professor Tabbac admitted and somehow thickened slightly, that is, became even more unctuous in his tone. "The early Renaissance has a whiff of decadence about it. What's the play called, Sasha?" Alexander confessed that the play didn't exist yet, but that he could write it in a month. His younger colleagues, almost killing themselves to be tactful, began to remonstrate with the newcomer. Dante—it's always a forbidding subject, too serious, you know. We're dealing with students, after all, all they want are the usual bread and circuses. You still need to assemble your troupe, after all, don't you think, Sasha? They didn't tell him, of course, that for Dante they'd have to invite some Italian, after all, and not a Russian. Korbach immediately underwent a chameleonic change. My colleagues are probably right. We need to find something else for the students. Let's say, Petersburg in the early nineteenth century, Gogol's *Diary of a Madman*—that would more fun, simpler. We'll even stick in "The Nose" and at the same time some Shostakovich. We'll play it with a company of ten.

"Enchanting!" the department chair cried, and Sasha got to see what his "enchanted" shade looked like.

The entire department threw itself enthusiastically into working on Korbach's show. Throngs of students turned up for auditions. A.Z. was dashing off his "Gogoliana"—that is, something that the Party critics in Moscow, without beating around the bush, would have labeled "a mockery of our classical heritage." A dozen copies of the script were immediately run off for the students, and they rehearsed and discussed it. Students rushed around on the staircases of the Black Cube. Tabbac attended these near-riots with a paternal smile. "Sasha, your Dostoevsky won't let me sleep," he would say. "Gogol, Nigel, Gogol!" A.Z. would correct him for the tenth time. "It's all Dostoevsky to me!" the classicist stubbornly insisted.

The students, of course, fell in love with the uncontrollable Russian genius. They had fifty purple T-shirts printed with, on the front, a picture of Sasha taken in a moment of directorial exaltation, with all the details exaggerated—a distended mouth, bulging eyes, and extraterrestrial jug ears—and the words BUFFOONS OF THE POTOMAC on the back. Forgetting about everything in the world, he rehearsed as he had in the glory days in Moscow's Presnya. At times, words failed him, at which point he would bellow or wave his extremities to point out the effect they needed to strive toward. Things were even more comprehensible that way than with words. Sometimes he even forgot that he was working in America. At particularly daring points in the script he would look around: were there stool pigeons from the Repertoire Commission anywhere in the darkened theater? "What's happening to you, Sashka?" Nora would laugh. "You look ten years younger. It's only your baldness that saves me."

She was exaggerating, of course, but he was indeed seething inside, even though he stopped going to his former extremes of self-expression in bed. That's what he's been missing all these years, the poor boy, she thought, kissing his head during their revelations, just as lengthy and sweet as before, but, alas, no longer as irregular, if we may say so. I'm lucky that he didn't have a theater when we met, even a fleapit like the Black Cube. He sublimated everything to me, and gave me a sort of love that I'd never known before. Now these Homeric delights are going to be squeezed out by the theater. Mama was right—he's one of them, a *cabotin*.

Oh well, she would go on—pretty soon he'll have to get acquainted with the role that I play—and would leave for Houston. Along the way she continued squaring her accounts with Alexander. We're each other's closest friends, but we've hidden so much from each other for so long, and we're still hiding things. He tells me almost nothing about his sons, doesn't say much about his former family life, never mind about women in Moscow. He kept quiet for so long about that damned Westwood parking garage and about the Hotel Cadillac, and even now he seems to be hushing up something from that period. I'm one to talk, though: even if I've told him a bit, there's still a lot under wraps. Just like now, I'm keeping him in the dark about Houston. "What're you always running off to Houston for, clever Nora?" he asked one day, as though he wasn't even expecting an answer, as though he didn't attach any importance to it, and rustled a few of his Gogol papers. Well, if you're not very interested, then there's nothing to tell. "Oh," Nora answered, in the same matter-of-fact way as the question, "some people are working up an archaeological project down there," and it seemed as though she weren't lying, though in fact she was lying through her teeth, and then she left for Houston.

2

OTHER SPHERES

*N*ora got fixed up in Houston by her cousin Mortimer Korbach, Air Force colonel and American astronaut. Back at the memorable Korbach gathering on the Maryland estate, Nora, tearing herself away from thinking about the Russian faun for ten minutes, had struck up a conversation with Mort about archaeological research in space. It would be good to have a look at the areas of ancient civilizations from orbit, say, at the Fertile Crescent from the Euphrates to the Nile, or at the Cuzco region of the Andes. Why don't you include an archaeologist in the shuttle crew one day—let's say Nora Mansour, Ph.D.? Mort had squinted and said that he didn't see anything crazy about the idea, though it was proposed by an insanely beautiful woman—on the whole, a compliment entirely in the style of our Air Force.

They had their chat and then forgot about it, all the more since on that night of owls and bats she was thinking not so much about outer space as about the meadows along which she would need to gallop to take the faun alive. Six months had gone by when Mort called to say that Houston was interested in her project. "Project? Did you say 'my project,' Mort?" "If you're such a reckless woman," the colonel said with a chuckle, "then you need to go to the NASA office on Independence Avenue tomorrow and get them to agree to your 'proposal.' "

For some reason, all her thoughts began to turn not around the Earth but around Sashka. Now he'll think that I'm a raving feminist. As though I've got something to prove to him. Should I forget about this nonsense? Or should I write the proposal after all? What the hell—why not write it, why not test the hardiness of our bureaucracy? And not say anything to Sasha about it—what does he care about my studies, after all? He's all caught up in his own complexes.

The bureaucracy turned out to be alive and kicking, which was confirmed by its long, dead silence. All at once, a year before the events described in this part, some barriers were lifted, and the whole business—wonder of wonders!—moved ahead! That's how it goes, good sirs—ten pages ago we weren't even entertaining the idea of sending our Nora into space, and all the while her candidacy was being given serious consideration in governmental, military-space, intelligence, financial, and scientific circles. Various committees began to invite her to their sessions, at which her ideas, among other things, were discussed. At congressional hearings on science, one of her statements excited particular interest. "Archaeology, gentlemen," she said, "has more to do with space than with present-day biology." All seven gentlemen sitting on the dais looked at each other—that is, the three on the left and the three on the right all looked at the one in the middle. Our society pricks up its ears when it hears a one-liner. The lethargy of received wisdom needs a few blows of the whip from time to time. The chairman of the committee removed his glasses. Everyone froze: How should we interpret this movement? The chairman said: "In the name of present-day biology, allow me to thank you for your sincerity, Mrs. Mansour!" In America, a good laugh often decides things. It seems that that's what happened in this case.

Nora understood that she would be investigated, and didn't rule out the possibility that her student past could come back to haunt her as an argument against her candidacy. She also imagined the arguments in her favor: now, gentlemen, the daughter of Rita O'Neill and Stanley Korbach simply had to play the revolutionary when she was seventeen. The important thing is that right now we're dealing with a serious scientist, the author of the much-talked-about book *The Hygiene of the Ancients*. This person is also a well-educated, pretty face of the female gender, and she will demonstrate the progress made by that recently still enslaved segment of society.

Finally, the presidium of the American Archaeological Society meets—people who are no slouches in the domain of breaking from the existing world into the spheres that lie there motionless. In the majority of cases, unexpected experiments produce unexpected results, gentlemen. Many archaeological discoveries have been made with the aid of aviation. Satellite photos are widely used in geology. Some of the subject matter of the supermarket tabloids could take on a scientific character. Observation of the Pyramids from orbit, for example. Dr. Mansour is proposing her own method of investigation of the zone around the city of Ur. There's one more important factor in favor of the Mansour expedition. The appearance in her person of the first archaeologist in outer space will attract an enormous amount of attention to the problems of our scientific community and could lead to greater financing of our expeditions and publications. In a word, Good luck,

Dr. Mansour! At this point we'll add a certain observation concerning mores. Americans always approach legal tender with their mouths hanging open, making no attempt to close them, unlike the Russians, who loiter, pretending that their "filthy lucre" doesn't even interest them particularly, because, as they say, there are higher spheres. What one's to make of that, I don't know—I leave it up to you, ladies.

Going for her first physical examination in Houston, Nora said nothing to Alex. Only after her return, with a laugh: "You know, I just had a physical the other day, and the doctor said to me: 'You're in excellent health, you could even go on the space shuttle.' " Just at that moment Alexander Zakharovich was adjusting her in one of her favorite positions and panting in his best style. "I never doubted it, darling," the insolent stud answered. "Every meeting with you is like a rocket launch."

Again and again she went to Houston: one time to become familiar with the equipment, the next for a week of training, but he didn't even seem jealous. From time to time he would ask entirely formal questions like "So how are you getting on in Houston?" accepting her equivocations without any doubts. He was already completely caught up in his show, at that damned Black Cube, where those Pinkerton sluts were virtually lap-dancing for him in his office. Finally, Nora decided once and for all: I won't tell him anything about it to the end—let him find out about it from the TV!

In imitation of Vladimir Nabokov and his Tolstoyevsky, and considering the literary orientation of his department head, Alexander invented an author for the play: Lieutenant Gogloyevsky. The poster advertising the show looked rather odd, intended as it was to intrigue the enlightened inhabitants of northern Virginia, southern Maryland, Georgetown, Downtown, and Federal Triangle: "The Black Cube presents Lieutenant Gogolyevsky's play *Mr. Nose and Other Allies of Common Sense,* staged by Alexander Korbach under the aegis of the Pinkerton University Theater Department. Sponsors: Alexander Korbach Department Stores, Inc., Doctor Duppertutto, Dolls for Grown-ups Co. People with no sense of humor are requested not to bother."

The last line brought an objection from Professor Tabbac. "That's a rude thing to say. The people to whom it's addressed will get offended and won't come." The *artistes* were naively surprised. "But who could think that it's directed at them?" After thinking about it for a while, the professor agreed, "All right—so long as it's not addressed to me, I won't object."

A week before the show, A.Z. began to torment himself. It'll be a flop! These kids aren't professionals, they'll get scared, they'll get all my "biomechanics" mixed up, the sound system will break down, of course, we never did get the lighting entirely sorted out, the "demiballet" that we thought up and rehearsed will turn into the meaningless shoving of some suburban boneheads—oh, and then the sets will fall down.

A.Z. had underestimated modern youth. The show went off smoothly, without a single departure in tempo or rhythm, virtually without a hitch. The kids didn't show the slightest inhibition—as though they played before a house packed with the beautiful people of Virginia every night. At times it even seemed that they'd had a bit more than their fill of this crowd. Maybe they'd sniffed a bit of "powdered sugar"? As a man not entirely naive where such things were concerned, A.Z. knew that after a good snort any fiddler in a restaurant could play like Paganini, then melt like shtetl dough an hour later. In the same way, the marasmus of "The Nose" is going to start in an hour. After the second act starts, I'm out of here.

"Everything okeydokey, boss? What's the matter?" The kids tried to reassure him at intermission. "Why're you so pale, Sasha? Having a bad hair day?" Beverley, Kimberley, and Roxy Moran, the inhabitants of the female roles, joked cheekily. Our Alexander Zakharovich had overlooked the fact that these children had grown up under the watchful eye of their parents' home video cameras and weren't afraid of the lens. An entire generation of artists had sprung up who behaved perfectly naturally in front of spectators, and no worse than Dustin Hoffman or Julia Roberts—maybe even better, ladies and gentlemen, maybe even better.

Not only did the troupe not fall apart in the second act but it began cooking up something that he had only dreamed about at the rehearsals, something rhythmic and dodecaphonic, bubbling like Louisiana soup, a demiballet with flashes of bas-relief—"Let the moment be frozen!"—and in two or three places improvised these stops so fortuitously that A.Z. even pumped a fist triumphantly in the air. The students roared their approval. Harry Pons was riding in circles on Akaki Akakyevich's bicycle, his Overcoat in one corner of the stage was singing one of Cavaradossi's arias, Pannochka momentarily turned into a witch and then back again, and the Nose, Robby Rook, was calling for democratic reform from the podium of a candidate for governor. There was a real feeling of *Gogolyevshchina* coming down from the stage. Everything was falling into place that night, and even the almost impossible finale with its moment of "incurable sadness," when all the characters began dying out, like Maya Plisetskaya as the Dying Swan, turned out so well that Mrs. President Millhouse had tears in her eyes.

In this country, clapping in unison and endless curtain calls aren't the done thing—especially in a university theater, where a show, after all, is part of a course of study. And yet the familiar intoxication of success was already buzzing in its veins. My God, I'm not dead yet, then, am I? Backstage the whole company was lying on the floor, weakly handing cans of beer to one another. "Sasha, we did it!" "I'm proud of you, guys!" Then began the reception, which lasted two hours, which was also a measure of their success. Incredible, they said to them—just fantastic! Through the generosity of Art Duppertat, some pretty classy champagne was brought around. Jumbo shrimp were cooking on the grill, bouquets of crab claws were thrust at the guests, filets mignons were offered. Where there are Korbachs, there is success, there is victory! Here and there in the crowd he met the pensive and uncomprehending eyes of Marjorie. It had been ten months already that her husband was on the run. Next to her perched the patently insincere but amiable Norman Blamsdale. As for the chief benefactor, Art Duppertat, he was behaving like a Moscow actor who had finally attained the free booze and grub he had so long dreamed of. He was strutting about like a peacock. With half a finger he uncorked a bottle of Mumm and let a stream fly toward the ceiling. "You won, *starik!*" He had brought the word back from Moscow, obviously.

Journalists were coming up to him: a stickler for accuracy from *The Washington Post,* a slob from the *Times,* a girl from *The Village Voice.* She turned out to be on special Korbach assignment. New York wants to know who he is. Alexander roamed through the crowd as though he'd put some sort of rubbish up his nose himself. He took no notice whatsoever of those whom, according to the Pinkerton rules, he should have noticed, in particular financial bigwigs from Virginia's high-tech corridor. Instead, he spoke for too long—about what, you won't understand—with the eternal rivals from the neighboring huge university, George Mason. Suddenly he was gripped by a feeling of unease. There's somebody missing! It was only when he was nervously surveying the room and already jumping up and down for a better look that he detected the catastrophically absent Nora Mansour. She's lost her head, he thought. She didn't come to the opening night! She wants to chuck me. She's had enough of me. She's got a lover in Houston. It's the end of the celebration. Farewell, *dolce stil nuovo!* And at that moment he left the Black Cube and moved off into the slushy expanses.

―――――――――

Trudging along through the slush, he cursed his wretched fate and his own stupidity. I let a woman like that, a messenger of calm skies and stormy, bubbling earthy depths, get away! In aid of some school theater, I abandoned my love to the mercies of Texas sex maniacs. Farewell now and forever, my youth named Nora! "Farewell, youth"—I can't help but recall those lousy Soviet felt boots that were called Farewell Youth. Now my whole life will turn into just that sort of "shit-stomper" with mold on the inside that you can't scrape out even with a fork—even with a fork, that's it, even with a fork.

The wind was scattering wet leaves across the path. Two crystal eyes swam up slowly behind him. He stepped to one side. It was some sort of *"est-ce que vous avez du Grey Poupon?"* The window lowered. The face of a serious doll looked out of the Rolls. Margie Korbach—she rides around at night alone. "I don't know why, but I didn't see Nora today," she said. "Who the fuck knows where she is— she's probably buggered off to Houston," he answered in Russian. Love's step-mother nodded, as though she'd understood more than just "Houston." "What are you walking for?" she asked. "Get in the car with me."

"What the fuck do I need your car for? My Saab is over there under that cunt of a lamppost." With uncharacteristic seriousness she nodded again, as though she'd understood more than just "Saab." The Rolls speeded up, and soon its two rear rubies had disappeared in the slushy gloom.

3

COME DOWN FROM THERE!

*T*he next morning, in his de-Nora-ized burrow—if one can put it that way, playing with prefixes and suffixes—in his small apartment in the middle of the gay quarter, he found out what had happened. None other than Omar Mansour called him up. "Eh, listen, can I congratulate you?" he said, sounding almost as though he were speaking Georgian.

"What, you mean you were there?" Even on this Grand Guignol of a morning Alex found it hard to imagine that young fellow at a show at the Black Cube.

"Why did I have to be there?" Omar practically shouted. "I saw it this morning on TV. Turn on the TV yourself and you'll see it on almost any news broadcast."

"It's incredible," Sasha muttered.

"Exactly! Incredible." Now Omar was shouting. "My name's in space! It's going around the world!"

With the receiver cradled under his ear, Sasha Korbach amortized the air with both hands, as though repelling an absurdity crashing down on him. "Of course, sometimes a whole city can go for something overnight, but just what are *you* talking about?"

"Why, what're you saying, Sasha—it's an event of huge importance, especially for the Arab world, pal! For all progressive Muslims! Our retrograde types can go on mocking women, they can cauterize the clitorises of little girls, and here we've got a woman in space, a lady archaeologist photographing ancient civilizations from orbit! And the biggest blow to these reactionaries is that the woman's got an Arabic name! Okay, so she's American, but she's Nora Mansour, the wife of Omar Mansour, who's not unknown in Lebanon! No, I was right in not rushing into a divorce. We've hit you where it hurts, reactionaries! And I congratulate you, Sasha Korbach, as her boyfriend, as her de facto husband—greetings to you, a good Jew and a good American, from the husband and an Arab, from a Phoenician and everything that goes with it!"

After executing a few caterpillar movements, Alexander moved the soles of his feet in the direction of the television and turned it on with a big toe. The words "Special Report" immediately appeared, followed by the anchorman, as always seemingly on the point of belching up something tasty and as always with a badly knotted tie. The latter condition always got on Alexander Zakharovich's nerves. Even now, a second before Nora's appearance and with Omar's voice in his ear, he had time to think his usual thought: They pay you all this money, you hack, and you can't even learn how to tie a necktie. Just then, the images from Cape Canaveral came on, and, unable to believe his eyes, he saw Nora in a space suit, smiling, with her hair flying in the wind, boldly striding along with the whole crew to board the *Atlantis*. "For the first time in history, an archaeologist is taking part in the expedition—Professor Nora Mansour of Pinkerton University," the one with the badly knotted tie said. A shot of the launch was edited in: streams of fire beneath the bunches of rocket fuel tanks, the pulling back of the transporters, and finally the remaining dot of flame quickly moving away from the Earth. Nora's there! She's going away from the Earth, my little one! He immediately choked up. A shudder began to tear through him, starting at the crown of his head and concentrating in his heels. With horror he remembered the quite recent tragedy of one of the shuttles, the explosion right before everyone's eyes, an abracadabra of fire. There had been two girls aboard, one of whom reminded him of Nora. God help her! God carry her through! The prayer was heard—they were already showing pictures from orbit: the happy faces, weightless bodies floating, there's his beloved drifting by, thin, her little behind up, hair following her head like a calmly streaming banner, she's smiling at the camera, waving, as though to him personally. End of special report.

The progressive Arab was still shouting away in his ear: "We need progress everywhere . . . in space, in the bedroom, in the drinking glass!"

"What did you say? 'In the drinking glass'?"

"That's right, dear Korbach! We have to have a drink together today, to our Nora! Why shouldn't we drink champagne? Let the Shariat ban vodka and whiskey, but there's no need to ban champagne, so that every Muslim can drink to his wife who's taken off into space! Isn't that right, Sasha?"

He went on yelling something, this time about the greatness of the America that had bred such extraordinary women as Nora Mansour, but this was intended for the benefit of the FBI's tape recorders. Alexander put the receiver down. Merciful God, Almighty God, I don't want to hear about anything else, I can't think or talk about anything else until she comes back from up there. Just let her come back from there, as the Americans say, in one piece!

―――――――

Nora still hadn't come down from there—the flight was scheduled to last a week—when, five days after opening night, Alexander had occasion to taste of his own success—not as cosmic, perhaps, but success all the same. The famous film director Stefan Chapski called. He spoke Russian with the giggling undertones characteristic of Poles. Way back when, in the fifties, he had graduated from the State Film Institute in Moscow, and even shot a coproduction at Mosfilm studios. By the end of the sixties he was in the West, but he didn't end up there, the way the Soviets did, with charges of "betrayal of the motherland" and a lot of KGB hysterics. In Poland, after all, they took a somewhat gentler view of defectors; okay, so he stayed in the West. It's not the best news, but we'll live.

At first, Chapski was lost and starving in the forests of Hollywood, like a large number of his predecessors, but suddenly he emerged in a bright clearing and made himself a name among the new wave of Slavic directors: Polanski, Kosinski, Forman, and now Chapski.

"Hello, Mr. Korbach, *dorogoi tovarishch*! [His "hello" sounded like Liza Minnelli's in *Cabaret:* "hell-ooo!"] Chapski speaking, Stefan Chapski, don't faint. There's a good offer, Sasha, you know. You and I as one generation will make a movie. You don't object? Fine! Can you take a plane today? You can't? Then can you hold? Two minutes—hold!"

Imagining that the verb *hold* was being used as a direct translation, Alexander held on to the receiver. Exactly two minutes later, Chapski, jumping over from another line, said that he would fly to Washington. Right now he's turning from Sunset onto the San Diego Freeway. The flight's in an hour and ten minutes, he'll make it. Should he pick up some vodka? "You've got it all? Brilliant! *Chef d'oeuvrable!*" he said, shouting out the most popular exclamations of his student days in the fifties, and then he was gone.

He flew in toward the end of the day, not at all what one might have imagined after their jovial conversation. A heavyset and seemingly half-blind Jew, or more likely half-Jew, like everyone on the scene. Alexander would subsequently get used to quick changes by this Chapski. Periods of heavyweight torpor alternated with an attacking style when he even seemed to be dropping the pounds.

Naturally, they were on a first-name basis before they'd even finished their first glass of vodka. It turned out that Chapski had been put on to Korbach by one of his friends who had been at the opening night of "Gogolyevsky" at the Black Cube. One of those great *khlopaks,* a rich guy, but still of our crowd, an artistic type. Why, Art Duppertat, of course—who else? Chapski was stunned. He hadn't known that Korbach was in America. Of course he remembered his songs, he'd followed the Buffoons saga, all that fucking Communist scandalmongering, but then everything had gone quiet: the Buffoons and Sasha Korbach had disappeared from the correspondents' dispatches. There's so much of everything going on, blood flowing everywhere, one avalanche of news buries another, only the spray flies around. Listen, we got two tapes of your monologues, one from a show in Moscow, and the other from one in some English Gothic hall—in the States, it seems. "You know, I've just been engrossed," he said in English. "I just went crazy about it, your artistry knocked me out, Sasha, but most important of all I remembered your films of the last years—you were considered one of the top five Russian directors!" Korbach was astonished to learn that Chapski's efficient staff had gotten hold of even those museum pieces for him: he'd been sure that the "competent authorities" had wiped those films off the face of the Earth years ago.

Chapski was not just a director now but the head of the nascent cinematic empire Chapski Productions. From this position, he had decided that it would be simply idiotic not to use Sasha Korbach in the American movie business. Tell me, old chap, can you write a screenplay, put together a film, on your own or with me, and act in it? Of course you can! What kind of film? We'll talk about that in a few days.

Right now I'm flying to Paris, one of my *équipes* is shooting there, then it's back to L.A. I'll come back to D.C. in a week. There'll be a deciding meeting of the interested parties here. Yes, there are some already. That's all—let's put business aside. Let's drink to what we used to drink to when we were in the dorm at the Exhibit of the People's Economic Achievements.

Let 'em croak! "And let 'em not be born again!" Korbach said, completing the popular Moscow toast.

On Connecticut Avenue, running for a taxi, Chapski dropped his briefcase. Flying out, among other things, was no small number of Trojans, condoms in packages with pictures of seaside sunsets. They gathered up all the case's contents from the wet pavement, swearing in Polish and in Russian. Blood, dogs, mother, what a lot of . . . , frigging . . . ! People looked from passing cars at the hulking old man in a heavy coat and a svelte pseudoyoungster who looked like one of the local homosexuals. In order to "get themselves back to normal," they burst into the Timberland, where, in almost complete darkness in the American style, several who had already reached the norm were sitting. Chapski, tired of all that half-forgotten Slavic crap, went over to English.

"Listen, Korbach, are you happy in America?"

"Not at this particular moment, Chapski."

"Why not?"

"How can I be happy when my girlfriend is in space?"

"In what space?" Chapski yelled, looking off at one corner of the bar as though he were looking for the answer to his question there.

"In outer space." Korbach rocked back and forth on his stool like the well-known Humpty-Dumpty. "She's so far away, my love, she's orbiting our planet, she's losing her gravitation, she's not my love anymore, a weightless baby. . . ."

"That's great, Sashka! It's a great proposal. He's drunk in the bar, she's weightless in orbit! You're a generator of proposals, you fucking Soviet Sashka Korbach! We'll make you rich and famous *sous les drapeaux de* Chapski Productions!"

It was not more than a week later. Nora was already back on Earth and undergoing postflight tests in Houston. Their telephone bills increased with cosmic rapidity, since the conversations consisted mainly of sighs and pauses. Suddenly, Chapski turned up, shaved and in a blue suit of the best quality. With him was a female assistant, in whose eyes was that same Trojan seaside sunset, the most popular sort in our part of the world. "Let's go, Sashka—today you'll see that the Central Committee of the CPSU has nothing on the Synod."

In the car he thrust a sheet of paper at Alex. It was, of course, the proposal. Naturally, you can rewrite it later or just throw it in the trash. The important thing right now is to get the ball rolling. It was a short ride, and A.Z. didn't have time to read anything. The only thing he noticed was that the action began in Afghanistan. In those days it was difficult to find a script that didn't start in Afghanistan.

"Well, here we are," Chapski said. "We jump out, and Nora takes care of the parking." Sasha shuddered. "What Nora?" "You know, my assistant." "My girl-friend's Nora, too." Chapski shrugged. "I guess both of their dads devoured too much of Ibsen." Before them stood a gray building the height and width of a city block, decked out with numerous columns and bay windows, of an indeterminate architectural style but with a certain resemblance to the Paris d'Haussmann school. It was the well-known Old Executive Office Building, the second most im-portant in Washington. It was ringed with fences, gratings, and concrete barriers with the look of flower beds, which had appeared there after the compatriots of Omar Mansour developed an enthusiasm for trucks loaded with explosives.

Chapski and Korbach went up the main steps, opened the doors, and immedi-ately found themselves surrounded by stately, keen-eyed officers, both black and white, who flowed rather than moved. After a brief check of a computer printout, the visitors had buttons pinned to the lapels of their jackets; it was not beyond the realm of possibility that in these buttons was some sort of magnetic strip by which their movements in such an important structure would be monitored. "Second floor, gentlemen—you'll be expected," the older guard said.

Chapski came to a stop on the marble staircase. "Listen, I just had an idea; the last time, you were babbling something when you were drunk about your weight-less girlfriend, and just now you said that her name's Nora. You don't mean to say that she's Nora Mansour?" Korbach didn't have time to answer: two young func-tionaries were walking briskly in their direction. Sasha was struck right away by a silly thought: these kids make a pittance compared to that guy on TV who didn't learn how to tie his necktie, but their ties are perfectly tied. It just takes concen-tration, that's all—fiddlesticks. What opera is that from, anyway—fiddlesticks? Fiddlesticks, fiddlesticks—what sort of abracadabra is this that's bothering him? We invite the reader to leaf through a bit of what he or she has already read, to dis-cover this verbal scarecrow. A hint: Chapter 4, kind ladies and gentlemen.

They walked down a broad corridor with high ceilings (they don't make them like that anymore); doors, wide and high as well, were opening right and left, and highly placed officials were joining each other. They'd seen the faces of these peo-ple enough times on TV; otherwise they might have taken them for guests at some nineteenth-century German spa—fiddlesticks. Finally they came to the appointed place. The two immigrants were met at the door by an American politician of the sort whose name is preceded on official lists by "the Honorable," a term that in Russian translation conveys a certain image of fat-bellied excess.

Edmund Peabody gave the appearance of a perfect example of well-balanced external and internal qualities. Though his hail-fellow-well-met manners did little to distinguish him from his staff, he nevertheless bore the stamp of upper-echelon politics, both foreign and domestic; the latter was perhaps more important for him than the former. Mr. Peabody stopped just short of giving the visitors a hug. "It's a great honor to have you here, gentlemen! Before you stands a great admirer of your movies, Mr. Chapski! Oh, Mr. Korbach! My wife saw your show at the Black Cube. We're neighbors of the president of your university, you see. Nancy Mill-house all but dragged my Andie to the opening night by force, and she came back in seventh heaven! She was just swept away by your talent. You're fairly new in Washington, aren't you? Well, welcome to our provincial capital!"

He turned to his aides. "Everyone's here now, we can start. Let's all go to my office, folks."

Just before the meeting got under way, Chapski had time to whisper to Korbach: "I'll tell you who's who later. For right now, just sit there with a thoughtful expression; that's all I need from you."

It wasn't all that dissimilar to a meeting at the Central Committee, given that some of those present were sitting on the arms of couches, and two were even on the floor, showing off their perfectly pulled-up socks. Everyone called everyone else by their first names, and nicknames at that: Ed, Joe, Phil, Rex. In Soviet "Party protocol," a similar element of informality was introduced by tacking the tail of the patronymic onto the names.

Chapski was first to speak, and the situation became steadily clearer as he went along, as though he were wiping a decal clear with his sharply bent thumb. The matter under discussion was a big-budget action film about Soviet POWs in Afghanistan. "Everyone knows that it's a hot topic, but we at Chapski Productions aren't just rushing to keep up with the times. We want to create a real human drama through the power of modern—I'd like to stress that word—art. It ought to be a hard, authentic film that has almost the look and feel of a documentary. No Sly Stallones with their phallic machine guns, no blah-blah with saber-dancing mujahideen, no girls with eyes burning from behind their chadors. At the same time, our film has to be shot through with a certain postmodern aesthetic, with moments of the grotesque, and of nostalgia for Soviet decay. Taking all these elements into account, guys, we've decided to offer the director's chair to Alex Korbach. No one else in America can do what we want, Mr. Peabody."

All those in the room—and there were no fewer than two dozen people—nodded in understanding, as if they were the film specialists on this political committee, and when Korbach's name came up, compassion and sympathy were added to understanding. Has "Gogloyevsky" really earned me that kind of favor in Washington? Nonsense—it's all due to Mrs. Nora Mansour, of course: the goings-on in the life of this superstar of the moment were being discussed all over Washington, naturally. Later Alexander would find out that in addition to the "guys," some big guns in foreign policy had been taking part in the meeting, as well as a couple of high Pentagon officials (in civilian clothes, but with their government boots) and experts from the CIA.

Chapski went on: "We could, of course, get along without the government. It's not a Hollywood tradition to ask for government subsidies. After long discussions, however, we've decided to give you the chance to participate in a coproduction, which would include taking part of the financial risk. Don't think, however, that we're considering only economizing on our own means. Hollywood isn't interested in economy, it's interested in profits. It might seem paradoxical, but we're turning to the government out of artistic considerations, in particular for the embodiment of principles of documentary authenticity, which would help us to avoid anything smacking of a Broadway show."

Short break, in the form of a good laugh and an exchange of understanding glances. No one was in a hurry to ask for the floor, and Chapski went on a little further. "Don't think, either, that Sasha Korbach and I are pursuing some political ends as victims of totalitarianism. Artistic problems before everything else for us. Soviet prisoners—ethnic Europeans, by the way—in the hands of indomitable Muslims, that's just what is called a 'marginal situation.' " Now in one of his active phases, Chapski was jabbering away in what to Korbach's surprise was less than ideal English, yet everyone understood him perfectly: Americans are thoroughly trained in the barbaric tongues. At hearing the word *totalitarianism*, many of those gathered pricked up their ears. Certainly looks like they don't care for it, thought our hero. Or maybe they have respect for it as their object of constant study.

Someone had already begun to raise a finger to the chairman of the meeting. "A couple of words, Ed, if you don't mind." Peabody slowed everybody down with a gesture of his palm and spoke first himself. "We're very grateful to Steve Chapski for his appearance. A very interesting project, thank you. I don't think that the government ought to shun film production; at the end of the day it's one of our biggest exports, after all. It's time to break down stereotypes, my friends. Before we proceed to a discussion, I'd like to ask our talented friend Alexander Korbach a question. Alex, I hope that you fully share Steve's enthusiasm? Do you see yourself in the director's chair?"

You can't say he doesn't have experience, this bigwig, Korbach thought. He must have noticed how out of it I looked. That damned fool Chapski didn't even tell me that the film would be about prisoners. "Of course, Ed" was his adroit reply, giving no hint of doubt. "It's all Steve and I talk about day and night. I'll do everything I can."

Chapski spoke up again at that point, saying that they planned to "use" Sasha Korbach on three fronts: "First, he'll write the screenplay; second, he'll direct the film, either with my help or, still better, alone; and third, he'll play the role of a paradoxical character, a Soviet general who hates Communism and dreams of becoming president of a free Russia." Saying this, Chapski glared over at Korbach: Understand? Got it, Sashka? Korbach nodded and smiled. It looks to me, pal, like you're not so independent of these guys after all, and you're using poor old Korbach here as bait. With a nod, he said: "I'd like to lower the rank of this person to colonel. He's a flier, he ejects himself in flight over a mountain range to get back to our people."

"To our people or your people?" one of the men in the government-issue boots asked. He was very serious and was making notes in a little yellow ruled notebook.

"When I said 'our people,' I meant 'your people'—that is, the American observers," Korbach said for the sake of precision. "In other words, our colonel wants to defect to our representatives. . . . Excuse me, I mean their general wants to defect to our side—in other words, to your observers, sir; sorry, I got a bit mixed up about where yours are and where ours are."

The entire room laughed heartily, and as we pointed out earlier, in America a good, generally shared laugh is often the sign of a favorable decision to come. Chapski was overjoyed.

The participants in the hearing began to make statements. Everyone enthusiastically supported the project. The basic task, of course, was to create a powerful, high-quality work of art. The involvement of the government will help to break down the stereotypes of the market. It will create a precedent. If we manage to make an international hit like *Dr. Zhivago,* the outlay will pay off, too. It will more than pay for itself. The most important thing is still artistic quality, though. Great art of high quality, indeed. It will pay for itself in financial terms. And in other respects, too. In other respects, naturally. A thing of high art can influence the public's state of mind. The government, of course, will have to participate in the financing, but chiefly in the search for sources. To use our leverage in the big corporations. For the creation of a work of high-quality art. The soldier with the notepad spoke up with determination: "We're for the creation of a high-quality work of art, too, because it will do more to influence people's thinking than a low-quality work. In the present case, such a work will help stop the Russians' dangerous meddling in the oil-producing regions."

Just before time ran out, Peabody moved to create a working group to liaise with Chapski Productions, wished success in assembling a full budget, and thanked everyone who had been present. In leaving, he shook Korbach's hand firmly and said that he hoped he would see him soon near Pinkerton—that is, in his own house. "I promise not to invite anyone from Mason." Those around them laughed, because everyone knew about the traditional rivalry between the two schools.

Korbach was joined at the door by one of the young participants in the hearing, a lad who had obviously received good all-around training. "By the way, Sasha," he said to him in Russian, quite informally, "your songs have become hugely popular in the Soviet Union again. And in the Fortieth Army, too—in Afghanistan, that is. The political officers chase down the cassettes, but the soldiers keep on rolling those old classics from an 'enemy of the people': 'Purgatory,' 'Figure Skating,' 'Chekhov's Sakhalin,' 'Swedish Pea Jacket,' 'The Dolphins,' 'The Ballad of Dombai,' 'The Ballad of Butyrka Jail,' and 'Kolya Brugnon,' which is absolutely tops." The youngster obviously derived pleasure from dropping the titles of these songs, completely unknown, as he supposed, in this country. A.Z. meanwhile was thinking to himself: So even here there were a couple of specialists studying Sasha Korbach's songs. No, Stanley's right—this country really is a citadel of freedom!

Two days later Nora flew in. The girl had strangely changed somehow after her space flight: she had contracted into herself, pulled her head down between her shoulders, as though she were trying to inspire in him protective feelings and tenderness rather than what had been the day-to-day norm of their relations— "punishment of the mangy mutt." He responded to this innovation and pitied her without letting up. In the pauses between these sessions of pity she would tell him a few strange things about her trip, which had been unusual enough as it was. Things had happened to her while she was in orbit that she hadn't really been sure were happening even while they were going on.

4

FELIX

*E*xternally, everything was going as expected. Time and again the Fertile Crescent emerged from lunar shadow onto the glittering surface. Nora was taking countless pictures, focusing mainly on the already mapped "intersections of caravan routes." Through the lenses, it seemed to her that at the presumed location of the six-thousand-year-old metropolis of Ur she could see the topography of city blocks. These shots would of course be studied and discussed at conferences after her return.

In addition to these studies, which were her main purpose for being there, she, like all the other members of the crew, did exercises with medical sensors attached to her body and ate space food that was "stronger than Goethe's *Faust,* as you would put it, Sasha," and even played cards with the guys—something that you had to learn to do all over again in conditions of weightlessness.

Rest periods, however, turned into something quite indescribable for her. Stretching herself out and getting into a comfortable position, she would look through the small, round window in the opposite direction from Earth. Something unthinkable began to appear to her. I'll try to describe it, but I know it won't even come close to how it was. First of all because these phenomena had nothing to do with the concepts of "was-is–will be." She understood it perfectly well at the time but doesn't understand it at all now. Well, maybe I could call them incredibly large faces. They came into view one after the other, and each one embodied all the rest. And they moved away one after the other, as though because of the fluctuations of the light like the one in the third part of the *Divine Comedy,* but without end. It's only now that I call them "faces," but they weren't faces, Sasha; it's impossible to say, in the end. Sometimes she pleaded with them: Show yourselves! Show yourselves! And then, as though in reply, there appeared likenesses of angels. Yes, that's right, Sasha—with wings; as though they were human, but with wings. Then everything changed into an all-encompassing paroxysm. She herself seemed to become a part of the joy, and everything was contained in it—the end, the beginning—and the only thing left to do was pray, about what, I don't remember. Suddenly, she realized that she could see Christ; not in a human form but rather in one that was both invisible and grand—if one can put it that way, except one can't put it that way at all.

All at once, in one spot, there was some sort of drilling, as if with a probe. Inside, at an unimaginable depth, appeared a little box with incrustations on the lid. She opened the box and found herself on the brink of a precipice, above a Gothic city with brick rooftops, facades in ruins, the crosses and gargoyles of a large church. In short, there turned out to be inside the box an episode that had happened in her life—even before Sashka—on the island of Gotland.

She was walking on a path along a precipice. In front of her was a mowed green field, edged on three sides with flourishing rosebushes, and on a fourth with boulders that seemed to hide the edge of the precipice. In a clearing, looking up at the sky, lay a young woman. Alongside her sat a man with a handsome, melancholy face. Meanwhile, a little boy who could not have been older than three was running around the meadow in a round hat with a plastic brim. One of his feet was angled sharply inward—it was undoubtedly a birth defect—as a result of which his running form could have been compared to a rowboat on a steep wave in a lateral wind. This in no way prevented him from being the very picture of life's joy. He would pluck from the grass a blue flower, then a yellow one, cry, "Papa! Papa!" and then hobble smartly with his gift over to the downcast man. The latter would take the flower and immediately lay it down in the grass without looking at it. The toddler, laughing, would rush back and snatch up another flower dangerously close to the precipice.

Nora felt her knees buckling at the sensation of this perilous edge. "Hey!" she shouted, and the boy, after plucking his next flower, turned at the shout. Catching sight of Nora, he would now rush to her, a laughing cripple, not yet knowing what life would have in store for him with a leg like that. Drawing near her, he held up a forget-me-not to Nora. "Thank you very much—allow me to shake your hand," Nora said. He held out his left. "No, give your right hand." She laughed. She was bubbling over with happiness at her contact with the child. Cackling, he extended his right hand. They shook hands with each other and laughed. Just then, the boy's mother turned up beside him. Their eyes met. The young woman smiled uncertainly. "What a wonderful boy you have," Nora said. "What's his name?" "His name is Felix," the mother answered, as though in disbelief at the idea that someone could like her son. Nora clapped her hands together. "What a wonderful, sweet, enchanting Felix!" The little boy clapped his hands together as well and laughed even more loudly. Nora gave him a kiss on his cheek with its rosy though none too healthy blush, then immediately walked away, so as not to burst into tears in front of the others out of deep feeling for Felix. Looking back over her shoulder after a few steps, she saw that the whole family was gathered: the mother with her timid and grateful smile, the beaming Felix, and the gloomy Viking, who seemed nonetheless to have softened slightly. "Take care, Felix—there's a cliff!" Nora cried out. The boy once again jumped up and down at the sound of the unfamiliar voice. His mother looked in the direction of Nora's gesture and opened her mouth in horror: she had clearly thought that beyond the boulders was nothing more than a slope. She immediately took Felix in her arms and silently formed a thank-you with her lips to the stranger. The man gave an "Everything's under control" sign with his hand.

Perhaps everything wasn't under his control, particularly when he fell into a blue funk at the realization that life had dealt so unfairly with him, bestowing a deformed son upon him. Perhaps the whole time Felix was running after flowers, the father had been feeling out that area, and in some corner of his mind an appeal to fate had made its nest: This precipice has to do with you, against you we're powerless. He will never admit it to himself, just as he will never admit that the woman who happened to be passing by, some American with a strange glow about her, had endowed him with a lifelong love for his son. For Felix.

That time Nora, of course, had forgotten about this scene within an hour and never thought of it again. The box that contained this meeting, which had appeared out of unknowable depths, turned out to be full of surprises for her. Now, back on Earth, she was whispering in the ear of her lover: "You know, it seems to me that all the contents of my life were in there, as though I had been born only for that purpose, for that momentary flash. For Felix. I don't know what was engraved on the lid—perhaps it was just my name and the dates of my birth and death. Then again, maybe it all only looked like a box, so that I'd understand, and in fact there was just the incomprehensible gist of something connected to me there."

He had one arm around her shoulders and with the other hand was stroking her head. The more she feels something corporeal and ordinary, the faster she'll come out from under nonbeing. What were they thinking about at Mission Control in Houston? Approving for a flight a woman with a history of drug and alcohol use like hers! She had gone through something like the experience that Dante had just before he began to write the *Divine Comedy*. Whatever the impetus—illness, a wound, some strong poison—one thing was clear: he had been where it was forbidden to be. Something similar had happened to Nora while she was weightless.

"Okay, then, let's go out to eat. On the way we'll get tickets to the cinema next door, to a film at the 'Two-Faced Janus.' Even better, I'll buy you some high winter boots. I see you in boots like that. Look over there, someone's opened a new bookstore, and there's just what I need, a new translation of the *Odyssey*. While you were off flying, someone went out of business around here—the Revolutionary Posters store, as a matter of fact—but someone came into the world, that is, the Dupont Underground wine cellar. They've got everything-must-go prices on Veuve Clicquot: twenty-five dollars for a bottle, and in Paris, you remember, I paid thirty-five. How about forty?" She smiled, and he was delighted at this brisk reaction to world prices. "Let's take half a dozen at these everything-must-go prices and we'll drink all night. It's good not to deny yourself, isn't it, Nora Mansour, née Korbach? So here we are trudging along, heavily laden, like donkeys in the mountain passes of Sardinia: your boots, the *Odyssey*, six bottles of champagne. Do you feel how heavy these things are? Gravity is coming back to you in the guise of luxury items and fountains of poetry. Now we're rolling into Vincenzo's: Do you like your shrimp grilled or fried in butter with rusks? We don't need this garlic sauce. Yes, I'm a Jew, but I don't like garlic! I'm ready to renounce my Jewishness, just so long as they don't stuff me with garlic sauces. What do I want with the

Odyssey? For a paraphrase—I'll go into the details later. For a start, let's decide—pasta or risotto? Red wine or white? Parmesan or Gruyère? After eating out, decent people go to a jazz club. You and I are upstanding young people, after all, and jazz is what we ought to cling to. If we had a child, I'd call him Jazz. Jazz Alexandrovich Korbach—I can just imagine how happy Stanley would be.

"You see him—admit it! He's somewhere around here, your dissolute father. I wouldn't be surprised if he walked in right now. There's a rumor that he's starting up some huge philanthropic fund. Do you like the saxophonist? His sound's too sharp. I'd play differently for you." "You mean you can play the saxophone, too?" "Sure! A real jack-of-all-trades, harvesting corn and blowing a horn at the same time, or something along those lines." "Way to go, Sashka, my blue-eyed daring boy, merry friend of my Pushkinian diversions. Saashkaa! You're stuffed with snatches of things, scraps from your pop culture. Like all Russians, for that matter." "And how do you know all Russians?" "I slept with them all." "I knew it—finally, you've confessed!"

They left the jazz café and their jaws dropped: everything was covered with snow, which was still coming down in abundance. The snowflakes were oversized, some as big as half a hand; the patterns they described in swooping down to earth were as intricate as those of butterflies. Nora gave a little shriek of delight. Just look, madame guest from outer space, what wonders are produced for us by simple combinations of oxygen and hydrogen. And we still wax poetic about such things, my lady. He pulled a wet *Washington Post* from a trash bin, twisted it into the shape of a saxophone, and began to play just what she wanted to hear: Come to me, my melancholy baby, cuddle up and don't be blue. . . .

5

THE STARRY EIGHTIES

*M*eanwhile, the wheels of the film project had begun to turn in small revolutions. Chapski Productions sent Alexander an official letter stating that now, after the (theoretically) serious hearing at the Old Executive Office Building, all the interested parties were waiting for an outline—a "pitch" of two to four pages—from Mr. Korbach. After that, the company would sign a contract with him, as the writer, for a more detailed description of the story—a treatment—and then would come a contract for a full screenplay. The steps of the numbers offered in the letter were fairly impressive but still not so impressive as, if it had been a silent movie, to make him freeze openmouthed, followed by an intertitle of "I'm rich! I'm rich!" in vignettes on a black background. The phrase "in vignettes" would be reserved for the day when admiring humanity would be lining up at theaters from Toronto to Djakarta.

And he still didn't know what to write about yet. Having come up with the idea of the downing of a flier, whom he was supposedly dreaming of playing, he was ready now to brush this character aside. Too much would have to be explained to the Western moviegoer to make him real. This military stuffed shirt and Soviet boor could be out there on the periphery, but the basic plotline would have to be something else. All right, so there are prisoners, but what's going to be the basic thrust of our story? For all its surface similarities, we mustn't draw a parallel with the Vietnam epics of the American cinema. There's got to be something profoundly Soviet, or, strange as it might seem, something European about it. Chapski had tossed out a sensible definition at the time: European boys held captive by Islam. The ideological gulf notwithstanding, Russians were still a part of the European ethnic community. Islam was resisting them by its indomitable nature but also by its still valid original meaning: "submission," fear of God.

Something began to glimmer through the phraseological fog of the project. A cave in the Afghan mountains not far from the border with Pakistan. The mujahideen are holding some Soviet prisoners there. Most of the authenticity comes from the stories of three eighteen-year-old kids. One of them is from Siberia, another from the Volga, and a third from a group of Leningrad street musicians. Hey, it could even be something like that story about the three kids that kicked up such a fuss a long time ago—*Starry Ticket,* was it? No, *Ticket to the Stars*—that's it. What a lot of ink was spilled over that harmless little thing! How many lances clashed over such a simple story! And it clearly wasn't without reason that the Party, that stinking old lady with its Komsomol gigolo, went into such a rage. I was twenty-two then, but I still identified with the eighteen-year-old heroes of the novel. Why, I even met the author, you know. He was living somewhere near the Kropotkin Metro station. The Party's attacks made him famous. One day I spotted him. A fellow with a baby carriage was standing by the *Komsomolskaya Pravda* kiosk reading an article with the headline A TICKET, BUT FOR WHERE? I approached him with a light step. Hi! I like your novel.

Listen, what are you playing at twenty-six years later, anyway? As if you hadn't met him lots of times at parties in attics and cellars, as if you didn't have loads of mutual friends, as if Stepanida Vlastevnaya, as they called the Soviet regime, hadn't booted this V.A. out of her stinking hut a couple of years before you. As if you didn't know that he lives somewhere around here, in Georgetown, and teaches at the rival university. As if you hadn't ended up in his new novel as the main character.

Whatever the case may be, my story could be a paraphrase of *Ticket to the Stars.* The driving force of that book was flight, and it even indicated a direction—to the West! The Komsomol, on instructions from the Party, was always playing up "romanticism" in the East (they need "feats of labor" there), and the "starry lads" take off for the West, even if it is only for Estonia—that is, the border of the USSR—but still for the Gothic—for the remains of the Baltic Hanseatics, just a stone's throw from Gotland. The characters of *Ticket to the Stars* were boys from intellectual families; the heroes of our film will be children of the Soviet mob—the only way for them to run from "mature socialism" is into the bottle or into dope. The only border crossings for them are in tanks or armored personnel carriers. Soldiers in battle are essentially a return to the horizontal position, a repudiation of human beings' primal act. Only rout and captivity can make them look at the sky again. From the opening of a cave high in the mountains, beyond the forms of their guards with their pancake-shaped hats, they saw their fatherland for the first time not as the USSR but as a sea of constellations.

Loneliness at its outer limits. Constant burning fear of some monstrous torture—say, castration. No one and nothing to hope for except for Air Force Colonel Dmitry Denisov, who ejected himself from his undamaged plane right into the hands of the mujahideen. The idea of defection to the West had been occurring to him regularly since 1961, but it hadn't been a matter of ideology or caprice—rather a purely existential moment. Colonel Denisov knows that Soviet helicopter pilots have been given the order to wipe out Soviet prisoners whenever possible. What is surrender in the unconscious sense? he asks the youngsters, in whom he sees himself and his friends twenty-six years ago. The man who gives himself up isn't stark raving mad; he is rather the man who is counting on a small scrap of humanity in the heart of his enemy. The longer a war goes on, the less remains of this naive calculation. Only the West, that ever-beckoning land of freedom, is left. In the end, they escape and reach their goal—everyone except the colonel, obviously. His time has passed once and for all. The *okhlo*-boys, as he called them in the cave, are strolling down the Champs-Elysées, but that already looks like the sequel.

Having discovered the existential meaning of the idea of fleeing, Alexander wrote an "outline" with little difficulty, sent the page off to Los Angeles, and soon received his first check, in five figures, from Chapski Productions. The motor was beginning to turn over faster. Stefan, who was now calling almost daily from the most unexpected places on the globe, liked Korbach's working idea, with its two denominators. The colonel, who will of course be played by Sasha himself, represents a complete break with the illusions of the post-Stalin generations. The subject of today's young generation will stun the West, the audiences will see that Soviet soldiers aren't mysterious fanatics of Communism but are the same as their Western counterparts, dwellers in the worldwide "swamp," thumping out their rock music and crazy about the audio and video images of their pathetic hedonism.

We'll shoot the basis for the Russian flashbacks behind the I.C. What "I.C."? You know, the Iron Curtain. We'll send a team through some third party in the guise of making a film about the beauties of the Russian land, and then we'll edit the shots at the studio. Basically, then, full speed ahead—don't spare the horses! The excess product of your imagination we'll give to a museum later, for a tax write-off. Never throw out your rough drafts, Sashka, give them to a museum and deduct their value from your taxes! And how do you feel in general, anyway? You don't need anything else? I don't know, some superexpensive vitamins? Of course they exist in nature. You think that all vitamins are sold in drugstores? You're mistaken—some vitamins aren't sold in drugstores, so as not to annoy the public. No, I haven't seen them myself, but I know for a fact that half of Hollywood lives on superexpensive vitamins. Otherwise we'd be down in the dumps all the time, my dear man! What got me started now? I just want you to have everything you need.

Alexander knew from the example of friends, and for that matter from his own long experience, that the business of directing or, in Chapski's case, of producing, brings one into a strange mind-set, like that of the whore-pimp relationship. The director-producer falls in love, in a way, with the person he works with. He lives for his/her interests, is concerned about his/her daily existence, intervenes in the complications of his/her personal life, can spend a whole day looking for some "supervitamins" or spare parts for the typewriter of the adored colleague. This infatuation evaporates as soon as the beloved has finished the job. You can fly to the object of your passion on gossamer wings as before and find a new love already there. Don't look for constancy of feelings in a director, and if he insists on it, then know it's all a sham. But, of course, he won't insist.

6

IDEOLOGICAL POTHOLES

"*W*ho is it you're always on the phone with?" Nora asked him one day. She had the key to "Sashka's" apartment, naturally, and this fact seemed to give her pleasure. You come without any preparation, whenever it feels right, as a surprise, you find your beloved in a natural pose, in a natural mood. Even if he loves to sit with a Russian newspaper in a remote toilet, then that's part of his being, too. In the interest of reciprocity she offered him the key to her apartment as well, but he refused. I don't see the sense of it. Your doorman will give the game away to you over the phone while I'm getting to the door, and you'll have time to show out your lover, some big lump from the Redskins' defensive line—you'll push him into your sitting room, and from there he'll jump onto the roof of the next building.

Often she found him slumped on the couch with the phone under his ear and with his brow furrowed as though from a headache. "Yeah," he would periodically grunt, or "Well, you know . . . ," "Are you sure? . . ." "Really?" "Where to? . . ." "Oh, there . . ."—such an eloquent participant in an obviously substantive dialogue.

One day, after hanging up, he answered: "You know, it's about the film. We're about to start shooting." "Why didn't you say anything?" she cried, in a way that she herself didn't care for, somehow: there was an imitation of something about it—of joy maybe. "Well, you know. . . ." He got up from the couch and shrugged his shoulders. "With whom?" Nora asked, adjusting her pseudojoyful tone to pseudodry. "With Chapski," he said. "Oh!" she said, and that was the end of the conversation about the film.

In this way, unaware that they were doing it, they laid traps for each other. Alas, kind ladies and gentlemen, it often happens that people can't find any reason for their growing irritation; they blame everything, let's say, on the fact that their cohabitant is "too highbrow" or, on the contrary, "too lowbrow"; on his crudity in bed or, on the contrary, her lack of crudity; on the incompatibility of their astrological signs, and so on; however, my friend, you and I both know, sad to say, that a lot has to do with childish pride and hypersensitivity. Let's say, for example, that Alexander Zakharovich starts throwing stones at his darling: she thinks that I can't achieve anything because it's she, not I, who gave a jump start to my dubious success. And Nora, meanwhile, gets cross with A.Z.: he doesn't want to talk about his success with me, because he writes everything off to my connections as a daughter of rich parents; in his mind he cherishes the image of the persecuted immigrant, the unrecognized talent—well, I'm not going to ask him about anything, then, if he's that much of a fool.

One day, however, she did have occasion to say something. "You know, you didn't come with me to the Bertrand Russell Human Rights Memorial reception, and I got into some unpleasant conversations about you. Or, rather, about Chapski's movie, and about you in connection with it. Is it true that you're making a movie about Russian POWs in Afghanistan? And is it true that it's all happening with the patronage of the administration, the Pentagon, and the CIA? How strange! I always considered Chapski a talented guy, independent enough in the commercial swamp out there these days, and suddenly he falls into the political swamp! I realize that both of you hate totalitarianism—who likes it?—but do you really have to . . . well, let's not quibble about words—do you really have to rub elbows with our 'ultras,' with our strutting toy soldiers, with the unprincipled spooks from our intelligence establishment, eaten right through with cynicism, all for the struggle for human rights? What's that got to do with art?

"I don't know what Chapski's game is, but you, Sasha, are going to have a permanent black spot on your name in the eyes of the American intelligentsia. You'll never wash yourself clean! And it'll mean your artistic ruin, for your information. You might not know it, but they're already suspicious enough of Russian intellectuals as it is, because of their flirtations with the government.

"Sasha, you've got to distance yourself from this 'Cold War' project right away! I hope you haven't taken any of their money, and if you have, you've got to give it back. I'll help you—we'll get any amount. You'll get a movie to do, don't worry. I've already told you—all Rita has to do is spend half an hour on the Hollywood phones, and you'll have a full contract. Just tell me what you want. A film about Dante? *Dolce stil nuovo?* Why not? The most important thing right now is to refuse this political order, and flat out at that! Or even without any theatrical gestures, but you've got to refuse!"

"I won't even think about it," he said briefly in answer to her monologue and, with that, ended the discussion.

While she was talking, though, pacing around the room, he could not help admiring the orator. Nora was striding, slim-figured, reinforcing her words with enchanting gestures, now flushing with sympathy for the intelligentsia, now dying down and aging out of animosity to the forces of reaction, only to flare up again and regain her youth. And suddenly she came to a dead stop, as though she had run into a tree frog—his answer.

No sooner had he so harshly replied to the emotional harangue, occasioned not so much by appurtenance to the camp of the left as by genuine concern for him and alarm, than he began to feel deeply wounded in his amour propre. Cut it short, you high-handed American, he began to think almost with spite. You're a cultivated creature, after all—you even read my unconscious thoughts sometimes, your almost Dantesque revelations were in space, and you can't understand simple human psychology! You ascribe primitive hatred for Communism to me and Chapski! My dear, that means that you simply don't know the man you've spent four years with! For all your fine sensibilities, can't you tell hatred from revulsion? You draw a primitive equal sign between the CIA and the KGB? Why, all of your guardians haven't committed as many abominations in their whole history as the Gee-Bees have in an hour!

And what, if I may, do you make of your own collaboration with the government, Madame USA Astronaut? Where did you get permission for the flight from? From Amnesty International? You'll forgive me if I bring up your interpretation of artistic success—no, no, forgive me, but I'm going to bring it up! In your opinion, a flop in left-wing circles means an artistic flop? And unless it's recognized as such by your gang, a masterpiece doesn't exist? And you propose that I should return any sum that I've received from a movie studio? You say that to me, who only recently was pushing little bags of powder at Colonial Parking? You're telling the Buffoon who was thrown out of his country to push away the producer, the only one in this country who recognizes him as an artist, and not just as Nora Mansour's lover? Do you really not understand that you're humiliating me? And you promise me that your mama will put me in the director's chair for a film about Dante? And you can't figure out that it's an outrage, Nora Mansour, wife of a terrorist?

Dear reader, given the abundance of *r*'s in that last sentence—at least in Russian—you can imagine how it resounded in his mind in Russian and in English, not softened even by the feminine cushion of *wife* in the last instance. She was already long gone, having, in fact, slammed the door right after ". . . won't even think about it," and he had carried on for some time with his mental thundering, accompanied by the overturning of pictures, the splashing and spraying all around of several huge drops of whiskey in a glass, and the crushing of several innocent (though who knows, really?) cigarettes. Enough! This has been going on for too long! What the hell did I come to America for? To become the court buffoon for the pretentious local branch of the Korbachs, this lice-infested aristocracy? Even Marjorie is looking me over now! I should have stayed in France, should have gone to Israel, I never should have met them and their nightmarish fortune! I would have stayed an honorable Soviet plebe, a twig, a bud [*sic!*] on the tree of the victims, the insulted and humiliated! Mrs. Mansour, you're simply pretending to be my dream, when in fact it's only my member that draws you to me, only your vagina concerns you!

That last adage forced the whole roar out of him. It was the end of the aforementioned glass of whiskey, too. It flew into a wall, soiling its irreproachable whiteness for a long time to come, and down to the next tenant. We now offer the female half of "our dear reader" the floor to answer, on Nora's behalf, Alexander Zakharovich's furious invective. I'm sure there won't be a single clause left of it! In our present state of enlightenment, though, it's not likely that even the male half would be able to restrain himself from smacking down the barking man-dog. We, however, will make an attempt to reconcile both sides. After all, one can look at love between a man and a woman as an endless Greco-Roman wrestling match, too! Remember the Russian proverb "Sweethearts who curse each other are only having fun"; just think of the national optimism contained in that one!

A couple of days after the scene just described, Nora pulled herself with the tenderest and silkiest of creations, something like a caress, from beneath the still puffing and panting Alex, and wrapped a bare arm around his head, that likeness of Nike, whom she already knew from her work on Ptolemy. "Darling, what would you say to going to a reception for Klunie Kudela today? You'll see all of our liberal beau monde there. And you'll stop wandering in the wilderness, you reactionary!" Maybe she's right, thought Alex, as he entered the ballroom of the Mayflower Hotel. Maybe liberals are better than conservatives. After all, the former have a sort of connection with *libido* in their name, and the name of the latter reminds me, whether I like it or not, of *sterva*—bitch. From the look of the crowd, though, one probably couldn't make such nice distinctions: the men were all in black, and the women in pastel shades. No need to pun here, we mention in an aside to the Russian reader. *Pastel* doesn't necessarily mean "bed."

"Tell me, please, just who is this Klushi Kudel?" he asked Nora, pretending that he'd never heard of the heroic woman. "Stop your posturing," she said in a serious tone and in the next instant burst into a smile that was addressed to everyone everywhere, since many in the throng were looking at them. Even though A.Z. had had his little joke about Klushi Kudel, we'll say for our part that he himself was an adviser to the well-known society named in the memory of Bertrand Russell. Not long ago the society had asked him which Soviet hero should receive their annual prize of fifty thousand dollars. He immediately offered them a choice of two swimmers: one had buggered off from the "motherland of all hopes" and floated across the Black Sea in nine days on an air mattress. The second, even better, had jumped without a thing from a Soviet steamer and swum for three days surrounded by sharks to one of the Philippine islands. "We normally honor people who have displayed civic courage," Alex Korbach had written to the committee, "but in these cases it was combined with physical courage as well." Alas, neither one got the prize; instead, it went to the woman who was being honored by the reception, Klunie Kudela from Namibia. That is, it was the prize that made her the guest of honor of the celebration under way. That's what I mean. Fiddlesticks.

People around Nora called to her and hurried over. The usual exchange of kindnesses got under way: You-look-great-you-too! For some reason, no one asked her about her expedition in space. Perhaps because the government is mixed up in it, A.Z. guessed. Drinks in hand, they sat down at one of the numerous round tables. Waiters swooped back and forth with large trays, offering guests lasagna, spinach salad with scallops, chicken cacciatore. Everything was simple, very simple.

There were no fewer than eight gathered around their table: enchanting oblong faces, the self-effacing smiles of the East Coast intelligentsia. There was one black couple, visibly not claiming any special attention. The special and visibly positive attention, it must be said, was directed at Alexander Zakharovich. It seemed to say: You'll pardon us for our curiosity, but we all know Nora, and we don't know you. We like you, Sasha Korbach, but say something, please, anything, even a sneeze in your napkin, and then you'll be a friend!

Across the table from them sat Klunie Kudela, a woman with a powerful, hungry form and a face with something of the Gypsy about it. For that matter, her clothes had a certain similarity to the ensemble of a "queen of the nomads' camp." Suddenly she fixed her gaze on Alexander Zakharovich, and so intently that he bridled a bit: Go away, little mother, you and your crystal ball. In the group they struck up a conversation about the prizewinner. She's so sweet, this Klunie Kudela, don't you think? Oh, she's so nice! After everything she's been through she looks simply marvelous, doesn't she? You know, guys, I was talking to her today. How are you feeling in the States? Upright and courageous, she just winked and said: "We shall overcome!"

Then there began a dialogue that subsequently, in confused form, would come back to Korbach at night like an indistinct echo of his own fate.

Someone asked: "Do you like her, Sasha?"

Surprising even himself, he answered: "Not very much."

Nora gave him a sharp kick just under the knee.

"Stop kicking," he said calmly.

"What are you talking about?" she simultaneously asked and exclaimed, as though combining humor and indignation; that is, offering both him and herself a chance for retreat.

"I mean I want you to stop kicking me under the table in my sensitive knee. Your signals, Nora, even those as out of place as that one, won't make me keep my mouth shut about a very simple fact—I don't much like this Klunie Kudela of yours."

"Take it easy, Sasha," said someone at the table—a man, it seemed. "You might not like her personally—that happens, cases of inexplicable hostility—but you can't deny her contribution to the struggle against apartheid."

Korbach nodded in comprehension but then suddenly slammed the edge of the table with the heel of his hand like a sailor of the Kronstadt commune.

"Excuse me, but I wasn't even thinking about apartheid. What I said has nothing to do with apartheid. And I'd like to add, buddy—"

"Jack," his opponent put it gently.

"Thank you, Jack. Excuse me, Jack, but it seems to me that people like you and your friends can't possibly like a woman of that sort."

"You're out of your mind today," Nora said to him fiercely in Russian.

"Not at all, my love, not at all. No." He felt like a complete idiot but still for some reason couldn't bite his tongue. "And you, my friends, why don't you just spit the hot potato out of your mouths? Do you mean to tell me that you can't see the decadent, lustful, corrupt, and faithless nature of this Klunie Kudela of yours? I know, you'll say: She's suffered, her husband is in jail to this day. I don't know how she suffered, but I feel sorry for her husband, particularly now that I've seen his wife. Yes, ladies and gentlemen, particularly after meeting her eyes in this room."

At that moment we hear the clattering hoofs of a horse galloping away. Nora was tapping her high heels, flying away, vanishing. He watched her go, wondering at how women can move so quickly and gracefully on heels. Then he got up and went after her, but first bowed to the entire group. It's too bad, guys, that you can't see something a hedgehog would spot. Just one glance at that broad and you can tell that you can't give her a prize named after a person of dignity. Having said all this, he realized that it had been in Russian, but he wasn't going to repeat it in the local gobbledygook. Klunie Kudela continued to look at him, not taking her eyes away for a moment. Not even her delighted admirers distracted her. He sharply thrust one hand in her direction, palm out and fingers spread, as though trying to cover the lens of a TV camera.

Nora was standing on the corner of Connecticut Avenue and a short segment of L (for "Love" or for "Lust"?) Street, at the end of which, perpendicular to the pavement, hung a sign reading ABC NEWS. Meanwhile, on broad Connecticut Avenue, a sparse flow of traffic was winding its way through a gently swirling snowstorm, much as it might have done on Moscow's Gorky Street. Look at these skinny little figures wrapping themselves in fake fur stoles (real fur, after all, is a crime against humanity), or at those on the corners at night by the hotels (Sasha Korbach's thoughts, as you have undoubtedly noticed, kind sir, had a tendency to go off on a tangent at moments of crisis), or at the ladies waiting for taxis they've called—they might be taken for prostitutes, wouldn't you say?

"Leave me alone, Alex," she said without turning around. Well, now I've got to say something to justify myself. "But what did I do?" he asked. "Nothing shameful except tell the truth. This new passion of yours, Klunie Kudela, is just short of being a bandit, and that's all there is to say about it. I know you think that Russians in their anti-Communism rub shoulders with the Western 'right,' with racists, with the pillars of exploitation. Oh, how wrong you are, Nora Mansour, née Korbach!"

A car pulled up. Nora opened the door. "Leave me alone, Alex!" I'll try one last variation: "When should I call you?" She finally turned and faced him. Gravity, sadness, trembling lips, Darling, don't go! "Don't call. I need a break from you, Alex." She drove away. Yes, that blow was like that of a boxwood walking stick to his head. But not fatal, all the same, not fatal! After all, she said "a break"—that means not forever, right? I'm asking you, hags of the snowstorm: Isn't that right?

7

REPLY, NORA!

Several weeks without Nora went by. During that time, Chapski flew in several times. Together, they visited the capable lads at the "Old Exec." One day Ed Peabody gave Chapski a gentle scolding for bringing up their project at every interview. There's one consideration, Steve, not a very important one, but just the same. . . . The subject of the film is a very touchy one for the Soviets even now, and their network of agents of influence is spread throughout the world. Many people in this network don't suspect that they're helping the Bolsheviks, and some are even convinced of the contrary. Premature publicity could kick up an undesirable fuss in the Lubyanka—that's the problem.

Chapski said: We'll keep that in mind, Ed. Thank you. We take it seriously. He laughed. His general impression is that things are starting to fall apart in Moscow. They don't give a damn about anything, is the way it looks. He'd been there recently, on a flight from Tokyo, for the first time in twenty-three years. No one had paid any particular attention to him, even though not long before that he'd been called "the notorious Chapski, the zoological anti-Soviet." They'd slipped him a transit visa for 120 bucks and told him to take a walk. In Moscow, people are standing in long lines for bones in cellophane wrappers with "soup selection" printed on them. You don't see hungry people on the streets, though— it's only everyone's eyes that are hungry, prowling, questioning. The people are the same surly boors that they're used to being, but at the same time they're even looking into each other's eyes: maybe someone knows what's in store for us? There was this one song in an old Soviet film: *V Vozdukhe pakhnet grozoi.* Sashka, translate that for Ed. Uh-huh, that's right: The air smells of a thunderstorm. Ed Peabody coughed modestly. " 'The Vyborg Side,' you mean?" Alexander was dumbfounded. "So, you know our language then, Ed?" The big cheese shrugged and spread his arms, palms up. "Well, what do you think, Sasha? That I could sit in this chair without a knowledge of the Russian language?"

Chapski went on sharing his impressions of Moscow. All their basic totems are under question. Even the stonelike guard at the Lenin Mausoleum has flinched. The soldiers quietly talk among themselves and snigger. "They're fucked" was Alexander's comment. Peabody exulted: "That's what it means to be a man of the arts—he gives so many details in just a few minutes! I'd like to have staffers who are that observant!" He went on: "All the same, hold off on the publicity, Steve, for the moment. It might not even be a bad idea to let the word out somewhere that the project has fallen through." "No way," Chapski growled. After his Moscow reminiscences, he began to shift from the lightness of his "Mr. Steve from Warsaw" role into his heavyweight mode as a famous, morose director.

The meeting went on nonetheless. The mujahideen, even though they're getting money and arms from us, categorically refuse to cooperate on the question of prisoners. Taking hostages is an unchanging part of war for them. Even so, sometimes we manage to pull out a few lucky ones. A group of five just arrived in Peshawar. From where I sit, guys, you'd do well to take a ride over to Peshawar. Chapski brightened. What a question, of course we'll pop over to Peshawar. We'll go for a ride along the Afghan-Pakistani border. Peabody smiled. Just don't say anything about it in your interviews, Steve.

The prospect of traveling to the other side of the world, in Peshawar, struck Alexander strangely, somehow. He thought to himself that in his years in emigration, he had never been out of the United States. For Soviet sensibilities, the States passed for some sort of final frontier. Where else could one possibly go from the American home? To Peshawar, as it turned out. To cross the border into those dreadful mountains, into a land where one could catch up with a Soviet or a Muslim bullet, where one might even be visited by a few Dantesque revelations.

––––––––––

Nora wasn't calling. Several more "de-Nora-ized" weeks had already gone by. As though she'd never even been with him. Several times he left messages on her answering machine—at first pseudolighthearted, then jokingly pleading, then simply desperate—but no answer was forthcoming, sad to say. Coming into his apartment and seeing the flashing red signal on his answering machine, he would dash to the receiver and collapse with it right on the rug, still in his overcoat: So talk to me, talk! The little cassette only played back some rubbish from the Black Cube or from Chapski Productions.

One day, he saw Nora on campus. In a leather jacket with a big scarf over her shoulder, she was carrying several poster tubes with maps or diagrams from one building to another. He was running at an angle across the lawns to intercept her before her entrance into the building, but he suddenly realized that she wasn't alone but surrounded by a whole crowd of faces. Obviously some sort of conference was going on. They all had name tags on their lapels, and everyone was in a fine mood. Including Nora. She was laughing. So that's the way it is, madam? You're cheerful? You've already had your rest from Sasha? You've quite recovered from your ruinous passion? And he sharply turned on his heel.

Well of course she saw, kind ladies and gentlemen, how he broke off the chase—that was why she had begun laughing it up with the other participants in the interuniversity colloquium Intersections of Caravan Trails and the Mutual Influences of Paganism. That was as it should have been, anyway: a person who specializes in human remains ought to have a sense of humor, right?

Several times he sent lyrics of the troubadours to her, in the yellow intracampus mail reuse envelopes, which don't seal but rather are tied shut with strings that wind around stiff paper buttons, as strange as that may seem. "En Elias, shall we say / Of those whom love attracts / He who never lies to love / And who himself is loved without betrayal; / Say, if you have regard for us, / The law of love, what honor is there: / To become a lover or the husband of a noble lady. / Whom should we choose?" The sending of these epithalamia also seemed to involve a sort of unobtrusive humor but in fact was more like a prayer: Reply, Nora! She didn't reply. By now he was ready, in the spirit of the young Blok, who had followed the rosy-cheeked Lyubov Dmitrievna through the streets of St. Petersburg, to wander in circles around her building in the West End, where they had spent so many happy hours together, but there would be no point in that sort of wandering. You won't even so much as catch a glimpse of her: she tools around in her Benz, and when she comes back she dives right down into the underground parking garage and then soars straight up to the penthouse; not a hope, my friend, not a prayer!

Fortunately, the most outrageous idea of all, that of turning to Mr. Mansour for help, never crossed Alexander Zakharovich's mind; for that matter, friends, you and I aren't going to rehearse any vaudeville sketch as dirty as "The Husband and the Lover in Search of the Woman." All that remained was to become the laughingstock of Pinkerton University, to turn into a Pierrot with a gloomy mug, sprinkled with suffering—"*muka*" in Russian; moving the stress to the second syllable, which changes the meaning to "flour," would be a direct invitation to *commedia dell'arte*—to hang around the archaeology building, where she, as we all know, doesn't spend much time, or to turn up at her lectures, which would obviously mean retiring the age-old cavalier's principle of "The less we love a woman, they more she likes us."

He would sit for hours in an armchair by the window, watching the Dupont Circle homos slide by on their bikes, and the fire-breathing Cyclops coming out of Vesuvius Pizzeria and gloomily wrapping himself in his huge overcoat. Without Nora there was no sense in writing, singing, or putting a film together. It was only in the theater that he still came to life without her. I wonder why she doesn't even feel any pity for me, it's a curious thing. She was filled with pity and love for little Felix, but not for me. There you have different forms of love. Her feeling for Felix must be close to the one that Beatrice spoke of to Dante in Paradise. It's clear that compared with these joinings of ours, nothing is worth anything—funny, isn't it?

All right, enough about love, there are other areas of life. Even on TV, occasionally, in between discussions about sex, they show Gorbachev's Washington adventures. The *gensek* turns up in the most unexpected places in the Capital City. For example, just go to the window of a bookstore. There's his picture as turned out by the Soviets, that is, without the birthmark on his head. With a sigh, he says to Vice President Bush, who is accompanying him: "I don't recognize myself in this, George—there's an image of Socialist Realism for you." With the same George, the Gorbachevs stroll nonchalantly through the Georgetown Park shopping mall, like people of the world. With his experienced Soviet eye, Sasha Korbach spots some nervous reaction in Raisa Maximovna as she looks over the price list. The official guest, however, is satisfied and is not without a flash of wit. "I wonder, George, what this shop will look like the day after our visit." One more drawing. Obviously having had a drink somewhere, the party rolls into Blues Alley, where none other than Dizzy Gillespie is blowing on his horn made from a drainpipe. Gorbachev is amazed by the Americans' ingenuity. Why, that's him, the very same one—you know, the great one, the one who's for peace. He goes over to the musician, arms open wide. Hello, hello, my dear man, our whole country loves you, old pal, *Polyushko-pole!* Dizzy's jazzy head is spinning. Look what a guest we've got tonight, fellas!

A crude editing job, Alexander Zakharovich notes with his pro's eye. Gorbachev and Gillespie are chatting about the fate of modern art. Both have come to and look terrific. The former pulls on the ancient Soviet wily saw inherited from the first *vozhd:* "Tell me, what message would you send by your music to your admirers in the Soviet Union?" The latter sternly intones a great thought: "Music has no messages, sir!" Gorbachev shakes the trumpeter's hand and heads for the door. Suddenly, a good shot comes on the screen: an old, heavily made-up lady standing at the bar and shrugging her shoulders. Korbach switches off the television. Darkness takes possession of the room for a minute, then begins to retreat. The first thing to shine forth is, of course, the white telephone, the bastard, which can at any moment gladden the body lolling in the armchair; it can, but it doesn't want to. Wait, it sounds like the moment has come: the raucous ring of the telephone passes as a convulsion up and down the previously mentioned body.

It seems hardly likely to us that even the most inveterate optimists among our readers will think it's Nora. We will, however, applaud those who decide that, according to the ignoble logic of things, another woman ought to come into the picture now. That is, in fact, the case. A husky woman's voice, the sort that is called inviting, even come hither, asks for Mr. Korbach. You guessed it, friends, she's calling from around the corner, from a pay phone. The oval of her face is partly hidden by an expensive fur. There she is, the anti-Aksyonovites in your number will say, another beautiful broad! This author creates a false feeling of reality, he indulges in wishful thinking. With him, every woman's got to be a beauty: Anis, Sylvia, Marjorie, Lenore, Nora, her mama Rita O'Neill, and so on. There's even a hypertrophic beauty in the character of the Californian favorite Bernadetta Luxe. Even if a plain woman turns up—against the author's will, obviously—she'll have to be dragged off to the periphery.

And now, no sooner has our main female character Nora Mansour, "the stars of our eyes," as they would have said in Russian literature of the Byronic school—from which, in point of fact, she had arrived in these pages—displayed a tendency to drop out of the narrative; no sooner has the need for a new woman arisen, than, on the spot, from head to toe, into a telephone booth dashes one more—well, obviously—beautiful woman. And this babe of the Hispanic persuasion, partly concealing her oval face in an expensive fur, is calling up our Alexander Zakharovich in her perturbing soprano. All of this is somehow at odds with the real state of things in the District of Columbia, where the number of unattractive women is significantly higher than the number of candidates for the position of our heroine; where, as a matter of fact, expensive furs aren't much to be seen, and if "ovals" are wrapped in anything, it's in the collar of an anorak; and where legs don't appear in the light of these expensive furs, like heroines of Offenbach operettas but only modestly trudge to work showing off badly pulled on tights.

All this is the way things are, my friends—we're trying to defend ourselves, but the fact remains that fictional reality is oh so different from real reality: in it, the author gives free rein to his caprices, for the sake of which he even risks his place in "serious literature," where these days you won't find so much as a pretty little face, much less a pair of legs worthy of a nymph. By way of a conclusion to this argumentative and not terribly pertinent passage, we will take the risk of reminding the reader that he is the coauthor of a work of prose, and if he has a need for realism, then he can lengthen the noses of our heroines, or make their ears stick out, make their behinds sag, or put in question the straightness of their legs. For our part, we'll say forthrightly that our "babe"—you know, the one who's talking to A.Z. from a phone booth just next to the Janus cinema—was the very embodiment of a fandango.

"Sasha Korbach, this is a future friend speaking to you, and she's very near you at the moment," the soprano sang out. "Well, come on over, then," said A.Z., his baritone slipping into a descant. "Write the address down." How imprudent, thought Mirelle Salamanca—it was she (the first mention of her is in Part 4, Chapter 3)—and she sighed in a way that made the telephone in Alexander's grip turn into a languid tropical parrot. "I don't need the address. Open the door, and I'll be at your place in a minute."

Exactly a minute later, she was already leading him with all her bodies and furs up the stairs to his own bedroom—she was laughing, flashing the whole spectrum of colors in her eyes, and holding herself back only to give him a good tickling with her tongue, and then, leaving pieces of her wardrobe on the stairs, she whirled her way right into the bedroom; that is, she was clearly sweeping aside all other variations on the beginning of a friendship: a cup of tea, talking about the weather, the past, and so on. And now our hero is already sprawled on his bed, which had previously been set aside only for Nora's caresses, and the feminine visitor, as she was, in furs from the hard-currency section of GUM, in a cloud of Obsession by Calvin, or Clyde, or something like that—we're not going to be precise—and humming something by Bizet, is ascending his perpendicular throne and offering him her breasts for acquaintance, now one, now the other, now a third—fiddlesticks.

"Well, Sasha, do you recognize me?" she asked when the feast was over. "From where, kind stranger?" he asked in surprise. "What are we going to do with you!" She laughed. "And a dissident, too!" Just then he realized that they were speaking Russian. "Did *they* send you, or something?" At that moment, the little flame held up to her cigarette dramatically illuminated the outline of her nose. She laughed amicably. "You're clever, anyway. Allow me to introduce myself: Captain Mirelle Salamanca, Department N, KGB, USSR. Does that name ring any bells, you dissolute artist?" He sighed. "Absolutely none at all, beautiful agent provocateur."

"What, do you mean that Burevyatnikov didn't tell you about our whirlwind in Nicaragua, about the volcanic avalanches of poetry that rained down moonlit mountainsides on us, while owls and hawks circled over our heads like cherubs?" While Alexander gathers his wits after this avalanche, we'll send our faithful coauthor and reader back to Part 4. For that matter, we recommend that you dip into Part 4 from time to time: a number of roots are hidden there.

Thus it was that the same poetess with whom Tikh had undermined the film crew surprised Korbach. Right now, as luck would have it, Nora will decide to come over to make up, open the door with her key, and see the "captain of poetry." It should happen right now, according to every law of dirty trickery. "You should at least take off your fur coat, comrade, and put on . . . er . . . other items."

"Yes, I'm a well-known poetess," she confirmed with modest pride, following him from the bedroom into the living room, taking off the fur coat, yet without being in a hurry about the other items. "The winner of an international competition at Knokke–Le Zoute. Mikhaloshchenko himself presented the award to me. And in addition to that I'm a member of the Bolivian Communist Party in exile." "Sure, and in addition to that you're also the chairwoman of the International Union of Prostitutes?" Korbach inquired politely. "Or just a member of the Central Committee?" She laughed. "Our chairwoman is someone else, a person you know very well!"

She wandered around the apartment as though she were at home, opening a cupboard, taking out a bottle of whiskey and two glasses, and an ashtray. She knew where everything was here. The only thing she doesn't know is that I'm about to let her have it over the head with the bottle, the KGB twat. But he didn't do it. Anyone can understand the cause of A.Z.'s indecisiveness by putting himself in his place.

"So, Sasha, let's have a serious talk," said Salamanca, settling down on the carpet, smoking and downing Chivas in healthy, military gulps. "Have a seat." The invitation was made in the new, civilized style of the beloved "organs." She used the Russian proverb almost correctly: "The foot has no truth." "Neither has anything else," Sasha noted as he sat down. Her eyes narrowed. "First of all, your family sends greetings." She smiled. The blow struck Alexander Zakharovich in his most vulnerable spot, that is, the forehead. The dissident, as she had contemptuously called him—and there was no more contemptible word in Department N—was all at sea, and without a wheel at that, floundering and taking chaotic gulps of air. "Take it easy, take it easy," she said, obviously enjoying herself to the hilt. "Nothing has happened to them yet. I saw them yesterday at the estate of Chapeaumange, Baron Vendredi, in Haiti. Albert and I are old friends, after all. Before he met Anis, we used to read Saint-John Perse together frequently. Well, what can I tell you? Your wife has put on quite a few pounds, even though she's as pretty as ever. As the Russian people say, 'A woman thrives at forty-five.' [Again she screwed up the folk saying!] Lyova and Styopa, they're your masterworks, Sasha, not some songs with a dubious spirit, and even a few plays with their dirty anti-Soviet hints. They're good-looking—they take after Mama. Their build would be the envy of any homosexual; they'll be athletes. Not long ago they won the surfing championship of the tiny little region where that Haitian bourgeois swine lives, okay? French has become a second mother tongue for them. Chapeaumange is thinking about their going to the Ecole Normale in Paris. They have a wonderful relationship with their new father—don't twitch like that, Sasha, it was all your fault. They even help him during rituals. Not long ago, his dead aunt came over from the Dominican border—she is known far and wide for her ability to swallow a live rooster, so the boys and their father did three voodoo rings around her."

The bitch is sitting on the couch at an angle that makes it impossible to get her with the bottle, thought Sasha, in desperation from the mocking treatment. How can I make this cunt shut her mouth? Did she really see my kids? As if in answer to this disbelief, Mirelle produced a gift, a photo of a garden party in front of the villa; among the guests were the fifteen-year-old twins in white jackets. In the background Anis could be seen, too, with her magnificent shoulders, in a dress the color of the backside of an ink blotter. It was hard to tell where Baron Vendredi was: everyone present looked like an aristocrat. It seemed to him that Lyovka and Styopka were looking right at him, though at the moment of the taking of the photo they had been looking at that bitch with her tiny Minolta. It used to be that I'd carry them on my shoulders, one on the left and one on the right. Anisia would shriek: "Put my children down!" At the same time, the lecherous woman would be glad when I picked them up and took them to Koktebel. We'd knock around the bay for weeks on end, climb up Karadag. They grew up as my friends. Even after I left that disgusting Central Committee of a homeland, the kids went on loving me and boasting at school: "That's our dad, all right—the notorious Sasha Korbach!" That damned government took all their early teenage years from me. And now they're being raised in the family of a witch doctor.

"What's all this, then—you're a strong man, and you're whining?" Salamanca said. "You can see that they're fine. Of course Haiti's a dangerous country, but we've got a strong, reliable network there. If we want it, they'll go on being fine." "What's the point of this blackmail?" he asked. "Come on, spit it out!" Clearly, she had been preparing to go on swaggering, when all of a sudden the subject at the heart of the matter came up. Her breasts, none too snug in her bra, became agitated, as though they wanted to take part in the crucial discussion.

"All right, then, listen. You'll stop screwing around with Chapski and Ed Peabody. You'll refuse to direct this anti-Soviet film. All the materials that have been gathered for the screenplay you'll turn over to me. These demands are not negotiable. When you've met them, you'll have ensured the protection of your children. Otherwise, they'll remain unprotected. As for the rest, you have a choice. The first option is total silence. In that case we'll keep the story of your labors in Westwood under wraps. The second option is a step toward us. You'll get support, and even—"

"They've been talking about me?" he asked. She burst out laughing. "You can be sure that *they* talk about you. A whole group keeps track of you, you traitor." "The children have been talking about me?" Alexander asked, stating his question more precisely and immediately put a lid on it: look who I'm asking! "What a jealous father you turn out to be!" Mirelle neighed again. It should be pointed out that this entire conversation had been accompanied by her specific array of evocative sounds: humphing, clucking with her tongue, even muted derisive howls when the man she was talking to said something she didn't like. "Alexander Zakharovich, would you like your boys to come for a visit in a week? Everything will be 'great,' as our chief, General Bubtsov, says. Or maybe not so 'great,' and you'll never see your offspring again, you motherfucker—Sasha the piece of shit, a bitch's pup, beaten with a stick, Korbach's bastard; that's what Soviet officers say about you!"

Exactly what had caused this new outpouring of Gee-Bee filth from her mouth, which had been created if not for the *dolce stil nuovo* then at least for sugary kitsch, it was hard to say, unless one chose to delve into the fact that she was shaking and glowering at him like some kitchen maid who was getting stripped naked again behind the house. What is this satanic temptation? was the thought that suddenly struck A.Z. Pure temptation of human nature by the forces of the devil. "Do they pay you well for this work, Captain?" he asked, trying to go over to the counterattack: Don't forget, he was saying, you hired hand, that you're sitting before a man who's never sold out! "Very well!" she shouted. "I'm richer than all of you, elders of Zion! My Leninist ideology is always with me! You think you've already demolished the fortress of socialism? You're celebrating too soon! In perestroika we're cleansing ourselves of Jewish filth! The backbone of dedicated volunteers will deal a crushing blow to the bourgeoisie! We won't forgive you your attempt to turn back history!"

He looked at his watch, and she looked at her watch. He stood up, and she stood up. He took a step toward her, and she took a step toward him. He was turning back history, and she used her back to help him. "Elbows and knees position," he commanded her. "You see, you bitch, it's time for full docking," he muttered. "I hate you," she was muttering in return, "I hate the thing you rule me with!" A sulfuric secretion dashed forcefully around the room. In the dark window, on the other side of which the peaceful intersection went on bustling, a scene of the basest sort of temptation was reflected. I'll never wash myself clean of this, he was thinking. Right now I'm going to suck you in, bald head and all, she was thinking. The comrades had given her the right suggestion: work the perversion angle hard. Just don't let Nora come in now, he thought in desperation, and as a result of this desperation went into even more of a rage. If that little slut of yours comes in now, she thought longingly, that'll be the end of all your "new sweet poetry." Sweetness is just oozing out of her, he thought, the sweetness of infinite disgrace. She was bellowing: "In the mines below, or the sky above / I long for but the scent of love!" She finally called out, and a powerful shudder rolled through her body like a Red cavalry squadron. Shut up, just shut up, he commanded himself, but he repeated her "scent of love" until the convulsion of the frontline detachment lifted their battle straight into the air, in order to crawl down into the murkiest possible après.

For ten minutes or so, silence and semidarkness reigned in the room. The white of her raised haunches, which would soon come down to one side in a rapid motion, was the only thing visible. Not far away was the droning of Connecticut Avenue, as always dropping its middle c in the buzz. Through the wall, weakly but clearly, music could be heard. Some normal person was listening to the "Serenada

Notturno." A.Z. buried his face in his hands and said: "Now leave, Captain!" He heard her go into the bathroom, and when she came back the fragrance Mme Rochas went about the business of crowding out the sulfur. Acting within the framework of her instructions, she gathered her things ably and quickly. She stopped in the doorway and said softly, humanely: "Think everything over, Sasha. You've got no way out. I'll call you in a couple of days." The door closed. Fiddlesticks.

8

THEY WERE DRINKING COFFEE, EATING CAKE

*T*he good thing about our mid-Atlantic states is their autumn. You can forgive them anything for this season, filled with sunny, blue air seemingly crunching with light frost, filling the huge bronchial networks of tree branches finally purged of tired leaves with new, invigorating oxygen; and beyond the translucent groves, so modestly and appropriately, stands a white church with a sharply sloping roof, or a pseudo-Hanseatic row of town houses—which loses nothing by the prefix *pseudo-,* since it has long been a question more of style than of trickery—or some glass monument to advanced technology, or some other object, like a stone behemoth, or anything else you like, but always in measured portion and in keeping with the proportions of the landscape. You'd be hard-pressed these days to find any citizen who wouldn't stop for at least a moment and sigh: say what you like, but they're nice, our mid-Atlantic autumns! Even those young people who come out into the parking lots in the morning, drinking coffee with one hand and chatting on their mobile phones with the other, even they, setting their mugs down on the roofs of their cars so as to unlock them, say offhandedly to the autumn "Nice!" and only then dive inside and with nimble hands collect their steaming drinks from the roofs of their high-speed thrones.

It instills vigor in you, the autumn does, as you walk across the campus to your theater, vigor and a feeling of being cleansed of indecency. Working metamorphoses, autumn itself often changes. Yesterday it seemed as though it were over, as though the disheveled locks of the arctic witches were already lashing at the peaceful streets, as though the power of disgrace and melancholy were wailing in the ventilation ducts, and then the next morning blessed autumn renews itself, and along with it individuals who seemed razed to their foundations. That's what our mid-Atlantic autumns are like—let us thank our Only Lord for this blessing, given in equal measure to the Jew, and the Catholic, and the Mormon, and the Orthodox, and the Muslim, and even the worshiper of Baal, whose presence in the greater Washington area cannot be doubted.

A.Z. was marching along on such a morning to his seminar on biomechanics. At first he trudged along in exhaustion from the previous night, then his feet moved along more happily, and his lungs breathed more deeply, as though they had joined the bronchial wisps of the university trees. He had come back to life after the previous evening's repulsive peep show had taken place with his own participation, that sex-kitsch prepared by the KGB crowd. Just then a rejuvenating thought occurred to him: You're a part of nature, after all, and even though your time of flourishing may have passed, there's no reason at all why you should fall into decay before your time. Go straight to the archaeology building now. Curb your pride. Seek out Nora without any put-on nonchalance, don't be afraid to show living feelings, even if it all turns to tragedy. When you meet Nora, don't show her any sexual feelings, take your mind off your uncontrollable penis, throw yourself at her feet, hug her shoes, put your nose between her shoes, ask for help. Whom else have you got to ask for help if not your Beatrice?

In the office of the archaeology department, they were drinking coffee and eating cake: it was Fran the secretary's birthday. The atmosphere was one of low-key excitement, partly brought on by an excess of sweets. Everyone who turned up was offered a slice of cake with all the hospitality expected from ladies of Virginia (no play on words intended with regard to damsels of this fine Confederate state, all you good wags out there). The director in residence was pleased to drink the coffee and took a healthy chunk from the cake that reminded him of the dearest person of all those who had ever been close to him, Grandma Irina. For all the distance separating the pierogi of the Arbat from the cakes of Virginia, they still have common roots in Strasbourg. If I'm wrong, then correct me: that's the much-loved expression of a Soviet adolescent, with the help of which many lackadaisical types managed to avoid deserved punishment.

All the ladies present told him what an unexpected surprise it was to see Dr. Korbach, the star of our theater, at our little get-together. Many in the university called him Dr. Korbach, and oftentimes he wanted to answer in the popular style: "Stick out your tongue!" He managed to lead Fran, "the party girl," a skinny Scot about whom Nora and the whole department said in one voice, "You can always rely on her," off to one side. They stopped in a corner beneath a poster with a picture of a hundred-million-year-old fossil that by the will of the elements had turned out looking like an Egyptian toy only six thousand years old. It was the intention of the designers of the poster that these two numbers should say something to the human mind and heart.

Alexander Zakharovich didn't try to stretch things into a tragedy this time either. On the contrary, he began to babble: "Beg your pardon, Fran, for this intrusion into your celebration, but I'm looking for Nora Mansour, you see. I had to go on a rather long journey, and I've lost track of her, and now a mutual friend of ours just arrived from London, and he needs her advice on an important scientific question." A.Z. had known for quite some time that the secretaries loved to be entrusted with details, even false ones. "Do you mean you don't know, Dr. Korbach?" Fran began, only to be corrected straightaway by Dr. Korbach: "Sasha, please." "Yes, Sasha, thank you. Listen, Sasha, Nora left for Iraq the day before yesterday. She plans to join the Lilienmann expedition there. What? You didn't know about it? Sasha, you're all pale! Take an aspirin!" These Americans, he thought, going more and more pale—they believe in aspirin as a panacea.

Fran, a good soul, taking his wrist seemingly by chance—or was it in fact to check his pulse?—went on imparting information. Nora had begun a two-year sabbatical. How long will she be in Iraq? At least three months, I think, but then I think she wants to start her own team. In any case Fran had sent out a number of letters under her signature for that reason. You understand, of course, Sasha, that with her name all the doors are open to her now. Seeing Nora Mansour is all anyone dreams about. Fran's neighbors can't believe that she has coffee with Nora every week at the faculty club. Of course, we'll all miss her. And you too, I can tell. What can you do, Sasha—a lot of our professors live like vagabonds. As far as I can tell, it has to do with some serious excavations at the crossroads of the caravan routes. In other words . . .

"In other words, she's gone for a long time," he said quietly. "She left without saying a word to me. Okay, it's my fault, Fran, but it's so sad, Fran, unbearably sad, when a part of your life ends, and everything gets ground up like undelivered mail." This time, a tragic mood showed clearly on his face. Fran clenched her dry little fists on her chest. A living opera was being played out in her eyes and with her participation. If Sasha wants, she'll try to find some way of getting in touch with Nora. In any case, she'll keep him in mind if Nora calls, which is entirely possible, if only because several of her students still had incompletes.

The greater the innocence, the greater the sympathy. For some time already, the ladies present had only been pretending to be interested in their cake. In fact, they had been paying attention, almost holding their breath, to the dramatic conversation taking place in the corner of the not very large room. "Thanks, Fran, I don't need anything. You've got a big heart, but I'm sorry to say that not even it can help me. As the Russians say: *Chto bylo, to proshlo*—What was is past. Happy birthday." He walked away, but looked back from the doorway. All the women, shaken, were watching him go: what a program, without a television! On the wall behind them was the fossil, which a hundred million years ago under the influence of an unknown process had assumed the form of a rider on horseback. It looks like I've played the buffoon again, and if that's so, then there's no forgiveness for me. Dismissing even this thought, he left the chapter section, and it immediately disappeared from the screen of the laptop.

9

HOW CAN I, IF I JUST CAN'T?

*S*hould we take Salamanca's threats seriously? Without a doubt, she, or one of them, had seen his family in Haiti. The snapshot of his sons still lies before him—maybe it's a focal point for his love, maybe it's a reminder of blackmail. Then again, Anis is no slouch either. Most of our audience must remember the rather ticklish mission that she carried out at the beginning of the book. It's somehow hard to imagine that she settled on an exotic island without a "green light" from the committee.

That's the theory—in reality, everything might turn out to be a repugnant misunderstanding: one sector is looking out for Mrs. Chapeaumange, while another is blackmailing Korbach with his sons' lives. They're pushing all his buttons with the help of their well-trained cunt. They'll say, though it's not likely, that the "Committee" isn't what it was in the days of Efron, Merkator, Sikeiros, Eitigen, Sudoplatov, and their other fanatical killers. Hasn't the scope for such possibilities increased? Why, Salamanca herself could knock someone off with her "fury of the female."

For that matter, how can there possibly be any art when the Party keeps the pressure on the way it does? thought Korbach. In Moscow, they considered the Buffoons obstinate, but still theirs—homegrown. They made a show of solidity, conducted inspections and held meetings of all sorts of repertoire committees, adopted resolutions. Now that they number me among their undisguised enemies, they can set the "cloak and dagger" stuff in motion—outright criminal provocation. Well, what do I lose in the end? our unhappy artist agonizes. And as it is, everything *is* lost. I've lost the love I was living for, even though I'd never expected to find it. Have regrets about some film? But what else have I got to have regrets about now except work, the blissful "outpouring" and the quiet orchestral piece that follows? How can I not feel sorry about the loss of maybe my last chance to say what I have to say? Admit it to yourself—even when you were working at Colonial Parking, you were counting on that chance, hungering for a miracle, for the moment when they would come and say: Go ahead, Sasha, show us your stuff. In the artistic world, where everything is saturated with the shit of ideology or commerce, the chance to be a real artist comes along less often than a jackpot in Atlantic City. Andrei Tarkovsky managed to drive both beasts, the one from the East and the one from the West, behind the curtain. I won't forgive myself if I let myself just get lost along the way.

Again, for the umpteenth time since the meeting of the two branches of the Korbach family, a childish idea came into his mind—to rush to Big Brother, that is, to his fourth cousin Stanley Franklin Korbach. If he'd been swaggering before, now God was giving a command—they're threatening the little Korbachs, after all, the Russian bearers of the Jewish gene of the house of Kor-Beit, traced by Fuchs's office right back to the time of Nebuchadnezzar. With his pull in this country, Stanley could bring the local secret services in on it, and they'd just say to the "Knights of the Revolution": If you hurt us, we'll hurt you even more; better if you hold back, and we do the same. They have a simple name for it: reciprocity.

Moaning as though he had a toothache, Alexander called up Miss Rose Morrows, office manager at Halifax Farm. She wasn't there, as it turned out. She doesn't work here anymore, sir. It was only then that he remembered: that's right, the Fourth Disappearance is under way, after all! His petty troubles had made him forget about the historic event! Halifax Farm must have been occupied now by King Kong, Norm Blamsdale. There'd probably been a shake-up of the vanished president's whole staff. "May I ask who's calling?" a kind female voice asked: Maryland wasn't yet wanting for kind secretaries. Having received in reply the name Alex Korbach, the voice faltered for a moment but didn't lose its balance. "Excuse me, sir, but I have instructions on what to do in case you call. A member of the family wants very much to talk to you. Would you mind holding the line for a moment?"

Now it was his turn to falter, but, unlike the secretary, he almost did lose his balance. Had she really left the phone to make a connection? With these newfangled cellular devices you could call anywhere, right up to Hammurabi's tomb. Her phone's ringing right now, in her rucksack, at that moment when she's cleaning the dust off the tablet that reads: "A woman who abandons a man is subject to the lash. . . ." No, the other way around: "A man who forces a woman to leave is subject to the noose."

"Hello, Alex," he heard on the phone. "This is Margie. Do you have any news?"

Another stumble. An outrageous plucking of the taut wire of his own sciatic nerve. No, I'm going to grab at it with both hands anyway. I went a bit bowlegged, but I'll straighten up. "That's just why I'm calling, Margie—to find out if you know anything."

"Come here. I'll send a plane for you."

"Just where are you?"

"On Corsica," came the reply.

"No, Margie, how can I?"

There was silence for several seconds, and then a trembling voice said: "Have pity on me, Alex! Please come!"

"No, Margie, how can I, if I just can't?" He put the phone down.

10

FIDDLESTICKS AGAIN

*A*ll at once, a few days later, the situation with the film resolved itself, and in the most unexpected possible way. A new high-level scandal in the administration broke out. Something on the order of Irangate, only with the difference that this time everything came out all at once. Once again authority was skewed in the democratic superpower. It turned out yet again that an empire cannot exist without secret operations, while at the same time the structure of a democracy demands complete glasnost.

This time it was a matter of secret violations of trade sanctions against the apartheid regime of South Africa in exchange for substantial favors to the pro-American rebels in Angola. The agent of the unmasking was once again *The Washington Post,* which over the decades had managed, despite the high humidity of the Potomac valley, to hatch out a powerful brood of investigative journalists. In the first installment of the story, which took up half the front page, and two entire pages of the first section, Edmund Peabody's name was mentioned at least two dozen times. There were even pictures of him: a headshot, one of him at a committee meeting in the Old Exec, one with the secretary of something important, and even one of him with a pleasant-looking woman and a magnificent dog.

Unlike Marine Colonel Oliver North, Peabody, who to Alex's surprise turned out to be a colonel in the Air Force—that is, a counterpart of Colonel Denisov in the script that was taking shape—made no attempt to keep anything in the dark but rather at the first opportunity made the following statement: "There are some circumstances in which some agencies cannot bring their operations before Congress for discussion. There are some actions against apartheid that we could not present for public discussion either, so as not to render them pointless. The demand for uncompromising openness in the work of certain bodies makes questionable the very existence of those bodies. Period." In the present context, it would be entirely appropriate to add the expression that we've already grown so fond of: Fiddlesticks. Fiddlesticks, period!

The public, already tired out by Irangate, reacted sluggishly to the new scandal; the newspapers and networks, though, reported, not without a certain schadenfreude, that the Old Exec was shaken to its foundations. How deep those foundations were, however, no one knew. There was a news flash that Peabody had been impeached but wasn't losing heart. Some corporation has already offered him a post in which he would earn three times what he was making in government.

That's why people leave the government in such a good mood, Johnny Carson commented. All they do is dream about being driven out in disgrace. Such are the peculiarities of democracy, ladies and gentlemen: the pillars of the fatherland tremble, critics and scoffers build up their authority.

Farewell, Peshawar, Alexander thought, as soon as he had read the first story blowing the lid off things. And yet, over the last few days, Peshawar had seemed to him like the equivalent of Lermontov's Caucasus. Leaving for Peshawar—there's the ideal answer to a certain someone's departure for Iraq! There, in Peshawar, all this muddle in my head will clear up, and the only things left will be mountains, the border, the war, a tape recorder, a video camera, a laptop. No one will know where I am. Maybe I'll even be able to put one over on that poetic bitch Mirelle. I'll make a date with her, give in once more to temptation, then fly straight to Peshawar. Kiss your Peshawar good-bye now, he told himself, turning the pages of the newspaper. Now everything is going to start slipping out of your hands. Melt, stink, and slip away.

National Antihero Peabody called him up one day. "I just wanted to say, Alex, that I'm very sorry about what happened. Believe it or not, what I'm going to miss more than anything is my modest contribution to your remarkable project, yours and Steve's. I still believe, though, that it'll see the light of day. Chapski is a real idea mill. And you're simply a one-of-a-kind artist. All the best to you, and a big hello from my wife. She shares my feelings completely."

There was only Chapski left. According to the logic of things, he, too, should have started melting, stinking, and slipping away. And sure enough, Chapski, in the best directorial tradition, dropped off the map right after the scandal broke. The calls in the middle of the night with the outpourings that had overflowed his fat belly of ideas, with the jokes in the best Warsaw-Chicago style—"Hello, old chap, this is your old Chapski!"—came to an end. Swallowing his pride, A.Z. himself called L.A. The kind secretary told him that the boss was "overseas" at the moment but that he would be informed of Mr. Korbach's call as soon as he turned up. Alexander detected a note of pity in her voice. Then again, what possible emotion could these robots of politeness have?

Finally, Chapski called. From Athens, for some reason. He was obviously in a gloomy mood: no jokes, no diminutives, no swearwords. His flight was in an hour, and the next day at noon he would be at Dallas–Fort Worth International, and from there he would be continuing to California three hours later. At some point over that time, you and I can talk *O tempora! O mores!* Come if you can—I'll be waiting for you in the Diplomat Bar. In such a strange state of freedom from obligation, he could simply not go, but all the same it seemed necessary to dot the *i*'s. He arrived in Dallas at the appointed time and spotted Chapski right away in the bar, sitting at a table in a cloud of cigarette smoke. The heavyset physique of the Slavic émigré. The bags of his shoulders in a burlap sack of a sweater. A drooping, sarcastic lip. Well, now you see, Sasha, what a goddamned mess everything's become. Everything at the Old Exec fell apart, and our investors, those whores, scattered in every direction right away. There you have it, the movie business subconsciously longs for a strong hand.

The atmosphere in the bar was uncomfortable. Scatterbrained waitresses were hauling trays of salads and beers around. A basketball team showed up, twelve towering lads who gathered at the bar and whose protruding backsides hung over our heroes' table; in their number was a genius of the game whose name would later echo throughout the country after a fatal overdose of crack.

I didn't call you because I was hoping for another approach. The Putney Company brought up our project for discussion at a meeting of the board. The majority were for it, but then this bastard with a fat share of the stock showed up. You can imagine the rest. That's how it is. All things considered. Sorry, the thought got away, went off to the loo. At the end of the day, it's just Jewish luck. This guy says: The Russian project flies only over my dead body. That's the insurmountable obstacle, the carcass of a horse preserved in spirits. It seems they offended him in Moscow by dumping your shit all over him. He was expecting them to roll out the red carpet for him—he was a rich man known all over the world, after all, who'd come expecting cooperation—and no one even met him at the airport. You know those motherfuckers at Goskino better than I do. He went to the best hotel, and they weren't expecting him even at the worst one. So, a multimillionaire found himself alone in the barbarian horde. Rather a stinging feeling, wouldn't you say? Have you ever felt it? When was that, then, Sasha? Okay, you don't have to go into detail. The main thing is that's how the Commies, in that idiotic way, pulled the rug out from under your *Starry Ticket of the Eighties*. Chapski looked at his watch and downed the rest of his beer. Time to board. Korbach paid the tab, and he didn't try to stop him.

11

TEMPORARY OR FINAL?

*A*ll these circumstances led our A.Z. to do a temporary, if not final, tallying of accounts. The love affair is finished. The film project is finished. The Black Cube has gotten itself twisted around, as though it had lost its edge and settled for the banality of surfaces. His colleagues on the faculty keep giving him strange looks. Maybe Salamanca had already been singing to someone about the "happiness powder"? By the way, where was that Mata Hari of the world revolution? Maybe she committed hara-kiri in her prostitution. Believe me, comrade, it's not for a thrill, not for the sake of fat royalties, and not in the expectation of any prizes that we mention this—yes, that's right, dear reader, it's only for the rhythm. Even that broad had vanished, although it wouldn't be a great bother if she were around now that the hot question is off the agenda. She promised to surface after a couple of days, and she's been out of sight for a couple of weeks already.

But now the phone was ringing in the night: it was her! She was a bit hoarse from vodka, or maybe it was from an excess of growls and rumblings in his mother tongue. "Where are you calling from, Comrade Salamanca?" "From Peshawar." She laughed. "We're sitting here waiting for you." "Don't wait up, we're not coming. You'd do better to come to my place, we'll get together." She's an illusion, this damned spy! Is she a real object of present-day biology? Did Alexander Zakharovich just dream her up? Just a nightmare of that twisted sexuality that forever flows through his veins in the form of Chekhovian consumption?

"So you've given in, then, Mr. Korbach? The children mean more to you than an internationally recognized masterpiece?" It was a strange sort of disenchantment that was now flowing from Peshawar, or from the phone booth next to the Janus cinema. She ought to have exulted, it seems: that's how renegades tremble before us, she should have said, but the female officer was dissatisfied, as though some project of hers had fallen through, too.

"That's right, you can tell them that: the children are more important."

"Even so, we're not going to let you off the hook!"

"No objections here, madam."

"Stop your provocations, you scum!" rumbled over the line with such force that it was as though the Afghan-Pakistani frontier had trembled.

"Are you going to tell lies that you did it with me? No one'll believe you! If you want your children to live, then think about your whole life! Wait for a rendezvous, and stop looking at the revolution and jerking off!" Click. Hell, through which, without a doubt, all telephone lines run, had howled.

Alexander Zakharovich was howling himself. Woe is me, a Jew who denies his family and who has brought shame on his Russian military family, too! White Horse, pour through me in an uncontrollable stream, connect me with at least something dear to me in the world! Tapping out the country code for the Republic of Haiti, he did not remove the bulky bottle—though it was becoming lighter all the time—from his mouth. A most kind and ingratiating voice, perhaps a girl's or perhaps a jaguar's, inquired as to whom such a prodigiously drunk monsieur might be calling. I'm calling the residence of Mr. Chapeaumange, *mon chat actuel*. I'll connect you with the minister of the interior. But I'm not calling the minister, I'm just calling the husband of my wife, goddamn it! Hello, Minister Chapeaumange's residence. Listen here, what's all that wailing in the background, that moaning and crowing of roosters? Styopa and Lyova, two Komsomolists from the land of the Soviets, have got hold of two drainpipes. Don't worry, Father, it's just Granny Furan, who's come with her *chanteclair*. And is it true, Dad, that you've become a millionaire in the USA, *c'est vrai*? *Ce n'est pas vrai*, good-for-nothings! That was how they had once romped with each other, joking: crook of a father, good-for-nothing kids. Beg your pardon, but do you know a lady named Mirelle Salamanca? Mrs. Minister at that moment picks up a third drainpipe. Relax, Sasha, we've had Mirelle Kollontai Salamanca on our books for a long time. Baron Vendredi himself picks up a fourth pipe. Good Georgian accent. Listen, Monsieur Sasha, if you want to have a good feed and some good drinks, come right away. We've got lots of good things piled up here. Not much good stuff all around, but here inside there's loads. Thank you for the invitation, I wouldn't have expected anything different from you. The tropics give birth to expansive natures, great souls settle there. The North, for all its philosophy, lacks the brotherhood of the ancient caravan routes. For example, I've found myself all alone here, now—*odin kak perst,* as we say. No, not a Persian—*perst* is 'finger'—alone like a finger, it's a figure of speech. An allegory, correct, man. Not then one who's got nine mobile brothers, but an allegorical one, like Gogolyevsky's *Nose.* All right, then, I'll come to your place in the role of the ex-husband—that is, like one of your zombies.

Before I leave, I've got to say good-bye to the monuments of my love. That's the way it's done in modern Byronic circles. That's how it was in the days of the *dolce stil,* and even before that. Long before. We'll soar up in the elevator to the bastion of King Solomon's tower. All the windows of these penthouses were smashed long ago, a gang of winds strolls around, tossing around the remaining curtains. Bathrobes wander from room to room, like your Haitian specters. The toilets, stuffed full of some unknown shit, smell like death. In one corner of the bastion sits his brother in love, Omar Ibn-Kesmet Mansour, bent over and suffering. Sasha, I got the official divorce papers, he weeps. That's unfair, brother! It's an act that somehow goes against the Hammurabic code. Even if I wasn't loved, I kept her secret all the same. Listen, brother, just hold on—any moment now you'll blow away along with the secret! And there it all goes. The secret of Nora Mansour, absurdly flapping its terry-cloth wings, tries to join a flock of geese and dissolves into the twilight.

Your last hope for something wonderful is waiting for you in the hills of Maryland, where noble horses blew currents of air on their first meeting with their silken manes and tails. But what's this? Only skeletons of horses picked apart by Egyptian vultures now graze on the blue slopes, and even those remains are slowly crumbling into dust before your very eyes. The gelded sire with whom you had your dialogues in 1983 drags himself out of a grove. In his devotion to existence, that is, to fleshiness, he's become huge, like Alexander III's dray. He slowly turns his giant hindquarters to you and bows his legs for a shit. A fire hose of grayish excrement bursts out beneath his tail, breaks up, falls like apples, then forms into a hose again. And he shits and shits. Resting his elbows on that very same fence, Alexander Zakharovich just cries and cries with that same excremental slowness.

12

GET UP, LAVSKY!

*W*ell, enough of this shit! He can still come back to life, to the deep translucence of the Florentine skies. The one who intends to save him is taking his time, simply out of a sense of tact. You have to let a drunken man sleep it off. He has to get up, be horrified by his face in the bathroom mirror, squeeze half a tube of toothpaste into his mouth, muck around there for a long time with a droning electric tooth-brush, shake his head, chuck out the things that happened and the things that didn't from the night before, suddenly be incarnated before the mirror with the feeling that the incarnation is no relative of his, mutter "Oh, fuck, oh, fuck," throw up pro-fusely, and moan over his emaciated stomach.

Finally, when he gets to his coffee, the doorbell rings. Our hero drags his body down the stairs. Probably some more course work, goddamned midterms—what else could it be? He opens the door. A February day in 1988 is looking him in the eye and full in the face. The snow that fell in the night offers him the gift of the smell of his childhood and motherland. On the front stoop, in an incorrigible cow-boy pose, albeit in a cashmere coat, his eyes no longer young but with a subdued twinkle and full of humor, stands the savior of the perishing individual, the fugi-tive tycoon of our trillion-novel (according to *Forbes* magazine) business, Stanley Franklin Korbach, in the flesh.

"Get up, Lavsky! Collect your limbs and all drops of your consciousness! It's time to do real things!"

VIII. THE BORDER

You ask how I see him. Now in the form of a cloud,
Now like a field on which rain is falling.
Sometimes he's a hand holding out an apple,
Sometimes a passing Venetian doge, his gown rustling.
Now he's flowing like the channel of a mighty river,
Now flying like a cherub in the branches of a Rococo pattern,
Now crumbly like a measure of wheat flour,
Now curly-headed, like a Jewish Red Army major.
My son, he is silent, and I understand the unseen father,
Though we've never met on the roads of this earth.
I see a temple before me, either the facade or a side.
Is the color from a cherry tree or a blizzard?
The question "Are you here or there?" is absurd.
"Judaic or Hellenic, that is, Jew or Greek?"
He walks through the fields and leads his horse by its bridle,
And behind him like a sunset our sin rises in the fields.
This is what remains between us and what forces us to pray
For forgiveness, for mercy, for the insatiable sadness of love.
As Israel stands, praying, before a handful of olim,
So he and I gaze on the lacework of dark print.
You ask: Where does that sin make its nest?
Darkness is gathering, faces are coming nearer and nearer,
The rain beats at the window like peas,
Two starlings have nested in an abandoned paneless hothouse,
And Father sails away like a rustling plane tree in the morning,
Or like a spinning oar presenting the river to us as a gift,
Or like the knocking ties of a railroad bed,
Or like a curly-headed Red Army officer executed by firing squad.

PART IX

1

GALAXY-KORBACH

$\mathcal{B}$y the beginning of the last third of our story, we can already discern a certain encouraging regularity: the chronological gaps between our sections are made up of approximately three years. A tendency toward realism, then, is growing. The unfriendly critic, of course, might sharply object—and she'll do it, of course—that this chronological regularity is only a smoke screen for events leaping around with the chaotic abandon characteristic of modernism. Pshaw, madam, don't make us point out that the device of literary reminiscence was used even by Turgenev. Having once opened someone's mouth in amazement, we didn't forget to shut it, after all, and as for how many reminiscences we let out through that mouth, that's between us and the reader.

In this part, the role of the open mouth will be played by the expanse of the Atlantic Ocean on a night in December 1990, and we swear that this expanse will not be left unsupervised until its timely intersection with a chapter toward the end.

And so, we're onboard Stanley Korbach's private jet, which has taken off from New York's La Guardia Airport heading for the old countries. Visibility is unlimited, and all the heavenly bodies are shining upward as well as downward, with their reflections in the distant waters. The airplane is one of the Galaxy family, of Israeli manufacture, though this particular example was made to order for the Korbach Foundation and is distinguished from the mass-production model by its more impressive dimensions, its more powerful engines, and its capability of flying twice as far without refueling. "Not a bad dolphin," says Captain Ernie Rotterdam, patting the airplane's belly before each flight. In his opinion, this machine stuffed with the most advanced technology has already approached the intellectual level of the thinking animals that walked the earth.

The engines were already humming quietly, that is, doing their own sort of thinking, while the four men in the cockpit were engrossed in their own thoughts. Captain Rotterdam, a forty-five-year-old veteran of the U.S. Air Force, looking at the spherical instrument panel, was thinking about women, naturally. He'd had one or two sweet pieces of ass near the base. Since he had started working for the fund, his circle of girlfriends had widened immeasurably, inasmuch as he flew all over the world now and made stopovers in Rome, or Djakarta, or Jo-burg, sometimes for a few days, or even for a week. He hadn't been to Moscow yet, but he'd heard good things about it.

Meanwhile, his navigator, Paul Massalsky, sitting behind the captain and pretending to study the course, was reading the latest novel by one of today's passengers, Lester Square. The book was called *The Pianist's Fingers* and told a story that would make the reader's blood change course in his veins. A jazz pianist and British agent in West Berlin had been kidnapped by some Gee-Bees led by a man with the strange name of Zavkhozov. In order to squeeze the secret code out of the pianist, they started to chop off his fingers, phalanx by phalanx. The sweetheart of the pianist, an MI-5 major in whom it was not difficult to recognize the author, took the matter of revenge into her gentle but resilient hands. What a talent, after all! Massalsky thought. To write a book on sale in any airport in the world that gives even navigators the shudders!

The seat next to the pilot's had been specially built for the boss. It gave enough comfort to his substantially oversized body. On a small table in front of him, Stanley had his reading glasses, a small notebook, a laptop computer, the *Decameron,* and, of course, a glass of whiskey. If he hadn't been flying in his own jet on his own course, one might have taken him for an eccentric pensioner whiling away a sleepless night in his modest condominium. At the moment he was busy looking up needed telephone numbers in his address book, entering them into his computer, interfacing the computer with the chief thinking instrument of the airplane, and adjusting earphones and a microphone on the corresponding parts of his head.

Just behind him in a semirecumbent posture was his fourth cousin. Alex Korbach was heading for his motherland after an eight-and-a-half-year absence. Sitting in the skies, he was trying not to think about the rapidly approaching meeting with Moscow. Sad to say, he couldn't not think about it. Okay, he said to himself, getting irritated, I'll think about it. Alas, not a single worthwhile idea came into his mind. He felt nothing but a tiresome, all-consuming unease. What am I going to say there? What will I see? Who will be there for me to love? What am I racing there with such strange, jet-engine speed for? The unease crossed over into his deep sleep. Through the humming of the engines the invigorated voice of Stanley reached him. The energy that elephant has—you could really envy him!

"Hi there, Juan!" Stanley said to someone via his system. "Glad to hear your voice, buddy! I hope I didn't wake Your Majesty? . . . In full uniform? . . . You were inspecting the guard? Sorry I wasn't there with you. I love to watch you inspect the guard. . . . Oh no, no, I was calling to chat. I'm on my way to Europe and I might be able to fly by in a week. . . . Straight to Ibiza? Okay! Will Slava be there? . . . Great! You and Slava are really suited to each other, somehow. . . . I am too? Well, we'll play a trio!" The longer the chatter went on, the clearer it became to Alex that the person on the other end of Stanley's conversation was the king of Spain. After that conversation he called some Charlie and asked him, by the by,

"How's that old bore of yours?" which made one suppose that he had great concern for royal families.

Then, after a bit of fiddling with the computer, he said, unexpectedly, in Russian: "*Privet,* Mikhail!" and then in English: "It's Stanley, remember me? Yes, Stanley Davidovich, at your service! *Shto? Shto? Nye ponimati. Tozh ne ponimati?* Do you have an interpreter at hand? *Ne ponimati?* Oh, shit!" Alexander raised his seat to its upright position. "Stanley, I can help you with this guy." Stanley guffawed. "Why didn't I think of it before? Take this extra headset and help me talk to him. He hasn't got an interpreter there right now."

"*Zdravstvuite,*" Alexander said into the microphone. "Stanley Korbach sends greetings."

"Good to hear from you, Stanley," said Mikhail. "Where are you calling from?"

"From an airplane," Alexander explained. "We're flying across the Atlantic."

"What, have you got a Russian there with you?" Mikhail asked.

Alexander translated Stanley's answer: "No, only Americans, but fortunately, one knows Russian."

"Hmm . . . ," said Mikhail, and from this *hmm* Alexander gathered that Stanley's relationship with this Mikhail wasn't as warm as the ones he had with Charlie and Juan. "How can I help you, Stanley?" It was always possible that this Mikhail was afraid of bugging.

Stanley began to explain. "Listen, Mikhail, we're heading for Moscow. Our fund has been invited to one of 'Memorial's' meetings. For reasons that I can't understand, the visas weren't ready in time. I decided to fly anyway. I hope we won't run into any obstacles in Moscow, all the more since we're bringing a project of enormous importance for the Soviet Union. Perhaps you remember our conversation in Rome two years ago?"

"Why didn't you let me know earlier that you were coming, my dear Stanley?" Mikhail sighed. "Such important, fundamental things ought to be announced ahead of time. They expand our horizons, after all. They demand serious preparation. We'll give you a first-class reception, of course—why, even in the time of the czars, Russia was known for its hospitality. How many people are in your group?"

"There are ten of us," said Stanley, and then added jokingly: "All Jews." Mikhail paused imposingly, indicating that the joke was not apropos. "Everyone is a Jew, after all, at least partly," Stanley said with a grin.

"In America, maybe, but in our country, not everyone," said Mikhail. It wasn't clear whether he was joking now in Stanley's tone or whether he was deadly serious.

"I've always liked your sense of humor, Mikhail," Stanley said anyway. "You know, there's one hitch in the list of our group. I've got Alex Korbach, my friend and relative, here with me. He was stripped of his Soviet citizenship eight years ago. Brezhnev had no sense of humor, Mikhail. I hope that it won't be difficult to resolve this thing in the perestroika era, am I right?"

"I don't quite understand." Mikhail sighed. "How can it be that your relative was deprived of Soviet citizenship?"

"He'll explain it to you right now," said Stanley. "Who?" Mikhail almost shouted. As often happens with such people, he'd forgotten that he was speaking through an interpreter.

"You're talking about me," A.Z. immediately put in. "About your interpreter . . . er, Mr. Mikhail. I'm Sasha Korbach, perhaps you've heard of me? From the theater."

"Sasha Korbach?" Mikhail exclaimed. "What on earth are you doing there?"

"Where's 'there'?" It was A.Z.'s turn to be astonished, absurdly, somehow. The meaning of the word *there* was unclear to him for some reason.

"Well, you know, over there, not with us, abroad," Mikhail intoned with growing indignation.

A.Z. was already bridling. "At the moment I'm translating a conversation that my relative Stanley Korbach is having with a man named Mikhail."

"With Mikhail Sergeyevich Gorbachev."

"I'd already figured that out. Very pleased to meet you."

"Well, I'm not that pleased."

"How's that, then?"

"We lived by your songs, after all, Sasha, and dreamed about change for the better. And now you're over there with the American tycoons. People like you ought to be working for our perestroika, ought to be the flagships of the process, and you're playing the interpreter."

"May one ask how I can be a flagship when my citizenship was taken away?"

"That's no excuse."

"Well, I don't need any excuse."

Brief pause. Something is rustling. Papers, maybe? Or do thoughts rustle? Gorbachev's or mine? Most likely it was something in space that doesn't normally rustle rustling.

"No need to hold yourself in opposition to the motherland," Gorbachev said, using that nauseating Soviet expression. "Obviously we were mistaken when we took you for one of ours." He seemed to realize that he'd said the wrong thing. "Somehow we associated you with newness, Sasha Korbach. With the romantic spirit, with values shared by people everywhere."

"You have me confused with someone else, Mikhail Sergeyevich," A.Z. responded coldly, bringing the conversation to a close. It was good that at least he hadn't told the creator of the collapse to shove it up his ass. Maybe he'd been making a recording, talking to some Gee-Bee tape? All at once, everything that he had delighted in to the point of tears over the last two years, the sight of hundreds of thousands of Russians marching across the world's television screens under banners calling for democracy, had turned into a slimy fake, into a cheap attempt to inveigle "flagships."

"All right, then, tell your boss that people from my office will meet him at Sheremetyevo."

It was only now that Alexander noticed that Stanley, having turned his chair 180 degrees, was observing the expression on his face. The weighty hand of his fourth cousin settled on his shoulder until he had finished the conversation with this wary guy Mikhail. "See you soon, Stanley!" "See you, Mikhail!"

Alexander freed himself from Stanley's hand and went into the cabin. The only light was from a row of small lamps along the aisle. Everyone was already asleep, lulled by the mighty Rolls-Royce engines: Leibnitz, Square, Agasf, Duckworth, Piu, and also the "stewardess" Bernadetta De Luxe, who, as the reader can see, had managed in the course of the last chronological break to add a *particule de noblesse* to her surname, which was already sumptuous enough as it was, and to drop thirty pounds from her generous form. Everyone knows that weight loss is a substantial plus in our age; in any case, it had helped her to become one of the best-known hookers in New York. Alex went to the bar, poured himself a whiskey, and sat down by the window. The confounded rotgut had the taste of a life sold off for no reason at all. How many times have I told myself not to drink this stuff with the fat-assed optimist striding forth on the label? Gorby is filing some sort of claim on me. It turns out that I still owe something to this bitch of a motherland. It would never cross the mind of this bitch or those of any of her children that they'd ruined someone's life. I wanted to puke all over you scum! I don't belong to any Russia anymore, just as, sad to say, I can't belong to the States, either, no matter how United they are. What a shame that I don't belong to the ocean that lies in the middle, that I belong only to the moment, which has no past, no future—it's just black nothingness. He drained his glass and corrected himself with a smile: there are stars, at least, and the reflection of the stars; this sleeping band flying east, anyway; and that little red light on the wing of the Galaxy.

We'll leave him dozing over the ocean in order to make use of the novelist's license and enter into the domain of reminiscence to recount what happened with our characters from the moment Stanley Korbach appeared on Alexander Korbach's snow-covered front stoop.

2

HOW STANLEY KORBACH SOLVED ALL OF ALEXANDER'S INSOLUBLE PROBLEMS WITHOUT EVEN SLOWING DOWN

*H*is Majesty Stanley usually solved his own problems approximately in the manner of his favorite literary character, Gargantua, who combed cannonballs out of his hair, absolutely certain that they were only lice he had picked up on the dirty streets of Paris. Alexander's problems didn't even seem like lice to Stanley. They were just dandruff that one could brush away with a single hand movement. The bloodcurdling story of the demonic KGB blackmailer simply made the giant laugh. Moreover, he was delighted by some of the details of Alex and Mirelle's copulation—in particular by Alex's confession that a strange feeling had shot through him when the female adventurist had mounted him wearing a fur coat. "I held on to her mink ass, and it seemed like the skin she was born with," the sinner muttered. "At that moment I had nothing against the notion that all women should turn into fur-bearing animals." Stanley, who, following his operation, had been constantly worried about his virility, decided to immediately begin a series of experiments with different types of furs. Congratulations, Brünhilde, thought Alex.

As for the blackmail itself, Stanley simply rang up one of his most valued aides, that very same Square-Rooted Lester in fact. The latter promised to find out everything he could about the matter right away. It ought to be said that Lester's familiarity with secret operations throughout the world had increased two-, three-, perhaps even tenfold since he had decided to leave the intelligence service and plunge headfirst into the writing of exciting political thrillers. Before the day was over he called back to say that Alex wouldn't have to worry anymore. How was that? Nothing could have been simpler, my enlightened friends. He simply found a certain Sergei, aka Pathos, one of the influential KGB "residents" in North America, and let him know that AK & BB, Inc., did not wish to see this operation continued. The respect that agents corrupted by perestroika feel for the multimillionaires of American corporations significantly surpasses that which they feel for their own organization. Particularly when this respect is reinforced by a check for twenty thousand dollars deposited in the personal account of Pathos. One way or another, we've already received confirmation that the Department N operation against Sasha Korbach under the curious code name of Mink Coat has been terminated. Sasha's boys are already "out of hot water," if one can use that idiom in light of the general situation in Haiti.

So, what else have we got on the agenda? The catastrophe with the film project, which sank our sensitive artist into the depths of depression? Stanley had long ago learned from Alex a Russian expression endowed with a multitude of nuances: *mudilo greshnoye,* the closest literal approximation of which is "sinful jerk." It was with this very term that he now addressed his cousin: "You, Alex, *mudilo greshnoye,* have fallen victim to your '*mudilo greshnoye*-esque' feelings about the American business process. If you'd thrown away your Russian megalomania and all that standing on ceremony, you'd have become a well-known figure in the movie business a long time ago. Fortune, you *mudilo greshnoye,* gave you connections of the sort that would make anybody in this country happy, and you rudely turned your nose up at them. Just sit there now with your vodka tonic and listen."

To Alex's utter amazement, Stanley asked the faithful Rose Morrows to put him through to that very same Putney Productions that Stefan Chapski had been trying to bring in on their project. "I'd like to talk to whoever's there, with Iceman, or with Magaziner, or with Ted Lasagna—better yet, with Putney himself or Walt Ridgeway." A few minutes later Ridgeway was on the line. It was only then that Alex realized it was the very same guy who had torpedoed his *Starry Ticket of the Eighties*. "Hey, Walt, old buddy, how's it hanging out there? Listen, I've got this great Russian director with me, my namesake and distant relative Alex Korbach—you've heard the name, of course. You haven't? How can that be? They're talking about him from coast to coast these days." Stanley covered the mouthpiece with his hand and started to relay to Alex what the Russophobe had said. "He says he'd be very happy, says he's always had a lot of respect for the Russian potential, says he's all ears." Taking his hand off the mouthpiece, he went on with Ridgeway. "This guy is preparing a huge film about the life of Dante Alighieri. No, it's not about ancient Rome, it's about the Middle Ages, or the early Renaissance, really. . . . Well, now it's clearer, that's exactly it. Just picture it, Walt—it'll be so beautiful on the screen: Florence, castles, poets in knights' armor, the uncorrupted Beatrice. . . .

"Well of course I'm going to invest in the project. I'm going to invest pro-fusely. . . . No, no, Walt, we're talking eight figures here. A megabudget, a huge packet, everything's got to be highest level!"

At times, Alexander began to flagellate himself when he thought of the "Russo-American hillocks" of his life: you wallow at the bottom of a garbage pit, right down in the slime, then you soar up to the peak, where you have to catch your breath at the view—really, isn't it just a frightening, irritating, provocative, amoral, insolent, and intoxicating metaphor for existence?

The Gargantuan carnival began to spin around and around at a dizzying pace. Alexander Zakharovich didn't even have time to get through all the messages left on his answering machine in a day. The Putney people were clamoring for a syn-opsis from him. Send us a photocopied draft, Alex, as soon as possible. We need a piece of paper so that we can start working up your contract. It's imperative that we get in touch with your agent, too. Who's your agent, sir? Borchardt, Goldberg, Cynthia Cannell, maybe even Andrew Wiley himself? Shit, he's never had an agent. He's been agentless in a world rich in agents. Stanley grinned. You ought to give them Enoch Agasf's name. The Eternal Jew is potentially the best movie agent in the world. He knows every existing language, and some that don't exist. I'm not sure that he's seen a single film in his life, but what's important is that he knows how to say yes or no without beating around the bush.

At this point we would like to say in advance that the history of the represen-tation of artists has never known a better agent than Enoch Agasf. With enviable efficiency, he penetrated right to the heart of Hollywood intrigue and even became the supreme authority in such complicated matters as "risk allocation," "project packaging," "collateral revenue," et cetera. In the course of making the film *Radi-ance*, Alex thanked heaven more than once for having sent down such an agent. Agasf, it must be said, was always very happy when he realized that his new oc-cupation in the silly, bustling, and diverting movie business could help him to while away the coming centuries.

3

THE EASTERN CORRIDOR

*O*ne day, Stanley said: "Alex, I know that you've got huge pangs of conscience eating away at you, that your latest good fortune is making you crazy. Your screwy mind tells you that the presence of Gargantua the Benefactor casts doubts on your own potential for artistic creation. Cool it, pal! This time your fourth cousin's pursuing a very pragmatic aim in pulling you out of the shit you're in. The fact is that, unlike for the previous three meaningless 'disappearances,' I've found a meaning to the fourth, the one that's under way. It's in my giving my money away to others.

"It's all very simple: in this world, where there are a large number of vicious circles spinning and pushing each other on, one circle is suddenly opening and stretching out into a straight line. Even in this simplicity, though, just like in the whole fucking dialectic, there's a trap hiding. Even a repentant fat cat is still a fat cat. I'm deeply troubled by the idea that the desire to give everything away to others is just the flip side of the desire to grab everything for oneself. Generosity brings you blessings, which means that in being generous you become self-satisfied. I need an antithesis to myself beside me, a close friend who'll never be shy about saying *mudilo greshnoye* to my face. That's you. You'll be my right hand, in the sense that I'll be your left, if you'll estimate my modesty. It's only with you that I'll know my money is going to those whom I hypothetically call others, or the rest, if you think about it in English. Now I'm sure you can understand the reason for my meddling in your artistic career."

"No, I don't understand," said Alex.

"Okay, the left hand is interested in the welfare of the right. And vice versa, isn't that so?"

Alexander laughed. "It's simple, but there's more to it than meets the eye!"

Stanley nodded. "I know that you can't live without being able to do something creative, whether it's a song, a show, or some huge movie project, particularly if it's got something to do with the *dolce stil nuovo*. So then, full speed ahead, work any way you like, and I'll guarantee you a green light in every direction—except your own blind alleys, my friend; there, I'm powerless."

This conversation was taking place in the half-empty carriage of a Metroliner on its way from Washington to New York. Low, leaden skies were hanging over the whole Northeast Corridor. From time to time a few snow flurries would fall. The train crossed over half-frozen bays with their yacht moorings abandoned until spring, which gave the landscape a specifically mid-Atlantic, strangely cozy melancholy. The feeling was only heightened by the flickering sight of tiny towns with their grocery stores and invariable neon "Bud" signs. Reading the little word with the Russian pronunciation—*bood*—it is not likely that our melancholy Russian would have been able to avoid the temptation of forming the word *buduschee*—"future."

"Speaking of my 'blind alleys,' Stanley, you've obviously got my breakup with Nora in mind?"

"Not necessarily. Everyone has blind alleys. I'm just judging by myself. Believe me, I've been known to drive love into an impassable spider's web."

"You've hit it on the nose. All I think about is your daughter, and I beat myself up for what happened."

"I'm sure that she's more at fault," Stanley said dryly. "I know my daughter. She can hit a man right in his pride with terrible force and not even realize it herself."

"I don't agree. Nora's the most sensitive person I've ever met. She understands all of our screwy subtleties. So all the blame rests on thick-skinned me."

The short winter day was fading. The inclement weather outside the rushing windows was quickly turning to darkness.

"Have you ever had occasion to see Robert?" Stanley asked cautiously.

"What Robert?"

"Bobby Korbach, her son."

"Hey, you know I forgot that he has—er—the same last name."

Stanley thought: He meant to say "our last name" but lost his nerve. "Well of course he's got our name, what else?"

"She and I never talked about Bobby," Alex muttered. "For that matter, we never talked about my kids either, to tell the truth." He looked at Stanley and suddenly confessed the thing that he was perhaps more ashamed of than anything else. "I was crazy with jealousy, Stanley. I was jealous of everything connected with her, and most of all, the way it seems to me now, of America. That is, of her life without me. In America." "It's a shame you were never completely open with each other," Stanley said. He looked Alex directly in the eye, as though asking him if he ought to reveal something else of great importance. Alex didn't want him to. Suddenly he put on another record, as it were, and asked with a smile: "What are we going to New York for, anyway?" Stanley sighed with evident relief. He hated divulging secrets, all the more when they concerned his own family. "First of all, we're going to dinner. I've reserved a table at the most exotic restaurant in America. Just imagine, instead of reducing calories, they take pride in piling them on."

4

YOUR GRANDMOTHERS' DINNER

*T*he thing that always strikes you about Manhattan is how built up everything is. After all, until quite recently it was still just a badly cleared forest. A fox or two a day would dart past in broad daylight in Times Square, and nothing else was going on, apart from the swarming of insects. In a trifling space of time the island became overgrown with stone, iron, and glass, heaping up loads of absolutely everything, not to mention a polyphony of food.

The word *food* contains within itself so much that is not directly connected to the concept. The simplest nibbling, the tearing off of a piece from the whole, the grinding up of what has been torn off with the hard protuberances especially arranged in the mouth for that purpose, this whole range of the most basic of actions has been transformed into a manifestation of culture, into a celebration not only of the flesh but of the spirit as well. Many patriotic principles are bound up with ethnic cooking. Take, for example, the dumpling wars. Russian and Chinese armies, you see, have fought each other in fierce engagements for dumpling priority. And in spite of these battles and ingenious peace conferences, ask any Russian—even the academician Likhachov, even Neizvestny the sculptor, or, for that matter, the author of these lines—what the primary, age-old Russian dish is, and any Russian will immediately answer: the dumpling!

Quickly, before we get caught, let's skip over to the Russian question. For some time, the magnate Stanley Korbach had been noticing certain strange pro-Russian moods in himself. There exists, he would say to his entourage, the stereotype of the Russian as a pathological anti-Semite. That's a mistaken view, guys. There is, of course, the word *pogrom,* and, yes, it is of Russian origin, but on the other hand, why don't we ask ourselves how it happened that over the centuries Jews were booted out by the Spanish, the French, the British, and the Germans, and all the time kept heading east, for Russia?

Of course we always got ourselves worked up about the ignoble Pale of Settlement, but why did the Jews, from the time of Catherine the Great, settle there in the hundreds of thousands? Doesn't it mean that they received some, paltry as it might have been, protection from the Russian administration, created, possibly, by a subconscious desire to see these strange outsiders next door? Look at what happened at a rapid pace in the development of Russian Jewry. Yesterday's pathetic money changers and pawnbrokers, cobblers, innkeepers, and shtetl dwellers who huddled around crumbling synagogues and dark *kheders* managed to achieve great success on Russian soil. New generations of Jewish engineers, doctors, pharmacists, merchants, and bankers made the notorious Pale almost invisible to themselves. And that's not to mention artistic endeavors, ladies and gentlemen! Jews made no small contribution to the great Russian artistic revolution. It's enough to mention Mark Antokolski, the sculptor, a distant relative of our Korbachs, as well as Levitan the painter, Nadson the poet, Rubinstein the musician—and they were all in the nineteenth century. In the twentieth, there were even more great names: Mandelstam, Pasternak, Lifschitz, Chagall, Lissitzky, Meyerhold, our Alex's grandfather Ruvim Korbach—there were lots of them in the avant-garde.

By 1914 it was clear that the Pale of Settlement had aged beyond salvaging. Of course there were the "Black Hundreds" and Purishkevich; Russian society, though, turned out to be mature enough to reject the Beilis Affair as pure provocation. What I'm saying might sound paradoxical, but it seems to me that the first decades of our century saw the beginnings of a strange sort of mutual understanding between Russians and Jews. Yes, but what about the brutal Jewish commissars during the Civil War? people ask. First of all, the cruelties of that war were motivated not by ethnic but by purely political considerations; second, who knows— maybe the presence of Jews in the ranks of the victors made the proletarians' treatment of the annihilated classes ever so much gentler.

If you want an example, you've got it, to put it in a shtetl way. In 1921 the Bolshevik government was greatly irritated by the activities of the Free Philosophical Academy, or the Volfila. Lenin, as an honest-to-goodness Russian revolutionary, proposed the quickest and most effective action: a nighttime roundup and execution of all the bourgeois pseudophilosophers, but Trotsky, a Jew who worried about international opinion, held out for exile. As an experienced demagogue he would say: There's no need to make martyrs of these chatterboxes; no need, comrades, to give our enemies a propaganda weapon. As a result, 1,220 brilliant Russian intellectuals were forcibly loaded onto a steamship sailing for Germany. Jewish common sense helped to preserve an entire Russian philosophical school for Russia.

Now allow me to leap a quarter of a century forward, to the end of World War II. Whatever the motivation, it was the Russians who liberated the remnant of the Jewish contingents doomed to the gas chambers. We mustn't ever forget those officers and soldiers who opened the gates of Auschwitz and Maidanek. And we mustn't ever forget those hundreds of thousands of Jews who fought in the Soviet Army as equals. No one knows how the Russians would have behaved toward the Jews if Stalin had managed to set his plan for genocide in motion, but, thank God, it didn't happen.

There are people, even entire peoples, who are absolutely without any feeling of gratitude. We Jews, I hope, are not among their number. We ought to think about Russia, my children, particularly now, when her screwed-up utopia is collapsing. "What the hell are you talking about, Stanley—'your children'?" Bernadetta De Luxe asked at that moment. "Come on, don't make yourself into some kind of patriarch, baby." As if in confirmation of the relativity of all scales, Cookie, whom everyone knows by now, popped his tiny head out of Bernadetta's bodice and gave a little yelp.

All those present burst into laughter—though not everyone expected had turned up yet—that could have brought down the walls of the Fimmy House restaurant, at the corner of Seward Avenue and Orchard Street on the Lower East Side of Manhattan. It was here that Stanley and Alexander had come directly from the station. The restaurant's theme was East European nostalgia. "Welcome to the dinner of your grandfathers and grandmothers!" the menu said in English, Yiddish, and Hebrew. At the center of each table was a decanter containing an amber-colored liquid. God forbid that you should take it for anything refreshing! In the decanters, ladies and gentlemen, is nothing other than pure chicken fat, without which the dinners of your grandfathers and grandmothers would have been unimaginable. Well, how could we do without it—judge for yourselves! Take, for example, chopped liver. They bring you a tin basin containing the item that was ordered, and then the amber-colored carafe goes into action. No less than half its contents go into the basin, and there mix with the chopped liver. The delicacy is ready. With a ladle worthy of the kitchen of an artillery brigade, the liver in the chicken fat flops into the customers' tins. And can you imagine *mamalyga* not mixed with chicken fat? We'll answer in the style of this whole dinner: Not a chance!

And what sorts of mashed potatoes, someone will pipe up at this point, for example, are even imaginable without chicken fat? You say that "mashed potatoes" is unthinkable in the feminine grammatical gender? No, it's unthinkable without chicken fat! And that's not's even mentioning *knyeli,* blintzes, and so on and so forth.

This sort of lipid centerpiece stands in the midst of salad-fruit-fiber America as a reminder of the days when gaining weight was considered a sign of good health. Well, what can you say—Fimmy's Beefsteaks isn't just a place of gluttony, it's part of a cultural heritage, and the aforementioned delicacies are just the overture. The opera itself starts with the serving of the steaks. Steaks at Fimmy's come in three sizes: small, medium, and large. The Small Steak is a sprawling piece of meat nine inches long and two inches thick. Taking it by one end, any of Stanley Korbach's gang could give any one of Norman Blamsdale's underlings a good lashing across the face with altogether stunning effect. Better for birds to stay out of the trajectory altogether—they'll fall dead! But then again, all things considered, good people, better just to eat these things piece by piece, seasoning them with mustard and topping them off with chicken fat, their passion for which has earned Jewish folk the particular hatred of indigenous populations.

In contrast to the Small Steak, the Medium surprises one by its rotundity. It covers an entire large platter by itself and shoots the hefty bone off to one side, thereby reminding one of an oversized Ping-Pong paddle. And finally before us we have the crowning achievement of the Lower East Side, Fimmy's Large Steak, which puts us in mind of the courts at Wimbledon! You can't find a plate large enough for it in Manhattan, so it's served on a board. A viscous juice streams from the board onto the tablecloth, putting in doubt the strictness of observance of the kosher laws here. Full-blooded Jewish youngsters, who a century ago were New York draymen and who now have become lawyers and movie directors, create a Rabelaisian feast, cooling themselves with ice cubes from which protrude the necks of vodka bottles, "cooling" themselves into a fury.

They were used to this sort of thing here, it must be said. Any successful meal concludes with an unknown quantity of fractured skulls, smashed jaws, punctured stomachs, torn-off ears, and crushed scrotums and egos, particularly when, toward midnight, the establishment is besieged by the dregs of King Picrochole.

For the time being, they were dancing and singing. The crowd was dying to put on its own show. A rock band of Hasids that had just flown in from Israel was pounding out any rhythm to order, only the payess flying around. One folk singer requested "Hava Nagila," another asked for "Rachel, You Are Like a Tear in My Eye," while a third came jumping out enthusiastically with the Russian White Guard tune "Cornet Obolensky." Again and again the establishment was shaken by a mass of dancers, among whom was an old man who had eaten too much and, with his large thumbs jammed underneath his armpits like Lenin at the triumph of his electrification plan, was invariably seen cavorting. Also present was an attractive little lady who had taken her clothes off with the deftness of a sea lioness.

That evening the place was particularly noisy, so Stanley asked that the edible treasures be brought to his party in a private room. Following on the heels of this latest parade of our characters, we have to confess that we haven't got a very clear picture of how this meal, fraught with something, is going to end up. Oftentimes in the construction of a novel, plans drafted ahead of time are completely discarded. Coming under the influence of his heroes, the author refuses to write according to the plan; what the hell—it's just not interesting. Taking our eyes off professional activities and contractual obligations, we have to admit it: if it weren't interesting for us to write novels, we wouldn't write them.

In the private room, Stanley turned to all those present. "I hope, gang, that you appreciate the fact that I brought you here and nowhere else. Fimmy's, you see, is part of our common heritage." "What, you don't mean to say that everyone here is a Jew, do you?" exclaimed a greatly surprised Alex Korbach. "That's exactly what I meant to say, my dear Lavsky!" Stanley laughed. "Everyone here can boast of a few drops of what they call Jewish blood." Alexander looked over the group gathered around the several round tables. In the subdued light they looked like a group portrait done by a Flemish hand. Zion thrives, particularly in the person of General Piu, that little crocodile from the Mekong Delta.

"Yes, yes, Lavsky." The General giggled. "My mama's mama's mama was a Jewish governess in the family of Huong Ksian Nguem."

Alex's eyes turned involuntarily in the direction of Benjamin Duckworth, a fine black specimen: all clear here, at least, it seemed. His lips formed a reserved smile. "My mom's maiden name was Vysocky. Grace Vysocky—Stanley Korbach won't let me tell a lie." "Sounds more Japanese than Jewish," Alex objected. The ex-Airborne soldier took a napkin and wrote out on it his mother's maiden name—*Vysocky.* "Vysotsky?" Alexander shouted. "My respect, sir," the department store security specialist said with a click of his heels.

"As for me, I'm one hundred percent Jewish," Bernadetta De Luxe announced, for some reason shaking her shoulders like a Gypsy. Before getting to know Stanley, Bernie had never been "real stuck" on her Jewishness, if she'd remembered it at all. Now, with a clarity that surprised herself, she remembered scenes from her childhood: Papa the Talmud scholar and Mama the wailer; on Saturdays the whole family sitting around wearing ritual *taleses* and muttering prayers, not daring to get up and turn on the light lest they anger the All Highest. Right on cue, her beloved Cookie yelped from his cleft. Cookie, little ghetto boy, go walkies around the table, everybody here loves you. Cookie recoiled in horror from the ethnic restaurant's pieces of meat the size of shovels but happily licked the melting ice from the dripping vodka bottles.

After this announcement from Bernie, whom, before this, most of the members of her circle had generally assumed to have come more from the Hellenes than the Judaists, excitement reigned among the company. Everyone was trying to assert his or her Jewishness, though, alas, truth be told, the most compelling argument belonged only to Bruno Kastorzius from Orthodox Budapest. The others had somehow managed to keep their foreskin intact. Stanley happily listened to the general hubbub and blissfully surveyed this group of people he was already calling his "gang." With this gang, he was thinking, I might be able to fulfill the idea of the Fourth Disappearance, that is, giving my money to others. He was probably the only one who had ever managed to finish a Fimmy's Large Steak. Trying not to lose the thread of the conversation, with a huge knife that would have been useful for "negotiations" in the castles of Ashqelon and Caesarea, he cut off pieces, larded them with kosher mustard, and washed them down with gigantic gulps of the kosher beer Maccabee, named in honor of the mighty brothers who, twenty-two hundred years earlier, had risen up against Greek decadence for the glory of the One God.

It had been a long time since he had gotten so much pleasure out of food, drink, observing faces, and conversation. Having finished with the matter before him, he raised a hand and asked for everyone's attention. "Pay attention!" Rose Morrows, who knew her business, cried sharply, and attention was paid.

What was the nationality of Abraham, the Father of us all? We know that he was the son of Terah, of the generation of Shem, that he lived in the region between the Tigris and the Euphrates, in the city of Ur, which means that he was a Chaldean, or a Sumerian, or an Assyrian, which amounts to approximately the same thing. The Jews simply didn't exist at the time, and no one considered Hebrew shepherds in the deserts a people. Two millennia before God appeared to Abraham and commanded him to begin a new race in the Fertile Crescent, there existed developed civilizations, the Sumerian in the east and the Egyptian in the west. There were trades there, arts, and even codes of laws. Everyone, of course, remembers the Pillar of Hammurabi, on display in the Louvre.

The leader paused and passed a significant glance over those present. Perhaps the question of precisely who would make up the "gang" was being decided. Each of them, by either mannerisms or expressions, confirmed his or her acquaintance with Hammurabi. Bernadetta, for example, raised her right shoulder and her left eyebrow: How, she seemed to say, can one not know an outstanding pillar of humanity? Piu gestured with his cigarette as if to hint at something highly significant: the question reminded him of the courses at the general staff college under the Ngo Dinh Diem regime. Bruno Kastorzius, with both hands over his head, was depicting an ascension to the heights of jurisprudence. Alex knocked back a shot glass of vodka and held up three fingers: I learned about the Babylonian code in the third grade, he was saying, and that speaks for itself. All in all, in one way or another everyone present displayed his familiarity with the article under discussion; only Matt Shuroff remained as motionless as a stone. "Maybe someone can enlighten our friend?" Stanley asked. " 'Course I know," said Matt, finally unclenching his teeth. "I spent the night at a police station in Paris 'cause of Hammurabi's pillar." Everyone, naturally, was intrigued beyond words: details, details!

It turned out that ten years earlier the company Matt had been working for at the time, Great Pacific Communications, to be precise, had rewarded its most productive employees with a trip to Paris. There, on the first day—no, I tell a lie, on the second, a Wednesday, to be exact—Matt saw the Pillar of Hammurabi in the Louvre, and he had an irresistible urge to give it a hug. He was even ready to die with the Pillar of Hammurabi in his arms. Maybe not everyone understands, particularly the frivolous representatives of the female gender, but Matt was in tears from this overwhelming desire. You'll just go ahead and die, guys, without ever having hugged the Pillar of Hammurabi, he explained to his fellow outstanding employees and raced along the squeaky floors of the Louvre toward the exhibit. The tears in his eyes prevented him from seeing the bulletproof glass surrounding the rare object. He hit it forehead first and in his enthusiasm squeezed the sides of the glass box so hard that it shattered. He didn't remember the rest very clearly. The guard in charge of the floor paralyzed him with a stun gun. Then, at the station house, the cops taught him to appreciate their homeland with their nightsticks. Considering this item in his biography, it was somehow strange for him to answer a question about the Pillar of Hammurabi.

Brother of mine, Stanley Korbach thought lovingly as he looked at the powerfully built trucker, who was a chip off the same block. You and I are similar, we like the same things, jealousy has no place. The same sort of passion for the P. of H. has come over me any number of times in the Louvre. I don't know what it is that held me back from taking such a wonderful step.

He went on. You will begin a new race, the Lord said to Abraham, and the Covenant was established. Why of all the inhabitants of that delta had old Abraham been chosen? Obviously because he had a deeper understanding of the futility of paganism and of the indivisibility of the One God than anyone else. He was one of a multitude of Chaldeans, and he became the first Jew. That means that our people came into existence not as the result of an ages-long ethnic process but as the result of a mystic revelation. An unorthodox thought begs to be voiced here: Maybe even now the concept of Judaism is more a matter of spirituality than of ethnicity? Abraham was an apostate who left his home and his people in order to find a new home and begin a new people? Maybe in four thousand years the process has yet to be completed? Why is it that we're always leaving for somewhere: for Palestine, then Egypt, then Babylon, then Rome, Africa, Spain, Europe, Russia, America, and then Palestine again? Maybe the unfailing performance of the ancient rituals isn't as important as the preservation of the spirit of this journey, of cosmopolitan Judaism as such?

Why does anti-Semitism always come from the musty racial depths of different peoples? Why is the basic idea of anti-Semitism a worldwide Jewish conspiracy, a blood oath? Anti-Semitism is obviously a subconscious attempt to turn the tables, to ascribe to the Jews their own ideology of the primacy of blood over the spirit, to destroy the mystic Covenant.

The old couple Abraham and Sarah were not ideal producers of offspring. They were lamenting that they would never have children. The Lord brought Abraham out of the tent beneath a starry sky and said to him: "Look now toward heaven, and tell the stars, if thou be able to number them: and He said unto him, So shall thy seed be." That's an example for all of us, the descendants of Abraham, how much stronger than the flesh the spirit is. Abraham and Sarah lived another thousand years or so after that, and from their loins issued entire peoples.

Having said his piece on this not entirely simple topic, Stanley seemed distracted, not to say embarrassed, and even looked at his watch, as though he had slipped back into the role of corporation president. Bernie De Luxe immediately perked up his spirits with a tender look. "You know, honey, age isn't always an obstacle in this sort of thing." The daughter of our Gargantua, the sweet Sylvia, sitting next to her husband, closed her eyes for a moment: she was flabbergasted that this unbelievable woman, with her arms decked out in small tattoos, should address her father in such a familiar tone. And he's smiling back at her! And everyone around, including Art, just sits there looking deeply touched. Stanley drank down a glass of Romanian vodka—brr! "This idea, guys, ought to stick in your minds while you work for the fund. You understand that this is a conspiracy of the 'Crackpots of Zion': the giving away of one's own money to others. We'll work on a worldwide basis, but priority will be given, for obvious reasons, to Eastern Europe and the Soviet Union. All the people of the Earth, whether they be children of Noah, Deuklen, or Gilgamesh, must remember the Great Flood."

"That's what the politics of the United States are based on," noted the former master sergeant of the 101st Airborne. Stanley Korbach looked affectionately at Benjamin Duckworth's face, with its chiseled features. He looks so much like his father! Peering at the guy, he forgot his age, and he felt as though he had gone back to 1946, when he and Roger Duckworth had served together in the U.S. occupation forces in Japan.

5

JAPANESE DIVERTISSEMENT

*I*n point of fact, they served in the same Marine battalion and sailed together for the shores of a vanquished empire on the aircraft carrier *Yorktown* in 1945. A friendship at the front, you'll say, and immediately begin picturing the landing at Iwo Jima; two lads, one black and one white, up to their chests in emerald green water, directing fire on the short yellow guys, and then, as experienced baseball players, tossing grenades into machine-gun nests. Then one of them—the black one or the white one, it's always hard to decide—drags the other, wounded one to safety under fire. A couple of chords from an orchestra complete the deeply affecting scene.

Nothing of the sort had happened in the lives of Stanley and Roger. Their friendship had started on an entirely different footing. A year and a half after victory, Corporal Duckworth and Private Korbach were sent from a base on the coast in the Nara region to see to the installation of some sort of radio antenna. It turned out that the area had been a fashionable holiday resort before the war. A towering old hotel in the British colonial style adorned the slope of the mountain. The two soldiers took a room in it. They didn't see any other guests, but the hotel was in full operation. Silent, smiling servants were standing around everywhere. In the main hall, in a marble niche, sat a white cockatoo. One day, however, aspirating the vowels in the British way, it asked: "How are you getting on, old chaps?" The chaps took their meals in the dining room with its lancet and stained-glass windows, the latter showing a tournament of the Knights of the Round Table. A squad of waiters fanned out in a half circle behind their backs. All you had to do was pull out a cigarette, and right there in front of you was a match made from the finest Japanese wood.

The overall feeling was dreadful. It felt like someone was going to bop you over the head with a bamboo stick at any moment. "Hey, Roger, where are you, you motherfucker?" Stanley shouted. The echo made its way down the enfilade of reception halls with their portraits of the emperors of the Meiji dynasty. Duckworth suddenly popped up from the depths of the swimming pool. The water, which seemed thicker than usual, made polite waves around him, as though asking in the name of the vanquished country: What? What? What do you wish?

"We can't live like this—let's bring in some hookers," Roger proposed one day. He was five years older, and an idea of this sort was supposed to come from him. Stanley looked sadly through the window, outside of which clouds stuffed with wet ice dragged themselves over the pine-covered hills like an invasion squadron. "Speaking of hookers, do you mean she-wolves or she-bears?" Bear in mind, ladies and gentlemen, that there was not even television at the time, much less MTV. Roger approached the manager, who paced the lobby from morning until night, as though he were expecting the arrival of a post stagecoach carrying Victorian-era travelers. Shaping the index finger and thumb of his left hand into a circle, he thrust the index finger of his right into it, forming an eloquent gesture. The manager nodded gravely and with his eyebrows asked: How many? During the war, everyone at the Mountain Palace except for the white cockatoo had forgotten whatever English they once knew. Fingers, though, could play at anything. Six, Roger indicated. Stanley came rushing up with one index finger raised. It wasn't clear what he wanted: one more or only one. Roger almost fell over laughing at the sight of the hulking, redheaded kid still wet behind the ears, in his Marine combat boots, rushing around with a finger in the air. Even the manager, the very picture of inscrutability, was unable to keep from smiling.

The girls arrived at the end of the afternoon, seven *maiko-san*s with beehive hairdos decked out in flowers, combs, little silver bridges, and garlands of bells. "Everything about these chicks is different from ours," Roger instructed him. "The main thing with ours is their tits, but with these girls it's their backs, the triangle between their shoulder blades." He wasn't entirely correct, though: these chicks resembled ours exactly in lots of ways. Stanley rolled on the carpet laughing. The maze of red hair on his chest and his muscular forearms sent the girls into raptures of amazement. The black sovereign Duckworth sat in an armchair, two girls on each knee. Outside, some extraordinary creature was tossing around among the trunks of the trees, now plastering its entire muzzle against the window, now hanging over the crowns of the spruces like a phantom of the rising sun. Even now it's difficult somehow to get to the heart of the Japanese enigma.

On the whole, serving on this mountain was no easy matter. Fortunately, it also included trips in a jeep to the building site, where one could take a break in the open air from the stunts pulled by the jinxed hotel. In the end, the mast was raised, the wires strung up, and the lads went back to their barracks, where several hundred mouths rhythmically consumed hot hamburgers three times a day. What can you say? That sort of combat experience isn't forgotten either, and it was not for nothing that, at their chance meetings in the years that followed, Stanley and Roger would burst out laughing and fall on the floor, or the deck, or the pavement, or whatever surface happened to be under their feet at the time.

Stanley, of course, was immeasurably richer than Roger, but the latter didn't waste time, ending up as a big-time boxing promoter. Unfortunately, his personal life was nothing to write home about, but then, when does it ever work out any other way for men without restraint? One girlfriend followed another; children, some of a pronounced negritude and others almost white, grew up in various cities. Grace Vysocky would weep bitterly. Her husband called her the American tear champion. At times, Stanley would have to console the beautiful woman all night long. In utter confusion, in the sweaty atmosphere of locker rooms, amid fountains of room-temperature champagne, in the presidential suites of an endless round of Sheratons and Hiltons, in meaningless bargaining for big money, Roger Duckworth's time slipped away; and in this way he slipped out of it, too, without even having tried to make sense of any of it. The phantoms of the mountainside hotel had pursued him even more closely than they had his young friend, yet maybe he had once dreamed of becoming just what his Benjamin grew into: strong, sedate, a fervent supporter of the American Constitution, a man at whom Rose Morrows—not the most unattractive girl in Maryland by a long shot—looked more and more dreamily with each passing year.

6

LET'S GET BACK TO THE

"GRANDMOTHERS"

*T*his sad memory has occupied no fewer than three of our pages, while in Stanley's mind it was just a flicker, like a peacock feather that had burst forth, floated by, and disappeared immediately into darkness. He was on the point of continuing his speech, describing how all of those present might apply their strengths, when suddenly the door of the private room opened with a bang. At first the strains of "Two Crooks Skipped the Odessa Clink" reached them from the main room, then the smells of the crowd letting its hair down burst in—sweat, garlic, fat, Elizabeth Taylor perfume—and then finally everyone saw a short man in a black suit of a somewhat old-fashioned cut, a London City bowler, and, in his right hand, a pair of white kidskin gloves that he was nervously smacking against his left hand standing in the doorway. His compressed mouth and large spectacles made one think of dueling pistols. What else could there be in the polished burgundy-colored boxes in the hands of the two powerful companions of the dramatic little man, who was none other than the first vice president of the AK & BB Corporation, Norman Blamsdale. "There you are, finally!" the aforementioned cried out in a voice like a rooster. "I came to tell you that your plans aren't going to come off! You, the unworthy husband of a magnificent woman, know this: the board is planning to have a meeting and divest you, the so-called president, of your power, and your ridiculous creatures along with you!" *"O mamma mia!"* Vice President Art Duppertat cried out at that point. He took up one of the remaining Medium Steaks and began to fan himself with it. Norman thrust his hand forward, and the gloves flew up with it. "Stanley Korbach, you're not worthy to bear the name of our corporation!" Stanley's reply was a booming laugh. "Taking the wife, he takes the name, too!" He was standing in front of Norman now, hands thrust in the pockets of his trousers, which were so wide that they would have served for Pantagruel, had they had the fly so vividly described by the *maître* Rabelais. Norman went on shouting: "We won't let you encroach on one of the greatest enterprises in American business! You're crazy! A megalomaniac! You think you're the Messiah! The place for you is the nuthouse!"

Now Bernadetta rose beside Stanley. "My little bumblebee, so even you get insulted in this world?" "Ah, there she is!" Norman howled. "The very picture of decadent erotica! How much does he pay you for your services? He's not even a man! They cut everything off him!"

"That's funny"—De Luxe snorted—"who is it, then, that makes me cry out like kidnapped Europa?"

"Like who?" asked the astounded Blamsdale.

"Stanley does it to me like Zeus!" wailed the insulted native of Oceania.

"I don't believe it!" Zeus's rival, having lost all self-control, was about to slap His Majesty across the face with a glove, but at the last moment—that is, just in front of the nose—the offending accessory was intercepted by the absolute ruler's daughter. Norman's bodyguards immediately produced pump guns from their two boxes. The terrible weaponry put an end to the possibility of a peaceful outcome for the historic meeting. "Freedom! Dignity!" General Piu shrieked and, displaying the fighting shovel blades of his hands, which were so well-known to Alex, plunged into battle. Behind him, breaking everything around them and swinging the uneaten, spade-size pieces of Fimmy's beef over their heads, the strike force of the new humanitarian fund, Ben Duckworth and Matt Shuroff, went over to the attack.

At the height of the battle, Stanley drew Alex into a corner and showed him an antique daguerreotype in a frame held with screws. The more-than-a-century-old photograph showed the staff of a newly opened kosher temple of meat. In the middle were two young men, identical and somewhat insolent in appearance, wearing long aprons and bow ties. "This is what I dragged you here for," the president said with a grin. Alex wiped away a sort of emotional perspiration from his bald dome with the first napkin that hit him. "Is that really them?" "Nathan and Alexander in person," Stanley exulted.

Meanwhile, the struggle in the room was coming to an end. The bodyguards were carried out of the restaurant onto the wide open lower eastern shore of the island, which was swirling with a primordial blizzard. The body itself suddenly took up a position at the elbow of the target of his invective. "God knows how long it's been since I've seen you, Stanley," he was saying now, in the country-club manner. "It would be great to play a round sometime."

On the street, Blamsdale's escort extended the length of the block: three stretch limos, two racing-speed Porsches, and an urban Jeep with a machine-gun turret on its flat roof. No sooner had our gang rolled out onto the street than the doors of the limousine opened and a brigade of fighting men emerged. Our guys, of course, were not to be outdone. A unit deployed there ahead of time by Duckworth immediately descended from the roof on rappelling ropes.

Those who have seen the film *Die Hard with a Vengeance* or thousands like it will have no need of a description of the scene that followed. We'll just add the personal note that they do a great job in these movies of punching people in the mouth but a lousy job of shooting. That is, they shoot well but hardly ever hit anything. From a creative point of view this is understandable: if they were better shots, hardly any of the characters would survive to the middle of the film. From the point of view of verisimilitude, which filmmakers supposedly hold dear, if a good soldier shoots at the hero, how can he survive? Give him his paycheck and carry on without a hero.

On Seward Avenue, fortunately for our story, they were bad shots as well, though they managed to knock off no small number of innocent bystanders. American citizens killed: 18,493; resident aliens with green cards: 7,548; recipients of political asylum: 4,004; illegal aliens: 28,697; foreign tourists: 678; just passing by: 18. No shortage of broken bones, either: 840 jaws, 18,600 ribs, 618 skulls, 65,111 long bones of all sorts, 300 pelvises, 115 collarbones, 240 sternums—and that's just the bones. As for soft tissue, statistics are unreliable; the count doesn't distinguish itself by its accuracy, since New Yorkers, concerned with saving face, don't show their bottoms in hospitals.

To reassure the reader, we'll say right away that not a single bullet hit our heroes, even though it was precisely they who were the targets. The weather conditions may have been to blame. The "Battle of Norman and Stanley" took place in what was essentially zero visibility. The white hags sent the giant, top-shaped snowstorms spinning over the Atlantic crashing down on New York with a breadth of several miles each. We can regard with admiring surprise the durability of our towering structures, which lost half a million bricks and a quarter of a million windows in the storm occasioned by the battle. We sing the praises of the steadfastness of our police force. One hundred and eighteen patrolmen froze into ice statues overnight, though we must say that over the afternoon of the next, well and truly bucolic, day, they melted, fortunately.

Korbach—Alexander Zakharovich, that is—fifty years old, drifted around on the streets for several hours, skirting the fire zones cordoned off with yellow tape, avoiding the automatic weapons fire and the grenade explosions, shaking the ice off his overcoat, skidding and whispering: "Can it really be that even on a night like this I won't meet you?" He didn't.

7

LET'S SWING FROM THE CHANDELIER

*S*oon after the noteworthy dinner at Fimmy's, the official inauguration of the new fund took place at Carnegie Hall. It was a real society event, of the "black tie, off-the-shoulder gown" sort, that is, evening dress required. "Everybody who's anybody," as the saying goes, was there. Try to translate that expression into Russian if you can, ladies and gentlemen—the best I can offer is a personal variation that amounts to something like "anybody who's not an idiot."

Like all those present, Alexander Zakharovich Korbach was decked out in his society uniform, including even a cummerbund, something he'd never heard of before coming to America. The guests turned to look at A.Z. He was completely unknown in these "stardust" circles, and this made him noticeable. The announcement of Stanley Korbach, who without batting an eyelash introduced the stranger as his right hand—that is, the number-two man in the new humanitarian organization—lit a fire beneath this curiosity.

"Mr. Alex Korbach," he told his somewhat baffled audience from the stage, "was invited to participate in our work to come not only because of his name. His name, ladies and gentlemen, is not his principal asset, though it's not, I must admit, his chief liability either. His principal value to us in our search for real reality is his inexorable striving to see the world through new eyes, a quality that he developed in the course of his struggle for fundamental artistic values in the Soviet Union."

The crowd was slightly shocked when Stanley went on to say that the Korbach Fund was looking for people who were unspoiled by their position in society, excessive salary, or lifestyle that looked like one long holiday. The members of the audience chuckled nervously and exchanged glances, preferring not to understand that the eccentric tycoon was referring to them. Stanley, however, found it necessary to state his meaning exactly—namely, that for all his deep respect for those present, they were good only for society gatherings, a bit of meaningful chatter over bubbly drinks, and that "we need people who have nothing, who've come from nowhere, but who have principles and thoughts concerning the destiny of the human race."

"And what about yourself, sir?" came a shout from somewhere in the hall. "You don't have anything either? You've come from nothing, too?" The voice apparently belonged to a television talk-show host who received fifty thousand dollars for a half-hour appearance that wasn't even very funny, five days a week, year round.

"I belong to the genus of giants," Stanley replied with disarming simplicity. "Gargantua and Pantagruel are my forefathers. Even further back, the Maccabees are my ancestors. I'm the last Byronite among the rich—after all, ladies and gentlemen, without what we call Byronism, creativity is impossible." The public was quite simply flabbergasted by such a clear declaration of abnormality, but just then Stanley made a small comic bow, showing to the relief of everyone that he wasn't serious.

The biggest sensation of the evening, however, was the business report, given by one of the most important members of the fund, Dr. Leibnitz. He read out a first draft of the list of stipends, grants, and prizes, then modestly said that the enormous range of the fund's charitable activities would be guaranteed by a pre-scribed capital in the amount of $15 *billion;* that's right, ladies and gentlemen, 15,000,000,000; no, no, you didn't mishear—fifteen plus nine zeroes, ladies and gentlemen. A forceful shudder ran through the room. From the stage, which had known so many world-class artists, beginning with Houdini the escape artist, and not ending with Miss Ella Fitzgerald, that captress of all our hearts, one could see gaping mouths and bulging eyes, as though the roof had descended on them like a raven and the floor at once had risen like a bear—as some poet said. After that oc-curred an event that many were inclined to consider a mere figure of speech, while many others maintained that they had seen with their own eyes Art Duppertat, vice president of AK & BB, swinging from the chandelier of the historic building.

What's certain is that as soon as the amount of founding capital had been an-nounced, hostilities were renewed in the area around Carnegie Hall. Not even the thick walls could deaden completely the hubbub of soldiers' boots and triumphant shouts.

Alexander didn't stay for the concert. After walking several blocks along Fifty-seventh Street, he went into a coffee shop and took a seat in a corner. An old man sitting at the counter looked at him attentively, his eye obviously caught by his tuxedo. Then he went up to the sharply dressed gentleman and offered to sell him the silver bracelet from his own wrist. It was cast in the form of two monkeys with their tails intertwined, a splendid bit of kitsch. "It's a good deal, young fella," the old man said. "Only one twenty for this one-of-a-kind item." "A hundred," A.Z. said, and immediately received the bracelet for his full delectation. The old man, very pleased, took his bag of doughnuts from the table and went out onto the street. Nothing symbolic, A.Z. said to himself. Just two monkeys, an old con artist and a middle-aged idiot, that's all.

Fifty-seventh rolled by, paying no attention to the military action. People car-ried their purchases along in brightly colored shopping bags, hailed taxis, slid along on roller skates, whistled simple little melodies, blew little bubbles from the principal orifices of their heads, gulped the news down on the go from the head-lines of newspapers, counted dollars in their hands and inside their pockets. Mean-while, the fighting men of the Korbach and Blamsdale sides were raising and storming barricades, firing bazookas and recoilless rifles, and clashing again and again in hand-to-hand combat. From time to time, people covered with blood would poke their noses into the coffee shop, then stagger away, dragging either a wounded friend or plastic bags filled with fresh organs for transplants.

Alexander was glorying in his solitude. He undid the bit of black silk at his throat, pulled off his starched shirt, and put his tuxedo jacket on over his bare torso, immediately changing himself from an irreproachable comme il faut into an ordinary New York "wacko" with a monkey bracelet as the most attractive item in his wardrobe. It's coming to a close, he was thinking, moving forward with rapid strides beneath the banner of the fourth shiz-cousin. Korbachs of the world, divested of love but with unlimited possibilities, unite! All the way to the end!

8

WITH A FLATIRON OVER THE HEAD,
RIGHT?

On the surface, A.Z.'s Washingtonian life had not changed at all. As usual, he drove his Saab along I-77 to Pinkerton twice a week. Every time he saw the hodge-podge of Gothic spires and postmodern structures rising among the towering poplars, maples, and oaks, he felt a comfortable sense of belonging to something salubrious, tranquil, reasonable, and gratifying to him in the bargain. He liked campus life and—you can spit in my face en masse, ladies and gentlemen—the educational process in and of itself. He loved the faculty club and his lunches alone amid the hubbub of the student cafeteria. He even loved the Committee of the Subcommittee of the Committee on Committees and university routine, when all the participants painstakingly chew every morsel of this or that topic, having as their chief aim to show that their jaws are working on the matter at hand, too. The wholesome karma unquestionably rolled over him in waves along the paths and quads when the young people, stuffed with the excrement of their own slang, paraded day in, day out from the parking lots to their classes and workshops and back. The Black Cube was still his favorite place. One season he proposed that they put on a play he had found in a cobwebbed corner of a trade union library in Paris on the advice of Vitez. It was an Irish remake of Chekhov's *Seagull,* called, naturally enough, *The Heron.* That's the Irish imagination for you—to exchange the romantic bird of the elements of air and water for the offspring of the local swamps, a heron-maid, a working girl in a knitting mill. The action of the play occurred on an emerald green plain just on the south side of the Ulster border, sealed off by British troops. The inhabitants of these places feel cut off from the whole world. They don't even dream about crossing the frontier. There is, however, one person who manages to go back and forth across the covenanted border with no problems—the maiden from the knitting mill. By night she flies from "our swamp" to "their swamp" for a romantic assignation. Local society is split over this question. Some hate this bird; others are staggeringly and alarmingly in love with her. Rejecting because of her avian nature the limitations established by the powers that be, and repudiating also the prejudices that have hardened over the centuries, she gives off nothing but a sensation of pure love and becomes thereby a sort of angelic creation. She is killed by a gun that hangs on the wall throughout the action. In keeping with the famous Chekhovian aphorism, such a gun has to kill. In keeping with the Irish tradition, any heron with two gnarled legs, modest tail feathers, and something under them has to lay an egg. The play ends with the resurrection of the heron; she perches to lay an enormous egg for her lover, an American Byronite of incurably Irish ancestry.

The theater faculty was delighted with Sasha's choice. Above all because it wasn't a Russian play. Having rejected the Dante theme in their time, they were afraid lest the Black Cube be turned into some sort of Russian fief. Sasha showed himself to be very tactful, guys, by choosing an Irish play. It'll be closer to the hearts of a northern Virginia audience, after all, and the educational process will gain by the widening of the theater's repertoire.

He went to work with a huge, if not actually lupine, appetite. The impenetrable border was a metaphysical theme for his generation of Russians. The awkward flights of the heron, as it seemed to him, linked the Irish bogs to thirteenth-century Florence. The boys and girls from the Gogloyevsky cast were very keen to land parts in the new project. They were ready to hang around at the rehearsals run by Wild Sasha, as they called their respected professor, until morning. Particularly active were his pets Beverley, Kimberley, and Roxy Moran, the three mischievous girls who danced as they walked. He predicted for them the great future of three Moscow actresses: Yablochkina, Turchaninova, and Pashennaya (three old hags, just between us).

Naturally, no one at Pinkerton knew where the director spent his free time. Actually, he whiled it away in his old, almost nostalgic, California stomping grounds, or more precisely in Hollywood. One day there was great excitement on campus. A rumor was going around that a film crew was at work there with two idols of the new generation, Quentin Landry and Goldie D'Argent. Students rushed to the shooting location with an envious enthusiasm that reminded the aging professors of the good old days of the campus uprisings. All of a sudden, everyone saw that the man in charge of the filming was none other than Wild Sasha.

Perhaps it's time for us now to disclose another of Sasha's secrets. Sometimes after class hours he would wander around campus alone, imagining himself finally meeting Nora in one of the numerous passageways or catwalks, in the galleries or beneath the arches where clusters of unrepentant smokers gathered, and where her heels would tap as they might have done on a Florentine street between Borgello and Badia. One day he happened on a place, some cylinder of architecture and air, that immediately told him it was only here that the meeting of Dante and Beatrice could occur. It had a quality all its own: in the background, a cypress, a section of a high cathedral window; in the foreground, steps leading up to a fountain with a statue of a lion; still closer, the strands of a weeping willow; taken all together, a pseudo-Renaissance design, perfectly appropriate even though part of the eclectic Pinkerton surroundings. At that moment, the scene by its scope seemed to come directly from the parchment of the first edition of the *Divine Comedy* published in Urbino.

The business-minded people at Putney didn't like Alex's choices for the lead roles. They were planning to pay the lead couple no less than $5 million, while Landry's price—and here was the rub—was significantly lower, to say nothing of that of D'Argent, who was still more or less unknown in America, her huge success in Europe notwithstanding. Alexander succeeded in convincing the management to give the two performers a screen test, which was why the film crew had pitched their gypsy camp on the Pinkerton campus. He was sure they were the only pair he would film.

The flights from Washington to L.A. were, of course, recorded in his very genome. Once upon a time he had trembled with romantic feeling on this route, but over the past two years it had become routine. Settling himself in the first-class cabin, he immediately began to think about the new draft of the screenplay, which he would have to discuss with a swarm of editors at Putney, and he switched on his laptop as soon as the plane had reached cruising altitude. In L.A. there was invariably a limo waiting to take him to the Belle Age Hotel on Sunset Boulevard. The staff of Chicanos in Russian collarless jackets with sunflowers and roosters à la Natalya Goncharova greeted him and his suitcase at the entrance. The hotel had been designed in the twenties along the lines of the Parisian style of the Russian emigration. There, one of the presidential suites was invariably waiting for the director from the line of Korbach. An account was opened, everything was paid for by the company—that is, in the end, by Stanley, who had already made no small contribution to the budget for the "Radiance" project.

On one occasion, Alexander decided to gather his old Russian gang together under the roof of the Belle Age. A crowd even larger than the number that had been invited showed up gladly. It turned out that the majority of them had not even suspected the existence in this Los Arkhangelsk of such a stylish Russian place, where the murals of Bakst and Benoit for *The Rite of Spring* hung on the walls, and where the music of Stravinsky was even piped into the rest rooms. There were, of course, a few permutations in the sexual games that were forever being played. Stas Butlerov, for example, came with Dvoira Radashkevich. Shirley Fedot, his faithful girlfriend for the first half of the decade that has elapsed to this point in the novel, was accompanying Gary Hornhoof, aka Tikhomir Burevyatnikov. Also present were "our Russian doctor," Nathan Soloukhin; "our Russian lawyer," Yura Zimbulist; the retinue of epic heroes of "our Russian cosmetolo-gists," Felix Boim, Edik Shengelyan, and Ilyuha Popovich; a couple of them with aesthetically tense wives, one with a new filly who didn't give a damn about anything because of the bloom of her youth.

The sitting room of Korbach's suite gurgled with English, and only occasion-ally would the bubble of Russian obscenity burst forth: "Tell him to go fuck him-self!" and so on. One man there, a rather unexpected guest, was trying out his Russian: the old parking-garage boss Tesfalidet Khasfalidat. "Russka brothers," he would say, "Ortodoxa! Kazhdy everybody na borba! Fuck off nasha kommunista!" Gabi Lianoza the shift man showed up a bit late, as befits a rich man. As soon as he came through the door, he began to imitate his favorite instrument, the tuba. Puffing up his cheeks and then blowing out as he played the *Carmen* overture, he made such a good job of it that all the slim-figured girlfriends and even the chubby wives broke into a dance. Keeping one foot out, he wouldn't let the door close, and when he had finished his number, he bellowed: "Fucko Russo, look who I've brought—the two in-laws, Terzia and Unzia!" The two surprises burst in from the corridor, two full-figured quadratic *donnas,* from whom one might expect any sort of art in the magical realist style. There was a smell of age-old Riga elegance when Dvoira Radashkevich, elegant thanks to Anne Klein II, sidled up closer to the host, glass in hand. She had the sad gaze of a woman with a past worth remembering.

Stas, as it turned out, had managed to get his qualifications accepted and had been working for three years now as the mouthpiece for a gang of Odessa bandits who bought heating oil and sold it as diesel fuel. It appeared as though Butlerov's success had stripped him of his sense of reality; in any case, he told the regular of the luxury accommodations of the Belle Age Hotel: "I'm rich, Sasha—you can't even imagine how rich I am!" He liked contact with male bodies as much as ever: when he wasn't resting an elbow on your shoulder, he was resting his belly against you—not like a homo at all, though; obviously, it was just his version of the reck-less traditions of the Kazan University chemistry department. "Hey, Sasha, you know, sometimes I just want to sit with you on the roof for a while, drive in a few nails, and suck down a few beers afterward." Apparently he was under the im-pression that Korbach was still mending roofs.

The influence of that universal philanthropist Shirley Fedot clearly showed in the appearance of Tikh Bur. Instead of his bandit togs by Gucci and Versace, he was now outfitted in the country gentleman style; even his jaw quivered slightly. Letting himself be hugged with his arms like an albatross, Alexander expected to smell some sort of *adzhika* spice on his breath but instead caught a whiff of good mouthwash. "Everything's falling apart," Tikh whispered almost tragically. "The hydra of Bolshevism is on its last legs. It's dragging our Leninist Komsomol down into the grave with it. We'll all be in jail soon. You know how Rosenbaum sings, 'And the geese are already flying far away'? Makes you want to spread your wings and take off after them. Allegorically speaking, of course."

"And how's your personal life?" A.Z. asked, and smiled at Shirley Fedot, who was observing them with great attention but with genuine amicable delight as well. "She's put me on a diet!" Burevyatnikov guffawed and for some reason slapped himself on the nape of the neck. "Isn't drying out herself, though—right from the morning she's on the Click!" A.Z. supposed that he was referring to Veuve Clicquot. "Please, Sasha, don't believe a word you hear about me!" the woman of aesthetics and common sense put in, blazing forth with all the jack-of-diamond colors of her palette.

Also among the throng was Aram Ter-Aivazian, arm in arm with Sally Sullivan, secretary to the Hornhoof office; perhaps some of our readers still remember her irreproachable—that is to say, it hasn't stuck in anyone's mind—passage. Now, when she stepped over the threshold, every electronic device in the large suite went haywire for some reason: the hands of watches began to run backward, the image on the television screen froze, and the Vivaldi on the turntable started to sound like Sofia Gubaidullina. Aram cut an even more severe figure than he did formerly. He was already doing the balance sheet of his years in exile. They had not been wasted; a basis for independence had arisen in the diaspora. No small amount of literature had been sent to Urartu. It was time for him to get himself ready. Azerbaijan wasn't sleeping. The motherland was threatened with danger.

Alexander led the whole crowd to a restaurant. The menu also was maintained in the Russian style: Yasnaya Polyana salad, Peredvizhniki fish stew, Art World borscht, Stray Dog Cabaret meat soup, Kremlin meat pies, Winter Palace ice cream, Firebird soufflé, and so on and so forth. While the large party was downing all these delicacies, Alexander Zakharovich was exchanging rejoinders with Burevyatnikov.

"I happened to come across a certain Mirelle Salamanca here, Tisha. Does that name ring a bell with you?"

"The muse of poetry," Tikhomir recalled somberly.

"And of the Lubyanka," A.Z. added for greater precision.

"You got it off together?"

"We engaged in a polemic," A.Z. replied.

Their conversation was being followed with great interest by a guest whom no one recognized—a man without a face, unless you count the eyes, brows, and all the other details, plus a rudimentary nose. A guy like that would just as soon break your head as look at you, Sasha thought. He answered the stranger with a movement of his chin. "So who is that, Tikh?" The boss of Hornhoof, evidently in a state of hungover misanthropy, gave the succinct explanation: "Zavkhozov. A partner."

The bill came. Without even a glance at it, Sasha signed with a flourish. Zavkhozov's rotten peepers sparkled with delight: that's how we ought to live in the new Russia!

It might have seemed like time to go, but the group wasn't moving. Russians are easy to invite and difficult to show to the door. They went back up to A.Z.'s room to lay waste to the private bar. Before long, the majority of them were rolling on the carpet and on the couches. They shut themselves in the bedrooms and in the bathroom by couples, and even by small groups. A whole platoon of them sang popular songs they knew: "A Combo of Hope" and "Right On, Maestro." Their English-speaking girls listened uncomprehendingly: somewhere in the midst of the off-key choir they heard the familiar word *Mozart*—where had it come from?

"Butlerov, you won't object if I stay with Korbach, will you?" Dvoira asked. The host of the sparkling soiree started to say in a low moan: "No, don't, Dvoira, I'm not that man anymore . . ." Someone thrust a guitar at him anyway. "Go on, Sasha, show us your old stuff!" All at once, surprising even himself, he launched into "The Old Woman Fidel," a near paraphrase of an old hit of his called "The Old Woman Izergiel." The new composition delighted no one. Along with the condescending glances he heard a whisper: "He's lost it living abroad." A.Z. made his way over the carpet and rolled up to Zavkhozov. "How were they planning to liquidate me, Comrade Zavkhozov?"

"Oleg," the faceless one corrected him.

"All right—how were they going to do it, Oleg?"

"Different methods were discussed," Zavkhozov recalled. "Poison. Grease. Radiation. Letter bomb. The usual." A.Z. was looking into the Soviet face, now and then resting his chin on the shoulder of the executioner. The latter was sitting on the carpet, his arms wrapped around his knees. His wrist, sparingly and touchingly covered with hair like Slavic steppe grass, was decked out with a twenty-five-grand Cartier. "Who am I, anyway, Sasha?" he said with a shrug. "Not much depended on me, you know. But on the whole I was in favor of traditional methods."

"With a flatiron across the head, right?" Korbach asked, peering at him inquisitively. The grassy brows rose as if to say: There's a guess for you! "I like your sense of humor, Sasha."

Just then Tikh sat down beside them, holding three little glasses containing some high-octane mixture. "Whadda ya say, boys, look lively! Three shots at the Reds!" He was obviously feeling merrier: he'd managed to take on a load while Shirley was billing and cooing with Tesfalidet in the depths of the presidential suite beneath a portrait of Alexander Blok suspended in the half-light.

A telephone rang. Someone tossed a mobile to A.Z., and when he caught it he heard Stanley Korbach's voice: "Sasha, I've been looking for you all over the world! Turn on CNN in ten minutes! The Berlin Wall's come down!" "Good news for Zavkhozov!" Sasha yelled and started poking at Sally Sullivan with a finger, meaning: Get her out and switch it on! It turned out that Stanley was there on the spot. He'd just brought in Rostropovich and his cello on the Galaxy. Slava's already sawing away. The Wall's falling. In pieces. People are climbing into the holes from the West and from the East. Fountains of Soviet champagne! History is being made! The Belle Age Hotel was shaking as though a new tremor were running along the California coast—a possibility that, incidentally, couldn't have been ruled out. "A Combo of Hope" thundered out like a giant Soviet Army chorus.

It was only toward morning that the party began to break up. Sasha watched as they dragged themselves across the parking lot to their cars in a Felliniesque procession. In the center of the lot, the young women and the old women alike formed a dance in the round. Three iguanas, four raccoons, and five coyotes emerged from the manicured shrubs and stared at the dancers. All of living nature, apparently, had grasped the seriousness of the times to come.

9

AN ATTEMPT AT A GENEALOGICAL
JOURNEY

*O*ne day, Fuchs showed Alexander Zakharovich some of the results of the research he had obtained with computers and the latest generation of software. An enormous amount of information is filtering through. Numerous other lines will appear concurrently with the Korbachs', and in this way a mass of data on the whole history of the diaspora will be summed up. You're all in a hurry, Sasha, and for no reason. I could show you, for example, how our Korbach-Fuchs line approaches branches of the Colón family, into which Christopher Columbus was born in the middle of the fifteenth century. I can see that you're not as surprised by Columbus as you are by the connection between you and me. Ha, ha . . . that's just one of a thousand surprises we'll meet along the way.

Their conversation was taking place on the fourteenth floor of the new Korbach Center, a skyscraper rising at the corner of East Fiftieth and Lexington Avenue to the same height as that of the publishing firm Random House just down the street. The researchers, having exhausted their day's supply of genealogical enthusiasm, had gone home, and now only Fuchs, who looked like a miniature Mark Twain, was twisting around on his chair among the computers, turning his face now to the parallelepiped of the gleaming sunset, now to the trapezoid of the murky sky, in which the moon had already risen. Neither of the two geometric forms had yet convinced Fuchs of the futility of his exertions.

If the future Hollywood celebrity has half an hour to spare, Fuchs can invite him to take a journey from his great-great-grandfather Gedali Korbach into even more distant times, if one can put it like that. It's well known that Gedali established his thriving fur business himself. He was born in 1828 in the family of a furrier from whom he inherited nothing except the knowledge of how to turn hides into fur, to scrape and tan, and even inherited the smell of the acidic mixture that would not leave him even when he had become a man of means.

This was what Lionel Fuchs—who, judging by his name and sideburned appearance, had something to do with things furry himself—was saying.

"This craftsman, your great-great-great-grandfather Mordecai Korbach, is the first man in the line whose surname is exactly the same as yours. The -*ch* at the end was added clearly as a result of the family's move from Holland to Germany, more exactly to Leipzig, where the large and well-respected Bach family lived. The future furrier was born at the end of the eighteenth century, in either 1795 or 1798. His father was Jeremiah Korbeit (in some records, though, he is already called Korbach), a fairly powerful banker; add one more *great-* to the word *grandfather* for him. He moved to Leipzig from Amsterdam seven years before Mordecai's birth, from all appearances in connection with the division of the inherited property. The family's move from Germany to Poland was more like a flight. There exist fairly clear records documenting the seizure of the bank by the Saxony authorities, and less clear ones of a pogrom in the Korbeit house. It's entirely possible that the whole catastrophe was instigated by the banker's highly placed debtors.

"As a result of this collapse, the banker's sons fell several rungs on the social ladder. The name Korbach became firmly attached only to Mordecai the furrier, while his two brothers appear in the Lodz archives under the name of Korbat. From them, to judge from all appearances, come the Eastern European surnames of the Korbach, Korbachevsky, Korbabutenko, Korbut, Korbis type. We haven't turned our attention to those branches yet, but we'll get to them soon.

"Let's stay with the main trunk. We can say that the Korbeits, and the Korbeit-Levits of the seventeenth and eighteenth centuries, who were very close to them, were Dutch. The bulk of their progeny can be traced fairly accurately thanks to the commercial and financial records of the time. You can just string out the *greats* like beads on a rosary. From Jeremiah's father, Khalevi Korbeit, on back: Moses—Nisson—Magnus—Jehuda—Emmanuel—Elias—Leon—Santab—Ezra. They dealt with the shipping contracts for the royal fleet and for commercial boats as well, and that was big business at the time, in Holland. Where did Ezra Korbeit come to Amsterdam from? From Spain, naturally. He was from a family of *anusim,* or Spanish *marans,* but a generation later, thanks to the extremely liberal atmosphere of Amsterdam, the Korbeits returned to Judaism.

"At this point there comes into being a significant joining of different cultures: the Arabs of Seville, Sephardics, and those who later came to be called the Ashkenazi. Without computers, of course, we would have lost the trace of the Dutch Korbeits; sifting through a mountain of information, though, including the archives of the Inquisition (just imagine the cost of this work, and you'll say 'thank God for Stanley!'), we stumbled onto an account of the departure of a certain Ezra Korbach, supposedly for Holland. This discovery brought lots of others in its wake. For the first time we saw the hyphenated name Kor-Beit, and we found it on the lists of the Barcelona synagogue written in Hebrew. This confirmed our theories about the origins of the name in the ancient nickname Cold House. In countries with a hot climate, that sort of nickname carried more positive connotations than negative ones.

"I'll go on! You're not looking at your watch anymore, I suppose? At the time of the Spanish-Arab-Jewish 'golden age . . .' Ah, now you're looking at your watch!"

"I'm sorry, Lionel, Stanley's waiting for me at the airport. We're flying to Budapest for an on-the-road session of the fund. We'll come back to the 'golden age' later, I hope."

Fuchs sighed. "Well then, at least take this as a parting gift." From the printer he tore off a six-foot length of paper containing a complete family tree from Gedali to Ezra, branches and its veins of biblical names and all. "In the German bit you'll find the point of the joining of the Korbeits and the Fuchses," the researcher intoned sadly.

"I'm very glad to consider you a relative, Lionel!" A.Z. was already heading for the exit, weaving his way among the little computer tables as though carrying out the task of exiting the menu. He looked back from the doorway. A slight figure with a pipe (Fuchs could take it out only when the antinicotine squad had gone home) was standing there with a cooling, westward-looking window as a backdrop. A moment of keenly felt sadness flitted by. Sasha had always avoided fortune-tellers, having no desire to know his own future. At that moment he felt something along the lines of that aversion in the presence of this man who was dragging such distant ancestors of his up out of the past.

"What are you looking at? Do you think I'm ridiculous?" Fuchs asked. Sasha shrugged. "My friend, who isn't ridiculous these days?" And he cleared out of the center feeling slightly ashamed but rather relieved as well.

10

CRACKING NUTS WITH A MONGREL

"*I*'ve already seen this film in my mind I don't know how many times without any Putney Productions. In pieces and in rows of pieces, in a hodgepodge of shots and in strict order, in verse and in prose, to jazz and to old violas, and once, starting on Venice Beach surrounded by the cardboard boxes of bums, and carrying on in the plane on the way to Washington, I ran the whole thing, from the epilogue to the finale, with a symphony orchestra accompaniment, with Nora in the lead role and with my monkey's mug instead of the noble faces of Dante and Blok.

"It doesn't look like I'll be able to make a damned thing come of it. This subject is so private that it can't be made in the flashing round of faces of a movie set, among the people who are intending to make this film with me. The director has to be able to protect his inspiration—that is in principle, he ought to know how to hide it. There are some things that I just can't say to 'outsiders.' I can't tell them that this whole business of the *dolce stil nuovo* sprang up in me as a premonition of what we helplessly call true love, that this premonition lives in me as a strangely restrained, youthful, girlish feeling, a thirst after inexpressible tenderness. I've gone through adolescence, cursed, led the dissolute life, and when I look at myself I still see a little boy who hasn't been kissed, which means he hasn't fucked around.

And without this constantly trembling background I wouldn't get ahold of the metaphor.

"How can I tell the people who want to and will make this film with me how this metaphor shone before me with new strength after I met Nora? And how we in our 'true love' got tangled up right away with sex, with convulsions, with her and my depravity, with all the happiness of fucking, the poses that we played up, the instillings, the mergings, the torments of obscene jealousy?

"And what now? All of my loves are in ruins. Dante's sunrise doesn't shine on me anymore, and neither does Blok's sunset—I'm fifty, I came too late, the train's gone, I'll never be able to bring to life on the screen what I've been dreaming about for so many years, and what, it seems, fate is bringing to me on a silver platter now. At best I'll add my two cents to 'entertainment,' win a gilded statuette of a mongrel: crack nuts, gobble them down, get fat, sprinkle everyone around me with the shells.

"If I want to preserve myself as an artist, I've got to get out of the game, finish the contract. And reduce the influence of my dear Stanley and the whole Korbach world, its philanthropic lunacy, and its mad numbers to a minimum."

Such were the thoughts that Alexander Zakharovich Korbach confided over a lonely lunch in a small restaurant in Georgetown, which had recently become a favorite haunt. It was March 1990. La Belle Ruche had arugula salad on the menu. A sign from a well-known Paris street hung over each table. The *vins de maison* here were of excellent quality, though they were served in carafes. The little restaurant had been discovered by A.Z.'s friend here, a journalist from Radio Liberty. From time to time they gathered here as a small Russian group: A.Z., the journalist, a jazz musician, a souvenir merchant. Sometimes they were joined by the author of this novel. He would sit there quietly, looking around with indifference, as though he had no business there, the little shit.

One of the subjects of their discussions was, of course, the mind-boggling spiral of the news from the Soviet Union: hundred-thousand-strong meetings and demonstrations for the repeal of the Sixth Amendment and for the expulsion of the CPSU and for the creation of new parties as well, the de facto abolition of censorship, the outbreak of war in the Caucasus, the personality of Gorbachev. Who is he, so roundheaded, with a mark on his forehead in a mysterious combination of pigments—a shrewdly maneuvering Commie saving his own groaning ship on the point of cracking up or, on the contrary, a shrewdly maneuvering anti-Sov who has decided to run his rowboat aground on a sandbar and smash it to bits? These discussions often ended with voices raised, chairs thrown back, and dollars flung down, followed by a dash to the door; later, however, the five of them would get together again as though nothing had happened.

On ordinary days, Sasha would pop in for just a bite to eat. Some time ago, hot food had acquired for him a sort of added meaning, had become as it were a philosophy of "hot food." Any man who hasn't let himself go entirely ought to have hot food at least once a day—that was the credo by which he lived, come what may. Along with the arugula salad (God knows where they found plants like this) he would order flaked crab soup and a healthy wedge of quiche—in other words, a genuine "hot meal." To just chow down and not think anymore about any mega-movie projects. Only a handful of directors in the world had found a way simultaneously to express their vision and keep the studio and the team making the film right where they wanted them, even play the tyrant. Tarkovsky could show up at Goskino with his tortured metaphors, and there, even though everyone was fairly farting with feelings of Party responsibility, he was revered; no one wanted to go on record as a stifler of genius. It's not likely that Hollywood would have let Tark make *Stalker,* whose main theme was water, slowly flowing, dripping, stagnating—a translucent liquid oozing from everywhere.

Sasha was already on the point of asking for the check when the headwaiter, a Creole from Guadeloupe named Pascal, came up to him and said in a melodramatic half whisper: "Alex, there's a lady asking for you over there. I stress, a real lady, one of the beautiful people. She asked me in French: Can I speak to Monsieur Korbach? I've never seen any ladies like that among our clientele."

Sasha turned and saw Marjorie Korbach. She was sitting in a corner beneath a fake but attractive palm plant and looking as young as her waist was slim. Sasha, with his penchant for improper thoughts, immediately began to reflect on why some American women looked like hippopotami while others were more like delicate nanny goats, even when they were well past fifty. Marjorie was one of those. No bodyguard and no escort! Very modestly attired, just a very simple Celine. No jewelry, kind ladies and gentlemen! In the urban jungles, wearing jewels is not in the least de rigueur. A member of high society can also get in step with the times and understand egalitarian ideas. Everything must be the way it is for everyone else, or at least must look that way, and your Celine suit has to look like . . . well, like I don't know what.

She was sitting with a bottle of beer and was thinking with some apprehension that she would have to order something else now, and she didn't know what to order or how in such places. In a way, the ladies of the upper echelons of the Kremlin nomenklatura experienced the same feelings when they found themselves out in the City, as they called the frightening outside world. Once, Soviet Minister of Culture Ekaterina Furtseva—Marjorie, by the way, reminded Sasha slightly of this minister by way of an expression of veiled suffering, and even more often outright confusion, in her eyes—having decided to show a gathering of leading artists that she possessed the common touch, began a sentence with: "In any trolleybus, you pay your ruble and off you go," and was interrupted by enthusiastic applause—she didn't know, the poor dear, that a trolleybus ticket cost five kopecks—that is, twenty times less than she thought.

Nowadays in America, of course, there are more atypical fatties than typical well-turned WASPs, A.Z. said to himself, carrying on with his absolutely inappropriate train of thought as he approached the stepmother of the beloved woman who had run off to Iraq. It's too hot and humid in this melting pot. Bodies swell from generation to generation. Only in New England, and right along the Canadian border at that, do the descendants of the pioneers manage to keep in form. Marjorie, of course, is one of those. Enough lousy humor, he thought, coming up to her. It's not enough to remember the old Soviet saying "In the rear a young pioneer, up front a pensioner." And he stepped up to her. "Marjorie!" "Oh, it's you!" Her blazing eyes cast her into the ranks of ageless, model youth. A first-class babe, that's all there is to it. An enchanting doll of a lady. He sat down opposite her and found himself beneath a Boulevard Saint-Michel sign.

"I wanted to say something important to you, you know," she said in a rush.

"Excuse me, Marjorie, but how did you find me?"

I'm not quite sure how this question will appear to the enlightened reader: far-fetched, purely informative, entirely outside the norm? I'm going to insist on it stubbornly, though. If you, dear reader, were English, wouldn't you be surprised to see one of the Buckingham Palace princesses in a Covent Garden pub? If you were Russian, wouldn't you be surprised to see Alla Pugachova in a crowd of com-muters at the Kazan station? To an American it's all perfectly clear as is.

She gave a not entirely guileless smile, and it suited her face. "Do you really think it's that easy for you to hide, Alex, given your popularity?" "Given my popu-larity?" "Given your popularity with ladies of a certain age?" He thought, Why is she using the plural? Perhaps she even means Nora? She thinks she has joined her stepdaughter in her victory over age. No need to carp about some dryness of the fingers and some parched skin just about the clavicles; Marjorie Korbach is a won-der of nature! "All right, then, what have you got to say that's so important that you even got up the courage to come to a café?"

"Stanley and I have divorced."

"Now there's a bit of news!"

"My husband is Norman Blamsdale now. A man whom you hate."

"Well now, that's a bit strong."

"Now you can punish him in grand fashion, and any way you want."

"Margie, I'm an old man."

"You, old? That's ridiculous!"

"Margie, what are you thinking, getting stuck on me? Find yourself a younger gigolo. I've even got my eye on one, the ideal stud." Her eyes widened foolishly. This doll-like, empty-headed look has been her cover her whole life, he thought. "That's interesting! Maybe you can write down the name and phone number of this walking cock for me?" He wrote on a napkin: "Matt Shuroff, 213-information, Venice area." She took the napkin and stood up. "Well, let's go! We're not going to sit here all day."

There was no chauffeur in the Rolls-Royce—could she really have driven her-self? She walked by the car, not even looking at it, and noticing even less the pink parking ticket under the windshield wiper. Let's go for a stroll along this murky, muddy canal. A touch of romanticism, Alex. You know perfectly well about my love, you big merciless ape. Sasha Korbach was suddenly seized by a desire to step off to one side and disappear beneath one of the decaying arches of the narrow, humpbacked embankment with its two or three pathetic streetlights in front of some eateries and a shoe-repair shop. "How wonderful," Marjorie whispered. "I had no idea that Washington could be so romantic, so inviting to do something mad. Look at that dark corner beneath those huge elms! What is that piece of shit standing there with such winning unpretentiousness?"

"It's a feeding trough for mules, ma'am."

"Alex, your Russian accent makes my head spin. A feeding trough for whom?" "For m-u-l-e-s, madam, for that bastard race of horses and donkeys. They take people for rides here on a rusty old eighteenth-century barge. It's the best tourist attraction in the Old Town."

She went up to the feeding trough and even rested her elbows on it in such a way that her bottom nearly protruded from the Celine outfit, albeit not entirely, merged entirely with the night, so that a nearly ideal *Au Bout de la Nuit* figure resulted. "Well, Alex, what would you do to me now if you were a bit younger?" "Just what you're asking me for, ma'am." She gasped. "You mean here, at the mule feeding trough?" "No, right *in* the trough. *Kak? Kak? Kak?*" "Is that the Russian way?" "I'd set your backside right here in this trough all covered in mule drool. I'm just imagining how many oats would stick to your buttocks." She gave a moan. "That would really be something, oats sticking to my buttocks, from which you'd yank the panties, tear them off in two yanks." "One yank, ma'am." "You know how to do it in one?" "What can you do, life has taught me a few things." "And then what? Would you start ramming it to me?" "That's right, ma'am, that's just the word—ram!" "Wha——?" "As though the whole meaning of my life were summed up in ramming it to aging beauties, ma'am." Margie seized him by the lapels. "And your hands, Alex, what would you do with your hands?" "Well, they'd be pulling out your not badly preserved tits." "And then what, then what?" "Now, Marjorie, I didn't know you'd go so far. You want a finger up your anus, don't you?" She stifled her howl with both hands, but it, even silently, shook her body for no more than a minute. Then she was hanging on A.Z., looking around with unseeing eyes, as though she was making her way through some foggy zone between imagination and reality. There was a strong smell of burnt hair. That's the way it ought to be with mules, when their tails are too tired to chase away horseflies, and the animals begin rubbing up against the walls.

A few minutes later the respectable couple emerged from the zone of philological gloom and burning and passed over to a more civilized stretch of the embankment of the Georgetown canal, more precisely, to the Foundry gallery of shops with its windows of antique booksellers and art galleries.

"Look here, Alex, we're not strangers to each other any longer, so I'd like to give you a warning," the lady said with quiet melancholy. "The fact is that the war between Stanley and Norman is entering its decisive phase, and it doesn't look as though Stanley has much chance." "All the more since in all probability he hasn't even noticed the war," said Sasha Korbach.

She was silent for a while, then took out a small pair of reading glasses and leaned over toward the shop window, as though checking a price. As though she knew something about prices. "That's just it," she finally went on. "He doesn't notice it, and meanwhile the main blow is being prepared, from an unexpected direction." "Your husband must be Napoleon, is that it, ma'am?" He stopped by an automatic teller machine. "What is that?" she asked, examining with unfeigned interest the faintly glowing apparatus with its screen, keyboard, and different slots for pulling out and sticking in money. He drew out a packet of springy, crackling bills. "Poor child of the nomenklatura," he said with a smile at this on the whole not-so-bad babe. "So many discoveries in one evening!"

11

NORA DURING HER ABSENCE

*I*t's well known that no small number of unhappy occurrences have resulted from love, in life as well as in literature. There have been incidents that have left a strong impression as well, but alongside them have been those that were pathetic, absurd, curious, and really worthy of treatment only in the minimalist style. Our present chronicles, even if only obliquely, and through a series of mirrors, both ideal and distorting, are nonetheless a reflection of another style, one that was announced as long ago as the thirteenth century as *nuovo* and *dolce,* and as such we will try at least not to put our lovers in any completely ridiculous positions. On the other hand, of course, we can't forget that the ridiculous—a tendency to depart from the best possible tone—runs alongside even the most grandiose symphonic system and not infrequently exercises an influence on the interpretation of events in the domain of love.

Allow me to remind you of what happened once to one of the bards of our Russian *dolce stil,* echoing the Florentine some 650 years later, the young Boris Bugayev, aka Andrei Bely. Refused by Lyubov Blok after a series of heart-wringing trysts—traces of them are scattered through the first half of *Petersburg,* the Russian *Ulysses*—having lost everything he valued in this world that is perishing: his friend and cocrusader, his traveling companion through the fields of mysticism, and also the wife of his friend, the embodiment of Sofia—alas, an all too fleshly, rosy-cheeked embodiment to abstain from the temptations of the carnival—he was trudging through the muddy expanses of St. Petersburg, where only cast iron stands with any dignity, everything else acquiring a slimy coating of tiresome moisture, and was heading for the Neva, which even at that time, before the Acmeists had gotten up a full head of steam, was linked with one of the rivers of the sad Netherworld, most frequently with the Lethe. It would have been hard not to figure out his intentions, looking at his nervous walk, with his knees angled inward; with his arms now waving like those of a navy signalman announcing an artillery attack, now groping before him in the hopeless air of Peter's city; with his eyes like those of Adam having suddenly realized that he is banished forever, in the sweep of a man's cape, indifferent to the sufferings of the master, for it lived by its own dramatic twists, flapping away in the wind; it would have been difficult not to figure them out, but the guardians of the city's peace pretended that they couldn't, since they didn't give a damn, the lousy cops, that our *Ulysses* hadn't even been created yet, and that in a few minutes' time it might turn out that it would never be created, and would simply fly by the planet in unbegun form and vanish into a black hole. Whew, what a paragraph!

On a bridge—the Nikolaevsky, I think, though it might have been the Troitsky—one leg ending in an English boot had already been thrown over the balustrade, his gaze looking over the arc of the columns and spires of the miragelike city one last time. For a second it lingered on the unread announcement of the dying sunset, and in a final moment of terror fell to the tin ripples of the all-engulfing water. The ripples suddenly went dim. Sailing right under the bridge was a large, formless boat loaded with coal, or perhaps with something worse. I don't want to fall into that! I didn't come up here to make a laughingstock of myself! I just wanted to sink, that's all—you know, into the Lethe! His leg drew back in a reflex reaction, back onto the walkway of the bridge. At that instant the idea of the novel came into the mind of Boris-Andrei-Kotik Bugayev-Bely-Letayev, and he froze on the bridge, over the liquid "teeming with bacilli," and raised to the setting sun not only his own face but the pale mask of Kolenka Ableukhov as well. Thus the creative instinct overcame the ridiculous state of affairs that was threatening, beat back the death-dealing kitsch of an affair of the heart, saved for us the heap of remarkable pages that is our *Ulysses*. I would be a very poor Russian philologist if I didn't point out at this juncture that "our" *Ulysses* appeared in print nine years before "theirs."

I'm not about to maintain that this story somehow influenced the survival of our characters, but I'm not going to rule it out, either. Their surface calm might have had nothing to do with fin de siècle sexual cynicism but rather merely reflected some unconscious refusal to come crashing down on a dirty barge instead of dissolving in the Lethe. As paradoxical as it seems, this barge is in fact a saving force. That's why we parted with such apparent ease, for such a quantity of pages and over three years of the story line, with our heroine. It doesn't mean at all that we've forgotten "our Tatyana." We love her so much that we even find similarities to her in the stars of world cinema, particularly in those of Swedish ancestry, like Greta Garbo, Ingrid Bergman, Ingrid Thulin, and Ingrid Sterling.

Sorry, that last name seems to come from another opera altogether. It's from one of Igor Severyanin's poems, you see: "Ingrid Sterling has a pallid face, she's a brunette, has violet eyes and a sorrowful mouth." It was in just such a state that we found Nora one day during her absence from the pages of the novel, in the Palm Beach Hotel on the south coast of Cyprus. She emerged from a phone booth, and her face was pallid. She sat down in a corner and was a brunette, though with that slight bleaching of hair color that always happens during archaeological digs. A waiter brought her something strong from the bar, and when she'd drunk it she turned her violet eyes in the direction of the sapphire—from the name Sappho— sea, but her mouth was sad between swallows.

We never learned why she was pale when she came out of the phone booth, we just couldn't get up the nerve to approach her. We ambled in circles, watching more and more of the bloom come back to her cheeks with each shot of Scotch, her brow darkening, burnt by the sun of the ancient world—in short, we didn't behave much better than the two inveterate hotel womanizers who noticed this "stunning woman" right away. However, something kept them from approaching her as well, and meanwhile it was getting dark. Nora glanced at her watch, stood up, tucked her white shirt into her trousers, hitched up her belt, and, with the height of self-assurance, made for the exit, the heels of her sabots tapping all the way. One could see through the glass door how she took her seat in her waiting Jeep. With that, our extranarrative nonmeeting ended. It's probably for the best that things turned out this way. Any less straitlaced turn of events might have infringed upon our authorial freedom. Freedom has been preserved, so we're going to go on however it suits us.

She often asked herself what had provoked her breakup with Sasha, and then her abrupt departure to join the Lilienmann expedition in Iraq. There were no words for it—she'd been damned angry with her sweetheart. He's self-assertive, always trying to show his authority over the "American airhead," the spoiled scatterbrain. This idiotic gap between cultures! He would condescendingly point out my American habits, typical gestures, mimicry, all that rubbish that no one pays any attention to. For example, if I patted him on the back to say good-bye, he would ask, without missing a beat, what the problem was. What do you mean, what's the problem? Your slapping me on the back, what does it mean? Why has it got to mean anything other than good-bye? He shrugs. It's interesting that after so many tender kisses you slap me on the back, as though you're breezily approving my performance: "Not bad, not bad, old boy." What a lot of nonsense!

Oh, and here's one more example. If he sees me in a crowd at the airport with suitcases in both hands and my ticket in my mouth, he starts to laugh: Look at the American girl! What's the matter, Alex? What is it that you've found so terribly American about me now? Of course, in order to ask the question, I've got to put down one of the cases and take the ticket out of my mouth. I do it automatically, dear readers. Automatically, *vous comprenez?* He laughs, and it turns out that that's how he spots the American women in a crowd at an airport—they're the only ones who carry their tickets in their mouths. Then he goes into greater detail. It's interesting that you use only the outer, dry part of your lips for this carrying work, the mucous membrane isn't involved in the process, which means that the ticket doesn't go limp, and hygiene doesn't suffer. You're our specialist in the hygiene habits of the ancients, after all. Say, do you suppose they carried cuneiform tablets in their mouths?

If he didn't have anything else to laugh at, then he'd make fun of me for being left-handed. What is this strange American mania for writing with the left hand. I'm sure it's connected with the leftist inclinations of "our intelligentsia."

At first I didn't notice these signs that we were getting a bit fed up. I joked in reply: look how observant this guy is! He lives among us like one of us, even sleeps with one of us, and he's still keeping up his anti-American vigilance! Even so, I tried to spare him. These Russians, I thought—their eternal inferiority complex is intertwined with an odd complex that they're *superior* to other peoples, particularly Americans. I didn't realize that with him it wasn't about America but about me. How strange to turn out to be so insensitive! Usually, I was too refined where he was concerned. In bed, I was often overwhelmed by a feeling of complete understanding. A sharp, alarming feeling, to tell the truth. Sometimes it seemed to me that I knew all his poetry ahead of time. I didn't let him know it, but I had the feeling that I was overcoming any number of barriers, not to mention the one of language. Once I got the impression that he'd sensed in a dream the presence of his father, a man who had died before he was born. It was some incomprehensible act of repentance, a sensation of higher love that existed in his secret places. I waited for him to confess to me, that is, for him to tell me about this "dream"—which he remembered, I've no doubt about it—but he didn't. On the contrary, I sensed a strong feeling of irritation coming from him. And maybe I'd just imagined the whole thing? Maybe I was the first one to feel some slight irritation, because he didn't want to tell me about his meeting with his father? Perhaps I changed my gestures or the tone of my voice without realizing it when I spoke to him?

After being in orbit, even I couldn't bring myself to open my mouth and tell him about those mind-boggling revelations of angels as big as all the heavens and the little box with Baby Felix. It was only the nearness of loving, a strange feeling that this time he would somehow protect me through sex, that loosened my tongue. I sensed that he was shaken, he was trembling all over, he was overflowing with love and tenderness at the time, and understanding. I was sure that he'd tell me about his father and let me understand from whom that strange feeling of repentance had come, and he was on the point of opening his mouth, but he didn't.

I'm sure that he fell into the trap of the male stereotypes that are typical of Russians. Like all of them, he subconsciously drove the slightest idea of my potential superiority out of his mind. Over there, they say, "He fucked her," while the expression "She fucked him" seems unnatural to them. The woman is always pictured in a subordinate, not to say enslaved and humiliated position beneath the all-powerful stallion. Subconsciously, and perhaps even consciously, he thinks that if he enters me from the triumphant position, as though into a prostitute or a concubine, then I really am a prostitute or a concubine.

Am I right, or am I always finding fault with him? Isn't it true that I myself want to feel like a prostitute sometimes? Doesn't he read to me from Guido Guinizelli, and don't I realize, in spite of his ironic tone, that he's ready to die for these "arrows of love"?

Well, all right, but how do you explain his venomous remarks that became the constant refrain of the last month of our relationship? He hated every sign of my protection of him, while for me there was nothing more natural than helping the man I'm in love with. Of course I made a few faux pas, especially with that awful party in Malibu, but what mistake did I make with Pinkerton or with the BRF? He seemed to derive some sadistic pleasure from provoking me and my old friends, mocking all our ideals, our struggle with our domestic right wing, with the plague of capitalistic corporate society. That's what these Russian liberals are like. We consider them people who stand up with us for democratic values, but they in their anti-Communist fury think that we're playing into the hands of the CPSU and the KGB. For Alex, our whole movement, our sixties—it's all just the pranks of the spoiled children of rich society. As he used to ask with his permanent condescending smile: "I wonder, do you understand that Trotskyism and Stalinism were just factions of the same fucking Communism—let's call it Red Fascism so that it'll be clearer to you—with different window dressing."

I understood what he was getting at. He just didn't say it aloud—that I and my friends from Berkeley in '68 were closer to fascism than the spooks and the stool pigeons of the CIA. Oh, no, Mr. Korbach-from-abroad, I'll never sell out my youth, not even for all the nights of our love together! Perhaps I'm not understanding something essential, but you're missing one very simple thing: it wasn't for your Russian business that we were fighting, whether it was Trotskyism or Stalinism or any damned thing you like! Whatever it may have been called at the time, we were fighting for our right to confrontation, for a way of life that was an alternative to the hackneyed American dream, with its dollars, bonds, mortgages, Cadillacs, and suburban comfort. I spit on you, my chosen little Sasha! You didn't value our closeness, and all the while it was getting watered down with smirks, smiles, looks askance, and fits of badly concealed, vulgar jealousy. If you ask me a dozen years from now when we're old and worn out why I ran away from you to Iraq without saying a word, I'll only tell you this: I wanted to save that *dolce stil nuovo* that descended on us from the autumn skies of Maryland in November of 1983.

Meanwhile, she'd hit forty—that is, she'd "changed another tenner," as the Russians say. Her Russian, incidentally, had been getting steadily better, thanks to almost systematic study of that idiotic language. In addition, after Iraq the Lilienmann team had shifted to Israel, where the majority of the workers on the excavations in Caesarea turned out to be Russians.

Almost two years had gone by since she had left Pinkerton. She was as beautiful as always. More beautiful than ever. Archaeology, dear readers, helps aging girls to turn back the clock. And no special effort is required. Just work in a trench day after day, scramble up hillsides in the desert or on the seacoast, let your hair fade in the fierce sun, wet your skin with the water of ancient springs, spend the nights in tents with the flaps up—that is, in a constantly blowing breeze— change your partners without regard to their intellectual level: that's the formula for staying young.

You won't have time to think this formula through before we tell you that an archaeological expedition is no picnic. At times Nora grew tired of wandering around in the footsteps of the ancient patriarchs, from tents and decrepit old dwellings, where a dodgy shower was like a gift from God. Then she took off for a short while for the parallel universe of five-star hotels, swimming pools, and cool, dim bars. Cursing herself for her incurable bourgeois tendencies, she would go shopping in the hotel galleries with their prices aimed at "piggies" and after lunch would appear looking now like a Saint Laurent lady, now like a Sonia Rykiel bohemian.

Tel Aviv, Athens, Corfu, Venice—there she is, entering some soporific, elegant hall. A slight earth tremor sends a ringing down crystal glasses. The aging populations of these cities look agape at the lone impeccable beauty walking along passages like a ghost from "those years of ours." She takes a table in the corner, orders a bottle of champagne. The maître d'hôtel, agitated and serious, stands alongside asking questions about the menu. He has already seen the name embossed on her credit card and knows who she is. Maîtres d'hôtel of the Mediterranean follow the society columns and know about the lives of the Korbachs and the Mansours.

She would say that she was staying in these hotels only to cheer herself up with the help of any vulgar adventure with some twat-chasing playboy, of the sort who go digging in these places in search of high-class whores. Alas, where are they, these sexual conquistadores devastating everything in their path? Not a single one piqued her imagination. After some champagne, she would admit to herself that she was only looking for "Sashka," though the chance of meeting him in these places was about equal to that of a meteorite hitting this very restaurant.

Out in the field, it had often seemed to her that she was over Sashka. After screwing some curly-headed kid in a tent, she would mutter: "Let your whole *dolce stil nuovo* vanish into thin air! I can cope with it! I don't need you!" In some strange way, any return to civilization summoned up a long series of memories of their meetings and partings with glass walls around them. She would see the terminal of an airport, deserted because it was nighttime, with a lone figure winding his way toward her past closed stands and souvenir kiosks. He still doesn't see her, but they're approaching each other in an endless, slightly curving corridor of what he called "our comfortable Purgatory." He hears the tapping of her heels and raises his head with a vigor unexpected in a body dragging itself along in baggy trousers. His forehead in its full sweep reminds her of a Boeing 747 head-on. At the sight of the figure running toward him, the lower section of the cockpit opens into a one-of-a-kind simian smile. What a face!

She would often dial the number of his lair on Dupont Circle. She knew nothing about how incredibly busy he had become after her departure, and his constant absences, announced by a hurried, ungrammatical recorded message, drove her to distraction. That louse, where has he gone? And with whom? Maybe it's one of those shameless Pinkerton bimbos? Or maybe he's joined the Dupont Circle "fag division"? She was stunned and saddened by a simple fact: he'd never once tried to find her in two years of separation! As the saying goes: "Out of sight, out of mind"? That goddamned bit of clichéd wisdom turns out to be true.

In the course of her infrequent but lengthy conversations with her father, she didn't mention Alex even once. Sensing this deliberate determination, Stanley didn't mention his name either. Only very recently, that is, as Nora's return to the territory of the novel was already approaching, he mentioned in passing that Alex had been chosen as one of the vice presidents of the Korbach Fund, and that perhaps in the near future they would be going to his "magnificently crumbling motherland" together. Then again, he'd immediately bitten his tongue, having encountered her stony silence. He was suddenly saddened by the circumstance that Alex and Nora were not about to give him the gift of a little "twofold Korbach."

One day at her hotel in Cyprus, a sharp feeling of proximity to Alex shot through her. He was somewhere right nearby, no doubt about it! She rushed to a phone booth and dialed the Washington number. If he picked up, she wouldn't say a word to him, but at least that way she'd know that her intuition had led her astray this time. The recording came on again, but then a terrible thought flashed through her mind: While she was sticking her finger in the dial of a Cypriot telephone, Alex had walked past the booth and vanished into thin air! She threw open the door and jumped out. A middle-aged man wearing shorts and a Panama hat leapt to one side, as though he'd been trying to listen in on her conversation. He couldn't take his amazed eyes off her. What happened? Maybe he was some friend of Sasha? Or maybe this guy remembered her picture from the papers two years ago? Her own reflection flickered before her eyes. She was struck by her curious pallor, and even more by a strange violet light in her eyes.

No question about it, he was around here somewhere. Perhaps he'd been sitting in the bar with this one in the Panama and had spotted her on the beach. Maybe he'd said to this friend: See that woman? I loved her once. Or maybe something in greater detail, the way men love to talk in bars, with meaningful smiles and smirks like characters out of Hemingway.

She sat down at a table in the bar and ordered a martini. Why not just ask the reception desk whether or not there's an Alex Korbach here? Not a chance—I'll never lower myself to searching. I'm only sitting here because it's nice to sit around with a martini after a month in filthy caves. Of course we might run into each other, but it'll only be by chance. Sit here, wait for a coincidence, order another martini.

The guy in the shorts took off his hat, stuck it under his belt, and sat down at the bar itself. He was drinking tea. What a loser—drinking tea in a bar! He was glancing at her out of the corner of his eye from time to time. Do I ever know these phony paternal looks! But why do I get the feeling that if this guy is here, then Sasha must be somewhere nearby?

"*Excusez-moi, vous êtes* very lonely I see tonight?" a voice that was at once insolent and cowardly said behind her. She turned to see a tall, ungainly type in a shiny silk suit. "*Poshol na khuy!*" she replied politely. The shiny suit moved away in horror. The shorts at the bar nodded approvingly. Through the revolving glass door she glimpsed Jacob Palsadski, who had just pulled up in his Jeep to take her to an archaeologists' party in Paphos. She stood up and walked out of the hotel. Outwardly without hesitating, inwardly, if one can put it this way—and why not, the tea fancier shrugged—in a pose of classic desperation.

Finally, she got through. One day, almost as though it were a ritual, she dialed his number with her little finger and suddenly heard a smoky voice: "Hello?" It was ten o'clock in the morning in Jaffa, which meant that it was 3:00 A.M. in Washington.

Alex was in bed. He hadn't been able to get a wink of sleep. There wasn't any hope of it. The endless flying had muddled the hands of his internal clock irreparably. He'd be unable to close his eyes all night and then fall asleep just before a workshop at the Black Cube. At that moment he was indulging in his not entirely healthy habits: pulling on a bottle of Jack Daniel's, smoking black cigarillos, and thinking about whom to invite to L.A. for the screen test, Beverley or Kimberley. Maybe both? Roxy Moran had just left, which meant that she was already invited. An all-pissed-out fifty-year-old asshole. It's ridiculous to start all over again at that age, even if you are backed by Stanley Korbach and his billions. Sprawled out among the pillows and blankets, he couldn't move his hands or his fingers. Nevertheless one wandering finger from the group on the left began poking the remote from the TV. The VCR started to display its offering of what it had recorded in its owner's absence. Well, a talk show, of course—a group of sadists meets a group of masochists, laughter all around, the exchange of innocent jokes.

At that very moment the telephone rang, the damned toad. He turned off the TV and picked up the receiver with the gesture of a well-sated man taking one more shish kebab. Hello. Silence. Well, here we go again. Of course he had long since given up waiting for Nora to call. "Listen," said the voice, which at first he couldn't even place. "I'll be in Paris in a week." Recognizing her voice now, he refused to believe it. "I'm staying at the Lutèce, on the corner of the Boulevard Raspail and the Rue de Sèvres." And again, he didn't even understand at first that she was setting up a rendezvous with him. "So, come if you can." After a pause: "And if you want to." She hung up.

And fell to the carpet, wrapping all ten fingers around her own throat and howling with shame at such a kitsch performance.

Alexander Zakharovich meanwhile was surprised to find himself not in bed but by the windowsill. A measured wail came from the telephone receiver, which a few lines back we inappropriately compared to a shish kebab. It was April, if you've no objections. The night modestly bloomed in purple alongside the ingeniously curved illuminations of words. Priapus Videos was still—or already—open. One could see a dense crowd of devils with neat horns, elegant hooves, and spring tails getting cassettes for home use. "I'm flying!" A.Z. suddenly roared like a love-struck schoolboy. "To her! To the Lutèce!"

12

INTERSECTION, PARIS

*N*ineteen ninety. End of April. Summer heat. *Crépuscule*. Early sunsets. Telegraphic style. And something is waiting around the corner.

Nora was sitting alone on the terrace of the Brasserie Lutèce. A tea service and a piece of *tarte aux pommes* had been set before her. No alcohol—it could spoil the image of a dazzling beauty sitting alone at a Paris café table. A thin wisp of smoke winds over the ashtray. A cigarette doesn't spoil the look of a beautiful woman. On the contrary, it accentuates something in it. A camera lying beside the pastry on the table adds a particular note to the scene, all the more since from time to time the dazzling woman raises the device and clicks it once or twice without changing her position. Just what could be the object of her interest? Nothing in particular, just an ordinary Left Bank intersection with its boutique display windows, a couple of traffic lights, a typical Parisian *poteau d'affiches* with a sharply sloping top in the Belle Epoque style, its contours augmenting the broad face of Gérard Depardieu, and of course with tables, chairs, and umbrellas on every corner.

She was relishing every moment that she sat there. Over the last few years she had been catching in herself an inclination for certain clichés. This is my favorite cliché—a Paris café. I'll leave Amman and Baghdad to the snobs. I prefer Paris.

Nothing in particular was happening in the intersection. The rush-hour wave had subsided, the rhythm of the street had slowed. Then again, the girls in their clingy slip-dresses were still walking briskly, their big, white running shoes flashing. As for the middle-aged men, they were already undoing the top buttons of their shirts, pulling their ties down, unhurriedly moving in the direction of their cafés, stumbling for a moment at the sight of these girls attired in what still quite recently would have been considered undergarments and enticements to intimate occasions.

Nora raised her Nikon and snapped a picture of two sixty-something men, elegant and slovenly, who were crossing the street and heading for the Lutèce, and who were completely engrossed in their friendly banter. They looked like people from Paris literary circles. One might be the senior editor at some old publishing house, whose pen might have journeyed over manuscripts from Sartre and Camus. What publishers were located in this neighborhood—Gallimard, Fayard? The second, of course, was a writer; his novels had won him a solid reputation, in large part thanks to the former's amicable editing. They love each other and have never betrayed one another. And they never shall, as long as they're alive and having drinks together once a week at the Lutèce.

All at once a feeling of being in sympathy with these two came over Nora. They belong to those who prop up the world, a group to which I belong. Every moment of their lives, already on the downslope, does its bit for the upkeep of a phenomenon known as Western civilization: books, clothes, art exhibitions, self-indulgence, dissoluteness, vitamins, tranquilizers, long-standing habits, including this friendly banter on the way to the café. They're already too old for these girls in their slip-dresses and white sneakers—and maybe they're just the right age for them. Either way, they're no longer paying attention to anyone except the beauty all by herself on the veranda.

The pair took notice of Nora and exchanged significant glances, as if to say to each other: You see, she's still here, this woman, the heroine of our literature, she's still of this world! Then they opened the door, and from the café flew the main theme of the first movement of Grieg's Concerto in A minor. Just what the doctor ordered.

Nora was waiting for a man here. For the first time in her life she had come to a rendezvous before her partner. Those of you guys who are thinking that she was waiting for Sasha Korbach are mistaken. She'd come to Paris this time to see another individual of the male gender, her son, Bobby. He was turning eighteen this year; he'd finished his boarding school in Switzerland and was beginning to think about a new phase in his life.

Bobby had spent the Easter holiday with his grandmother, Rita O'Neill, in L.A., and now he was on the way back to school. Sitting in the café, Nora was daydreaming about how her six-foot-something son would emerge from the crowd and how she would snap him with her camera. Instead of Bobby, another one of the guys in her household spread throughout the world appeared on the other side of the street. This time you've guessed right—it was our indefatigable Alexander Zakharovich. He got out of a taxi just opposite Nora's observation post, and she immediately admitted to herself that it was him she'd been waiting for here, not Bobby.

When he had clambered out of the cab, Alexander Zakharovich (she always said his full name with a certain sardonic tone of voice) froze, as if bewitched by the lights and shadows of Paris, its smells and sounds. Or maybe he was enchanted by a young, nubile creature in a black, skintight slip-dress and white running shoes, who rapidly strode past and threw a feigned haughty glance at him over her shoulder? Nora caught her breath.

Well, here I am, Sasha Korbach thought at that moment. Eternal Paris is all around. Who said it was eternal? Beg your pardon, it certainly wasn't me. I always stay clear of clichés like that. It's a different level of refinement, you understand. Mind you, I love it. I love this Paris that's forever slipping away. I can't picture the world without Paris. This eternal Earth without this eternal Paris. Everlasting planet, everlasting city, everlasting intersection, everlasting *poteau d'affiches* with its everlasting actor's mug, everlasting young girl forever ready for anything, two everlasting literary old-timers nibbling on their *fruits de mer* on the other side of the window, everlasting woman on her own in a corner of an outdoor terrace, a beautiful piece of work with a rich past, and right alongside an everlasting Paris kiss to fill out a hideous couple—but look out, a clatter of iron hooves, the deadly metal appears from around the corner, a mortal metal, an imperial centaur with steel *facesta* shoved up its backside; isn't sculpture getting ready to destroy this everlasting world, to carnivorously fuse flesh and metal, why does it drag itself down the side streets, this embodiment of mortality? Alas, not even Paris is eternal, was the profound conclusion reached by A.Z. at that moment. Put that thought out of your mind and take inspiration from the fact that there is something eternal here, that is, something that's forever slipping away, at this moment. He picked up his shoulder bag from the pavement and walked toward the Lutèce.

She saw him approaching, and it seemed to her that he could walk right by without recognizing her. She noticed something new in his face, a sort of self-conscious squint. The people at the next table looked in surprise at the independent woman in the baggy, stylish clothes: why was her teapot knocking so hard against her camera? She raised the camera and turned on the motor drive: Alex Korbach comes up with his quasi-lunatic expression, stops, drawn by the clicking of the shutter, puts on his glasses—he's got spectacles on his nose, unbelievable!—finally, he recognizes the photographer.

"Excuse me, sir," she said, "can I count on your company for this evening?"

"I'm all yours, lock, stock, and barrel—giblets and all, that is," he answered, in the proper tone. He was a director, after all, and knew better than anyone else how to avoid bittersweet kitsch. He sat down next to her; neither of them said anything for five minutes, looking at each other intently, as if studying every wrinkle on each other's forehead and around the eyes. Then, embarrassed, he extended a hand and pushed a lock of hair aside to uncover the birthmark on her temple. Finding it, he smiled, and she remembered how he had joked that this was a sign of the Brahman caste that had just got a bit lost in this fairy-tale country. In reply, with a movement of her fingers like the lightning thrust of a fencer, she undid a button of his shirt and saw the mast of the little ship on his chest. That tattoo had been done thirty years before in the barracks of an artillery brigade where Sasha and his classmates were receiving their course of military instruction or, more accurately, their monthlong courses in human degradation. Nora had said more than once that the boat had taken him too far.

Soon after this exchange in the café, Bobby Korbach, a lanky young "Anglo," having nothing in common with the "rap-style" of his generation, appeared—just another preppy aristocrat. "Imagine, Bobby, I was waiting for you, and out of nowhere my friend Alex pops up like a jack-in-the-box," Nora said with *mauvaise foi.* Bobby looked at Alex with cool reserve. "How do you do, Mr. Alex!" A.Z. shook the strapping tennis player's hand. It's funny, he thought—this lad could be considered a Jew as well, even though by my calculations there's only seven-thirty-seconds of our noble genes in him, and his features have nothing to do with the Warsaw furrier.

"How do you like Rita?" Nora asked. The boy laughed. "Couldn't be better. Getting younger, as always. She says: 'Unfortunately I missed one important moment in my life and so I got old. Since then, though, I'm always on my toes, and I never miss a chance to get younger.' You know, Mom, she almost persuaded me to go into the movie business."

"What does that mean, for God's sake?" Nora asked in alarm.

"Well, for a start I might take a one-year course at the USC film school."

"You're not serious, I hope, Robert?" Nora turned to Alex. "Just last December my son applied to Bennington. He was going to study political journalism and classical philosophy. It was his own choice!" Now she turned to her son. "Mr. Alex, as you call him, has certain connections with the movies. No one can explain to you better than he can that the film business is a vanity fair."

Bobby gave one of his thin smiles. "I realize, Mom, that Mr. Alex Korbach isn't just one more clown at that fair, particularly in connection with his super-project that there's so much talk about these days." Nora turned back to Alex in near shock. Her eyes have started to bulge a bit, he thought. And the skin at the corners of her jaw is drooping ever so slightly. But my God, how beautiful she is, my darling!

"What project of yours is there so much talk about these days, my friend?" With the palm of his hand, Alex made a silent gesture in Bobby's direction: Ask him, he seemed to say.

"Radiance," Bobby said modestly. He was clearly proud to show off his access to Hollywood inside information. Alex grinned. "I like your word *clown*, Bobby. I really am a clown by nature. I'm no political journalist or classical philosopher, that's for sure. The cynical and vainglorious crowd—that's my world. I've got no choice. But what about you, young man? Are you sure you love the sideshow tent, too? It's too bad I can't give you a try on the stage with my old Moscow troupe."

"You mean the *Shuty,* sir?" Bobby took pleasure in saying the group's Russian name. Nora brought her hand down on the table. "What's going on? How do you know so much about Alex?" "He's all Rita talks about," Bobby said and winked at his mother's friend. He's got quite a friendly wink, Alex thought. It's not likely he gets it from his papa.

"God in heaven!" Nora exclaimed. "If Rita's little club is talking about you, then that means you've become a real star in my absence!" "In your absence where, Mom?" Bobby asked innocently. And all three burst into uproarious laughter, after which all ambiguity disappeared and fairly natural connections were established in this small company: the eternally beautiful and still young mama, her grown son, and her former lover. Former? Well, it doesn't matter either way— the important thing is that he's stayed a real friend, which means her son isn't a stranger to him.

Those readers who have even a passing familiarity with the other *romans* of the present author might be justified in supposing that after the burst of friendly laughter the trio went off to dinner, and at the Coupole, of course. However small the circle of these readers might be, we'll say that they're right, and that our respect for them is measured in inverse proportion to their numbers. It's a sure thing that they will now take off on the heels of our threesome for the temple of Montparnassian gobbling. We in our turn will not follow in the footsteps of the highly respected maître François Rabelais and pepper the readers with superlative nouns and adjectives like "drunks, assholes, gluttons, shitty bags of grease or greasy bags of shit"; we suppose that we'll maintain a sterotypically polite tone, though even we would insist that they not keep company with our heroes, or that they not display any *amis-comme-cochons* behavior. Even the author, as the respected readers have seen, pretends that he doesn't know this trio, even though he's sitting right next to them, all ears. It's not impossible that Sasha Korbach recognized the author—in any case he shot him a sidelong glance and a crooked smile that seemed to say: What's it all for, these constant attempts to listen in on other people's conversations? Do you mean that spying really is second nature to those of your profession, shameless novelists?

As for our beautiful lady, she took no notice of anyone else around her and simply savored the unexpected simultaneous meeting with the two dearest people in the world to her, and only occasionally felt inexplicable pangs of anguish. For his part, Bobby Korbach, feeling no pangs of sadness, was happy, as a genuine young man of all times and all people, to sit in a famous restaurant on an equal footing with his mom and her boyfriend, about whom he'd heard so much from various sources. Chatting casually, he did his best to impersonate the leading lights of his grandmother's inner circle. "Look, Nora!" Alex said with excitement. "Your boy isn't without acting talent! You ought to rethink his future!"

Nora made a show of irritation. "Do you really want to corrupt my 'stern youth'?" In her turn she told funny stories about her recent archaeological dig, also taking the parts of the characters, particularly when Professor Lilienmann, the "whale of fieldwork," came into it. At the beginning of each period out in the field, he would stop shaving and getting his hair cut. The deeper the expedition got into the layers of the cultures, the richer the deposits of artifacts got, the more ancient and majestic Lilienmann became. Like a biblical prophet in a soiled tunic, he would sit on a hilltop, tossing out one, then another phrase in Latin, Hebrew, or what he considered Sumerian, depending on where they were working. The most remarkable metamorphosis, though, took place in him when the "field" was finished. Painstakingly shaved, with a crew cut, wearing a well-tailored suit, he would appear in the scientific crowd at a conference and get terribly irritated and distressed when his coworkers didn't recognize him.

Sasha Korbach was not to be outdone. He began to recount his dealings with the professionals at Putney. One time, they had brought a whole crowd of fencing experts. They were flabbergasted when he told them that there wouldn't be any fencing in the film. A film about the thirteenth century with no steel in the hand, no rivers of blood? A session of the board of directors was called to discuss these contradictions. There, he told them that the closest thing to the traditional Hollywood idea of swordplay would be a group of Guelphs bumping into a group of Ghibellines in a narrow side street. After exchanging curses, both parties would go for the hilts of their swords. The battle would not occur, or else it would take place offscreen, yet the sequence would be more dramatic than your barrelfuls of cranberry juice, ladies and gentlemen. After that, one of the producers handed in his resignation. He refused to work on this "deliberately depressing, rotten, pretentious, and decadent example of so-called high art." You see, then, Bobby, even with all the money and influence of your grandfather, it's not likely that Putney will ever make "Radiance."

At that moment Nora noticed that her son was sitting stock-still, his mouth wide open. It seemed as though he had wanted ask a question but had become frightened at his own impudence. The next instant, Alex staggered the boy completely. "Listen, Bobby, do you think you could find a few hours to read through this and make some comments about it?" "Alex!" Bobby exclaimed in a whisper. "You mean your screenplay, don't you?" Alex unzipped his bag and drew out the weighty screenplay with the Putney Productions seal on the cover. Disbelieving, Bobby muttered: "And you're giving me this to read through, right?" "Well, of course—I've got two copies with me."

Nora realized that the copy Bobby was now holding in his hands had been intended for her. Now Bobby had received it. *The maître wants to know what the tastes of the young generation are. Poor Sasha, don't you understand that Bobby Korbach isn't representative of the broad masses of moviegoers? Well, let them exchange views. They obviously want to pal around together.* For the second time that evening, the motif of the Grieg concerto floated over her head. She looked around and noticed that at least a dozen people were observing her with a sad sympathy in their eyes. A sweet and aching melancholy seemed to take the place of the smells of haute cuisine in this gastronomic palace. The two men at her table appeared to have forgotten about her presence. Now they were engrossed in a conversation about the nature of the Renaissance. *What was it: the rebirth of a great tradition, of classical art and literature after a nearly inexplicable millennium of degeneration, or a new triumph of flesh over the spirit of timidity, of original sin over the original purity of the heavens? And if the latter is true, then what relation does Dante bear to the Renaissance?*

Bastards—they don't even think that a woman also has something to say about this subject, if only about the archaeological background of the Renaissance. Right now I'm going to choose one of the men who has been making eyes at me and I'll flirt with him. She glanced around and was disappointed: no one at dinner was paying any attention to her, everyone was engaged in the gently measured chewing of their food.

Everyone knows that the French make a holy rite out of their meals. What sort of conception of the Renaissance is at work here in this huge Belle Epoque hall? If restaurants are a sort of church for them, then this must be a cathedral. Which means that one can look on the graceful, beetle-browed maître d'hôtel who walks along the aisle as a bishop. It looks as though he's about to make some important announcement, to summon the clientele to some even more reverent state of bliss.

"Attention, mesdames et messieurs!" The beetle-browed type raised his hands in the manner of an ecclesiastical ringmaster. "First of all allow me to say that I am overjoyed to have the privilege of thanking you on behalf of the management and all of our staff, including our two culinary wizards, Monsieur Pussant and Madame Faton. Immeasurably esteemed guests, we are entirely aware that from time to time our historic institution serves as the setting for one novel or another,

often written in foreign languages. That, incidentally, is what is happening now, dear guests. We know that present among our regular customers are people who do not have any particular estimation for food prepared with inspiration, for all of the art and cult of La Coupole sur Montparnasse, being concerned instead with conversations about the contradictions of the Renaissance. We are also in a position to suppose that present among the ladies today is one whose laughter is something less than a manifestation of absolute delight, and whose eyes are filled behind their irises with sadness.

"Dear friends, I hope that I will meet with general approval if I say to these unexpected guests, so skillfully discovered by our own secret service: Welcome! In keeping with our world-renowned tradition, we say to them: Foreigners, you are no burden to us! We are certain that sooner or later you will enter the secrets of our temple. And in order to show our hospitality, we are taking a collection today. Each is invited to do his or her part! *Allez-y!*"

The small but well-honed orchestra began to play a medley of timeless favorites, such as "The Shadow of Your Smile," "Dream a Little Dream," and "Over and Over," which brought Nora to the point of sobbing. Two small Annamites rolled in an enormous, heavily gilded collection plate. They slowly made their way down the central aisle, making forays into the side streets among the tables as well. There was not a single parishioner who would have tried to get out of making a donation. A few of the ladies even stood up with a sudden jerk, while the gentlemen fully maintained their dignity. Some did it with half-ironic smiles, others with tears in their eyes. Some put a small vase of Persian caviar on the plate, while others offered a simple gherkin. Imagine the price range—just imagine! The first stratum of offerings quickly covered the gilded plate and continued to grow, turning into a veritable fragrant pyramid.

There was no shortage of dishes that had already been dug into by others: strips of salmon and fillet of sole, little mounds of mashed potatoes in mushroom sauce, tiny skeletons of marinated herring, anchovies that looked like little worms, the remains of oxtail soup, lobster claws and tails, *homard* and *langouste* alike, silvery oysters looking like something that had been blown into a handkerchief, sand dunes of cauliflower with umbrella-shaped broccoli, one personage who somehow escaped definition—is it animal or vegetable? (in fact it was a sea urchin)—and its closest relatives in the gastronomic caves of Paris; we mean, of course, lemons sliced in half, horned snails, seaweed that reminded one of mermaids' hair; and also the big contributors to the overall olfactory bouquet, cheeses of various types, and the remains of our carnivorous delights, calves' kidneys, lamb vertebrae, scraps of filet mignon pretending to be not a part of anyone's flesh but simply a delicious dish in the abstract sense; fowl, too, no small number of birds, in pieces like turkeys and pheasants, or in whole creatures, like crunchy chicks, or quail, some of them having already lost a leg or two in the course of the feasting interrupted by the charitable ceremony.

It would be dishonest not to mention here those who were already finishing off their dinners, and who therefore could offer elements of their dessert, mostly disfigured by teeth and tongues—all sorts of *tartes aux pommes, crème caramels,* currant sherbets, mille-feuille cakes, and so on. It would have been impossible to judge the value of a contribution in the given circumstances according to the degree to which it was untouched. Far more important was the impulse. We saw a literary mademoiselle in a wig whose Soviet-made dentures had gotten stuck in a slice of Jordanian halvah. She nonetheless yanked the whole gear out of her mouth and planted it on the summit of the pyramid, which earned applause.

Horrified, Nora watched the pyramid grow. Sooner or later the circle would be completed, and the sacrificial plate would come in the direction of the person for whom it was intended, her. Her patience finally snapped, and she rushed at the beetle-browed master of ceremonies. "What's the meaning of all this kitsch?" she shrieked, her voice rising hysterically in a tone she had never noticed in herself before but whose existence in her inner depths she had guessed at.

"You know, madam," the gleaming monster answered with a bow.

"You're proposing that my love come to an end here in this hideous way?"

"Your words, madam." The whole restaurant, several hundred diners, burst into applause. The gargantuan heap of leftovers was getting closer, seemingly opening its aromatic embrace to Nora. Worthy of surprise is the speed with which the heap began to go off, spreading a suffocating stench of decay. All right, that'll be enough from you, the author—you've wasted enough paper on all this crap!

They finished their meal and after coffee left the Coupole in a fine, friendly mood. At the corner of the Boulevard Raspail, Alex showed Bobby a small example of his Buffoon professionalism. A mime was at work there, falling into step with citizens and imitating their movements: hailing taxis, reading newspapers, kissing girls, eating a hotdog with the inevitable spurt of ketchup. Alex slipped in unnoticed behind the mime himself and began to imitate his imitations. Bobby laughed like a madman. Well, they're friends now, Nora thought, looking at them and trying to wipe the appearance of a maternal smile off her face.

"Come to see me tomorrow at four," she whispered to Alex.

"Why so late?" he whispered in reply, showing definite impatience. "At four," she repeated, and they went their separate ways.

He headed for the Place Saint-Sulpice, where some time ago he had noticed in the shadow of the large church a little hotel that for some reason seemed to him the very embodiment of literary Parisianness. I hope they'll have a room for me, he thought, and crossed himself in the Catholic manner. It helped. At the very moment he entered the small lobby, with its winding staircase and a statue of a shy nymph, the desk clerk was on the phone with one of the guests. The man was letting him know that he would be detained for a couple of days by the police and so was canceling his reservation.

A.Z. went into the tiny room with a window looking out on an imposing fountain decorated with marble statues. The streaming water created an impression of a bygone time. He sat down on the bed and began to look at the stern bishops, powerful lions, and rather lewd sea creatures. All three groups constituted in themselves a challenge to the inhuman laws of materialism. At the same time a certain humility wafted from the composition as a whole: what was, it said, is past.

She wanted to save our love, and she's done it. Saved love has departed, into the past. Irretrievably. It's preserved somewhere outside of our time. For Dante, Beatrice was a messenger from heaven. Blok would tremble in the shadow of a high column as the image of the *prekrasnaya dama* descended to him from the cupola of a church. Both of them were young at the time of their mystical adventures, their souls as yet uncorrupted. Unlike the greats, Nora and I met when we were already a sad pair of profligates. We hungered for a great love, but we couldn't imagine it without screwing, without mad coupling, so that our great love was doomed until she saved it. Irretrievably. These thoughts kept on coming endlessly into his mind until he fell asleep in the Parisian hotel, in the room a soccer hooligan from Liverpool had so ineptly reserved for himself.

The next day at 4:00 P.M. he knocked at the door of Room 609 at the Hôtel Lutèce. The door opened, and on the other side of the threshold he saw a youthful creature who was a stranger to him. Sorry, I must have made a mistake. The creature stretched her arms out to him. No, no, you haven't made a mistake, sir! Come in and do whatever comes into your head. Well of course it was she, in spite of the short, boyish hairdo. She was wearing a clingy black dress with two fine straps over her bare shoulders. Her chest was barely covered. Her hemline was practically at the level of her pubis. The only solid items in her ensemble were a pair of large white running shoes and white kneesocks.

Seized by an instantaneous, uncontrollable desire, he burst into the room, took Nora by the shoulders, covered her mouth with his, and laid her down across the wide bed. She wasn't wearing any panties, so his penis met with no obstacles to rapid and maximum penetration. Finding herself under him, whimpering and crying out, she continued to play the role of the streetwalker. "Would you like me to take my shoes off, sir?" she whispered when they had gone over to their well-loved knees-and-elbows figure of speech. "Don't you dare!" he growled in reply. The half-light of dissolution prevailed in the room.

I wonder how many people are getting off together in Paris at this moment, he thought, as inappropriately as ever. Just then he noticed that Nora was looking somewhere off to one side; following that direction led to a dark mirror. In the dim reflection he could make out a bald old profligate forcing himself on a pretty schoolgirl. He lightly bit her skin just above the shoulder blade. She gave a squeak of complaint, entirely in keeping with her character. She, too, had acting qualities. The fact is that everyone's acting qualities fade away in the course of their normal behavior. In every person lies sleeping a good actor, who, given the right circumstances, can be awakened—in this case, in the circumstances of a tirelessly pounding cock. There were, by the way, mouselike scents of cocaine winding all over the room.

At the next change of positions—Nora was on top this time—he started a new round of inappropriate reflections. What strange creatures we are! We're so strangely compact, we've got so many organs laid out so near one another. Why weren't we created in some less confused, some airier, more ethereal way? Why does it work out that the highest manifestation of love can't be obtained without sticking a certain shoot (sounds like the Russian word for *buffoon,* doesn't it?) into a certain elongated cavity? Why can't it happen in some less animal way—by, let's say, bringing some surfaces together, by breathing from one mouth into the other? We are a combination of processes that are strange to look at. Everything we eat, even the tastiest dishes, turns into shit that comes out of us from an opening very close to the organ of love. What is that if not a consequence of original sin? Perhaps the original concept was something else, but then it strayed from the path for a while? And we, poor creatures, turn out to be nothing other than the curious phantoms of this "while," which without us would not exist?

Strangely enough, the fundamental ideas roaming through his mind were not reflected in the least in his performance below the waist. After every ejaculation—and there had already been thirty of them in the course of his "deflowering of a schoolgirl"—his phallus immediately returned to its battle station. Let's be frank, he looked at the time and now with a vacant smile noticed that 370 minutes had already gone by, and no one could say how many such blessed minutes still lay ahead.

Finally the "schoolgirl" wrenched herself from his embrace and with a half-crazed expression on her face tried to save her exhausted, bleeding zone from the next round of merciless banging. It would have been difficult to make him, or someone else in him, any happier than by offering him the opportunity to chase the poor thing around the room and catch her in the doorway of the only possible refuge, the bathroom. She curled up on the floor in a corner and stretched out her hands entreatingly. Please, that's enough! Stop! I can't do it anymore! He sat down next to her, took her hands, and began to kiss them as passionately as if they had been the most sensitive parts of her body. Then, without encountering resistance, he parted her legs and entered her again.

The clock was ticking, he was watching the movement of the hands and thinking with dull satisfaction by what a wide margin he had broken his own record. I wouldn't be surprised if I've broken the record for the Lutèce. Must ask the desk clerk on the way out what their record is. They say in Ochichornia that there's a record holder who could hold out for over two hours on one screw. Even he is covered with shame now, and all his tourniquets and hypodermics of Papaverine. All the same, though, I ought to express some sympathy, show some compassion for my partner. According to Schopenhauer, compassion is the only thing that distinguishes us from the animals. He squeezed her hips and with a long howl finally injected his inner substance into her, without any remainder. The two bodies separated, and he immediately fell asleep.

When he awoke, he saw that Nora was sitting in an armchair, in her usual jeans and sweatshirt, a cigarette in one hand and a drink in the other. Nothing about her except the boyish hairdo reminded him of her recent turn as a schoolgirl slut.

"You don't love me anymore," she said sadly.

"Is that what you think?" He felt awkward at his own nudity. His organ looked like a forlorn little sparrow now, not like the triumphant eagle it had been at last sighting.

"It wasn't me you were doing it with," she said. "It was another woman, and you know who."

He went to the bathroom and came back with a towel wrapped round his waist.

"You know that there's no one closer to me in the world than you, Nora."

"I know."

Then she added: "But that's another matter."

He fell silent. Sadness sucked out of him what little he had left. Then he said: "Please, have pity on me, darling."

She whispered: "I have pity on you."

And she laid a hand on the bald crown of his head. "Poor buffoon. Tell me about your father."

He shuddered. "What can I tell you about a man whom I never laid eyes on?"

"You know what," she said.

He told her.

She gave a sigh of relief. "Thank God, that's almost exactly what I'd imagined. Do you remember what I told you after the shuttle flight, Sasha? It wasn't easy for me to reveal that hidden little drawer even to you. Then I expected you to reveal yours to me. I had the feeling that it was something connected with some sort of fatherhood. At first I thought that you considered yourself a traitor to Styopa and Lyova, and it was only later that it dawned on me that it went back to Zakhar Korbach. In every man, there's always living a little boy, and that boy wants to know his father. Someday Bobby will need an answer from me about who—" Alex cut her off: "Don't worry, he won't. Bobby knows perfectly well who his father is." Nora sensed that they were entering a zone of turbulence. "What are you talking about? How can he know something that even I, his mother, don't know? It's just that at the time, out there in that damned crazy life, I suddenly wanted a child, period." Alex put his lips to her hand. "You know, let's close this chapter of our soap opera. I realized a long time ago that your first husband, Danny the revolutionary, dropped in on you when he was on the run from the FBI on a charge of killing those two cops. He's Bobby's father."

The next five minutes passed in silence. Her hand reached out several times in the direction of the night table, obviously for a tranquilizer, but broke off the gesture. Several times she tried to throw back her long hair, then realized that it wasn't there anymore. Finally, she said: "How could Bobby know? I've never talked to him about it." Alex shrugged. "Barthelme could have visited his son at his Swiss boarding school." Nora's voice rose to a shriek: "He told you himself? Yesterday? While I was in the toilet?" He carefully took her hand in both of his. "Please, Nora, calm down. Bobby didn't say a word to me about his life. We were talking about the Renaissance." She jerked her hand away. "Then how do you know?" He saw before him her narrowed, almost hostile eyes. "How do you know about my dreams about my father, Nora? How did you come up with that chick-in-white-sneakers routine? It's hard for either one of us to keep a secret from the other." Then she said calmly: "Get dressed and leave me by myself. I'm falling asleep. Let's not see each other for a long time. Go wherever you need to be—Hollywood? Russia? Kiss me one last time and then disappear!"

He hadn't yet even left the room before she was asleep, having fallen into a dark pit without a ray of light. She awoke to a sensation of complete immobility. She couldn't move her arms or legs. Her son Bobby was sitting before her. He was looking intently at some point above and behind her head. In the unfamiliar mirror on the unfamiliar wall she saw his back in a checkered shirt, and then herself, sprawled out among the piping of the bed, and behind the bed a large metallic box with flickering red lights. Then she heard the excited voice of her son. "Monique, her pressure's coming up! Eighty over forty-five. It's still rising. Ninety-five over fifty-five. She's going to pull through!" The next instant, a feeling of boundless love for her only son gushed through Nora.

13

DECEMBER 1990, SVO

*W*e ought to remind our reader that we're still within the parameters of Part 9 of the novel, more precisely in the Korbach Galaxy, which has already made a night flight across the Atlantic and is presently penetrating deeper and deeper into the airspace of the European continent. Time, as everyone knows, is gobbled up a bit by astronomy in the course of this sort of movement, and a plane that takes off from New York at midnight arrives in Moscow in the evening, as though it has flown not ten hours, but seventeen.

Everyone was still sound asleep or dozing, except for General Piu and Colonel Square, who were tossing cards back and forth at each other, when the voice of Captain Ernie Rotterdam was heard from the cockpit. "Good morning, guys, or rather, good evening! We're approaching our destination. In an hour and a bit we'll be landing at SVO. Madame De Luxe [the way the Americans say it, it almost sounds like "lox"], the crew would like to remind you that there's an excellent coffee machine at your disposal."

After the higher retired ranks, which, as we have seen, were already up and about, Master Sergeant Ben Duckworth (USA, ret.) arose, immediately ready for any vagary of fate, up to and including the Siberian salt mines that he'd heard so much about when he was a young soldier in boot camp.

The stewardess of the aircraft, and in a certain sense the proprietress, the incomparable Bernadetta, was stretching her every extremity as well. "Damn," she said in a voice that was now hoarse from sleep but that would be transformed into a highly effective contralto by the middle of the day, and that by night sometimes rang out in the coloratura range. "Damn, I hope I get to take my minks for a walk in Moscow!" In New York she was a constant target of one of the groups of defenders of animal rights. Outside Korbach Center, where Stanley and his *prekrasnaya dama* had a modest penthouse with a mere three hundred square meters (to get it in square feet, you need to multiply the figure by eleven) of floor space, there was nearly always a patrol from the group standing watch. No sooner would our *p.d.* emerge from the lobby in one of her thirty-three fur coats than the activists would rush at her with their placards reading: STOP THE MURDERS! HANDS OFF FUR-BEARING ANIMALS! YOU'RE DRIPPING BLOOD! and with shouts even more scathing than their written slogans. From time to time, some youngster—let's give noble impulses their due—would run along just behind her and spray the marks left by her feet with indelible red dye.

At that point, Bernadetta, opening up her fur coat and planting her hands on her hips—that is, offering to the city what, as she put it, now belonged only to Stanley—began to mouth off in her onetime style as a building manager on the Pacific coast: "What sort of morons are you? What've you got on your feet, you bastards? Leather! What ran in that skin before it got turned into your shoes? Go fuck yourselves! You—you're carrying a leather handbag, and what did that used to be? Piss off! And you—what'd you have for breakfast this morning—bacon, sausages, chicken? Take my fur coat, tear it up, you barbarians, motherfuckers! Go on, eat my coat—ha!" In short, New York. In Moscow, she hoped nothing like that would happen.

The whole expedition team was gathering around an oval table for breakfast now. They greeted one another in the manner that was new but already well-enshrined in the president's inner circle—instead of "How are you doing today?" they would say, "How are you dying today?" with an eye to the philosophical aspect of human existence as a ceaseless process of dying. One was supposed to say laughingly in reply: "I'm dying fine!"

When their descent began, Sasha Korbach took a seat by a window and tried to detach himself from the merriment of the "dying" group. He was trying to catch a glimpse of a motherland opening to him for the first time in eight and a half years.

Ernie Rotterdam was doing a first-class job of guiding the craft through the mile-high layer of cloud covering the land of the Soviets. Visibility was zero, and twilight was approaching. Obviously we're going to land in total darkness, Sasha decided to himself, and at that moment, through the long, disheveled strips of felt, a land with the large, dust brown and white pelts of the Russian landscape came into view. The bowl rocked, here and there the lights of little villages flickered, then the imposing Muscovite skyline began to appear on the horizon.

Sasha Korbach nestled up against the window: the skyline, towering development as far as the eye could see, an agglomeration of kitchens, garbage chutes, all sorts of window shades, chairs with shaky legs, Sever brand refrigerators and

Rubin televisions, chopped and marinated eggplant and pickled pigs' feet, house slippers, unkempt cats, bottles with wet stoppers, torn-off little tinfoil hats, bits of Viola cheese fattening up the new nationalism, concerts of light music, all sorts of dumb scenes of kitchen discussion, a warning finger pointed at the ceiling, strumming of guitars, chords, "From Suomi to China," "The Motherland Holy Everywhere," telephones with vandalized, missing receivers at the entrances to buildings, elevators in which your chances of crashing down were almost as good as the odds that you would step in shit, that immortal quotidian question "Where did you get these chickens?" all sorts of Tarasevich textbooks with their borscht-colored ink stains, tobacco filters chewed by nervous mouths, cigarettes sucked until the cheeks fold inward, "Say, won't you lend me a ten till payday?" the calming effect of figure skating on the TV—5.8, 5.9, 5.9, 5.7 (he's not one of ours, the bastard!), 6.0, 6.0—hurrah, another gold medal for our children, and here's a *Shokolat Shokolatovich* for you, this one's got nuts, a Fantasia, I guess, you know, with a ballerina, or a porous one, a bittersweet Slava, almost Rostropovich, that is, the cozy feeling of curling up with a cup of tea and a "sh, sh," now the transom window open, frost and the night waft in, someone's waiting for you somewhere, the "Dance of the Little Swans" goes across the frosty sky like the apotheosis of everything that has survived, everything chocolate. A whole master of ceremonies' potpourri went by—it's not for nothing, after all, that we spoke French for two centuries; even with a Chekist mop you won't manage to sweep away all this from the metropolis.

The metropolis, after rocking back again, fell away beneath the wing, and Sasha Korbach nearly burst into tears. Rolling away from the window, he saw that the whole group was looking at him, and standing out among them were the eyes of the "raise your glasses to" loony patriarch of the Korbachs, with whom they had been conceived in a single Jewish egg cell 130 years earlier. Stanley immediately turned away, so as not to embarrass Alex as he returned to his motherland, and everyone else did the same, as though they had just happened at that moment to be looking at their friend pressed up against the window.

On the runway at SVO (the abbreviation for Sheremetyevo Airport that now appears on airline tickets), some Western machine was scraping at a frozen puddle with its iron brushes. A cheerless border guard was standing with his nose drooping. The Korbach Galaxy taxied up to an exit tunnel. The sleepy, postprandial atmosphere and low level of activity were surprising for the chief international port of the Soviet Land of the Setting Sun.

In the passage immediately outside the aircraft stood an "auntie" of indeterminate age. It had been many years since Sasha Korbach had seen a Soviet woman, with her indifferent yet always slightly hostile expression, with her head encased in a crumpled mohair kerchief, in a short overcoat with angled flaps, and down-at-the-heel half-length boots like dead ducks. What's she doing here in the holy of holies, why is she the first to meet the foreign passengers? Hello there, dear comrade woman who hasn't changed over all these years. You can't even imagine what a wind of things unheard of blows from you on a prodigal son of the fatherland! Behind the "auntie" stood a stone-faced border guard major. It seemed as though he didn't even see anything, as though he were only there to represent a state power that was weary but not yet ready to surrender. Other people, military and civilian alike, lined the walls as the group passed, and one of them made a strong impression on our hero. The figure was striking in its pallor and in the ecstatic blinking of its eyes. Perhaps it was lunatic pride that was reflected in them, or perhaps they were tortured by the terrible complexes of the empty-eyed young man. Everything's fine, thought Sasha: at first the "auntie," then the "underground man," and in between a major, as motionless as the Urals.

The expedition team of the fund entered the terminal. A rather striking group: the diminutive Piu in his bright "moonsuit," carefully chosen for him in the Schwarzie-Morzie children's store by Bernadetta; the Rabelaisian Gargamelle herself in expensive furs, enlivened by Cookie's tiny protruding head; Enoch Agasf in a black London City hat and a heavy overcoat with a karakul collar that was as Soviet as anyone could want; the president himself, towering over the rest with his enormous pelican's beak, in which all the promises of the repentant capitalist seemed to nestle; and so on. The reader can easily picture them without any further description.

Some people speaking fluent English appeared—in all probability, staffers from the International Department of the Central Committee. "Mr. Korbach, on behalf of the leadership we welcome you and your group to Soviet territory. At the present time your schedule of meetings is being worked out in accordance with your needs." Someone made a joke about the weather: "A blizzard is blowing up," he said, "but it won't be strong enough to blow away our friendship." Their number increased as they neared the Hall of Deputies, in which there was a crush of people. It even seemed to Sasha Korbach that Mikhail himself was floating around, only in a wig and a fake mustache—that is, in the same form in which the man whose books he still read before going to sleep had run around St. Petersburg in the summer of 1917.

The Soviet visas, looking like fine strips of quality ham, were brought fairly quickly. Piu and Leibnitz downed some "Soviet champagne" and stared at each other bug-eyed in amazement. Now all of them were led onto the sacred territory that, we dare to point out, profiting from our authorial liberty, had exactly three days short of eight months left to exist. While they were proceeding through the glass corridors, a view of the main waiting hall opened before them several times. A.Z. thought that it looked much shittier than before. The last time around, that is, in the summer of 1982, it had still been new—the West Germans had built it for them on the occasion of the Olympic Games only two years earlier—and now it was already old: panes of glass were missing here and there, and the floor was stained with something that wouldn't wash away, and clouds of wintry steam entered it along with the ponderous crowd, creating an atmosphere of flu and raw vodka. As a sign of things new, however, at the end of the hall stood a densely packed throng of demonstrators carrying signs. "The public is waiting for you there," the man from the International Department told them with an indefinite but creepy smile. "Look, folks—there's a whole crowd waiting for us there," Stanley said jauntily. Bernadetta ran a comb through his piebald hair as she walked.

They went around one more turn and through a boarded-up door, then came out into the crowd that was standing as though waiting to launch an assault. Sasha Korbach was nearly blinded even before the television lights were turned on. The bright flash of the crowd. Dozens if not hundreds of dear faces burst forth with unimaginable joy. "Sasha-a-a-a!" the expanse gasped. Signs, of which there were dozens, repeated his name: SASHA KORBACH, HURRAH! WELCOME BACK, SASHA! SASHA, WE'VE GOT YOU BACK! SASHA, WE'RE WITH YOU! SASHA, PETERSBURG BELONGS TO YOU! SASHA, YOU'RE IN THE ARMS OF THE ARBAT! and even KARABAKH WELCOMES KORBACH! but the biggest and brightest one, with a laughing monkey's mug of decade-old vintage, said, SASHKA, YOUR BUFFOONS ARE ALIVE!

Then the lights of several daring pro-perestroika TV programs—*Vzglyad, Vid, Pyatoe Koleso*—blazed up, and several new, young "anchormen"—Listyev, Lyubimov, Molchanov, Svetlichny—rushed at him with their cameramen. The interviews were not a particularly successful venture. The crowd pressed in without paying any attention to the media. The hero of the day was rocked back and forth by embraces like the cruiser *Aurora* by the waves during its flight from the Tsushima Strait. Suddenly everyone pulled back. Into the freed area, to the accompaniment of the music from their old show *A–Z (The Telephone Book)*, leapt the Buffoons' pioneering lineup: Natalie the Battery, Elozin the Bronze Wizard, nutty Shurik, Lidka the Rattler, Tiger Cub, Port of Odessa, Boozy Mark, and the rest I can't remember because of the agitation of the moment. They turned somersaults with no fear of osteoporosis, then pulled off a few more with no regard for vascular instability, did splits, and gynecological and urological problems be damned. Look out, Sashka himself is taking off his English overcoat that's been through the wars (he walked around in it when we were still here, can you believe it?) and joining the bacchanalia. "Film it! Film it!" the perestroika-era opinion makers shout at their cameramen. Someone thrusts a guitar into his hands. "Sashka, it's yours, I took it from you in 'seventy-five, it's got new pegs!" From the crowd come the shouted names of old songs: " 'Sakhalin,' Sasha!" "Cut into 'Purgatory'!" "Give us 'Delicacies'!" And he gives them, joining in the general, if not mad, joy of his beloved public.

Looking on from one corner of the described scene, with its jets (no puns, please, gentlemen!) of "Sov champagne," pushing a cat's-fur hat down onto a face, even though it was contorted enough by makeup, M. S. Gorbachev was thinking. No, we weren't mistaken about Sasha Korbach. He's unexpectedly found himself on the cutting edge of the movement. Many in our fossilized Politburo, however, fail to properly appreciate the elemental enthusiasm of this moment of perestroika. Maybe I was wrong to lurch to the right, promoting Yanayev and relying on Yazov and Kryuchkov. It really was quite unpleasant to stand on the sacred tribune on May Day and hear the tactless shouts from the crowd: "Red swine out of the Kremlin!" It was a ticklish moment, awesome, the sort that can reduce things to ashes. Even so, perhaps I was wrong to lead my comrades off the reviewing stand and veer to the right? Maybe I should have rushed forward along with the wave, heading the decisive phase? Everything is so complicated, and there's no one to ask for advice! Not this American billionaire Stepan Davidovich. What circles are backing his aid program? Oh, it's all so complicated!

At that point, Sasha Korbach was being triumphantly lifted onto the shoulders of the crowd. On his first upward flight, he glimpsed a threesome of Soviet citizens, so familiar in some way that it caused him pain. Flying up a second time, he glimpsed the delegation of the Korbach Fund with the president at its head. They were standing in the midst of the exultant crowd like poor relations. Soaring into the air a third time, he snatched a bubbling bottle flying by and managed to take a drink from it, sinking into arms of love. Then the crowd swept him toward the exit, into wet, blizzard-swept Moscow.

"How'd you like our Lavsky? Isn't it sensational?" De Luxe cried.

"It's exactly what I would have expected where Alex is concerned," noted Lester Square.

Stanley silently covered his eyes with a glove, and the rest in one way or another followed his example. In the distance, the eyes of the trio of briefly glimpsed Soviet citizens were brimming over. "Sashenka, Sashenka," his mother muttered. "Not a bit, not a bit, not a bit . . ." "Not a hair, not a hair," his half sister and half brother sniffed.

"Had it not been for perestroika, a meeting like this would never have taken place," said M. S. Gorbachev, noticed by no one as he walked past. He was keeping mum about the fact that it was from his office that the leak about Sasha Korbach's return had originated.

IX. THREE POINTS OF VIEW

There was a man of a most noble nation
Who could stand a modest quotation.
Once he'd guzzled his beer
He shed many a tear—
For lost tenure, and not termination.

Once a pirate was freed from a jail,
Who did grumble while hoisting his sail.
He saw sense in the end of detention,
But no cause to make here of it mention,
Much less remember the snails in the ale.

Mused a huge crocodile in the Nile
After loading his capacious file:
There are no onsets or ends
And you never get bends,
Just completion as long as a mile.

PART X

1

AT THE HIGHEST LEVEL

On August 19, 1991, Alexander Zakharovich Korbach was making one of his regular trips—it was perhaps the eighth one that year—to Moscow on the Pan Am direct flight from New York. To the regular deformity of my life between the university and the film business there's been added the deformity of an existence between two countries, he was thinking. Time for me to be pottering around in the garden, watching sunsets, waking up at dawn, dozing off during the day over Plutarch's *Morals,* and I'm rushing back and forth across the planet like a young tennis player. Then again, elderly violinists do even more racing around than the young tennis players.

For some reason, the flight schedules often brought him and Oskar Belvedere, the world-famous virtuoso, together. They would both have lunch in the first-class section, get quite drunk, and then Oskar would drop straight off to sleep, barely having to time to say: Excuse me, Sasha, I've got to play in seven and a half hours. While staying in, say, Japan on a monthlong tour, he still managed to fly to Zurich or Adelaide according to the demands of his agent. Waking up in his electronically controlled seat almost parallel to the floor of the plane, Belvedere would immediately begin shaving and spouting normal Jewish pearls of wisdom like "As long as a man lives, he's incorrigible, my friend—no, no, don't argue!" "I guess you're right," A.Z. would answer. "We Jews, in any case."

At the time of that first visit eight months before, Stanley had offered him the chairmanship of the fund's Soviet program. "You're as popular here as Elvis is in our country. But there's something besides popularity. One young journalist in Moscow said to me: 'Sasha Korbach, he's one of the few people in our country with any right to speak on this subject.' To the Russians, you're one of them, not an American Jew at all. With you as chairman, no one will be able to say that the

Korbach Fund is a branch of the CIA and that our aim is the destruction of Soviet potential."

The current situation did not seem to give any such cause for concern. The first visit in December had been a smashing success. The newspapers and the television stations had called the American magnate a friend of Russian enlightenment. The meeting of the Korbachs with the Kremlin leadership had stunned the television-thinking country. On one side of the table, alongside Gorbachev, sat Ligachev, Yanayev, Lukyanov, all the Party scoundrels, all more or less exactly alike. On the other side sat a remarkable collection of individuals, of a sort that had not hitherto appeared before the Soviet people: a polished kind of lawyer, whose every smile seemed to invite the Party men not to try anything clever—we'll find out about it just the same, no matter what, it said; next to him some inscrutable Annamite, clicking his tongue in a way that made Genka Yanayev start every time; then a nobly independent-looking Negro with splendid shoulders, obviously not from the Lumumba University; an old man with clearly marked Jewish features, according to rumor a Hollywood agent, gazing at the Slavs as though from the depths of Judaic centuries; and finally, the two most staggering ones—a high-class whore with a very serious pair of mammaries but wearing a professorial pince-nez, and then the head of it all, the richest of the rich, but more like an old Tarzan than an Ilya Muromets. Far from numerous among those watching were the ones who realized that before them were the characters of our novel.

The negotiations concluded very favorably for both sides. The Soviets welcomed the desire of the capitalists to pour half a billion dollars into the sinking domains of socialism, namely into science, education, health care, the printed word (the saving of the Soviet "fat journals," that priceless asset of world literary culture), and art (the self-immolating Soviet film industry). In exchange, the Korbach Fund received permission to open its Moscow branch, for which offices of the accustomed worldwide standard (and at a corresponding price) were offered in the ComEcon building, where the Hungarian leather armchairs had been languishing for a year after the series of buoyantly executed velvet revolutions. They'll say it's expensive, but what can you do? The market economy is on the march. Finally they gave a series of banquets concluding with a grandiose presentation of the fund that saw the arrival of individuals who sent the Muscovites into a stupor: Stella, Luka, Arsene, Mana, and still others with two-syllable names numbering two dozen at least. Just who invited them? A.Z. wondered in surprise. No one, as it turned out. They'll come without an invitation, and if they don't come, the game's up.

In short, things are going just wonderfully, if one doesn't count strange hints occasionally dropped during conversations with official figures. For example, the minister of culture, a Siberian of a well-known type, with broad cheekbones, asks if it's true that the Korbach Fund is the bearer of some Jewish idea. With a smile, though in earnest, Stanley starts to tell him about the "Conspiracy of the Crackpots of Zion." The minister gives an enlightened smile in reply but then says that it would be better not to emphasize this specific character. We can't accept your funds if this specific character is emphasized.

These are Soviet instincts at work, A.Z. explained. Someone gives them money in an open envelope, and they need it in a sealed one. And no one expresses any particular gratitude for the help—have you noticed, guys? Many of them are still thinking the old way, that the capitalists are pulling them out with the rope with which they'll hang those capitalists later. Lenin taught them that, Ben Duckworth put in. Long live the 101st Airborne.

One day a certain presumptuous Russian, a former Soviet "agent of influence" who in the years of the Cold War was forever turning up in the States supposedly on some cultural matter, or in connection with the "struggle for peace"—you know the type—invites himself into Stanley's room in the old-fashioned luxury of the Hotel National. Remember, Stanley, how you and I went to Cyrus's place, for tennis—it wasn't bad, was it? Well, this is along the same lines! From that place where pugs were washed, an extragovernmental dialogue—Pugwash Village, New York, where the conferences were held. Norman Cousins urged them to talk to the Russians. You have to talk, talk, talk to them, and they'll abandon their evil designs. Russians did most of the talking. The Soviets brought scientists over by the planeload, and they told loquacious lies and ran off to the shopping malls at the first opportunity. And this one walked around independently. I don't remember playing tennis with him but do remember that he was hinting at something the whole time, winking away, and then suddenly sat down at a piano and belted out something heartrending.

Now it all makes more sense. He's letting me know that he'd be useful in the position of chairman of the Moscow group of the fund. A lot of these names ending in -ov, -ova, -in, -ina, -enko, -atsky flash by—right, sorry. He takes a little book out of his shoulder bag and signs it "For my deer frend Stenly." The second d already looks like a z, and that's not half bad the way it turns out—"deer frenz," that is, almost "Stranley the frenzied deer." The "frenzied deer" sticks a finger in one of the little books. One great mass of anti-Stalinist revelations. I'll never read a heap like that in my life unless it's Plutarch's *Morals.*

We've all gotten older, and this big iron fox is a bit moth-eaten too. Even so, the "frenzied deer" is no friend to the "moth-eaten iron fox." The guest seems to grasp the general mood. Well, all things considered, he wasn't really counting on it. He's keeping aloof, ha, ha. By the way, they say in certain circles that the Korbachs were sent to Moscow by the CIA. Stanley passes his Pantagruelesque hand under the little reading table and pats the fox's knee, which is sticking out like a Max Ernst sculpture. You've done so much traveling in the States, Gene, and you still haven't figured out our hierarchy.

In one way or another, the warning signs were tossed out and the main idea became as plain as the nose on one's face: don't imagine that you're the masters just because you're giving us money. Stanley, however, as an expert chess player, replied to the intrigues on his flanks by putting his queen in motion: he named his fourth cousin chairman of the Moscow group. There were any number of factors in favor of his candidacy. First, he's still a Russian and almost an American. Second, he's not just a Russian but a national idol. Third, he is, in the words of the young journalist, "one of the few people in our country with any right to speak on this subject." Fourth, even though he's a Jew, no one thinks of him in those terms here: our Sasha Korbach! With a chairman like that, who's going to buy the disinformation about the CIA?

"You know everyone here," Stanley told Alex, "including the shady characters. You've got the gift of reading facial expressions. With you as chairman, we won't have nearly as much wood to chop. I know that Lester wanted the job. I can see now that it's not likely the local creeps would tolerate that guy in Moscow. He spent too many nights watching the Kremlin walls from across the river at the British embassy. Besides, have you noticed something strange in the way his nostrils are constructed? They seem to say to those around him something along the lines of: You, Russian cuckoo, I know every inch of your stinking guts, you can't hide from me! The apparatchiks won't stand for that kind of arrogance here, and as I see it they're not about to let go of power. They're going to cling to it right up until the final collapse. I feel for Russia almost as much as you do, but I doubt Lester does very much."

"Your Royal Fuck Your Truck," Sasha Korbach pleaded. "It's too much for me! I can't abandon the Black Cube at Pinkerton, and Beethoven Street in L.A.! Putney is ready to put my film into production tomorrow; it all depends on whether or not they can sign Quentin Landry. Our Eternal Jew is negotiating now, and he knows better than anyone that time is money. And then how can I just spit on my Buffoons, on that good devil with its mouth open in laughter and thirst?" "You're in good form today, a Korbach monster with its mouth open in laughter and thirst!" Stanley said with a laugh that made a young mug spring out of the aging spotted beak like a young kangaroo out of its mother's pouch. "You've made so many promises here that you won't be able to manage everything anyway, whether you become chairman of our Moscow branch or not. Let me tell you a little story from my days as a soldier.

"It was a Marine Corps base in the Aleutians, we were training for a landing there. Frost thicker than you can imagine, and my friend Galsworthy was going to see his Eskimo girlfriend, Cordelia, every night. He never made it back for taps, but every morning I'd see him snoring away on the cot next to mine. Hey, fucking Galsworthy, how do you manage to get back into the barracks without going past the checkpoint? The fences are so high and always so covered with ice that not even Tarzan could get over them. How do you even stay alive if it's thirty degrees below here every night? That's what saves me, Galsworthy says. I throw my jacket over the fence, and then I've got no other choice but to get over the damned obstacle."

"A wise parable." A.Z. nodded. "I really like the idea that stupid war stories can turn into wise parables and help a billionaire dispose of his dollars. All right, then, I'm throwing my jacket over, too!"

Thus began the very curious but, as it turned out, entirely possible life of the "Moscow shuttle period." The Irish play, meanwhile, was going great guns at the Black Cube, which allowed him to diddle a "flexible schedule" out of the administration. Now he turned up on campus whenever he liked, though still at least eight times a semester. Alexander had cleverly managed to join the Buffoons and the Theater on Beethoven Street in what he called an American-Soviet theatrical cartel. These two widely separated groups set about preparing a *spectacle de choc* called *Four Temperaments,* adapted from a play by the Mexican apostate Marxist Chapai Bonaventura. At Putney everything seemed to be humming along like a well-oiled machine, but at this point we need a larger chunk of the narrative to show how the oil was spread through the rather complicated mechanism.

After endless talks—everyone at the studio needed to show that he was on the job, after all—the screenplay was finally accepted. Both sides—that is, the director's and the producer's camps—hoped to shovel everything off in opposite directions during the actual production. Meanwhile, casting of the actors who could play alongside the only possible leading pair, Quentin Landry and Goldie Belle D'Argent, was being conducted. Basically, they were marking time, since these youngsters were gaining ever greater popularity and were, as they say, sought after on all sides.

Nonetheless, even on that front things were going extremely well, assuming we're not overly picky in our expectations. Things are even going so wonderfully that there's something suspicious about it, our hero thought—inclined, like all members of his class, the Soviet male, to mistrust good fortune. Sometimes it seemed to him that he could detect flickers of ambiguity where he was concerned in the hustle and bustle of the huge Putney office. Let's say he comes into an elevator and immediately notices that two whiz kids are exchanging ironic glances at the sight of him. And who are you, then, you little shits? I could understand it if Bertolucci and Forman were winking at each other, but just who are you, you money-grubbers?

The secretaries at Putney jump to their feet as if he were a close relative who'd just gotten out of jail: Alex! Dick is dying to see you! Sorry, he's got Bertolucci and Forman with him right now, but they won't be talking for more than twenty minutes—maybe you could drop in on Ed while you're waiting? Ed's dying to see you, too! As he walks toward Ed's office, he can sense them exchanging looks behind his back. What's the meaning of these unseen smirks? Maybe they think Stanley pulled a few strings for me, or maybe I just don't fit in here with my rumpled trousers?

While he's walking to Ed's office, who should come out of Pete's but Norman Blamsdale. What's our enemy doing here? Where are the machine guns hidden? He ought to be concerning himself with Alaskan oil, the bastard, and not with the California film trade. A dry nod from a distance, like a helicopter reconnaissance. Ed jumps out of his office, the classic Jewish cowboy. Alex, I'm so glad you're back! Let's do lunch! As though it were for lunch that I flew here from Moscow.

I have a hunch this ain't going to be free, as they say in America. And Dick's going to join us afterward. All things considered, the people here are as simple as anywhere else. As soon as they arrive in the morning they start getting ready for lunch. Then there's the postlunch exodus from lunch. Dick Putney, Ed Putney-Krieger, Edna Krieger-Nakatone mill around Japanese blocks with sashimi and quartered octopuses on them. Listen. Alex, could you tell us how the work of the

Korbach Fund in Russia's going? Glad to, Dick, Ed, and Edna, but first of all let me ask you, have you seen our screen tests?

Well, here it goes again—an exchange of these imperceptible glances that are perceptible all the same among these three important whales, or rather two males of the species and one she-whale. Screen tests, Alex? Why, they're just great! You've turned out to be a real master of the film medium. We'll talk more about that in a bit—right now, tell us, what criteria do you use for distributing the money?

What does "you've turned out to be" mean? They give me a film with a huge budget, an army of professionals as assistants, and then they're surprised: it turns out he's a professional, too. Does that mean that if Stanley Korbach brought a goat here, they'd give it the green light as well? You can bet your last dollar that none of them has seen the screen tests. They limit themselves to empty compliments, while what really interest them are the subsidies of the fund. Has Norman been spreading octopus venom around here? Too bad I didn't punish him the way Margie suggested.

But what the hell do I care about their glances, unseen smirks, words let slip accidentally, and lack of interest in my screen tests anyway? I'm in my fifty-second year, and I still haven't managed to get through Homer or Moses. What, am I just going to drop dead one day with no Aeschylus and Virgil, with no Kant and Nietzsche? How many coals of the old fire kindled by the *dolce stil nuovo* are still glowing? And how many imitations have piled up, supermarket, chemical-fed firewood? I occupy my time with everything and nothing, skimming off the cream. From an oppressed Socialist jackal I've been transformed into a dubious pet of the bourgeoisie. I should just chuck everything and go with Nora to a small Greek island. Let there be an archaeological dig nearby, and let her get deeply into that. It's possible that a child was started in her at the Lutèce. Maybe she's even given birth? There, on the island, to sit on a terrace over the sea, reading the *Iliad* with my left hand and drinking wine with the right, rocking the cradle with one bare foot. To try to hold on a bit longer, so that the child will grow to manhood with a living father. Or to womanhood. In short, to become an independent drachma grabber. Eh, what rubbish I'm talking!

Nevertheless, things were going well. "His" three theaters were exchanging ideas, sketches, music, and—most important of all—actors. At Pinkerton they'd given him the title distinguished professor. Dick Putney sent a personal, excited letter about the strong impression that the Korbach screen tests had made on him. The board of the Moscow section of the fund, now made up of numerous prominent local liberals—which meant that the atmosphere was always ripe for a squabble— greeted his appearances with applause: the chairman somehow always found a quick solution to the most complicated philanthropic problems.

Moscow society as a whole adored him. "You know, Sasha," an old musician friend said to him one day, "when you walk around here as though nothing happened after so many years of a disappearing act, we, your audience, start to think that maybe all's not lost, that we're going to pull through somehow—Sasha Korbach is back, after all." Alas, there was no small number of traitors among those in proximity to him—that is, the ones he knew had betrayed him. Not infrequently these people, considering themselves natural candidates for a Korbach stipend, would make straight for him with outstretched arms: "Sasha, my dear man, we learned about freedom from you, you know!"

Sometimes he would be unable to restrain himself. "What are you doing crawling up to me, you swine? After all, you know that I know. After all, it was you who demanded that the extreme measures of a period of martial law be applied to the renegade Korbach." Or to another one he would say: "I'm sorry, my worthy man, I'm putting my hands behind my back—they simply don't wish to come into contact with 'ten authors of letters of denunciation.' " "Sasha, God have mercy, with what 'authors of letters of denunciation'?" "Why, with your fingers, sir, unless you've got eleven." He would turn away from a third, who had sworn friendship on so many drinking binges, and write a letter of recantation himself and help others to find the right expressions. And then with a fourth he would have to play the hypocrite, even exchange theatrical kisses—the man had already gotten too close. You have to pretend you don't know that after you were expelled with a KGB disinformation label he called you Gapon, after the czarist agent provocateur, and you only allow yourself to look deeply into his eyes from time to time and think: Were your eyes really always so nasty, my eccentric friend?

All these flying commutes, trivial problems, and tugs at the emotions were going on against the backdrop of the real drama of Moscow, whose population was standing in endless lines for "soup selections"—that is to say, for sorry lumps of rotting bones, and was sloshing through the salty mud looking at each other and at Sasha Korbach as he passed by, with a silent question that sometimes emerged as a wail: What's to become of us now?

The underground passages beneath Pushkin Square were turning into more and more ill-reputed caves. It was in them that punks with dull stares and with their backsides drooping in jeans padded for extra warmth waited out the winter; anarchists and monarchists waved their little newspapers that looked like lists of rules for a public bathhouse; the first entrepreneurs trafficked in some yellowish palm-oil swill; the lady Yeltsinites walked around unabashedly with pictures of Boris Nikolayevich on the chests of their quilted jackets; readers of the *Moscow News* would let Communist power have it with every sharp sound they could find in the Russian language: "The disgraceful bastards, they've devoured us, puked all over us, the cocksuckers, scum, swapping our whores for computers abroad!" There, a Dem Union would daringly unfurl a tricolor Russian flag and charge upward, headlong, to die for freedom in the open air; they wouldn't die, however—just reinforce themselves with a few allies: "Down with the Reds!"

Junkies, winos, and codeine heads urinated in corners, but the broad mass of people buzzed with excitement like the chorus in the hold of a ship stirring with mutiny. Everyone was for the Lithuanians: Let them live the way they want to! In the city, a second government came into being, the Supreme Council of the Russian Federation. Of the two cardinal Russian questions—What is to be done? and Who is to blame?—the answer to the second was already clear, while the first, puffing itself up to Homeric proportions, howled beneath Pushkin Square as though in a wind tunnel and cackled in a mocking echo.

Summer came. Things were ever so slightly less vile. Girls' knees were bared. People got their minds off politics from time to time. A.Z. went on flitting back and forth across the Atlantic and one day suddenly found himself landing on the Island of Crimea, where at one time he had been in the habit of fleeing with his girlfriends from the Bolshevism of the mainland.

There she is, the Yalta coast, with her sunsets and rolling surf of elemental freedom. A chic article that summer was the Western plastic bottle. They would pour any homebrew into it and then suck it down as they walked. As ever, Lenin is thrusting his black palm into the blue sky. On TV, Colonel Alksnis is condescendingly letting it be known that there won't be much longer to wait, soon real Soviet men will retake power.

Some beneficiaries of the fund, specialists in pulmonary illnesses, were giving a hilltop barbecue, in a park called Red Stone, which had once belonged to the Party but had now passed to the municipal authorities. Those scoundrels had slaughtered all the native deer, the present owners explained to the Americans. Just breathe in this plateau's unique air, in which you'll find maybe two disease-causing microbes per cubic kilometer. Sasha Korbach stood on the edge of the Yaila, a towering rock face falling away into the sea. Two illness-causing microbes twisted through the air over him, trying to fly into his nostrils.

> *Magical Crimea, there in years past*
> *As even now, as always*
> *Through the almond trees flew the hoopoes*
> *Through the fingers flowed the years*
> *And the old buffoon like a friend of freedom*
> *Prayed: Shine, my star!*
> *And the steamships saw him off*
> *Not at all like trains.*

That evening he flew off to Los Arkhangelsk via Moscow and Helsinki, in order to come back to Moscow early on the morning of August 19, 1991.

2

MOSCOW ACTS

*H*e was met at the airport as usual by Rose Morrows, who had already been working here as a manager for six months. Remarkable changes had occurred over the course of the novel in this simple girl from Yornoverblyudo County. Now, when she walked through the main terminal of SVO in her business togs, the gazes of all the permanent male fixtures in the place followed after her. One couldn't say that this was much to the liking of Rose's assistant, Ben Duckworth, but for the time being he was patient, out of diplomatic considerations.

During the drive from Sheremetyevo to the Leningrad Highway, Rose laid out on her attaché case a pile of documents requiring the signature of the respected, but hard to get hold of, chairman. She was in luck: on the highway that morning there was an endless column of armored vehicles, the traffic flow was almost at a standstill, and Alex, who had not yet even reached the city itself, scribbled his signature on everything that required it.

Movement still was not being restored, and the pale sunlight was reflected from the badges of military policemen posted at the crossroads. A.Z. could not take his eyes off the armored personnel carriers and tanks rolling slowly toward the city. The motherland, clanking with Caterpillar tracks. It's a wonder that she hadn't started a dreadful war. For forty-five years she had been increasing the might of her battering ram. To smash every castle in Europe with a single blow! In theory, the motherland had no alternative. Fashioning this battering ram and laying waste to her own body, she seemed to live in expectation of a gigantic plundering raid when, like the khans of Horde, she would fall upon the West and return with spoils! Leave ruins behind, let them be rebuilt for our next campaign. It was a miracle that this logical chain had not been closed. Where is this disgraceful armored mass dragging itself to, to what meaningless maneuvers?

Suddenly the cops began letting cars pass. In single file they trickled past the halted column. The fund's Taurus had the good fortune to be near the front of the pack and soon reached the city's outer districts, whose rooftops still blazed with red ledges now bearing ridiculous slogans like "We will reach the triumph of Communist labor!" Just then everything came to a dead stop again. The highway, pedestrian walkways included, was blocked from one side to the other by tracked vehicles. The sirens of police cars and ambulances were wailing; no one was letting them through. From time to time there would be a crosswise surge of motorcycles mounted by absurdly bellowing traffic cops. Next to the Byelorusskaya

Train Station there was gridlock. The Taurus was solidly hemmed in on the hump of the thoroughfare running into Gorky Street. It, too, was jammed from end to end with vehicles. "It's incredible," said the chauffeur, Mark Goldberg, who until recently had been working at the Burdenko Hospital, where as a surgeon he had earned, according to the unofficial exchange rate with the dollar, fifty times less than his present American salary.

A.Z. got out of the car. From the bridge the all-embracing scope of the stupor was visible. The lights of a few traffic signals were changing meaninglessly. Fumes from idling engines rose into the air. Like a Valkyrie grown heavy yet still implacable, a dark cloud moved in over the area and hung there. Suddenly, it was as though everything had been bared for an instant, revealing thousands of people in attitudes of desperation. Rain began to fall. Several lads were standing among the cars, smoking cigarettes that they had been keeping up their sleeves. He made his way over to them to listen to their embittered words: "The fucking Garden Ring is closed, the cunts. They must have a fucking screw loose!" "What's happening, guys?" A.Z. asked. One turned his head. "What, you haven't heard? The SCSE is in town, they've thrown Gorby out!"

Alexander immediately rushed back to the car, took Rose Morrows by the hand, and drew her out along with her papers. "Rose, we're walking! There's been a coup! We've got to get to the fund as quickly as possible!" To the driver he said: "Stay in the car for now, but if any shooting starts, leave it and make your way to our place!" "Shooting where? What shooting?" Mark muttered. He hadn't left for Israel, after all, because there was shooting there. The idea of shooting in Moscow was beyond his understanding. Just then there was a loud report nearby, but it wasn't a shot, just a truck backfiring.

They quickly got to Gruziny. All quiet here—there didn't seem to be anything going on. The usual pathetic bazaar on Tishinka. They began to hear strange sounds as they approached Presnya: a roar and the trumpeting of trunks. It wouldn't have occurred to anyone just then that it was the sensitive animals in the zoo getting agitated. The usual morning human streams were coming out of the Metro. People quickened their steps toward the trolleybus stops. Only on a few faces could the timid question be read: Did everything in Moscow stay where it was while we were rushing along underground? Meanwhile, two youngsters in jeans, drawing generous scoops of whitewash from a bucket, were finishing writing in meter-high letters on a wall: DOWN WITH THE SCSE!

Korbach stopped. "Say, guys, can you explain what SCSE stands for?" The young men answered without turning around: "Shitheads, Communists, Spooks, Eunuchs." Suddenly a sort of spasm of delight seized A.Z. by the throat. He put a hand on each of the backs of the graffiti writers. What do you think you're doing, Dad? They turned around and recognized him. "Sasha Korbach, you're with us?" "Of course I'm with you, guys! Who else would I be with?"

The closer they got to the ComEcon building, the more often they saw the ominous abbreviation on the walls of houses and other construction sites, drawn in by the word *doloi* (down with), chased after by the club of an exclamation mark. They came upon knots of people heatedly discussing the situation and waving their arms. The groups were already growing into small crowds beside the building of the government of the Russian Federation. Suddenly, a part of the crowd moved off to one side. A chain of black Volga sedans was rolling down into the underground garage of the White House. The shout went up: "Yeltsin's here!" Scattered shouts of "Hurrah!" quickly fused into a chant of "Hurrah, Boris! Hurrah, Boris!" The police set up their rickety barriers around the building. In one place several lads rolled metal barrels into the middle of the street. A dump truck pulled up and unloaded sand. Broken-off sections of building site fencing were dragged in. Two large street-cleaning trucks were parked against either end of the barricade that had been erected. They're not thinking about resisting, are they? And again, this time as a powerful shiver, he was shaken by a joy that he had never known before.

From the balcony of ComEcon, he saw a column of APCs gingerly making its way toward the White House. Right, that's it, the game's up, he thought, then suddenly noticed—God! My God!—a tricolor flag, weakly lifted by the slight breeze, flying from the lead vehicle. Eight armored vehicles stopped as if forming a line of defense. The crowd all around was seized by joyous excitement.

In the main hall of ComEcon, an atmosphere of senseless activity prevailed. Overloaded elevators were going up and down. The police seemed to be checking documents with particular severity, while any Tom, Dick, or Harry was walking through doors right nearby. A large crowd was standing in a corner watching a television in expectation. On the screen the imperial Soviet ballet was dancing with a measured kicking of legs. Someone walked by with a small radio pressed to his ear saying "The Echo of Moscow" to those with him. "Taman and Kantemirov guards. Fifteen hundred tanks, APCs, and AMVs." Rose Morrows made her way through the crowd with dignity, pronouncing the first Russian phrase that she had ever learned in Moscow: *"Paaazvol'tee, tovarishchi!"*

The first person they saw in the fund's office on the nineteenth floor was Sol Leibnitz. He was sitting at a table by a window with a view of the river and of that masterpiece of the Stalinist wedding-cake baroque, the Hotel Ukraine, and was looking the epitome of American informational efficiency. Impeccable shirt, impeccable haircut, one buttock, as usual, significantly drooping from his swivel chair. All the communications apparatus around him was going full blast: the telephone receiver against his ear, the E-mail summaries on the computer screen, the television screen to the side showing not the ballet, as in the rest of Moscow, but a CNN announcer breathless with excitement, sheets with the letterheads of various organizations emerging from the fax. Spotting the new arrivals, he gestured at the window with his fat Mont Blanc pen without interrupting his conversation. On the other side of the river, around the Shevchenko monument, some sort of motorized infantry unit had formed. After saying, "Please keep me posted," to someone on the other end of the line, he threw up his hands to Alex. "I'm afraid the Moscow carnival has come to an end, my friend." He handed a pile of news bulletins to him. Gorbachev deposed from power. Under house arrest in the Crimea. He's dead. He created the situation himself by taking cover behind Yanayev. He's been sent abroad. Yeltsin's whereabouts unknown. Under arrest. Gone into hiding. Fled to the Urals. Ostankino seized by the military. The State Committee for the State of

Emergency (SCSE) is expected to give a press conference. Its members include all the ministers who had troops at their disposal. One more curious news item from a *Libération* reporter: According to reliable sources in the KGB and Ministry of Internal Affairs, 250,000 pairs of handcuffs were ordered for today's date, but it is not known whether they arrived in time.

Alexander held the last sheet of paper in his hand for a long time. Two hundred and fifty thousand—that's more than enough. A tenth of that number would have sufficed. Then again, just in case, let them have ordered as many as they did. Sol and Rose were looking at him with worried expressions. Why is he keeping that bit of paper before his eyes for so long? The cloud stopped just opposite the window on its way by and sprinkled the expanse between the ComEcon building and the White House with rain. Well, what are you waiting for? it asked. He got up and put on his raincoat. "Sol and Rose, excuse me, but I've got to go. I need a gulp of fresh air. If the situation gets worse, go to the embassy. Don't worry about me. Everything will be all right." Rose nodded, and Sol handed him a mobile phone. "Let us know at least every two hours where you are, Alex. We'll give your number to Stanley. He's in Bangladesh right now. Be careful."

With the first shock of the Moscow air, he ceased to be chairman of the Moscow group of an American humanitarian fund and lost his present professorship and his future Hollywood star status as well. He stood there for a few seconds like a statue, then felt as though he had been carried back in time to the autumn of 1956, as though the hairdo he'd had at the time was flying in the wind, as though he were dashing into a crowd of Hungarian kids with Molotov cocktails in their hands waiting for Soviet tanks by the Korvin cinema. "To fight for freedom on your seventeenth!" That was what he'd been dreaming about all his life. To stand against "them" with a gun in his hands! To smash this dull-witted, lard-belching, vodka-gorged Bolshevik junta right in the face, to stand opposite it on the barricades "on your seventeenth," if only to shout: "I'm not afraid of you, you swine!"

From the entrance to the ComEcon building he stepped out into the crowd, which had grown noticeably larger while he had been reading the dispatches. The faces around him were surprisingly cheerful. One might even say that he had never seen such a number of beaming faces in Moscow—as though everyone had decided that he would be seventeen years old today.

Two lads were wrestling with a sturdy piece of timber that they had decided on as a support for the barricade. A.Z. set to work helping them. With a few curses they hoisted it onto their shoulders and headed for the barricade, looking like figures in the famous Socialist Realist painting *Lenin's Communist Saturday in the Kremlin.* "The bald one is bringing up the rear, as usual," one of the guys, who also remembered the painting, said to him tactlessly but good-naturedly. Sasha bubbled over with the happy laughter of a child.

For at least two hours they worked on this barricade, hauling up sacks of wet cement and fixtures from building sites; anything that came to hand was pressed into service, even though every one of the builders knew that their amateur obstacle would in the best possible case manage to hold up a rampaging T-72 for a few minutes. Nevertheless, everyone worked efficiently. These were ordinary Moscow folk here, not from the university faculties but not hayseeds either. The man in charge was also a well-known type, the Soviet "geologist-mountain-climber-deep-sea-diver." Everyone called him Sery—gray—which had obviously come about because his name was Sergei, and not at all because there was anything gray about him, since the fellow had a copper-toned tan and a set of teeth that sparkled like the ivories of a piano, remarkable in a country where gum disease was endemic. His T-shirt identifying him as a fan of the rock group Time Machine spoke for itself.

Suddenly he stopped A.Z. and asked: "Say, has anyone ever told you that you look like Sasha Korbach?" "More than once." A.Z. nodded. Together they swung up a bag of cement and threw it into the middle of the heap. Then some women appeared with hot coffee, fresh bread, and long Soviet sausages. The lads joked that they shouldn't eat the sausages but use them to beat back Yazov's tank drivers.

Someone dashed in with the news that they were signing people up in units and distributing arms at Entrance 5. The barricade fighters clustered around Sery began to make their way through the crowd. All of a sudden the weather cleared. The clouds moved off beyond the Hotel Ukraine, as though to assure the illumination of the historic event. It was obviously drawing near, and hundreds of photo and television journalists sensed it with their hunters' instinct. Activity began to seethe around "our" armored vehicles. Young men in neckties with small submachine guns beneath their sport coats leapt onto the tanks. Onto the lead vehicle climbed the president of the Russian Federation, with his magnificent shock of silver hair. "Boris! Boris!" the crowd thundered. As though at the podium at a Party conference, the president straightened his tie, checked that his jacket was buttoned, took up his text, and read a statement that a few minutes later would stun the world with its boldness. Russia hasn't given in to its own tanks!

Where Korbach was standing, no one could hear a thing, only waves of cries of "They shall not pass!" "Long live Russia!" "Long live Boris!" "Down with the SCSE!" and he waved his beret crumpled in his hand along with everyone else and wept beneath the fluttering tricolored flags. The clouds moved in again. Those who had them put up their umbrellas. Sery started a bottle of vodka going around the circle. Have a snort and pass it on!

Slowly making his way through the crowd, Alexander saw a familiar tall figure in an Aquascutum raincoat. A few hairs neatly combed over the balding crown of his head. It turned out to be the former agent of Her Majesty Lester the Quadratic. "Les, I didn't know you were in Moscow, too!" The writer turned around. "Alex, I spotted you a long time ago." Lowering his voice, he spoke in Russian: a strange way to have a secret conversation in a Russian crowd. "Listen, any minute now, there could be a terrible massacre, yes, a slaughter. This could be a second Tiananmen, only worse. An Alpha team is moving itself here. One Alpha officer is like a small tank—don't doubt it." Then in English: "Armor all over, gas, spinning bullets, flamethrowers . . . er, how is it—*ognemyoti* . . ." And in Anglo-Russian: "*Strashny* grenades! Total *besposhchadnost!*" Then back to English: "So we should make ourselves scarce! Let's go upstairs, to Rose!" Alexander replied: "Tell them I'm fine, will you?" Square looked at him with attentive and, as it seemed to him, somewhat sardonic eyes. Then again, what we take for a sardonic glint in the eyes of an Englishman might in fact be the depths of emotion.

"So you're staying?"

"Yes."

"With your people?"

"Exactly."

"Take care of yourself, Alex."

"See you later, Les."

"I hope so."

Taking his time and still snapping pictures, Square headed for ComEcon, as the West called the Union of Mutual Economic Assistance. One must give him his due—by his calculations, after all, the Alpha attack could begin at any minute. And we will give him his due.

Interestingly enough, A.Z. received almost exactly the same advice from his commander, Sery: "Listen, you're a foreigner, am I right? An émigré? Yeah, I thought so. Listen, you might want to take off. Everything here could get . . . well, you understand. The KGB bastards won't stand on ceremony with the likes of you. They wouldn't spare even the real Sasha Korbach." A.Z. burst out laughing. "I *am* Sasha Korbach, Sergei, but I'm not about to hide behind that."

Astounded, the fellow stared at him wide-eyed. His happiness at such an unexpected meeting with a living legend slowly spread over his entire face. And Alexander Zakharovich, casting off all inhibitions, suddenly began to pour his heart out to him. "For me, Sergei, to die fighting the KGB people would be the summit of my existence. Listen, you're a mountain climber, you understand what a summit is. There you are, you've climbed up, you're ecstatic, and at that moment you catch a bullet—ideally on your left side, between the ribs, so that you've got a few seconds for your mind to take in that peak you won't make—seconds, that is—if they shoot you in the head. Either way, if the peak and the bullet are inseparable, then I'll never step aside. After all, I stopped believing a long time ago that that peak—crudely speaking, freedom—exists. For a long time now, you see, I've considered my Russia a blind horse in a forgotten mine shaft."

Astounded by this monologue, Sergei, who was indeed an instructor at a mountaineering camp, looked at Korbach with the pearly cave of his mouth, with its single, almost unnoticeable little stalactite of metal alloy, wide open. Obviously the lad had the feeling that, like Ulysses, he had fallen into some stream of miracles. To come to Moscow on business and to find himself in the middle of a revolution, on the barricades, to meet Sasha Korbach himself on them, and, to top it all off, to hear a little speech that might later become a popular song addressed directly to him.

They kept making their way toward the government building. Finally they emerged at the sign-up point. The fellows from their barricade were already there, the forty-fourth hundred-man unit was being formed. Our mountaineer Sergei

Yakubovich was chosen as commander on the spot. They weren't handing out any weapons, though some captain or lieutenant in full Navy uniform was calling with a megaphone for anyone who had served in a military unit to step forward. Someone with a red armband jumped up. "Are you Korbach? Please, stay in this sector. Someone will come for you shortly."

More and more familiar faces began to pop up in the crowd. Many of them were theater folk. Igor Kvasha from the Contemporary Theater asked him crisply what unit he was in. You're going to stay? I'm staying until the end. I've had enough, you know! All my life it was impossible, and now I've had enough! Some young actors and actresses from the Tabakov studio came up. They were laughing, as if what was going on all around them were just one big party. A pun that someone had tossed off based on a line from Lermontov was already making its way through the crowd: "I put a bomb in Pugo's bum!" Here and there were bursts of laughter: "Oh, I'm dying, Pugo's bum!" Everyone was obviously picturing the minister's Baltic Communist physiognomy at the moment when the explosive charge of Lermontov's bombardier was shoved up his backside. At this point it is worth pointing out an important detail that made this rather forced pun entirely appropriate: the monologue of Lermontov's bombardier comes at the point when he is expecting to die on the battlefield of Borodino. The day of August 19, 1991, was already approaching the time of dusk and head colds. In the crowd of artists standing on the wet steps, they were telling the story of how their former comrade the minister of culture of the USSR had lost his nerve and come out in support of the SCSE, thereby freeing up one pair of the 250,000 pairs of handcuffs that had been ordered. Now the Buffoons began performing: Natalie the Battery, Elozin the Bronze Wizard, nutty Shurik, Lidka the Rattler, Tiger Cub, Port of Odessa, Boozy Mark—you can't remember everyone at moments of historic perturbation. They began a performance on an age-old, Rabelaisian theme about the minister of culture who had got the wind up. The free people of Moscow, including numerous ladies with little dogs who had come out at this hour to walk their darlings, some of which were even bigger than they were, enjoyed the farce, particularly when U.S. Citizen Sasha joined in—yes, that's right—*that* Korbach—he's performing along with all of them, yet he wheels and deals in huge sums from the American budget!

Toward the end of the concert, people from "our government" began shouting in the crowd that there wasn't enough paper for the propaganda battle with the junta. Please, anyone who's got any paper, do your bit! We thank you in advance! Sasha Korbach took three of his mates from the barricade and headed for the ComEcon building to fetch some paper.

In the Korbach Fund, all the offices were blazing with wonderful electricity. In the conference room no fewer than two dozen people were gathered around the table, Russians and Americans alike, eating Tula cookies. Matt Shuroff, manager of the office, brought in a three-bellied samovar in his powerful arms. It must be said that he wasn't missing his eighteen-wheeler in Moscow, and that even the wound inflicted by the dramatic departure of Bernadetta still gave a twinge now and again, as he put it, but had stopped bleeding. This incorrigible Byronite from the ranks of the American working class had already fallen in love again, and we can probably guess with whom, can't we?

"All of us decided to stay," Lester Square explained. "The feeling of being under siege is something incomparable. The strongest such feeling I ever experienced was in 1969 in the Comoro Islands, at the Hotel Florida, when Bob Dinard's motor launches were approaching the islands in the dark. Now have a look at those lights winking on the other side of the river. I'm sure that's Alpha sniffing around."

Rose Morrows was inimitable in the role of besieged American lady. Who would have thought that fate would lift a postal worker from Yornoverblyudo County to such heights? "We're always sending out protests and calls for solidarity to every humanitarian organization in the world," she was saying. And we get a huge number of replies.

"I want to limit these activities somewhat, Rose," Alex said. "The expropriation of paper for purposes of resistance. Yes, yes, thank you very much." He fell asleep as soon as he sat down in a chair. Jet lag after the long flight and the high excitement that had had him in its grip for several hours already had taken their toll; he was dead to the world.

He woke up as though he had just nodded off for a moment. The room was empty and dark, with only a camper's lamp, the flame on low, burning in one corner. Someone had put A.Z.'s feet up on a neighboring chair. It was quiet, with only the indecipherable chatter of some information apparatus audible in the distance. He got out of the chair and went over to the window. For a few seconds he was unable to make sense of what he saw in the deep violet semidarkness. The moment of confusion immediately made itself felt in his breathing—he began "drowning" in the air. Panicking, he looked at his watch. The position of the hands dealt him a blow somewhere around his ear: five minutes to eight. Then it dawned on him: I still haven't changed my watch from the flight. Then everything fell into place. I'm in Moscow. In Moscow there's been a military coup. Send yourself seven hours ahead for Moscow time, and it turns out to be five minutes to four on the morning of August 20, 1991. The picture of the world was reestablished and even took on a feeling of coziness, as though it were the eve of a birthday and the arrival of "our people" was expected.

The sky was crisscrossed with helicopter lights. On the asphalt below were large puddles. It looked like the rain wasn't stopping anymore. There seemed to be fewer people standing in the square now, but there were still a good number. Speakers were making speeches here and there. Campfires were visible beside the masses of the barricades. A whole floor of the White House was lit up. I hope that they left the lights on as a diversion and that they themselves are sitting in darkened rooms. They say Boris is transformed at times of crisis. The flabby muzhik turns into a genius of the counterattack. Tricolor flags are hanging everywhere. That means the coup didn't end while I was asleep.

Hurriedly he tossed a few sandwiches and cans of beer that had been left on the table into a paper bag and dashed down the stairs—for once the elevators were stopped. There was a stench of something melted in the air outside, as though the

Hotel Ukraine had been transformed during the night into a soap factory. Slinging his bag over his shoulder, he approached the crowd. "Have any of you guys seen Seryozha Yakubovich?" They waved him in the direction of the Novinsky Passage. The commander is catching a few winks under an arch over that way, they said. He went there.

Beneath one of the arches of the large Stalinist building, a group in hooded jackets was sitting. A quantity of rucksacks and sport bags were gathered in a pile. The butt of a submachine gun was protruding from one of them. "Say, guys, you haven't seen Sery by any chance, have you?" A few gloomy faces turned to him. One of the men made a gesture that said: Go on, scram! "What's the problem?" he asked. "You can't tell me?" "Get lost or we'll rip your Jew face off," one of the hooded figures said. Someone sniggered. Some surface of tough hide swelled up behind the backs of the men and immediately went back down.

"These guys are cuckoo," explained Yakubovich, who had just appeared from behind them. "Monarchists." He was fresh, ruddy-cheeked, and white-toothed, just as he had been the evening before. "You've come just in time, Sasha! We're ready to act!" "Strange to see so many mongrels here," A.Z. said loudly so that they would hear and repeated: "Mongrels!" No one was looking at him anymore, and the faces were no longer visible beneath the hoods.

A small bus had been made ready for the action. What sort of action—conceptualism? More like normal activity—we're going to the Lenin Hills to demoralize the troops. A.Z., without asking any more questions, jumped onboard. In front of them a section of one of the barricades was pulled aside to make way. The trembling and shaking bus came out onto the bridge. They were afraid that a patrol would stop them on the other side, but they got through. They blew past rows of sleeping, if not actually dead, tanks and down the embankment in the direction of the Mosfilm studios. They used to return this way from government shoots to give the footage to the production department.

On the bus along with the men from the barricades were deputies to the Supreme Soviet and even one member of the national government, Professor Nikolai Nikolaevich Vorontsov, minister of the environment—the only one of Gorbachev's cabinet, incidentally, to condemn the coup. Sasha Korbach's presence was an inspiration to everyone. The young people know you, and the soldiers are those very same young people.

What are we going to do in the Sparrow—er, make that the Lenin—Hills? A big-time scoundrel doesn't attach much importance to small fry, he's only got one dirty trick left up his sleeve: to take the Russian word for "sparrow"—*vorobei*—and make a pun out of it: *vor-ubei* (thief-kill) or something along those lines. On the esplanade and farther along in the direction of the university, APCs were parked in large numbers. It was clear that the undermining of morale was already under way in this unit without any outside interference. The rear hatches were open. From the armored bellies came the sounds of snoring, chatter liberally sprinkled with obscenities, and even singing accompanied by a guitar: "Driving the

bayonet in with a smile, I run it into the taut chest of the *dushman*'s robe." Many
soldiers were ambling by the heavy vehicles. Here and there, not in the least worried by the presence of officers, some were listening to Western Russian-language
broadcasts on transistor radios. A voice that Korbach knew from the Paris studios
of Radio Liberty was exhorting soldiers not to take up arms against their own
brothers. No one was paying any attention to the party of civilians that had appeared out of the night. Beyond the esplanade, all across the horizon flickered the
lights of Moscow, fraught with meaning.

Finally, a commanding voice was heard: "What are these people doing here?"
Some important-looking colonel was standing in a circle of subordinates. "Who
are you?"

"We're from the White House" came the answer. "Deputies and a minister.
And Sasha Korbach, the singer."

"Seriously?" one of the officers exclaimed. "Sasha Korbach is with you, too?"

"Of course he is! All honorable people are with us!"

"Are you sure about that?" the colonel asked.

"Are you sure of yourself, Colonel? Why did you come into Moscow with such
a load of armor?"

"We came to save the country from anarchy. To prevent a general collapse."

"It doesn't seem to you, Colonel, that this is just a coup? The president has
been arrested. Don't you think the whole business smells of civil war?"

"Well, we can argue about it," the colonel suddenly offered and even adopted
a more comfortable pose, leaning against a balustrade and taking out a pack of
cigarettes.

Soldiers and officers gathered around. A discussion began. One of the deputies
cleverly paraphrased one of the Stalinist formulae: "Communists come and go,
but Russia, our motherland, remains." "Not badly put," the unit commander commented. One of the soldiers raised his hand, as though he were at school. "Permission to put a question to Sasha Korbach? Sasha Korbach, did you know Volodya
Vysotsky personally?" Laughter went up. There's a grunt for you! Even on a night
like this, he's got nothing but guitars on his mind! What a greenhorn! The first
question was followed by a second: "Whose side would Volodya Vysotsky be on
now?" "On ours," Sasha Korbach replied, and he said nothing more, though nothing else was needed. The crowd stirred. Someone shouted "Hurrah!"

Suddenly a major and two soldiers carrying submachine guns leapt smartly
from a jeep that had just pulled up. "What's going on here? Stop this agitprop business and come with us!" Seryozha Yakubovich pushed away the man's overbear-
ing arm. "You've no right; the deputies are inviolable!" At that point one of the
submachine gun bearers hit him full in the face with the butt of his "paratrooper
model." It—Yakubovich's face, that is—was immediately transformed into a pulp.
He fell over on his side and began spitting out clots of blood and fragments of
his once—a second before, that is—magnificent teeth. Sasha knelt beside him.
"Seryozha, are you okay?" he yelled in English for some reason. Seryozha moaned
something along the lines of "Everything's fine" but then fell silent. Korbach took
him by the legs. "Pick him up, guys! Let's run over to the Sklif!"

A few minutes later the crumbling bus was racing through the deserted streets of Moscow to the Sklifasovsky Institute. The minister and the deputies stayed in the Lenin Hills surrounded by the entirely friendly troops. As a general rule, feelings of guilt rarely contribute to a collapse of military discipline, but that was exactly what happened in this case.

There was no better place than the Sklif for getting a feeling of the presence of the ponderous Soviet Army in the city: one patient had got his legs crushed by a tank, another had been accidentally pinned against a wall, a third had simply been spattered with the snot of a burning kerosene lamp—well, you get the picture. "I'm afraid to think what it'll be like in here tomorrow," Korbach was told by Professor Zulkarneyev, the doctor in charge of the emergency unit, who, as it turned out, was an old acquaintance, a fan of the Buffoons. Yakubovich was transported to the jaw surgery center. His eyes were clear. He couldn't speak now. He indicated Korbach with his eyes to his men, as if to say: He's your commander now. "Don't sweat it, Sery," A.Z. said to him. "Later on, we'll make teeth for you the likes of which neither the Caucasus nor the Pamirs have ever seen!"

3

COMRADES-IN-ARMS

On August 20, around midday, Marshal Yazov was riding in his armored Zil from the Lubyanka to the Ministry of Defense on the Arbat Square. He was facing the most important decision of his life. A quarter of an hour before, Kryuchkov had told him that all attempts to come to an agreement with the "handful of adventurists" had failed. The comrades don't want to lay down arms before the Party. Who would? thought the marshal. Who wants to twist around under blows with his hands behind his back, be transformed into a living pork chop? If I were on that side, I wouldn't want to either. Being on this side, I could lay down arms, though: democrats wouldn't beat up an old man, after all.

The limousine drove by endless columns of demonstrators, walking with vigorous strides from a rally on Manege Square in the direction of the White House, that is, to support the renegades. The order to block Kalininsky Prospekt, the marshal noted gloomily, had been carried out by no one. That's strange, he mused. Orders are given to be carried out. Before, it was unheard of that orders should not be carried out. Maybe they made a shitty job of it, but they carried them out. I can't think of a single instance of a failure to execute an order.

On the signs in the hands of the demonstrators, in addition to the slogan "Down with the SCSE," which he was already thoroughly fed up with—and after only twenty-four hours!—were insulting and crudely drawn caricatures. They represented the qualities of the personages of the country's supreme leadership: the puffiness of Prime Minister Pavlov, the ferret-faced look of chairman of State Security Kryuchkov, the stupor of Minister of the Interior Boris Karlovich Pugo, the distinctive alcohol-soaked quality of Interim President Yanayev, the minister of defense himself with the look of a strange, ugly bullock. It's in bad taste, comrades, it isn't funny! You ought to look at yourselves! All these demonstrators will be held responsible for their rowdy behavior. Right up to the point of the supreme measure, if need be. Don't you realize that Kryuchkov's people have orders to carefully photograph all the ringleaders? I hope that their orders are being carried out, at least?

On the whole, there was something strange about Nikolai Fyodorovich. A sort of shrill quality. Why was it necessary to lay everything on the ministry of defense? Haven't you got your own detainment and liquidation forces? Where's your vaunted Alpha? Playing cards in entranceways? You're ordering us to crush such large contingents of our own people with tanks? They're not Hungarians, after all, or Czechs—they're not even Afghans! What are you squealing about, why keep shoving that atypical episode in the Lenin Hills under my nose? Colonel Mylnikov is a highly decorated combat officer—for the time being there's no reason to suspect him of violating orders.

"Have we got a line to Mylnikov?" the marshal asked his adjutant, Lieutenant Colonel Chaapaev. The latter turned his none-too-proletarian face all the way around. "No line, Comrade Marshal." Heartburn momentarily ravaged the entire digestive tract of the minister of defense. "What, the whole brigade has disappeared?" "Looks that way, Comrade Marshal," the adjutant replied and withdrew behind his pseudoaristocratic set of features. Yazov pulled a cream-colored curtain to one side. The impudent mugs of the out-of-control crowd immediately surged up into his field of vision. You missed out on a whole generation—they slipped through your shitty fingers, Comrade Komsomol, dear secret policemen of the motherland! Some runts who don't look the least bit Soviet are poking their tricolored bits of White Guard trash into the side of the Zil—pederasts! I'd like to fire a burst from the hip at that bunch myself! On that point, of course, Kryuchkov is right: One can do away with a few degenerates for the sake of the happiness of millions. But how do you separate them from the thousands who've led astray?

"Comrade Marshal, Varennikov is on the line," Chaapaev said in an expressionless voice and handed the radio-telephone receiver to Yazov. For some reason he couldn't place the name of his comrade-in-arms right away. That is, he did in fact remember it, but apropos of something else, as it were. "Varennikov, Val. Iv. (born 1923), Sov. military leader, General of the Army (1978). Party member since 1944. In Gr. Patr. War commanded artil. regiment. Since 1973 com. Carpathian Air Defenses. Dep. Supreme Soviet USR since 1974." This was the entry in the *Soviet Encyclopedic Dictionary,* 1980 edition, in which the present minister of defense had not warranted a single line. Marshal Yazov never revealed his outrage to anyone, but to himself he called Varennikov "that Stalinist upstart."

"Listen, Dimitry, what's going on?" a grumpy Varennikov asked. "We agreed, after all, that Yeltsin would be liquidated on the first day, and he's still gallivanting around, giving interviews to every PPC correspondent that comes along!"

Yazov bridled. "You're talking to the wrong man, Comrade Soviet Military Leader, born 1923! Why should the army concern itself with the removal of a criminal? We haven't got law enforcement bodies? Have you called Yanayev, Pavlov? All power is in their hands. And then there's Pugo—where are his units?"

"Yanayev and Pavlov have drunk themselves unconscious. Pugo is having a personal crisis. Kryuchkov is blaming everything on you. Have you lost your minds, fellows? You're destroying the state's power!"

"How dare you talk to me like that?" Yazov roared like a bear so powerful as to make even the unflappable Chaapaev look at him out of the corner of his eye.

"I dare!" the deputy to the Supreme Soviet, USSR, since 1974 shrieked back. "Did you know that Mylnikov's entire brigade has gone over to the enemy?"

Yazov threw the receiver to the floor in a rage. At that moment, Lieutenant Colonel Chaapaev asked the driver to stop and got out as soon as his request was granted.

"And just where are you going, Pyotr Yakovlevich?" the marshal howled at the young man's back. "I know you don't believe in Russia's historical destiny, but at least think of your career, you little turd! You're not even thirty yet, and I've made you a Guards lieutenant colonel! You've got the whole system of coordination on you, the motherland's nuclear shield! You philosopher-pricks, you've got into the upper ranks! Think about your tarts, about the library! You're risking your life, Comrade Lieutenant Colonel Chaapaev!"

The back, without a reply, quickly moved away and was soon absorbed into the unbelievable rabble of the enemies of socialism around the Khudozhestvenny cinema.

At roughly the same time, Kryuchkov, the country's chief secret policeman, and General Karpukhin, Alpha commander, went into the gymnasium of a secret base. No fewer than 120 officers in the aforementioned unit turned to face the new arrivals. To the outsider it looked like a gathering of soccer players: everyone there was wearing a warm-up suit except for Kryuchkov, though even he could have passed for a burned-out head coach in his grease-stained suit.

"Comrade Officers," Karpukhin began. "I've reported your decision not to get involved in the power struggle to the leadership. The leadership categorically rejects your conclusions. Will you allow me to formulate them one more time for Nikolai Fyodorovich?" The officers, each of whom could transform himself into a small tank, to use the expression of the literary spy Lester Square, in a few minutes, nodded to their commanding officer: Formulate, Karpukhin! Many of them were standing with their arms folded across their chests but were still rocking back and forth on their springy legs—that is, working their Achilles tendons, on which ever so much depends during an attack with the lower tier of the body. The headquarters' mascot, Kotofei the cat, was perched in a window devouring a pigeon. Now and again his remaining eye widened, like a night vision device.

"The basic problem is posed by the unusually dense crowding of the populace around the White House. In order to bring the attack to a successful conclusion, that is, arrest and removal of the leaders of the Russian Federation, we will have to sacrifice a minimum of thirty thousand people of our nation. In view of the fact that all this is happening in the capital of our motherland, in the hero city of Moscow, and not in some abstract foreign area, the Alpha team prefers not to advance in battle formations in order not to stain its colors in the historical perspective. That, on the whole, is the resolution." Karpukhin shrugged his uncommonly broad shoulders, as if to show that he was preserving his professional impartiality.

The officers were looking at Kryuchkov, whose name was never uttered among them, since it was replaced by a single syllable that laid waste to everything in its path: the Boss. This was the tradition in the unit: no matter what asshole the Party appointed, once in the commander's chair he became "the Boss" without any reservations. Basically, the first reservations in the seventy-four years of the existence of the "fighting arm of the Party" were being expressed today.

Kryuchkov turned his head and ordered his escort to take action. All the doors of the gymnasium were opened, with members of Kryuchkov's personal guard—including the three Zavkhozov brothers—their instruments of slaughter trained on the men of Alpha, standing on the thresholds. "Everyone lie down on the floor! Facedown!" the commander of the platoon ordered. The Alpha men obeyed. The meaning of the order was perfectly clear to them, although, in refusing to exterminate thirty thousand "people of the nation," they still could hardly imagine how not to obey the Boss.

Kryuchkov and his adjutants—Bubkov, Buitsov, Buinov, Brutkov, and Bruschatnikov—had a glint of sadness in their eyes as they looked over the 120 not at all bad backs and heads of their own Praetorian guard. Until that moment the minds of these generals in mufti, like the godfathers of international crime, had imagined an entirely different scenario. Yeltsin's band facedown, noses in the ground, and with these very men, their mighty charges, the pride of the all-Union spooks, holding their weapons over them.

"Comrades! Officers!" the Boss said, addressing the men lying down. "I'll give you one last chance. Those who return right now to their unit for the execution of the battle plan will be forgiven their violation of their oath. Those who persist will be subject to the law on the state of emergency. You have thirty seconds to think about it!" It seemed to him that all the steel of the regiments of the proletariat rang in his voice. Sometimes he thought about himself: It's a shame that my appearance is rather ordinary. Not like that of, say, Yuri Vladimirovich Andropov, that sinister bird on guard for the revolution! Unfortunately sometimes I look like a KGB pensioner playing dominoes in the park. Well, history has seen quite a few examples of individuals whose personalities were out of scale with their outward appearance—that's the way it is here. The great Lenin, for example, didn't make a dramatic effect with his features, but he gave off an aura of unbending will.

Now he was standing with his fists clenched in the pockets of his drooping jacket. The seconds were ticking. The officers lay there, though they were raising their heads now and then to see who had stood up. No one was getting up. Kotofei was dripping pieces of his pigeon from the windowsill onto the floor. Why are they just lying there calmly? the exhausted Kryuchkov asked himself. They're sure that even the Zavkhozovs won't shoot. Well then, the game's up. At the end of the day I can't push the nuclear button that has been taken away from Mikhail Sergeyevich . . . Yuri Vladimirovich would have pushed it. And Nikita Sergeyevich would have. No one else would have. Leonid Ilyich wouldn't have pushed it. That's how it goes, the decay of the steellike body of socialism. With a slight grunt, General Karpukhin lay down alongside his own men.

"Traitors!" the KGB chairman exclaimed, clearly, forcefully, like a sturdy rooster, and immediately left the hall. His adjutants—Bubkov, Buitsov, Buinov, Brutkov, and Bruschatnikov—followed him, already weighed down with worries about their futures. Not even the men of Alpha, a bunch of keen senses if ever there was one, noticed the disappearance of the personal guard. Top-secret supersubmachine guns, each bullet from which would produce a miniature atomic explosion in a body, were scattered around the would-have-been site of the massacre. Naturally, the officers examined with interest these weapons that they had recently been promised but still not issued.

Meanwhile, the Zavkhozov brothers were already heading for the hills. They had to clean out their flats in time: burn the Party cards, melt down the secret badges, flush the poisons down the toilet. They also needed to rid these flats of their own presence. As for the generals, their muffled steps were already sounding along the windowed passages through the top-secret suburban Moscow pine forest. It wasn't the first time they were fading away in the gloom, though here and there Kotofei's infrared eye lit up their backs. To make the symbolism complete, O Theophilus, we'll add that the pigeon half-devoured by the cat flew away to pursue his own business.

At approximately the same time, or perhaps an hour or two later, S. V. Mikhalkov, chairman of the Union of Soviet Writers, sat down in front of the ultra-Japanese television in his apartment. Attired in a cashmere cardigan and camel-hair slippers, he turned on the disgusting, not to say anti-Soviet, CNN channel. S.V.'s building was quite near the center of the events being observed by the enemy's eye. It would be enough to cross the Garden Ring at the point where it swells out into Uprising Square, walk past the towering structure that was a monument to a strong and generous power that had illuminated Mikhalkov's youth with its triumphant gleam and turned him from a children's versifier into the state's number-one writer, turn left, and there it would be—the White House standing like a ghost of the glorious thirties, now become the uprising of the nineties. That structure had always seemed to him the very embodiment of solidity, a bulwark of the Union's essence, and now it had begun to waver.

Without understanding what the American newswomen, overly familiar yet not without feminine charm, were chattering about, S.V. gazed at the swaying mass of faces, at the White Guard banners waving back and forth. It was incomprehensible that the "democratic gang" had endured the whole night, issuing their challenge to common sense for the second day running, putting the brakes on the armor-encased wheel of history. It was, in fact, in support of common sense that secretaries of the Writers' Union had signed their historic declaration the day before.

Suddenly a painful thought flashed through Sergei Vladimirovich's mind: They'd signed, all right, but what if they suddenly found that they'd miscalculated? They'd burst out of there all at once, a crowd would come from the river and go through the building unit by unit looking for deputies, laureates, f-f-functionaries? The old man's train of thought was interrupted by the ringing of the telephone. On the other end of the line was a colleague in every sense of the word: Kuznetzov, Felix Fedosyevich, descendant of Revolutionary Democrats. "Sergei, I'm calling you from the street—no, not from Povarskaya, from Vorovsky. There's an important discussion going on—can you come out?" Mikhalkov was intimate with many of his colleagues from the secretariat, but he and Felix were united by more than an outward show of official solidarity—it was something that went beyond the facade, a profound feeling of comradeship.

He went out as he was, in his camel-hair slippers, which immediately got soaked. The burly figure of Professor Kuznetzov was standing beneath an umbrella by the iron gates of the once reliable writers' colony. The professor's familiar beard looked like a crookedly applied disguise. He pressed himself up against Mikhalkov's left side, took him firmly by the arm, and exhaled on him with fetid breath. "You know, Seryozha, I've been up all night, I took Lenin, Rozanov, and Blok down from the shelf. I was tortured by thoughts of Russia, of what awaits us in the way of ethnohistorical circumstances; you understand all of this, of course. Against Bely and his 'Enough, don't wait, don't hope, scatter, my poor people,' we set the well-known 'mare of the steppe'; she'll carry on until the end, she'll make it!"

"G-g-get to the point," Mikhalkov said.

"Fine," Kuznetzov said, but he was unable to stop his civic discourse right away; it rolled on. "I was thinking about our resolution of yesterday, I was proud. We had enough courage not to be taken in by demagoguery, to take a stand against literary debauchery, to rise up with our . . . well, you know, with the people, with the patriots of the government. Yes, yes, I'm getting closer to the point now, of course." He gave a strange, almost sinister giggle, looked around, and then forcefully, from below, whispered directly into the cartilage of Mikhalkov's ear: "And what if all of a sudden . . . ?" Without missing a beat he whispered: "We can't get caught, we've got to think about saving our intellectual and creative riches, we mustn't let the achievements of our grandiose historic experiment be erased, those of our positivist philosophy. It'll still be of use come the joyful hour of sunrise! Okay, okay, here's the point: Have you got your own people with you, strong people?" Mikhalkov sniggered. "Just like you have, Felix, don't be so modest. But if your 'and all of a sudden' happens, these strong people won't bother their heads with polite niceties."

Kuznetzov grabbed at his beard and gave a moan. "That's not what I mean, Sergei—that's not what I mean. I'm talking about China, Cuba, the Democratic People's Republic of Korea. About Vietnam, even! Our extremists think that they're destroying Communism, but the Asian bastions are unshakable. Chernyshevsky's dream is coming from the East this time! You've got friends in the embassies of fraternal countries in case we have to save ourselves, to emigrate, haven't you? If they start sending people away ..." His face warmed with a smoldering heat, and with a little smile he looked at his old comrade, eyes lowered. "... people like you and me, Sergei?"

Mikhalkov immediately flared up himself from this heat. "What are you getting at, Felix? Six generations of children in this country grew up on my 'Uncle Styopa' and you're trying to drag me off to Ch-Ch-China? Not a chance, go off to China without me! We Mikhalkovs come from Russian merchants of the very first guild, we don't sell out to Asians!"

The stunned Kuznetzov sat down. The old man Mikhalkov, as he was in his camel-hair slippers, was walking away from him, straight ahead, not going around puddles, toward the very middle of Uprising Square. " 'Union unbreakable of free republics,' " he muttered the lines of his creation, the Soviet national anthem (which he had been commissioned to write by Stalin himself) and then corrected himself immediately. " '... of eternally free fighters for democracy'—that doesn't sound so bad. 'Mighty Rus has joined together forever ...' doesn't sound bad, either, even now. Beg your pardon, something's not quite right. My instinct for style has never let me down yet. 'Eternally free' and 'forever' in the next line, that won't do. Let's try something else. 'Fighters for democracy, strong and free/Mighty Rus has joined them together forever! Long may it live, created by the will of the peoples'—we'll leave that line as it is, it won't hurt anyone. Now there's another snag. Well, forward, inspiration!"

The gloomy clouds resembling the sails of a sizable fleet encouraged the poet. With his long beak like that of a woodpecker and his sturgeon's gills behind his ears (in connection with which he had once been slanderously but eloquently described by Valentin Petrovich Katayev), he was catching the scent of the new Russian wind. And so:

Fighters for democracy, strong and free,
Mighty Rus has joined them together forever!
Long live the society, created by the will
Of the peoples, by whose freedom I swear!
Be glorified, our free fatherland,
The firm bulwark of our thoughts and words!
Tricolor banner, national banner,
Let it lead all to prosperity! [Well, now that's more like it!]
Through the clouds the sun of freedom has shone on us.
And the great Pushkin has shown us the way!

Sakharov was our power for many years,
And with him Solzhenitsyn inspired us all!
Refrain.

He was standing now in the very center of his unshakable world, getting spattered by mud as empty trucks roared past and proudly singing the anthem of the new democratic Russia in a screeching voice. "Hey, Uncle Styopa!" truck drivers brought up on the good policeman's poem yelled at him as they raced by, and the state's chief versifier knew: I'll hold out, we'll get through this, too, and still we'll be standing and rumbling away!

4

ARDENT HEADS IN CLEAN HANDS

*W*asn't Sergei Vladimirovich being a bit hasty, and wasn't he overdoing things a bit? After all, the situation in the capital toward evening on the twentieth of August was far from clear, and the majority of the military units were ready to carry out "any order from the motherland." Everywhere in the crowd of defenders of the White House—we mean the unarmed mass of people who were standing in the tens of thousands among the barricades and on the steps of the marble and concrete hulk—conversations were under way to the effect that the hour of the final assault was approaching, that snipers were sitting on the rooftops of the surrounding buildings, ready to pick off anyone in the crowd—even you, my dear citizens—and that soon helicopters would be coming to release the tear gas.

A strange phenomenon was spreading through the crowd, however. Everyone was talking about the assault but somehow with a sort of detachment. Everyone was virtually certain that there would be an attack, but for some reason no one was even afraid, as though the people did not understand that it would be over their bodies, and no one else's, that the Red Army would break through to the White House.

The sunset displayed a sort of combination of quasi-Suprematist purple and scarlet figures, which no one could decipher. At twilight the rain returned. Sasha Korbach felt little streams trickling down his face but didn't wake up. He was back in the land of jet lag, but this time the off switch had been tripped not when he was in a soft armchair but beneath a plywood awning among the heaps of junk of the barricades, where he had crawled for a quick smoke. Later, remembering these blackouts, he would think that perhaps there had been something metaphysical about them: his energy contour had momentarily abandoned the heat of history in order to rest in some cool astral sphere. He woke up only when the mobile phone in the bag beside him chirped. A man's voice said in English: "I'm looking for Alex Korbach." "That's me," he replied, still not entirely sure whose voice was speaking. "Thank God, you're alive!" Stanley said.

The news of the events in Moscow had caught up with him in Calcutta. The day had been spent fiddling with the visas, and now they were in the air. "We're over the Himalayas now. There's a colossal moon, twenty-five-thousand-foot shadows right next to us, under the wing. Two of Norman Blamsdale's fighters attacked us an hour ago. We chased them off with a pacifying rocket. We'll be in Moscow in about five hours. Everybody sends you a hug: Bernie, Ben Duckworth, the pilots. Where are you? Well of course, Bernie, you were right, he's right in the middle of the hell. Hold on, Lavsky! The wire services say that everything will be decided tonight. Is there anywhere in Moscow to buy champagne?"

Alex put the telephone back in the bag and suddenly heard applause. His shelter was surrounded by a group of his admirers, men and women of the sort that Americans call aging children. He could pick out these late sixties types in any crowd. Right now they were giving him a touching round of applause, as though he had just played a scene entitled "Conversation in English with an Unknown Person." One woman said to him with a laugh characteristic of this sort of crowd: "We know it's stupid, but it still does us good to see you here with us now, Sasha Korbach!"

Two men with tricolored armbands made their way to him through the crowd. "Finally we've found you, Mr. Korbach." Lowering their voices, they said that they had come on a mission. If he wants them to, they can take him to the White House. The leadership was very glad to learn that he's here too, among the partisans of democracy, if it's really him. Well, you understand. Something could happen at any moment. But if you wish. That's all. Boris Nikolayevich, too. They'll be happy to see you.

In the corridors of the ground floor a crowd was seething; armed men were everywhere. Some walked through in bulletproof vests and helmets. Others were sitting on the floor along the walls, some nodding off, some drinking tea from thermoses and unwrapping sandwiches. The higher they climbed on the broad, frankly apotheosized staircases, the more often they glimpsed shoulder straps of field grade officers, including generals' stars. Commandos in full battle dress went by. The majority, however, was made up of bureaucrats in the uniform of protocol: coat-and-tie types.

They entered an enormous room with a metal cast of the RSFSR seal on the wall. There in one corner stood Yeltsin in the company of somewhat smaller men. A submachine gun of the very same type with which Yakubovich's teeth had been knocked out was hanging on Rutskoi's shoulder. Around a table in a part of the hall that could have accommodated one of Columbus's caravels sat a multitude of people. They were shuffling papers and tossing them back and forth to each other, but there were also some who were sleeping, their ardent heads on their clean hands.

Someone was eating something tasty. Waitresses from the buffet were plying back and forth, gathering up plates, setting down new ones, setting down bottles of Pepsi. At every window, slightly open, Mylnikov's commandos were posted, weapons ready. It was cold and damp, with an odor in the air of people who hadn't bathed in some time.

Yeltsin was told of Korbach's arrival. He handed a telephone receiver to someone and went toward Sasha with his arms outstretched. "Sasha Korbach, we couldn't get through a single tourist outing without your songs! Welcome! What a way for us to meet!" He radiated energy. It was obvious that these hours were the greatest of his life, and it was no accident that from time to time he cast a shadow on the white wall that was now a square, now a combination of triangles, now an outright parallelepiped; no one but Sasha noticed it, or stared, in any case.

"I have a great deal of esteem for the work of the Korbach Fund," the president went on. "The new Russia needs the help of the West, my friend Sasha! Now we'll be part of the civilized world!" He looked like a typical Soviet muzhik, this "our friend Borya," but there was something humane showing through in the outline of the lips. And there's something Suprematist that shows up in these reflections on the wall that no one sees, A.Z. thought. "Do you play tennis?" Yeltsin asked and gave a playful wink. "Well, anyway, Sasha, let's spend some time together, if you don't mind!" No fewer than half a dozen video cameras around them were capturing this additional moment of the general telehistorical revolution. Yeltsin solemnly raised a hand Siberian style and brought it down for an entirely civilized handshake.

I don't know if our reader can now see the full extent of this political theater—perhaps he can pause along with "our Alexander Zakharovich" for a moment before a few surprising circumstances and notice, for example, how in one wall there opens a piercing corridor, at the unfathomably far end of which are imprinted the images of a lion and a deer, an eagle and a cockatoo, a rosebush and an agave, and, finally, a unified—that is, not yet divided by sex—Adam, burning with eternal fire.

The action of the drama, however, does not pause even for that second. Yeltsin, in the breezy style of fifties volleyball—"Come on, boys, let's get ready!"—is back on the phone laying into the generals who are still wavering. In another corner, Rostropovich's cello is singing like a bass nightingale. Spotting his comrade in exile, Slava, helmet, bulletproof vest, and all, rushes over with kisses. "Sashka, you're here too! That's great! I love your talent, Sashka, goddamn it! I sobbed when I saw your film about Dante, it was brilliant!" Sasha gently corrected the internationally beloved artist. The film hasn't even started shooting yet, Slavochka. Having overdone it with the best of intentions, Slava kept up the friendly pressure. "I love your songs! I adore your music! You're a first-class melody writer, Sashka! Come on, accompany me on the flute! Say, lads, democrats, has anyone here got a flute? Korzhakov is already hurrying over with a flute on a tray. And Filatov here brought me a cello from the House of Pioneers! Bugger me if it doesn't sing like a Stradivarius!"

Korbach blew into the flute for a laugh and suddenly began to whistle like

Jean-Pierre Rampal. What do you know, we've got ourselves a duet in an encircled pavilion! Many of the rebels stopped what they were doing, deeply touched, and a group portrait of the besieged but audacious souls was suddenly flashed on the wall. "You see," Slava whispered to Sasha.

They were unable to complete their concert as they would have liked, however— as a flowing upsurge. In the city a cacophonous rumble broke out and began to increase in volume. A chaotic rush of uncovered heads and steel helmets alike was set in motion. Lighting was reduced to a minimum. The windows were opened wider. Figures with grenade launchers knelt down beside them. Korbach flagged down an officer hurrying by. What's going on, Major? The latter smiled. What we were waiting for, Comrade Musicians. Better if you go down into the cellar.

There's a remarkable sight for you: Rostropovich the maestro exchanging his cello for a Kalashnikov! Korbach hugged his old friend around the shoulders. "Slavochka, I've got to go to my unit. We'll finish playing tomorrow." The musician's thrust-out chin trembled with resolve. "You bet we'll finish playing, Sashka!"

The epicenter of the rumbling of tanks arrived on the Garden Ring in the area between Uprising Square and the Arbat gates. It was louder than any other sound and still could not drown out the chant: "Rus-sians! Rus-sians!" Young people were standing shoulder to shoulder above the tunnel into which the tanks and APCs were disappearing. Boys were waving tricolor flags from lampposts. The hellish elephants were pursued by flying bottles, not always empty, judging by the trails of fire snaking along the armor of the vehicles. No one was about to run away. Several times the crowd, swaying, rushed somewhere. It looked as though they were panicking, but no, it turned out that they were racing off to the first trolleybus they could find, getting the passengers off, and diverting the city transport to the barricades for reinforcement. A mass action of this sort, of course, was not without its jokers: someone started singing Okudzhava's "The Last Trolleybus Floats Through Moscow" at the top of his lungs.

Suddenly several of the tanks, instead of following the others into the tunnel, moved upward into the lateral passage—in other words, into people. A shrill voice cut through the roar of the engines: "Russians, are we scared of them even now?" And the crowd replied with a mighty chant of two syllables like a Greek chorus: "Ne-ver! Ne-ver!" A boy with his head swathed in bandages leapt onto one of the vehicles. Only small holes for the eyes and in the area of the nose and mouth protruded. He pulled the tank crewman who had thrust his head from his hatch with such force that the latter could only flail his arms until he had been removed entirely from his armored shell. A crowd was standing directly in front of the tanks, as if they had not the slightest intention of retreating, and several of the boys lay down on the asphalt. Well, what are you going to do, you bastards, crush your own people?

The tank drivers were braking, their machines barely advancing, which gave the daredevils the chance to roll out from under the treads at the last moment. Many jumped or clambered up onto the armored vehicles and, standing there on the backs of their enemies, continued to shout: "Russians! Russians!"

Meanwhile, a tragedy had occurred on the slope leading down into the tunnel. One of the APCs had broken formation, spun its wheels, and hit a concrete wall, in the process crushing three of the most vigorous protesters, young men in the Moscow uniform of jeans and white running shoes. "You've killed them! Murderers!" Moscow thundered aboveground and belowground, from sidewalks and balconies. The young lieutenant in command of the vehicle opened fire with his pistol. Kid soldiers spilled out of the rear hatch and disappeared with absurd leaps into the roaring night, that very night of the twentieth and the twenty-first of August, in the course of which, twenty-three years before, their fathers had driven into shaken and humiliated Prague and established their presence with steel wheels.

All through the night, the colossal encampment on the banks of the Moscow River waited in a ceaseless rain for the attack, but the attack never came. The roar of tank engines went up and then died down at once, then went up at another end of Moscow, creating the impression of a strange storm at sea, as though Neptune were now stirring the waves with his trident, now pouring olive oil on them. Meanwhile, on the periphery of the square, at the junctions and in the side streets, more and more tanks—whether they were "ours" or "Yazov's" was not quite clear—were gathering. The engines were shut off, and the crews climbed out onto their vehicles. It was not a rare sight to see Moscow girls sitting beside these "demobilized," as it were, soldiers on top of their tanks. The knots of people were smoking and singing a song by the female rock group Kombinatsia that was a hit that summer:

> *Two scraps of sausage*
> *Were lying on the table in front of me*
> *You were telling me fairy tales*
> *Only I didn't believe you.*

The soldiers were solicitously covering the girls with their overcoats. The populace, true to the age-old Russian tradition of taking pity on those under the colors, were handing rolls, pots of yogurt, and sticks of relatively edible sausage up onto the tanks. Goddamn, boys, this hasn't worked out too badly. We headed off on some half-assed mission that we didn't want to go on and landed in a pretty nice place: we've met some attractive chicks and had a party on some chow they'd never give us at the barracks.

"Boys, you've got no right to aim your guns at your own people!" two war veterans, each with a row of medals on his chest, said to them.

"We're not about to," the tankers replied.

"How dare you agitate among the troops?" a matronly woman, also wearing

medals, shrieked, interrupting the dialogue. "They took an oath to defend our Soviet motherland!"

"Get lost, Shura, you fucking snitch, or we'll give you one in the mouth," the
veterans admonished even this hysterical woman.

"Ruslan! Ruslan, my darling!" a touching feminine cry went up. It was addressed not to the well-known speaker of Parliament Ruslan Khasbulatov, but to a
skinny soldier in a tanker's helmet sitting against the barrel of a main gun. A stunning woman with bright red lips came running up. "Is that really you, my dear little Ruslan?" "Mama, Mama, come on now, what're you doing? Don't shout like
that, Mama!" the embarrassed tank crewman said. "I've got a little bag of candy!
I just knew it would come in handy! Take it, Ruslan!" The woman kept on crying,
while everyone around smiled, deeply touched.

Dawn had barely broken when a column of tanks began advancing onto the
bridge from Kutuzovsky Prospekt. It was heading straight for the barricade. What's
all this, then? The punitive monsters appeared out of the cold mist one after another like rolling flower beds. They all turned out to be covered with youths waving tricolor flags. And with furious energy, the masses of the human night watch
began dismantling the barricades. Victory!

Alexander Zakharovich Korbach burst into tears. His body shook now and
then as though he were in a state of religious ecstasy. More likely than not it was
in fact religious ecstasy, since never in his life had he expected to be witness to the
miracle of a real "spiritual revolution." Insubordination to tyrants will finally blaze
up like dry grass was the way that Lev Tolstoy had imagined these days. And now
the grass had blazed up, and all of our moments of desperation and powerlessness,
all of our humiliations, had gone up in these flames, if only for a moment. Even
if all of this be remembered by history, with the passage of time, as merely the
date of a failed coup, and even if things don't go entirely as these hundreds of thousands dream at this moment, all the same, these three days in August 1991 will remain the most glorious days in a thousand years of Russian history, a miracle on
the order of the Manifestation of the Mother of God. And maybe this *was* Her
Manifestation?

He handed his "Kalash" to one of the lads around him—fortunately, he hadn't
had to fire to a shot—and began making his way to ComEcon. Everywhere people
were laughing, shouting, and singing something entirely inappropriate to the occasion, since none of these people, who as recently as the day before had still been
Soviet, knew anything suited to it.

Incredible but true: the elevators in this run-down skyscraper had been fixed again.
The first thing he saw when he opened the door to the hall of the fund was Stanley's huge back. Next to this gigantic back, even the dorsum of Bernadetta De
Luxe looked like a little spine plus an ass. At that moment the first lady had assumed the form of an irresistible curve, since she was leaning slightly on the
shoulder of her protector. Other spines were stationed on the couple's flanks: Ben,
Les, Sol, Matt, Rose, Fuchs, and so on and so forth, count them yourselves. A.Z.

stood in the doorway and looked with a sort of fresh nostalgia on this American band now pressed up against the glass wall and having a lively discussion about the events taking place below. Farewell, America was the thought that formed in his mind as the result of this flash of nostalgia. Then someone turned around and let out a yell at the sight of "Lavsky the barricade fighter." Everyone rushed over to him, but Stanley got there first, to give him a Pantagruelesque hug. Sol Leibnitz, not letting the moment slip away, was taking one snapshot after another. Several champagne corks popped immediately.

5

THANKS FOR EVERYTHING!

*A*fter saying good-bye to America, Alexander returned there almost right away. Putney had scheduled the final negotiations for the budget. He was almost glad to tear himself away from the feverish atmosphere of Moscow and to land in the monotonous comfort of international first class. You go into the spacious, half-empty salon of a 747. In the middle of it they've already set up a buffet of luxurious drinks and hors d'oeuvres. An air conditioner buzzes softly. The air of Russia won't get in here. You pour yourself a glass of Clicquot, down it right away, and then head for your seat with another. Naturally, Oskar Belvedere is already sitting nearby. He's flying from Japan to New York. "Alex, what happened with you people in Moscow? Tell me about it, please!" And he added: "In a nutshell," which admittedly sounds almost brazen to a Russian ear in the post-August days.

Ten hours of semiwakefulness over an ocean lie ahead of you. In this half-conscious state you return to your normal life. For three days you haven't given this life the slightest thought. Not even Nora crossed your mind once. Well, now you can spend ten straight hours remembering her.

For a long time after their meeting at the Lutèce, he had castigated himself for being such a bastard to her. At times, though, he had begun to justify himself fiercely. Didn't she treat me dreadfully too? Wasn't she the one who played the part of the streetwalker? Since then, that is, a year and five months already, she'd not called him once and he hadn't looked for her. One day a bit of news reached him.

Beg your pardon, but at this point we're going to take a short time-out, leave our A.Z. alone with his thoughts, and engage the reader in a dialogue. It goes without saying, kind sir or madam, that we could hold off with this bit of news, postpone it until our twelfth and concluding part, in order to—how should we say?—stun you with its unexpectedness. There's another temptation besides this one: by delaying until the finale, we could charge this news item with symbolic meaning. No, kind sir or madam, we're not going to do things that way, if only out of respect for you as a reader of the creative sort, which you undoubtedly are if you've got as far as this page and haven't forgotten the ones that preceded it. As a reader of this sort and having got this far, you, of course, understand perfectly well that the author isn't looking for plot twists or stereotypical symbols. Our novel has nothing to do with the thriller genre, or as they say now in Moscow in neo-Russian, the *triller*. The rather strange pun contained in the correlation of the two words might provide us with a way out, however. If we translate the Russian word back we get the English word *trill*. As a matter of fact, it is indeed a "trill" that we're trying to put in place of a "thrill," that is, a keen sensation, but a no less superficial one for all that.

Let's go on now. One day, a bit of news reached him: Nora had given birth to a child, a boy. The timing coincided, or almost coincided, with the nine-month period after their passionate encounter. Does that mean that the conception occurred as a result of an access of lust, amid decadent draperies and mouse trails of cocaine? Be that as it may, a new continuer of the male line that Stanley called "double Korbach" had come into being. Just try to distinguish love from lust! Where is the face, and where the goat's mask? Had the modest essence of a human being, God's little worm, spent the night there?

Can one ever be sure about anything with Nora, though? Maybe the child has nothing to do with me at all. Maybe her age-old revolutionary ideal has distinguished himself again? After all, he's probably prowling around somewhere in the vicinity of those archaeological trenches. Or maybe it was just some ship passing in the night, in a hotel in the Middle East?

Once again he tried to find her. He even called up the Archaeological Society of North America. They told him there that, as far as they knew, Dr. Mansour had finished her work with the Lilienmann expedition and was in all likelihood compiling her results for publication. "Dig and publish!"—he had learned this archaeologists' precept eight years earlier.

And maybe she just went back to Pinkerton? It was a half mile or so across the rolling fields of the campus from the Black Cube to the archaeology department. He dropped in at Alfred Ridder Hall, one glance at the pseudo-Gothic towers of which summoned up amorous excitement in him. Just passing by, wanted to drop off "a Russian manuscript" for Nora Mansour. The secretaries in the office treated him with great feminine kindness. Unfortunately, Alex, we've got no news of Nora's whereabouts. All we know is that she extended her sabbatical for another year, without pay. Without pay? How will she get by without pay? They smiled and looked at him meaningfully. They probably know about the kid, but they think it's not quite proper to talk about it with the ex-boyfriend.

Stanley obviously didn't know anything. Caught up in the whirl of global philanthropy, he clearly had no time for individual newborns. He used the word *child* only in the plural, with visions of orphans in Karabakh, or victims of starvation in Somalia and ethnic cleansing in Yugoslavia, or the ones at home in the United States who were not receiving their mandatory vaccinations.

All the more stunning, then, was his recent (just a day before the flight in progress) revelation of his fourth cousin. In the bar of the Moscow Inter-Continental, he'd told him, sheepishly, that Bernadetta was expecting a baby and that it would be a boy. I have to admit to you that this old stud was beside himself with joy. First of all, I'm pleasantly surprised that my genital capabilities are still intact. Second, I'll be glad to shake off the image of King Lear. Third, I'm happy that the male line will be renewed. I'm already old, of course, but Bernie's still young enough to raise the boy.

Young and healthy like Pantagruel's mare, A.Z. thought in the semidarkness of the Soviet bar decked out with a large number of top-of-the-line prostitutes. Healthy if you didn't count the megaton of Scotch and the megaton of gin that she'd knocked back at the First Bottom, and also the crack that she indulged in prodigiously so as to make her Homeric copulations all the sweeter; and, of course, not counting trivial things like gonorrhea, herpes, and crabs, which hadn't given the receptive body a wide berth either. He tried to drive away these uncharitable thoughts and slapped the magnate approvingly somewhere in the outer regions of his titanic back. It would have been stupid to bring up the subject of Nora's child at that moment.

In the end he even called Bobby Korbach, who by now was studying at Bennington College and surprising his classmates with his literary English. The boy was very glad indeed to hear from him and asked him if he could work on his technical crew during the holidays. I'm ready to do anything, even carry lights. Alex didn't tell Bobby that lights were carried only by members of the lighting technicians' union but still promised to arrange something. As for Mama, Bobby, who wasn't particularly used to her company, supposed that she was okay. She called once a week, but where from, he didn't know, because as usual she was on the move. The impetuous youngster didn't say a word about a little brother, so he didn't know anything.

Confirmation of the rumor came unexpectedly, but from the most reliable source possible. One day, looking through photos of the actors who had been signed, he paused over the wondrous, seemingly always radiant, face of Goldie Belle D'Argent. Her face and elongated figure held him spellbound: there's no better Beatrice in the movie business anywhere in the world! In his face-to-face meeting with her, he had to admit, the girl didn't give that impression. She had the facial expressions and the manners of a cheap London bimbo. Well, that's what I'm there for as the director, to turn this little slut into a Florentine angel. Suddenly he was struck by the resemblance in several of the photos to Rita O'Neill in her earlier incarnations. All at once the idea for a new plot twist sprang up. Beatrice didn't die. Frightened by Dante's love, she staged her own funeral, disappeared from Florence, and lived to old age somewhere in Urbino, in complete and ascetic solitude. And the role of the elderly Beatrice would be played by Rita O'Neill, the mother of his beloved, the head of a Hollywood "shadow cabinet." Already imagining the howls that would go up at the studio over an unexpected rewriting of an accepted script, he called up his almost-mother-in-law and requested an audience.

"Alex, I think about you so often," said the faded star in a very young and resilient voice. "In connection with the film?" he asked rather stupidly. "No, in connection with Philip," she replied. "With Philip, Rita?" "Yes, with Philip, my little grandson and your son, my friend."

He raced to her home on Bel Air Hill, and she, "just like in a movie" against a backdrop of the flickering fluff of Los Angeles, told him about her recent flight to Europe to see her second grandson, Philip Jazz Korbach. The stunned Alex immediately remembered one happy night, and a wet *Washington Post* that he had twisted into the shape of a saxophone to play for Nora. Philip Jazz Korbach, I like the sound of that! Nora said that you're the father, my friend, but that she isn't going to foist paternity on you. He yelled that he loved Nora, only Nora, and that he already loved Philip Jazz Korbach too! He's not young anymore, you know! Rita noted with a thin smile that his age obviously wasn't slowing him down, and from this first-class small-talk smile he gathered that his almost-mother-in-law had been let in on a few details. He went on about his curious relationship with the only woman in his life (at that point, Rita made a perfectly proportioned gesture with her hand, palm down, as if telling him not to overdo it). He didn't want anything more than to devote the time he had left to her and to Philip Jazz. But he didn't even know where she was. Nora seemed to think for some reason that he was encroaching. On something. On her independence, maybe. This was immediately followed by: "Does that quality in a woman seem strange to you?" After saying that, that is, having registered her progressive views, Rita, with great sympathy, promised her almost-son-in-law to help arrange a meeting for him with "the best little boy in the world," and, naturally enough, with his mama as well.

Only after all this did he reveal to her the reason for his call. He was afraid she would be shocked: so then, he's thinking about the film and not about her daughter? He needn't have worried—this professional of the kingdom of fantasy instantly forgot about everything else in the world except the possibility of once again appearing on the screen in a colossal, not to say epochal, film. Of course she'd do it, but there's one condition, without which we can't do business. A long time ago she vowed never to play old women, which means that Beatrice has to be sent to heaven as a woman, of a certain age perhaps, but still in the prime of life. "Look at me, Alex, and you'll see that I'm not asking for anything ridiculous. I'm still perfectly capable of playing love that's platonic but ardent all the same. Believe me, I've got something to say about this domain." He beamed with delight: it wasn't the first time that this vain and worldly veteran had struck him with her ability to cut through to the heart of the matter.

One day he remembered that Gumilyov had a poem about Dante and Beatrice. The whole Silver Age in St. Petersburg—not in Moscow—had gone by in the presence of these two shades. The Symbolists and the Acmeists were all obsessed by Dante and his universe. Alighieri roamed through the arid classicism around the Stray Dog Café. He reached up to his shelf and took down his four-volume set of Gumilyov published by émigrés and bound in rough paper covers. He found what he was looking for in the very first volume.

> *Muses, cease your sobbing,*
> *Pour your sadness out into songs,*
> *Sing a song of Dante*
> *Or play the flute.*
> *Off with you, bothersome fauns,*
> *There's no music in your call.*
> *Do you not know that not long ago*
> *Beatrice left Heaven?*
> *Strange white rose*
> *In the quiet coolness of the evening.*
> *What is this? Again a threat?*
> *Or a plea for mercy?*
> *There lived a restless artist*
> *In a world of deceptive appearances,*
> *Sinner, rake, one of the godless,*
> *Yet he loved Beatrice.*
> *The secret thoughts of the poet*
> *In his capricious heart*
> *Became streams of light,*
> *Became a rushing tide.*
> *Muses, in* sonneti-brillianti
> *Take note of the strange secret:*
> *Sing me a song of Dante*
> *And Gabriel Rossetti.*

Theoretically, that's what I ought to film. That's my synopsis right there—everything else is just window dressing. Each one of those Petersburg folk saw the prototype of Dante in his own fate. Modernism and the *dolce stil nuovo* merged into one. Bryusov challenged the Symbolists:

> *You ought to be proud like a banner,*
> *You ought to be sharp as a sword,*
> *Like Dante, an underground flame*
> *Should singe your cheeks!*

And whose step was it, if not that of Beatrice, the Blok felt in the high temples of Roman-tinged Orthodoxy—who was it if not she who walked in the chasubles of the Majestic Eternal Woman?

Proclaimed "the central man of the world," Dante remained a man—that is, a victim of the universe. In him, as in Rossetti, as in Blok—as, indeed, in all of us sinful people—a longing for heavenly love was mixed with earthly desire; that is to say that happiness became mixed with lust. Beatrice had once walked the same streets as his legitimate spouse, Gemma, as well as Fiametta and Pietra, two high-spirited *signoras* of the time whom he had made a rather crude attempt at winning. The act of merging, all of its sensuality, became for him a sort of longing for Adam united and whole; *dolce stil* reminds us of what he was cast out of by original sin.

Something else was originally conceived—something incomprehensible to us. Then there occurred in it some kind of warping, and we are the children of this warping process. All the world's biology, including human history—that is, biology elevated by history—is nothing other than the process of overcoming this distortion, an effort to return to the ideal. And it is for this incomprehensible ideal that the poet forever longs, bound like all living creatures with the chains of chromosomes and DNA. Not a word about any of this at the Putney Productions board meeting, otherwise they'll throw us out, Stanley's investment or no Stanley's investment. In saying "us," he had in mind, of course, himself and Dante.

––––––––––

All right, all right, what am I doing fiddling with these high-flown ideas for so long? he thought, pulling himself together. As in that old joke, a real scream: "What the hell do I know, anyway?" Me, the child of a Soviet Army officer stood against the wall and an archives clerk afraid of her own shadow; a boy dealt a staggering blow across the head with the boxwood walking stick of a Central Committee member; the pathetic offspring of Russo-Judaism; the bard of young and unlearned Soviets who gulped down so much crappy vodka in sleeping compartments and dormitories, who opened up so many tins of stuff you wouldn't feed a dog, who shuffled along in the midst of the age-old Soviet spirit of snitching and denunciation and misery, in the midst of a permanent stench that they don't notice anymore, and that to notice I had to be away from, away from home, for eight years, and then come back and gasp for breath among the outhouses of the motherland, and her piss-reeking entranceways—what the hell do I know?

What the hell do I know, anyway, imagining myself as a creator of high art, all of this Okudzhava-Galich-Vysotsky-Tarkovsky-Lyubimov-Kozlov-Paradzhan-Korbach renaissance? Just what the hell do I know, always dreaming when I was there with them about some castles in Spain? About some "Island of Crimea" where you can hide from the Red devils, about all these fleeting images of the Greco-Judean primal homeland among olive groves; what the hell do I know?

Oh well, any one of us can ask himself questions like these, any of those people I spent those three days with—those mountain climbers, chauffeurs, doctors, journalists, Afghanistan veterans, teachers, librarians, construction workers, doctors, puppeteers, and so on—what the hell do we know?

And what the hell do I know anyway, Korbach, Alexander Zakharovich, b. 1939, place of birth Moscow, Jewish by heritage, who has got so well acclimated in America, "as snug as a bug in a rug," as they say, as though I belonged to her, and not to the land of the Soviets. What have I got to do with this country, with, say, its blacks, to whom, as it turns out, I don't have any connection, in spite of their jazz and their basketball? What have I got to do, for example, with a package of Gillette razor blades, from which a plastic card good for a five-minute telephone conversation falls out when you open it, courtesy of MCI in cooperation with the Athletic Federation under the aegis of the aforementioned razor company? What have I got to do at all with this continent, when I fly to it at the height of its summer, more accurately when it reaches the boiling point, and see from a great height its coasts languishing in clouds of hot steam? What have I got to do with the hides of its forests, where, no matter how you enter them, you're gripped with a feeling of noninvolvement with the strands of impassable barbed wire and the branches hanging motionless? You haven't got anything at all to do with its Victorian houses either, standing in rows beneath leaves drooping in the damp heat like bundles of Virginia tobacco or the multitiered skirts of Spanish matrons, under which are planted the oak- or elmlike legs of these females of magical realism.

Speaking of realism, a few words ought to be said about fucking, too. The American woman doesn't play entirely straight with you, you old goat. Nora told you more than once that you didn't do it to her quite the way their billy goats did. The equality of partners isn't built into the structure of your language—that's the reason for it—and it's precisely out of the structure of their language that all feminism and political correctness flow.

So, let's be direct, then. When I come into a five-star hotel, have I really got anything to do with it? Those who have don't notice the splendor, while I, in bubble baths, standing in front of mirrors the perfection of which even old Venice would envy, in front of a window with a view of whatever ocean it happens to be at the time, answering a polite question about what time to send an opulent Lincoln with an efficient, unobsequious chauffeur, I keep thinking that I don't have anything to do with all of this; on the other hand, I definitely have something to do with another type of hotel—for example, the Sailor's Rest, in Kerch, where in the luxury room a sturdy nail, pointed end out, protrudes from the parquet floor for the greater comfort of those who want to rip their trousers; where in the bathroom, in addition to a no-water sign there's no light either, because someone carried off the bulb, and where instead of toilet paper there're a few issues of the local Communist fish wrapper stuffed in a bag; where in order to turn the nightstand lamp on or off you have to crawl out of bed, cross the room, climb onto the back of the couch, since that's the only way to get to the outlet; where in the morning you wake up all spotty from the visits of those ladies of the night, flies from the neighboring dump; where the Bolshevik floor lady comes into your room without knocking to count the towels and ask in a bass voice if it was you who gobbled up all the waffles— that, when you come down to it, is the sort of hotel you've got something to do with, Alexander Zakharovich.

Well, I guess it's time to come full circle and go back to my own people. Thanks for everything, America, you're all right, and what the hell do I know, anyway?

6

THE GLASS WALL

In New York he took his time walking from one airline terminal to another. He had two hours until his flight to L.A. He walked along the endless glass corridors, along the moving sidewalks past newsstands, snack bars, cafés, bars, shoeshine boys' high chairs, garlands of T-shirts with so much nonsense scribbled and drawn on them, past bookstores, lined almost wall-to-wall with bared fangs and incisors. There's another good question: Why is this country so fascinated by Dracula? There's not a hint of vampirism in its everyday life, but in its spiritual life there's this endless bloodbath, sniffling as it flows along to an accompaniment of romantic—must be Romanian—music. He was walking along in one column and looking at the stream of American passengerdom coming toward him. He got the impression that he was in a crowd of vaguely familiar people; the basic social types, of whom there aren't that many—three hundred, let's say—were going by. Over there, dragging along in this direction, was a familiar sort from the academic milieu, some playwright on a university salary, one could tell by the careless way he was dressed; he disappeared behind the looming mass of some fat people—how many male and female fat folk have we got here in the land of baseball!—and then reappeared, displaying the haughty chin of the unrecognized genius, an utterly typical American not-quite-American; and then went by. A.Z. passed the glass wall without having realized that for a few seconds he was observing his own reflection.

In order to conclude this highly significant section within the space of Part 10 allotted to it, we'll have to resort to a device that we would characterize here as the "one day." This is being done not in order to conceal any chronological inconsistencies—far from it; rather, we're hoping, with these two little words, to smoothly lead you, the reader, through the waning years of the nineties up to the very moment when you, having laid down a small pile of rubles, dollars, or francs, open this book.

7

THE ZIGZAGGING TOTEM

*O*ne day, Dick Putney called Alexander right on the set. It happened at the moment the director was explaining to his *acteur fétiche* Quentin Landry that the latter was not "horny" for D'Argent at the moment of their meeting on the Ponte Vecchio, only in a state of mystic exaltation.

"Excuse me for not letting you know earlier, Alex," Dick said, "but how about lunch together? . . . Yes, today. The fact is that my old man, who's been dying to meet you for a long time, just showed up at my office unexpectedly. I doubt that there'll be a better chance for all of us to get together."

Alexander finished the morning shooting schedule and said to Quentin in parting: "Don't eat meat. I'm begging you, don't eat steaks while we're shooting *Ponte Vecchio.* Can you do that for me?"

The lunch took place right in Dick's office on the twelfth floor of the company building that protrudes among the tops of the palm trees on the slope of Bel Air Hill, and the windows of whose upper floors look out on the architectural rubbish of the endless sprawl of Los Angeles. It seems as though we haven't even yet sketched for you a portrait of Dick Putney, that all-powerful producer of various sorts of cinematic junk, and for that matter there's no real need to. Suffice it to say that he presented all the typical features of the financial bigwig, and that his eyes often had an expression of the "you're not going to catch me napping" sort.

The figure of his daddy, however, who was successfully approaching his eighty-fifth birthday, merits a more detailed description. This Abe Putney, who at the dawn of the century, in the little town of Lutzk in the Kherson district, had been known as Abrasha Putinkin, looked the model of healthy old age cultivated at the desert springs of California. Dark red dye did a fine job of concealing not only his gray hair but also the broad, richly hued age spots. Two veins beneath his chin clearly characteristic of old age had an ascot wound around them. Abe always had a cigar between his excellent false teeth—it was a habit acquired at the beginning of the golden age of Hollywood, and one that he was not about to give up, regardless of the cardiologists' orders. Sometimes he would even light a match and bring it toward the cigar, yet the little flame would come to a stop a fraction of an inch from the favored object, then go out from a careless, seemingly absentminded shake. The patriarch was wearing a noxious brown blazer with a long slit and jeans a light shade of blue that closely fit his trim legs. His shoes were by-the-piece cow-boy boots encrusted with gems of some sort. Such was his exterior, to which we'll add eyes that matched his jeans for blueness; perhaps naturally, perhaps artifi-cially—in any case, certainly perceptive enough, as the discussion that follows will show. As far as his interior is concerned, at this point our pen begins to spin its wheels, as it were, not even daring to broach the subject in the concluding phase of the novel.

Waiters from the Maupassant Restaurant, which was on the first floor, brought two menus in leather bindings that looked as if they might contain a welcoming ad-dress to the celebration of an anniversary at the General Staff College. The menus were intended for Alex Korbach and Dick Putney. The old man slammed down his favorite McDonald's meal: two hamburgers, fries, a large salad, and a small plas-tic packet of ketchup, with which his napkin became smeared almost immediately.

Alex watched carefully to see if Abe's mouth would be able to open far enough to become intimate with the hamburger. He always underestimated the springy plumpness of these historical-cultural rolls. The fingers and jaws of a skillful man transform even the thickest burger into a convenient, edible construction, and Abe Putney happened to be just such a one.

"So, Alex, tell us how things are looking for you," Dick asked. "How the first of the filming is going, and all that." Alex immediately launched into a palaver about the enormous significance that Dante was now acquiring in the context of the European culturopolitical challenge. "The Balkans show that we are observing a sort of ebbing of the Renaissance; however, our film, set against a backdrop of the unexpected advance of Russia, could turn out to be the manifesto of a cultural front. The West is still alive, civilization won't give up! Europe isn't going to re-treat from the front of the stage as long as humanity still lives, Mr. Putney!"

"Abe," the old man said.

"Pardon?" Alexander didn't understand.

"Call me Abe," the old man said. He had already dispatched both burgers, all the fries, and two-thirds of the salad, while the "young people," sipping a fine Mer-lot, had only started on their filets mignons. Now Abe was already getting up—to go to the toilet. "You're Alex and I'm Abe," he said with a giggle. "*Po-russku* Sashka and Abrashka, okay?"

He was rather a long time in coming back. Meanwhile, Dick and Alex had managed to finish their lunch and talk about the female extras from the crowd scenes. "The guys say that you've got lots of beauties—is that right?" By the time Abe came back, Alex himself was feeling the need to take a piss. Entering the lava-tory, he discovered in the toilet bowl a large, dark green mass attesting to the good condition of the corporation president's digestive system. A thick newspaper was lying on the tiles, stock market report up. Absorbed in his favorite reading, Abe had forgotten to flush the toilet—well, that happens.

Over the coffee, there began a conversation that, though rather strange, clearly went to the heart of the matter.

"It's been ages since I've seen Stanley," Abe said. "Is it true that he's married a black woman?"

"First of all, he still hasn't got married, and second of all, she's not a black woman," a surprised Alex replied.

"They told me she was a black woman," Abe mumbled.

"No, no, Abe," Alex said, renewing his objection. "She's a typical Irish Jew, descended from the Blooms."

"The Blooms or the Blamsdales?" Dick asked sharply.

"Her surname is Luxe," Alex explained. "It's a branch of the Bloom family tree."

"Well, it doesn't matter anyway," Abe said, with a wave of the five fingers of his right hand and four of those on his left. At least seven rings shone on this squad of wrinkled but still reliable soldiers with their bitten-down nails. "Black women can be great girlfriends, in bed and out. I know from personal experience."

Alexander started: on the tablecloth, not far from the selection of jams, sat an emerald green lizard no longer than a teaspoon. His emerald eyes peered at our hero with curiosity. A forked tongue shot out for an instant. A surprising degradation of fire-breathing dragons. Putney the elder tried to bring his hand down over the lizard. So it's real, then! The reptile had no trouble darting off to one side and hiding behind the coffeepot.

"They write such an awful lot in the papers about the Korbach Fund." Dick sighed, sounding as downcast as if he had read the Book of Ecclesiastes the day before yesterday. "They say that the Velvet Revolution was financed by Korbach."

"What rubbish!" Alex laughed. "It was Gorbachev who arranged it all. The Soviet spooks stationed in Berlin, Prague, and Budapest went into action, and everything happened all in one go."

Abe quickly slid a hand behind the coffeepot. The lizard immediately took refuge behind a napkin folded in the shape of a pyramid. Abe asked: "And who's this Gorbachev? Does he work for the fund too?"

"If he does, then it's not ours!" Alexander exclaimed. "Where did you fish that one up, Abrashka?"

Dick Putney shrugged. "Well, it doesn't matter anyway. They just talk about these things in the papers sometimes. Once I read somewhere that those August days in Moscow were pulled off with Korbach's money." "What papers do you read, Dick?" Alex inquired coldly. Putney shrugged again. "The *Post* and the *Times,* that's it." Now it was Alex's turn to shrug. "I read the same papers, and I've never seen anything of the sort." Suddenly it turned out that his reply had cut Putney the younger to the quick. "Forgive me, Alex, but there's something I've got to say to you. You know, we treat our directors as though they were family. We even allow them to share in our family life in some ways." With a sidelong glance that was barely noticeable, but noticeable just the same, he looked in the direction of the toilet, and then in the direction of the starched little pyramid, from behind one slope of which an emerald head was now protruding like a tiny totem. Then he went on. "That gives me the right to set you straight, old man. The fact that you don't see something in the newspapers doesn't mean that it isn't out there. You're a man of the arts, a poet, they tell me—a musician, right? Well, forgive me, but you don't know how to read the papers the way we businessmen do. We extract lots of information from them that's hidden from . . . well, artists."

At that moment Alex noticed that old Abe was eyeing him with a hard, unblinking, and secretly mocking stare. As a matter of fact, he was the focal point of three pairs of eyes: those of two Putneys and of one lizard. "I've been hearing, Sashka, that Stanley's spending one hell of a heap of money in the 'old countries'—is that true?" the old man asked. Alex said nothing in reply. Dick put in with a smirk: "From the same papers, old man. There are reports that the amounts spent by the Korbach Fund are reaching monstrous proportions, and that tensions have arisen in the AKBB organization as a result."

"Maybe, but it doesn't seem likely," Alex answered calmly. "Either way, Stanley's still a financial genius. In any case, I try not to involve myself in what doesn't concern me." If they knew Stanley's philosophy, they wouldn't be asking such questions.

"And right you are, my boy," said the old man, and treated the newest "member of the family" to a cigar produced from the pocket of his blazer. If it could also have been said of this jacket that it had "seen better days," then the cigar was obviously not from those days, being rather of the $2.99 per half dozen supermarket variety. Then he banged his palm down on the table, and the lizard immediately darted up his sleeve, past the cuff link.

"That creature's at least sixty years old," explained the forty-five-year-old Dick. "She appeared in our first feature—that's right, *Putney and Lizzy* itself. She brought in a container of dollars." Very pleased with himself about something, he stood up with an outstretched hand. Alexander shook it. It was difficult not to ponder that proverbial saying of the American God-fearing folk: "There's no such thing as a free lunch."

8

OFF-SEASON

*O*ne day in the late spring or early summer of 1993, Alexander Zakharovich was sitting in his office, that of the chairman of the Moscow branch of the Korbach Fund, and signing documents prepared for his arrival by Rose Morozova, as the Maryland lass in the eternal bloom of youth now preferred to call herself, after three years in Moscow.

The fund's business was doing better all the time, in the sense that they were spending ever-increasing amounts of money. Greater means were flowing into various domains of Russian science through the Working Intellect program. In order to slow the brain drain, the Korbach Fund was trying to approach scientists directly, particularly those in the fundamental disciplines, offering them monthly stipends on the order of four or five hundred dollars, which at the time, in that half-starved country, was a sinecure. In this way they succeeded, if only partially, in supporting the work of a good number of laboratories, and geneticists didn't develop the urge to inject some chromosomes into a North Korean leader or, even worse, into the greedily munching hippopotamus next door.

An extensive education program called HUG for short (High School, University, Graduate School) was getting under way. The rules for competitions among teachers and students had been worked out. They were such that only layabouts would receive nothing, but they still needed to keep an eye out for the real go-getters.

Though they couldn't get their arms around the entire gigantic, crumbling health-care system, their "Emergency" project was taking off, through which financial reinforcements were going for emergency facilities in major cities. From the Korbach Fund came ambulances, equipment, and also bonus stipends for doctors and staff.

An important sector of the social budget was aid to refugees, of whom there were more and more: people were fleeing the newly independent states, as well as Chechnya, with its government of bandits, and hotbeds of fun and iron games in Abkhazia and Prindnyestrovye.

Alexander Zakharovich, though aware that he was here as little more than a figurehead, derived satisfaction from his presence in the fund. These are the matters that a man ought to occupy his time with, not chasing phantoms of self-expression in the place least suited to it in the world, the Putney studios. It would be better if those movie-business millions went to refugees than as pearls to swine like Quentin Landry.

The aforementioned was striking in his affectation, with the caprices of the stereotypical fairy, even though he was also known for his countless conquests of women in the film business. It's hard to understand how this poseur managed to come out in the image of the pensive and severe Dante in the footage that had been shot. From time to time in front of the camera, this "Actor Actorovich," gorged with his multimillion-dollar fees, reached into some bag of tricks and produced just the right effect. If only the blowhard wasn't always pulling dirty tricks with his schedule. Almost every month it turned out that he was filming somewhere else. He ran in a state of hysteria. Alex, are you my friend or just some dirty sock? Do you value me, your alter ego? My agents, the bastards, the parasites, have got everything in a tangle again! It turns out that I've got to shoot for two months in Sydney, otherwise I'm done for!

As a result, filming had to come to a halt, all the union members had to be paid huge forfeits, you lost the rhythm, you got heartburn. And that nympho wasn't far from her partner's pretensions. She recently left her boyfriend, by the way. He wasn't sleeping with her for some reason, and of course she was in a rage: he was a "megastar," you see, and she only a "superstar," which meant that he could get away with things that she couldn't, right?

Having worked himself up into a fury from the waves of cares that were coming over him from across the ocean, A.Z. left Rose Morozova and walked over to the window. What did I get involved in all this megalomania for? What can I add to what already exists in the world under the sign of Dante? I'm weak and vain, I can't resist temptation. In the end, Stanley's money corrupted me. I'll never get back to the purity of those early years in America, to the blissful decrepitude of the Hotel Cadillac, to the queues for the Catholic breakfasts, to being in love with Princess Nora, sitting in her archaeological tower three thousand miles from her bald admirer. That's why she hid herself from me, and why she doesn't show me Philip Jazz either—it's just that she sensed the corruption of my entire inner makeup.

Below, in the square, a Communist rally was going on, as there always was lately. A few hundred of Anpilov's swine were standing beneath red flags and pictures of the Red-Haired Ferret and the Black Cat. Alongside, not joining them, but not going away either, some passionate young folk stood beneath black-and-gold monarchist banners. Hatred for those they call "the Jews" unites these two forces seemingly inimical to each other. Is this really the sort of freedom we stood on the barricades for? For freedom of hatred?

He took up the pair of binoculars that had been there invariably since the August days of '91. He focused on the faces of the demonstrators. Human scum, the embodiment of everything about his homeland that he hated to the point of nausea. They're considered poor, old, driven into a corner by predatory capitalism. Tell that to those who don't know them. I know these mugs and these pigs' snouts, former camp guards, apparatchiks, SMERSH agents, bureaucratic bigwigs, parvenus still shitting themselves, sponging Party members, milk-skimming bosses, and most important of all—snitches, snitches, and snitches! At first they kept themselves hidden, afraid that they'd be dragged out into the light, in front of God and everyone, and then they saw that the new government wouldn't even beat them back with clubs, and began to gather in the thousands. The bloodthirsty old-timers back themselves up with youngsters just the right age to be executioners. Their newspapers are multiplying, their agents provocateurs are always turning up on TV. Some Parisian Bolshevik hack is making a pseudomessianic speech, his lips puckering from the acerbic lemon essence that his entire round, fucking Soviet mug is shot through with; he howls: "To your weapons! To the ax!" The Red rabble is already hurling itself with its iron on the Moscow cops, who lose their nerve in the face of their red banners. Journalists are comparing this summer with that of 1917. The definitive upheaval, the storming of the Kremlin, is expected in the autumn. The hyenalike generals, without shame or fear, lead meetings of reliable officers and promise to "give the democrats a bath in their own blood"—in other words, to kill "Yelts," slaughter the young government, and launch an anti-Western terror.

And the members of the government race around town in the limos that used to belong to the Central Committee and pretend not to notice the graffiti in letters a yard high on the walls calling for their destruction. Cynical smiles are gaining currency in the circles of the pro-democratic press. It's already become awkward to bring up August, so covered is it in the crap of disinformation, so deformed by knowing Gee-Bee winks.

What're we doing hanging around here with our "despised dollars"? A.Z. thought. Who are we helping? The Russian people? The Russian intelligentsia? The Commies are going to grab everything again, and they'll just spit in our offering hand, charge us with espionage. The feeling of gratitude is not exactly the most pronounced trait in the character of the Russian people, and as for the Bolsheviks, don't even think about it. Bolshevism has taken root here as permanently as booze in an alcoholic.

"Alex, are you all right?" Rose asked him in an alarmed voice. And at that very moment, as if summoning him to tear himself away from his gloomy antipatriotic thoughts, a telephone call came that went straight to his heart. On the other end was none other than his ex-wife, Anisia, now the Baroness Chapeaumange.

"My Sashka, dear Sashka, forgive me, I'm out of breath," said the same sweet voice as once upon a time, save just one difference: whereas before it had streamed out like crystalline sugar, it now clung like molasses. He stood with the receiver in his hand by the full-length mirror, and all of him was reflected in it: the youthful figure in a well-worn sweater, with an old top. How old is she now, this Anis? An instantaneous calculation: my God, the woman's half a hundred! "Why aren't you saying anything, my witty-bitty darling?" "Just lost my head for a second," he answered and took a step toward the mirror. What was this? On his sharply sloping forehead a small galaxy of age spots was visible. Well, now you're off, the bald spot will start to go yellow like a canary, then take on the spots of a leopard; looking at it will be enough to make anyone say: What's this guy hanging around for?

Where was she calling from? From Port-au-Prince, I hope? The bubble of hope burst right away—she was calling from a phone in the neighborhood. "We've come back to Papa's old flat, Sasha, in Yuri Trifonov's house on the Embankment, can you imagine? You remember how it was there, those nights full of fire even before we were married, and Andrei, and Volodya, and Seryozha, Lenka, Tamarka, how we would sing, Sasha, just think back, Sasha . . . all right, I won't."

They just arrived, the entire family. Yes, yes, Styopa and Lyova too—you won't recognize them, Parisian students, handsome young men, and the other members of the family, even the pets, you won't believe it. Of course we have to meet, spend time together, we're not strangers to each other, after all. They could come over to his place right now. As it turned out, there would be no need to wait: they were ringing the doorbell downstairs, and they were all coming in. He whispered: "Rose, please stay!" The office manager didn't need to be asked twice—to see such a surprising meeting!

Both twins were wearing white sport coats. They had identical haircuts, shaved at the back of the neck and with a fringe in front, long, blond locks that still had a wiry Jewish curl about them. They hugged without worrying about formalities. Hello, *Papasha!* They pronounced the remarkable word with the stress on the last syllable, which made it all the more remarkable: papa*sha*!

Anis had gone quite plump, which wasn't surprising considering her Haitian chicken diet, but she was as attractive as ever. Her stay on a tropical island had not affected her taste; her outfit was restrained as always, in bright, yet well-coordinated jack-of-diamonds tones. Her sexual tail always made itself known as it lay between her legs when she was sitting down. Looking at this downy appendage, Alexander Zakharovich could not help thinking: Good sex does contribute to good offspring after all.

The Baron Chapeaumange said hello with all the kindness of a deaf-mute gentleman. Emphasizing the somewhat relative character of his connection to the Korbachs, he sat down slightly to one side of the seating arrangement. This position, as well as a complete absence of movement on his part, helped all of those present, including the employees of the fund who seemingly chanced to be dashing through, to survey his figure in all its striking character. His exceptional aristocratic slimness was surprising. He seemed to be an anachoresis of a well-known twentieth-century bit of wisdom: "You can never be too thin or too rich." An even stranger phenomenon was the decadent monochromaticism of his face, from the dark violet shades beneath his eyes and in his sunken cheeks to the gentlest of lilac pastels of his suit. The way his head gathered to a sharp point made the baron look like a steel No. 86 nib, which even today is used in calligraphy.

"I guess he doesn't speak any Russian?" Korbach asked.

"Not yet," Anis replied, as if reassuring her former spouse. "He will."

Meanwhile, those two efficient workers Rose and Matt had already sprung up with refreshments: coffee, tea, crackers, a selection of soft and hard drinks. Alexander gestured to Albert: Help yourself! The latter delicately pointed with a little finger at a bottle of Ballantine whiskey. Right away, like a symbol of American imperialism, Matt Shuroff loomed over him with a glass and a bottle: Say when.

"Why's he so thin?" Alexander asked the mother of his sons.

"He's dying, Sasha," she answered simply, almost in the neorealist manner, and of course lit a cigarette. Even before this Alexander Zakharovich had more than once caught himself unconsciously imitating anyone who was putting on an act for him. Just as now, instead of showing bitter amazement, he simply raised one eyebrow—"Oh, so that's how it is"—in the neorealist manner. The furious Anis, however, immediately switched over to full-blown melodrama. "Albert has fallen victim to love! It's devoured him, a pagan priest of love rituals!" "What am I supposed to understand by that?" A.Z. asked, still in the old style, not having switched over in time. "Take it any way you like," she said, and turned away, struggling to hold back sobs.

Korbach looked Chapeaumange in the eye. The other bared his decrepit teeth in a grin and raised his cup: *A votre santé, monsieur!* Right now you pour yourself some of the amber liquid and toast him in reply: Hold on, brave islander! Anis's voice seemed to reach him from some great distance: "And I'm going with him!"

She was sitting with her rounded chin turned away to the window. She was watching the sour clouds of the gathering Soviet revanchist storm float by. "Excuse me, Anisia, but what're you talking about, and, what's more important, what style are you saying it in? Allegorical? Metaphorical?" He was looking at the spot where his sons had just been sitting. They weren't there. A door to the corridor was open—there, Lyova and Styopa, their dental keyboards gleaming, were playing on two computers; there's a quartet for you!

"Ah, Sasha dear, always endlessly beloved in spite of everything, my sincere, direct man unprotected in his artistic nature. How can I survive if he dies, Sasha, this Negro whom I love to the point of convulsions?" The obviousness of the tragedy was plain to see, yet she, at the spate of Belorussian birch sweetness, seemed to have ceased to be a tragedy. Nevertheless, that strong intonation, our actor thought, seems to belong in some *Dame aux Camélias*. "He opened the whole universe of the wisdom of voodoo to me, and all of our—like theirs over there—plasma and amoebas circulated together again and again," Anisia said, continuing in the earlier style.

"There's no need to exaggerate," the Baron Chapeaumange suddenly said with a creak in his voice, but in Russian. Dumb scene. Everything froze in midmovement, in midsentence, only Anis managed to open her moist, even slightly foamy mouth to its full width. She was the first to whom the gift of speech returned. "So you knew everything, then, understood everything?" "Not everything, *ma chère*," the baron answered briefly. "Almost everything." "Bastard! *Merde!* Walrus prick! I just knew it all along, you were going to the meetings of this Salamanca's cell, of that KGB cunt! And for this shit I sacrificed everything, children, a talented husband, the purity of my womb!" A pot of begonias flew at the baron's head like a volleyball, but upon striking, unfortunately, lost this lightness and flew into small pieces. There was nothing left for the baron to do but stand up and walk away to a corner of the capacious room. Anisia, again with success, threw a Korbach chair after him, but he was already tracing Veves symbols on the white wall with a lilac felt pen.

"You don't scare me, you animal!" She shrieked with incinerating force. Everyone was quite shocked, except for the twins, who were now laughing and dancing around in the common room. "*Papasha!* Look out! Any minute now the spirit of Loa will come out!" The baron, meanwhile, was modestly tracing a mysterious line that reminded one of a rainbow intertwined with a serpent. "Oh God, oh God!" Anis cried, raising her hands. "You, Loa and Veves, come and help me!" The boys, imitating sports announcers, said in affected voices: "And any minute now, Granny Furan will appear! In life she was the Supreme Mamba!"

Granny Furan had already been there for some time. No one had noticed her coming, perhaps because everyone was distracted by the growing smell of carbide. And all at once everyone saw her standing like a pillar between Matt Shuroff and Dr. Fuchs.

For all the confidence that we have in the reader, we still can't bring ourselves to describe Granny Furan's appearance. Literary practice has more than once disproved the old saw "paper can tolerate anything." No, kind ladies and kind gentlemen, even paper has limits on what it can bear. It's not by chance that it began to force some authorial filth directly onto celluloid. Stop, the paper says sometimes, and bends beneath the unrestrained pen—remember, good sir, the "rules of good society," as they said in an earlier age. Stop, it growls, jamming at times in your printer, I beg your pardon, sir, but the fact that I was subjected to Communist violence in no way gives you the right to smear on me all the muck that has accumulated in society. I have the right to a time of cleanliness, even if it's only for a little while!

All right, then, given what we've just said, we will restrain ourselves from describing the appearance of Granny Furan and limit ourselves to just one detail, even if it is a fairly striking one: a living rooster was sticking out of her stomach.

We'll leave this chronotope. With their pure hands Lyova and Styopa picked up their father, who had nearly fallen victim to the magnet of the voodoo religion. "Let's get out of here, *Papasha*! They'll sort out everything themselves."

They went out into the fresh air, if one could say that about the Moscow summer of 1993. Not far from an agitprop truck a lady Bolshevik from the Komsomol was engaging in elegant but furious ravings, her graying blond locks flying in unison with her red flag. "Scoundrels!" she was howling. "You've robbed the people! We'll take every square inch of floor space back from you! We'll give a flat to every kindergarten graduate!" Alongside, a meaty-faced country sort with a lock of hair falling over his forehead was bawling away on an accordion: "When Comrade Stalin sends us into the fight and Makashov leads us into battle!" Several women were chasing a little old man with a big nose with cries of: "Stool pigeon! Stool pigeon!" He nimbly turned away from the sharpened points of their umbrellas, then sprang onto the bottom step of a trolleybus, waved a small tricolor flag, shouted, "I'll die for democracy," and he was off. The women came to a halt and turned right around to a speaker expounding from a chair. "Comrades, I'll teach you to read the Jew press! They've got the number 22 hidden everywhere in them! The number of Zion, that's what it is! It's no accident that Hitler attacked our country on the twenty-second of June!" The crowd breathed noisily; here and there shouts went up: "They ought to be strangled without any respect!" "Drop 'em all through a hole in the ice!" Someone asked, perplexed: "Why a hole in the ice, comrades? What, we've got to wait until winter?" Meanwhile, four teams of workers were toiling away on the edges of the square putting up huge billboards: OLBY BANK. I'M ALWAYS WITH YOU! MMM. FLYING FROM DARKNESS INTO LIGHT! CASINO EL-DORADO. LEMONTI CLOTHES. COMME IL FAUT.

"It's interesting here, too," Styopa said.

"Even more interesting than it is there," Lyova said.

Papa Korbach was taking his sons for a ride in a Mustang convertible with the top down. "Wow, what a car!" his delighted sons exclaimed. "Gonna let us drive, Dad?" Alexander Zakharovich wanted to become friends with his sons. He asked them what it would take. Just think about it, Papasha. He couldn't think of any better way than to buy each of them a Jeep. In a new dealership on Tverskaya Street, with an American Express Platinum card, they picked up two Cherokees, one dark blue and the other red. Together with the youngsters' clothes, the result was a statement in favor of liberty. "Always at your service," the salesmen said. His sons were delighted. "You couldn't have come up with anything better! We can see that you're the greatest, Papasha!"

They spent the evening at the flat by Patriarchs' Pond Park, which the Moscow K.F. had rented for its chairman from the former Soviet minister of bread production. The latter was waving a broom by the gates, in the getup of an ordinary janitor; it didn't take him long to become a good capitalist.

The boys told their father that the baron was one of the chief *hungani,* that is, the witch doctors of Haiti, and that even "Mamasha" over the years of their life out there had grown into a real *mamba,* i.e., a sorceress. The conflicts that come up between them should not be considered mere family squabbles but rather a struggle between two powerful elements, which the people of the republic treat with unwavering respect. Suddenly, for no apparent reason at all, the boys burst into tears like small children. "Daddy, why did you leave us? We want to live with you in the simple art world! Don't chase us away, please!" He was crying, too, an arm around each pair of broad shoulders. Maybe I've been in their dreams the same way that Zakhar had been in mine sometimes. With a plea for forgiveness—not for leaving them but for fathering them.

Suddenly, the sound of a woman's tender singing reached them through the window: "Garden, you, my garden, eternal dew"—with a Belorussian accent. "There you go, they've made up," the kids supposed. A.Z. went to the window. Baron Chapeaumange was strolling back and forth on the bridges over the pond with a guitar. Mamasha Anis was singing, ambling after him. Granny Furan was standing beside them like a pillar. The rooster that had been let out for a walk gave a cock-a-doodle-doo and sniffed at the impurities of the celebrated literary intersection. And that was twenty-four hours in the life of Moscow in 1993.

9

WHAT'S A HUNDRED YEARS?

*O*ne day, in 1994 as we recall, Dr. Lionel Fuchs arrived from an expedition to the back of beyond. He was very excited, scattering pipe ash everywhere, trying to tug on the zipper of whomever he was talking to, as his grandfather Peisakh Fuchs in his day had probably seized the buttonholes of his interlocutors' vests—in short, he was happy. To tell the truth, Alexander Zakharovich had already forgotten (or pretended to have forgotten) about the existence of a rather sizable rudimentary organ in the K.F.'s bowels, namely, the "genealogical section"; nevertheless, not only had it not ceased to exist, it was even growing. Do you mean it isn't clear, Dr. Fuchs would say, that our research is directly linked to the humanitarian goals of the fund? If it doesn't realize that it's a galaxy within a galaxy, then mankind spends its money in vain. Am I right?

In short, however foggy his conception of things may have been, particularly if one considered that it involved Fuchs's deeply rooted atheism, our researcher was ready to rush off at any moment to anywhere from Dublin to Durban, if the slightest spark of the Korbach-Fuchs "molecule" had shown up. This time he was coming back from Samara.

Well, guess what? The Volga had made a strong impression on him. He hadn't expected it would look like it did. But that's not the thing, Alex! What's important is that we found quite a few Korbach milestones there, in particular your great-grandfather Nathan's paper factory. Yes, it exists and even makes paper from time to time. In theory, it's your factory, Alex, but more about that later.

It turned out that, studying the line of Amos Korbach, the natural brother of the Warsaw inhabitant Gedali—that is, the great-great-uncle of Alex and Stanley—the computers of the genealogical section began periodically coming up with a certain Khesia Teodorovna Korbach, b. 1894, native of Samara, formerly Kuibyshev—no, no, Alex, not *khuy*-byshev, Kuibyshev it is, later appearing in various documents as Asya Fyodorovna Sukhovo-Korbach. For some reason they never came up with the date of her death. All inquiries were answered with a straight line. Then, suddenly, it occurred to one of the researchers—it's not absolutely necessary to say exactly who, although it goes without saying that Fuchs would not have failed to point it out had it not been himself, the most modest of men—that Asya Fyodorovna might simply still be alive.

Just imagine, that's the way it turned out. A hundred years isn't so long, Asya Fyodorovna said to your correspondent. She was smoking, sitting on the balcony of her flat in a building beside the Samara river port. Not more than half a pack a day these days—before, not even two were enough. She smoked everything but the kitchen sink. Not even this lousy balcony has collapsed in a hundred years. When she was a child, everyone said that it was going to fall in any time, but she's still up there, puffing away, she noted with a hoarse laugh.

She had somehow managed to get through her century without any particular disturbances in her life. I just watched the Volga flow by, that's all. I read dictionaries, guidebooks, and encyclopedias and became a real fountain of information on the scale of the current of the Volga itself. Here's another pun for you, gentlemen from America. Take any dictionary, open it to a page at random, and ask me a question. We pick up a heavy object bound in leather tatters, bits of gold leaf, a currant jam spot half a century old. Asya Fyodorovna, what is mint? She raises her Ashkenazian eyes that had not lost their blueness over a hundred years to the sculpted ceiling that hadn't fallen down over that time either, and tossing aside her cigarette with a gesture that is not devoid of elegance, remembers: "Did you say 'mint'? The plant *Mentha*. Curly mint, ordinary, wild, or Russian, sour mint. *Mentha crispa. Mentha viridis,* baby's breath, peppermint, English mint. *Mentha piperita,* cold mint, wild mint, deaf mint, horsemint, *Mentha arvensis, Moribus vulgaris,* horehound, catnip, gill-ale, marjoram, basil, *Origanum, Mentha Pulegium,* spearmint . . . Well, is that enough?"

They underestimate Russian culture in the West, the endurance of its Jewish element. What's a hundred years? I haven't lost my hair the way I'm supposed to, although my famous relative, they say, was bald from birth.

No, she didn't have to go to jail, but let's present a few facts in their proper order. In the twenties it wasn't easy for girls from banking families, especially if your brother had run off to Persia with the Whites. Fortunately Sukhovo the engineer had offered her his name. Asya Sukhovo had a respectable sound to it, even in an anti-Semitic context. Well, then the Economic Institute, all sorts of things, the Komsomol. After the institute, *ach,* a bit of this, a bit of that, everything but the kitchen sink. And suddenly, Mr. Fuchs, just imagine, they offer the young lady a job at the Volga Communist, a large factory, in the economics division. I'll reveal a secret to you—the bourgeois connections helped, kitchen sink and all. The factory had once belonged to a second cousin of the brand-spanking-new Komsomol girl Asya Sukhovo named Nathan Korbach, a big paper manufacturer. In 1918, two of the most powerful Samara Korbachs, Nathan and Asya Sukhovo's own uncle Girkan, a banker, disappeared from the city after the expropriation of their property. It seems they tried to get to Finland, but alas, they got nowhere. It was said in town that they were robbed and killed by two soldiers, who were then robbed and killed by the commander of the train himself.

Even among the Samara Bolsheviks there were people who took pity on the Korbachs, since they'd given no small amount of money for the revolution in their time. One of these people was Comrade Shlyakhtich, an old technician from the Korbach Paper Factory that became Volga Communist. He set Asya Sukhovo up with a job in the bookkeeping department, he did, where she worked almost without stopping for fifty years, doing this and that. This factory is a unique enterprise. Yes, Mr. Fuchs, it exists to this day. There's not another production line in the country that turns such "laid paper," or Eaton, Whatman, tracing paper, et cetera. You can be sure that it was all allocated to the Central Committee. No small number of letterhead, documents with terrible stamps on them, small notepads of special manufacture intended mainly for the congresses and conferences of our Party, passed before Asya Fyodorovna's eyes. The unique English equipment installed here by Nathan Korbach is still considered unsurpassed. Yes, that's exactly right, Messrs. Fuchs and Duckworth, your interpreter understood correctly: these machines are still running.

Our immense thanks, Mrs. Sukhovo, but let's leave the factory to one side for a while and come back to your relatives. Do you know anything about the French branch founded by your brother Vladimir, aka Volya? "Why, of course, comrades! Volya's grandchildren, Lily, Lazare, Yannick, Antoine, Marie-Thérèse, and Hippolyte, are always helping me to stay afloat, that is, they send me aromatic teas, biscuits, and these Gitanes. And now brace yourselves, historians, I'm going to tell you the most exciting story of my life!

"In 1945 I was mobilized to work as an interpreter in a POW camp. It was in the Zhiguli Mountains, the third most beautiful preserve in all Europe. The Germans, of course, didn't notice the beauty in the stone quarry. With one exception, it's true, and that exception was the twenty-year-old, blue-eyed . . . let's call him Siegfried Wagner. He fell in love with Zhiguli and with the fifty-year-old Asya. But what's fifty years when your head spins from the waltzes that this boy plays for you on a kazoo? Alas, it lasted only for half a year. In 1946 Siegfried signed an agreement to work for State Security, and they gave him his release on medical grounds and set him home to Germany. I don't rule out, gentlemen, that a child was born to me in Germany. Well, they arrested me, of course, but I was soon free, after signing a document saying I'd work for State Security, blah-blah. Oh, it was all nonsense, they were just trying to get everyone to sign up to collaborate, because they could get promoted for it.

"I often long for those days, Mr. Fuchs and Mr. Duckworth, you know—every Tuesday political information, everyone gets together, there's some feeling of coziness, warmth, big music, theater stars putting on free shows for us, and little boxes of our Kuibyshev chocolate on the eighth of March. Now they say the city has become a dangerous place. But I've got supplies of aromatic tea for another five years, after all—I want to live. So then, I don't go out on the street, I prefer the balcony. If it falls in, then it falls in—we're none of us going to live forever, after all."

From Khesia Teodorovna's place Fuchs and Duckworth went to the Volga Communist factory, which had long been snuggled on the banks of the Volga between Stube Brewers (1898) and the Mamonov electrical power plant (1912). Everyone there, naturally, was overjoyed at the arrival of the Americans. Men who were papermakers like their fathers before them took it for granted that they were Korbach men and were proud of the mechanisms of the old English forge. From generation to generation, at first in a whisper and then loudly, the dream that they would one day be bought by Americans had been transmitted.

Well, help yourself to what God has sent. Fish—salted, smoked, and boiled. Here's some vodka for your odds-bodkins and a few brews for your fish stew. The representatives of the K.F. made a striking pair: the tiny Fuchs with his Einstein mustache and Ben with his athletic, dark-skinned good looks, his smile flashing now and then like the flash of a well-made camera.

A month had already passed since the factory was privatized and transferred to the control of the former District Komsomol Committee, now the Utyos Co-op. The first secretary, or rather the president, Gleb Koloborodchenko, a stocky young man in an Italian jacket, arrived lugging four pistols. Ben went to the toilets and, holding his nose through his handkerchief, called his own president via satellite. Buy it, said Stanley, without even waiting for the end of the story about the old Korbach factory. Let our Alex become a Volga capitalist who inherited his pile.

They began to negotiate. They'd wanted to offer Koloborodchenko a million, but no sooner had they opened their mouths than he asked for five hundred thousand. They settled on two fifty. Romantic little fires began darting in Gleb's alcohol-fogged eyes. He was already imagining how he would invest this windfall. Suddenly a weighty consideration stopped the signing of the contract. Koloborodchenko slammed a fist down on the antique table. "The Korbach comes only with some extra baggage! Without Post Office Box 380, I won't let it go!"

It turned out that in the heat of privatization, the Utyos Cooperative had not even noticed that it owned a secret munitions factory for shells. Deprived of state orders, the factory was a millstone around the necks of the Komsomolists. "I'm handing you a gold mine, boys," Koloborodchenko said to the Americans, his wily Cossack eyes shifting back and forth. "Convert the whole show into anything you want, even if it means firing the shells back!" Ben began to poke at his pocket-size two-way radio with a none too steady finger. Where are you calling to, you two-legged minus sign? Gleb asked. Jamaica, I think, the ex-Airborne soldier replied. It turned out that Stanley had flown from Jamaica to Mexico City while they'd been sitting at the banquet table. From the excited voices coming over on the receiver, Duckworth gathered that one more of Norman Blamsdale's units had been smashed and regretted that he hadn't taken part in the glorious action. Take it, of course, Stanley said apropos of the factory, only without the gunpowder. It won't do our Alex any harm to have a little pots and pans factory to go with his paper. That's all I needed, Alex, who was next him, moaned. The satellite connection was working perfectly.

10

A FREEBIE

*O*ne day—it must have been toward nightfall in 1995 by then—a semiunderground Moscow club opened its doors for the first time. "Semiunderground" not from a political standpoint but by way of its situation. At ground level it gladdened the eye with its eighteenth-century pavilion, on which someone had done a first-class restoration job. It extended downward, deep underground, as a large postmodern palace with staircases, pipes, niches, transformers, alcoves, boilers, offices, and arched corridors, one of which, it was said, ran into the secret Kremlin Metro. In keeping with the ambiguous style widely popular at the time, the club was in fact called the Semi-Underground.

A. Z. Korbach, who by this time was fifty-six, didn't feel drawn to this gala party, but he went anyway. The opening was shaping up as a celebration for everyone who was anyone in Moscow—that is, the business and financial communities, the artistic crowd, the press corps, political circles, and, of course, a squadron of beauties. The owner of the club, a certain Orest Sorokarorsky, whose way of pronouncing his name with French *r*'s made it unintelligible, greeted A.Z. with the most respectful of embraces. He was simply delighted to welcome the pride of our culture and, moreover, a representative of the great Korbach clan. Without your presence, old man, we simply wouldn't be able to show off our new Moscow fin de siècle style.

The upper floor of the Semi-Underground was brightly lit. From the French windows opened a vista of the illuminated churches of Zaryadye. The crowd was standing noisily around the tables charged with excellent *zakuski*. Stretching a hand out to one side, one could get any drink from the trays dashing by. Our "devils" were certainly being quick about acquiring the art of living well.

A.Z. was already sick of parties, yet not a week went by without him delivering himself into the hands of Moscow the lady swindler, and she "partied" him into her deck with its stuck-together cards. Almost the entire deck was present here— a carnival of all four suits. Among the windbags there were some friendly faces as well, "our" people; figures from the sixties crowd turned up now and then, too, having started on the final stretch of their travels. Let's heap compliments on each other, he thought, remembering the old song. The updated refrain of the singer was If you're late with a compliment, you might never get to pay it.

He saw the actors' contingent. Old guys with young girlfriends. Old girls by themselves. An age-old injustice that by itself would be enough to make you join the feminists.

He was thinking about pushing his way through to them, but just then he was intercepted by a cry of "Look, girls—it's Sasha Korbach!" and was surrounded by a flock of unbelievably beautiful creatures. Well, you know, if this generation is producing girls like this, then I'm all for it! I'm on their side, wholly and entirely! What height, what suppleness, what exquisite dresses! I'll bet Paris himself must have worked on their hairdos! Adonis was their trainer, from the looks of them! Here are two possibilities for your future, my people: a gloomy Zyuganov cobblestone or any of these maidens, a little locket illuminated by the muses. I choose you, young women! Lead me into your dance in the round! I'm even ready to run along the bas-relief of an ancient vase with you forever. I'm yours completely, and here are five of my *cartes de visite* for you; any of you can get a stipend for beauty maintenance. Flee the small, hirsute "new Russians," seek out a proud real Russian from the European family of peoples, don't avoid a brave Jew, either!

The girls were laughing loudly and, strangely enough, without a hint of vulgarity. Their family origins unknown, they all seemed like the fruit of highly developed civilizations. A strange phantomlike quality, almost an example of mutation. It looks like I've talked too much again and found myself in front of the TV cameras one more time. The latest scandal is brewing, just wait for it, an attack of the neofascists: the Korbachs are asking the prices of our girls!

Just then, a young man resembling nothing so much as a jackal walked quickly past in a well-cut suit. He was saying something to someone on a mobile phone. Without interrupting his conversation, he gave an order to those who were "illuminated by the muses": "Circulate, girls!" The lovely giantesses, as it turned out, had been hired by the Semi-Underground for the evening, but not as tarts, as any hidebound sexist with a one-track mind might think, rather to distribute themselves evenly around the room, to create an aesthetic picture.

A.Z. had not had time to still his beating heart, as it were, before the dramatic flow of the evening cast him down into a state that was the contrary of his present one: behind the bare shoulders, he glimpsed Zavkhozov's face. That creep shouldn't be allowed to grow old, he thought. Before, the smoothness of his skin had given him a general lack of expression. Now, though, the leper within him is oozing out from every wrinkle. Soon the people will begin to puke at the sight of this monster, if they don't elect it president first; then they'll get used to it.

Gee-Bee General Zavkhozov had begun to pop up quite unexpectedly in the context of the Moscow branch of the Korbach Fund. Yet the man should have been hanged on that glorious August night. For all its absence of violence, that night still should have ended with the hanging of Zavkhozov. Maybe not to death, but he should have dangled upside down for a while. A measure like that might have beaten his desire to run for president out of his system. It didn't happen that way. The revolution as a whole didn't take place. Zavkhozov mingled with the peaceful crowd. And now, four years later, he resurfaced as a respectable businessman, aspiring to participate in the work of an American humanitarian organization.

To begin at the beginning. In 1992, the homegrown Russian Scouts Fund came into being. They turned to the Korbachites for help. In A.Z.'s absence, the delighted philanthropists handed over a tidy sum and drew up a plan for monthly payments, but even though A.Z. might not have known a hell of a lot about philanthropy, he saw that something was rotten: behind the "Scouts" was hiding the bureaucracy of the All-Union Leninist Pioneers organization. He was about to raise a fuss in the press when he spotted the names of several respected liberals on the list of the body's sponsors.

The liberals came to the Korbachites for a conference. Yes, we know that there's Communist and KGB trash there, they said, but we think that for the time being we need to keep the old structures. After all, Sasha, there are hundreds of thousands of kids that we've got to pull out of a desperate situation—this is no time for moral crusading. Look here: kids with TB, runaways, victims of racial confrontations, kids in alcohol rehab, health camps in the south, gifted and talented competitions, groups for the retarded. Who's going to take care of them all if we drive out all the old scum? We need a gradual, soberly balanced process. Such conversations on the territory of the fucked-over motherland were typical. The mass of the population may have been phonies, but they were still Communists, O Theophilus.

Time passed. A.Z. had even begun to forget about the Russian Scouts in the midst of his other activities, when suddenly an extraordinary event took place. A certain repentant Pioneer organizer named Boris Razdryzgalnikov turned up. He was shaking a red folder produced by the Kuibyshev Volga Communist Factory imprinted with gold letters reading, "To a Participant in the All-Union Leninist Pioneer Jamboree. Be Ready! Always Ready!" Sasha Korbach, I can't keep quiet!

J'accuse! Swindlers, scoundrels, defilers of pure ideas! I'm not afraid of anything!
I'll expose every last bit of it!

It turned out, of course, that many of the Korbach dollars had not gone directly
to their intended recipients—that is, children. No, no, there was no outright stealing, God forbid! Some of the leaders said just that—"God forbid!"—and crossed
themselves. Others swore on "my honor as a man," and one, forgetting himself,
even roared: "And I'll lay down my Party card!" Most of the money had got
through, but only after the execution of a few procedures in the system of free enterprise as understood by the members of the organization. The Korbach subsidies
simply enjoyed a handsome turnover rate for six months, or even for a year, in
newly created banks, giving the members tenfold or even twentyfold profits to rake
off. Once these operations were complete, the American philanthropy—well, let's
say the bulk of it—reached the "Scouts," sick and healthy, as well as their "scout-
masters"—specialists from the disbanded Pioneers, the majority of whom could
not have come within a rocket's flight of joining in on any rake-offs. The truth-
seeker Razdryzgalnikov was among that number.

"So what's the matter, Mr. Korbach?" the leaders of the Scouts asked in surprise. "Your money is intact. Here's the proof. The Scouts got everything. And the
income, sir"—whenever our people say "sir," you can always hear a loud whack as
the edge of the entire deck of cards smacks you across the nose—"went for the
broadening of our movement. Here, if you please, are the repairs in Tuapse,
restorations in Pavlovski Posad, just look for yourself."

A.Z.'s attempts to drive home to his clients the idea that charitable donations
should not be used for cooking up profits were in vain. You, Sasha Korbach, separated yourself from our life. That sort of snobbery won't fly with us. We've got our
own *know-how* now. They even raised their voices and banged their fists not even
on the table but on the arms of their chairs. Sad to say, this attitude to foreign aid
could not be called unusual. In our country, you accept help with a haughty and
gloomy expression on your face. As far as "know-how" was concerned, that term,
in gaining currency among the former Komsomolists, had undergone certain mu-
tations. For us, *know-how* has come to mean on the one hand something downy
that might be used to make a fur coat, and on the other hand something bracing,
like the *feikho* fruit, with its reputed aphrodisiac properties, that the members once
gulped at the sanitoriums of Abkhazia to help them get it up better. As for "snobbery," which they stick in every hole in a sentence these days, it looks almost like
something derived from Gogol's "Nose"—a way of saying, "There's no need to
stick your nose in the air!"

Using the same Gogolian style, then, we'll say that the well-entangled A.Z.
"faxed himself two 'Inspector Generals,' " namely Sol Leibnitz and Lester Square.
And you call him an impractical artist! He couldn't have made a better decision. Beneath the steely-eyed stares of the North Atlantic gentlemen, the Komsomol elements began to go to pieces, reminding one in olfactory terms of a pack of
skunks swarming around. It turned out that the "Russian Scouts" could not produce even the most nominal sums, buried as they were beneath the ruins of pyramid schemes, or carried away in the clutches of a new plague of locusts—namely

the ephemeral butterflies of a certain Mr. Mavrodi, who created a tremendous pyramiding financial empire to hornswoggle the naive man on the street. It also appeared that the R.S. had now become one of the numerous fronts for the huge financial trust Viaduct, whose offices, by an irony of fate, were located only two floors up in the very same skyscraper, constructed, during the period of "mature socialism," in the form of an open book, as the Korbachites'. We'll allow ourselves to point out here that there is no "fate" in this "irony," just as there's no "irony" in these "fates"; the only thing present in this state of affairs is the usual bloody mess.

"Well, then, we're closing the Scouts program and bringing a lawsuit against you, dear comrades," A.Z. wearily summed matters up. He had been dreaming of retirement from his high position for some time and felt himself drawn toward the pastoral settings of the Pinkerton campus, not worrying in the least about his soliloquy to us a dozen or so pages ago. The specialists of the Scout movement began thrusting their chins forward. "We wouldn't advise it, Mr. Korbach. We would advise you to talk to our curator first. He's waiting for you, by the way." Criminal fingers pointed at the ceiling, as the fathers of those fingers had once pointed at the cloud that was Stalin hanging over the country.

A.Z. went upstairs. There was no need to go, but curiosity was drawing him: What is this Viaduct that everyone in the city is talking about so much? He didn't notice anything in particular there, just the usual thugs in expensive suits smoking in the corridors. In the city, meanwhile, it was claimed that the old Lubyanka had moved over to Viaduct, under the leadership of the very same Bubkov, Buitsov, Buirov, Brutkov, and Bruschatnikov: they all had the title vice president now.

Yes, yes, Mr. Korbach, the president is waiting for you. A.Z. comes into a gigantic office. A distant corner of it is embellished with a bronze reproduction of Rodin's *Thinker*. Behind the president's desk was an inhuman mug, that of Special Agent Zavkhozov, who had aged a good deal. "Oleg, isn't it?" "No, Oryol. Oryol Ilych. It's strange, Sasha—we're neighbors, and we can't have a couple of snorts of vodka together." "Let's get down to business, Mr. President." "Right, let's." "We've just been looking over your budget charts, and a number of questions have arisen." Five men, getting on a bit in years but still healthy devils, move up a bit closer and station themselves around the guest. They intently study every wrinkle of the buffoon's face. "Beg your pardon, but I didn't come up here to talk about our budgets but about forgeries fabricated by the R.S., your charges. As a matter of fact, not even to talk, but just to let you know that we've shut down their program."

The reply was a burst of Homeric, even carnivalesque laughter. The surrounding gentlemen shook their heads. Well, whadda ya know! Someone even grunted: "That's Sasha Korbach all over for you, comrades!" All of them came even closer, somehow, and one, standing up from his perch on a windowsill, took up a position behind him. Are they going to beat the shit out of me? A.Z. sized up the situation— any way to slip away? The smile on President Zavkhozov's face was terrifying. "Why, we're just having a neighborly chat, Alexander Zakharovich. We thought perhaps you could use a little help? We've got some very experienced people here, at your disposal." "I'm very grateful indeed, but I think I'll go. I've got nothing to talk to your experienced people about." A new burst of almost good-natured laughter. "That's Sasha Korbach for you, comrades, that's him all over!" "And you're all comrades here, gentlemen, as I see?" "Yes, yes, we're all comrades, from our days at the institute. Tell me, Sasha, what does your name mean in Hebrew? Cold house, or something like that, isn't it? And is it true that your cousin Stanley has lost his marbles? And is it true you're with his daughter?"

Korbach stood up. "So long, gentlemen-comrades, I'd advise you not to waste your time paying such close attention to us. Better if you take those chiselers from the Russian Scouts in hand, let them return the money to the growing generation." All of them, including President Zavkhozov, came along after him, and, overtaking him, moved to the door. An awkward little crush of people, not to say a roadblock, formed there. "What, do you mean to tell me, Alexander Zakharovich, that you move around our dangerous democratic capital without bodyguards? How strangely frivolous of you. Some Jew walks around here and pretends that he isn't afraid. But democracy isn't just standing still, you know, it's developing!" A small commotion was heard in the antechamber of the president's office, and immediately afterward two broad-shouldered fellows, one black and the other white, added themselves to the mise-en-scène in the doorway. Two of ours! Alexander sighed with relief at the sight of Ben and Matt. "Alex, we were worried. Where were you for so long!" Now both sides were bowing to each other politely—pluralism of a sort that had never yet been seen within these walls!

Suddenly the walls swayed. The floor was buzzing as though tanks had reentered Moscow. This time, however, it was not steel but bronze that was in motion. At the backs of the Viaducters the local Thinker stood two heads taller. "All this hubbub, and no brawl?" he asked. "Go on, go, Misha," the president said to him, and smirked with his Guignol mouth. So long, neighbors!

Now that Guignol mug was smirking at him in the smartly dressed crowd at the Semi-Underground. A raised shot glass. One eyebrow, a dried-up grasshopper, arches on the spotty forehead. Everything hunky-dory? A.Z. didn't reply to the greeting. Zavkhozov was already hissing something into someone's ear from behind, something obviously anti-Semitic.

Suddenly, beside and slightly above Alex, rang out a cheery, angelic little voice: "Alexander Zakharovich, I've been assigned to you this evening, if you don't object!" There, smiling divinely, stood one of the tall girls of a few minutes before. "My name's Lasta." "Vlasta?" he asked, surprised by the Czech name.

"No, just 'Lasta.' " The girl laughed. "You know, like last but not least. Don't you like it?"

"On the contrary, I even like it too much."

"Well, you understand everything, Alexander Zakharovich." With humor in her gestures she snuggled up to him for a moment, her chin sliding across his bald head.

"Lasta, you know, I'm old enough to be not just your father but your grandfather." She countered heatedly: "Maybe as a foreigner you don't know this, but Sasha Korbach has no age in our country. Come on, let's go down into the mine! That's where all the action is!"

Leaving the sparkling hall, they began to descend into the basement, which looked like the set of some Hollywood blockbuster about the twilight of civilization, with crude masonry walls with protruding girders and huge pipes, from which here and there something was oozing. The space of the room was broken up by staircases that looked as though they were falling down but were in fact perfectly safe. Mountains of crates and wet cardboard boxes added to the atmosphere of decay. From time to time, however, the whole cave blazed in a whirlwind of multi-colored lights. "It's a lighting check for the cabaret program *Apotheosis*," Lasta explained. Nostrils were catching contradictory smells: perfume and perspiration, vomit and good coffee. The eyes were adjusting. One could see that young people were standing around everywhere, at least two hundred of them. The girls were towering over the shaved heads of the guys. At the far end of the room a cozy cave of a bar was lit up. The beam of a searchlight was trained on a crumbling, ancient five-ton truck. Standing in the bed, its sides thrown down, were four musicians stripped to the waist, as gaunt as prisoners in a Bosnian concentration camp—it was the group Umum. Hammering the strings, they were bawling:

Sorry that I was completely smashed,
Darling!
Sorry that I kicked you with my boot,
Darling!

Lasta clasped her hands to her chest. "I just love these guys!" At that moment Sasha Korbach spotted the *prekrasnaya dama* walking by the repulsive intestines of some piping. In the first instant he didn't realize that it was she, though he thought, in the most hackneyed style imaginable: The years take nothing away from her. The next moment, the light moved away from the level of the cave where the lady had been walking, and it was only then he realized that it was Nora.

"What's wrong, Alexander Zakharovich?" Lasta asked.

Now the whirl of colors began spinning again, and Nora, with her infinitely sweet and intelligent face, was flickering before him like a figure in a cartoon. Forgetting about Lasta, he came rolling down from his level toward her. The whirl subsided, and in the half-light between the tables they saw each other. Behind her stood a companion, a young man with an abundant, long blond mane wearing a light-colored jacket—the white knight of the national movement, Dima Pletoyarov. Even recently, democratic Moscow had still been referring to him as "the fascist swine" but now had condescendingly dropped the adjective: "He's a swine, of course, but there's something about him."

The durable phenomenon of forgetfulness had developed in post-Soviet Russia. What hadn't Pletoyarov written in the days of his spindly youth in the Fascist rag *Tushinsky Pulse* and for Prokhanov's *Day* (more like the night in this case)? He would flash his now Nazi, now Bolshevik buttocks through the transom window!

Everyone knew him—tall, handsome, with a very red (it suited him perfectly) mouth. People say that he stuffs himself with some chemical, but who can be sure; he hasn't been caught at anything, unless you count the things he's published, but who's counting now? Well, for what it's worth, here's one of them—judge for yourself.

On the third anniversary of the Great Soviet Crash, Pletoyarov published an article in Prokhanov's paper in which he called the junta Decembrists, after the romantically inspired uprising of 1825. Alas, he lamented, they, too, turned out to be far from the people! They allowed that Moscow rabble, all those full-blooded, half-, and one-quarter Jews, to seize the initiative. They didn't have the nerve to put on a good Russian Tiananmen. He'd tried at the time, the brave kid, to influence the officers of the general staff—it wasn't for nothing, after all, that he was known as the nightingale of the Supreme Soviet, after his rousing television appearances. Well, all right, he'd exhorted them—if you're afraid to spill blood, then spill paint! What strange ideas you have, Dimitry, the generals had said, screwing up their faces. Listen here, Your Excellencies! Some agents get sent secretly into the crowd around the White House. Each one of them has some stage paint in a plastic bag under his jacket. Sirens start howling, a few fake explosions go off, the agents pull the stoppers, the blood comes gushing out, the Jews scatter in a panic. You can take Yeltsin with your bare hands. The generals had roared with laughter. What a strange head you've got on your shoulders, Mitya! That's how they lost their power!

All this came back to A.Z. in the few minutes it took him to get to Nora. It returned to him in a flash and was just as quickly forgotten. What does this whole Russian madhouse have to do with us, with her or with me? Now she saw him, and flushed with excitement, just the way she used to in Washington when they met at the airport. "Sashka!" "Norka!" They sat in a corner and laid their joined hands on the top of a little cocktail table. "You've taken so much of my time again, you louse! Four years! Four years and four months!"

"What brings you here?" "We're working nearby." "Who do you mean, 'we'? Where?" "My expedition. By Elista. We're excavating Khazar burial mounds." "And why did you come to Moscow?" "Just for old times' sake." "Do you remember how you were jealous of me because of Moscow? And now there's this Dima." "Do you approve?" "Oh, to hell with Dima! It would be better if you told me about our son!" "About whom?" "About Philip Jazz Korbach!"

She withdrew her hand from the friendly embrace. Tossed her scarf over her shoulders. A white beam fixed itself on her, as bad luck would have it, illuminating all her wrinkles, her suddenly thrust-out chin, and a small but noticeable goiter. At the same moment, another beam, this one yellow, helpfully lit up Pletoyarov, who was dancing with Lasta; postmodernist youth! "My son has nothing to do with you." "That's not true!" "Nora, are you done with your secret conversation already? Can we join you?" the young man with the Fascist leanings yelled from the whirlwind of knees-and-elbows dancing. Nora turned away from him without a reply. After a moment of reflection A.Z. decided to deal his beloved an answering blow. And a strong one, too. "Where'd you pick up this Slavic Apollo?" She burst out laughing in the very way he hated, with a whore's laugh that heaped the whole dumping ground of his jealousy up into a mountain. He was interested, you see, in our excavations, and in the Khazars in general as a possible tribe of the Israelites. A young man with a great deal of curiosity. Ah, my little Nora, you unreasonable Berkeleyite, you don't seem to know who he is. You're sleeping with this country's chief anti-Semite, a Fascist everyone knows about.

The two dancers, breathing hard, came and sat down. Two knees immediately raised themselves above the edge of the table: the bare one belonged to Lasta, while Pletoyarov's was encased in white denim. The young people looked inquiringly at the professional philanthropist, expecting hospitality. A.Z. disappointed them greatly and offered them nothing. Nora was sitting beside him, her eyes on her own cigarette. Pletoyarov gave a puzzled smirk. Obviously, he had promised the gangling beauty that during the dance he would find her a sugar daddy.

"What'll you have?" said the barside mercenary, who had come over to them.

"Champagne all around!" Pletoyarov said to him. "Only make it ours, not French."

"Have you got money?" the mercenary asked, but obviously realized that he had and moved off without waiting for a reply.

With an encouraging gesture that went unnoticed by the others, Lasta tapped her fingertips on the back of Korbach's perspiration-covered head. Don't give up, maestro!

"Mm . . . ye-e-s, Mr. Korbach," the nationalist drawled with a languor that in our country often goes hand in hand with impudence, "you made a mistake, after all, in throwing away your only successful beginning. Your Moscow theater, you know, even though it had a certain inescapable odor about it, still turned out to be a milestone. A milestone, my dear man! You should never have gone crawling after money, old boy! Money's a cruel thing, not everyone can pull its weight. It's really too bad." He was glancing back and forth between Korbach and Nora the entire time, as if trying to work out whether or not he had managed to tell her who Dimka Pletoyarov was. Nora didn't look at him so much as once and never favored him with her smile, which—we'll reveal one of the Fascist's secrets—he called "a ray of light in the Khazar kingdom."

"Yes, it's too bad, Alexander Zakharovich, that our cesspool drew you back. They say that your name is already on a contract, and it's a great pity."

"How about if I shove that pity up your ass?" A.Z. said, surprising even himself. Pletoyarov rocked backward like a flabbergasted log. The mercenary was popping the cork over them then. Foam streamed into the goblets. A.Z. raised his. "Here's to us!" Everyone clinked glasses.

He saw that Nora was on the verge of tears. As was he. My little girl, my Maryland equestrian! You're forty-six now, and in your desperation you're ready to cling to any good-looking cock. Do you remember at least that copper-colored dawn, the seething purple leaves, the shy hooves of your Gretchen, the way your body was smothered in kisses and the way mine was covered with them, all the *dolce stil nuovo*? Get up and leave with me now! We'll live out together the time we have left!

Without a word, and without waiting for a reply to his unspoken words, he stood up, tossed some quantity of fifty-thousand-ruble notes on the table, and headed for the door.

"It's interesting, A.Z.," Lasta was saying thoughtfully. "The hair that remains on the back of your head looks quite young, but there are gray tufts growing out of your ears. In the card game of life, A.Z., you were dealt an interesting body. There's a lot about you that's young, and here your neck is all wrinkled."

"Tell me, Lasta, what does 'on a contract' mean?" he asked the girl, who had managed to follow him to Patriarchs' Pond.

She laughed. "It's a list of people to be got rid of, I guess. Contract killing. I remember Dimka saying that to you, but don't you believe him, the big blowhard. Do you mean you're not surprised by this nonstop chatter all around?"

As a matter of fact, A.Z. was surprised. He reared up so far from surprise that the girl stopped counting his tufts of hair and wrinkles. It is surprising, after all, to have a contract out on oneself in one's motherland!

From the window, the pond and the tree-lined walks around it were visible in the half-light of the spring dawn. A large, mangy Ussurian tiger was plodding along the damp earth among the tree trunks. It was yawning like a retired marshal of the Soviet Union. "And what's this, then?" A.Z. asked, surprised once again. "Maybe you can explain it to me, a foreigner?" The girl was already yawning—not at all like the tiger we've given the literary treatment, though, rather like some new creature, the longest of flippers. "Why, that's a tiger, Alexander Zakharovich—you mean you don't recognize it? There's a zoo near here, after all—my, my . . ."

X. AT NIGHT ON THE PIAZZA CICERNA

The sensitive Dante picks his way among lacework in stone.
In the gallery a stone donna,
Whose face was given to him as a temptation,
Stands in luxurious Lyons silks.

They approach each other, he raises up
A piece of the moon driving him mad.
San Gimignano covers the sin
And opens a valuable drawer.

He's happy that he wrested a cry from the stone
And alarmed even the edge of the forest,
That he didn't break the rules of the game
And turned granite into living flesh.

And Beatrice looks at that moment
And tenderly sighs: O, my rake!

PART XI

1

ART

*D*isappearing characters—isn't that the novelist's greatest worry? The flow of inspiration—isn't it a treacherous route for our unhurried caravan? Caught up in this current, rolling along the road in the bubbling foam of ingenuous delight, you can easily lose your professionalism and characters without which you couldn't have imagined your narrative a hundred pages earlier along with it. Such a thing could have happened even to the author of the present work were he not shrewd enough to anticipate a rebuke from the Highly Esteemed and Perceptive Reader (HEPR).

In particular, the HEPR is justified in asking: Where's that nice guy of ours, Art Duppertat? After all, the last time we saw him was half this book ago at the gala presentation of the Korbach Fund, swinging from a chandelier, perhaps in a figurative sense, perhaps in a literal one. I thank the foremost group of my connoisseurs, including you, O Theophilus, whom Andrei Bely, and Vladimir Nabokov after him, quite correctly called creative readers. From time to time, in the light of your attentive eyes, I look over a list of characters, and sometimes, I admit, I allow myself a certain feigned absentmindedness. In fact, I realized quite some time ago that Art had been left by the side of our road and undeservedly forgotten. Feeling pangs of conscience, I kept trying to slip him in somewhere, but nothing came of these attempts. Any possible return of his created a strange awkwardness, as though there was no place for this brilliant young man among our eccentric philanthropists. There was a feeling that he hadn't dropped out of the text just by accident, that there was some important novelistic reason for it. And then it suddenly dawned on me that there really hadn't been a miscalculation but rather a sort of maneuver on the part of our young activist.

By the way, about his age, how old is he now? Let's see: if he was twenty-seven at the beginning of our story, now, gentlemen, he's exactly forty. Let us refrain from sighing over the implacability of time's passage; we have, after all, only ourselves to blame. Anyway, forty is a great age for belles lettres. And that's all I want to say about that.

Sometimes things work out very strangely in modern thick novels! The author gets all wrapped up in figuring how to move his bulky creation along, and in the meantime one group of characters is rebelling against another. It gets scary for the author when he realizes that such conspiracies undermine the very foundations of his miniuniverse: the subject, fundamental structures, and even the central offices of giant corporations with their unequaled charitable trusts.

One evening in late autumn of 1995, in the very heart of Manhattan, in the AK & BB Corporation building, on the fifty-seventh floor of the central offices, two gentlemen had stayed late in front of their computer screens. They were both in their shirtsleeves, and we can easily make out their sculptured shoulder muscles. Since we're seated behind them, we can easily discern that baldness poses not the slightest threat to their crowns. On the contrary, the short crew cut of the one and the lion's mane of the other bring us back to the novel's first chapters. The reader has probably already guessed that one of them is the corporate vice president Arthur W. Duppertat, and the second is none other than Director of Research Mel O'Massey. The latter's face, as we can see, with the years has acquired a lionish aspect to go along with the mane, but this is not, as you might think, a symptom of leprosy, simply the result of the same major masculinization experienced by the heads of so many major corporations. To be sure that some tiresome critic won't carp about this point, we're obliged to note that even though we're standing behind them, we can also see the faces of these two people, since they're reflected in the large, dark window of the skyscraper. That's all—that'll be enough out of you, tiresome Skameikin.

More important at this point is to say that five years earlier Mel married Stanley Korbach's middle daughter, who was five years older than her half sister Sylvia Duppertat. Cecily, a divorcée with two children, wasted no time, and quickly gave Mel a son, Chris, and twin daughters, Lavonne and Amy. At times, when the Duppertats and the O'Masseys got together at Halifax Farm, or anywhere else on the planet, and if in addition the older half sister, Walker, showed up with her progeny, there was created the impression of a large clan from the cat family (Are they lions? Tigers, maybe?) with their young at varying stages of development into capitalist predators.

What joy there was during these gatherings of kindred souls and bodies—it was like a carnival! Laughing, singing, chatter, dancing, teasing, the hurling of cream pies into dearly loved faces, but it was the competitions between the fathers, Mel and Art, that turned into the main events on these days. These two were uncontrollable in their desire to beat each other. Neither could live without testing the strength, skill, training, luck, and endurance of his brother-in-law. For example, if Art saw that Mel was buttering his toast, he would say to him without fail: "Listen, I bet I can butter a piece of toast three times as fast as you can!" Battle would be joined immediately, and soon the table would be covered with dozens of buttered pieces of toast.

We won't even talk about tennis, swimming, high jumping, and so forth. As far as kick boxing was concerned, the children had long been accustomed to the sight of their fathers covered with sweat and trickles of blood, and coming out with "Shit, shit, shit . . ." and other more or less printable words. All the members of the tribe were quite used to bloodstains on the patio or in the living room, and no one would call the police at the sight of them.

Of course, there were some domains in which competition would have made no sense. Mel, for example, couldn't even dream of outplaying Art on the guitar, or imitating his repertoire of Dylan, Simon and Garfunkel, Vysotsky, and Sasha Korbach, never mind the ballads and blues of his own composition. These spontaneous concerts forced the onetime merman, now transformed into a lion, to go off to a corner and sit with a sardonic smile on his face that rapidly turned into a series of nervous little yawns. On the other hand, whenever Mel got near a computer, Art threw up his hands and signed an act of surrender. Mel was the undisputed lord high wizard in this sphere of human endeavor. "That O'Massey is awesome!" was the word on him on every floor of the corporation. It was said that the head of the Special Research Center could break through the code systems of even companies with the best security measures, like IBM, Chase Manhattan, General Dynamics, and the Central Bank of Russia. He could calculate the strategy of AK & BB for years in advance and was never wrong in his estimations, strategic or tactical, of development in the world. There were rumors that it was he and his Special Research Center, and not Chairman Blamsdale, that the company had to thank for its huge successes over the last few years. Then again, people said, who but Blamsdale could hire such valuable people? It was no secret that it was Norman and no one else who had found the young genius in one of California's shady seaside bars, where for whole nights at a time he was "staffing" (staffers "staff," what else?) fat-bottomed, half-horses, half-hookers like the grotesque Bernie Luxe, now the girlfriend of Stanley Korbach, who, though right out of his head, was still the nominal president of AK & BB. One way or another, rumors that his sparring partner would be promoted to the vice presidential level had already reached Art's ears. The guy earned it, Art thought. He's a genius of modern, aggressive marketing. His indisputable calculations are enough to give you the shivers! It's only thanks to him, after all, that we've managed to gobble up McDonald's, Mitsubishi, Lockheed, Coca-Cola, and CNN in the last few years, and to open our jaws for Putney Productions.

Mm . . . yes, we have to say that with the passing of the years, Duppertat, our favorite, has begun to feel burdened by his high position. Not long ago he opened the door of his wardrobe, saw several dozen of his three-piece suits, and felt sick to his stomach. Is it really my calling in life to chair countless, endless meetings? Or to sign a paper mountain on my desk? Or to deposit always more and more millions in my bank account? Isn't my calling to drive an old Jeep along Mediterranean roads, to sit behind the wheel in worn-through velvet trousers, to take puppet shows to kids in godforsaken places, and, last but not least, to look after my own Pulcinelli nose and eyes, which, I hope, haven't lost all their sharpness and hunger for life?

God knows he never wanted to become a shark in the business world! When he fell in love with Sylvia, he thought that they would be a carefree and, up to a point, artistic young couple, collectors of some sort, the sponsors of exhibitions and uncommercial films, fixtures at bohemian gatherings, and not boring yuppies with nothing on their minds but financial success. Well, all right, so it's my lot in life to make opening the business section of *The New York Times* my first task every morning, but all the same it's unbearable to see my love, glasses on her nose, studying the market indicators and NYSE CP figures over her first cup of coffee.

At the risk of our reputation (which, for that matter, became a hopeless case a long time ago), we should at this point add to Art's lamentations the fact that sometimes even during the performance of her conjugal duties Sylvia would try to occupy such a position as to continue flipping through the pages of *Forbes*. Approaching her thirty-first birthday and the mother of three delightful children, Sylvia Duppertat remained the very picture of the American beauty, graceful, gentle, with a romantic expression on her still schoolgirlish face, in spite of her discovery two or three years earlier of a dry and immutable stock-market operator beneath its surface.

Sometimes, draining glass after glass of one of his beloved Merlots, Art would think: It's too bad I stayed with the ship, too bad I can't be with my friends Alex and Stanley, and that whole merry band that gathers around them. Spending money really is more fun than making it. Sad to say, I've got to stay at the head of the corporation, to protect Stanley's affairs from encroachments by Blamsdale. The only problem is that my friends, and the author of this novel as well, forget about me too often. This thought filled him with sadness. He began to have the feeling that "life was passing him by," as they often sing in folk songs. Somehow he had pictured his relationship with Stanley Korbach, the man who had been his idol from the days when he had worked as a cabin boy on his yacht *Rita*, differently. Of course he was playing a critical role these days in Stanley's struggle against Norman Blamsdale's ferocious appetites, there's no denying that. As long as the vice president was sitting at the table of the board of directors, everyone could see that the Blamsdale forces would not overcome the Korbachites. Art knew perfectly well what bloody battles were raging out on the peripheries of the empire: over the Himalayas, in Mexico, Chechnya, Bosnia; in the headquarters in Manhattan, however, everything still looked quite on the up and up. The slaughter on the East Side and in the environs of Carnegie Hall that had begun it all was considered an unseemly topic of conversation here. Here, the most powerful weapon at Art's disposal was humor. After each meeting of the board, E-mail added fuel to the highly significant conversations taking place on the floors of the building. "Art Duppertat put Norman Blamsdale in his place, calling him a 'representative of the majority.' " Some analysts from the fortieth and fiftieth floors supposed that Duppertat was getting close to taking the top position on the board. The know-it-alls from the thirtieth to the fortieth, with the impudent nonchalance typical of such people, started to call the holy of holies, the sixty-fifth, King Arthur's Round Table. All those swine are capable of is running off at the mouth. One day all this chatter will come back to haunt you, youngsters of the "Duppertat team"; you see, Norm's staff never stopped collecting all the jokes and little exchanges concerning their boss. Okay, at the end of the day, Art had a big advantage in this never-ending quarrel: a readiness at any moment to take off from this confounded pyramid seething with intrigues. Then my friends will realize that they expected too much from me!

In giving himself over to these reflections, Art didn't know that the decisive moment was approaching and that quite soon—on the very evening, in fact, that we're talking about—Mel O'Massey would call, and in his usual outwardly lackadaisical manner ask him to drop by his office, just to have a look at an unusual configuration of numbers and statistics that had popped up on his screen. Well, of course I could bring the whole thing to you, Mr. V.P., but then I'd have to make it an official report, and I'm only asking you to take a look and tell me if I should write up this strange layout as a report or just chuck the whole damned thing. Of course, Art, any time, but this evening would be better. It'll take you ten minutes to realize how urgent it is. Well, shit, I wish it weren't urgent!

When he came into Mel's spacious office, the windows of which were looking out on a late sunset over the Hudson, a strange feeling of unexpected chromatic balance akin to what one feels when one stands before a painted masterpiece went right through Art. He didn't realize right away what it was that was completing the picture. Everything seemed the same as ever: the endless skies with their gold dust over the skyline of Manhattan and the emerald-colored vault of the heavens in which stars at an early state of washing their faces could be distinguished. In other words, everything was irresistible and incomprehensible, as was always the case when one looked from the large, half-darkened room. In the next instant he found the moment of unexpectedness. It was the screen of Mel O'Massey's personal computer, so personal that he wouldn't let anyone even dust it. The screen showed a combination of simple geometric forms: a circle, a square, a pair of parallelepipeds, a handful of triangles of different sizes. In addition to the shapes a combination of colors was shown—simple, vivid hues: red, black, sky blue, lemon yellow. The overall effect was similar to that of the elements of the simplest chromatic materials displayed to the public in the era of the great openings, in particular at the first Suprematist exhibition of Kazimir Malevich and his pupils in October 1915.

For a minute or two, Art stood there as though hypnotized, in the middle of the room, behind Mel's back, while the latter rocked lightly in his chair, his fingers interlaced behind his head. After that immeasurable "minute or two" had ticked away, the vice prez realized that the chromatic celebration signified nothing other than Stanley Korbach's final sentence: his reign had come to an end!

"Understand?" Mel asked without turning his head.

"Yes," Art replied, and immediately assumed a pose of defiance, arms akimbo. "Whatever your fucking thing shows, I'll never betray Stanley!"

"Why don't you sit down next to me, Mr. Vice?" Mel suggested gently.

"Listen, Art," he began, as his friend and brother-in-law rolled a chair up to the computer. "God knows I didn't want to blow up the old son of a bitch! I'll admit to you that he was my idol when I was a kid, with all his teams of rowers and yachtsmen, with his girls and his Vince Wilkie cars, with his Marine Corps past and his aristocratic upbringing, with his brilliant financial operations and his scandalous 'disappearances,' and now finally with his worldwide charitable crusade. Of course I hated him for making the girl of my dreams, the queen of the Pacific coast from Santa Monica to Marina del Rey, into a slave, but I saw pretty quickly that she hadn't changed much since the days of our get-togethers at the First Bottom. Still the same fast filly that I knew, and she always comes galloping toward you as soon as you call her.

"In a word, I didn't have any scores to settle with Stanley, and I certainly didn't want to get into investigating his financial dealings. I knew what Norm and his majority on the board were expecting from that sort of investigation. I was even getting ready to quit, when one day Norm called me in for a chat. He said: 'Try to show what Stanley's credit capacity is. Use any information you need toward that end, break any codes—I'll take the responsibility—hire any outside people. Just show how much credit he really has, and I promise that nothing bad will happen to you. What's more, you'll get a raise earlier than you expected. And what's more, I'll stop all combat operations against Stanley and begin negotiations. However,' he went on, 'I'm one hundred percent sure that not even you, O'Massey, will be able to square his balance, no matter how you try. On the contrary, you'll blow away the whole smoke screen that Sol Leibnitz has put up along with Enoch Agasf—who, they say, counted talents and shekels for Pompeii itself.' I'm sorry to say that he turned out to be right, brother-in-law of mine! Stanley's going through his assets so fast it's like he's blown all his gaskets. I've seen a lot of nutcases in the business world—our great pragmatist Norm doesn't take last place among them—sometimes it seems like he wants to settle scores with every guy for three generations who's done it with Marjorie. No, just think about it—stick a finger in any of the biggest political and financial schemes in the world, and you'll find some babe; we're getting close to the world of great logic, but we can't enter because we're out of our minds about sex."

"Get to the point," Art said dryly.

Mel was getting more and more nervous. "I just wanted to say that even among those idiots, Stanley and his philanthropy takes the prize for sure. Here, judge for yourself!" He put his slightly trembling fingers to the keys and started to clear the images from the screen. Then, with an occasional significant glance at Art, he began doing operations with columns of indexes and figures. Each stage of the operation he converted into colored graphics. The screen was now ablaze with Suprematist shapes. Art's head began to spin when he saw the interaction of the AK & BB data with that of the NYSE, the correlation of these figures with those of the IMF and World Bank, and with the figures of some unknown companies in India and Russia, and with the secret files of the IRS, and with the results of current operations in Tokyo, Jo-burg, Hong Kong, and London. All these information units circled around the solid columns of the Korbach Fund until the fund turned into a sphere of pure red. "Alas," Mel said almost sadly, with almost a gleam of human nostalgia, and in any case without schadenfreude, alas, alas, in the dark space around the red sphere, some outwardly innocent-looking cylinders, cubes, wedges, and rhomboids began to form, now swimming along separately, now rising chaotically in the corners of the screen.

"Now you see, my friend, that this heavenly body hasn't got a chance anymore." Mel sighed and half-turned to Art. "Well, do you want me to do the final click-click?"

Art nodded silently. Mel did the click-click. All the small parts began a rotary movement around the red sphere, periodically attacking it from their orbits. After a minute or two, the sphere collapsed into a formless stew of red dots. Mixing with the basic elements, the stew gradually, but with increasing speed, began to form one kaleidoscope after another. At first it was impossible to grasp the meaning of these transformations, but soon it became clear: the picture was losing its original bright colors and taking on more and more pure black. Finally, all the other colors disappeared and Art saw before him an ideal, vivid black form, the "Black Square" itself, a material equal to less than zero, nothing, with a tendency to suck in anyone who looked at it too closely. This was the final result. Postmodernism. Post-everything. Deconstruction. The death of Stanley Korbach as the hero of his generation. The complete overthrow and banishment of Byronism.

"I wish the damned thing would suck me in, too," Art said. Mel burst into laughter. "Forget about all that commedia dell'arte stuff, Duppertat! Chin up, Pulcinelli! We're still here, in our virtual reality, after all!" He clicked the mouse one more time. The Black Square immediately changed in flight into Tartarus, and there, in the "tartaries"—that is, in that kingdom of ancient mythology—was transformed into a tiny, invisible dot. In its place a conference table with familiar faces sitting around it appeared on the screen.

By this time, the sunset over the Manhattan skyline was almost finished, with only a cupola of light rapidly fading on the horizon like a descending parachute. An enlarged projection of the computer screen with all its familiar faces and life-size bodies appeared on one of the walls of the SRC operations center.

In fact, there were only members of the Korbach-Blamsdale clan here: Norman and Marjorie, all three of Marjorie's daughters—namely Sylvia Duppertat, Cecily O'Massey, and the celebrated operatic diva Walker Rossellini and her entrepreneur husband—and then Norman's ex-wife Pontessia, and their son, the roly-poly, good-natured Scott, two or three cousins from each side (their names don't matter, since they don't figure anywhere on our list of characters), and—wait for it!—the hit of the season, the patriarch David Korbach, looking at least a decade younger than his ninety-six years.

Mel rolled his chair closer to the wall and "virtually"—that is, in fact—turned into one of the participants in the gathering. He beckoned to Art: "Join in!" Unwillingly, but without objection, the latter moved toward the wall and found himself next to his wife, who was smiling at him with the usual tenderness that immediately preceded one of her no less usual capitulations.

Then began the meeting, in the course of which all the members of the so-called family—fuck their genealogical tree!—tried with all their might to talk Art around to an act of betrayal. Stanley's finished! He's a madman, obsessed with self-destructive ideas. He's squandering billions on his useless philanthropy campaign that's bringing nothing but disgrace. He has to be purged once and for all from the leadership of a great corporation, and isolated. And isolated! At that moment, all those present looked at the patriarch, and the stinking schmuck pointed his thumb down in unison with the rest. All of Stanley's personal accounts must be frozen immediately!

Art, you've just seen more than convincing proof provided by an undisputed expert and your best friend, Melvin O'Massey. Our legal experts are working on the question; they're already close to a final resolution. All the American and world financial communities are on our side. The proper government authorities and the people on the Hill are ready to support our decision. For the sake of your family, for the sake of our corporation, for the sake of the stability—we're not afraid to use these words—of our entire country and of the whole civilized world, you, Mr. Vice President, have to join us in our decision, which, believe us, was not an easy one to make, taking into account the personality of old Stanley, whom we all love dearly.

The least active voice in this chorus, strange as it may seem, was Chairman Blamsdale. He was pretending to be a more or less neutral financier, as though he had not recently been seized in his fortress on Aruba by Stanley's Marine commandos and then set free in exchange for Colonel Bernadetta De Luxe and her baby, captured after a bloody battle on the south wing of the butterfly island of Guadeloupe. And only after the rhetoric had begun to die down did Norman put in a calm—calm on the verge of hysteria, one might say—word for the attention of all. "Of course, we would prefer a unanimous decision at a meeting of the board. In view of the present circumstances, however, we can get along without one. I hope that Mr. Duppertat understands what this means for his personal career."

Art's first instinctive reaction was a desire to grab his wife by the hand and drag her away from this collection of creeps. He even reached out for her but realized immediately that she was unattainable. In Sylvia's eye he read the same question that was weighing on the minds of all those around the table. Refraining from any sudden movements, he asked in a businesslike tone, surprising even himself: "When are you expecting this decision from me, ladies and gentlemen?"

All the faces around the table shone with joy. How wonderful that this great guy, this—*entre nous*—symbol of success for all of AK & BB, seems ready to sacrifice his dubious friendship for the good of the corporation, and his family, and the growing generation! "The sooner the better, honey," Sylvia whispered, and the breeze of her sex, having penetrated even virtual reality, stirred in him a feeling of happiness that was so familiar. After all, in saying "honey" to him, she didn't mean a normal form of spousal address in this country—she meant that he's the sweetest of all the lovers in the world.

All their favorite ways of foreplay came to his mind as he looked into her eyes, particularly one of their latest. She's an adolescent wearing a bra for the first time. She's very proud of the fact that her tits are in a bra now, but she suddenly realizes that she can't unhook it, and she needs to change to go swimming. She looks around in desperation for help, but there's no one at hand except an aging (around forty) gentleman from next door. As a man with a good heart and worldly manners, he can't refuse to help. Who'll answer for the consequences? He's trying as best he knows how, and his attempts are so gentle, so slow, oh, how slow they are and how gentle! The final removal of the brassiere comes like an apotheosis, she's squealing and farting, puff, puff, puff. Oh, honey, and they both fall asleep.

He leapt to his feet and made for the door. It seemed to him that he had left his own body in some senseless attempt to wrench himself free from this silly illusion, while at the same time he sensed that the only action of his own volition left to him was to drag this body to the door as quickly as possible. In the elevator, in the enclosed cube of air, he gave a twitch like a salamander and then felt like himself again. "Mongrels, shit eaters, assholes, pukes," he hissed in his rage. "Trying to make me into an electronic zombie, are you? Trying to turn the woman I love into one of your ghosts, slippery as an eel? To hell with you—you spy on us in our bedroom, but you underestimate my endurance, my courage, my faithfulness to my love and to my friends, and for that matter to the whole world full of feelings, smells, motifs, colored pollen, to everything that doesn't exist in your fucking virtual reality!"

As usual, his Bentley immediately calmed him down, body and soul. With its taciturn power it carried its owner along the Long Island Expressway in the direction of the Hamptons. In actual fact, it wasn't so taciturn, Theophilus, if you take into account the Beethoven's Fifth that the automobile was playing in order to lift Art's spirits.

In the dark sky, one after another, transatlantic aircraft descending toward JFK appeared. They shone brightly with floodlights, landing lights, and blinkers, as though their chief purpose was to provide illumination. Looking at the airliners and listening to the sounds of the Beethovenesque rising and falling, Art was crying. I'm a weak, pitiful, blubbering wanker. I've got nothing to do with these great air routes, any more than I have with the storm of this brass section and the soaring swarm of the strings. How can I run from these swine and their "v.r."? If only she were with me, my darling, my only anchor on this Earth!

The night watchman opened the gates of Art's seaside estate. What a repulsive mug that guy has! Every time he sees Sylvia and me, he smirks like he was watching a peep show. I ought to fire the S.O.B. The tops of the cypresses and the junipers swayed in the ocean breeze. You're my only angels, cypresses and junipers! The windows of the children's rooms were dark. You're my wings, kids, and at the same time you're my shackles. He drove around the house and saw Sylvia standing on the balcony. Getting out of the car, he heard her joyful voice: "Art, I'm so happy that you're going to be with us, with us the whole family! Enough is enough, you know! Dad's just gone off the deep end ever since he hooked up with that filly! And enough of you and your double role on the board of directors! Oh, I'm so relieved! It feels like I'm breathing in a whole new way after that historic 'v.r.' session!"

He tossed his jacket on the hood of the car and slowly walked toward the roaring ocean. Darkness swallowed up more and more of him with each step. The surf struck the breakwaters and rolled over them, forming figures of foamy lions sur-prised and furious. Art sat down on the sand, still warm from the heat of the day. He wasn't thinking about anything but those foamy lions. How'd you like 'em?

"Sir," Sylvia whispered, sitting down beside him. Barefoot, in a bathrobe. "I don't know what's happening to me. My husband's waiting for me at a high-society do, and I can't get my bathrobe off, can't get my bikini off. Would you be kind and help me, Mr. Stranger?"

2

LAVSKY

*T*hese film studios in North Hollywood look like frozen chicken storehouses—well, all right, we'll raise the bar a bit and say frozen ostrich. You might say, of course, the author is exaggerating—a certain section of the readership does have this strange habit of finding fault; he's inflating some far-fetched images, you say; still, you've got to agree that these studios on their best day look like abandoned garment factories, and that only the flashy cars parked along their walls give one the idea that they're soundstages.

Either way, these long structures built from fire-resistant materials remind us of anything but the *dolce stil nuovo,* of Italian poets from the thirteenth century, of the city of Florence, where a conflagration of words and passions blazed forth from a divine spark. They don't even have anything in common with the Silver Age of Petersburg, with that crowd of Symbolists and aviators, ballerinas and cav-alry guardsmen, enchanted by the slow sunsets and the heavy roll of the northern waves. And what have they got to do with the singing poets of the reborn New York City of the last third of the twenty-fifth century, with their hysterical swing fore-telling the ruin of Utopia?

Beg your pardon, one of our readers will say, but what's the connection between these ostrich storehouses and your Alexander Zakharovich, aka Sasha Korbach, former Soviet "protest bard," to whom you sometimes give the degrad-ing nickname Lavsky? He himself supposedly keeps renouncing the "dream fac-tory," and you just go on your way, sticking him within these fire-resistant walls.

Come on now, let's be objective. Let's try to take a look at the whole situation and at our A.Z.'s place in it from a position of detachment. How many Russian filmmakers, émigrés, and refugees from the seventies, eighties, and nineties were drawn to Hollywood! They all dreamed about making a masterpiece, about real-izing their always unique cinematic ideas, and they all flopped. They lived on the fringes of the enchanted kingdom, took any job going to live, toiled away as taxi drivers, masseurs, chiropractors, waiters, pizza deliverymen, hotel busboys, truck drivers, and used every second of their spare time to write proposals, outlines, treatments, and finally scripts, and none of them ever stopped shrugging his shoulders: why is there no reaction, no interest in the Russian potential, in all of our "Dosto-Tolsto-Pushko-Goglo-Chekhoviana"?

A few of them timidly approached the city of the wizards and occasionally even entered, hoping that refined manners and a British accent acquired from private English teachers in Moscow would make an impression on the Hollywood aristocracy. Others tried storming the fortress, playing the "Russian spontaneity" card for all it was worth, and looking just short of boors. Allow me to point out that Alex and I met one of them at a party at Jeff Crappivva's. With these types, their English was so broken as to be unrecognizable, and their Russian was full of filth. They would fill their plastic cups to the brim with vodka, and then, showing off their "Russian bravado," throw them against the wall. Any one of them was ready to bang any veteran actress who could open the magic gates for him. Alas, both types flopped. Not a single Russian managed to mount an honest-to-goodness, full-budget Hollywood motion picture. Unlike their Czech and Polish colleagues, they were congenitally lacking in whatever it was they needed to know here.

Well, here's one exception for you: Alex Korbach, his particular case. Who of the millions of immigrants over the course of the colossal exodus to the new world didn't dream of finding rich and generous relatives here? The lucky ones, however, could be counted on the fingers of a single infantry battalion, and among those fortunate few, the most fortunate of all was our A.Z. Just imagine, good sir, such a cosmically rare stroke of luck—unexpectedly, with no idea that such a thing could happen, to bump into a fourth cousin who not only admits his relation to you but even foists it on you with an unimaginable amount of money, right up to and including massive subsidies for producing a film in which you dream of making your odd—to put it mildly—artistic intentions a reality. Surely Alexander Zakharovich isn't going to get everything handed to him by means of a boxwood walking stick across the head, is he? Don't you think so? Well, we can't renounce such a chance simply for the sake of psychological realism, which is as ephemeral as anything else.

That morning our child of fortune was getting ready to shoot his last soundstage scenes. After that there remained only the expedition to Europe for filming on location: four weeks in and around Florence and three weeks in St. Petersburg. Then he would remain with his miles of film in the editing room. Not long ago he'd been struck by the thought that something worthwhile might come out of this undertaking. The wind of success blew through the clumsiness and general chaos of the production period. Or was it just a momentary flicker of something artistic? Either way, at some moment he was caught up in a storm of inspiration. Was it really possible? Will my old dreams really come true, the reflexes of my adolescence, the masturbatory impulses of my immaturity, flashes of turbid revelation . . . in other words will my whole life be fleshed out on the screen?

Above all, I need first-rate music for this thing. The editing will be geared to the score in many respects. There are three names that could be of use: a Russian, an Italian, and a Swede, Pyotr, Pierro, and Per—three geniuses unrecognized by the modern world. Their telephone numbers are in my laptop. The clever thing will make the call itself. We'll start with the Russian, of course—he's my countryman, after all. Hey, Petya, what're you screwing around with up there in Bremen? Jerking off your flügelhorn, bowdlerizing your diary for posterity? Want to make a quarter of a million bucks? Yes, Pyotr the genius replied laconically, and the deal was done. Pierro and Per never found out how close they'd been on that day to a quarter of a "lemon."

A.Z. was sitting in the classic director's chair beside a camera mounted on a tripod. On his head was a classic tweed eight-paneled cap that gave him the look of a New York City cabdriver, and around his neck a classic llama's-wool scarf. All in all, a "classic" indeed!

The people around him were in chaotic motion. Union representatives were showing up to reach agreements with management on per diems for the lighting and sound technicians. They were shouting at and advancing on each other in the same way that baseball managers and umpires shout at and advance on each other and even kick dirt with the toes of their shoes but never come within an inch of a real collision. Goldie Belle D'Argent turned up with her entourage, including the current boyfriend, two bodyguards (by Hollywood standards she rated only one), a makeup artist, a pair of hangers-on from her native Sardinia, and the inevitable "suit," who intended to respond to management's carping about chronic tardiness by kicking up a fuss of his own about their constant underestimation of his client's star status. Meanwhile, in the parking lot, through the open gates of the service entrance, one could see "Dante," that is, Quentin Landry—who was pretending to chat with the studio chauffeurs about his 1936 Hispano-Suiza, but in fact was simply stretching out the time so as to arrive on the set five minutes after his "Beatrice," that "cheap, cheap, *cheap,* come-to-me bimbo," as he referred to her between takes. As for "Beatrice in later years," that is, Rita O'Neill, she, displaying her class, had arrived right on time and was now sitting near the director and reading the *Divine Comedy.* Assistants and assistants' assistants, meanwhile, were just running back and forth shooting guilty glances at their czar, sitting there motionless like a figure of silent reproach.

Now we've come to the moment of action, and as such we need finally to say something, if only a word or two, about the plot of the film. We have to confess, Theophilus, that we didn't do so earlier simply because we didn't know how to outline it. The only excuse that we can make to the demanding reader is that even A.Z. himself, endless discussions and approvals of different versions of the script notwithstanding, had reserved right up to this moment for himself a sort of poetic license to make changes in his chef d'oeuvre. Now, however, it's time.

At the end of the thirteenth century, there lives in Florence a young knight from a "White Guelph" family. He wears knitted tights of finely spun wool. His graceful legs delight modest girls and irritate the crude *ragazzi,* who love to start noisy brawls in the arched passageways of the fortress city. The most repulsive of them, of course, are the Ghibellines. The youth is well-trained for such eventualities, and his mastery of the sword cedes nothing to his mastery of the dagger. He does not like to kill, though, and even on the field of battle, clad in armor, prefers simply to unhorse a rider with a spear and not kill him. Only a handful of people know him to be a poet; the rest see in him only the young head of the once dreaded Alighieri family.

One day, at a moment of exaltation brought about by an inspiring church service, Dante meets a girl who stuns him with her inaccessible beauty and the radiance emanating from her face and eyes. Nor is Beatrice Portinari indifferent to the person of Dante. From that moment, the two young souls enter into a cycle of painful and pleasurable relations. Dante, who, as the head of his family, has already long been married to the faithful Gemma and has fathered sons, makes of Beatrice a cult of Divine Beauty. Day after day he follows her as she walks along the streets, buys things from merchants, prays on her knees in chapel, or embroiders on her balcony. He worships her as the angel of his verses but never once dares to approach her and strike up a conversation. As for Beatrice, she dreams of him as a lover and a husband. She in her turn follows him and hides in the shadows when the young poet begins to discuss the *dolce stil nuovo,* the "new sweet style" in poetry.

One night she sees him drunk, trying to seduce an actress on the market square. She flushes with jealousy. At that moment, a quarrel arises on the square between the Guelphs and the Ghibellines. Dante rushes by with dagger and sword, his profile filled suddenly with demonic passion. She flees, having lost control of herself, and breaks down in sobs.

Not long after that, Beatrice marries a good man of property with the best recommendations. The newlyweds leave Florence, traveling no one knows where. Dante is staggered and broken when he learns that his inspiration has vanished. He races from province to province on horseback looking for traces of her. At times it seems to him that he can see a strange radiance over the rooftops of the little towns or over the tops of the olive trees, and then he gallops in its direction in absolute certainty that it is Beatrice giving off this glow. His old friend the poet Guido Cavalcanti is sure that Dante is going through "the madness of love."

Meanwhile, Signora Beatrice knows all about Dante's attempts to find her. She trembles before the image of this wild romantic poet, sword in hand. She fears that he will challenge her husband to a duel or commit suicide. Her passion for him is becoming unbearable.

Suddenly, the unthinkable news of Beatrice's death strikes Dante like lightning. The poet's consciousness orbits in a void until he finds new amorous joy in the tragedy. Beatrice was so perfect that she must have been summoned to heaven to fill an empty place in the ranks of the angels. Henceforth she is his Eternal Bride, his Heavenly Maiden, the Image of Supreme Femininity.

He becomes a stern young man, one of the leaders of the White Guelphs. He challenges the powers that be, takes part in various conspiracies, writes poems (*La*

Vita Nuova), reflects on the Golden Age, religion, and politics with his friends, philosophizes about Earth and Water, carouses in the cellars of Florence, falls in love with and seeks the favors of ladies (Fiametta, Donna Petra), yet never forgets to peer at the sunsets, trying to interpret them as the "Radiance of Beatrice."

At the very end of the century, his faction is once again defeated in the struggle for power in the city, and he is banished to the plague-infested provinces. The Black Death does not spare him either. Cut off from his friends, deprived of any help, he is in his death throes in a dilapidated hut on a hillside from which the towers of San Gimignano are visible. All around is the dreaded forest, which will later become the setting for the first canto of the *Divine Comedy:* "In the midway of this our mortal life / I found me in a gloomy wood, astray . . ."

The audience, meanwhile, will be astounded by the abrupt change of scenery. St. Petersburg, the spring of 1914, the zenith of the Silver Age. A young officer in a cavalryman's overcoat—his features remind one of Dante—enters an enormous and nearly empty cathedral. Standing in the shadow of a pillar, he whispers not a prayer but "Verses About the Beautiful Lady" by Alexander Blok. A young woman in a fashionable coat walks up the aisle and kneels before an icon of the Mother of God. There is no disputing it, she looks like Beatrice. The officer watches her from his hiding place. The defenders of the motherland are handsome men.

The streets are those of the modernized European capital that Petersburg was at the time. The young woman is walking along the Neva with a brisk step, an upturned nose, and a haughty expression on her face. A young officer catches up to her and pleads with her to hear him out. He simply cannot live without her. She shrugs. It seems to me that you've already got what you wanted out of me. Stop being such a pest, Lieutenant.

Now we are in the artists' cabaret the Stray Dog. Smoke, noise, music. A group of poets in one corner are talking about Dante. How is it that the "time of Dante" has come again to Europe and to Russia? Why is everything decked out in lilac and purple? Someone is saying that the third part of the *Commedia* was written, in fact, only about the incomprehensible fluctuations of the light. Someone supposes that Dante really was *there* and came back—that is, he was sent in order to try to put it into words. Well, which one of us would have the nerve to undertake such a journey, someone jokes. And who among us would dare to fall in love with Beatrice, says another with a grin. No one except you, Alexander Alexandrovich. Everyone turns to A. A. Blok, the "king of poetry," about whom it is said that he is the embodiment of Dante. Blok turns away in annoyance.

A young officer standing next to the group is nervously listening to the poets' conversation. His eyes, meanwhile, clouded over by love, are searching the stage. His passion will appear there. She is barefoot and wearing a Greek tunic. To the delight of the audience, she is doing a seductive dance and singing a risqué song. Someone sends a bouquet of roses up to her. She tosses one of the roses to Blok. The latter catches it with a sardonic grin, dips it in a glass of champagne, and sends it back. The officer is trying to hold back tears.

White night, deserted streets, illusory contours of the city. The poets, men and women, are slowly making their way toward the Neva. Among them are Blok, the young officer, and the dancer, whom everyone here jokingly calls Bumble-Headed Psyche. The group reaches the embankment and sits down on the marble stairs that lead down into the turbid waters. The endless sunset is languorously playing out its drama on the western slopes of the Baltic firmament. Engrossed with the encoded signs in the sky, the poets meditate silently. The officer tries to touch the hand of his beloved with his fingertips. The lady moves closer to Blok in exasperation.

One after another the poets begin reciting poems about Eternal Femininity and about the Apocalypse. Blok is smoking, saying nothing. Then he stands up, bows, and hails a coachman. He does not say a word to the dancer, but she follows him and springs into the open carriage. The officer rushes after them, but to no avail—the coach has already vanished without a trace. One of the well-wishers in the company gives him the name of the hotel where Blok usually takes infatuated young ladies.

Toward the end of this endless night, the officer shoots himself in the park just across the street from the small hotel. The beautiful lady comes out early so as not to be late for work: she is an operator at the Central Telephone Station. She sees the young man dead and falls to her knees before him as though in church. Blok is looking out the window at this scene. It seems to him that he is in his last agonies himself after the death of this man whom he has noticed for the first time.

Dante is delirious. He does not see that he is not alone in the isolated woodsman's hut. A woman dressed in black is trying to ease his sufferings. She changes the damp cloth on his head and tries to get him to drink milk. But he goes away again into the terrible forest of the First Canto. He peers at the alarming tangle of branches, twigs, and twisted trunks as if attempting to distinguish what is out there peering though the gloom. From that direction, finally, appears yet another vision of Dante's wandering spirit.

New York, the twenty-fifth century. The city has not changed particularly since "our era." The same skyscrapers around Central Park, though some of them bear unfamiliar, even strange slogans on their facades. Tanks and armored vehicles roll slowly down Fifth Avenue and Fifty-seventh Street. From time to time one or another rises noiselessly, as if to look into the windows on the top floor. Hundreds of fliers in individual flying craft soar over the vast crowds gathered in the park and on its adjoining streets. The city is in rebellion against the rest of America. It is under siege. The decisive battle is approaching. The ultimatum of the All-American Army is spread across the whole sky by means of the new technology.

On one of the platforms in Central Park we see yet another embodiment of Dante—a popular singer-songwriter who invites comparisons with the singers of our time, including John Lennon, all the more since the platform is located next to the Dakota apartment building of sad memory.

People around the platform are passionately debating the surrender terms.

There are a fair number present who are in favor of laying down arms. Listen, guys, they promise they won't punish us. In the final analysis, we're historically part of the same country. Our languages have many common roots. The majority, however, refute the arguments of the "defeatists." We can't trust these proper types, they'll carry out mass executions, and they'll drive the ones left into concentration camps in Nebraska. New York must remain free! We still have a chance! If Washington will join us, we'll establish an aristocracy from one end of the continent to the other.

Our singer, the idol of the city, has the power to stir huge crowds with his rough, wheezing voice. Today's "gig" has been feverishly awaited by millions of the city's defenders on the streets, rooftops, and bastions. The ranks of the All-American Army are waiting for it as well. The high command is worried lest their soldiers fall under the influence of Alti Tude—that is the singer's name.

The rebel leaders try to dissuade the singer from appearing at an open venue. There are All-American commando teams operating in the city. We can't rule out the possibility of an assassination attempt. Alti Tude dismisses the warnings. What're they gonna sing out there in the States if they annihilate me?

Near the stage stands a group of young people. They look like the usual rock music fanatics, but in fact they are saboteurs. Among their number is a woman who looks like Beatrice, only with her head shaved. She cannot take her eyes off Alti Tude, and he cannot take his eyes off her. A passing cherub strikes their hearts with an arrow of love.

He begins the concert. The first song is the anthem, hoarse and terrible, of New York in rebellion. Then he extends a hand to the girl and helps her jump up onto the stage. He embraces her and begins to sing a delightful new song, the origins of which are a mystery, entitled "God, She's from Kentucky." This time he sounds like every tenor in the world. And she, a trained terrorist, suddenly begins to harmonize with him in the voice of an absolute angel.

The crowd is staggered by the beauty of the duet and gripped by the feeling that trouble is close at hand. The fighters, pretending to clap their hands over their heads, raise their tiny annihilators. At the last moment, the girl covers Alti Tude with her body and melts in his arms.

Dante, shaking off this vision, continues to wander in the gloomy wood. Ghosts from a nightmare, a panther, a lion, and a she-wolf circle around him. He rushes about in horror and then notices the lone figure of Virgil, his favorite ancient author. Virgil has been sent by Beatrice to help Dante pass through this circle of Hell, through Purgatory, and to stand before her in Paradise.

Dante, his face afire with happiness and love, follows his guide with absolute confidence. They slowly descend the slope of a hill, until the steep path leads them to a dismal gorge, in which might be the Gates of Hell themselves. Having slowed his pace and glanced at Dante, who, unlike the dead still casts a shadow, Virgil, in his majestic severity, continues the descent. Dante follows him in hope and expectation. They disappear.

Meanwhile, Dante's body writhes in the agonies of the plague. The aging Beatrice, dressed in black, sits beside his bed. She is weeping: the object of her dreams is dying, the proud poet who made of her a cult of Divine Femininity, is dying. How could this be Beatrice, whose funeral we saw? But who except Beatrice could so passionately express Dante's love? Once, in order to flee from his adoration, she had married Simone de' Bardi, an ordinary man. Alas, the respectable citizen was little given to expressiveness in the conjugal bed, while her passion for Dante grew keener from day to day. In the end she realized that there was only one way out of this unending sin: death. As a devout Catholic she could not commit suicide; therefore she decided to stage her own funeral and afterward to vanish and to dissipate her flesh in complete isolation, in a distant locale, in the forests of Urbino. Her husband as her "true friend" is made aware of all her sufferings but soon after the sham funeral disappears without a trace himself. For many years Beatrice has lived alone and incognito on the very same mountainside where she has recently found Dante near death in an abandoned hut.

As she, and we along with her, remember these sad doings, she suddenly notices that her beloved is no longer dying but merely sleeping. The crisis has passed, his breathing has become even, the color has returned to his cheeks, he is smiling in his sleep and sometimes mumbling lines of poetry. She understands that he can awaken at any moment and see her, but she is horrified at the thought that he will not know her, since her beauty has faded with the years. At the same time, the possibility of being recognized seems unthinkable to her, since it could dispel the mystery and deprive her of the "sweet sorrow" from which she is inseparable. A minute before he regains consciousness, she leaves the hut.

He wakes up and looks around, not recognizing the dismal shelter in which he was nearly overcome by a terrible disease. The small hut has been transformed into a cozy little cottage: a fire is crackling in the hearth, a large, downy carpet is spread on the floor and generously decked with wine, bread, cheese, and vegetables. Swaying from weakness, he reaches the table, drains a glass of wine in one gulp, and sees the inkwell, goose quill, and pack of good Bolognese paper so clearly prepared for him. Forgetting about food, he begins to write down in cantos what remains in his human consciousness of his meetings with Virgil and Beatrice beyond the boundaries of the Earth.

Another fifteen years go by. The exiled poet continues his wanderings through the cities of northern Italy. He lives now in Verona, now in Pisa, now in Ravenna. True lovers and connoisseurs of literary creation consider him the greatest figure among living writers, perhaps the greatest who has ever lived. His native, beloved and despised Florence in the end grants him an amnesty, but he finds the conditions humiliating and refuses it. In reply to such "haughtiness," Florence sentences one of its former seven priors to be burned at the stake.

One day in Siena, Dante, a tall, upright, middle-aged man in a long, dark purple cape, goes into a rarity shop. The proprietor, who is known to him as Don Simone, usually offers him books that he has obtained from Milan, Venice, or Lyons. That day he finds Don Simone in a state of great excitement. When he asks what has happened, the proprietor divulges an unimaginable secret. He is none other than Beatrice's lawful wedded husband, Simone de' Bardi. This morning he received word from her. She is coming and could be here any minute. No, Signore Dante, not from heaven, from Urbino. He tells Dante the story of the sham funeral and of Beatrice's self-denial. He has not seen her since and is trembling as though she really was going to come down from heaven. He proposes to Dante that he, Dante, meet Beatrice here, in the shop, and that he himself would probably do better to disappear.

Don Simone, of course, does not know that Beatrice is going to entreat him to arrange a meeting with the poet. Her health is worsening. She is certain this will be the last time they see each other in the land of the living. She is wandering along the narrow streets in the direction of the merchants' quarter. Her heart is pounding, her soul is filled with unthinkable consternation. She feels as though the most important event of her life is about to occur without any agreed-upon conditions.

Seized by the same feeling of alarm, Dante rushes from the shop. Trying to get away as quickly as possible, he stops dead in his tracks on a little stone bridge over a canal lying underneath as peacefully as a marble slab. The lone figure of a woman is approaching the bridge from a side street. Old verses from *La Vita Nuova* ring out in his memory. He sees the young, luminous Beatrice coming up the bridge.

And before her is revealed a miracle of equal magnitude: the monumental figure of a patrician is transformed into a youth, trembling from overpowering love and mortification. At the time, thirty-eight years earlier, they did not dare to reach their hands out to each other. Now two people advanced in age gasp for breath in their first and last kiss.

A gigantic radiance rises over Siena. The inhabitants of the city are astounded at the glow in the sky. All the weather vanes begin to spin, windows are flung open, flags flap in the wind, and a strange formation of shiplike clouds cuts across the sky.

The faithful Don Simone comes running up, out of breath. He is ready to do anything to help his lawful wedded wife, Beatrice, and her beloved, the great Dante, but they are no longer among the living.

That, in its broad outlines, was the plot of the script that was finally approved for production. In that form we can still do something with it, the professional grumpily agreed. Anyway, it's better than your early versions, Alex—admit it. It was the lovers of fencing who put up the most resistance. One of them, the rising young star of the production group, a certain Clipperton, had worn down Alex with nighttime phone calls. "Listen, Alex, in 1301, Karl Valois arrived with his whole army at the walls of Florence and fomented a first-class revolution in the city. And your pet Alighieri was up to his neck in that brawl, wasn't he? Listen, how can we let a chance like that slip away? Can you imagine how a five-minute battle scene will tighten up the entire project? Well, there'll be blood, of course, there's no war without blood—come on, Alex, don't play the fool!"

On another occasion Clipperton was telling him that he hadn't been able to sleep for the last three nights—he kept on thinking about the final sequence. "What the hell do you mean, Clip, you can't sleep, when everything's already been thought through, and a long time ago?" "No, Alex, listen, in the last scene, everything ought to shift to passionate sex. It'll be a triumph of humanism, Alex, do you get me? Yes, yes, an old couple, right there, on the bridge, in the presence of the city dwellers! It'll be a triumph over all prejudices, the dawn of the Renaissance—are you taking this in? The end of the Dark Ages, along the lines of the end of the Soviet Union—you ought to get into this, Alex!" A.Z. politely thanked this connoisseur and enthusiast. That's "awesome," Clip, really "awesome"! Where did you study history, Clip? Ah, that's what I thought—Harvard!

One way or another, everything was coming to a close. He couldn't believe that two months after the expedition to St. Pete (as the Americans had quickly renamed the former Leningrad for themselves) he would part company with those two mangy business types Quentin and Goldie and be left alone with only their images on film.

Everything was running smoothly that day, with, of course, the great Rita O'Neill setting the tone. Without any doubt, she had prepared herself wonderfully for the filming, and she looked perhaps even too fresh to be the fifty-one-year-old Beatrice. All of a sudden, though, everything almost degenerated into a squabble. Goldie Belle D'Argent, who had appeared on the bridge with her aura of eternal beauty, did not find there the object of her passion, Quentin Landry, who was supposed to have exchanged his "grandeur" makeup job for his real age by then. "Am I going to have to wait much longer for this idiot?" she asked so loudly that everyone on the set heard her. "Look at that slut!" Quentin yelled. "She's taking away my right to take a leak between makeup sessions! The small-town airhead, she doesn't understand anything in our Lavsky's system! She's a cretin of a woman, guys, and nothing else!"

Fortunately, a quick-witted soundman named Guillaume turned on the musical backing as if by accident and drowned out Landry's words in a roar of brass. As far as the first sentence was concerned, we should say forthrightly that Goldie never took offense at the word *slut*. In short, everything was set to continue when Dick Putney came into the studio.

At first Alex took no notice of the bosses. He had only just said the fateful word "Action!"—the camera went to work and began to roll slowly along its track toward the bridge—when someone behind him gently but firmly seized the director's microphone and gave a contrary command: "Cut it!" Turning around, Alex saw a group of the highest-ranking people in the company: Dick Putney, Ridgeway, Ed, Pete, Ed Putney-Krieger, Edna Krieger-Nakatone. "What do you mean, 'cut'?" he asked and gave a cough.

"Everything, 'cut!' " Edna said in the best Japanese style—that is, not allowing any chance for a last-minute reprieve. In saying this, she handed him a copy of that morning's *New York Times*—i.e., the very paper that he had kicked from the porch onto the lawn in the morning as he hurried to his car. The first page displayed staggering headlines: END OF AN ERA, FALL OF THE KORBACH THRONE, AK & BB IN WHIRLWIND OF REVOLUTION. Right alongside were the photographs, larger ones and smaller ones: Stanley Korbach in his heyday; Stanley in his period of decline, with the details of that decline emphasized by wrinkles and a crop covered with age spots; Norman Blamsdale, the implacable leader of the coup; Stanley's three daughters, who had taken up arms against their father (the fact that they came from different mothers didn't stop the journalists from making allusions to Shakespearean drama); Mel O'Massey, a new name rising like a rocket; Art Duppertat, whose departure from Stanley's camp had played a decisive role in the "coup of the century"; and, of course, Marjorie Korbach, whose doll-like face not only displayed the latest achievements of cosmetic surgery but also looked like the mask of a latter-day financial Lady Macbeth.

In addition to the front-page headlines, the entire business section was full of analyses, calculations, and predictions of what would happen to the money markets in light of Stanley's removal from the president's chair. Also discussed were questions about the certain crash of the Korbach Fund, a humanitarian organization the likes of which history had never seen, and the future of Stanley's personal assets, already seized by the appropriate federal agency.

Alex tossed the newspaper away, took out his mobile phone, and dialed a number known to only a handful of people in the entire world. "Shalom!" he heard a sepulchral voice say—one that would have scared any of you had it not been that of your agent.

"Hi there, Enoch! It's Alex! Where are you guys at the moment?"

Enoch Agasf snorted. "It looks like an island. Either one of the Greek ones or it's in the Caribbean. Stanley just went down to the beach. Ernie and George are waiting for him—they're going fishing."

Alex didn't even ask who Ernie and George were. For all he knew, they might have been Hemingway and Byron. "Has he seen today's papers?"

"Of course he has. He flipped through a cubic yard of them, then said, 'We've lost,' and went down to the sea—Ernie, George, and Charles are waiting to go fishing with him."

"And who's this Charles?" Alex asked.

"Charlemagne," the Eternal Jew said for greater precision, and went on. "And why wouldn't they? The guys still get pleasure out of it."

A.Z. knew that if he didn't stop Agasf, he would dwell endlessly on his favorite subject: the infinite boredom of all the world with its banal sunlight and the silly trembling of its shadows, how one can get fed up with it, if even working as a film agent has already worn thin, and you desire only one thing, and you know what that is, sir. He thanked Agasf and put the phone down.

"Let's have a talk, Alex," Dick Putney said to him in his best voice of steel. He was visibly saddened and upset, however. All six—sorry, make that seven—of them sat down in big chairs and formed a circle alongside pieces of set decoration that now seemed loathsome to A.Z. Fucking vanity, he said to himself, fu-u-cking vanity, trying to conceal an uncontrollable yawn.

"At your service, gentlemen," he said, and supposed that the form of address was not entirely the correct one. Then he made a small bow in the appropriate direction. "And ladies, of course. Excuse the plural, but it's just a figure of speech." Everyone looked at everyone else with glances of the sort that people exchange in the presence of an incurable alcoholic. "Obviously, you've already realized that we have to shut down the production of 'Radiance,' " Dick said. His teeth seemed to be chattering slightly. "You have to know that it was a difficult decision for me, Alex. Stop yawning, sir! You know that it's been a tradition in our company to treat our directors like family. You know how much we like you, how much you were loved by our honorary president, my father, Abraham Putney, don't you?"

"What happened to him?" asked Alex, who, having stopped yawning, shifted suddenly in his seat. "I hope he's all right? Is he alive?"

"Let me finish!" Dick barked with inexplicable fury. "I hope you understand how sad we all are about having to close down your enchanting project in view of the lousy circumstances that have arisen. It isn't a matter of financial gains or losses. Certainly, Putney could afford to set aside a budget that could help you finish your work even without Stanley's investment. What's important here, however, is the principle of worldwide solidarity. Look around you, my dear man, and in every financial community in the world you'll see a fever of activity unprecedented since the great stock-market crash of 1929.

"Even people like you, Alex—modern Byronites and friends of Russian literature—have to understand that the business brotherhood was outraged by the wild squandering of money in places like Russia and Bangladesh! There's no such thing in the modern world as private capital! Money doesn't belong to anyone—on the contrary, we belong to money! Money needs to work, and to make money—I'll be damned all to hell if that isn't so!

"I tried to convince my dear Abe, my father and my friend, that we had to shut down 'Radiance' as a result of the protest against the way Stanley was handling money, just to distance ourselves from a bankrupt anarchist, but Abe stubbornly insisted on his own way. 'Hands off Sashka!' That was what he liked to call you, Alex." Dick Putney sniffed. "Now it'll be easier for you to understand why I was forced to kill him."

At that moment, Alex noticed the tiny emerald head of the lizard darting out from behind the cuff of Dick's sleeve. That, of course, was Popsy, whose acquaintance we had the honor of making quite recently.

"Hey, Popsy," he said, and chirped at him like a bird, or like a lizard, or whatever else chirps in this fucking world.

"You mean you killed Abrashka?" he asked.

Dick nodded, holding back a sob.

"Figuratively?" Alex asked.

"Literally." Dick sniffled.

"Really?" asked Alex in his "man of the world" tone.

Madame Krieger-Nakatone squinted so hard that her eyes turned into two horizontal wrinkles. "Dick had to take Abe's life with a Japanese bamboo pistol from the seventeenth century. We were all impressed by his courage, and also by the message that he sent by this action to the entire business world. All of the board of directors hopes that you, too, Alex, appreciate this sacrifice."

All the Putneys, Putney-Kriegers, and Ridgeways sighed. "Oh, yes—it's a drama of biblical proportions, you see!"

At that moment, Popsy slipped out of Dick's internal sphere and into Alex's, that is, up his sleeve and even deeper, beneath his T-shirt. Surprisingly, Alex did not even give a shudder. He sat there without moving, wet and limp, as the reptile raced with lightning speed along his skin. It crossed his chest several times, administered a small sting to his left nipple, then to the right one, made a few circles beneath one of his armpits, and only after that dove down across his stomach toward his genitals. The elastic of his underpants proved no barrier to it.

Alexander Zakharovich fell of his own free will into the "chasm of humiliation," as a poet once called it. The Putney family, meanwhile, ordered coffee. When their order came, he unzipped his trousers and pulled Popsy out by the tail. The company mascot was insulted in its best intentions. Chirping indignantly, it left its tail in A.Z.'s fingers and darted back into the irreproachable sleeve of the new president. Only then did A.Z. get up and walk away. Popsy's tail went on dancing on his palm for some time.

3

STANLEY

I'm surprised that Darwin's theory of evolution and the idea of Creation are considered irreconcilable concepts, even ones that cancel each other out. I daresay, Theophilus, that this irreconcilability is based on a ridiculously simple misunderstanding. Allow me to engage you in a Bakhtinian "dialogue from the threshold"; some people think that I used to do fairly well in that genre after a quart of Scotch. I'll consider all the pauses between my sentences your wise contributions to the discussion, Theophilus. Or just your smile, Theophilus—thanks.

It seems to me that the chief disagreement between the two camps lies in the disproportion between their reckonings of time. In the Old Testament, time is measured in thousand-year periods—it's now six thousand years and a bit since the creation of the world by the Jewish calendar—while the theory of evolution operates over millions and hundreds of millions of years. There's one thing that this theory doesn't take into account for some reason: the biblical years are allegorical—that is, poetic in nature—while the evolutionary years are linked strictly to physics, to calculations of the earth's revolutions around the sun. Having accepted this, we can suppose that biblical "thousands" are immeasurably greater than physical millions.

In saying "greater," I'm resorting to the simplest of simplifications. The concept of "years," biblical and physical, was given to us, the living, so that we might somehow adapt ourselves to that periphery of the incomprehensible in which we have to exist.

The Creation that we try to understand (sorry for the parentheses, Theophilus, but in saying "we," I'm generally referring to myself and my fourth cousin Sasha Korbach) occurred in a "space" (how can we avoid quotations and parentheses in this case?) where there was neither time nor air. The Original Concept was entirely different, and entirely beyond comprehension of us, children of air and of time. This conception was left to us only in the form of a timorous memory to which we attach the word *heaven.*

We can't picture the Original Concept, but we can imagine that somewhere in the outer reaches there occurred a certain act of rejection, perhaps the result of what we call the struggle between Good and Evil. The moment of Temptation— any allegory will do here: a serpent, an apple, nakedness (maybe Adam and Eve, in their substance of something other than air, didn't need clothes)—happened, Original Sin and Banishment—that is from the Original Concept—followed. Creation "from the dirt" or "from the dust" occurred—that is, from the primordial mixture of the elements with oxygen and carbon.

We could say that Temptation and Banishment occurred at one and the same time, had time existed then, but it didn't. Time *is* Banishment, exile, it created this world of ours, the sphere of mortals. Time/Banishment created biology, or maybe vice versa—most likely, they created each other, and thus we can consider DNA to be the formula of banishment from Paradise. Naturally, a world of creatures couldn't exist, and for that matter couldn't have been created, without the substance of the air and its derivatives, water and earth. Air, earth, and water formed the elements of every living, and consequently mortal, thing. Time, then, came immediately after that. The countdown from Banishment began.

I hope you'll excuse us, Theophilus, but Alex and I arrived at these reflections after endless telephone conversations at the expense of the Korbach Fund, which, to translate a Russian expression word for word, "commanded us to live long"— that is, departed this world. So then, there is Creation, and there is this digression from the Original Concept somewhere out on the periphery. And here, in the course of this digression, millions, billions of years may have passed from the primordial amoeba to the human being, but that in no way disproves the existence of the Almighty, inasmuch as in the context of the Original Concept longevity doesn't mean a thing. "A long time" doesn't exist there, and neither does "a short time"—for that matter, the verb *to be* isn't even in use; they use some other verb, unknown to us and unknowable by us. In the attempt to make this more understandable, we say that even a billion years couldn't cover one inch on the path of the exiled Adam, but even this attempt sounds like nonsense, since in the Original Concept there are neither billions nor inches. So it's not important, then, the question Did man come from the apes or not? and how long the process took, since it happened within the framework of Banishment, and is still going on. Right now it's carrying on in the form of human history and everything connected with it, and will continue until the end of history, which, obviously, will be the end of Banishment.

All these *Australopithecus anamencis, Australopithecus ramidus,* and other "hominids" of the Upper Pleistocene and Lower Pleistocene, which lived 5.5 million years ago, and even *Oriopithecus,* which lived 25 million years ago, can't disprove so much as an inch of Adam's path out of Paradise and, consequently, of his path back to Paradise.

The evolution of species existed, exists, and will continue to exist as a digression on the periphery from the Original Concept and, clearly, will cease to exist only when Banishment comes to an end and all forms return to the world beyond comprehension, where there is neither time nor air—in other words, when biological life completes its cycle.

As far as modern man is concerned, as soon as we had assumed vertical posture, we glimpsed the starry sky and were gripped by some vague memory of the Original Concept. This memory, that is to say, what we call the Holy Spirit, led us to activities rather strange for a purely biological organism—namely, to religion, to a sense of beauty, to creative imagination and an inclination toward a slightly comic walk.

Schopenhauer said that the feeling of compassion for those who share the road of one's life is the only quality that distinguishes man from other participants in the biological cycle. It would be good to add to that the gift of humor, which, wonderfully, lives in us alongside the awareness of unavoidable death. These qualities, which perhaps in some strange way coincide with a peculiar hunger for immortality, might from time to time help man to overcome the blind "will to live," as Schopenhauer would have it. In other words, "vague memories" help one to overcome the feeling of meaninglessness. God has not abandoned us, in view of our return toward the Original Concept. The evolution of forms is simply a *temporary* digression from Creation beyond understanding—isn't that right, Theophilus? The Holy Spirit doesn't leave us, and so that man will not feel himself to be the sacrificial lamb of the universe, the Lord sends us His Son in the flesh, showing that He shares our sufferings of birth, life, and death. Along with Christ there will appear other messengers of the Holy Spirit, avatars, like Mohammed and the Buddha, whose traveling companion, a lion that doesn't prey on other animals, might also be a glimpse of the Original Concept.

Sometimes poets are chosen for an attempt to transmit the Incomprehensible. My fourth cousin and I have talked at length about Dante. Alex is sure that he, Dante, visited those spheres that are beyond understanding. Perhaps under the influence of some substance, but more likely as the result of an illness, he crossed the boundary between Banishment and the Original Concept. After returning from this "journey," he tried to set down his astounding impressions in poetry, but words were not enough, no matter how much force his talent lent them.

This painful insufficiency of expressive force, those material walls in which he was imprisoned—these were perhaps the things that made him call his opus a "comedy." Nevertheless, he leads us through the sufferings of writhing flesh into the severe, purifying sphere of the heavens and even further in that direction, where among the blinding fluctuations of light, that is, joy, he meets his own image of Beatrice and is able to touch the sense of the Primordial Love.

Listen, Theophilus, Alex once sent me via Federal Express a Penguin edition of Dostoevsky's short stories. I was in Cairo at the time, and not long after that he called me from Helsinki. Stan, he said, read the story "The Dream of a Ridiculous Man." It's usually considered an example of utopian satire, but it seems to me that even the great literary scholar Bakhtin got it wrong with that definition. Fortunately, Alex and I were in the same time zone, so we could call without being afraid of waking each other up. We talked about this strange story several nights in a row.

What's it about, in brief? A certain man in St. Petersburg has decided to commit suicide. He lays his pistol down in front of him and falls asleep. He dreams that he's killed himself. He sees himself in his grave. After he says a few passionate words to God, the grave opens and a dark figure takes him flying through the galaxies to a distant star.

The star resembles Earth, but an aura of some sort of lofty triumph prevails there. Ideal beings, filled with genuine love for everything around them, live on this celestial body. He recalls that there were men and women there, that they loved each other, but that he never noticed any outbursts of cruel sensuality, which is almost the only source of our sins. The place had not been tarnished by the Fall; these creatures had not yet gone the way of Original Sin. A great many things there were beyond his understanding, and beyond the boundaries of the "rational" scientific approach. Obviously, then, before him stood the Original Concept; that's how it seemed to us, O Theophilus!

After that comes the story of how he corrupts these ideal people with his earthly vices, but that part actually is something along the lines of a moralistic satire. That's not the point. When the hero wakes up, he realizes that there are no words with which he can express just what happened to him in his dream. All the same, he feels a persistent desire to at least try to put it into words, because maybe it wasn't a dream but something staggeringly real.

Dostoevsky, as everyone knows, was an epileptic. The illness tormented him from childhood to the end of his life. There were periods when he would be exhausted by blackouts and furious convulsions, yet he confessed that he looked forward to the next attack, because it was in these attacks that there often came a fleeting moment when it seemed to him that he could understand everything within and around himself with uncanny sharpness, and that he could grasp the "causality" of what was happening. After the attack, however, he wouldn't remember anything—nothing remained but a dark hole. It's not impossible that one of these "moments of causality" left a greater impression in his mind than the others, and that then he, like Dante, tried to put his vision into words—that "nonlife" that was immeasurably higher than biological existence. Either way, he succeeded in saying that during that fleeting moment he had sensed some reality beyond understanding, without time, and without the air in which everything decays, and cannot *not* decay. That's the conclusion that Alex and I came to, and we also decided that the images of corruption were nothing other than signs of the awakening of the "Ridiculous Man"—his return to earthly consciousness.

We beg your pardon, but we forgot to say at the beginning of this chapter that Stanley Korbach was carrying on his "dialogue from the threshold" while sitting in an International House of Pancakes at the corner of Bonaventura Boulevard and 1056th Street in densely populated San Teofilo Valley, in the state of Ochichornia. At this point, he had already dispatched his thirty-third stack of oat pancakes, accompanied by a small jug of maple syrup. Tasty, he thought, in a rather playful departure from his philosophical exercises. Damned appetizing! Just think, if I hadn't been dethroned as president, I would never have tried such terrific eats, never mind the unique international atmosphere of this pancake heaven! Very cozy. A little place where the gemütlichkeit goes all through you. Cozy and warm. The whole state of Ochichornia was caught up in some freezing high-pressure system, and outside the glass walls of the IHOP clouds looking like gaunt beasts of prey were rushing across the sky, while here it was warm, as though we really were in "Sunny Ochichornia." The people on the other side of these walls weren't losing heart either, though. Crowds were trooping down Bonaventura in shorts and T-shirts, stubbornly supposing that this was the very same place that they paid for at the travel agencies. Everything was running with the mood of a resort: convertibles with the tops down and buses air-conditioned to an arctic cold rolled by, a feeling of unconcern prevailed in the crowd, people were moving along with any business or direction, and dogs, too—in particular this pair, a German shepherd and a golden retriever.

Stanley noticed that these "man's best friends" were out for a walk without a friend—that is, by themselves—joined only by a leash. It looked as though they were walking themselves, then, or, more accurately, as though one of them, the powerful, broad-chested German shepherd with a rather sardonic smile at the corners of his triumphant maw, was walking the exalted and impetuous blonde, whose tail was wagging nonstop over them in a show of joie de vivre and boundless friendship. For example, if this "blonde" saw some interesting character across the street, particularly one of the female gender, regardless of her breed or size, and immediately got ready to dart across the way to her, the "brunette" dug his paws into the asphalt with all his force, thereby nipping the romantic impulse right in the bud.

Stanley Korbach continued to watch the intersection full of cars, people, dogs, signboards, flags, palm trees, and clouds for some time, until he suddenly caught his breath from a feeling of love that was permeating his entire being. Listen, Theophilus, I understand the futility of this world, and all the same I can't help but be delighted by its diversity. From time to time, my fourth cousin Alex, as though he's testing himself, reminds me of Schopenhauer's stifling concept of the eternal return. To be honest, I can't be convinced of it. I long after the Original Concept, and I hope that someday the door to the Incomprehensible will open for all mortals, but unfortunately, I'm a sinner, still so drawn in spite of my age to this peripheral, truncated, pathetic, dissolute, and sensual world of "digression," with all of its history and its thick, bubbling concoction, that I'm observing right now from this International House of Pancakes, that I can't imagine myself outside this world.

Alex usually smiles when I talk to him about this. Listen, Stan, he jokes, it sounds like you're afraid that you'll be bored in the world of the Incomprehensible. It's naive, of course, but I still think that the Creator needs every moment of our pathetic existence, even these forty minutes that I'm spending here polishing off stacks of pancakes, first with caviar, as the Russians do, then with eggplant, like the Mexicans, and then finally with maple syrup, the homegrown way.

He asked for the check and thrust his hand beneath the table into his money bag. He had come into possession of this bag one fine night during the time his assets were frozen, when they had begun peppering him with subpoenas. The butler Enoch Agasf had summoned him under cover of darkness to the park at Halifax Farm, to the gazebo under which they had once hidden bottles of booze. Stick your hand in there a little farther, my son, he invited him. Feel something soft? Now squeeze your fingers together and pull! A rather heavy bag of rather moss-grown leather came out. There are several million in there, exactly how many I don't know, said the Eternal Jew. When it runs out, let me know, we'll get some more from somewhere else. Stanley's greatest fear was that he would not pull a hundred-dollar bill from the bag but a thousand, or even a ten thousand. Something of the sort had happened not long before in a drugstore, and he had been deeply embarrassed by the panic that had reigned in the establishment as a consequence of such a simple mistake.

Fortunately, no one recognized him in the USA anymore. It's surprising how careless our people are about even their favorite celebrities. Not long ago, every tabloid of the sort whose ink comes off on the reader's fingers was printing his picture on its front page under huge headlines: THE UNEXPECTED FALL OF STANLEY KORBACH'S EMPIRE, BIG STAN'S FINAL DISAPPEARANCE, and so on. He'd had only to grow a white beard and cover his famous "pelican's craw" for everyone to stop recognizing him.

He walked out of the pancake temple, joined the crowd, and moved slowly along Bonaventura Boulevard in a northerly direction. He didn't know what to do. As a matter of fact, he hadn't known what to do with himself since the "fall of the empire," apart from think about the mysteries of life. All things considered, it's not such a bad thing to think about the mysteries of life, particularly when you're close to the end of your seventh decade and have nothing else to do.

Scantily dressed people, often shivering with cold but still preferring to enjoy Sunny Ochichornia as though it were summer, were giving him strange looks, though no one recognized him as "Big Stan." It was just that he was "something"—a gigantic prophet with a bushy white beard, and, most surprising of all, wearing a warm tweed coat.

On the corner of 1059th Street a strange vehicle, half limo, half delivery van, caught his eye. It was parked in the spacious lot next to the Safeway. Two dogs were sitting on the roof, a German shepherd and a golden retriever that looked like the very same ones that had been walking along the boulevard by themselves just a short time before. An odd-looking type got out of the van and stretched, as though still asleep. His appearance merited description. He was tall, but not as tall as Stanley. Then again, his beard was much longer. As far as his mane of hair was concerned, it was now flapping over his head in the cold wind like the plumage of some unknown species of bird. He wasn't as gray as Stanley, and didn't look so much like a prophet as like a dervish in his Middle Eastern burnoose. On his chest hung a massive Orthodox cross, a weighty Star of David, as well as various pagan amulets, including bird claws. So as not to forget: he had a large, bony nose, and his navel, though unseen beneath the burnoose, was similar to a chess rook in its dimensions and hardness.

He noticed Stanley and motioned him over. Stanley approached him and they shook hands.

"Ty tozhe ptitsa?" the stranger asked in Russian.

"I don't think so," Stanley replied, but, noticing the slight disappointment that rippled through the other's generous coiffure, added: "In any case, not yet."

"I'm a bird," the man said with an avian smile.

"As in 'free as a bird'?" Stanley asked.

"Free as a bird, strong as a bird, clever as a bird . . . so, I'm a bird!" He laughed, and held his hand out. "I'm Tikh."

"Stan," said the magnate by way of an introduction and winked at the two dogs, who were following the scene from the roof of the vehicle.

"Those are my friends, Smartie and Dummy," said Tikh, or, as you have of course already guessed, Tikhomir Burevyatnikov.

Stanley produced a flask of whiskey from one of his bottomless pockets. "Want a snort?" Tikh sampled the drink like an expert taster. "I like Glenmorangie more than any of the others. You know, Stan, I used to be a rich man." "Me too." Stanley nodded, and asked: "Where are you guys headed, you two dogs and a bird?"

"For Swistville," Tikh said. "A buddy of ours is in a concentration camp there. Want to come with us, Stanley?"

"You bet!"

And they set off.

4

DE LUXE

*I*t's time to remember my first and only lawful wedded husband, Mister Luxe—thanks for the name, you son of a bitch; can you imagine me with my maiden name of Fief? He gave that million-dollar name, the dirty old man, even though he fiddled the papers. I was fourteen when he wanted to marry me, but I looked twenty-five, and he forged an ID for me. I loved that asshole all the same, though.

Well, it's because he would have breakfast in bed and munch on his eggs in the middle of our deluxe pillows, and then moan like he was going to barf them up as soon as he swallowed. His first wife, Babelka, would drop by on her way back from the synagogue. She was religious because there wasn't a single man who wanted to look at her more than once, and even so that fucker Luxe would try out his jokes while she was around. Hey, Babelka, this kid's got no sexual technique—show her that "yellow thumbs" trick of yours that you like. Her dog, Extrakvin, would sniff "my furs"—that's what Luxe called that winter coat that he picked up for me at some flea market. We were living in Boston then, where people have icicles up the ass. Those French furs were called *les sobakis*. It wasn't until later that I figured out they were just dogs, the same breed as Babelka's Extrakvin.

Even so, that kid Fief was really proud of her husband; she tried to turn him on in bed so that he'd tell her all his dirty secrets, the way old men do. He was forty-five, and he seemed like Noah to me. When he got turned on, he'd get all hysterical and start kissing my cunt; he'd pretend he was getting his second wind, and then he'd start snoring right on me—so *voilà*!

Just picture this, friends, folks of my generation—one day I found a long gray hair in his underwear. A week before that, some old hag named Signorina Giulietta who was supposed to be his aunt came to see him. She loved oysters. So eat your snot, watch your *I Love Lucy* and Johnny Carson on the box, but suddenly one night I wake up and someone's screaming. *Voilà*, my ex-husband is doing it doggie style with his "auntie," who's even older than he is! The next scene was enough to make you piss all over yourself. I stood in front of them like a young fury from the rebellious generation. You love to jerk off your libido on grannies, Luxe—all right, I'm going to go out on the street now and give it up to the first guy who comes along! Enough about him.

I know how guys feel when they look at me. They want to see me as the biggest whore on the planet. There was this rich doctor—a gynecologist, naturally—who taught me this long, warm kiss that goes right down to your womb. The joy of my long body and of my shy young girl's heart came close to paralyzing me. And I shouted out what he wanted to hear: Yes, I'm a slut, I'm a big, horsey slut!

I confessed everything to the Lord, whimpering and pleading: Merciful One, Blue-Eyed One, forgive me these dolphinlike convulsions!

It was interesting to be in really posh places like the Century Plaza and the Waldorf. Studs in white blazers open up one bottle of champagne after another. What're you so worried about, I can serve you all in a row; all of a sudden the ceiling falls in with a noise that sounds like the end of the world. What happened up there? Oh, just some prick that fell from space and went right through all the floors.

He says: You've got no soul, only gray matter. It's just the other way around, I said to him—just the other way around. I wonder where he found any gray matter in me. And who was it who said that? There was something special about him. Stanley Korbach, who had more of some quality all his own than anyone ever, Mr. Massive Moneybags, MMM. Then again, they're all unique in their own way. Actually, there was one who was even more unique than Stanley. Ten years before Stanley, I worked for an outfit called the Pink Flamingo—it was an escort service for suckers coming to Ochichornia. That guy was skinny, a bit taller than my Piu, a sort of medium-height gorilla; he was waiting for me with no pants on, but with a big red thing that I was supposed to "escort" into my hole. Let me tell you, it was like a fat crowbar, and when he started to drive it into me, he had a sort of evil smile on his face; I kept seeing it in the mirror. What made him be such a bastard to me, and what was I taking it for? And what else are we supposed to do with a big hole in our middles? I'll never allow myself to be their hole again, I thought. It's going to be me that thrashes them. I'll take control of their things, that's all there is to it. Sometimes they've got so much come in them that you feel like you're getting all their secrets out of them. Well, whip it out and come on me. One of them squirted all over my body and the sheets, too. And one, with the most exotic piece I ever saw—it looked like some sort of Malay with a tuft of hair—kept making me swallow. Creeps like that always want to dominate you. Stanley was different—when I told him I thought he had gotten me pregnant, he was so happy that he danced with me all night, as if I were some star in an old movie. I told him that there was going to be a little boy, and he said, "In that case, I'll marry you, you'll be Mrs. Korbach." Well, what do you want from them? They're not satisfied until they've thrashed it into you so hard that you swell up like an elephant, or like I don't know what.

Jesus jake, the kid turned out to be colored—a huge black boy, Clemens, at your service! S.K., of course, was out of the country, in his dirty Russia, where else? When he came back a month later, the first thing he did was screw me under the staircase. Then we had a big argument about politics—that "Russia, Russia" business again—and then he gave me a present, a book of Mr. Byron's poems, and three sets of gems from the Kremlin. Well, then he yelled at the top of his lungs: Where's my boy—where's Clemens? He kissed that innocent little black child and said something in a foreign language like *que grand tu a!* Just look, Bernie, he shouts, he's a chip off the old block! This is my first son! I had four daughters, Bernie—as if I didn't know all these bitches, I thought—and I've never had a son! How about taking a closer look at him, I said—you mean you can't see what color he is? I don't care what color a man is, he says. Your Negroid gene, Bernie, turned out to be dominant. What the hell are you talking about? I ask him. It seems that Fuchs and his bums worked out that I've got one-thirty-second Negro blood. I mean, I really lost it.

Over the last few years I haven't had more than six black guys—make that eight. One was a shoe manufacturer, he loved shoes. I loved stripping down to nothing and having that guy in his whole suit and in his jewel-encrusted cowboy boots. And another one was a virtuoso musician. He played his clarinet like an angel, and I played his other clarinet like a devil. Sometimes I'd even start yawning because it was getting on my nerves. Come on, Vint, please stop playing—you're with a woman, after all. I don't remember if it was him or another one who brought me a book by some François. There was a story in there about a woman who delivered a baby through her ear because all her plumbing had fallen out. No, it was Lavsky that gave it to me. Wow, memory, tell me about how Lavsky drank champagne out of my shoe. Instead, memory starts sucking on my nipples. Who was as gentle with them as Mel was? He made them stand up, and he purred over them like a cat with a lion's mane.

They say "big, big," but my tiny little general would blow into me from behind like a flame. True, my Matt was still working on me down below, while that Asian devil was riding my backside—whew, I'm coming every five minutes, and that Hungarian tramp is still waiting his turn. Lavsky, where are you, why don't you join the fun? Arrogant bastard!

And meanwhile Mister Luxe, who gave me such a classy name, kicks the bucket. His last "wife," some old queen, brought me a cassette with his dying words on it. He was making a list of things he was leaving to me, whom he called "a little flower plucked by me": a silver coffee service, a mahogany buffet, and a little Chihuahua that got under the covers on the very first night and started licking my clit.

When all's said and done, I knew more about men when I was fifteen than most women know when they're fifty. And guys felt that right away, from their first look at me.

When I was a little girl, I would just die for a blancmange with black currant jam. My mama, Mrs. Fief, spoiled herself with it all the time, and a bit would come my way. Philosophically speaking, I got enough sweets down me to last me for the rest of my life! Then Jock the Cook started dropping in on my mama. Sometimes at night, he'd scratch at the door like a beggar wanting a crust of bread. Sergeant Fief, with a lamp in one hand and a poker in the other, would go off thinking he was dealing with a rat, and he'd pull out this hippie from the state of Ochichornia: granny glasses and a top hat on his head like a critic of the regime, and in front his thing was making his trousers stand up like a tent. As soon as I looked at what was going on, I knew that there were sweeter things in the world than blancmange with black currant jam.

Merciful and loving God, I hope peace will come to me at least when I'm laid out in my grave!

A couple of years later this hippie showed up in a spotless suit to see me, not Mama, and it's my turn to get plowed, and he's plowing away, and I'm pretending that it's not me but some other little girl that he's plowing, and the whole time he's looking down at me through his glasses and talking about Spinoza.

Once, an idea came to me that made me sit right up. Why shouldn't women run this world? Powerful and generous women? They say that women ruled Russia the entire eighteenth century. They chose a personal guard for themselves, dressing the whole army in tight-fitting pants. They'll say I'm just a nutty nympho, and I'll answer that if they're doing it to the empress twenty times a day, then the whole country wins.

Believe it or not, I dreamed my whole life about a prince who would satisfy my needs. And then he appeared, Stanley Franklin Korbach, a son of a bitch and a motherfucker. His tongue's seven miles long, and his stallion's penis is even longer—it is with me, anyway—and he wrote me checks of matching proportions. With checks like that I'd walk into a ritzy boutique and nobody would laugh behind my back anymore. That's how my taste for the finer things developed. One day he invited me to a party at an embassy, the Brazilian one, I think it was. "Hey, Stan," I asked him, "what if I pin a white rose right here?" "Well of course," he says, "who else should wear a symbol of purity if it's not you?" "You know," I say, "I'd like to see this whole place, life, I mean, swimming in white roses." "Well, then let it swim in white roses just the way you like. Maybe you, Bernie De Luxe, really are the biggest slut at this reception, but none of the respectable public has the right to cast any stones: I know them all from financial dealings. They're all afraid to go to Hell because of their unclean consciences, and your conscience, Bernie, is a white rose, even though it lies a bit off to one side on your body."

One day we were lying in a field of rhododendrons on the edge of a huge cliff. It was in the Crimea—that's in the Indian Ocean, I think. Daybreaks and sunsets took each other's place every five minutes over there. And the fig trees were still in bloom, and in all the little towns there were geraniums and jasmine growing by pink, blue, and yellow houses, and fields of white roses with the wind streaming down them like a raging river. I pressed my tits and the hill between my legs against his chest and his genitals and whispered: "Yes, yes, I will, yes, I am, I'm your other half, but I don't want to die before my time." And he said: "Go ahead, white rose, give birth to it, yes, yes, go!"

5

NORA

I was never closer to my father than in January 1987, when he, like Odysseus, was wandering from island to island of his ontological archipelago. Unlike Odysseus, though, he seemed to be the sailor and the sea at the same time. I came to his hospital room and sat on the edge of the bed for a long time, listening to the whisper of his pharmacological babble with my mind a blank.

A thought that reduced everything else to ashes kept occurring to me. It seemed to me that my all-powerful "daddy" might at any moment of his mysterious travels cross that threshold that no one returns from. It was like coming close for a moment to that which exists outside of space and time, like what I experienced in orbit later on. I never said anything to anyone, not even Sashka. I was just trying not to miss a single opportunity to visit my father in the urology ward.

From that room there was a view of the roofs and treetops of Foxhall Palisades. Beyond them, breathtaking Virginia sunsets would change the colors and forms of illuminated clouds. Oh, these Virginia sunsets, Sashka's idol Nikolai Gogol would say. What bird would not fall to the ground dead from delight at the sight of them? One might suppose that they extend out over the uncharted ocean and over undiscovered islands, but certainly not over endless blocks of American dwellings with their law-abiding inhabitants, these "aunties" and "uncles," as that malicious Moscow buffoon calls them.

Sister Elizabeth would look into the room from time to time and smile at me sympathetically. I started listening to my father's barely audible whisperings and mutterings, trying to catch at least some meaning in them. I even brought a tiny Dictaphone, and then played the tape over and over again at home, until I suddenly realized that he was on a journey far from his own life. He was talking about a man by the name of Kor-Beit, which means "cold house" in Hebrew.

In the old days, Stanley had made several not particularly successful attempts to master the language of our ancestors. Now I was stunned to hear genuine fluent Hebrew flowing out of his subconscious. I tried to decipher the recordings myself, but then I realized that I wasn't up to the task and took the tape to my close friend Ruth Rosenthal, from the Jewish history department at Pinkerton. Somehow or other, I worked out that the man named Kor-Beit was a tanner of a sort in a small seaside town. He ran a business that had a tannery, a warehouse, and a leather goods shop. I got shivers down my spine when Stanley began briskly inventorying skins and hides of various sorts, sizes, and qualities, and counting up the money in ancient Hebrew denominations, all these *assaris, drachmas, didrachmas, shekels, statirs, dinars,* and *talents.* These inventories and reckonings took up the largest part of the tape, but here and there were snatches of phrases addressed to other people: to family members or servants, and once there was something along the lines of an admonition to a tax collector.

Here and there, a fleeting description in English of some landscape had worked its way into these ancient mutterings: there was "dazzling sea," and "wild roses on the fortress walls," and "winding path."

One day, Nora found her father not in a horizontal position, as usual, but sitting up in bed with a pile of pillows behind his back. "Hey, Daddy!" she exclaimed. "Are you all right today, then?" To tell the truth, she was a bit disappointed that the excursion into the past had come to an end. He didn't answer, and she realized that he didn't see her, and hadn't heard her words. At that moment a hunched-over figure appeared in one corner of the room; it was none other than the butler, Enoch Agasf. "You were here the whole time?" she asked him. He nodded and made a gesture with a long finger that said: Sit down and shut up!

Sister Elizabeth appeared briefly to bring the long spout of a teapot to Stanley's parched lips. Politely, he declined to drink and raised his palm, as if calling for their attention. The nun, crossing herself before the crucifix, left the room.

Stanley was still with Kor-Beit, but now he shifted from counting hides to an important historic event—namely, the Destruction of the First Temple. This time he saw the streets of Jerusalem and his tanner in a crowd of captives being driven into slavery by Babylonian whips. The deafening crack of these enormous knouts. Suddenly I heard a "click-click": it was Papa turning on the TV with the remote control. Miami Dolphins and Washington Redskins were flashing in his eyes. "They'll never get anywhere unless they get a new defensive line. Manny Brown and Bennie Fields have got to be replaced, no two ways about it," he said in an authoritative tone. My incorrigible daddy!

During the course of the next few days I racked my brain over these recordings of mine. What were they—just ravings brought on by intoxication? In that case, where did the ancient Hebrew come from? I gave Lionel Fuchs and his genealogical group a call and asked if there had been any other tanners or furriers in the Korbach ancestry, besides Gedali from Warsaw, my great-great-great-grandfather whom everyone knows about. What do your computers say, Lionel? He didn't say anything for a while and only made a sort of moaning sound, as though some pain were tugging at his heart. "I've got a tanner," he said finally, "but he's so far back, Nora, that I simply can't talk about him, and I won't say a word about this man, Nora." "Why not, for God's sake?" I shouted. "Because I'm still a Marxist, and therefore a tenth-generation materialist!"

One time Ruth Rosenthal called. It turned out that she was working night and day on my "projects" and that she was dying to press on with the "research." She was one of those university women who divide all human affairs into two categories: projects and research. I think they even classify a hot date as a "project" and screwing as "research." I offered to meet her at my office to do a bit of research.

"It's a terrific project," she exclaimed. She was obviously excited by this invitation from "this Nora Mansour of ours."

All right, then, old lady, she said, spreading out the cassettes and transcripts. First of all, we've got to separate the wheat from the chaff. Everything, or almost everything, that's said in English here is chaff, just a reflection of the popular literature, stuff like Ruth Samuel's *Trails of Jewish History*. I can't rule out the possibility that all of these scenes involving the burning First Temple, King Nebuchadnezzar, Zadkia's sufferings, and hordes of Jews driven into Babylonian captivity came right out of that book. All of this, obviously, showed up on your father's road back up out of the abyss that he'd fallen into.

The wheat, as it were—if we can use that word for such things—comes up in the Hebrew. It's not likely that Mr. Korbach could get these hazy commercial calculations of his ancestor's from a book. This phenomenon is beyond the realm of science, and we have no way of explaining it. The only thing that's clear is that Kor-Beit the tanner lived much later than the destruction of the First Temple, let's say about five hundred years later, judging by the names of the money mentioned there. As an archaeologist, you know that better than I do. In all probability we're dealing with the era of the Judaic War.

I don't think I'm making a mistake if I tell you, Nora, that as a professional you're thinking more about an archaeological hypothesis right now than you are about your family tree. Schliemann based his plan of excavations on lines of poetry, and you can lay down a challenge to common sense and try to work out the disposition of a place two thousand years old on the basis of a drug hallucination. There are lots of details scattered through these mutterings that can help. There's mention of a deep cellar and steps leading upward. Jerusalem can be ruled out, because this is somewhere right next to the sea. I'm not afraid to say that it was some sort of storehouse located in a fortified city by the sea. Walls and towers, and beyond them a coast with wild roses and bright yellow shrubs. Then he shares with someone—with himself, even, perhaps—some strange, I'd say even poetic, observation. He sees a flock of small birds. They're flying with their movements so well-synchronized that it's as though they're one complete being. The flock turns suddenly in this or that direction, all together, as though it were held together by some secret laws of perfection. It's something along the lines of the expression of some higher avian happiness. How happy they are, your father whispers, every one of them, and all together as one. Of course, you could suppose that he'd seen a flock like that in his own life, if he hadn't been whispering it in ancient Hebrew, which he doesn't know.

Nora smiled, recalling the excavation sites along the coast of Israel, in Akko, Caesarea, and Ashqelon. There had been masses of wild roses and shrubs with bright yellow flowers along the precipices over the sea. To put it mildly, the information gleaned from the subconscious depths of the urological patient was insufficient to set in motion the scientific sequence that, according to the rules, should consist of three elements: formulation of a hypothesis, linking of arguments, and clarification. The meaning of science consists of the accumulation of knowledge in an upward spiral. Here we're getting into the twilight world of mysticism. My

God, what's waiting for us beyond the boundaries of the world of the air? she was thinking. Beyond the boundaries of scientific cycles . . .

Meanwhile, after finishing the fieldwork on the Khazar burial mounds on the Salsky steppes and a whole series of conferences, in Athens, Paris, Moscow, and Chicago, she headed for those very same Israeli shores to join the famous Volkeruge expedition, which had pitched camp between Tel Aviv and Ashqelon.

The expedition had been in existence for twenty-seven years. It still went by Volkeruge's name, even though Hans Volkeruge had died ten years earlier at the age of eighty-six. He called himself "the happiest gravedigger in the world," and why not? Sixty-six years of work in the archaeology field hardly interrupted even by wars. Even the legendary general Moshe Dayan had worked as archaeologist *sous les drapeaux* of the inspired Alsatian, but he'd had to interrupt his activities more often.

This time Nora decided to spend the entire fall semester in Tel Aviv and to return to her teaching at Pinkerton only later. The university administration had recently given her to understand that the academic community was very unhappy indeed about her endlessly being on leave.

The university was, of course, delighted to have such a brilliant scientist on its faculty, and with such a great name, the "cosmic archaeologist," the author of *The Hygiene of the Ancients,* a scholarly work that had also been a great popular success, an outstanding representative of the well-educated and progressive order of American women, and, to top it off, a member of the "Korbach clan," about which the papers were writing endlessly; however, the community would like to see her on campus more often as a participant in the educational process and of the university's development. She had solemnly promised to return in the spring and to stay for a long time. She still needed the autumn to wrap up her cycle of fieldwork and sorting through of materials for catalogs to be included in her definitive work on the caravan routes of the Fertile Crescent. It would have been difficult to find a better place for that purpose than the Volkeruge expedition, under the aegis of which excavations were going on simultaneously in several locations, and concerning periods ranging from 2000 B.C. to the Crusades.

In accordance with the modern methods of "predicting the past," groups of scientists from various countries excavated from their trenches not only artifacts like arrowheads, beads, pots, craftsmen's cutting tools, dice, effigies, fetishes, millstones, tanned hides, decorated shells, turquoise good-luck charms, decorative statuettes, amphoras, armor, weapons, stone flacons of perfume and aromatic oil, toothbrushes, and bronze jugs for everyday washing and ritual ablutions, but also so-called ecofacts, like grains of pollen, feathers, leftover bones, excrement, horns, insects, quartz crystals, snakeskins, rushes, seeds, veins, snails, and all sorts of bones—in other words, anything that could be put through the carbon 14 dating process in order to re-create the paleontological picture—that is, to prove or disprove scientific hypotheses.

Our creative reader understands, of course, that all of this was said in order to emphasize yet again—as we approach the end of our chronicle—that Nora Korbach-Mansour was not any sort of thrill seeker with a penchant for the superficial brouhahas of outdoor digs; she always was and remains a profound archaeologist, a workaholic, and an initiator of interesting projects. Under the aegis of the Volkeruge expedition, she had assembled her own team of men and women devoted to her, and the "V.E." leadership always treated her with respect, all the more since she brought generous grants with her.

Enough, she said to herself after bumping into Alex in some Moscow dive. I looked even more ridiculous there with that young prick, "the blond beast," than Sasha did with his "baby" the size of a basketball player. Stupid, old-fashioned, and hysterical. Every age group ought to sing from its own musical score. At forty-six, you ought to be first and foremost a professional woman, and then you ought to think about your maternal responsibilities.

In a departure from her "field" habits, she rented a three-bedroom flat in Tel Aviv, two blocks from the esplanade. Four-year-old Philip Jazz Korbach arrived, accompanied by his Irish nanny. The first thing he asked about was whether or not there were any "recreation facilities"—meaning a playground, obviously—nearby. Nora took him in a westerly direction, and when after two blocks there opened before them the esplanade, a wide, sandy beach, and the fairly vast expanse of the Mediterranean, she asked: "Do health establishments like this suit you, Jazz?"

"Quite," the child replied in the Irish manner.

One day, Nora got behind the wheel and headed south in the direction of Ashqelon. It was a mild morning in the Promised Land. Nothing but the weather forecast indicated the approach of the high winds of the khamsun. In her Volkswagen convertible she was soaking up every note of this Israeli overture: the breeze that ruffled her hair, the smiling faces of the cosmopolitan Jewish crowd, the light swaying of the palm trees, the roar of jumbo jets at the end of their transoceanic routes. I wish that I could always drive this way along a great expanse of water that doesn't need archaeological excavations to be aware of its connection with aeons of history, since it's already been rolling and foaming for millions of years. Thank you, sea, for always washing my libido and for always crashing against the rocks at the foot of the Jaffa, where Andromeda was chained and given over to be violated by the sea monster every day. If it wasn't me, then who else? If not for me, then who else would wait for Perseus, who pierced the monster with his spear and cut my shackles with his sword?

Israel, for all its remarkable diversity, is a small country: less than an hour's drive, and you're already driving into the cherished Park of Ashqelon. Eucalyptuses, cedars, and palm trees quiver in the wind, the smells of gasoline and diesel fuel have disappeared without a trace, your own tobacco smoke doesn't count. She drove past the ruined walls of Richard Coeur de Lion, past the restored ancient amphitheater with its poster advertising a recent rock concert, past the disparate columns of the Greek agora and the statues of the Roman baths. All these had now become tourist sites, but she remembered the excitement that had come over her and her friends when on one of their digs a sculpture of Nike nearly untouched by time had been uncovered.

Since then, the archaeologists of the Volkeruge expedition had moved closer to the sea, where according to the latest hypotheses the seaport of the Jews, the end point of a great caravan route, had been located as early as the time of King David. It was there that she had left her group two months before. Under the leadership of her assistant, Dave Rex, her gang was to have dug a shaft to a depth of forty feet, and if nothing was found there, to move closer to the sea and dig again.

She didn't find her people where she expected them to be. She came upon a few shafts and trenches surrounded by fences, and crudely fashioned roofs covering the more valuable sites, but for some reason not a living soul was around: at that hour no one was working in the excavations, no one was sleeping in the shade, either. For no less than half an hour, she wound her way along the dry, slight roads, one sight of which was enough to make her heart beat faster, because they had barely changed in three thousand years. From the top of one of the hills she saw some tents and decided to go to them on foot. The sea blinded her for an instant when she got out of her VW. A gust of dry wind blew her hair in the direction of the sea. Here, forty miles south of Tel Aviv, one could already feel the breath of the desert. She walked along the steep path that led to the foot of the ruins of the Crusaders' fortress.

Along the wall, the path went down and then up into the overgrown dunes by turns. In one spot she saw wild roses and a dense shrub with bright yellow flowers clinging to the crude brickwork of the fortress. A feeling of what in everyday speech takes the French name of déjà vu shot through her. The Canaan coast is scattered with thousands of places like this, but it was here that she'd stopped dead in her tracks and nowhere else. Not far off she saw the square entrance to some sort of archaeological mine shaft, obviously abandoned by a previous expedition for lack of data supporting someone's hypothesis. But she was not thinking about that, she did not even remember the recordings she had made at her father's bedside, which she and Ruth Rosenthal had racked their brains over. It was just that she was staggered by the feeling that the moment had stopped. And in this frozen instant a flock of birds appeared, silently overflew her, then made a sharp turn, all at once—a hundred starlings. They all came back as one and turned again over her head as if to fly away, and again came back and again flew away, and again came back, and this went on until the moment itself took flight, until Nora realized that she was still alive, that she was sitting on a stone, that her eyes were squinting in the sun, that she was on the Earth's surface, atop the cultural "strata" that cover Kor-Beit, the house of her ancestors.

6

OMAR MANSOUR

*A*pproaching the end of a sizable work, in point of fact completing the penultimate part, the novelist unavoidably comes to resemble the hen trying to gather together her entire brood, including the "ugly ducklings." In fairy tales it's assumed that ugly ducklings will grow up into irresistible swans; in novels, sad to say, things sometimes turn out the other way around. Some characters conceived as vivid literary types shrink down to complete insignificance, hobbling along on crooked paws. Fortunately, no such fate threatens Nora's ex-husband, whom the end of our chronicle finds in the fine form of a self-assured forty-something editor in chief of an influential liberal newspaper in the capital of one of the pro-Western Arab countries.

Omar Mansour—whom, incidentally, all the staff of the paper as well as the political and cultural elite of the capital now called Anwar Sha'abani—makes his appearance in this chapter devoted to him sitting in his spacious office, which is on one of the upper floors of a skyscraper in the city center, and from which he has a marvelous view of historic structures, including graceful minarets, the cupolas of ancient mosques, and the huge, hideous monument to the ruling president. His light gray suit, custom-made for him by a tailor in the Avenue Victor Hugo (Paris, sixteenth arrondissement), wonderfully takes into account the slightest nuances of his athletic frame. The very same thing could be said of his socks and shoes: they're a perfect fit for his ankles and all twelve toes of his finely formed feet.

No matter how hard I work, I'll never be able to afford togs like that was the thought of Henri-Claude Metz, a journalist from a leading French newspaper now sitting with his Dictaphone before our character, who was somewhat in the shadows, his obvious brilliance notwithstanding. The polished coffee table between them resembled the fossilized form of some mythical locust. The journalist had come on special assignment. This newspaper, *Al-Passawar,* and its editor were the subjects of numerous discussions in the centers of the world press. Unlike most of the other—it would be simpler to say all of the other—mass media in this country, which was under the control of an authoritarian, though pro-Western, government, *Al-Passawar* displayed a certain independence, a more liberal attitude toward Western culture, and even subtle nuances in its views on the touchiest subject of all, Israel. This singular position was bound up with the personality of the editor in chief, who in Paris was considered quite comme il faut.

Henri-Claude Metz was an ace of the political interview. He knew Anwar

Sha'abani's real name. He knew his ex-wife as well. A dozen or so years earlier he had often hobnobbed with the bohemian elite of the Left Bank, and now he was absolutely certain that at parties in those days he had often stood not far from this good-looking Arab who spoke French without an accent. He even remembered that some people had exchanged significant glances and knowing smiles behind his back. It was clear that Sha'abani remembered him, too.

"Excuse me, Metz," he said, dropping the *Monsieur* in the style of those days. "Your face reminds me of someone whom I knew rather well a few years ago." Henri-Claude smiled. "I'll bet it was Alex Korbach." He lightly touched the magnificently bald crown of his own head. They looked at each other intently and smiled at the same time, tacitly agreeing not to say any more on the subject.

At that moment, two young, chubby assistants came into the office carrying fresh galley proofs. Sha'abani excused himself to Metz. "We've got a rush job going on; five guys are working on this text next door." He quickly made several corrections and exchanged a few guttural Arabic phrases with his subordinates. "Can I ask what the hurry is?" Metz said. "Of course, of course," the editor in chief replied. "We're putting together a reply to the *Jerusalem Post,* which tactlessly criticized our president for his statements on nuclear issues."

"And what sorts of corrections did you make, Monsieur Sha'abani?" asked the Frenchman. The editor immediately made a photocopy of his galleys and tossed them over to Metz. Then he dismissed his assistants. Metz looked at the elaborate Arabic script. His Arabic wasn't very good, but he could see that the word *swine* had been crossed out.

Omar gazed at his guest with a polite readiness to explain anything he wished. These whores, he thought. They never took me seriously. They never really let me into their club. The whores, they were always exchanging glances behind my back and Nora's, too, the same way those whores at the court of Nicholas I in St. Petersburg exchanged glances behind the backs of Pushkin and his wife. Just look at her, they would silently say, those liberals and Marxists, she's sleeping with an Arab. A woman from our set is living with this rich, good-looking Arab shit. As if I were one of those fat-cat Arab sheikhs! Whores, fucking slimy Jewish scribblers!

"I want my people to learn a new language," he said. "They always go too far with the words they use with the Israelis. Brothers, I say to them, lower the temperature a few degrees! You're only giving them more stature than they deserve. Israel, at the end of the day, is just one small country in the Middle East. It's not worth making it a stumbling block to the leading forces of Arab civilization. Learn to talk about them condescendingly."

"Condescendingly?" Metz asked, by way of checking.

"That's right. Condescension is the first step toward better mutual understanding. For example . . ." He picked up the galley proofs with two fingers and shook them as though he was trying to pour some liquid from them.

"Do you read Arabic, Metz?"

"Not so well as to be able to make a judgment about something without a translation," said the journalist.

"Are you sure about that?" Omar (Anwar) asked, and then burst into none but the friendliest laughter.

"Cut it out, Sha'abani—you know me, after all," the journalist said dryly. "And I know you, cher monsieur."

Anwar (Omar) stopped laughing. "Okay, let's play by the rules. I just want to give you good material for your article. You see, my guys have prepared a rough draft of an open letter to the editor of the Jewish newspaper in connection with his venomous attack on our president. Here they write: 'This newspaper has the same qualities as the swinish Israeli leaders with their impudence that stinks like a gefilte fish.' Listen, guys, I say to them, you can reject Anglo-American culture, but here's something that you ought to take from it, and that's the principle of understatement. One well-placed word can be of more use than all your rabid salvos. So, we strike out *swine* and *gefilte fish.* The word *impudence* standing all by itself will work better.

"Then they write: 'The editor of the *Post* is a stupid, insolent, dirty Zionist.' Knock it off, guys, I say. Do you mean you haven't heard that too many adjectives can kill a sentence?"

Omar delivered this whole didactic monologue as though the Frenchman himself were responsible for the text of this important editorial. There was something hypnotizing in his voice and in the generous demonstration of several languorous gestures, even in his long left leg, which was using his right knee as a support in its triumphant rocking. Henri-Claude was angry with himself. What do I keep nodding to this motormouth for? Of course, these journalist's nods were designed to encourage the speaker, to invite him to ease up on the brakes, to allow him as many slips of the tongue as possible, but in this case it was difficult to say who was on the lookout for whom.

The editor went on. "The rough draft reads: 'The dirty Zionists will meet with the same fate as the bloodthirsty Crusaders, they will flee from our land. They will return to their malodorous ghettos in Warsaw, Budapest, and Odessa, et cetera.' I take out the annoying epithets and turn this manifesto of irreconcilability into the usual phraseology of a liberal newspaper."

"Liberal?" Metz asked, checking again.

"Well, of course," Sha'abani (Mansour) confirmed. "Here's one more example for you. The young hotheads call our opponent the 'Jewish anus,' which after my correction becomes 'Zionist backside.' Do you see the difference?"

"No, I don't," Metz said with a shrug.

For a few seconds they stared at each other in silence. I wonder if this Yid slept with Nora, Omar was thinking, just like all the other Yids I knew back then on the Left Bank of the Seine. You know perfectly well I didn't, Henri-Claude thought in reply. You know perfectly well that I adored her just like all the others whom you call Yids in your mind. She slept with only a small number of us, Sha'abani, and keep your hands off the woman of our dreams, *s'il vous plaît!*

"All right, Metz, I'll read you the full text of our editorial reply for your little Dictaphone. I'm sure that you'll understand it with your usual perspicacity."

Sha'abani began to translate from the sheet into English, from which Metz concluded that the "reply" was intended for international distribution. "This Zionist backside cautions our president against repeating the mistakes of Abdel Nasser in nineteen sixty-seven. The Zionist effendi thinks that the Arabs suffered a defeat in nineteen sixty-seven. It was not a defeat, however, hapless editor, but a many-headed conspiracy, in which even the American president Johnson himself took part. The defeat was dealt us by the conspiracy, and not the Israeli Army, the proof of this being nineteen seventy-three, when the Arab armies, fewer in numbers and with inferior equipment, defeated Israel. I say, then, to the Israeli journalist: A bit of humility is what you need instead of baseless bragging, and remember that if America abandons you for even one day, you will sail off into exile across the Mediterranean with hundreds of thousands of refugees just like yourselves.

"And America, for your information, will crumble into pieces one day just like every other empire in history. We wish only that it would happen in our lifetime. For the time being, we would advise you to speak politely about our country and our president, since you are nothing other than Washington's agent on Arab territory, and your army nothing but the frontline units of the American army.

"Forgive me, my Zionist, if I say *Mal'un Abuk* in your honor, but your prime minister is nothing but Washington's representative in Tel Aviv. Concerning our president, he is a great leader of a great Arabic civilization, and you are unworthy even to mention his name!"

He stopped reading and directed an intent, serious gaze at his interlocutor, as though he really wanted his opinion of what he had just read. Henri-Claude was slightly nauseated. He mumbled: "*Mal'un Abuk,* I think, means 'your father be cursed,' doesn't it?"

"It's just a figure of speech," Omar said. "A traditional saying, something like a formula of refutation. I hope that you understand the subtext of our message to our Israeli colleagues. They ought to be less arrogant with regard to a great Arab civilization. A large part of the whole problem, by the way, is their arrogance. At any rate, they've been coming and going since the time of the father of them all, Abraham, and we've stayed on our land. In principle, we were here even before Abraham, but Ismail was accepted by us because his mother was of our race."

Metz shrugged and proposed changing the subject. "May I ask you, Mansour—oh, sorry, Sha'abani—what you think of the *fatwa?*" The editor did not answer right away but first offered the Frenchman a beer from his refrigerator. "Metz, I know that son of a bitch Rushdie has become a litmus test for liberalism. But you can see, and you know, that I'm not such a devout Muslim. I find his blasphemous writings repulsive, but on the whole I'd prefer to leave the matter up to God on the Day of Judgment. In this sense it's curious to point out his collision with a garbage truck during his trip to Australia. As far as I'm concerned, the *fatwa* has already been carried out."

He laughed loudly, clearly pleased with his on-the-spot discovery of this metaphor, and Henri-Claude recognized his resourcefulness with a little smile. He was ready to recognize anything at all so long as he got out of this office as soon as possible. After asking a few more rather colorless questions, he began to take his leave. Sha'abani was surprised. "How can you leave, Metz? After all, I was planning on showing you a couple of nice little Western-style places in this stern capital today." "Thanks, Sha'abani, but I'm not feeling very well: the consequences of the flu, and I'm flying off this evening." "Flying back to flu, Metz?" "Bravo, Sha'abani, it's almost a pun! Give me your word that you'll call next time you're in Paris." "Why, I'll be there on Tuesday, Metz." "*D'accord,* Sha'abani, we'll have dinner in a nice little place, all right?" "It's a deal, Metz, thank you." "It's a very pleasant Jewish restaurant, Sha'abani." "Jewish, Metz?" "Well, yes, Jewish, Sha'abani." "No problem, I've always got my Pepto-Bismol with me."

The journalist had not yet left when the two chubby young men appeared in the office with the final version of the text. They cautiously showed the boss a sentence they had thought they might add. Omar could not believe his eyes: it was exactly what he himself had been thinking. "And I swear by the name of the Almighty that if I meet you, Mr. Zionist Editor, I will roll up your newspaper tightly and stick it up the stern of your craft, and no one will be able to help you then!" He laughed with pleasure, then took a pen and added: "I hope, dear sir, that you've not lost your sense of humor."

A few hours later, a fax arrived from Paris at the empty, darkened office of the liberal editor. Monsieur Metz was sending his regrets: he would be out of town on Tuesday.

XI. A QUOTE

"A quotation is a cicada." Mandelstam is a hot-air balloon, a Mongolfier.
A cicada is a water hemlock. And Socrates, therefore, is a crème soufflé.

The ways of rhyming are inscrutable.
You drag yourself across hummocked syllables,
And erect the Vendôme Column
At the entrance to a cheap sideshow.

Through the transom window you see a square by night,
Flickers and flashes of the clowns' mugs.
There, a dapple-blue horse
Slowly brings in your Amarcord.

You'll have a drink of wine. You go out
On the balcony to calculate the Apocalypse.
Instead of an answer, piles of leaves
Come rustling down from the heavenly Balkans.

PART XII

1

THE SILVER OF OCHICHORNIA

*S*o, here we are, rolling into Ochichornia, which wedges its spacious lands into the map of America by crowding California, Oregon, and Nevada. Another wave of authorial arbitrariness is rising, the tired reader will say, and mistakenly. Polyphony is in full swing in our story, the characters are marching to their own drummers, so what authorial arbitrariness can there be? Even the state of Ochichornia turned up quite by chance in connection with the spinning of an old Louis Armstrong record in the jukebox at the International House of Pancakes, since old Satchmo persisted in rhyming *Ochichornia* with *California.* We didn't even have time to realize what was happening before the new land was claiming full membership in the union of states, and already, you see, taking pride in its expanses of territory and its capital, Las Pegas; basically, like it or not, it has become a literary reality at the present hour of sunset beneath stunning desert skies with outlines of Joshua trees and the running silhouettes of ostriches.

What a strange creature the ostrich is—you can't compare it with an eagle or a horse, and where do they come from in such numbers, anyway? More about that later, though. For the time being, we'll say only that these powerful, if pointless, strides of these creatures gave the desert sunset an ancient appearance, even though the glass skyline of the city of Las Pegas was visible on the horizon.

And here's one more strange thing—an extraordinary vehicle is turning from a typical American straight-as-a-column highway onto a narrow country lane leading to the ghost town of Whistlestop, the city of abandoned silver mines. Whistlestop had once been a hive of activity, but the buzzing had died away when the silver ran out. For a hundred years it had lain in oblivion and then began to buzz with tourists, and then the buzzing died away again when tourists lost interest in that sort of curiosity. Refinement on a mass scale had now spread through the public; give them Vermeer and Vivaldi, they're fed up with bearded quasi bandits. The strange vehicle, however, was rolling stubbornly toward the ghost town. It was welded together from two disparate sorts of automobiles. The front was a Cadillac limousine, and the back was a Ford Explorer with a terrace instead of a roof. A strange jalopy, all right—the only thing left to guess at was whether it had been made to order or by mistake.

Now a word about what this carriage was carrying. At the wheel was Tikhomir Burevyatnikov. At that hour, without his ritual headdress, and with his wings unhooked, he looked like a typical American citizen, only a bit on the run from criminal charges. Next to him on the broad seat were his two friends, Smartie and Dummy. One had its ears pricked up, as usual, while the other's hung down like burdocks. He's a handsome guy, this Burevyatnikov, Dummy was thinking. He takes the prize among people and birds. Too bad he isn't sensible, thought Smartie. Blowing up the gates of that ostrich farm last night could have cost me and Dummy our tails, and Tikh himself could have lost everything that he's dug up here and there.

In the rear section of the vehicle—that is, on the terrace—two other passengers were playing chess. It was a rather cozy atmosphere. In the midst of Burevyatnikov's mildewed household belongings glowed a large television. Its flickering colors might have seemed a reflection of the sunset had the reverse effect not been at work. From time to time, skinhead NBA players ran across the screen like Tamerlanes.

The chess players did not resemble each other, though they were related. One was of superhuman proportions, the other just the right size. One had a head of hair like that of a biblical prophet, while the other had an entirely bald crown, but more in the style of Voltaire than of Tamerlane. Well, what's the point of beating around the bush: it was Stanley and Alex Korbach.

"Come on, cousin, give up," Stanley said. "I can't," replied Alex. "I'd like to, but I can't. Our country is falling apart, but we Russians still have the victor's mentality."

When they arrived in Whistlestop, the sky was almost dark. At night, in spite of the absence of silver in the mountain, there's still a strange argentine glow that spreads around the place. The black hole of the entrance to the mine into which the tourists once trooped presides over the clutter of the town. After leaving their vehicle beside the boarded-up post office, they walked along the street in search of a house where they might spend the night. There wasn't a soul to be seen; even the cats had scattered long ago. At an abandoned Citgo station, the only living thing turned out to be a pay phone. For reasons that were unclear even to him, Alex slowed down beside the apparatus. I wonder how many years it's been since anyone put a coin in that slot, he thought. Wouldn't it be funny if it rang right now? It rang. Gusts of wind from the desert were blowing bits of trash around. Alex picked up the receiver.

"I beg your pardon," a woman's voice said. "This is a call from Israel. For some reason, this number, with an area code for a state that I must admit I've never even heard of, just popped into my head. Tell me, is there a man named Alex Korbach anywhere around there?"

"Nora," he whispered. "That means that it's you that the desert has been singing about for the last few hours. Are you still the same? Does your Jewish hair still blow in the wind the same way, do your Swedish lips still tremble the way they used to?"

"That's not what I'm calling about, Sasha," she said. "I'm calling because I found our common ancestor during a dig. He was sealed in a natural sarcophagus of petrified honey. You and Stanley have got to see him before the state museum gets its paws on him."

"We'll fly out tomorrow," he promised. "I want to see you and our son so much!"

She, calling from a seaside pay phone in Tel Aviv, put down the receiver in a muddle of emotions. He, in a muddle of emotions, quickly walked down the ghost street past the empty bank, in which effigies of cowboy bandits had still recently imitated the holdup, that act beloved by millions.

Stanley was sitting on the flat surface of a rock with Smartie and Dummy. On the edge, meanwhile, Tikh was smoothing out his wings and making his plumage stand on end. "I'm the emperor of the birds!" he cried. "Prince Alkonost, Khan Gamayun, Burevyatnik the Unvanquished!" His audience, nearly three dozen African ostriches, was milling around at the base of the rock. An equal number were racing to the gathering along the hard surface of a salt lake.

The time has now come to tell the story of how the strong-legged, flightless birds came to be on the territory of the state of Ochichornia, the fauna of which had never seen any creature of the sort. Perhaps some lackadaisical reader will wave a hand in disapproval: it's all just something dreamed up by the author, who's gone right off the deep end now that his story about the two cousins is nearly finished. Such a reader will be wrong again: the mystery of the ostriches and its solution are contained in what all mysteries and their solutions in our society are to be found in—money. At the end of the last decade, there were entrepreneurs who decided to turn this inhabitant of African game preserves into an American domestic animal. Farms were equipped with the latest in incubator technology, and a big business was launched.

"The bastards are processing these proud birds down to the last cubic inch of their innards and the last square inch of their surface," Tikh Burevyatnikov would rage over a half-gallon bottle of Smirnoff. "Feathers, bones, spurs—everything goes on the books! They even use their intestines. Every bit of liquid in an ostrich is condensed into tablets. What do you mean, for what? As an aphrodisiac for screwing! And the most important thing, of course, is meat for ostrich burgers. They say it's like something between chicken and veal. In this way, boys, I give you my Komsomol word of honor, the whole bird is technologically processed down to nothing for dollars. Why, it's just like Auschwitz, brothers! It's the gulag of our democracy!"

At the beginning of his transformation into a bird, Tikh had registered a society named Free Birds of the Occident with the clerk of Birdland County, Ochichornia. Given the peculiarities of the English language, the first word could be taken for a verb or an adjective—that is, it could accommodate both a proud claim to existence and an ardent call for the liberation of feathered creatures. The second member to join the FBO was Stanley Franklin Korbach, about whom one still could have said, quoting the classic movie line: "He's seen better days." Our favorite, Alexander Zakharovich, having decided after the failure of everything he'd begun that things could only get better, became the third member in short order.

"You aren't birds yet, of course, brothers," Tikh told them one day. "Well, thanks for that much at least," Sasha said, tossing his once elegant suitcase onto the roof of the van. It's interesting to note that after the collapse of his undertakings, all his fine things quickly degenerated to the level of the usual vagabond's belongings. "I want to be quick about giving you hope, though," Tikh said. "Judging by everything, both of you have a chance to join our condition. The day will come when I'll give you both a set of wings, swear you in as birds, and we'll fly away." "Toward the shores of the Original Concept?" Stanley asked. "How'd you guess, Stan?" Tikh responded, his jaw dropping. "That's just where we're going, to those blessed shores. But first we must liberate our brothers and sisters from the concentration camps of the state of Ochichornia."

Like all freedom fighters, they didn't know any better means than explosives. In the course of seven silvery nights, seven blasts made seven holes in the fences of seven ostrich farms. The ostriches, having glimpsed the limitless expanses of the Culihunarie Desert, rushed out into freedom. The metaphysics of freedom have been set in motion, gentlemen. Several generations of these creatures had already been processed down to nothing by the state of Ochichornia; the present generation was already displaying all the characteristics of domestic animals—that is, they were marking time senselessly in fenced-in enclosures, copulating, dropping eggs, willingly going to the slaughter pens, and suddenly, the whole tradition crumbled at once; the population of the camps rushed into the holes that had opened, and the habits of slavery were broken in a flash. The ostriches rushed along, powerfully working their still far from atrophied extremities, without direction or purpose, as ever, but inspired by open spaces.

Tikh Burevyatnikov would gather his liberated masses every night for his speeches. Many of the runners were attracted by his pipe calls, screeches, and whistles. Sometimes hundreds of the creatures would gather. He would call them "representatives from the provinces." Now, once again, he was making a speech to the ostriches. "Birds, free children of the air!" He'd somehow failed to notice that such a form of address was not very appropriate for flightless birds. "Never again will we allow humanoids to process us into utilitarian substance! Long live our ocean of air!" With these words, he spread his wings and plunged into that very ocean.

"Have you known him for a long time?" Stanley asked.

"At least a dozen years," Alexander answered. "Actually, he claims that he was the Komsomol Central Committee watchdog over our theater even before that, but I don't remember him."

"And he's not bad at gliding," Stanley noted. "I wouldn't be surprised if he did learn to take off in the end."

"I've got news," A.Z. said, and he told his cousin about Nora's call.

"The cycle seems to be closing" was the reaction of the "king in exile."

"At least if you consider this novel a lyrical cycle," A.Z. agreed.

As they talked, they were watching Tikh, who, having folded up his wings, was walking to and fro among the ostriches and persuading them of something with the passion of a Komsomol leader. The birds were flocking around him, nodding, sending up a whirlwind of feathers. Scarcely restrained indignation seemed to show in their poses.

"I told her that we'd fly in tomorrow," A.Z. said and scratched that part of the back of his head from which, as a result of his wandering lifestyle, a graying pony-tail had begun to hang. "How can we make reservations on an international flight without it getting in the papers, though?"

"Panurge, my friend, even in exile, Pantagruel is still Pantagruel." Stanley reached into his rucksack and produced his mobile phone, which he hadn't used in, say, three months. He poked at it with a finger as gnarled as a ginseng root, and suddenly the clear voice of Ernie Rotterdam, the pilot of the Korbach Galaxy air-ship, was heard on the rock: "Stanley, is that really you? Over!" "Ernie-Pernie," the giant joyfully roared. "Where are you right now?"

"Over Saudi Arabia, a hundred and fifty miles north of Riyadh," the pilot replied. "I'm flying a charter for the Black Children of Moses group. Do you need me? Over."

"Sasha and I need you. Yes, of course he's right next to me. Sashka, say a few words to Ernie!"

"Fuck you and the horse you rode in on, Rotterdamsky, you loser!" Sasha yelled from one side and got a good dose of friendly cursing in reply.

"We're in the Culihunarie Desert," Stanley said. "Just outside the former town of Whistlestop. You can land in the bed of the salt lake. We need to get to Israel."

"Got you," Rotterdam replied crisply. "I'll have a look at the computer right now to see when I can get there. Hold the line, boss!"

While somewhere out there over Saudi Arabia the captain of the Korbach Galaxy was doing calculations on his computer, unexpected events were beginning to take place beneath a rocky ledge in the ghost town of Whistlestop. The ostriches were pushing the Emperor of the Birds into their crowd. His Majesty looked as though he were receiving pecks to the head and scratches on his backside. There was nothing for him to do to save himself but spread his wings and soar over the representatives from the provinces, which is what he did. The ostriches immediately scattered into the Ochichornia night. Landing on the edge of the cliff, Tikh petted his dogs and came up to the Korbachs. "Well, fuck 'em," he said simply. "That meat factory isn't even worthy of the name of birds. They want to go back to the farm. They took care of us there, they said. Sure, and they were processing you until there was nothing left, I said to them. Every bio-object eventually gets processed down to nothing was their answer. Bunch of fucking philosophers."

At that point the telephone spoke up. "Stanley and Alex, I can land where you are in twenty hours, eighteen minutes. A friend in Las Pegas is going to bring up a fuel tank. The crew'll be wanting lunch, but nothing too exotic. Scrambled ostrich eggs will be fine. Get ready to fly."

Three pairs of stunned eyes were now looking at the cousins. "Stan, Sashka, you're not going to leave us, are you, you lousy creeps?" roared the just dethroned emperor. Smartie, raising his muzzle, howled tragically. Dummy chimed in with a hysterical descant.

"We've got to get to Israel, guys," the cousins muttered in embarrassment. "Archaeologists have discovered the remains of our ancestor."

"Well, there are probably loads of my ancestors in the ground there, too!" Tikhomir riposted hotly.

"Buy you're not even Jewish, Tikh!"

"Beg your pardon," Tikh protested with the good manners of a Moscow flea market. "If I'm not Jewish, then who is? The Burevyatnikovs have been Jews for a hundred years, they've just kept it hidden."

Do we need to say how the conversation ended? Tikhomir, of course, got a seat on the Galaxy. In his turn, not to be outdone, he promised in businesslike Komsomol tones to find a free place in Jaffa for all of them to stay. It turned out that his friend Apollosha Stolpovorotnikov was working as a janitor in the Armenian monastery.

While the ex–bird fanciers were bedded down for the night in the abandoned Silver Bullet Motel, A.Z., who was relatively refined by nature, was the only one not snoring. To immediately diminish the image of our favorite we'll add: he wasn't snoring because he wasn't sleeping. The four other beings were pouring it on, each in his own way. In addition, Stanley was traveling in space and time, arguing in Hebrew and crying out Roman commands. As for Tikhomir, he was doing what came naturally, now giving an eagle's screech, now doing his best Khlebnikov number, imitating sparrows and wagtails.

Well, what can you say—if everything that's gone before our eyes and with our participation is a novel, then it must be reaching its end: such were Alexander Zakharovich's thoughts. If, of course, there is such a thing as the end of a novel. In the theater I bring down the curtain or I turn on the lights: that's the end, dear ladies and gentlemen, please go home now. In a novel, no one goes home, everyone makes up an epilogue.

What's to become of this character who throughout these pages has stubbornly opposed the author's intentions, unexpectedly turning into now a hopeless loser, now a favorite of Fortune; now impotent, now a world-beating lover; now a cynic, now an idealist; now a Melmoth, now a cachalot. Am I, Alexander Korbach, of whose life fourteen years have passed before your eyes, real, O Theophilus? Do you feel compassion for me, or do you consider me a cold phantom? Are you able to believe my grief at finding myself, in the fifty-sixth year of my life and wrung out by this novel, alone in the midst of my ruined ideals, in the vacant lot of my soul, along the fringes of which slip the shadows of those who were dear to me and those whom I lost so ignominiously in the ups and downs of an unpredictable genre?

Everything's lost, including my motherland, and I haven't managed to find a new home either. Did I have my people, apart from that one one-hundredth of a percent whom the Bolsheviks counted out so precisely? Three August nights flew right away into the background, and the machinations of the devils are throwing shit all over the scene again. Take your cynical bastard back. The highest degree of cynicism is shown not by the boys in the Mercedes but by the masses. After everything that's been revealed about the history of Communism, they vote for Communism.

I'm lying on a bare mattress in the Silver Bullet in the middle of a nonexistent state, in my nonhomeland, surrounded by people and animals who don't belong to any people except for the crowd of characters. This country doesn't offer strangers the land of their forefathers, but it does at least offer them a homeland. The country of your home, of our, my, your, their home. But instead of becoming a law-abiding apartment renter, a valet in a parking garage, a professor in a university theater department, I insist on remaining a character in a novel with its anarchic plot. Don't count on a happy love affair—in a novel it always turns out to be a vice, doesn't it? Success in this fucking polyphony dulls the senses like a drug before it crumbles into pieces. There's only one thing left on the plus side of the mental balance sheet, but it's no small thing: the theme of so many years of life, Dante and his love, never assumed concrete form—it survived!

And here's what's left of my *dolce stil nuovo:* a motel with holes in the roof, Scorpio in the night sky and scorpions on the floor, sniffing around our dogs, and out there, overseas, in our ancestral homeland, the mummy of Kor-Beit pulled from the stones, perhaps a figment of someone's imagination, perhaps a symbol, perhaps the reality of reunification. "Lord God! Look not upon the stubbornness of thy people!" (Deuteronomy 9:26).

———————

In the morning, when they went out into the open air, the Korbach Galaxy was already waiting on the ideal natural tarmac of dried-up Lake Ochos. A small black boy was sitting in the door of the plane, his bare feet dangling in the air. The captain of the ship introduced him as "our new steward, Mengistab Neurosis. A veteran of the Eritrean people's struggle for liberation."

In the salon everything looked as it had in the old days, unless one counted the cigarette burns on the upholstery of the couches, the smell of sour milk, and hard, round little droppings scattered here and there. The Black Children of Moses had managed in many cases to haul their favorite goats onto the plane during their evacuation to their historical, if not ontological, homeland.

Two hours or so later, their tanks filled with stolen fuel, they rose into the limitless skies of the state of Ochichornia, so as to enter the airspace of the United States once they were over the belletristic barrier. During their climb, the gates of one of the liberated ostrich farms flashed beneath them. They could see a line of gigantic chickens returning home. Well, what can you do, the bird lovers shrugged—we wanted things to turn out for the best, and they turned out the way they always do. And they sat down to play cards.

2

*A*nd here we are in Israel. The prophet Mohammed, who so desired peace but only caused everyone to quarrel, probably flew with no less speed. Do we dare, however, reproach the Prophets about anything? We're guilty of everything ourselves, biological mutants that we are. Such were Stanley Korbach's thoughts as he carried his own quasi-prophetic, though alcohol-sodden, head above the crowd on Tel Aviv's seaside promenade.

The whole group—five men (Stanley, Alex, Tikhomir, Ernie Rotterdam, and his ever-faithful navigator, Paul Massalsky), one boy-veteran (Mengistab Neurosis), and two dogs (Smartie and Dummy)—were walking in a slow and blissful procession from the Dan Hotel toward Jaffa, whose hilly profile with the church of St. Peter at the summit was still awash in the morning smoke, though the cross on the bell tower had already begun to gleam in the sun even before we finished this sentence. Smartie, as usual, was leading Dummy on a leash and was particularly alert in the new locale. Dummy, for his part, could not restrain his delight in the rumbling valor of the Mediterranean Ocean (no, that wasn't a slip of the tongue), which was why he made a good two-thirds of the journey on his back paws.

If this country were a bit bigger, even by a factor of ten, I'd wander around in it for the rest of my life, thought A.Z. Unfortunately, the country is too small to be a vagabond in, and the borders are hostile. A band of tramps freely spread out beneath a cluster of palm trees, leaves crackling in the wind, on a well-manicured lawn thirty feet from a rocky cliff overlooking the dark green, manelike surface of the sea might not have agreed with this mental conclusion of Sasha Korbach. One of them was cleaning his teeth, keeping to himself as he wet his toothbrush with an economical stream of water from a plastic bottle. Another was in an attitude of Eastern meditation, though now and then scratching one foot that happened to be turned toward the featherlike morning moon. Most of the group was breakfasting from packets labeled in Hebrew, which was so well-suited to advertising dairy products. Passing by, our group of travelers caught a snatch of the conversation of the breakfasting Russians.

". . . Nobody was ever as good on the double bass as Lavrik Briansky. He felt the sound. I worked with him in Lukyanov's crew, and then with Kozlov at the Armory. Lavr was born to play the bass, but he thumped it up too much."

All three of the names mentioned rang a bell with Alexander. He came to a stop and peered at the bearded faces of the typical jazz musicians. *"Slikha, adoni?"* one asked and took a bite from a long baguette. A.Z. was unrecognizable in his broad-brimmed hat.

Turning off the embankment and walking down a grubby street lined with dark, cavernous wine shops, Stanley's group emerged on another embankment; they were already in Jaffa, known in ancient times as Joppa, which was a couple of thousand years older than Jerusalem itself. A crowd of old Jewish and Arab fishermen were standing about. One of them tugged on a long pole and froze with an amazed and perhaps even insulted expression on his face. Instead of a fish on his hook, there dangled some sort of black growth that might have looked like an over-size trepang had it not been so similar to a waterlogged boot. No, I wasn't expecting that from you, Mr. Ocean, the old man's face seemed to say. Beg your pardon, really I do, but I wasn't expecting that at all!

Stanley Korbach was in high spirits. "Listen here, brothers—why, Andromeda might have been chained to this very cliff face beneath our feet, and it was probably from these spiraling waters that the sea monster emerged every morning to have his sadistic way with the beautiful woman. And right there, covering over space and time, was where Perseus the rescuer appeared!" One of the fishermen turned at these words and winked approvingly at the entire band. A.Z. was prepared to swear that it was none other than Enoch Agasf.

In the swirling waters around the abandoned Old Jaffa lighthouse, it felt as though time were ticking away according to some reckoning unfamiliar to us, if it was being reckoned at all. "Stan, you remind me of a painting by Piero di Cosimo, the fifteenth-century painter," A.Z. said. "I looked at it for a long time one day in the Uffizi Gallery. *The Liberation of Andromeda,* it was called. The sea monster in it was so ugly that it even made you feel sorry for it. Tusks not of this world and a tail in the form of a spiral. There were streams coming out of its suckers in different directions, as from a fireboat. The suffering but still magnificent body of Andromeda stood out brilliantly against the backdrop of the Joppa cliffs, which looked like the very ones that we behold now. The little form of Perseus was standing on the sea monster's mane, waving his sword sharply like a hussar; it's one of the few examples in the world of justice triumphant.

"The most surprising thing about this painting was that there were people scattered along the shore in it. When I was a child, it always seemed to me that the fateful triangle was cut to pieces without witnesses, simply among the raging elements. In Cosimo's version, though, there were lots of well-dressed people there, and it was more ecstasy than compassion that was written on their faces."

The fishermen on the embankment had already been listening to this discussion for some time. Grandfather Agasf coughed, trying to draw attention to himself. "Your artist is right, young man! The dealings of Andromeda and the Monster had attracted the attention of the local inhabitants some time before. The wails of the girl during the rape sessions, as well as the deafening grunts of the monster, struck their imagination. I myself was here that morning when Perseus suddenly leapt from the clouds. An enchanting spectacle—an avenging hero on a human scale!" With these words Grandfather Agasf bowed and moved off, carrying a small bucket with three fish tails protruding from it.

"What, didn't he recognize us?" Alexander asked in surprise. Stanley shrugged. "Maybe he was just pretending not to recognize us. History is coming to an end, he's looking for some new domain. And maybe it wasn't even our man: the shores of Canaan are full of 'Eternal Jews.' "

On the approaches to the port and on the other side of the gates, to the left, loomed the walls and terraces of Old Jaffa. The concrete here alternated haphazardly with basalt. Narrow ladders in the walls with those symbols of Mediterranean civilization, men's underpants hung out to dry, flapping overhead in the breeze, led up to the top of the hill, to the tourist zone and to Abrasha Park. Balconies of various shapes and sizes were suspended at different levels, now with watchful monks visible on them, now with epicureans in Hawaiian shorts.

From one of the Jaffa terraces, or more accurately from the flat roof of the Armenian monastery clinging to the precipice among the concrete and basalt arches, Apollon Stolpovorotniker, the guard of the religious establishment, was looking down at the approaching group. His appearance: head shaven, a cavalryman's mustache beneath a large nose, small eyes, a full array of shoulder muscles bulging from a tank top, no evidence of any waist muscles at all unless one counted a belly drooping like a bag containing a cat. In the Soviet art scene, Apollon belonged to the "generation of watchmen," which had hidden itself from Socialist Realism in caretakers' huts, boiler rooms, and spare quarters of all sorts. On the Israeli art scene he had remained in the ranks of the same generation, though he had changed the last two letters of his surname from -ov to -er and had moved from basements to a tower, where his face was constantly peeling from the Mediterranean sun. He was always glad to receive guests, and it was not a rare occurrence for him to roll a keg of Maccabee beer up to his bastion; this time he rolled up two.

Tikhomir Burevyatnikov was looking around happily. He was proud of the fact that even in this distant land it had turned out that he had such a good friend, and one for whom he had long ago predicted a bright future, at the time when the Komsomol police auxiliaries were raiding underground art exhibitions in Moscow. Suddenly his attention was drawn by a strange figure on a neighboring roof. "What's that, then, Apollokha?" "A sculpture," Stolpovorotniker said, and then explained. "A sculpture of an eagle."

The sculpture had been thrown together from remains of cement by the construction workers who had added an annex to the monastery. The eagle stood in an upright position, flinging wide what were either its wings or the sleeves of a roomy *lapserdak*. It seemed to have trousers on its legs, but semblances of claws still stuck out from the bottoms. The hook-nosed face registered sorrowful amazement, like that which had appeared in the expression of the old man who had fished something entirely unexpected up from the sea.

Tikhomir gasped. His antiornithological pledge was instantly forgotten. Eagles are living creatures, after all, and their cause lives, he thought. Seemingly by chance he spread his arms apart and threw back his head, rejecting the galosh that was being proffered in place of a fish.

Meanwhile, Stanley Korbach, after positioning himself in immediate proximity to the keg of Maccabee, was thinking aloud about the nature of mythology. "All of our heroes and antiheroes, Andromedas, Perseuses, and monsters were, are, and will be as long as the world exists and reflects fear, hope in bliss, and the humorous gesture. From divine meaning, man created a carnival of gods and heroes in his own image. Aristotle, Messrs. Vagabonds, wasn't so simple, even though he didn't reject paganism either. He knew that God couldn't be grasped, and realized that the throng on Olympus represented the clearest personification of the unfathomable that man could create.

"Judaism heroically renounced polytheism, but it couldn't limit itself to the Unfathomable, which is unbearable to man. The intermediary prophets—Abraham, Jacob, Moses, the prophet Jonah in the belly of the whale—these are human images of God.

"Christianity has its source at the meeting point of the comprehensible and the incomprehensible. In the minds of some, monotheism appeared a void. Perishable biology seemed a trap. Man saw himself in the loneliness of the universe as a sacrificial lamb for a rite that made no sense from his point of view. It was just then that God sent us His Son—that is, Himself in the flesh. The face of the God-Man is brought as close as possible to our powers of comprehension. His flesh speaks to the fact that God shares in our fate, our sufferings. We're not alone, we're simply on the road back from exile to true creation. Christ is followed by a throng of holy images: Apostles, the Mother of God, Magdalene, George the Triumphant, and other martyrs. Poets attach their ideals to them, as Dante did to his Beatrice.

"In other words, all of this is always with us, fellow wanderers, everywhere, and even in this keg. Through the air and through beer, the Holy Spirit flows into us, and if you start fooling around, don't forget that, and you won't do anything too swinish."

Soon roving Russian musicians appeared on the terrace. They tooted on flutes, strummed guitars, banged Bedouin drums with their hands. The Armenian monks were tearing themselves away from their sacred tomes, leaning out of windows and smiling. "The abbot has flown off to Echmiadzin," Apollon explained, "so we can make a bit of noise. But without women," he added. "Alas, without women."

"Listen, Apollon, where around here is there an archaeological expedition working?" Sasha Korbach asked.

"There are lots of them here," Stolpovorotniker answered. "Every free patch of land is divided up between soldiers and archaeologists."

"Fact is that an ancient ancestor of our whole family tree was found here." Sasha Korbach sighed.

"That happens here." The artist nodded. He began to bring out his canvases still in their frames and arrange them on the roof, along with pieces of pipe welded to each other—i.e., sculpture. Looks like Tikhomir the bird isn't the only crazy one around here, he was thinking. Maybe they'll buy some of my work. And he wasn't wrong, by the way. After the party on the roof he was a man of means.

How am I supposed to find Nora? Sasha Korbach thought. She scheduled the meeting in Israel, but Israel's a big place, you know. Guess we'll have to forget about logic and dial at random according to the laws of this novel business; that is, do just as she did when she gave Whistlestop a jingle. What the heck, let's give it try while we're still not too drunk.

He ran down the staircase, on which at one time a lone Jewish spear carrier could have held up two heavily armed centurions because there was no room for a third to pass. The crumbling streets of the old port were full of people out for a stroll. Others were sitting around the tables, masts swaying in the background. Fishermen were selling excellent marlin, octopus, and squid directly from their little boats. In huge dilapidated hangars in which the English and the Turks had once kept God knows what, art now reigned triumphant: endless variations on the Andromeda theme in oil and acrylic, along with paintings of just cliffs or waves; other sorts of Aivazovskian daubing; bits of jeweler's junk lying around like mineral deposits, including tiny Stars of David, crosses, and half moons uniting peacefully in the tourist business. Among these warehouses, rusting launches and small boats lay propped up for dry-dock repair in positions absurd for nautical craft. Between them an Israeli pay phone blazed in the sun with all the might of its metal. A.Z. poked it six times with his sinful index finger without even looking at the combination of numbers.

"Sashka!" Nora exclaimed. "Here you are, finally! And we're just leaving!"

"Where could you be going?" A.Z. asked in a Jewish accent. "How do you know where we are?"

"Everybody already knows," she replied with youthful animation. "The local paper *Nattahnam* announced last night: Stanley Korbach, after the biggest bankruptcy case in history, and after a miraculous escape from the pursuit of Norman Blamsdale's agents, is coming to Israel. Together with his entourage, which includes the well-known director Alex Korbach, whose planned Hollywood blockbuster fell through. He is staying on the roof of the Armenian monastery in the old port of Jaffa, where Apollon Stolpovorotniker, the rising star of the new generation of Israeli visual art, is caretaker. So, I'm coming, and I'm not by myself!"

"With whom, then?" he asked, this time like a vaudevillian.

"Guess!" she cried with a strange playfulness.

"Omar Mansour," he suggested.

"Idiot!" she said, and put the phone down. He couldn't call back: in the first place, he didn't remember the number, and in the second place he realized the absurdity of calling a second time in the last part of the book.

He sat down in the blazing sun and leaned against the wall of the Armenian monastery. A lizard ventured out from under his backside and perched opposite him, fixing him with his tiny, ruby red eyes—the spitting image of Popsy Putney! He held out a hand to it. Do you want to live in my sleeve? Want to become the lucky charm for an unlucky man? While it was thinking that over, Nora pulled up in a marble white Jeep. Next to her sat a little boy, the very image of Alexander Zakharovich: the same easily stretched buffoon's mouth, slightly protruding ears, wide eyes laughing with the same fire that Alexander Zakharovich's had once laughed with.

"Jazz, remember when you asked who your daddy was?" Nora said and indicated the man, no longer young, sitting against the wall of the monastery with sandals on his bare feet. The little boy sprang from the Jeep and ran up to his father. "You don't like to cut your toenails, either, Daddy?" he yelped triumphantly.

Sasha Korbach's eyes filled with tears. "What are you crying for, Daddy?" "Damned if I know, son." "Monsieur, your son isn't accustomed to such language." He cried even harder, and even his armpits, shoulders, and upper back poured themselves out. "Say, you're all wet, Daddy." His son laughed from his perch on the nape of his father's neck. "It's like you were swimming." They went up the narrow stairs that had been hacked from the rock face to the roof of the monastery. Taking the lead was his beloved, bounding ahead in white jeans that were also almost the color of marble. "I'm all wet because I'm so happy, Jazz. You're a bit heavy, and I'm weak after my bad luck in life and my sorrows." "Bad luck, Papa?" "And sorrows." Sashka, don't whine, your meeting with your ancestor is still to come, you've got to be strong!

They came out on the roof. The old giant towered there, wrapped for the occasion in a blue Tuareg burnoose. He was holding forth about something to the rabble packed around him, taking in the Mediterranean horizon and the Tel Aviv shore arch with the gestures of his arms. "I'm not seeing things, am I?" Such was the joyful cry of the little boy Philip Jazz Korbach. "So this is my grandfather?" "Jazz, my boy, heir to a fallen empire!" The grandfather, in the folds of his burnoose, stumbling slightly to the sound of the Russian syncopations, rushed toward his grandson. The mother and father of the small boy went off to one side, to the edge of the roof. A fresh keg of beer was making its bobbing progress toward them over the heads of the crowd.

"When will we see him?" he asked.

"Tomorrow," she answered. "There's going to be a state ceremony. We're all expected there, of course."

An Israeli Air Force helicopter gunship flew over Jaffa with a brigandish whistle. Displaying some secret quality all its own, it rose in the sky like a candle, then immediately dived toward the sea. No sooner had it scooped up some water with its rotor than it gained altitude again, only to go into another dive and play out this martial dialogue to the end. It was a display intended to intimidate: Hamas was in town.

"I'm a little scared," she confessed.

"Of what?" he asked.

"I don't know, but one way or another, things are coming to an end. Almost all of the pages have been turned."

He was annoyed. "You know, at the end of the day, only ink runs out, not life. And this is my story, after all, you know. It's ending, but all of you will carry on, that's all."

"And you?" she cried out and threw her arms around his neck.

"Maybe I will, too," he said. "That depends on me and you, not on the whims of any novel."

"Well, we finally seem to be getting near true love." She sighed.

"Tell me about Kor-Beit," he said.

She told him about her Dictaphone, with its recording of her father's postoperative ravings, and about the "shift in time" that she had felt at the sight of the flock of starlings in Ashqelon. Immediately after that, her group began an excavation, which was more like a rescue operation in its speed. They'd already dug on that spot, and they'd never found a thing. People who knew about such things tried to talk her out of it, but she stood firm. They used the latest technology in "geophysical diffraction tomography" and unexpectedly enjoyed stunning success with it. "They send sound waves into the ground with special devices beneath the surface. The 'geophones' measure the vibrations of the surface as the waves go by. The computer finishes things up, creating a three-dimensional picture of the empty spaces. In this way, we found something incredible at a depth that no previous expedition had gone to. We opened up the whole rock face, and found there the remains of walls, floors with two levels, one stone and one wood, a storeroom for finished hides, and lots of artifacts—in particular tanner's tools, chests of Roman, Jewish, and Syrian coins, whole amphoras of flour, olive oil, and wine, pieces of furniture and kitchen utensils, Roman weapons, menorahs, decorations, and the remains of a well and a good system of running water. There were a few skeletons there, too, of both men and women, in poses suggesting that these people had come to a sudden end. The skeletons of the other living creatures—that is, horses, dogs, and two cats—seemed to confirm this hypothesis. The biggest sensation, though, was still to come. In one place, where one would have expected the next increase in volume, the sound waves kept hitting something that appeared to be a monolith. We got through to that place and discovered some crude masonry work. In the end we found that it was a sort of natural sarcophagus, which obviously had been formed as the result of a major tremor by a shift of the rock. Over the centuries, neither air nor water got in, which is why the body found there, a man who died almost two thousand years ago, was so perfectly preserved. Besides the stone shield, he was also covered by a layer of petrified honey, which had obviously been poured over him from one of the huge, fragmented amphoras. In other words, he looked like a million-year-old fossil preserved inside amber. In all probability, he was covered in this way after death, since there was the head of a spear typical of an armed legionnaire lodged between the ribs near his heart. We also found there scrolls of parchment with business records in Hebrew and Greek, from which it became quite clear to us that the preserved body was that of the wealthy merchant Zeyev Kor-Beit, approximately forty years old, born in Jerusalem, which had opened a coastal market for its goods two years before the catastrophe, just outside the west wall of the fortress of Ashqelon, by the city gates. It's clear that his shop was one of the first to be plundered by the landing Romans.

"Here in Israel these days, archaeologists try to keep their discoveries a secret for as long as possible. Not long ago, some fanatics surrounded one of the Hasmonaean burial grounds that had been uncovered. They consider archaeology sacrilegious. Excavations disturb the peace of the dead, which will create a mass of difficulties when the Messiah comes. Thank God, the government doesn't think so, at least for the time being.

"We had to ask the Israeli Academy of Sciences for help right away, although we still haven't published the news of our discovery. Naturally, we couldn't guarantee the preservation of Kor-Beit's body by ourselves. The cosmic object—do you remember what we said about man becoming a cosmic object after death?—began to decay immediately on contact with the air. Well, anyway, Lilienmann rushed to the capital and raised a secret alarm in some highly placed circles. The question was discussed in closed session by a committee of the Knesset. The senators, naturally, were disturbed by the problem of whether our 'John Doe' might be a Philistine, or some other sort of pagan; after we showed them photographs of the parchments and other indications of Jewish descent, they were beside themselves with joy: the coastal region is indisputably ours! In two days, everything was taken care of, and now our ancestor is lying under glass, in a vacuum, like Lenin. He'll probably become one of the prize exhibits of the Israel Museum, and the site of our excavations in Ashqelon will be turned into a place of pilgrimage—and then . . . well, your wife will be considered the Schliemann of modern archaeology."

"Wife?" he exclaimed. "You called yourself my wife!" She was embarrassed. A glance upward with her head lowered, which used to drive him wild. Now, among small wrinkles and slightly drooping cheeks, it summoned up a deep, almost archaeological tenderness.

"Well, it was just a manner of speaking," she said.

"No, it isn't!" he objected vehemently. "If you meant it seriously, then all of history can come full circle back to that point. It's the final result of my whole theatrical school! It simply means that the *dolce stil nuovo* still triumphs!"

"Hold on, hold on," she said in a sly tone that would have been more appropriate somewhere in the middle of the book than in its final pages. "It's still a bit early for us to be coming full circle. It would be absurd to end the book with your Russo-Jewish exclamation points."

"We're on Jewish soil now!" he exclaimed. "I'm fed up to the back teeth with your mid-Atlantic English and its restraint. I reserve the right to brandish exclamation points by the barrelful in the land of my ancestors!"

"How I love you, Sashka! I'm not so old that you don't want to take my jeans off, am I?"

3

ABLUTIONS BEFORE THE END

Suddenly it turns out that they were not on the roof in the midst of the revelers at all but at a corner table in a small, three-walled café, sitting over mugs of Israeli mint tea. In the place of the fourth wall was nothing whatever; the café was open to the shore road with its heavy traffic, beyond which extended the broad esplanade, paved in an unobtrusive Jewish mosaic. Along it, on two different sides, paraded—that is, not seeming to parade at all but rather merely to sway—a crowd of Jews dressed for the hot weather. The backdrop of this attractive picture was formed by the interaction of the beach, on which the grains of sand must have been no fewer in number than the human fates that had been played out since the days before the Flood, with vestiges of the aforementioned Flood—that is, with the deep blue mass of the Mediterranean.

Every reader who has studied any geography at all knows that the seacoast of Israel is fairly rectilinear, so it won't be difficult for him to imagine an enemy flotilla arrayed before us on the horizon at sunset and ready to open fire on the densely populated shores. It will be just as easy to imagine this flotilla in the form of a string of campfires after a preemptive strike from our missile launchers and air force. But we'd better not. We'd do better to occupy ourselves with the couple in the small café over their mugs of mint tea.

"In this dark corner it's not hard for me to see you as a young streetwalker, the way it happened once on the Boulevard Raspail, but, you know, it seems to me now that we've crossed some frontier, and that our love has lifted itself much higher than sexual lust."

Nora smiled. "So you've decided to promote me, an adulteress, to the ranks of the angels?" It seemed to him that she was making fun of the failure of *Radiance.* He was afraid to ruin their new, unspoken tenderness with a tactless word. "I only meant that we've still not yet known true love."

She turned away toward the sea in annoyance, then burst into raucous laughter, jumped up from her chair, and clapped her hands. "Look who's walking along the seafront! Sashka, we're present at a stunning literary meeting!"

The staging that followed really was worthy of applause. With the stately grace of an unvanquished lioness, none other than Bernadetta De Luxe was making her way through crowds of astounded Israelis. Her dress, in a pattern of flowers and pheasants, trailed behind her in a train yards long. The slits, extending right up to her crotch, bared with every stride two legs, each of which looked like a perfect lass. The region of her shoulders, bared to the absolute limits, were reminiscent of Leni Riefenstahl's cinematic sports epic. As it had in better days, her mane of hair flapped in the breeze like the tail of Bucephalus, the horse of Alexander the Great, who had galloped along this very seafront in the same southerly direction 2,330 years earlier.

Next to Bernadetta, constantly taking his shiny black top hat off as a greeting to the Jewish people, walked Teamsters' Representative Matt Shuroff. As a matter of fact, all the old gang from Venice Beach was there in the company: Bruno Kastorzius, minister in the shadow cabinet of post-Communist, but still Communist, Hungary, who was calming the crowd with meaningful gestures while, still in keeping with old habits, pecking at something edible from a package of "humanitarian aid"; Melvin O'Massey, who had just completed the consolidation of several corporations and had received an honorarium of $500 million for his pains, was radiating youthful happiness, giving sidelong glances to the queen of his computerized dreams; Piu Nguen, who had recently become head of state security for the new bourgeois Vietnam; and even old Henry, the pianist from the First Bottom, with his ever-present cigar clenched in the bridgework that vaguely resembled his piano—all of them were moving effortlessly, as if in a dream, and were peering into the crowd with gentle smiles, as if to ask: Where's our Lavsky?

"Lavsky," as we know, was watching them from one side; meanwhile, moving directly toward Bernadetta and her retinue, that is, in a northerly direction, was another procession of our characters, headed by an aging giant in a blue burnoose, whose height was made even greater by his grandson, the son of his fourth cousin, sitting on his shoulders.

No doubt one of our malicious readers will not fail to pull the author up at this point: Here you are again, my dear man, dragging along your processions and losing characters at the same time. After all, don't we have the right to expect one more little boy in Bernadetta's entourage? Or were all of your allusions to his appearance of a strictly irresponsible, not to say "secondary," nature?

No, no, my spiteful friend, you don't understand. You, impatient as you are, couldn't even wait until the whole train of Bernadetta's dress had dragged itself across the page. It is after all her beloved progeny, the delightful Clemens, a swarthy copy of his father, Stanley, who is holding up this train. And in its lace, flashing in and out of view like a trout in Niagara Falls, is a male Chihuahua named Cookie, whom even you, dear sir or madam, may not have thought of in a long time.

But now these two delegations came together and mingled. Even if we were to use up every word at our disposal, we would not be able to describe this merging. We'll only point out that everyone on the esplanade was joyfully amazed: the *sabra,* and the *olim,* and the *galut,* and the trembling *falashi,* and the Russian atheist cynics, and the *daties* and the *khabad* and the plainclothes agents; the Hamas people with dynamite strapped to themselves forgot about what they'd come for and fell like chickens into the hands of their pluckers—which is to say that they were intercepted on the road to Paradise.

Meanwhile, the sun, as it almost always did, was preparing to draw an ideal

picture of a maritime sunset for the entire elongated city. The sunsets of coastal Israel—now there's something for us to be proud of! Not finding any way stations
such as rocky islets, the sun of Torah and Tanakh sank directly into the sea. In delicate modulations of bottle glass, in bands of purple extending over the horizon, in
puffs of cannon smoke scattered against the copper backdrop of the clouds, the
sunset offered anyone who wished the opportunity to calculate the proximity of
the Apocalypse.

"Listen, Natalka," A.Z. said to the proprietress of the café, "have you got any kind
of private room here?"

The former leading actress of the Buffoons theater, Natalka Motalkina, threw
the "legal" Kleofont Stepanovich Sitny, former KGB general with responsibility
for theaters, out of the private room, in which he'd been lying around long enough.
The latter, in spite of a trunk bulging with KGB hard currency, commanded no authority on the waterfront. "It's only all these fucking roles that are still bouncing
around in my head that keep me from telling that sack of shit to fuck off," Natalka
was saying in the intellectual jargon of the sixties and seventies. "Get up, asshole,
and piss off to your Zavkhozov!" she shouted now. "A genius needs the bunk to
fuck some American girl!" Comrade Sitny jammed a Chinese straw hat, an antique
from the Bolshevik golden age of the fifties, on his head and headed off to the
neighboring Opera House skyscraper, where his former colleague from the department of special assignments and now president of the major Russian concern
Viaduct Major General Zavkhozov had a $5 million penthouse on the twenty-
eighth floor.

Sitny knew a good deal about Zavkhozov, but not everything. In particular, he
didn't understand why an outstanding financier of our time sat in a Jewish skyscraper for month after month and couldn't even be bothered to go for a walk. We
know a good deal about the "financier," but not everything. We know, for example,
that one day in his Moscow office, President Zavkhozov decided to check the list
of those on whom he had contracts out: some actually had been eliminated—the
earth receive them gently—while some had had the impudence to survive. Some
genuinely curious things are going on, not to say curiouser and curiouser, as Alice
would have put it: some little man who was crossed off the list long ago suddenly
pops up on "live" television, and, as a live being talking to the living, pontificates
about the problems of national stabilization. This sort of disorder above all de-
means the authority of the "contract"—it gives any creeps the right to avoid responsibility; must look into this.

And so, that morning, having used a cipher known to only a handful of people
in Moscow, he brought up the Contract list on his computer screen and found his
own name there. The fear was so overwhelming that he didn't even try to get any
information. He simply grabbed his briefcase and raced to Sheremetyevo. The

next flight was to Ben Gurion. Let's go there, then! Under the protection of Shin-Bet!

The passage of this individual through the metal detector set off the mechanism's squealing alarm. All in a sweat, he nevertheless found the strength to put on a show of amiable absentmindedness. What a fathead I am, I brought all my keys with me: the one to the dacha, and to the garage, and to my locker at the tennis club. He tossed the metal ring to one side and then casually picked it up again. It would never have occurred to anyone that in that pile of junk were three keys to Swiss safes. At any rate, he escaped! And now he sits in a tower.

As always, Sitny was met by a Chinese servant who checked him with a magnet and let him into the flat. His friend came out to him from the balcony. Hello, Your Excellency! What were you doing? You know, doing what I always do—looking at the waves. I'm lucky that I can see only waves, and none of that—he wanted to say "crowd of kikes" but thought better of it—herd. You're just in time—that's what it means to have the KGB sixth sense! I'm expecting a guest, a top-of-the-line babe from our international department. Right now we'll have a few drinks and few snacks, too.

A dark-complexioned beauty in a fine chamois dress appeared. Her movements were full of femininity and her eyes of masculinity. Sitny felt a bit awkward in his threadbare jacket that, as a matter of fact, he lay about in day after day, rustling the latest issue of *Top Secret;* the lady, however, said to him in their own language: "Say, I know you, Sitny—you're from the Fifth Department, right?" Accompanying her as she came in was a man with the look of a Middle Eastern aristocrat about him who gurgled something polite but incomprehensible when introduced.

The lady began to make small talk with Zavkhozov, and the gentleman, as if to show that he had no personal relationship with her, went out to the edge of the balcony and stood there motionless, arms folded across his chest like a demonic sculpture. In all probability he was a rich Arab—Sitny had never seen an Israeli like him. The ocean, meanwhile, continued to play out its colorful overture to the sunset: the waves looked like chameleons as they rolled along.

"Well now, Comrade Salamanca, I invite you to the table!" Zavkhozov rubbed his hands together. Sitny could not recall ever having seen him in such a good mood.

A house in a dream
a wave on the water
why did it seem
that fate was my daughter?

The lady recited with her eyes half closed and gestured to the proprietor to lead her to the table laid in the far corner of the balcony. ". . . That fate was my daughter," Zavkhozov repeated, savoring each word. "Not half bad, not bad at all!"

The handsome demon came over, dispatched two shot glasses of vodka in rapid succession, and ate a spoonful of caviar. Suddenly he began to speak in a perfectly comprehensible language: "Here you are sitting at home, Zavkhozov, and down below a bacchanalia is going on! This embankment, I hate it more than anything else in the so-called state of Israel. They almost imagine themselves in Nice here! They're starting to drink without even waiting for the end of the Sabbath! They've made quite a cozy setup for themselves on someone else's land! All of their devotion to their ancient cult . . . nothing but lies! They sold out to the golden calf a long time ago! Youngsters sacrifice their lives, reduce their buses to shreds, and they just go on looking for ways to get high! Blind hedonists! Deaf gluttons!"

"Now, now, what's the sense in talking like a hothead," the owner of the flat began admonishing his guest, not forgetting to admonish the sensitive knee of Comrade Salamanca while he was at it. "Why not just leave it all up to history? Do you agree, Lyalka?"

"No, Zavkhozov, I'm sorry, but I understand Tamir's anger." The guest's face, which could not have been more serious, didn't look as though it had any connection with the sweet little knee at that moment. "The fact that you people in Department N are half gone to pieces still doesn't put an end to the national liberation movement. Out there"—she pointed down below with a finger like the hammer of a pistol—"at this moment two groups of outrageous characters are mingling. There you have the much-vaunted carnivalization of art, the Rabelaisian marketplace, all of this clowning around and hullabaloo headed up by that well-known loony American Gargantua. And at the very same time, Comrade General, there's that other Korbach nonentity, that former artistic director of the Buffoons or whatever they were called—it's not important—getting up to incest with a loose American woman. Did you know about that, Tamir?"

"I know more about that than anyone else in this whole story," the guest said gloomily. In his dark marble pose, he now cut a figure of implacability.

Salamanca laughed out loud. "Degenerate America, it sucks everything out of you! Where's your *dolce stil nuovo*? Where's your Beatrice? All sucked out! Now they're rolling around on a ratty couch and dying from happiness, the two old dolls!"

"What's the couch got to do with it? Why's it 'ratty'?" General Sitny was cut to the quick.

"Take it easy, comrade-in-arms!"

Zavkhozov continued to admonish the knee of the revolutionary fury and with the other hand filled everyone's glass with champagne of a vintage that you won't find in Israel, that great egalitarian country, even if you go over it with a fine-tooth comb. For the first time in all these months since his flight from Moscow, he felt the tension leaving him. It's good, after all, to let one's hair down among good friends. It was not for nothing that he had been taught from childhood the line "He sympathized with his comrade with a human love." Why, even this one, this birdman Burevyatnikov, now flying toward the balcony, was one of our "Kommsies"— the shithead; even if he did sell out to imperialism in his time, he's still one of ours.

"Where do you think you're going, Tikh?" he asked, letting him know elegantly that he shouldn't count on an invitation.

Burevyatnikov stopped in midair, gently flapping his huge wings, grinning from ear to ear at the unimaginable good fortune of the flying abilities that had just come to him. "Back to my own people!" he barked.

"You mean to the land of cheap polka-dot calico?" the former killer remembered with a melancholy warmth.

Burevyatnikov gave a guttural laugh. "To the feathered world of North America, General!" His plumage was blazing in the rays of the setting Mediterranean sun. Zavkhozov regretted that none of his guests, it seemed, could see this surprising phenomenon. "Give me a quart of liquor, friend, and it's good-bye to all your dirty giblets!" "And you'll make it there?" the general inquired with a Stalinist squint. "I'll make it, if they don't shoot me down!" With the quart bottle in his teeth he began gaining altitude and getting farther from the Opera House and from the Tel Aviv seafront, with every flap of his wings looking more like an albatross.

At this point, we'll add something that goes beyond the parameters of this book. He got there, though by his count 7,300 surface-to-air missiles were fired at him from various countries; got there after 5,118 days and 10,236 nights; got there after eating 44,897 fish and stealing 7,019 quarts of liquor from passing ships; got there in order to disappear in the twilight distances over the ocean.

Snow and wind and the night flight of the stars, my heart calls me into the troubled distances, Zavkhozov thought as he watched him go, humming a song of his Komsomol generation to himself; only then did he return to his guests. And he went on: "We mustn't forget, after all, that we're from there ourselves. From under the same cover, as they say. Everyone knows now that a positive hero can't get along without a negative one, and we are ideologues, all the same. The red-letter day will come, truth will triumph in the court of highest instance, but no one can take away some of the achievements of privatization in our country."

"You're always looking out for number one, Zavkhozov," Commandante Salamanca said with irritation, moving away from the opportunist, "though we're talking a complicated phenomenon like polyphony. There's a rabble down below, but there's a purposeful hero, too. Coming into this story, every one of us had the right to a display of individuality. I understand Tamir's historical indignation, and I reserve for him the right to take any revolutionary action. Just as I myself might at any minute commit an act that no one would even have thought of on the previous page. That's how it is!" With these words her starfishlike hand laid into Zavkhozov's shaggy paw and moved it from her lap up to her stomach. Time for action, she decided, to go with him into the bedroom. Polyphony is all well and good, but they don't fool around where contracts are concerned. The only question is whether to liquidate him before we do it or after.

"Well, all the best," General Sitny said, immediately starting to take his leave. His jacket pockets were crammed with excellent lobsters, and as a man not entirely unfamiliar with dramatics, he had already understood the direction in which things were headed.

Sasha and Nora lay sprawled on the "ratty" couch, feeling such tenderness that they could hardly move. Through the small window just below the ceiling nothing was visible but rubbish: the cornice of a cement wall, the ugly box of an ancient air conditioner, an ice-cream wrapper clinging to it. But they saw none of that. In those moments when the angel turned his face away, they saw only silvery emptiness in their minds' eyes.

Almost inaudibly, directly in her ear, he read to her again and again from Guinizelli's *Amour* with its surprising news, caressed her earlobes with his tongue and his lips. The sound of an explosion came from the embankment, but it was joy, not a bomb. "Why don't you dye this gray lock of hair?" "If you want me to I will, but people tell me that it suits me. What do I care about hair?" "You know, I feel like a young woman again." "And I feel like a doddering old man." "I hadn't noticed." The angel flew away, and through the silvery emptiness wafted a strong smell of pseudo-Siberian dumplings, a large pot of which Natalka the Battery cooked up every night for the acting fraternity. "Do you mean you didn't feel as though it were an old man lying on top of you? See how my Leninesque brow is covered with age spots the color of buckwheat?" "But my eyes were closed when you were lying on top of me. You were even sweeter than your *dolce stil nuovo* today, honey." From one side, a dense wave of pseudoborscht fumes began to come through, but in between the two edible currents, the aroma of a quasi-tropical rose penetrated and tickled their nostrils almost like a spindle. "Now that it's almost dark, I can't see any age spots on your forehead. You're the same Maryland faun that you've always been." The smell of roses was crowded out by the roar of a truck on Airekon Street. The smell of fuel oil swallowed up even the dumplings and the borscht. "When you're lying in cement huts like these, it seems as though there's no nature left around you. A hundred yards from us, nature is flourishing: a mass of waves, seaweed, fish both living and dead, monsters and sea gods. Did you know that this sea once saved the people of Israel?" "Is this about Jonah?" "No, this story is almost from our day. Caligula, that mad asshole, ordered his commander for Syria and Judea to put busts of him in the Temple. And for our ancestors this amounted to the end of the world. They hurriedly gathered in huge numbers and pleaded with Petronius, the commander, to refuse such a mission. Teachers and high priests rent their garments and sprinkled their heads with ashes. Petronius came out onto the steps of the Temple and said that the emperor had ordered that all the people be slaughtered if they resisted his deification. The people cried out that everyone was ready to accept death for the purity of the Temple. The shaken Petronius sent word to Rome and withdrew from Jerusalem to Antioch. Caligula, enraged, sent Petronius the order to destroy the people of Israel. A series of storms, however, held up the delivery of the order for three months. By that time, Caligula had been assassinated in Rome. News of this none too tragic event came by the calm sea in twenty-seven days. It had arrived before the cannibalistic decree. Such was the will of Poseidon, my dear! Thus we were all saved, and Adonai Kor-Beit could begin fathering children. Well, why don't you say something?"

"Mmm . . . ," A.Z. murmured. "I'm calculating the budget for the film."

"We'd do better to pray to Poseidon!"

The sun was already suspended like a large red something—choose any of a thousand similes, you won't say anything new—well, in short, like Chashnik's Suprematism it was hanging over the horizon, though there was nothing ominous to be seen in either the scene itself or the faces of those observing it. A fresh northwest wind was blowing, the surf was breaking evenly. In addition, little waves were splashing in between the breakwaters and the shore, and even in these splashings a certain synchronicity was felt, a gentle rhythm that on the whole was far from characteristic of the turbulent history of this riviera.

The mood on the embankment was ebullient. Russian and Moroccan orchestras were playing here and there. One man, having occupied a square of sidewalk, was doing a masterful job of running a puppet show, managing on his own to play out whole scenes between Colombine, Harlequin, Pulcinella, and Dr. Duppertutto. The audience was generous with shekels. Noticing the approach of two aging lovers with their arms around each other, he smiled his old dazzling smile, as if to say: I hope you recognize me? I hope you haven't forgotten me? I hope you love me as much as you once did? I hope my treason has been forgotten? I hope we'll have a drink this evening?

For some reason, a crowd of people was wading in the shallow water, some up to their ankles, some up to their waists. Many were sitting on the breakwaters. Eyes were turned to the open sea, from which an isolated yacht, a Star of David emblazoned on its huge spinnaker that was billowing in a tailwind, was approaching.

Sasha and Nora wondered: What's going on here? It looks like some sort of sensation is in the offing. Kicking their shoes off, they too entered into the water, and the farther they got from the shore with the setting sun in the background, the more reminiscent their still trim bodies became of their own youth. Just like that, taking each other's hands, they could splash through the shallows, through the pink patches of light, as though they were in an advertisement for those fine rubber articles called Trojans, twenty-five-year-old Sasha and fifteen-year-old Nora.

Standing in the water directly ahead of them and looking at them was a tall man dressed in white. The wind was tousling his long, white hair. "What's going on here, sir?" A.Z. asked him. "What, you mean you don't know?" the old man asked in surprise. "A remarkable world record is being established. On that yacht approaching our coast is a married couple, sea voyagers, Lenore Yablonsky and Anthony Arrowsmith. You've probably heard of them, they're our people, too. The couple have been plying the seas and having children for years now. The newspapers say that they've already produced eight hundred children over the ocean depths." Other spectators coming up to them eagerly volunteered details. "Lenore is forty-eight years older than Anthony, but she looks twenty-eight years younger." "During their first trip forty-five years ago, she gave birth to three sets of triplets in a row, and the really interesting thing is that they arrived at three-month intervals." "That's how it's gone since then: children, children, children, thousands of boys, no less, and thousands of girls, too." "They left them in care in various countries so as not to interrupt their never-ending voyage, and the finest people on many continents took this lovely time upon themselves." "Among those who raised the children one can count 115 prime ministers, 318 current and former presidents, 516 laureates, 604 dukes, 707 world champions, 80 virtuosos, 905 bishops, 1,008 film and rock stars." "All of the children grew up into splendid people (except for those who are still growing), received a first-class education and excellent physical and intellectual training. Among their number are no fewer than 300 highly qualified doctors, 600 advocates, 750 screenwriters, 880 composers and musicians, and 1,500 of these offspring work in television." "At least one-third of these children, to sum up, have gotten married." "The seagoing pair's first grandchildren have already appeared, 4,875 in number." "The increase of the family is proceeding not geometrically, but Homerically. It is not only an epos that is being created, though, but a new race is being born, enjoying greater freedom from the consequences of original sin than previous generations."

Impressed by this information, Sasha and Nora continued on toward the breakwaters, on which most of the welcoming crowd was clustered. The old man walked beside them. "Do you mean you don't recognize me, my brother and my sister? Why, I'm your former rabbi, Dershkowitz. It's twenty years now since I left the Fountain of Zion in Maryland and entered the New Essenes of Galilee sect, but you still ought to remember me."

"Twenty years?" A.Z. asked in surprise.

"At this point, no one needs any clarifications," Nora put in immediately. "Of course we recognize you, *rebe!*"

With a beatific smile, Dershkowitz began to move off to one side. He was heading for one of the rocks of a nearby breakwater, on which Stanley Franklin Korbach, deposed leader of the entire novel, having found time for a shave and haircut, and also to exchange his burnoose for orange shorts, was sitting like a twice life-size statue of the emperor Vespasian. Approaching, Dershkowitz produced two liter bottles of beer from a fold in his garment. He handed one to Stanley and kept the other for himself. "My first bottle of beer in forty-five years," he explained to his friend. "Who's arguing?" The latter smiled.

Beneath the rock on which the two old men were sitting, two small Jewish children were swimming in an inlet, towheaded Philip Jazz Korbach and black Clemens Dedalus Korbach. Sasha and Nora took the children and went with them toward the foamy passageway between the two breakwaters into which the yacht *Delmarva* had already sailed. The tanned figures of the crew were now visible. A very long beard tossed back over one shoulder and knotted to his belt really did make Anthony look older than Lenore. The latter had never grown a beard. Her cheeks sparkled like oranges from the Carmel Valley. He was lowering and furling the sail; she was at the wheel. Meanwhile, three girls, one of the celebrated sets of triplets, were dancing on the prow—perhaps they were the very first set.

Television lights came on; the whole beach rang with delighted greetings. The invulnerable helicopters of the Israeli Air Force released a huge quantity of balloons and fireworks. The sun had already sunk halfway into the dark, sparkling sea.

"We all need to become a nation of the sea," Stanley said. "The Philistines are pressing us from the mountains, but we're standing on the sea and we'll never go away from here!"

"Tell me, Stanley, are you an angel or a devil?" Dershkowitz asked. The giant scooped up a handful of water and shook it in his palms, which he cupped to form a Phoenician craft. The water flowed out, and in its place remained a tiny crystal of salt, gleaming like a star. "Open up your mouth, Dersh!" he said to his friend, and tossed the crystal into the open orifice. "Now do you understand who I am?" "I'm dying of thirst"—the Neo-Essene coughed—"and that's why I'm going to get drunk today for the first time in half a century!"

"All the stars seem like salt crystals to me today," Stanley said. "Oh, Pantagruel, it seems that you really were one of our race!"

Two hours or so after the enchanting aquatic spectacle, the entire clan gathered on the terrace of the Khadiag restaurant, an oasis of light and comfort among the crumbling warehouses and cracking-from-the-sun trawlers of the old port. Over our heads hung bunches of grapes and large balloons. The waiters were dead on their feet, bringing up large pans of St. Peter's fish crackling in olive oil; the fish came directly to the kitchen from boats rocking at the establishment's own small pier. All the tables were provided with fresh beer and inexpensive Mediterranean wines. The fortified port of Falerno, well-known from ancient literature, stood by itself. Blocks of cheese, mostly Gruyères and Roqueforts, sat beside stone-hard Tuscany sausages. No one here paid any mind to kosher laws, even though they all had the greatest respect for the ancient custom. No one seemed to notice the fresh oysters that they were consuming in abundance.

Waves were crashing somewhere out in the darkness just next to the long table at which all of our main characters were sitting. Droplets of seawater sometimes landed on the table, immediately sending crystals of salt rolling on it. The feasters would pop them into their mouths with a laugh and, dying of thirst, grab for a bottle.

Suddenly, the waiters brought out a thirty-two-liter bottle of vintage Clicquot. Someone had written over the label with a felt pen: "From our table to your table!" With chins, noses, hands, index fingers, and full turns of lithe bodies, the waiters indicated the source of the rare gift. Beyond the terrace, in the depths of the spacious cave of the Hadiaga with its white walls decked out with photographs of celebrities, sat a victorious party looking like yet another photo, blown up to life size: Norman Blamsdale, Marjorie Blamsdale-Korbach, three traitor sisters, various inconsequential riffraff, and finally the 103-year-old patriarch Dave with his new companion, a young Burmese girl named Yin-Yin. They were looking at our table with strange, not entirely impudent smiles.

"It's not a bomb, is it?" Stanley asked. The bottle was turning ponderously on its own auxiliary table like a heavy mortar. "It doesn't matter! Open it!" The bottle's mighty ejaculation soared and landed on . . . well, on whom else might the ejaculation of a bottle land? Why, on our quasi-mythical Bernadetta, of course, sitting there with the Order of the Star between her breasts, surrounded by her entourage, which that night had been enlarged to include Duppertat the puppeteer and a few other defectors. With laughter all around, the aforementioned container, as Soviet people used to say, was emptied. The Blamsdale party applauded with almost sycophantic loyalty.

"Do you think this is from the goodness of their hearts, from a pure desire for reconciliation?" Stanley asked. "It's just because that son of a bitch Norm found out that I'm going to get the backing of the Israeli armed forces soon, and then that'll be the end of him. The same thing happened in the early fifties with the Korean Red czar Kim Il Sung. He'd driven our side onto their last scrap of territory and was already celebrating his victory when there was a seaborne landing in his rear. The dumb Commie hadn't even figured out that the geography of his peninsula practically invited a landing. Norman blew it the same way. He never should have let me get through to Israel, and now there's nothing to prevent me from getting all of my money back and giving it away to the people who need it the most."

"It looks like my father is really in his cups," Nora whispered in Sasha's ear. Her whisper made every hair on his chest and under his arms stand up. He felt as though he had never loved her as much as he did at that moment. The libido is fading, love is in bloom. Maître Alighieri, could that be possible outside of Paradise?

"Oh, Sashka," she whispered, "I'm so happy that this is happening to us in the land of our ancestors!"

Well, what else can we offer you, our faithful readers, and you, O Theophilus, as a conclusion to this evening, as a conclusion to the novel? Where on our wall is Chekhov's famous gun hanging, the one that has to be fired? And can it be that this snake, immutable as it is, won't crawl into any crack it can find? Perhaps we can get along with just some shard of the same author's bottle, which, lying in a puddle by moonlight, completes the landscape. What in our scene on the terrace of the Khadiag could play this part? Maybe the empty magnum of Clicquot, or some unvarying tavern guitar strumming?

There it is now, a seven-stringed instrument in the hands of a dazzling Euro-Gypsy woman, now it's ringing out in time to the jingling of her bracelets and necklaces, there it is rumbling, emphasizing the knowing Gypsy singing:

The time of bad weather will pass, will pass!
The happiness of old will come back, come back!
The years have not bent us,
Our castle is not washed away!
Bullets don't scare us,
Dynamite either!

The time of bad weather will pass, will pass!
The happiness of old will come back, come back!

At that moment, a thin, nervous figure in dark glasses and a false beard and equally false pigtails dangling at his temples, who seems not to be looking at the Gypsy but who at the same time is keeping her under observation, and perhaps even in a gunsight, goes to the bar in a distant corner, sits down with his left buttock on a stool and his right leg planted firmly on the floor. He orders a pepper vodka and makes a speech in his mind to the bracelets and necklaces: You filthy woman, so you decided after all to end our story in your own repulsive style, with an explosion and the disintegration of our entire cast of characters into nothing but twisted printing signs? You bitch, you think I'm your accomplice, but I'm a man of ideas, after all, not terror! Bitch, bitch, Medusa-Gorgon, I won't let you blow up my youth on the Left Bank of the Seine! Such are the thoughts of Omar Mansour, in their hypocritical sincerity, as he goes on sipping his revolting drink.

At this moment—that is to say, at the moment when the thoughts of the nervous man filter through the pepper vodka to their conclusion, and when the Gypsy's singing is swallowed up in her own shrieking and in the ringing of everything jingling on her—Stanley Franklin Korbach, Alexander Zakharovich Korbach, and Nora Katerina Korbach-Mansour simultaneously raise their eyes, see the bunches of grapes, garlands of balloons, and an uncountable number of small birds and stars, and realize that in spite of all the sublime wonder of this moment, there will be an explosion in it. And the explosion goes off.

It seems to Sasha Korbach that he has been flung immediately up to a great height. Staying there, he sees his poor remains falling, and feels an unimaginable pity for the survivors. This feeling goes for the space of a moment without time and without air, but in the next ordinary instant he finds himself back at the same table among the same laughing people. It turns out that one of the balloons has burst, and that his stunning hallucination can be written off to vegetative neurosis. The explosive ending does not take place, and the latest triumph of our literary tradition makes itself known.

4

A MEETING

$\mathcal{T}$he next morning, the Korbach clan and their retinue, all in ordinary, respectable suits, piled into a chartered bus—the bill, of course, was paid by the bankrupt magnate with cash on hand from his usual bag—and headed for Jerusalem, for a meeting with their supposed ancestor.

Traffic on the main Israeli motorway was heavy. The cars were racing along at the same speed at which cars travel in America or in Russia, as though unafraid of suddenly ending up in Havlanitida, Bashanta, or Batanyei. The higher the multi-lane roadway rose, the more the surroundings, with their light gray and light pink boulders amid the fresh green of pine and cedar groves, and with their small towns perched on steep slopes in the distance, reminded one of this land's long history.

As he always did in Israel, A.Z. was beginning to feel a lifting of his spirits that was at once triumphant and soothing. The excitement of the previous evening in cosmopolitan Tel Aviv had immediately subsided, as though a year had passed since then, rather than a few hours. My head's clearing, he thought with surprise. All of these Russias and Americas just drift away in the wind. Perhaps now a good, healthy thought will occur to me.

It occurred to him right away, when around the bend there appeared a valley with little towns hanging on its slopes at various altitudes. To live here for the rest of my days. To get lost here. To forget all about the carnival tent. To forget about the brothel. To write poetry. To not read it to anyone except Nora when she comes back from one of her gravedigging expeditions. Unfortunately, she doesn't understand everything in this goddamned lingo that was given me at birth. That means I wouldn't read it to her either.

"You know, I'm really nervous," Nora said. He shuddered. Thinking about her, he'd forgotten that she was beside him. "How so?" She smiled. "How could I not be? I think of him as one of my creative children, after all."

"Who, for God's sake?" he asked, surprised.

"You seem to have forgotten where we're going!" she said indignantly.

"What do you mean? We're going to Jerusalem."

"And why are we going there? Just on a sight-seeing trip? Or with some purpose in mind?" She was seething, hardly able to restrain herself from giving him a whack on the head.

"Oh, yes, that's right—we're going to see your stiff, this Mr. Cold House dipped in honey! Ouch! What're you hitting me so hard for, Nora? I understand the importance of this event just as you do. A revolution in archaeology, in the whole gravedigging business. . . . All right, I'll stop. I was just thinking about how we'll live together on that hillside. We'll sit there and watch TV, you with your CNN, and me with Ostankino."

"Oh, cut it out," she said angrily and turned away.

Apart from A.Z., everyone in the bus seemed to realize the seriousness of the moment. The head of the clan was unrecognizable after his escapades of the night before. Wearing a sand-colored thin flannel suit—where he had produced it from, no one had any idea—and a long tie with a stickpin in it, he maintained a stern silence. Beside him sat his eternal servant, Enoch Agasf, who had appeared as mysteriously as the suit. With his eyeglasses and tweed jacket, he looked a Pinkerton professor from the Conflict Resolution Center.

The former chief advisers Leibnitz and Square were sitting in the middle of the bus, along with Lionel Fuchs, representative of the long-defunct genealogical group. They were chatting quietly and making notes on their laptops. Ben and Rose Duckworth, that married couple unnoticed by any of the readers the previous evening, were contributing their modest and serious presence. We must slip in a few words about how the story of this likable pair unfolded. Even at the time of their fruitful collaboration in the field of philanthropy, Ben and Rose had both participated in the variety of modern sports that is close to both art and philosophy, namely, that which for a logical reason is known in America as bodybuilding and which for no clear reason at all is known in Russia as *kulturism*. There was no one at the Count Lefort Foreigners' Health Center in Moscow who could outdo them in muscle development and synchronized movement. After the collapse of the Korbach Fund, they managed to return to the United States, where they almost immediately became champions at the professional level. For want of space, we'll just say that they derived great pleasure from considering themselves a model mixed-race and mixed-sex American couple.

Bernadetta De Luxe's group, now headed since the spectacle of the night before by the wandering and well-liked Middle East puppeteer Art Duppertat, was carrying itself in the bus with surprising solemnity. In particular, Art had taken it upon himself to entertain the children, of whom a dozen or so had accumulated as a result of various permutations of people. Their mouths open, the children watched as the numerous characters of commedia dell' arte popped up in one place on the bus, then another, and then disappeared again.

In short, they were making their way toward Jerusalem, and after ninety minutes they entered the city's suburbs from the west. West Jerusalem begins as a rather broad plateau on which a multistory Holiday Inn rises like the Lighthouse of Alexandria. To the east of this structure stand those masterpieces of neoancient architecture, the Knesset and the Israel Museum. It was for the latter that our expedition headed. It was there, in a specially constructed glass case, that the unique mummy of a tanner rested.

They had almost reached the last turn before the museum when the head of the clan suddenly stood up and ordered the driver to change course. "We're going to the Old Town first," he said, and no one objected.

Leaving the bus in a parking place not far from the fortress walls, they crossed the Kidron Valley—that is, the very same Jehoshaphat where the Messiah will descend and where the resurrection of the dead will begin. Then, along with a crowd of pilgrims and tourists, they entered the gates—where David and Solomon had reigned, where Nebuchadnezzar had destroyed the Temple and cut whips from backs, where the Maccabees had defended themselves against the armies of Antioch, where Herod had arrayed his Roman columns, where the whips had driven Christ on, carrying his cross up to Golgotha, where he had died and risen, where the legions of Titus had burned the Second Temple and where he had buried his gold—like Crescent Moon, Mohammed's horse, galloping up by night from Mecca to a meeting with the early prophets.

Oxymoronically, they took their places in an Arab café and ordered ice cream when they entered the Old Town. A platoon of soldiers on a patriotic excursion, their American semiautomatic rifles hanging, barrels down, on their shoulders, passed by on their way to David's Tower. Their sergeant was yelling *"Smelo! Smelo!"* to his charges, by which he did not mean an encouragement to great martial deeds in Russian but just an order in Hebrew of "keep to the left."

Refreshed by the ice cream, our people moved on farther into the Armenian Quarter and saw from a turn the huge expanse between the hill of the Old Town and the Mount of Olives, at the foot of which was the holiest of Christian orchards, the Garden of Gethsemane. Every time that A.Z. came here, it seemed to him a gigantic column of light was rising from the whole stretch of land. This was what happened now. He wanted to tell Nora about it, but he didn't dare. His beloved was walking along biting her lip, a pallor spreading over her face, her shoulders trembling as though taken by gusts of wind. What's she so upset about? Surely she hasn't got so much ambition?

The streets of the Jewish Quarter were lined with modern houses built from the local pink stone. Their architecture enveloped the ruins and seemed itself to have become part of antiquity. The huge square in front of the Wailing Wall was patrolled on all sides by commandos of the Gelavi Division sporting purple berets. Strapping guys in coveralls, festooned with weapons and radio-telephones, were standing beneath arches and making jokes with each other in Hebrew and in Russian. Their jaws dropped when Bernadetta the Modest passed by in her Parisian minisuit. One also noticed a few slightly built Hasidics trembling at the sight of our stern example of ultrafemininity. A wise law, however, divided the supplicants at the Wall by sex, and the temptation receded.

The Wall is striking in its dimensions, with its hewn stones fit sturdily to one another. Before you is only a small section that remains from the Temple—just try to imagine the whole Temple! Stanley laid his hands, palms flat, against the stone, and our entire team imitated the gesture. "At this moment, guys, everything that was Jewish in you is coming back!" Rabbi Dershkowitz announced triumphantly. Jews of various backgrounds were coming up behind our bunch: Uzbeks, Georgians, Dagestanians, Moroccans, Americans, Poles, and others—you won't be able to count them all. The reader knows that even the ten lost tribes will come here one day.

Next to the Israel Museum a crowd in long black coats was demonstrating. Their placards read: HANDS OFF OUR ANCESTORS! WE DEMAND THE BURIAL OF KOR-BEIT THE TANNER! ARCHAEOLOGISTS OUT OF ISRAEL! The security guards, pushing the protesters back, made a way through for the new arrivals. They had been expected, as it turned out: the opening ceremony for the new exhibit was supposed to start at any minute.

They walked along the polished marble floors in halls kept at a strictly regulated optimal temperature. In a hall with candles burning in the corners and a triangle of blue sky in the ceiling stood a small group of honored guests numbering no more than two hundred; among them was the president, cabinet ministers, rabbis, and several heads of state. Everyone turned at the entrance of the towering Stanley Korbach. The company was obviously intrigued by the appearance of the great philanthropist, one of the most controversial figures of the moment and, what was more, the descendant of the historic object of exhibition. A brigade of television cameramen and photographers were taking discreet shots from their strictly limited section. The director of the museum was already making a speech. The guttural sounds of Hebrew were accompanied by the aspirates of a simultaneous British English translation.

Nora was led up closer to the microphones. She was supposed to give a report on the historic discovery. No one was paying any attention to A.Z. Standing on tiptoe, he was trying to catch a glimpse of the display, but he could not see a thing. It was clear nonetheless that there was an open space in the middle of the crowd. Having made his way to the outer edge of the space, he saw what was going on. The crowd was standing close around a large glass rectangle embedded in the floor. Beneath it, in a brightly lit white cube, a dark brown mummified male figure was laid out. The fragment of a spear protruded from his lower left abdomen. A torn garment, obviously a light summer tunic, enveloped his chest and gathered in folds on his hips. It was the same color as the body, dark brown, like congealed buckwheat honey.

A strange sensation that he had never experienced before came over A.Z. Perhaps it was horror, perhaps delight—in any case, it was something unbearable. Drenched in sweat and shaking as from the cold of the grave, he stood over the supine body. He wanted to run away, but he was unable to move. He could not stay here either. It was absolutely impossible for him to take one more look down at Zeyev Kor-Beit. The blue triangle over his head seemed like an abyss. The faces around him offered a picture of unrecognizability. "My God, oh my God! How is it that I didn't see this before?" Nora's voice reached his ears. "Sashka, is that you? You're here, Sashka?" Even here, his penchant for inappropriate thoughts did not leave him. It's so hard much of the time to distinguish an exclamation point from a question mark in a woman's voice, he thought and took heart somewhat. He felt that the crowd was beginning to turn in his direction. There was nothing left for him to do but bend over the glass.

It was he himself lying down there. It was his own light, muscular body, and even the nail on the big toe of the right foot was a copy of his own toenail, which had once been called archaeological. The most important thing was that Zeyev Kor-Beit had Alexander Korbach's face. There was only a bit of skin that had flaked off the cheek just above the left lower corner of the jaw; otherwise, the features repeated A.Z.'s exactly: the shape of the bald forehead, and the protruding ears, and the elongated, simian mouth, and the eyelids squeezed shut as if in laughter—a two-thousand-year contraction over the eyeballs. Receding and approaching, a stunning mask of buffoon's laughter loomed before his eyes, resembling exactly the one that had appeared on his own face in moments of theatrical delight. He himself was receding and approaching, receding and approaching. And now he made contact with something that he could not yet understand. This means that this is me, this means that this is me, I, myself, this means that I've been here, too, in the form of this singer Sasha Korbach, he thought along with all of that. And receded, and approached, and receded.